# The SongBird's Love

## By Jenny Fox

Published by IngramSpark.
Made in the United Kingdom
2023 First Edition

First published in 2023.

Author Jenny Fox
Find me on Facebook & Instagram.

# Contents

# Acknowledgements

Once again, I am immensely grateful to my family and friends who have been supporting my journey as an author. I cannot believe I'm already in my fourth year on this path, and I am always so blessed for this unique chance to live my childhood dream.

I wish to thank the kind beta-readers & proofreaders who anonymously volunteered to help me prepare this story for its publishing.

Finally, I want to thank you, dear reader, for starting this new journey to the future. I hope you'll enjoy this story and start dreaming of a better, brighter future.

"*The Future belongs to those who Believe in the Beauty of their Dreams.*"

*Eleanor Roosevelt.*

# INTRO

The end of the gun was still hot when he lowered his weapon and put it down on the table. His long fingers traded it for the cigarette, bringing it to his lips. He took a drag, the end turned a fiery red for a second. Then, he sighed and walked back to the large, leather chair, sitting in it like a king on his throne.

Everyone else in the room had gone religiously silent. The pool of blood was slowly growing under the body, but no one moved to do a thing about it. Instead, one of the men cleared their throat, bringing the general attention back to the screen on the wall. The white silhouette had been captured in a single shot, frozen in movement from a weird angle, crouching against a wall. The lighting wasn't great and the image was blurry. The man clicked his tongue, slowly rubbing his index finger against his lower lip. His upset expression was frightening every man in the room. They were all standing tall and straight like soldiers, impeccable in their dark suits.

"...I suggest everyone think twice before giving me any more bad news."

His deep and cold voice sent another shiver down their spines. No one dared to look his way, but his amber eyes were riveted on the screen. It was his current obsession, the little annoyance he couldn't get rid of.

Finally, one of the younger men in the room stepped forward, the same one who had cleared his throat earlier.

"...We couldn't find any more information on Ghost, sir, b-but we managed to narrow it down to a location at least."

The boss' cold eyes went to him.

The young man suddenly felt all the pressure of that gaze. It was like facing a dangerous beast; those golden eyes were absolutely terrifying. Those were the eyes of a killer, an apex predator. A tiger.

He had never been in the boss' presence before, but now, he could see what all the others meant. He was on a whole different level. Some people in this world carried something in them that made them stand out, something that screamed to others that they were different, powerful, and fearsome. The Italian Tiger was one of those people. He had just cold-bloodedly killed their latest hacker because of one failure. It was hard to be in the same room or even to dare look his way. It was like a threat hanging right above their heads called death.

The young recruit could feel it at that moment; he had felt confident, cocky even, to be promoted higher and higher within their organization, but that confidence had just been thrown on the floor and smashed to pieces with one glance. Now, he could feel that cold drop of sweat going down his spine, and the cold spreading around him. The others almost stepped away from him to avoid whatever he was about to suffer. He took a deep breath, gathering all of his courage.

"I-in the Dragon's area. Each time they appeared, the beginning and end signals were emitted around the Dragon's area..."

He pulled again on his cigarette, the plume of smoke going up in the air. The room was dark, making the white smoke appear even clearer, like a ghost.

"...Find them."

Everyone in the room felt the pressure increase drastically. One of the men shook his head.

"Sir, we have tried already. Can't we just find someone else to..."

Before he had finished his sentence, the boss' eyes were already glaring at him, and the large, strong man went mute. It was like facing death itself. He could feel those eyes like a blade held against his throat. The man in the leather chair tilted his head.

"How many times has 'someone else' lost to Ghost?"

"E-every time, sir..."

"What does that mean?"

"Th-That Ghost person is the best hacker..."

"That's right," whispered the Italian Tiger, "and the best have to work for me or die. This is the last time I hear that we lost information to Ghost."

The big man who had dared to raise his voice gulped his saliva down and kept his mouth shut. The golden eyes would not allow another word, he could tell.

Another man, with white hair, who was the only one not looking distressed, sighed.

"We have tried offering money to Ghost, but it seems they refused to work for only one person. They take the highest bidder and the highest risks each time. This means our enemies can employ Ghost against us too, sir."

The boss remained silent.

His eyes had finally let go of the poor man, who regretted opening his mouth, to go back to that picture. He slowly scratched the little scar on his neck where his SIN was implanted. It had been corrupted and modified long ago, but sometimes he still felt an itch from that thing.

"...Isn't there anyone better?" asked the middle-aged, white-haired man.

"No, sir. In terms of statistics, no one on the market has been as good as Ghost. The speed of execution is exceptional, and they always keep it under twenty-seven minutes."

"That's extremely short..."

"Yes, sir. Ghost always completes their theft in less than half an hour, from the moment they appear in the Dark Reality until they go off the grid. They vanish as soon as the transaction is complete. No other hacker has been able to beat their record, even those who competed directly."

The boss suddenly took a big breath in and stood up.

Everyone else in the room immediately lowered their heads, getting tense again. He slowly walked up to the screen, as if he could see better from up close. Squinting his eyes, he stared at that white silhouette.

"...Why can't we get a better picture?"

"Th-they probably use some sort of jammer to prevent others from tracking them, sir. This is the best we've gotten in months... We are doing our best to get any information, but no one has been able to get any data. The age, size, race, and gender of Ghost are still completely unknown. The prices on the Black Market for any information are still high, but everything we've bought so far turned out to be fake..."

"Raise the price."

He turned around, facing his men with his golden eyes shining dangerously.

"Spare no means and no money to find Ghost. I want that hacker in my office, dead or alive."

"Yes, sir."

Dante brought the cigarette back to his mouth while most of his men used the occasion to leave the room in a hurry. He turned around, studying that picture again.

Ghost was going to be his, or die.

# CHAPTER ONE

"Eden, no. No, no, hun."

"Please," she insisted. "You can't do that to me. You said I'd be working at the tables tonight."

"You'll be working aroun' the tables, just as a hostess," he replied with his strong accent. "Sorry, honey, I ain't letting ya take any customers tonight."

"But I need the money! Jack, please!"

He sighed and turned around to look at that little piece of woman.

She was already dressed up in her brick-red dress and had put on some lipstick. Eden was almost ready, clumsily putting on the big jewelry pieces and following him barefoot into the waiting room. She was naturally pretty, but this old-fashioned look and those artificial curls didn't really suit her.

"Eden, listen. I know what I said, and I know you need the cash, honey. But look, tonight's bouncer is that idiot upstairs! What am I supposed to do? You know how bad that dummy is, right? And I got nobody else to take care of security inside, hun, nobody. You're the only one who's got the qualifications. Look at these chicks. Do ya think they'd lose a nail in a fight?"

Eden sighed, helplessly glancing around the room. All of her colleagues were busy getting ready, putting on their dresses, makeup, and jewelry, but she knew they all had an ear out for what was going on. Bella was sending her sorry looks in her mirror, and Xixi had been working on the same eyebrow for five minutes already. Sitting in front of the biggest mirror, Rose sighed loudly.

"Oh, just let it go and be happy, Eden. Be glad you don't have to sell your ass tonight..."

Eden glared back at her, but the two women remained quiet as Jack shook his head. He put a hand on her shoulder, adjusting one of her blonde curls.

"Hun, I'm sorry. I'll look for someone as soon as possible, but you know it's getting harder to hire staff around this block. If their stupid system allowed you to take on both jobs at the same time, swear to God I would totally put you on, honey."

"What about Dally?" asked Xixi with her chirpy voice.

"That idiot's brother got killed two weeks ago... and how about you chicks mind your own goddamn business!"

"Another murder?" said Rose, frowning and ignoring Jack's anger. "What the heck?"

The bar owner turned toward the ladies, crossing his big muscular arms. It would have been a bit more intimidating if they all didn't know him too well and if he wasn't wearing a turquoise, fitted dress and pink wig.

"You bunch of little..."

"What is Old Man Long doing?" asked Eden, getting a bit worried too.

Jack rolled his eyes. The girls barely got along, except when they were all ganging up against him. He sighed and gave up on his attempt at showing his authority.

"Bella babe, please help Eden do something about that shitty foundation she's got on. Girl, that contouring makes your nose too thin again."

The brunette nodded and jumped on her feet, grabbing one of the brushes on the tables to start sweeping around Eden's cheekbones. Yet, they were all waiting, so Jack started talking, grabbing his lipstick.

"Fine, fine... They say the old man ain't doing too well lately. That's why. Those bastards who already know about this are all leaving the area before it gets ugly, I bet."

All the girls began worrying for real. Next to Xixi, June dropped her kôhl, looking panicked. The twins exchanged worried looks too, and even Rose lost a bit of her usual haughty stance. Eden shook her head.

"What will happen, then? Will someone else take over this territory? What about the deals with the Core? The mayor can't do anything?"

"It's Chicago, babe. You know that the mayor ain't gonna do nothing! She probably doesn't give a damn what happens outside of the Core. We just gotta hope we're not going to get a piece of shit that's worse than Old Man Long. Either some young punk takes his place as the new Dragon, or–"

"Another one of the Zodiacs could take over?" asked Xixi, nervously playing with her braids. "If we get under the Russians, I'm leaving now!"

"...Or the Yakuza," whispered her sister Minnie.

"Hey, hey!" Jack exclaimed. "Everybody, calm down. Girls, the old man ain't dead yet. He's still alive, and everything is fine, a'right? We got a business to open, and I need all your pretty faces and booties ready for showtime. So everybody finish getting ready now."

He sighed and turned toward Eden, but behind him, all the young women were still whispering, forgetting all about their makeup and preparation. Unlike her colleagues, Eden was looking more sour than worried. Jack glanced at Bella, who got the message, and nodded before going back to her spot. He then turned to Eden, grabbing her shoulder.

"Come on, honey, come with me upstairs while we let the pretties get ready."

Eden nodded and followed him upstairs.

The bar was ready to be opened, the pink neon signs all lit up, and the tables were dressed up. Jack got behind the bar and took out a little box. It was as if a switch had been flipped once they arrived on this floor. His whole mannerism became more feminine, and his accent disappeared as his voice changed into something more polished and gentler.

"I've got a little something for ya, honey."

Eden frowned, but when he opened the box, her eyes suddenly lit up. She grabbed it, staring at the contents with a wide smile.

"Thanks, Jack!"

"It's nothing, honey. To be honest, these probably aren't going to sprout either. You know everything that comes from the Core is fucked up, all genetically modified..."

Eden didn't care. The little lemon seeds in front of her were enough to give her a little hope. Jack loved Eden exactly for this. Unlike him, she was one of those precious souls that still lit up at the tiniest bit of hope they could find. He was happier already just seeing her smile. He sighed and took out his bottle of whisky, pouring two drinks.

"...What's going on, honey?"

Eden's smile disappeared as she glanced up, knowing exactly what he meant. She and Jack knew each other too well already. She picked one of the stools to sit on, careful about her long dress, and took one of the glasses.

"It's Mom." She sighed. "I really need more money, fast."

"Oh no... What about last time?"

Eden shook her head.

"They said they're trying something else, more... costly. Of course, I agreed."

Jack sighed, grabbing his whisky and swirling the gold drink around, his lips pouting with a sorry look.

"Honey... you are the best daughter your old mama could have, but... that's too much, Eden. Too many sacrifices, hun. You're going to tire yourself out, maybe for nothing. You know that old mama of yours wouldn't want that."

"She's all I got left, Jack."

"It's Jacquie on this floor, honey. But, anyway... you got me too, alright?"

Eden smiled, but this one lacked a bit of warmth. Jack was genuinely worried for the young woman. Eden was too young, and she was literally sacrificing herself to save her poor mother. Kindness was a luxury that people

14

living in the Dragon's district couldn't afford these days.

"...Can you give me another shift?"

"No... you're full this week. That goddamn system ain't gonna allow me to give you anymore. Don't even try looking elsewhere, Eden. Your stupid SIN's gonna get all wonky again."

The blonde's expression got darker, and she touched her neck. The little piece of metal was pulsating under her skin, about the size of a coin. Eden scratched her skin nervously, but the device wouldn't suffer for this much. She hated this. The SINs regulated their whole lives. All of their personal data was entered within a system they had no control over. Eden hated having to scan this thing to be reminded of how penniless she was. The same device that wouldn't even let her work more.

"...I'll manage," she whispered.

Jack's black eyes got worried all of a sudden, and he leaned in closer.

"...You're not going to do the thing I'm not supposed to know about, right?"

Eden smiled a bit bitterly.

"You don't know anything, Jack–I mean, Jacquie. Don't worry."

Jack bit his lower lip. He could pretend not to know, but he knew enough to be worried about her, even if he couldn't say anything. He had his principles, and one included that the less he knew, the better it was. Which was true for his own safety, but it wouldn't prevent him from worrying about the young woman.

The truth was, even if he had agreed to let her work more, Eden wouldn't have earned much more than what she did as a hostess and bodyguard. She wasn't popular among their customers, despite her pretty face. Plus, it would create more tension between the girls as none could afford to share their customers. Every credit won was a little victory these days...

Eden grabbed her glass and finished her whisky in one shot, her hazel eyes shining again.

"Come on, Jacquie, showtime; let's get ready for those assholes."

Behind the bar, the man smiled and turned on the whole system.

The bar's lights lit up all at once and holograms of all the ladies appeared, either pole-dancing or simply moving around in short outfits. The digital doppelgangers all looked very real. Jack had invested a lot in this. It would have been hard to distinguish that those were fake just from sight. Yet, Eden knew their choreographies by heart. She had seen them dozens of times already. She could tell when Rose would send a wink across the room, or Xixi would split her legs around the pole.

She ignored all those fake ladies, there to keep the eye busy and add to the illusion of a crowded place, and walked to the little stand where an elegant gramophone was. Eden smiled, her finger dancing between the pieces of vinyl until she picked one and put it on. The jazz song resonated on the gramophone and throughout the bar's speakers.

15

"Now that's Chicago," said Jacquie with a little smile.

One by one, the girls came up to the floor, dressed up and ready for their customers. Rose sighed, grabbing her favorite bottle over the counter despite Jack's glare.

"Let's get the party started," she sighed, taking it in one shot.

The doors of the bar opened, letting a bunch of gentlemen in.

Most were familiar faces, the patrons that would come often. Immediately, the girls began smiling and chatting, each going toward their targets for the night. They all had their favorite customers and, moreover, no one liked to share a patron. Slowly, they took their seats on the pink and purple semi-circle sofas across the floor, each facing their own table. Putting on her business smile as well, Eden walked toward an older man.

"Evening, Mr. Charles," she said, putting her arm around him with a gentle smile.

"Evening, Miss Eden. What shall we drink tonight?"

"Isn't your doctor going to scold you?" she asked, tilting her head.

"What for! I'll order a new liver next week if I need to."

Eden chuckled.

"Alright then, how about your favorite: a good old brandy?"

"Ah, now you know how to make an old man happy. A brandy it is!"

She gently took him to one of the sofas to watch the scene and glanced at Jack for him to start preparing the drinks. Actually, the bar was preparing them as well. Half of what was really being prepared was automatized under the counter, but the customers couldn't see that. It simply looked like Jack was incredibly efficient and made some impressive bartender moves before putting the final touches and putting it up for the girls to collect. It maintained the illusion of a jazz bar stuck in the past, somewhere in the nineteenth century...

Eden left her customer for a minute to get their glasses and returned just in time to light his cigar. He opened a little box to offer her one.

"Oh, thank you, Mr. Charles, but I don't smoke."

"Oh, maybe in a few years, then!"

Eden smiled and watched him relax and glance at the fake dancers on stage. She liked Mr. Charles. She didn't know if it was his real name, but she didn't really care. He was a nice customer with a lot of money. From his way of speech and mannerisms, she could tell he was probably older than seventy, although he didn't look like he was over fifty, as expected from someone who came from the Core...

She kept entertaining the old man quietly until some ruckus caught her attention. A bunch of young men had walked into the bar, and she could tell some weren't sober by any means. She hesitated, but their bouncer shook one of their hands and seemed fine with letting them in. She glanced at Jack, who had spotted them too, but he shook his head, meaning for her to stay put. Eden saw Rose come from across the room with a large smile. It was her favorite type of customer: rich brats looking to brag and spend their money without thinking...

Although she tried to stay focused on Mr. Charles, Eden kept glancing over. Rose seemed to have the situation under control. She wasn't the most popular hostess for nothing... The redhead entertained the little group of four young men with her bright smile and fake laughs. She was truly beautiful. Her cream-colored skin was perfect, and she had recently done her hair in some gorgeous burgundy curls. Even her dress was one of the few not bought by Jack; a customer of hers had gifted her that short, sequined black dress.

Eden returned to chatting with Mr. Charles, thinking Rose had everything under control. Those weren't their first drunkards, and the redheaded hostess looked fine handling them. She already had two bottles of the most expensive gin on the table, which was a good sign too...

"Hey! I said I want that one!"

She sighed internally before turning her head. She just knew when customers were about to get troublesome. She had been in this field for too long not to recognize them ahead of time.

One of the young men was pointing his finger at one of Bella's holograms, the one that was dancing on the stage in a cute purple outfit. He stood up, staggering, and tried to make his way to the stage. One of his friends grabbed his wrist while laughing.

"It's a fake, you idiot! Come on, man, don't cause a commotion now. It's Justin's night..."

"So what! He's the one getting married! I just wanna play with that pretty slut... Get me a room with her. Now."

Eden took a deep breath in and glanced toward Jack. The bartender was already making his way across the room with his business smile.

"Sorry, dear guest, Bella is currently busy with another guest. Should I call someone else for you?"

The man grimaced at Jacquie's appearance, checking him out from head to toe.

"You fucking drag! You're the one who decides here?"

"I'm the owner, yes, dear guest."

Eden knew Jack ought to be boiling inside, but he was doing a great job of hiding it... The man suddenly waved his arms around, a bit weirdly, glaring at Jack.

"I-I want that girl! How much!"

This time, Jack lost his smile, and Rose was the one to stand up, putting her hands on the guest's shoulder with her most charming smile on.

"I'm sorry, dear guest, but Bella is under the age restriction for this kind of service... However, I'd be happy to take care of you if you want."

Despite asserting her words with a sexy wink, it fell completely flat. The man looked at her as if she were an idiot and started laughing.

"I said I want that one! Age restriction? What age restriction? You are all fucking outlaws anyway!"

A silence took over the room. Jack glanced at Eden, and she slowly stood up this time, giving a little smile to Mr. Charles. The old man sighed and picked up his glass, shaking his head. Those arrogant youngsters, he thought...

In the middle of the jazz bar, the drunk young man was smirking, looking amused by Rose's cold expression. The hostess had dropped her nice smile and was crossing her arms, expressionlessly listening to his rant.

"You think I don't know?" he continued. "I can do whatever I want with you. The law doesn't apply here! You're just trash, criminals! I can do anything to you and no one would care! So get that little bitch here now!"

Rose sighed, not impressed in the slightest. The lack of response from the staff surprised the young man, but no one around was batting an eye. Even worse, some of the guests looked at him as if he was a nuisance. A cold atmosphere fell on the room, and suddenly, the jazz music wasn't giving off such a pleasant ambiance anymore.

"Stop being an idiot, man..." whispered his friend, trying to pull him back. "Don't make a fuss now... We were having fun..."

"Seriously?" retorted the drunk. "Who cares! This isn't the Core; there's no laws here! You can do whatever you want to these people! Isn't that why we came here to have fun?"

He was half-smirking and half-aggressive, which was enough to make everyone uncomfortable. Some of the other customers were glancing toward the door, probably wondering if they should leave before things took a bad turn. Yet, all of the staff seemed extremely calm, as if they were used to these kinds of situations.

"This is not the kind of fun this establishment is offering, sir," said Jack with a stern voice. "I will politely remind you, this club is open to gentlemen only. We will have to escort you out unless you temper your attitude."

Rose sighed, waving her curls, and returned to sit with some other customers, leaving the young men alone at their table. Now, it looked like they were isolated from the other people in the bar, and everyone had turned their glares to them. The previously joyous atmosphere of the bar had turned a bit scarier and somewhat sour, even with the jazz still playing in the background.

However, this only angered the young men more, as they felt isolated. Out of the group of four, two were looking a bit concerned about their position at the moment, but one of them stood to come by the drunkard's side with an aggressive stance.

"Hey, you better show some respect," he said. "My friend is just a bit drunk, but this is a bar; you should handle it. Gentlemen, my ass. Aren't you just prostitutes... and a fag!"

"Those pretty chicks here are hostesses, and I'm a bartender. And a drag queen, darling. The 'queen' part is important," said Jack, with a smile that didn't go up to his eyes.

"You're just a bunch of trash living off others' money," hissed the man. "So now, you're going to take my friend's money, get that whore from wherever she is, give us a nice bedroom, and close your damn mouths."

This time, Eden stepped forward. Unlike Jack and Rose, she didn't smile once at those men, simply standing in front of them with an emotionless expression. She knew this wasn't even worth getting mad at. They had heard much worse before, and people from the Suburbs were stronger than that.

"This is the first and only warning. Please get out before we have to escort you out."

"What the..."

However, one of the friends who had been silent so far suddenly looked scared and jumped to his feet, grabbing his friends.

"Hey, hey, seriously, cut it out. Let's go."

The other two looked surprised and brushed him off with an angry expression.

"What the fuck! Why should we go? We came here to have fun, and yet they are giving us that shitty attitude!"

"Man, we can't make a fuss here if they call the mafia..."

"What?"

The man glanced at Eden.

It was clear those young men had come here knowing nothing about the rules. Just because they belonged to the Core, they thought of themselves as untouchable. They had no idea that just because their laws didn't apply here, it didn't mean that there weren't other rules.

Yet, he didn't feel threatened. Not by the drag queen or the young blonde woman staring at him with those cold, hazel eyes. She was half a head shorter than he was and looked rather thin too. He hesitated, his friend pulling on his shirt again.

"Come on, man, let's go back. We're gonna get in trouble..."

"What trouble? What mafia? They are nobodies! Who cares about those criminals!"

Eden sighed and glanced back at Jack, but the bartender was visibly done with them. He rolled his eyes and went back behind the counter, meaning he was leaving that situation to be handled by Eden.

"...So you're not going to leave?" she asked, her eyes going back to the duo of drunk friends.

"Call the mafia, my ass! You scum don't–"

He felt the pain before even catching a glimpse of the action. With a perfect rotation, Eden had suddenly raised her leg to hit the side of his face. The strength of her kick sent him to the floor, two meters away. The man whimpered loudly in front of all the shocked customers, but she wasn't done.

His friend had barely realized their mistake when Eden jumped on her other leg and rotated once more to send another kick right into his flank. The nearby guests heard the horrible sound of several bones cracking, and right after that, he was sent in the same direction as his friend, brutally landing on top of him. Now, the two of them were gasping for air with stupid looks on their faces, shocked and in utter pain. Eden calmly walked toward them, and the two men were horrified. Not by that woman, but by the incredible amount of force she had in her legs.

"Y-you... Damn..."

"I had warned you," she said, lifting her leg again.

She didn't need to use it again, however. Both men rushed to get back on their feet, holding their injured body parts, and scampered outside, whining and yelling insults from the street. Inside the club, the girls were all satisfied with this conclusion. The two other men who had stayed behind awkwardly stood up and silently made their way outside, taking the long way around the tables to carefully avoid Eden.

The other guests had smiles on, not so surprised about the turn of events. Aside from the guys Eden had just kicked out, most of the men there were regulars. They knew perfectly well that the people working there could fend for themselves. And even if they didn't, there were other powers in place.

Eden sighed and put down her leg, turned around, and lowered her head.

"Sorry for the commotion," she simply said.

"Alright, dear guests," said Jack from behind the bar. "Let's get back to all the fun, shall we? Who wants another drink? Half price on me!"

The club quickly went back to a joyful and pleasant atmosphere. Eden walked up to the counter and saw Jack's smile diminish while he prepared more drinks.

"What a bunch of assholes..." she muttered.

"It's alright, honey, nothing new."

"Maybe not, but if we lose the protection of the mafia and those people know..."

"We'll just need to hope someone will take over. ...Someone good."

Eden took the new glasses of brandy with a sour expression on. She knew what Jack meant. They were the people of the Suburbs and those living and working there. Everyone had a story, and they hadn't landed here by chance or mistake. There was nowhere else to go, even if things got worse. They were subject to the laws of who was stronger, where they lived. They needed that protection. If someone other than Old Man Long took over the area, they couldn't predict what would happen next.

Trying to hide her concerns, Eden walked back to her customer, chatting with Mr. Charles as usual.

"Those are impressive legs, young lady," chuckled the old man, bringing his drink to his mustache.

"They do get useful from time to time," replied Eden, a bit nervous.

She didn't like talking about her legs. She could feel stares from all over the room, curious guests, or those who had already guessed the truth.

Mr. Charles wasn't duped either, and he gently patted her knee.

"Don't worry, young lady. Back in my day, those were the norm. Times just change too fast for people to even be respectful of others' circumstances anymore..."

Eden smiled, but she didn't want to talk about that anymore. She quickly shifted the subject to something else, like the music Mr. Charles recognized playing in the background or his grandchildren who were giving him trouble. He was a nice man, just a bit too curious about a nameless hostess at times. This old gentleman was nostalgic about another time before the typical sterile and boring days in the Core. Eden couldn't tell him how he should have considered himself lucky.

"Evening, bitches!"

How much trouble were they going to get tonight? Eden glanced toward the entrance, but this time, no one in the bar felt confident anymore.

A young Asian man was standing there with the smile of a shark and flashy clothes. Everything about him smelled like trouble, from the large tattoos covering half his face to the guns he was wearing on his belt, which had attracted Eden's eyes immediately by reflex. She knew that model. They were produced by the Core and programmed not to shoot at any vital parts. Like most weapons the Core created, those were made for self-defense, but the bullets were still very real. This time, she got up before Jack said anything. The young man walked in confidently, followed by two Asian men, both as fat as pigs and extremely ugly. They were bald, with tattoos covering every inch of their visible skin. Their expression was that of someone who had just bit a sour lemon.

"Young Master Kris," said Xixi, jumping on her feet and forcing a smile. "You haven't come in a while..."

"Hello there, cutie," he said, wrapping an arm around her waist as if she were his possession. "Ah, I've been busy. Busy waiting for the old man to make some important decisions, if you know what I mean..."

As he said those words, his eyes went up to Jack. The bartender wasn't forcing himself to smile, staring at Kris with a stern expression. Unlike the earlier clients, they couldn't handle that annoying man so easily. He kept pouring drinks and remaining composed, although the situation was significantly more worrying.

"I hope Master Long stays healthy as long as possible," said Jack.

Those words didn't please Kris. His smirk disappeared, and he walked to the bar, slamming his fist on the counter. Eden didn't move, but she was ready to intervene at any moment. Jack had this under control, for now. They only had to wait until that idiot was done and gone.

"I can't wait to kick you fucking Parts out of here. I don't need semi-humans to work for me. You guys belong in the junkyard."

"Noted, Master Kris."

Jack's calm was impressive.

If it was anyone else, he might have responded with more spite, but this wasn't just anybody. Kris Yang was Master Long's nephew and only living blood descendant, one of his most probable successors. He could inherit this neighborhood soon. The old man had yet to name his successor, and that wasn't a good sign. Everyone knew being a blood relative wasn't enough to become one of the mafia lords around there. They needed someone who was able to stand among and against the Zodiac, the ten mafia lords of the Suburbs. Each had their own territory and their own rules; hence, tensions were bound to arise anytime there was a succession issue.

Moreover, many people, even inside the Dragon's district, were against Kris being chosen. Eden had already heard rumors about at least three other possible successors for the old man. No wonder that brat was acting more and more recklessly every day...

As Jack remained calm and ignored his provocation, the young man turned to Eden, who was standing a few steps away, staring at him. She wasn't doing anything but looking on. Yet, Kris put on an annoyed expression, glaring back at her.

"You too, you fucking Part bitch. You'll be gone as soon as I get that chair as the Zodiac. ...And stop staring at me!"

He suddenly took out his gun and shot at Eden's left leg.

She didn't move, only frowning and looking down. The bullet had put a hole in her dress, and a little piece of dark gray metal was now visible in that hole. Eden pulled her dress' skirt to hide the hole. That bastard had done that on purpose... This time, she couldn't hold back her glare, but her lips remained resolutely sealed. Kris chuckled.

"That's right, keep your damn mouth shut, you little pest. People like you are just trash..."

He laughed at her and leaned over the counter to grab a bottle. Jack worried for a second, but he only began drinking right from the bottle and walked upstairs, taking Xixi with him. The young woman only had time to give Jack a glance before she was taken upstairs.

Eden hesitated, but Jack let out a long sigh and shook his head, getting back to work. Hence, Eden walked back to her client. However, Mr. Charles was already getting up.

"I'm sorry, Mr. Charles. Are you leaving already?"

"Sorry, darling, but that's a lot of excitement for this old man. Don't worry, dear, I'll come back sometime soon. Here."

He gave her a little bill, which surprised Eden. No one used those anymore. She had only seen actual bills a couple of times before... The green piece of paper weighed strangely in her hand. Mr. Charles chuckled.

"I know you like old things like these. And me! See you some other time, Miss Eden."

Although she walked him back to the entrance, Eden had a sour feeling about her customer leaving so soon. She turned around, but everywhere else was busy. Two of the girls had already gone upstairs with a customer, and the ones remaining were doing a great job of keeping the atmosphere joyful and busy.

Eden walked up to the bar, and Jack handed her a glass.

"There you go, darling."

"Is Xixi okay?"

"Don't worry, he won't do anything bad while the Old Man is still alive and kickin'. Plus, he likes her. Xixi always said he never goes further than the usual services."

"What an ass..." growled Eden, grabbing her drink.

"More like a brat. Goodness, if that guy becomes a Zodiac, then we are really in motha-fuckin' trouble."

Eden nodded.

"I really hope the old man stays around for a while." She sighed.

"Tell me about it. I don't know what's the best option. Half the Zodiac will get rid of Parts like you and me. The Yakuza would kill the twins... Let's face it, Eden, half the chicks here would become targets because of their past customers. Girl, we gotta lay real low for a while."

Jack shook his head and poured another drink for himself, his bangs swinging sideways with his head's movements.

"Eden, honey, you should leave now before that jerk comes back down. That little piece of shit enjoys ruining your legs. If the guy shoots at ya again, you're going to have to repair them, and that ain't something you can afford, hun."

Eden nodded. She hadn't even dared look at the damage under her skirt, but she was a bit worried about that as well.

"...What about security here? I bet your bouncer ran off after seeing Kris Yang."

"Don't worry, babe, I still got my good old girl under the counter," he said, tapping the countertop. "Those babies from the twenty-first century make a mean job, and they don't care which part they're shooting at."

He smiled and gave her a little wink.

"Alright. See ya, Jack. Be careful."

"You too, hun."

Eden finished her drink in one go with a faint smile and walked downstairs.

Their dressing room felt too big, silent, and messy without all the girls there. Eden walked to one of the seats in front of the mirrors and slowly took off her makeup. The red on her lips disappeared to leave a pale pink, and her skin was whiter than the foundation she had on too. She only left the curls in her hair as they were, only brushing her fingers through them to push them out of her face.

Then, she sighed and spun the chair around, her eyes going down to the skirt of her red dress. The hem was at her mid-thigh, a few inches below the hole Kris' bullet had dug in. Eden slowly pulled up the skirt. Surely enough, a piece of the dark gray metal was showing.

The square area around the bullet hole was sticking out on her leg, the metal indented. Eden grimaced and grabbed one of the girls' tweezers to dig that thing out. The little piece of metal fell on the floor, and she glared at it. That part was going to cost a lot to repair. She'd have to cover it with skirts for a while... She took a deep breath.

"SIN, deactivate the camouflage."

Immediately, all the skin on her legs vanished. Instead, she was left with the truth: two dark gray robotic legs, without an ounce of flesh.

Eden grabbed her bag, taking out her clothes to change into. She quickly traded the red sequin dress for a long-sleeved turtleneck bodysuit and a pair of cargo pants. Putting her long hair into a high bun and grabbing her face mask, she threw her dress in the automated washing machine and got ready to leave in just a few minutes. Activating the oxygen flow in her mask, she stepped out of the bar and walked into Chicago's nightlife.

# CHAPTER TWO

The neighborhood where Jack's bar was located was abuzz at this hour. Many people came here to have fun and forget their troubles or real lives for one night. Most of these people were coming from the Core, and Eden could recognize them in one glance. Perfect haircuts, bright smiles, clean and brand new clothes. They had no need to hide their shiny, white teeth behind masks as long as they could endure the smell, pollution, and dust for a few hours. They would be back to their polished and worryless lives before dawn. For people like Eden, however, there was nowhere else to go back to. She walked to the bus station, before remembering she needed more money this month... Eden hesitated. She glanced up at one of the giant screens on the buildings. The air quality that night wasn't good... and her face mask probably only had enough oxygen for the trip back. If she made a stop by the shop to recharge her oxygen, that would be more money, but she needed that refill anyway.

Moreover, taking the bus saved time, but it was still costly. The blonde shook her head and changed her trajectory without remorse. Like every day on her way home, she was doing the math over and over in her head. Adding up the cost of what she needed to buy, subtracting what she had to pay. Eden had always been good with numbers, but no matter how many times she did the calculations, it never fell on the positive side.

Walking added an extra half hour to her trip back. Most of the streets were empty. No one wanted to waste oxygen with a trip outside. The few people she crossed paths with were on their way to work, probably not able to afford the

25

bus, like her. Although all but their eyes were covered by their face masks, no one lifted their eyes off the ground to look at her. Everyone was busy going their own way. Sometimes though, she'd recognize a familiar face and nod, but no matter what, Eden kept walking. No one had time to stop for a chat.

Finally, she spotted the little corner store. She walked in, deactivating her mask right away.

"*Namaste*, Miss Eden!"

Eden walked up to the counter, handing her mask to the middle-aged man behind the glass.

"How are you, Said?" she asked with a tired voice.

To her surprise, the man answered in Hindi with lots of gestures. Eden frowned.

"Did you deactivate your translating software again? I thought you had taken a full one this time?" she asked.

"No, no! No money!"

Eden grimaced. Every time his shop was in a pinch, the poor man had to deactivate his software to save himself some money. It was always bad news for him though, as most people wouldn't bother to try and understand him. Although Eden had no idea what he was saying, he kept talking in Hindi, so she nodded, aware that he only needed to vent. He knew enough English to understand his customers, but he most likely didn't realize he was using his native tongue instead.

"Pay?" he asked.

Eden nodded.

"Yeah, making the transfer right away."

She felt the little device in her neck vibrate and mentally accounted for the money that must have been taken out of her account. Said nodded and thanked her, or something along those lines, and she left the little shop, taking a deep breath before putting her mask back on.

She was already halfway home when she left the little shop. Eden had to live in a different neighborhood from the one she worked in. Not many places hired Parts for many reasons. Not only did people like her have a bad reputation in many communities, but they had more costs than others to maintain their cybernetic parts, and no one wanted a worker who could physically break down at any moment... She put all those dark thoughts aside and instead began to sing the lyrics of the song that was playing when she left the bar. It was one of her favorites, one of those old songs she could listen to and forget everything else.

"*Homesick, tired, all alone in a big city, why should everybody pity me... Nighttime's falling, folks are a-singin'... they dance till break of day...*"

She had heard it so many times, she could hum and whistle every instrument's part. She would swing her head and go on like this, forgetting how tired she was. It was slow, dreamy jazz that matched that time of the night. She liked the raspy, deep voice of the singer as if she could see him in an old black-and-white movie.

Just like that, with those legs that wouldn't get sore or tired, she arrived home in no time to the familiar, quieter streets of the Lower West Side. This part of the Suburbs wasn't really under any of the Zodiacs' watch. It was stuck somewhere between the territories of the Italian Tiger, the Chinese Dragon, and the Mexican Eagle. While the first two didn't really care for that territory, the last one was using it as an excuse to cause trouble. Sometimes, men wearing luchador masks and driving big vehicles would suddenly come down the streets and cause a ruckus for no reason just to see if they could annoy the bigger monsters. It never really happened though. Old Man Long was too busy to care, and the Italian Tiger didn't seem interested at all. In the end, only the people from Eden's neighborhood would suffer in silence.

"Evening, Miss Eden," said a man when she finally arrived in front of the building.

That man was middle-aged, wearing a bandana over his face to protect himself from the dust, and a rifle. Eden frowned.

"Evening, Manuel. What's going on?" she asked, pointing toward the gun.

"Ah, you know, the usual," he replied with a strong Hispanic accent. "My wife is grumpy, so I came down to stand guard. A kid was shot last week, and we heard gunshots two hours ago... but I'm happy you're okay."

"Thanks," said Eden, glancing toward the upper floors. "You be careful. ...How is the baby?"

"She's really cute, but she cries a lot. My wife and I had a fight again; she wants another one!"

Eden felt a bit sorry for him; the poor man looked exhausted. He would probably have been better and safer upstairs than standing here on the sidewalk.

"But you have that job at the factory now..." she said.

"I know! But you know how my wife is. She thinks we will all be condemned by God for using those. I try to tell her I can bring good money home now, but she doesn't like it."

He pointed toward his neck, where he had recently been implanted with a SIN. Eden sighed. Manuel was a good man, but he had struggled so much until he could finally get one, and it included some sacrifices as well. His wife was very religious, and she hated anything that modified their bodies. She wouldn't even talk to Eden and cursed or started praying in Spanish every time they saw each other.

"It will be fine," she said. "I'm sure she'll come around."

"I don't know, Miss Eden, but thank you. I hope you have a good night."

"Good night, Manuel."

Without waiting anymore, Eden walked toward the stairs. However, as soon as she found herself there, she hesitated. The stairs went two ways: up or down. She glanced at the stairs going down to the basement and hesitated. ...No, she shouldn't. She ignored it and ran upstairs. Her apartment was on the fourth floor. As soon as she got home, Eden let out a long sigh of relief and dropped her bag on the floor. She didn't have enough belongings for this place to be messy, but it certainly had a lot going on.

She had a table against the window, with dozens of little pots filled with dirt. There wasn't anything sprouting, it looked like they had just been left there. Eden walked to that table first, checking if anything had happened. She was so used to deception, though, she only glanced once and didn't look back again. She walked to the mattress on the ground and let herself fall on it. She wasn't really tired, but she did feel a bit... out of it. She regretted not staying longer at the bar. Being here, between four walls, was a bit depressing. If it had been a better day, she would have gone up to the roof, but she couldn't waste more oxygen today. She sighed and grabbed the little notepad that was left somewhere on her bed. She wrote down, again, all of the expenses for the week. She could skip dinner and save a bit of money there. Jack let her wash her clothes at the bar too, and she could go without water until her next workday. She scratched her neck, her SIN a bit itchy.

She wrote down what she had earned at the bar, and her work at the shop. The number she had in mind was still bigger, though. The usual costs for her mom's care were just a little bit under both combined. If she added the special care, and her own expenses... Eden took a deep breath and closed her eyes. She couldn't manage a third job. She had no time for it, and the first two she had already been lucky to find in her condition. She glared at that notepad, a bit annoyed. Why did things always end up like this?

She glanced at the window. Do those people have any idea of the struggles they faced on this side of the river?

After a while, she left the notepad on her bed, stood up, and walked back to the stairs. This time, she was resolutely going down to the basement. She hadn't been there in... what, a week? She arrived in front of the locked door and pushed the number combination.

"*Wrong code. Two attempts remaining.*"

Eden rolled her eyes. He had changed the code again?

"SIN, call Loir."

However, nothing happened. His SIN number too? Eden sighed and banged against the door, annoyed.

"Loir, open up, you paranoid idiot!"

The door opened right away and Eden almost fell forward, not prepared for it to open so quickly. She sighed and closed the door behind her.

The basement was completely dark. A bit cautious, Eden walked in silently, each of her steps echoing. It was like being in an underground parking lot, but a small one. After a while, a light bulb flickered in one corner. She heard a desk chair rolling toward her.

"Good morning, my little Eden."

She turned around, a bit annoyed.

Loir was the most unique character she knew, and that was saying a lot. She didn't know his real name. From what she had heard before, he had at least five or six aliases. She finally spotted him in the darkness, sitting on his desk chair, perched like an owl with his bare toes out, wearing shiny, blue nail polish. The rest of his clothes were all black, so dark it was hard to even know what he was actually wearing. He was bald, but he had so many tattoos on his face and head that it was hard to tell in one glance. Although he had dozens of tattoos, Eden could only read a handful of them. The most obvious one was the word "Anarkia" tattooed on the left side of his head, and she also knew the Chinese symbol on his neck meant pain. The rest of it was presently covered by his clothes. His skinny arms were wrapped around his knees as he was staring at her. It was a disturbing stare, mostly because she couldn't figure out where his pupils were; his eyeballs were completely tattooed.

"It's evening," she retorted.

"Maybe here."

She knew she shouldn't get into his little mind games. Loir was crazy in his own way.

He tilted his head and smiled, revealing two missing teeth. Then, he rolled his chair to another side of the basement. The screens lit back up one by one, all fourteen of them. Loir was seated in front of a giant table, his keyboards scattered all over in random order. Despite the number of screens, she couldn't tell how many computers there really were, as she'd see his mouse jump from one screen to another from time to time, with no logic either. It would disappear to the left side of a computer on the far right and reappear at the top of another one located at the other end. She couldn't even figure out if he had messed it up to play, or perhaps to confuse people who could intrude and try to use his things.

"Eden is not sleepy tonight," he whistled, his eyes back on the screens. "What is she up to?"

"It's too early to sleep," she said in a low voice, although it was half a lie.

"Mh... I can smell someone who needs money."

She glared at his back, but Loir wasn't looking at her. Eden crossed her arms and walked up to stand next to him, glancing at the screens. One was displaying a Russian news channel, two others the news of the various Cores throughout the world. Eden stared at the pictures and videos of places she had never been, curious. She wondered if all Cores were the same, living without a care about the rest of the world. Another channel was showing the Green Earth Party news, where images of the thriving forests were displayed. It changed into gorgeous, blue images of fish swimming in the aquamarine sea. She stared at that even longer.

"...It's fake."

"What?"

Loir pointed at the screen she was looking at without looking at it himself. His other fingers were activating like crazy spiders on one of the keyboards, sending coding information on a black screen.

"Those images. They took it from a documentary from the twenty-first century. This isn't the real current state of the Western American sea. They are just clearing the place to build three other Cores. The water is still too polluted for fish like that to be there. But fear not, they will make more artificial beaches."

Eden remained silent. She knew those images couldn't be trusted. She knew the other side. The Green Earth Party only had green as a word in its name, and that was it. They showed the people in the Cores what they needed to see to sleep soundlessly...

"By the way, a new job came in," he said with his scary smile.

"I'm not here to take another job, Loir. I just... wondered how you were, and came downstairs."

"Well. I'm still aliiiiiiiiive," he suddenly started singing.

Loir began singing some old song loudly, wiggling around on his chair and making some strange movements with his shoulders, as if they had a life of their own. Eden stepped back, careful not to get hit. He really was crazy... After a while, he finished with a spin of his chair, his arms spread with a big smile as if he was waiting for her to applaud.

"...Are you done?" she asked.

"Mh, yes! I mean, unless you want an encore..."

"I'm good. Now, the job?"

"...What job?"

"The job you mentioned two minutes ago, Loir!"

"Oh. That?"

"Yes, that. What about it? What is it?"

He started laughing.

"You'll love it... They are paying a lot of money for it."

"Who? The Russians again?"

"No, no, no, Eden. The Italians. Some nice, pretty Italian bills," he chuckled, rubbing his fingertips.

"How much money...?" she wondered, trying to tell herself it was stupid to even ask.

"Hm... *abbastanza per comprare tanta pizza*!"

"For fuck's sake, Loir, how much?"

His laughing turned hysterical, and Eden sighed again. She knew better than to answer his provocations, but she had given in again. She waited for him to be done laughing.

"Twenty-two million," he suddenly blurted out between two laughs.

"T-twenty-two...?" she repeated.

A cold chill ran down her spine. There was no easy job at this price, but it was... tempting. With such a sum, it would pay for her mom's expenses and hers for at least a few years, maybe even a decade.

"See? I told you. A lot of pizza!"

"What the heck do they want for that price...?" she muttered. "Some data from the Core? Or a hacking bomb?"

"Oh, no, no, little Eden. The Tiger just wants to play with a cute little mouse."

"...A mouse?"

Loir chuckled and tilted his head.

"The price on Ghost's head just went up, little mouse. Twenty-two million. Congrats!"

Eden's blood went cold in half a second. The Italian was looking for her? Ghost already had several bounties on her head, but the price had just been raised again! Was it because of the last job? She had worked for the Italian before, but in the last job, she had worked against him. Was he pissed? Eden's heart was going crazy with conjectures. If the Italian was looking for her, she wouldn't be able to go north again. No, maybe she was just paranoid. He had no way to know who she was, for now...

"When did he put that bounty up?" she asked.

"Oh, not a bounty; an offer," said Loir, staring at his painted toes. "It did specify he wants you alive, and he's willing to pay two million just for any piece of info. Maybe you should sell yourself if you need money..."

"Very funny, Loir."

"I know what I'd do with that much money..."

Eden reacted immediately. She took out the little knife hidden in her sleeve and pointed it toward Loir's head. He squinted at the blade.

"You better fucking keep your mouth closed shut, Loir. I could rat you out too."

He chuckled and stuck out his tongue, revealing the large piercing on it.

"Don't worry, Eden... I sell secrets. People pay me for secrets. ...But a friend's secret? Now that costs a looooot of money, little mouse..."

Eden lowered her weapon a little bit. Loir was a very strange character, but he had more to lose if they were found out, from what she knew. His bounty was much higher than hers, and Loir had one on each of his fake names. He was working with dangerous people behind all those screens. Moreover, he had never stepped out of this basement since she had met him here four years ago. None of the other residents even had any idea there was someone here; they all thought it was locked by the previous tenant.

She eventually put her weapon back, and he smiled even more.

"...Fine. But do you know what the Tiger's got after me?"

"Who knows? You probably pissed off the wrong kitty, meow meow... He does send out some minions to retrieve some things for him sometimes. Maybe he's trying to get rid of the competition or... get it for himself."

Eden frowned. She didn't like this at all. Having someone on her tail, one of the mafia lords at that? She'd much rather be left alone. At least, her identity was still concealed for now. No one, except for Loir, could connect Ghost to her. She sighed, crossing her arms with a sour expression. Maybe it wasn't a good idea if she returned to the Dark Web so soon after all. She had never seen the guy, but she knew enough rumors about the Italian Tiger. He was not someone she could afford to piss off, and if he was looking for Ghost, he probably wouldn't back down anytime soon. He was known as one of the most dangerous of the mafia lords. They all were, but the Italian had his own fame. She was cautious by nature, but he was probably on top of the list of people she didn't want to be associated with. Of all the different mafias reigning in the Suburbs, the Italian mafia was the one she hated the most...

Eden clenched her fist without thinking, her memories taking over. She'd never work for that kind of scum again if she was given a choice...

"Oh..."

Loir was watching one of the screens displaying video surveillance. Eden frowned and moved to his other side to look at it too.

"The Eagle's..." she whispered.

Those were men of the Mexican mafia indeed. Once again, their faces were covered by luchador or eagle masks, but it made it even more obvious. Those men were ruthless, even toward those supposedly under their protection... Eden recognized the narrow street behind their building. She squinted, trying to see what they were doing. It looked like they were shooting at something and laughing.

"You know if we really come from monkeys," said Loir, "those guys are proof that some people evolved faster than others..."

"Loir, open the back door for me, please."

He tilted his head, raising an eyebrow.

"Our Kitty is going out? Why?"

"That's where the dog is."

"You'll be in danger, though..."

"Open the damn door!"

He raised his finger and pushed a button on the keyboard.

Somewhere farther in the darkness, a door opened. Eden took a deep breath. She didn't have her mask with her; she couldn't afford to stay outside for more than a couple of minutes. Eden ran there, prepared for anything. She wasn't one to intervene in those kinds of things, but she just couldn't ignore it.

Every morning, she saw that dog in the back alley. It was a female, a big one, probably a mix of several breeds, with short hair. She wouldn't let the humans approach her, but she stayed around as the locals fed her. Eden liked that dog. It was rare to see animals around as they usually died young, from hunger or whatever disease they'd catch, being in the polluted streets all day. Most of the locals didn't have the means to care for a pet, but they still tried to look out for those living in their area if they could. Eden knew that dog sometimes slept in their building or the neighboring ones when someone let her in.

That door led her to another back street. Eden had to climb up some stairs and walked a few steps to get to the right one, but she could already hear them sniggering.

"Come on!"

She heard another shot and the dog growling. That was definitely the female. Eden got as close as she could, staying close to the wall and being cautious. She could smell the cheap beer, but it was clear those three were drunk even without that. Only three men? She hesitated. She had nothing to cover her appearance if they saw her. Plus, it was her building. They could find her any time...

"That bastard is still alive!"

She shivered. What were they doing? She slid a bit closer to take a look.

The dog was cornered in the dead-end street, growling furiously. However, she wasn't standing, but in a strange position, her front paws hidden, her back legs up, as if to play. However, there was obviously no play here. Because her fur was so light, a cream beige, Eden could see all the blood. Her anger rose in an instant. They had really injured her!

There was glass everywhere on the floor, and from the large foamy puddles, they had probably broken many bottles of beer on the asphalt. Eden clenched her fist a bit more. She just couldn't sit still.

"Hey, leave it alone, *cabrónes*."

The three men turned around. They were young, from what Eden could see of their eyes. However, with these kinds of guys, young meant stupid and reckless.

"Look at that little bitch showing up," one of them chuckled. "Playing hero? Is this your dog?"

Eden stood still, not answering. She wasn't moving, but her eyes were counting. They each had a gun. Two were referenced weapons, one was an older model. The last one was the most dangerous. No matter how fast she was, Eden knew she couldn't outrun a bullet. She glanced behind them. The dog looked about to collapse. She wanted to go there, but she wouldn't be able to without walking between those three idiots.

"Isn't she rather pretty," said one of them. "You got a name, lovely? Want to come with us?"

"My name is 'fuck you'," Eden retorted. "Go play elsewhere."

"Feisty, feisty... Should I fill your head with lead, bitch?"

Eden tilted her head. She wasn't really impressed. Those kinds of insults and threats were a weekly thing for someone living in this area. Especially a young woman. She was one of the very few who could walk alone in the streets.

Seeing that she didn't respond to a gun pointed at her, the men frowned. They could tell when something was off, and a girl unafraid of a weapon surely seemed like it.

"Should I zap them?" a voice suddenly chuckled in her ear.

"I told you to stop zapping people," she retorted.

Loir's voice in her ear giggled. She frowned. Actually, she had told him to stop hacking into her SIN as well. Of course, he wouldn't listen. Suddenly, one of the men who carried one of the modern guns twitched uncontrollably. One of the others asked him what was wrong in Spanish, but the guy seemed lost. His arms twitched again as if they had just gotten an electric shock.

Eden ignored them and walked toward them, aiming for the dog. As she reached them, one of the guys reacted.

"Hey, bitch! Where do you think you're–"

Eden had learned one thing about street fights: whoever attacks first has the greater chance of surviving. She flipped her body at the last second and sent a high kick into his face, her favorite move. The guy flew toward the other side, his face smashing the brick wall with a horrible sound. His two friends reacted immediately, lifting their guns and swearing in Spanish again.

She was ready, though. She jumped to the side, grabbed the other gun by its barrel, and pushed it out of her way. The shot fired and hit somewhere on the asphalt behind her. At this point, the other guy had his gun aimed right at her, half an inch away from her face. Eden turned her hazel eyes toward him, just in time to hear him chuckle.

"Die, b–"

Before he finished his sentence, his eyes rolled over, and he fell down on his knees unconscious. Eden grimaced, even if she was a little grateful. She really hated when Loir did that... The only guy remaining, whose weapon she had pushed aside, went livid.

"You're a hacker..." he gasped.

He wasn't wrong, but he wasn't right either. He probably didn't know how it worked, and hence he had no way to know Eden had a partner, but she wasn't going to explain. She took his weapon forcefully and turned it against him.

"S-sorry," he said. "I... I'll go..."

"Yeah. As if you bastards let anyone go."

Eden shot.

She had aimed for his stomach, and the guy fell to the side, pure shock on his face. He probably didn't expect she'd shoot for real. She wasn't going to let anyone who had seen her face and her skills live.

"...Loir?"

"Ding-dong. They are dead, dead, and re-dead."

She looked, but indeed the marks on their necks had gone purple or black, a sign their SINs had just gone off forever. She sighed. Eden didn't like killing by any means. However, she knew all too well what an unforgiving world it was for those who trusted the wrong people.

Pushing her blonde hair back, she walked past the bodies to go to the dog. The poor female was still growling, cautious of Eden, but she didn't have the energy to attack anyway. When Eden got closer, she began whining.

"It's okay... It's okay..."

As she caressed her for the first time, Eden felt her heart sink. From the injuries, she knew that dog wasn't going to survive. Her front paws were sliced open, the bones showing. Eden's soles were getting tainted by all the blood on the ground. She sighed and crouched down. The dog barked again faintly, but

Eden wasn't scared anyway. She frowned, looking at the dog's belly.

"You... You had babies?"

She had noticed the female had gotten fatter lately, but she hadn't realized the dog was actually pregnant.

"Eden!"

She turned her head. At the other end of the street, a young Hispanic man was standing there, out of breath and looking horrified. His sleeveless T-shirt was showing off his muscles and sweat. Eden frowned. She really didn't need him to show up now.

"*Madre de Dios,* what the heck did you do!" he said, walking toward her, careful not to trip over the bodies.

"They were torturing her."

"The dog? Eden, you just killed those men! What are you going to do if they send more here!"

She ignored him, looking back toward the mama dog.

"Lito, I think the dog's nursing. Did she have her babies yet?"

"What...?"

He stared at her baffled, and his eyes fell on the dog. At a time like this, she was asking about the dog? He hesitated, glancing down at the stray. He grabbed the cross on his chest, but he had a sour face while checking her overall state.

"Yeah, maybe... Anyway, what happened? What are we going to do about... this?"

"Don't worry, nobody will know."

"Nobody? Eden, we have three fucking bodies here!"

"Shut up, Lito. Or are you going to shout that even louder, so all the neighbors hear it? Anyway, weren't you ignoring me? Why are you talking so much now?"

He hesitated, but it was true. They hadn't actually talked in ages. Although Lito and Eden lived in the same building, he had been avoiding her on purpose lately.

"I heard the gunshots... I was worried it was you."

"Well, it was," she replied, very calmly.

Eden kept caressing the dog, but she was looking around. He realized she was looking for the puppies. He sighed.

"She must have hidden them. Eden, they're probably dead. Let's go back inside..."

"You go back inside," she retorted. "I'll look."

She got up and started rummaging through the mess of that back alley; Lito was frowning. Sometimes he couldn't understand Eden. She was risking her life by being out there so long, and for what? To look for some dogs who were probably dead already?!

Yet Eden was stubborn like that. He watched her look in every nook and cranny of that trashy spot. She wasn't afraid to turn over some trash bags,

35

check under the dumpsters, or inside some empty boxes. Lito sighed and began looking around too. The faster they found those dogs, the faster they'd be back inside.

"Here!" she suddenly exclaimed. She was somewhat crouched down, and half of her body was pushed between two large piles of trash, but behind them, she had found the puppies. She stepped back, carrying two of them, one in each hand. They were whining and wriggling around in her grip.

"Is there more?"

"No... the others weren't moving or breathing," she said.

Lito sighed and nodded. Those two were the lucky ones. One was dark brown, with a large white spot around his snout, and the other was brindle. They were quite ugly, in his opinion. They were probably a mix of pitbull and something else, a large breed. Eden put them down next to their mom, and they began suckling right away. The mom was lying on her flank, without much strength left. Eden sighed and patted her head gently.

"Alright... Let's go back inside now."

"You go back," she said. "I'll stay until they are done eating."

"What for?" he asked, annoyed.

"I can't leave them alone."

"Eden, you–"

"Fucking stop telling me what to do, Lito. Isn't that why you stopped talking to me in the first place? If you don't like what I'm doing, you leave me alone. Don't patronize me or tell me what to do."

"I didn't... Eden, this is a different matter. You're going to get sick out here!"

As an answer, Eden glared back at him.

"...Do you want me to zap him, Kitty?" chuckled a voice in her ear.

Eden ignored Loir and kept caressing the dogs. Behind her, Lito sighed, putting his hands on his hips, at a loss at what to do.

"Fine, I did say I don't like you working there, okay? I still don't! It's not a good place! You're selling your body, Eden!"

"So what?" she retorted, annoyed. "Are you going to pay my bills, perhaps? My mother's? We don't all have the luck you have, Lito. Yes, I work as a hostess, I'm a Part, and everything else. It's true, and I didn't want to lie to you about it. If you don't like it, I don't care. Now go back inside. I don't want to ruin a future doctor's lungs."

"Eden, I just..."

His words got stuck in his throat. It was useless, anyway. What could he have said that she would have actually listened to? Lito sighed and walked back inside, leaving her outside with the dogs and the bodies. Eden heard him leave, but she didn't look at him. She kept petting the dog until it really didn't move anymore. Then she grabbed the puppies as it looked like they were done eating and walked back inside.

As she returned to the basement, Loir was waiting for her, and his eyes lit up.

"Puppies!" he exclaimed.

However, Eden fell back on her rear, her head spinning a bit. It had been a little while since she had been out for so long without a mask. She put the puppies down on her legs and began coughing.

"You overdid it, Kitty..."

Eden glared at him, but she was too busy coughing to respond with something. Suddenly, Loir extended her a large mask. She recognized it. It wasn't just a mask; it was one of those very expensive oxygen converters. She glanced at him, surprised. This thing costs millions!

He smiled.

"Are you going to take it or not?" he asked.

Eden grabbed it, put it on her face, and began inhaling deeply. Having pure, fresh oxygen fill her lungs was an incredible feeling. Eden inhaled for a long time as Loir watched with a smile stuck on his face. The puppies were staring at her too, curious about what was going on. This was amazing, almost to the point she felt her throat clearing up. Once she had enough, she reluctantly handed the mask back to Loir and took another deep breath in the sanitized, filtered air of the basement.

"Feeling better?" he asked.

"Thanks..." she sighed, looking down at the pups.

"...You're welcome. I mean, if you can pay back the favor."

Eden frowned and raised her head, glaring at him.

"What?"

"I never said I'd lend it to you for free," he replied, tilting his head.

Eden was so shocked that she remained speechless for a while before suddenly standing up; the pups jumped off her lap.

"Fuck you, Loir! You never said I'd have to pay for that!"

"...I know."

His smile was annoying her to no end, but she should have known better. Loir was too calculating. It had felt strange that he'd simply handed her that mask without asking for something in return. How much had she breathed? It didn't look like he had checked, but he was asking for a favor.

"You wanted to ask me something from the start, didn't you?" she hissed, her fists clenched.

"Yes. However, I knew you'd refuse if I'd simply asked. Don't worry, it's nothing you can't do."

"I bet."

Loir knew her abilities very well. Having someone like Eden was exactly what he needed. Although he was a hacker too, Loir was more of a watcher. He doesn't dive himself; he'd send people in his stead and watch from afar. Eden didn't know why, but she knew it probably had to do with his SIN. Like most hackers, he was wearing a very corrupted one, so no one could get to him. At least half of the Zodiacs wanted Loir or another one of his names. Even

37

the government and some military organizations had bounties on his head, probably much higher than Eden's, but she had no idea.

"...What do you want?" she asked.

"Information."

Of course. It was always about money or information. Loir didn't lack the first one, despite his strange way of living. The fact that he had an oxygen converter mask and so much high-tech equipment was enough to assume that, despite his looks, he was probably the richest man a few blocks around...

"Do you know where it is?"

"Of course! I'd never send my best friend on a mission without some preparation!"

Eden grimaced. She wasn't his best friend, more likely his only one... She looked down at the puppies, who had begun playing with each other.

"...I'll do it," she said, "under one condition."

"Yes?"

"You help me get what I need to take care of the puppies. Everything. Food, toys, whatever."

"Oh, of course! I'll order them a lot of carrots!"

"Ca–...? They don't eat carrots..." she sighed.

Either way, she could always make him pay later. Loir was a weird guy, but at least he never went back on his word once he had promised her something. This wasn't because they made a deal, and it wasn't the first time he sent Eden to dive and retrieve something for him either. She slowly took off her shoes and pants, revealing her legs.

The circles were located right below her butt, and from there down, it was nothing but metal and circuits. It was good technology, but she hadn't been able to properly take care of her bionic legs. The dark gray metal was perfectly lustrated, but it still had marks of use, a few scratches here and there. Now only wearing her bodysuit, Eden resolutely walked toward Loir, and he smiled.

"Loir, the bounty..."

"Don't worry. I'll give you a long enough window. You'll have time to get in and out before anyone notices Eden has disappeared. I already have all the coordinates ready. A piece of cake!"

"It's never a piece of cake..."

"Well, there might be a few Russians on the playground with you."

"What? Russians? Fuck you, Loir! You never said–"

"Have fun!"

Loir moved quickly, extending a long cable and connecting it to the little device on her neck.

Eden went blind.

She woke up after what felt like half a second. By reflex, she jumped onto her feet and looked down.

Human legs. So he had sent her into the Dark Reality... She looked around, but it seemed Loir had dropped her in a waiting cell. There was nothing but mirrors around her, sending her reflection hundreds, if not thousands, of times. Eden stared at her other self. A tall feminine silhouette, with short white hair and golden eyes, in a white bodysuit. Ghost had her traits and her body shape, but none of her imperfections. Ghost had no wrinkles, no bumps on her skin, no color on her cheeks.

Suddenly, a robot-like voice began talking around Eden. She frowned. It did sound Russian, probably the server's automated welcome system. She agitated her fingers, checking that everything worked. They moved exactly as she had intended them to.

Eden took a deep breath and violently kicked a mirror.

A large crack appeared, and everything began blinking in red around her. The Russian voice became louder and more pressing, but Eden kept kicking until it came flying off. Suddenly, everything around her exploded in all directions. She began running before her feet touched the ground. A green pathway appeared in front of her, and a voice resonated in her inner ear.

"Welcome, Kitty."

"Stop messing up and help me!"

"Follow the white bunny!"

"...What?"

Eden kept running on the green path, trying to look around. The environment was forming in real-time around her. Walls suddenly appeared in front of her, like the universe was building in an accelerated motion. Those walls kept glitching, making her think the environment was unstable. She followed the green pathway, realizing she wasn't alone. She really did have competitors... Eden accelerated and kept looking around. Wasn't it ready yet?

Suddenly, she noticed it. Like a bundle of pixels, a white rabbit was down there, below the green pathway, hopping around. Eden hesitated. This server's defense system wasn't ready yet. Aside from this green pathway, there was nothing around her, just a dark universe. That rabbit looked like it was floating. As she felt more people coming up behind her, she jumped down.

For a second, she was scared Loir had tricked her, but then, her feet met something hard. Eden landed a bit unsure; although she couldn't see it, there was definitely something under her, keeping her from falling more. She raised her eyes. About thirty silhouettes were still on the green pathway above her, but the white rabbit was right there. She shook off her worries and ran after it.

A couple of seconds after that, the green pathway above her disappeared. All those silhouettes fell, most of them screaming. Eden ignored them and kept running, following the rabbit. The security system was almost done. She heard people falling on the path behind her, but she was at the front and kept going.

That's when an alarm rang, and she stopped. The rabbit disappeared, but there was no need anymore. The environment was done.

Eden looked around. She was in an actual room this time, a small one, almost like a closet. She opened the door in front of her, taking a glance through the opening. It looked like a library... and just as silent. She glanced around, but her opponents had ended up elsewhere. Eden slowly walked out of the closet, ensuring that no one saw her. She crouched down, making sure she was hidden behind a full shelf.

"...Loir?" she whispered.

"You're looking for row 34, the black book on the seventh shelf. Anthropology aisle."

Eden nodded and moved slowly, glancing at what was going on on the other side of those books.

This library wasn't empty. People were studying, or at least they pretended to. Eden knew those weren't real, but they looked very realistic. However, some mistakes were visible. A girl kept taking the same book repeatedly, like in a loop, and they were all reading books with pages filled with fake text. Not only that, but there were also inconsistencies, like the adult woman wearing a school uniform, or the dog at her feet.

Eden quietly slid against the shelves and tried to look up at the names; they were all in Cyrillic alphabet, making her grimace. This was going to take longer than anticipated...

She froze upon hearing someone else move, a couple of shelves further. She crouched down, waiting for the other to walk by. She hoped they wouldn't get noticed and trigger more security...

Just as the thought crossed her mind, an alarm began ringing loudly. Eden grimaced. That idiot had been busted. All the fake people in the room turned their heads at once, some to an abnormal degree. There was no more time to be discreet. If it wasn't the case yet, she'd be found too in just a few seconds. Eden began running again, not caring to be seen anymore, and jumped up, climbing on one of the shelves to get a better view. She heard a scream below and glanced down.

The security system of the server had been activated. The fake humans were slowly changing appearance, turning into giant creatures. Three of them had just changed into monstrous spiders. A tall girl was now some large snake, with a long reptilian body and fangs. Eden shuddered. The lady in uniform took the appearance of a clown with a scary smile, and the dog, a scary, growling wolf. Her heartbeat accelerated.

"Time for foul play," chuckled Loir in her ear.

Above her, a ruckus broke. Eden covered her head as debris began falling, the roof of the library opening to reveal a terrible storm. The wind blew her hair to her face, and the rain poured down into the library. She couldn't actually feel any water, but below her, it was starting to fill the room like a pool. Eden knew this meant she was going to run out of time. She looked around, ignoring the monsters down there chasing the other busted hacker or looking for more, and finally located a word on top of a shelf that could be Anthropology. It had to be it. She jumped down on the ground floor, ignoring everything going on.

However, the snake caught sight of her.

"Careful on your left, Kitty."

40

She turned her head just in time to jump to the side, avoiding the nightmarish bite. The beast stood tall above her, hissing furiously. Eden glared at it. She wasn't afraid of snakes, and she wasn't afraid of such basic security systems. Those were dupes meant to help the server win time, have the hackers leave their own, or trap them there. She turned around, ignoring it, and ran toward that shelf, trying to locate the black book. She glanced at the full rows.

"There's no fucking black book!"

"Oh... Did they camouflage it?"

She didn't have time to look a second longer. A scream came up from a nearby aisle, and Eden began running again, circling in that area. The snake's yellow eyes were still following her. She wasn't afraid of the simulation, but she knew the real deal would be coming soon. She didn't intend to stay for the security to increase. Rather than being kicked out, she was scared of being trapped and caught here.

She ran toward a wall in front of her, checking the sounds coming from behind, making sure that snake followed her. Then, she stepped up on the wall, jumping high enough to spin backward. She landed behind the snake, right on its tail. The beast that was going at full speed toward the wall suddenly stopped, frozen in motion, right in front of the wall.

"Oh, nice one, darling."

Eden turned back, running back to the shelf. She looked over again, checking the seven rows of books.

"You've got company, Kitty."

"What? Who?"

"Hm... One has a Chinese SIN. The other... Italian."

"Fuck."

Either they were coming for her or for what she was after. Eden glanced over the books again. None of them were black. She grabbed one of the books, and just as she touched it, the colors of the whole row changed.

"A fucking trick..."

This time, there was a black book. Eden grabbed it.

"What now?"

"Destroy it."

"What?"

"I said, destroy it."

Eden frowned. She usually had to retrieve information, not destroy it! It wasn't easy to destroy something in there. She took the book with her, but suddenly, someone began swearing in Cantonese.

She turned around. She had to figure out how to destroy that thing and get out of there. The snake was still stuck and glitching, so she ran past it, going back to her starting point. If the Chinese hacker had encountered the monsters, she had no idea what of the Italian one, and she didn't like it. Eden moved quickly between the shelves. She ignored the water, now up to her knees, running as if it wasn't there.

"You! Ghost!"

She looked back, nervous for a second.

"Loir?"

"Nope. Your camouflage is still activated, darling."

Eden nodded and kept running, ignoring the man pursuing her. If she could figure out how to destroy that thing, she would be out of there in a flash.

The Italian was still running behind her, but before that, something loudly creaked on their left. The two of them stopped, enough to see that the storm was getting worse, way worse. Eden grimaced. They were trying to shut it down. She looked down and opened the book, ripping the pages violently. They disintegrated into thin air as soon as they were ripped out of the book. She kept going, going, until the cover itself suddenly vanished.

"Loir!"

"Alright, extracting you in three..."

"Ghost!"

Eden turned her face, seeing the Italian hacker. He was too far to get to her now, but she still stepped back, cautious.

"...two..."

"The Tiger wants to meet you!"

"One."

Eden blinked.

She was on the floor of the basement, feeling a bit numb. She let out a long sigh, and Loir's face appeared above her.

"Thank you," he said with a large smile. "How did you escape the snake, by the way?"

"Data glitch. I figured the simulation would try to save both the snake and the wall and would be stuck if it had to make a choice between the two..."

"Oh, that's my girl."

He disappeared from above her, and she heard him roll his chair back to the keyboard. Eden sighed and touched her SIN, still hot.

"...How long was I in there?"

"Less than fifteen minutes. You're not far from your personal record. That wasn't such a big server, anyway... Oh, they really shut it down. A phobia simulation... Oh, so middle-aged, are they?"

"They looked real," sighed Eden, sitting up.

"Did they? It looked like an amateur job to me... I bet I could do better."

"Of course you could," groaned Eden.

The pups suddenly made some cute attempts at barking and walked to her, sniffing her. Eden smiled and grabbed the two pups, petting them. They began playing on her lap, but Eden's eyes went past them, to her legs.

"Hm... Having regrets?" asked Loir.

"...About the puppies. You promised, Loir," she retorted, ignoring his question.

"Of course, of course. Just send me the bills... They are so cute! Do you know what you're going to call them?"

Eden chuckled, looking down at them.

"Yeah. Beer and Bullet."

# CHAPTER THREE

Eden felt the pain before opening her eyes.

Like blades piercing her legs, fire devouring them. She whimpered in pain and opened her eyes, full of tears already. She tried to breathe, inhale and exhale, but her whole brain was focused on the scorching pain. She cried out loud and grabbed the mattress, using all of her arms' strength to sit up. She was sweating, shivering with a terrible fever.

As she finally sat up, Eden looked down and grabbed the upper end of her legs, or what was left of them. She glared at the empty space on the mattress.

"It's not real," she groaned. "It's not real, you fucking stupid brain..."

Clenching her teeth, she kept breathing, trying to fight the pain. It was still horrible. How could she feel pain when there was nothing there to feel pain from? Eden cried between her teeth and curled over, glaring at the phantom limbs as if she could convince them to appear.

Suddenly, a little sound on her left caught her attention. Amid the tremendous amount of pain she was feeling, she glanced to the side. Between her blonde locks, she spotted Bullet sitting down and staring at her. The pups... She had forgotten about them. She looked around, locating Beer curled up on the left side of the mattress. Seeing the little dogs so calm and quiet felt odd in comparison to the nightmare she was experiencing.

Eden took deep breaths and glanced up, trying to calm down once more. Bullet suddenly ran to her, climbing onto her lap and yelping. She looked down and grabbed the puppy, hugging him against her chest. Feeling his short fur and warmth helped her calm down a little. Unhappy, Bullet began growling and biting her hand a bit, but it actually made Eden chuckle. The pain slowly subsided. It didn't disappear at once, but it gradually faded as she was focusing on the pup instead.

Hearing his brother being so noisy, Beer woke up slowly and climbed on her lap too, wondering what was so interesting.

Once she calmed down enough, Eden sighed and put Bullet down, both puppies staring at her. She smiled at them, a bit relieved. So she hadn't taken them in for nothing, in the end... They climbed down from her lap and began playing together on the mattress, ironically where Eden's legs should have been.

Eden stared at her prosthetic legs, waiting on the side. Those damn pieces of metal were giving her more trouble than she had thought... Back then, she had believed it was a good deal to get a more expensive model, but now they were too expensive to take care of. She grabbed them and reattached her bionic limbs with a few movements. Her SIN sent a little tingle, and she tried moving her feet, which indeed followed each movement she intended. Eden was finally able to get up.

However, as soon as she got up, she raised her mattress, opening the little tear inside, and took out a little sachet. It only contained three little white pills. She grimaced and put them back. At least she didn't need one today...

"Beer, Bullet. Come on."

Following her voice, the puppies barked and came down from the mattress, running in circles and playing. Eden quickly changed into another bodysuit, a black one with a turtleneck and some jeans. She took her large jacket and left the apartment, her stomach a bit noisy. The two pups followed after her, excited to go out. However, Eden first stopped by the basement to see Loir.

"Evening!"

"It's morning, Loir."

"Oh... Hi, puppies! Hello there! You're so cute, and you're cuter! Yes, you two adorable cutie pies!"

"I'm going to buy them food," she said, putting her hands in her pockets, a bit nervous. "Give me some money."

"I'll transfer it to you as soon as you're out," said Loir, still making strange gestures at the two dogs.

"...Fine."

Eden turned on her heels and prepared to leave, both little dogs still following her. However, as she was about to leave, she heard Loir chuckling.

"...What?"

"You look grumpy today..."

"I'm fine."

"Eden, my little Kitty. Don't go buying something else."

She froze, resisting the urge to turn around to glare at him. He knew... How did he know? Was he spying on her? Probably. She wouldn't have been surprised if Loir had hacked her SIN again...

"...I won't."

"Good girl."

With a grimace, she went back upstairs and, this time, headed for the residence entrance, checking the information screen. Luckily, the air would be in the green today. The Core probably had used their oxygen supplies all day yesterday, enough to clear some of their air too. With a sigh of relief, Eden left the building, her dogs by her feet.

The air wasn't cleared enough that she'd take a deep breath, though. It still smelled of dirt, pollution, and something spicy too. Probably one of the Mexican restaurants around. Eden wasn't so foolish that she'd go back to that scene. Instead, she went in the opposite direction, heading to the grocery shop a bit farther away. She was careful, though. Whenever she heard a car coming close, she'd grab the two pups and carry them. There weren't that many people who could afford cars in that neighborhood, which made her even more cautious...

Indeed, another big car from the Mexican mafioso made a ruckus a couple of streets later. Eden knew they were only trying to provoke their neighbors.

In Chicago's Suburbs, the lines between the different territories were blurred, but the inhabitants knew where to pass and where not to go. Eden hadn't exactly chosen to live in that neighborhood. It was just the only one she could afford and one where she had the least chances of being found, although it was also one of the most dangerous ones. Out of the ten Zodiacs, the Eagle cared the least about who lived in his territory. Most of the population was of South American origin, but the rest was a melting pot of outsiders. The local gangs never bothered to check who came in and out, and from what she knew, they had no official hackers either.

Eden felt a little relieved when she turned onto a new street into the Rat's neighborhood. They were known as one of the most peaceful Zodiacs. Just like the Eagle, the Rat's territory welcomed strangers other than their South Asian inhabitants, but the local mafia was more active to ensure peace. They didn't care who came in, as long as they wouldn't disturb the locals and kept their business to themselves. It was easy to know when she reached it: the passersby went from mostly Hispanic to all Asian descent within two blocks. Her white skin stood out, but at least no one seemed to care. Grabbing her dogs, Eden stepped into Granny Duong's shop.

"Eden! How are you?" asked the old lady behind her cashier.

"Good morning, Granny Duong."

Granny Duong was incredibly old and so wrinkled it was hard to find her eyes on her face. She wore all of her white hair in a gigantic bun over her head and always had some very flashy pink lipstick.

"What are you going to buy today, Eden?"

"Do you have dog food? For... puppies?"

"Of course I do!"

"I'll take that, and if you have... I don't know, cushions for them?"

The old woman laughed with her high-pitched voice, but she helped Eden sort out everything she needed. Of course, the list was endless, but Eden put an end to it, knowing Granny Duong's business wasn't thriving by mere luck.

"Can you take the money from another account?"

Eden handed her a credit card, and the old lady took it, using it for payment. It wasn't a common way to pay, but Granny Duong knew not to ask any questions. Eden used that old system from time to time, always with a different card each time. As soon as the payment was validated, she'd destroy it and throw it away.

"Do you need anything else, darling?"

"Do you have... my candies?"

"Oh, the price for those went up, Eden."

"What? How come?"

"Tough times!" sighed the old woman. "The Rat is worried the Old Dragon will make a bad decision. We need to look out for ourselves, you know..."

"What about the Yakuza?"

The lady shook her head.

"Unless we get a strong new Dragon, the Snake will try to eat the Rat!"

Eden grimaced, but the imagery was fitting. The Yakuza head, known amongst the Zodiac as the Snake, had never gotten along with the Rat. If it wasn't for the Dragon acting as a mediator between them, it was unlikely those two would remain on speaking terms. The rumors of Old Man Long being sick was really shaking up all the territories...

"You're better without it," said Granny Duong. "Trust me, darling, I don't say this often, but that's one product I'm never happy to sell, especially to little flowers like you."

Eden nodded, but her throat felt tight when she remembered she only had three left. If she couldn't afford to buy more, how would she endure that pain next time? She grabbed her bags and left Granny Duong's shop.

Eden stopped outside to put her two puppies on leashes, although both hated it, and resumed her walk with her bags. Another thing she liked about that neighborhood was the cheap and good food. Eden knew exactly where to find the best street stalls. She sat down for her lunch and fed her dogs while waiting for her own food. Eden was no stranger to her favorite food stalls, but without interacting with anyone else, she just kept playing with her dogs and watching them fight over some pieces of chicken. She knew she was sticking out like a sore thumb in that neighborhood and shouldn't stay around for too long. The locals were still applying the Confucianism principle of hospitality, but she couldn't push it. Even the patron of the shop was just polite to her, as she was a regular customer.

"The Edge?"

She froze, hearing the two men at the next table whisper. Eden's SIN was translating everything they were saying for her. It was one of the perks of being a hacker; she could download most programs for free if she knew where to find them, and she had made sure to get one for Asian languages two years ago.

However, those men had no idea she was actually spying on them. How many White people spent money on Vietnamese translating software? Hence, they whispered for the other people not to hear them, but Eden was the only one they weren't cautious about.

"Are you an idiot?" said the other one. "If the Edge was hiding here, don't you think the Rat would know? Nah, I'm telling you, the Yakuza are hiding the Edge."

A shiver of excitement went down Eden's spine.

The Edge. The most wanted criminal organization and the only global one. An international league of hackers acting together, like vigilantes, shattering the Cores with each of their massive attacks. They had reportedly managed to have the Miami Core shut down for forty-eight hours four years ago, an unprecedented event that had made them famous but also put them as the number one enemy...

"No, no. I had some information. It said Ghost's signal appeared again, around this area."

"Ghost is part of the Edge?"

"Of course! The best hacker of the Chicago Server, why wouldn't he? He's got to be!"

Eden wondered if she should have felt flattered by those words, but truthfully she was a bit more worried that her last position had been pinpointed... She stood up, paid for her food, and left, a bit nervous.

She had never wanted to be Ghost. She needed money, and it was something she was good at. She had always been good as a Dive Hacker, and she had a unique configuration that made her the best among many, many others. That was it. She was curious about the Edge, of course, but she had no intention to look for them. Sometimes, she even wondered if the Edge was real. During the Miami Incident, their Core had claimed it had come from a malfunction, a technical incident. Of course, a lot of people hadn't believed that. Since when could the Cores' go out of power like that? Not only had their main energy source been cut off, but all the electrical support and extra resources had been cut off too, communications included. No other Core had been able to intervene, almost causing a major political incident between the Southern Confederation and the Northern States Republic Union...

As Eden went back to the Mexican territory, she suddenly heard gunshots from afar. She froze and, like everyone around, walked close against a wall, waiting a bit to see. It sounded like it came from farther north, in the Italian's territory... Were things going wrong? Or was the ruckus just caused by the Luchadores again?

She sighed, and as soon as things went quiet, she grabbed the puppies and hurried back toward her territory.

There was no safe territory in the Suburbs. Safety was something only the people living in the Core were allowed. The mafias were like a double-edged sword, protecting their citizens but also causing more fights.

A mafia lord's territory wasn't judged by its size but by how much their borders moved. The stronger ones had established their presence enough for the other Zodiacs not to mess with them... It meant nothing to have authority over several neighborhoods if they could lose them overnight.

Eden got home quickly. Once she had locked the door behind her and put the dogs down, she let out a long sigh, a bit out of breath. There really was no way to rest peacefully here... As the puppies went to nap on the mattress, tired from the little trip, she walked to her drawer, grabbing a picture hidden inside the little notebook she used to do her calculations. She smiled every time she saw that picture.

"...SIN, call Mom."

She felt the little device vibrate, and closed her eyes, waiting. It took a little while.

"Eden! Eden, how are you, my baby!"

A bright smile appeared on Eden's lips.

"Hi, Mom. How are you?"

"I'm fine! I'm at the restaurant with my friends! What about you, my baby? Are you alright? Your voice sounds different..."

"I'm great, Mom. I... Mom, I got two puppies."

"Oh, really? You always loved dogs. Eden, dear, you need to show me a picture of them! They must be so cute! What names did you pick for them, darling?"

"B... Berry and Bob," lied Eden, biting her lip.

"Berry and Bob? Oh, that is so funny! You should tell your dad!"

Eden's smile faded a bit, but she nodded.

"...I will, Mom. Are you okay? Are you eating well?"

"Of course! The food here is amazing, you should come! The restaurant's name is... What is it again..."

"It's alright, Mom. I'm sure you'll remember soon."

"No, no, wait! I'll ask the waitress! Miss! Miss, what is the name of this restaurant?"

Eden waited, a bit nervous.

"Yes, it's my Eden on the phone, my little girl! She's already twelve years old, can you believe that? Those children, they grow so fast! Anyway, darling, how are you?"

"I'm fine, Mom."

"Oh, really? Anyway! My friend, she was telling me, uh... What was she telling me again? Oh, never mind. But baby, we are at that restaurant, it's amazing! You... Where are you, Eden?"

"I'm okay, Mom, I'm... I'm at school."

"Oh, that's right! I'm so silly! When do I need to come and get you?"

"No, no, Mom, it's okay. I'll go home alone."

"What? What do you mean alone, of course I'm not letting my little girl go home alone! I'm coming! I'm coming! Wait, wait, where is my bag again..."

"No, no, Mom, it's fine! I... I'll ask Dad to come."

"Dad...?"

As her mom suddenly went silent, Eden sighed, rubbing her eyelids.

"It's alright, Mom."

"Yes... Yes, your dad... Uh... Excuse me, miss, where is this? Have you seen my bag? I need my bag, for... uh..."

"Mom, it's okay, you don't need your bag. Just... just sit down with your friends."

"Oh, Eden! How are you, my baby?"

"I'm fine, Mom."

The conversation went on again, but Eden had a little knot in her heart. It was hard to lie and pretend, making sure her mother wouldn't get too worked up. After a short while, she managed to have her hang up calmly and let out a long sigh of relief.

Once her mother's voice was gone, she suddenly felt a wave of loneliness in this little square room. She glanced at the puppies, sleeping like everything was alright in this world. Eden smiled a bit, looking at their cute little sleeping faces. She took a deep breath and put the picture back. Every time Eden heard her mother's voice, there were mixed feelings. She was more certain of her decisions, and at the same time, she had regrets. She wished she could go back in time, to when her mother could still be with her, take care of her.

It was strange how easily her mother talked about her dad too as if they had ever lived together, when that man had disappeared before she could even remember him.

She still had a few hours before starting work, so Eden slowly took out what she had bought for the puppies. There was an amazing feeling of relief in thinking she had gotten all of this with Loir's money. Her pups had almost more belongings than her now... She had given in to Granny Duong's legendary sales skills and splurged on a cushion for each of them to sleep on, some toys, and a lot of dog food. At least she wouldn't have to worry about that for a while.

Seeing the two of them sleep so peacefully, Eden smiled. She loved how animals remained innocent amidst this troubled world... After cleaning the room a little bit with the broom she had, she got up, and she went back to lying next to them on the mattress. Their hot little bodies somehow found their way to her and curled up against her, and Eden slowly gave in too, feeling sleepy.

She woke up to the pups barking.

By reflex, Eden opened her eyes and stood up immediately, ready for any danger. She quickly located Beer and Bullet, both yelping under her window.

"Hush, you two!" she said as she walked up to them.

Beer ran to her and she took the little pittie in her arms, but Bullet was still unhappy about whatever was going on outside. He was way too small to see, but he didn't need to. The ruckus was terrible. Eden got closer to the window, but she was careful not to stand directly in front of it, just in case.

As she had suspected from the noise, it was an Overcraft. She wasn't too surprised to see one here as they came from time to time... She opened the window slightly to hear the scene, although she was well aware of what was going on.

The engine landed in the empty parking lot a few streets away, and soldiers in black uniforms walked out, escorting some people in handcuffs. Eden frowned. She counted seven prisoners. Five men, a woman, and a woman who looked even younger than herself. While the three men that came out first were quiet with defeated looks on their faces, the next one was incredibly loud, shouting at the soldiers. Even Eden could hear him from where she was.

"...my rights! I'm not a criminal! I asked for another trial, you cannot treat me like this! I am an innocent citizen; I do not belong here! There was a mistake! You can't do this to me!"

Eden sighed. This was a familiar scene, but it had been a while since an exiled one had been so loud. The woman and young woman were crying and looked terrified, and she realized they ought to be that man's wife and daughter. The man behind him may have been his son or brother, perhaps. They were all wearing white clothes, and Eden grimaced. They weren't going to last long...

"I said, you can't leave me here! This goes against my rights! You, soldier? What's your name? I want your identification number! You'll see what I can do with my relations at the—"

"All of you are exiled from the Core from today on," announced one of the soldiers loudly, ignoring him. "You were judged by the Supreme Court as unfit to retain your rights as citizens of the Core. Your SINs, possessions, and rights have been confiscated. You are prohibited from visiting the Core as of today."

The older woman began crying loudly, and the soldiers suddenly grabbed one of the men, putting a little tool against his neck. He screamed as his SIN was forcefully removed. The injury was ugly, a little patch of skin was torn off and bleeding, but the soldiers moved on to the next one without care. The loud man kept protesting.

"See, Bullet? That idiot is going to die first." Eden sighed.

He should have been glad his SIN was removed. Otherwise, someone else would have attacked him to steal it and try to hack it... Eden knew that scene all too well, and she watched without feeling sorry for those people. If they were here, they had probably escaped a death sentence. Although, citizens of the Core being sent here had a very limited chance of survival...

She put her puppy down and glanced at the sky outside, deciding it was time to go. She packed a couple of things for work, put her jacket back on, and called out to the pups to follow her. Although they weren't fond of their leashes, Beer and Bullet seemed to have understood the rule that they had

51

to follow her. Eden quickly left the building, careful to take a detour away from the parking lot. As soon as the Overcraft was gone, those people were inevitably going to face rippers: people who had seen the engine and were lying in wait to rob whatever they had left.

"Eden!"

She stopped, seeing Lula running to her.

"Are you going to work already?"

"I don't have money for the bus," explained Eden. "I'll walk."

"Oh, just come with me. I'll pay for your ride!"

"No thanks, Lula, I'm–"

"Oh my God, those puppies are so cute! Are they yours? Can I pet them?"

After that, Eden couldn't really protest anymore against Lula offering her the bus ride. She didn't work the previous night, but Eden knew Lula was one of the most popular hostesses and made good money. Moreover, two of her older brothers worked for the Mexican gang, so she was one of the few girls who could walk around without worries.

The two girls got on the bus, Lula doing most of the talking, and completely fond of the two pups already. While Beer was acting all cute and curious, Bullet kept yelping until Eden put him in her bag and calmed him down with a few ear scratches.

"Did you see the Overcraft?" asked Lula.

"Yeah…"

"I really can't stand those people. They were given everything, and they were stupid enough to disobey and be sent here? I really have no pity for them. And thinking we are all criminals too! Do they think we are born with guns in our hands?"

Eden couldn't agree more. She had no idea what people were taught in the Core, but it's always the same scene whenever some are exiled here. They were arrogant and considered all the locals as savage criminals, uneducated bums. Although the gun violence and the pressure of the Zodiacs were real, a lot of the inhabitants were just regular people, doing their best to survive and take care of their families.

"The Eagle is so going to have them killed anyway," sighed Lula. "They are very riled up. Someone killed three of them yesterday."

Eden froze. She tried to hide it, petting Bullet.

"R-really?"

"Yes, so ugly! They found three of their boys in some garbage alley, all dead. I hope it wasn't one of the Rat's; we really don't need more fights… It's close to your block, actually! Didn't you hear anything?"

"Not really."

Eden was used to lying.

Covering her identity and keeping a low profile at all times, lying had become her main survival tool. Lula didn't even know Eden lived in that very building, and she had no idea she could kill so easily. To the girls at the bar,

Eden was just a Part with better reflexes than most and a few good fighting moves.

"Oh, well. To be honest, even if my brothers work for them, I don't really like the Eagle anyway… I'd rather live with the Italians or the Dragon. At least it's more peaceful there… Oh well, I was born in the wrong family for that."

Lula was a chatterbox, and Eden was fine with listening to her. The whole trip felt even shorter as she only had to nod and answer a little bit. Eden got along fine with all the girls that worked at the club, mostly because she was among the quietest ones herself. There were many catfights between the girls, as the rivalry was strong amongst them, but Eden was less popular and rarely involved. If one did arise, she would usually be the one to stop them.

They arrived early at the club, and only June and Bella were already there. The girls all greeted each other, and there was excitement about the puppies. Letting Beer and Bullet become the main attraction for a little while, Eden let them loose in the changing room. She and Lula grabbed their dresses before sitting in front of the mirrors, beginning their preparation.

"What are those?!" exclaimed Jack.

The girls laughed at his baffled expression. At Jack's feet, Beer was sitting and looking up at the large male figure, a curious expression on, while Bullet was still busy exploring the place.

"Those are my dogs," simply said Eden.

"Since when do you have dogs, and since when do you bring them here?!"

"Come on, Jacquie, they are so cute!" exclaimed June, grabbing Beer to show the puppy to her.

"I don't care that they are cute; this is a club, not a damn pet store! Eden!"

"Oh, please, Jacquie! We can take turns watching them!" insisted Lula, trying to pout cutely.

"…What's the ruckus all about?"

Just as Jack opened her mouth, they all turned their heads toward the entrance. Rose was standing there with her bag. Jack frowned.

"Girl, you ain't on the schedule tonight," he said.

"I put myself on it," retorted Rose.

"What?"

However, the redhead ignored them, walked up to the largest mirror, and loudly dropped her bag on her table. June and Lula exchanged a glance, but Rose started brushing her hair and opening her jewelry box as if everything was fine.

"Rose, what the heck?" repeated Jack, putting his fists on his hips. "I ain't payin' ya, girl!"

"Don't worry. I have a hunch I'll make a lot of money tonight anyway."

With her happy tune and the way she was picking out her prettiest jewelry, Eden understood right away. Some big fish was coming. Rose had a very strange talent for telling when someone with a heavy wallet would come to the club that night.

"But tonight was… Dalilah's…"

"Oh, tell that damn bitch to go home, Jack," said Rose, suddenly angry. "I'm taking over her shift tonight."

"You little bitches don't decide on the schedule!" roared Jack. "Who is coming, anyway? Like, what the hell, Rose!"

Yet, she ignored Jacquie, humming in front of her mirror and putting on her sexiest makeup. It had to be someone big. After a while, Jacquie rolled her eyes and went back upstairs. Eden said nothing, though. At least, he had forgotten about the pups…

The girls went on to get ready as more of their coworkers started showing up. As expected, a fight broke out between Rose and Dalilah as soon as the latter arrived in the changing room. The two most popular girls just couldn't see eye to eye. It got so bad that both Jacquie and Eden had to step in. She truly couldn't have cared less about their rivalry, but if she had to pick a side, it would have been Rose's. She had a terrible attitude, but at least she wouldn't scream hysterically, get violent, and attack everyone as Dalilah did. Eventually, Dalilah left after another one of her terrible fits, making everyone sigh in relief.

"Eden, your… uh… leg…" mumbled Bella, suddenly.

Eden followed her gaze, all of her colleagues looking down at it too. Her skirt had been accidentally torn while stopping the fight, and a part of her metallic leg was exposed.

"Gross," June muttered with a grimace.

"Hey!" said Bella, glaring at her.

"What? It's the truth…"

"Your face is gross too, and no one says it," retorted Rose, who was putting on her red lipstick.

"Fuck you!" angrily said June, standing up.

Since Bella and Lula were also glaring at her, June angrily left the changing room, slamming the door behind her. No one else said a thing, but Eden knew most of the girls actually silently agreed with June. Rose had probably only helped her as repayment for earlier and a way to pick at June, whom she didn't like anyway. However, Eden didn't really care.

"SIN, camouflage."

Her fake skin immediately appeared, but her dress was still torn. Eden took it off, checking the tear.

"Crap…"

"It's alright, I can sew it back," said Bella.

"You're going to be late for the opening…"

"It's okay. It'll only take a couple of minutes. Give it to me."

Eden was really thankful. Bella grabbed her little sewing kit from her bag and immediately began working on the dress. One after the other, all the girls left the changing room as the customers were about to come in. Only Rose was taking her time, checking her curls and lipstick over and over.

"Ignore June," said Bella. "She's so rude…"

"I'm fine."

"Alright, ladies, I'm off to get rich," whistled Rose, going upstairs.

Eden and Bella watched her go upstairs with a frown on their faces. The music was already playing loudly, and from all the ruckus coming from the upper floor, they could tell there were probably a lot of guests already.

"I wonder who we're expecting," said Bella. "She hasn't been this excited in a while. Here! Good as new!"

"Thank you, Bella. I owe you one."

Bella chuckled.

"You already did. We got to play with the puppies! I'll stay with them until someone takes their break; my client comes later today."

"Thanks," said Eden with a smile.

She went to pet her dogs a little, making sure they had food and water under her table and a couple of toys to chew instead of the girls' stuff, and quickly went upstairs. Eden never really knew when one of her customers would show up. She wasn't popular enough to have dates like the other girls did.

As she came up the stairs, she immediately realized the atmosphere felt a bit different than usual. Most of the customers had new faces, and despite their smiles, the girls were nervous. Eden walked up to Jack, who was also quietly wiping the glasses.

"Jacquie, what's going on?" she whispered, grabbing a tray.

"Trouble, babe. Trouble..."

Eden frowned and turned around, looking over the room.

It didn't seem like anything was wrong at first. However, the blonde quickly realized all the customers tonight were Caucasian. They were all perfectly shaven, wearing dark suits and shiny leather shoes. A chill went down her spine. Some weren't even with girls, simply standing in the corners of the room like watchmen. From their rigid stance and cold gazes going over the room, she could tell they were bodyguards.

Next, Eden looked for Rose. She had been right; a big fish was there... No, clearly, that was a shark. The Italian Tiger.

# CHAPTER FOUR

A chill went down Eden's spine as she laid her eyes on the man. He was seated on the largest leather sofa of the club, with Rose. It was the first time Eden saw that man in person, but she immediately knew who he was. Some of his tattoos were visible right above the collar of his silk shirt, and one could identify the paw of a large feline, claws out. Everything about him screamed powerful, rich, and dangerous. Without doing anything, he was clearly dominating the whole room. All the other men present had their bodies positioned according to his, watching his every move.

He was simply sitting, but even the way he was sitting had something imposing about it. It was like seeing a lion; although the beast was resting, he was still a predator. Eden averted her eyes for a second, grabbing another glass, but she was curious to see more of him again. His lean features reminded her of a feline. He looked younger than she had thought, with his clean-shaven chin and thin lips. Eden had to admit, this man was the definition of handsome. He had a long straight nose, perfect skin, and although he was sitting, she could tell he was probably toned and tall too. No wonder Rose was all over him. Even the girls busy with other customers were sending glances his way.

Suddenly, he raised his eyes, and without warning, he met Eden's. His burning, golden gaze shook her whole soul. It only lasted for a second, yet it felt like an earthquake under her feet.

Eden turned back toward the bar, unable to understand what had just happened. Her heart went wild in her chest as she tried to control her breathing.

He couldn't have found her. Has she been traced? The guy from earlier said her position had been pinpointed, but even so, the Italian shouldn't have been able to find her here! A drop of cold sweat went down Eden's spine under her blonde curls.

No, no, it couldn't be. She would already be dead otherwise. It just couldn't be. With trembling fingers, she took the glasses and adjusted them on her tray, taking discreet deep breaths. She couldn't have been found. If she had, she could always deny it. Who would think Ghost was a woman, and a Part too? No one could find out about her secret.

Jack had noticed the trouble in Eden's eyes but knew better than to say anything. Slowly wiping the glass, he sent a glance Eden's way, but the blonde put on a convincing smile and turned her heels.

Despite the seemingly joyful atmosphere in the bar, it felt like walking in a minefield. The Italians didn't belong here. This bar was on the Dragon's territory and not even close to the border. The Tiger had come here deliberately to piss off his rival. Eden didn't like that. If he hadn't come for Ghost, what was he here for? To stir up trouble? She started walking toward the table he was at, with Rose all over him.

"You should come more often," the hostess was meowing. "I'd love to have you as a customer any time..."

He remained silent, his eyes on Eden as she slowly approached them.

The tension was terrible around him. Although Eden had merely taken a couple of steps close enough to reach their table, she could feel a target on her head and a dozen eyes on her back. The pressure was on every inch of her skin, like walking on a very, very thin thread, or into a cage. Death was just lurking around the corner, looking for the wrong move to come claim her life. Eden had rarely felt that much tension, even in life-or-death situations she'd been in before. It was as if she had a leash around her neck; one wrong move and she'd be punished. Still, she dared to raise her hazel eyes and look into his.

Dante De Luca was watching her too. His eyes were glowing like liquid gold and watching her every move. He really was a tiger, and she was the girl lowering her head in front of him.

Careful with each movement, Eden put down their glasses. She could even feel Rose's stare on her, but that was the one she was least worried about. She stood back up and turned on her heels to leave.

This was almost a test for her. If the Tiger truly didn't react to her, then–

"Hey, you!"

Eden froze and glanced over her shoulder. One of the guys who had been standing next to the sofa walked up to her. He was a tall man with a large scar over his eye and a goatee.

"Are you busy, darling? You should accompany me..."

Eden hadn't expected that. She had almost forgotten that she works here. Sending a very quick glance to the mafia lord, she put on her business smile, acting charming as usual.

"Of course, dear guest. Shall we find a seat?" she said with her pretty voice.

The man smiled, a snicker that wouldn't have duped anyone.

However, before they could move, June suddenly appeared next to Eden, almost pushing her.

"How about you come with me instead?" she said seductively. "She's busy pouring drinks anyway."

Eden tried hard not to glare at her. June didn't care about the guest; she was clearly just messing with her because of earlier. Couldn't she have picked another time to act like a child? Unsure, Eden glanced toward the bar, where Jack was sending them daggers. He hated when they fought in front of customers.

"Well, I'll leave you with June then," said Eden, stepping aside.

However, as she did, the man suddenly grabbed her arm forcefully.

"Hey, I said I wanted you, blondie. Don't customers get to pick?"

June made a sour face but regained her composure quickly. She sighed and dramatically waved her hair in Eden's face.

"That's too bad. I guess some people do like Parts, after all..."

Her words sent a chill around the room. Eden's colleagues all glared at June, but she was clearly very happy with herself. The man let go of Eden's arm right away as if he had received an electric shock.

"Ew! A Part? Who would want to fuck that?! You should warn people you're a damn Part!"

Just as he had finished his sentence, a gunshot resonated in the bar.

Everyone froze instantly, and silence ensued. Eden's skin went ice cold, and the man fell to his knees at her feet. The blood under him began staining the wooden floor, and she took a step back, trying to calm down. As if she had just understood, June let out a panicked scream and stumbled away from the scene. Only Eden was still standing there, looking at the man. He was whimpering, holding his wounded leg, his hands not really stopping the flow of blood. It wasn't a fatal wound, but it ought to hurt. The bullet had transpierced it and was now lodged into the wooden floor. Eden slowly turned her head to look at the shooter.

De Luca had taken his weapon out of nowhere. It was one of those automatic weapons from the twenty-first century, which were sold for a fortune on the Black Market. He slowly handed it to the middle-aged man behind him, looking extremely calm. He didn't need to say a thing. Two of his men silently took the injured man outside. How he had just shot at one of his men without blinking wasn't the only scary thing: it was to witness how no one dared to even react to this. As if they were all aware this could happen, to any of them, at any moment.

No one dared to speak, but two people in the room had locked eyes, and everyone else had theirs on them.

Eden was strangely calm, but her blood had gone cold under her skin.

How could it not or how could it otherwise, when Dante De Luca had his eyes on her? The Tiger was staring right into her soul as if he was trying to decipher each of her secrets. It was a hot, intense, burning stare. His golden eyes were disturbingly deep, making Eden feel trapped. She shouldn't have looked back, but she just couldn't avert her eyes. She couldn't. She felt like he was choking her, judging her right to stay alive or not.

He had just shot one of his men for disrespecting her, and she couldn't understand that. What kind of man shot one of his own for a whore's respect?

"...What's your name?" he asked.

He had no need to speak louder. He could clearly be heard despite the music, and Eden was focused on him.

"Eden."

He didn't add anything else, but Eden felt like she had just lost something important.

She didn't want to give him any part of her identity. She didn't like him, and she didn't want to be involved with that man. Since he was the Tiger, she only cared about him walking out of there on his own two feet, for everyone's sake. As for the rest of it, she truly didn't care. Maybe he was crazy. Maybe he was a cold-blooded killer. She'd be happy if he walked out of her life and never appeared again.

He grabbed the drink she had brought earlier and slowly took it to his lips. It was as if everyone was hanging onto every drop he drank, waiting to see what would happen next. Although it looked like he had just been mad at his man for disrespecting Eden, no one could tell. He was the mafia lord and he had enough power to take what he wanted, even if it was a life. They were just some of the many lives hanging in the balance of the territorial feuds.

As the silence in the room got more awkward, Jack chuckled nervously behind the bar.

"H-how about a new round of drinks? On the house, gentlemen. Ladies, let's get this party started, shall we?"

The girls did their best to resume talking with whoever they were entertaining before, but truly, the atmosphere was too heavy for the smiles to be genuine.

Eden and De Luca were still staring at each other. There was a horrible feeling in her heart. She didn't dare to look away before he did, and he was scrutinizing her very soul. He wouldn't even blink. She felt like she was trapped in an invisible cage with him.

"Eden?" Rose suddenly called out, giving her a chance to shift her eyes. "...Why don't you entertain our guests?"

Eden slowly nodded and turned to Jack. Behind the bar, the bartender was quick to react. He nodded and touched the computer behind the bar.

Immediately, the lights of the bar changed.

From a joyful pink, it went much darker to an ominous red. The girls began to smile, knowing what was coming, but the customers were intrigued.

The atmosphere had shifted quickly, and a couple of them even put their hands in their pockets.

The jazz music went quiet, but a deep bass resonated in the background. Eden took a deep breath and closed her eyes, letting the music resonate inside. When she opened her eyes, they were shining with a new light. She began singing with a deep, seductive voice that called all eyes to her.

Yet, her eyes went back to the golden ones, as if she was taunting him.

*"You never make me stay, so take your weight off of me... I know your every move, so won't you just let me be... I've been here many times before, but I was too blind to see; that you seduce every woman, this time you won't seduce me..."*

She detached herself from him and turned around, slowly walking toward the stage.

*"I'll be saying that's okay; hey baby, do what you please. I have the stuff that you want, I am the thing that you need..."*

She brushed her blonde curls back in a seductive move, her eyes capturing the heart of a young man standing on the side. He swallowed his saliva, looking a bit lost, but Eden went her way.

*"Hey, look me deep in the eyes; I'll be touchin' you so to start,"* she kept singing, slowly climbing on stage. *"Let's say there's no turnin' back; you trapped me in your heart!"*

She grabbed the microphone, and all the girls began dancing at the same time. Some climbed on top of their customers, some standing in front of them.

*"Dirty Diana, oh... Dirty Diana..."*

Eden's deep voice resonated in the club, but the girls were working. All the men in the room were hypnotized by this new, sexy atmosphere taking over. As the music went on, their movements followed the suave, slow flow, moving each curve with incredible precision.

Eden kept singing, her voice getting stronger, echoing like an anthem to this sinful atmosphere. In a couple of minutes, the whole bar had turned into a siren's den, seducing every man in the room. As the chorus echoed again, the girls' outfits all suddenly changed, some pieces of fabric transforming. Some skirts disappeared to show more of their gorgeous legs, and some went from a short dress to a two-piece outfit. Impressed, a few men whistled, but the atmosphere was so hot in the room, it made throats dry.

The song had a low, slow, and seductive tone, but Eden's voice did most of the work. It was sexy, deep, trapping each heart and forcing them to get down to her tune.

Although all these men were hypnotized by the girls' gorgeous bodies, their ears were made slaves to Eden's voice. She was setting the mood, sending them back to their carnal desires, to their animal nature. They weren't as tense anymore, but like boys watching real women, confused by their desires. The girls weren't giving them any rest. They were caressing them, petting them with their eyes. Even without touching, even with their clothes still on, they were trapped.

There was one man still resisting. Rose was all over him, sitting on his lap and desperate to get his attention, but the Tiger wasn't shifting. He had his golden eyes glowing in the newfound darkness, like the liquid in his glass, and he was staring right at Eden.

The blonde kept singing, focusing on each word, each note, but she couldn't take her eyes off him. It was like two flames in the dark, two blades pointed her way. Her voice increased in volume again, channeling her anger into her song, throwing a storm across the room. She closed her eyes to sing louder, using her strength to bind them to her will. She wouldn't give up. Eden owned this place, at this very second. She was the one holding all those men down with her voice, setting the mood.

So why was he still there, looking that confident, when she had made his men into inoffensive kittens?

Eden kept going as if this was a challenge, a war against him. A war in which Rose was her partner, trying to own the mafia lord. The red rose was half-naked on his lap, caressing his torso, agitating her gorgeous crimson locks, and trying to capture his gaze, but he was looking at her like a king looks at some child. A giant, unmoved by all of her charms. He had that horrible smirk on as if he could toy with her, and not the other way around.

Eden's voice went lower and lower until she reached the peak and end of the song. She closed her eyes, using all of her strength into those last notes.

"...*Come on!*"

As the song ended and the last notes echoed in the speakers, the lights of the club turned dark purple, and Eden was out of breath behind her mic, still staring at the mafia lord. She felt defeated.

Rose too angrily stood and walked to the bar, pouring herself a drink despite Jack's glare. Eden wasn't moving. She was still a bit shaken and lost from her performance . The stare on her was sending her to the lowest levels of hell, and that man was even smiling. He didn't care that the most beautiful woman in the club had left his lap. He had his eyes set on Eden and his lips tainted by alcohol. He slowly put down his cup, and as soon as the glass hit the table, loudly resonating in the club, it was as if everyone had suddenly gotten a violent wake-up call.

All of his men realized where they were and sat up straight again, or stepped away from the girls, most blushing and a bit embarrassed. Some were even trying to hide the obvious bump in their pants, breaking in a cold sweat.

"...That's a pretty little songbird you've got there," chuckled De Luca.

His voice resonated like thunder in the bar.

All of his men, if not embarrassed, were trying to hide their trouble, despite the taunting ladies still next to them or worse, sitting on them. The girls were trained to entice the customers, and Jack had chosen them well. It was a silent war: the men held on to their dignity, and the ladies had their pride as hostesses to live by. A new song began on the speakers, something a bit less tense yet still sexy.

There was no need for Eden to sing again, and she didn't feel like it. She hated that grin on the Tiger's lips as if he had just won this battle. Rose too was looking furious at the bar. She hated when a man resisted her, and it was even worse when she was Eden's back up. Now not only was she being ignored, but this man had his eyes set on Eden.

The blonde slowly came down from the stage, Bella taking her spot to sing a cuter trot song, hoping to ease the atmosphere a little. Since they had been so easily enchanted by the hostesses, the men were now tense and on their guards.

Eden tried to ignore the golden eyes burning her way, but it was hard. She hadn't tried to catch his attention; she had done her job, trying to set the bar's mood for her colleagues to work, so why had it turned out this way? The young woman wanted to be as invisible as the music, yet powerful and loud. She didn't want to be seen, just to be heard. Holding her feelings in, she walked to Rose's side at the bar, but Jack clicked his tongue.

"...How did you know?" Eden muttered for her colleague to hear.

"Do you think I only sleep with customers for the fun of it? There are only three valuable things a man can give: pleasure, money, and intel. The Italian is just trying to piss off that dimwit Kris Yang..."

So he wasn't here for Ghost, but because of the territory war? Although this wasn't exactly good news, Eden was a little relieved that her secret was safe for now. It was merely a coincidence... or so it seemed. She was still a bit suspicious, especially since he just wouldn't stop staring at her.

"I wish he'd try to piss him off elsewhere," sighed Jack. "This is going to get ugly if Yang hears he's here..."

"He came here last night," retorted Rose. "Coming to his favorite spot is definitely a warning. Xixi is one lucky bitch. She may have been shot dead if she was here."

"...Maybe not. That guy looks like he respects women, from the way he defended Eden..."

Rose glanced toward the blonde with a snicker.

"Yeah. As if, Jacquie. Don't get your hopes up. It looks more like it's an Eden-only thing..."

She was obviously still bitter about being thrown away, but Rose knew better than to hold grudges against her colleagues. She could tell when there was another meaning behind it. Moreover, at the moment, the pretty redhead was sending deadly glares in June's direction, who had gone on the stage to dance.

"That crazy bitch... Let me know when she goes downstairs. I'm going to make her regret throwing a fucking shit show earlier. And put on my song next, I'm sick of Bella sounding like a strangled kitten."

"...Aren't you going to try again?" asked Eden.

At the bar, Rose sent her a glare. Eden had only hoped that Rose would distract the Italian from her, but obviously, she had already given up on him. Rose finished her drink with a sour expression.

"One thing I hate more than losing, Eden, is being a clingy slut. I'm done with that guy. He's all yours..."

After that, Rose swiftly moved on to another man near the stage, easily putting her professional mask back on. Eden liked how direct and cold-hearted Rose was. Although she was seen as arrogant and selfish by the other girls, at least she was honest about her intentions.

Still, Eden wasn't feeling too well about staying there. She wanted to go back downstairs, check on her pups, and hide for a little while. As long as it was somewhere far away from the mafia lord. Why did he have to turn up at Jack's bar with such odd timing? She just couldn't feel at ease with all this.

"...Eden. He's calling for you."

She frowned and looked over her shoulder. As if the piercing stare wasn't enough, now the Tiger was gesturing for her to come. Eden took a deep breath. If it had been anyone else, she could have ignored them. However, now all of the guests watched her actions, probably ready to shoot if she dared to make one wrong move. Grabbing her glass, she finished it in one go and snatched the two new ones Jack handed her with a glare.

"...Be a good girl," whispered Jack.

"I'll try not to bite."

With that, she turned around and prepared herself.

She knew how to act. It was something she had learned from experience. A slight smile, not too wide, or it would have been obvious it was forced. Never walk too fast, but keep her posture straight and her head held high. You couldn't seduce a man with your eyes on the floor.

However, this felt like the worst path to take. He was just a few steps away, but it felt like she was getting closer to a dangerous beast. She didn't care for his minions, but she could feel the pressure from the man himself, like a cage around her. Her heart was thumping, like a prey sensing danger. Eden tried her best to hide her turmoil, slightly squinting her eyes and thinking about her pups. Her gaze immediately softened as she thought about Beer and Bullet; to everyone else, it looked like she was making those eyes at the boss .

As she got closer, she could see his features a bit better. Despite his pale skin, she realized he was probably of mixed race, with his eyes slightly wider than the norm, somewhat almond-shaped. His body was on the thin but toned side, and his posture reminded her of a resting feline. His clothes too, Eden realized they were even more elegant from up close. She was no expert, but she would have bet it was one of those expensive custom-made suits, Italian, of course... It was fitted to flatter his body, with a white shirt underneath and a black jacket, with flapless pockets and buttons made of some really shiny metal Eden couldn't identify.

She carefully put the drinks down on the table for the second time that night, but then she cautiously sat down on the leather couch, leaving some space between them. He remained silent for a while, still staring at her. Bella's trot song ended in the background, and Rose took the microphone to sing something a bit slower and more seductive.

"...You're the quietest hostess I've ever seen," suddenly said the Italian.

"You're the oddest customer I've ever had," Eden answered calmly.

"Why odd?" he asked as if he was enjoying this.

"For coming to a place only to cause trouble and pick a Part out of all the women available."

"You're a hostess too. Why wouldn't I pick you?"

Eden frowned. His stare was too intense for her to remain as calm as she had hoped. Moreover, although she had been careful to sit reasonably far away from him, he still somehow felt dangerously close, too close. With his arm resting on the back of the sofa, his whole body was turned toward her. His fingers were playing with the little strands of tassels on her dress. He was too close. The movements were disturbing her a little, although they were barely touching the fabric.

"...Not as a first choice," she whispered.

He chuckled and tilted his head slightly, as if he was trying to decipher her. Maybe he had never met a woman who'd respond to him like this. Maybe he was one of those men who liked women who resisted a little. She just couldn't tell. His eyes were somewhere between playful and dangerous...

"You're the odd one, Eden," he said.

Her name on his tongue gave her the chills, and finally, Eden dared to look directly into his eyes. Just then, his smile widened.

"You're not scared of me," he said. "Most women are either afraid or attracted to me, but you're neither of those."

"Sorry for breaking your record."

He chuckled. There was nothing apologetic in her tone. Eden was clearly wary of him, but that wasn't the most interesting part. If anything, that was something he should have expected. No, the most interesting part was that she wasn't even trying to hide that little fire in her hazel eyes.

However, there was also something about Eden that sparked his curiosity.

"...Aren't you afraid of me?" he asked as if this was a trivial question.

"Death is less scary when you meet her every day."

He raised an eyebrow. Eden's swift answer spoke volumes about her character. The blonde hadn't blinked once or averted her gaze while saying that. She knew how dangerous he was, and obviously, she somehow didn't care. People were usually cautious around him, but that girl looked different. In the way she stared at him, she obviously had something else going on. No woman stared at him that way. They either feared him or wanted him.

However, Eden looked like she loathed him.

"So you aren't afraid to die?"

"I am. You're the one coming to the wrong place carrying a death wish," she retorted.

64

"Oh... so this is why I get the glare," he said, grabbing his glass of whiskey. Eden had a sullen look on, and she wasn't afraid to hide it.

No matter how terrifying that man was, she was much angrier at him for coming here, to begin with. He was putting everyone in danger for the sake of pissing off a rival. She couldn't get past that. The rest, she didn't need to speak about now. She watched him drink his whiskey and tried to ignore Jack making faces behind the bar, practically begging her to watch her attitude with a mafia lord.

"...Aren't you going to ask me why I'm here, then?" he asked.

"To chit-chat?"

Eden served him an icy smile, but it only made him smile more. His fingers moved on her leg, still playing with the fabric of her dress, but now closer. A hot chill went down her spine. How come this was shaking her so much more than if he were to actually touch her? Eden was used to the guests using her body as they wanted. There wasn't a place a man hadn't touched her before, and she thought she was impervious to those kinds of gestures.

Yet, seeing those long fingers of his playing with just a few loose strands of her dress was driving her crazy. She tried to control her breathing and, with trembling fingers, reached out for her glass to have something else to keep herself busy with. However, before she did, he grabbed her wrist and pulled her onto his lap.

That position took Eden by surprise. She was now straddling his legs, her hands grabbing the sofa's back behind his head by reflex, his face right under hers.

The suddenly-confused expression on her face seemed to entertain him. Eden looked baffled, angry, and troubled. She had been cautious not to touch him, but his legs were caught in between hers, and their faces were way too close. If Eden's hair had been just an inch longer, it would have fallen onto his shoulders.

She felt her throat go dry in a second and her heart go insanely wild. She wanted to get mad at him and ask him what he was playing at, but those words stayed stuck in her throat. She couldn't anger him, and she wasn't even sure what to say. Moreover, Dante De Luca was still smiling, like the devil looking upon her. She felt his fingers slide up her back, and a chill ran up her spine. She couldn't understand what he was doing. Men usually played with her body, not her reactions. Yet, the Tiger was going so slow and gentle that it was terrifying. As if he was toying with his prey. His other hand grabbed one of her wrists, and he silently guided her to hold on to his shoulder instead. The situation was escalating so fast, Eden couldn't understand what was going on. Despite her experience working at the bar, she had no idea how to react to all this.

The rest of the bar was gone, and Rose's voice over the speakers felt like a faraway dream.

Eden had to cling on to her hatred to not give in. She couldn't give in to him. Not Dante De Luca, among any others; not that man. Taking a deep breath and trying to regain control of the situation, she changed her attitude, playing along. She spread her knees farther apart, sitting on his crossed legs. She was a hostess, and he was a customer. Eden kept repeating that sentence in her mind like a mantra she ought to stick to. Her fingers on his shoulder relaxed a little, and feeling the change in her attitude, Dante squinted his eyes a little bit too.

"Playing along now?" he asked.

"Isn't this what you wanted?"

"We should make this believable."

Eden's heart skipped a beat. She wished he was a bit less handsome and his voice a bit less attractive. It was hard to get out of his game. Moreover, she was confused once again. Believable to whom? This probably looked like some sexy but not-so-unusual scene for a hostess club from an external perspective. She wasn't the first one getting on a man's lap tonight, and some of her colleagues were a lot busier already.

However, Eden couldn't have bothered to check how the other girls were doing. Dante De Luca was way too captivating at the moment. She had no idea how long this game would entertain him. She was just willing to play along until he left and hopefully never came back.

He put a hand on her neck, caressing her nape with a stronger grip than she had anticipated. The strength in his fingers was scary, and when he pulled her closer, Eden didn't resist. She felt exposed to him, too exposed. Her dress was one of the least sexy ones as it covered her legs, but it still had a deep cleavage and showed off her neckline.

When he pulled her in to kiss her neck, Eden felt her senses run amok. His lips were soft against her skin, yet it felt like her whole body was being caressed. The chills, again. How was he so good at throwing her off course?

"...I hope you don't die too quickly," he suddenly whispered against her skin.

"What?"

Eden suddenly sat up, understanding his words one second too late.

Right after that, the bar's door slammed open, and Kris Yang and his men appeared in the doorway. The music stopped right away, and all eyes turned toward the entrance. Some of the girls screamed and jumped away from the Italians realizing what mess was about to happen. Eden, however, didn't move. Even if she had tried to, she could feel De Luca's strong grip on her neck and back.

She understood and saw red right away. Sitting like that on his lap, she was right in between the Tiger and the entrance. That bastard. He intended to use her as a shield!

"De Luca!" Kris yelled. "You die today!"

Eden clenched her teeth, turning her head from the entrance to glare at De Luca with all her might.

"You damn bastard..." she hissed.

He smiled back, a snarky smile that made Eden hate that man even more.

She wished she could slap that smirk off of him, or insult him. However, she didn't have time for that. Those three men had guns and indeed, they opened fire right away without waiting. Eden was right in their line of fire. The sounds of their machine guns were deafening. A light above them exploded, sending sparks all over and lighting one of the old sofas on fire.

"Jack!" Eden yelled.

The bar lights were suddenly turned off, putting the whole room in the dark except for the light coming from the street through the large door frame behind Kris Yang and that fire. It sent silhouettes dancing against the wall, confusing their enemy. Eden had no way of knowing where Yang and his men would shoot, but they didn't stop. They were shooting blindly anyway. Yang hadn't even stopped to check where De Luca was. He had just opened fire right away and kept going.

That mistake of his gave Eden a narrow window for action.

She slid off De Luca's lap and dove to grab the table where their drinks were. In one large movement, Eden raised the heavy marble table like a shield behind them. Immediately, she heard a pair of bullets hitting it, carving dents into the thick table. She grimaced but kept stepping back. De Luca hadn't moved yet, shielded by her, but she didn't care. She could hear the girls as they began screaming from all around the bar. She soon realized it was even scarier when they suddenly stopped.

A couple of seconds later, she heard Jack's gun begin to shoot. It was a loud weapon that would only send one big blow at a time, but it was enough to send the attackers in disarray. Eden used those few seconds her friend gave her to glance behind the table, trying hard to think of a solution, a way to get out of this mess.

"SIN, call Loir!"

"Hi, Kitty, what's up? How is the... Are those gunshots? Woo-hoo! Party time!"

Eden didn't have time to answer his nonsense, but she knew Loir would be quick to react once he found out about her situation anyway. Indeed, a couple of seconds later, one of the weapons of Yang's men suddenly stopped and made a terrible sound. The automatic gun sounded like it was sizzling and about to explode. The man holding it screamed and let it go, the gun overheating in his hand. Eden felt that much-needed little spark of hope. She now had back-up. However, Eden was still in danger as long as she stood between Yang and De Luca. She groaned and threw the heavy table in Yang's direction, making him yell.

She didn't even wait to see if he had been hit or not. Eden dove to the left, hitting her back against the bar counter as she hid behind it. She could hear Jack's weapon shooting from time to time, but it took too long to recharge. The uninterrupted flow of shots coming from Yang's side was bad, and moreover, those of De Luca's men who were still alive had begun shooting too. The whole bar had turned into a war scene where everyone was shooting blindly.

"Eden! Do something!" yelled Rose's voice.

She grimaced and began by ripping the lower part of her dress, getting rid of all the fabric below her hips. She took a deep breath and jumped behind another table, closer to the entrance.

"Loir, full lights in two seconds."

"Yes, ma'am!"

Eden closed her eyes, and behind her closed eyelids, she saw the sudden difference in lighting. Many of the men yelled, suddenly blinded, but Eden was ready. She jumped, and the next second, she sent her leg flying, kicking Yang's weapon out of his hand.

"That damn Part bitch!" he yelled.

She didn't let him add another word and smashed her elbow into his face. The bones of his nose broke loudly, and he groaned in pain, blood splattering the man behind him. Eden knew the threat wasn't over. He wouldn't have come alone. She heard another gunshot and felt a slight push against her left leg, but no pain. Without hesitation, she spun her body, kicking the other man behind him in the stomach. If she hadn't been equipped with metallic legs, her kick would have bounced back against that enormous belly, but instead, the man's expression tore into a weird grimace. He retreated, looking like he was about to vomit.

Eden heard another shot, this time coming from behind her. She saw the other Chinese man whine, hit right on his shoulder.

"Loir!" she hissed.

"Hey, not everyone has a new generation gun..."

She glanced over her shoulder, and indeed, De Luca was standing there holding his old revolver at arm's length, shooting without hesitation. It was one of those old weapons Loir had no way to hack. Eden had never even seen that kind, but the mafia lord was holding it confidently. Even worse, he even had his other hand in his pocket! Eden only had time to glare, but for a second, she wished she had a weapon herself to get rid of all those crazy bastards...

"You damn bitch!"

Eden felt the sudden pain, real this time, and stepped back in shock, looking down at her wound.

The bullet had pierced her abdomen, staining her red dress with something redder that was spreading fast. She grumbled something, fighting against the pain. She knew she just couldn't stop fighting. No matter the pain, if she stopped, she'd die. Suffering was hard, but it meant she was still alive and conscious. It wasn't worse than dying.

She jumped back, and before Yang got another chance to shoot her, more gunshots came from behind Eden. She would be killed by De Luca's men instead if she didn't get out of there! This time, she ran to the right and hid behind one of the pillars. Things were spiraling into chaos. More Chinese men barged inside the bar to protect Yang with his broken and bleeding nose, and inside, the Italians began yelling and running toward the entrance.

Eden couldn't have cared less for those fights if it wasn't happening at her workplace. She just wished they'd finish soon. Why had she even attacked Yang? She had gone crazy, obviously. Her first instinct had been to get rid of the main threat without thinking there were two dozen more behind her, including one crazy bastard Tiger...

"Kitty, how are you doing? Having fun?"

Eden rolled her eyes and held her hand against her injury with a grimace. The gunshots weren't stopping. The bar was unrecognizable. Most of the furniture ripped by bullets, smoke everywhere, and bottles of alcohol exploding one after the other. There was glass flying from all sides, so much that Eden was scared she'd have another bottle explode too close to her. She glanced to the left, but Jack had disappeared behind the bar and was nowhere to be seen. Eden just wished her friend had found a place to hide and was fine. Still doing her best to remain behind that column and out of harm's way, she glanced around, trying to look for her colleagues. The first one she found was June, her body in a strange position on a couch. The flow of blood coming from her neck was a hint she had died quickly... Eden's heart sank a little lower when she saw a female leg coming from under one of the sofas, a blue shoe that belonged to Bella. That was all she could see. Too many men were standing, running, trying to dodge the fire left and right for her to see anything else.

At the entrance of the bar, behind her, all the mafiosos were fighting, but it would be over soon. It wasn't as if they were using their fists or knives. Most of them had guns. Things were usually over quickly when bullets were involved... Eden only had to hold on for a little while longer, but she was out of breath, in pain, and fed up. Even if she survived this, she would be in a hell of a lot of trouble for attacking Yang. She didn't really regret it because she hated the bastard anyway, but she didn't want to be killed. Now, she wouldn't even be able to work in the Chinese territory again...

"...You don't look like a Part."

Eden raised her eyes, surprised to hear such a composed voice at such a moment. Dante De Luca had somehow come to stand in front of her, almost too close. She froze, shocked and unsure what to do. She glanced down by reflex. His gun was still in his hand, but the other was now carrying a glass of whiskey as he slowly brought it to his lips. Eden wondered if this man was mad or truly didn't care about dying. There was a whole war going on a few steps away from them, yet he was standing there and drinking!

"You don't look like a hacker either."

Eden's blood went cold.

He had linked the disabled weapons to her? It couldn't be! Loir had only deactivated one. Or had he heard her? That was the only explanation but even that seemed impossible. The bar was thrown into chaos, gunshots were being fired behind them from all directions. Even more bottles of alcohol were exploding all around them. Eden couldn't understand that man. Who would focus on the actions of a hostess instead of caring about the armed men shooting at them? Plus, he was the main target, to begin with!

"Why do you care?" she hissed.

She just didn't have the strength to be polite or play along anymore. Her whole life was just about to be ruined because that man had decided to piss off his rival at none other than her bar, her workplace! She was in a hellish amount of pain from her injury and starting to feel like she was about to collapse.

De Luca chuckled but stayed quiet and drank some more. Eden was pissed. She wished he or Kris would get a bullet to the head, and this madness would be over. Everyone would run away and leave them alone. She didn't care about any of these men, and she was especially furious at De Luca. He was a huge storm of trouble that had hit her out of nowhere. And now, he was getting to her as if she was caught in the eye of a hurricane. Eden wanted to get away from this man, as far away as possible, and never see the bastard again. As long as she made it out of there alive, Eden knew she could survive. She just needed to survive. That was all she needed.

"De Luca!" yelled a voice behind them.

Eden glanced behind the column, and to her shock, Yang was still very much alive and well. He had half of his face covered in blood, but he was smiling and showing some of his hideous gold teeth, wielding weapons in both of his hands.

"It's your doomsday!" he yelled. "You provoked a Dragon, and you're going to die! And that bitch Part too!"

Eden grimaced from being linked together with De Luca. Meanwhile, the Italian put down his glass, raising his gun to shoot again, a smile on his face. Opposite him, behind the crowd of men fighting like wild dogs, Yang laughed hysterically, raising his guns too.

She had a scary thought in a split second. What if Yang survived, and De Luca was killed? He'd be the next Dragon, and she was going to die anyway. If De Luca survived, at least she had a chance. A slim one, but it was still a chance. Eden hesitated, hidden behind that pillar. She could stay there and let them die, and deal with the consequences later. Would she have a chance to, though? Once one of these two was dead, things were going to escalate quickly. Would she be able to evacuate Jack and whoever else had survived? What of the pups? They were still downstairs, and they needed her!

Eden took a deep breath, and as soon as she heard the first gunshots, she decided. She shifted her position and appeared next to De Luca, suddenly grabbing his shoulder. Whether it was because she had caught the same arm he was shooting with, or because he hadn't realized, the Italian didn't push her away. Eden raised her leg right in time to stop Yang's two bullets aimed right at De Luca's chest. Trying to shield herself, Eden raised her arm to cover her head and felt a third bullet entering her right flank once again, making her grimace. A fourth one hit her shoulder, and she thought this was it. She had made the wrong decision and was going to die.

She heard De Luca shoot, but Eden was already in a strange state, where

70

she was numb to everything else going on around her. The lapse of time she had lifted her leg to shield De Luca had been a split second, but it suddenly felt like hours, time stretching around her.

Eden heard Loir's voice, but she had no idea what he was saying. The irony was, although she was in pain, her legs were strong and smart enough to remain in position until the gunshots stopped. Only then did Eden begin to fall to the side and lost balance for real.

She waited for the second she'd hit the ground, but it never came. Maybe she blacked out for a second and missed it because the next thing she knew, she was on the floor. She could feel the hot liquid under her and her hair strewn across her face. She gazed at the ceiling, completely numb. The pain felt like shy waves trying to hit her, but she couldn't really feel them. She wasn't even conscious enough to regret her decision. She heard the familiar buzz of her legs, unhappy with all the bullets suddenly lodged in them. Eden was vaguely aware of the sounds going on around her, but she wouldn't have been able to tell if it was because her ears were failing or the fight was stopping.

She still had her eyes open somehow, and she heard someone scream her name. She thought she had recognized Jack's voice, but she wasn't sure. Just then, a face appeared above her, blocking the lights.

"...She's still alive," whispered De Luca, with a little smile.

"Boss, what do we do? We got Yang, but more will be coming..."

"Finish the job here. We're going back."

"Yes, sir."

"Take this one with us."

"Th-the Part, sir? Are you sure? She's... probably not going to make it by the time we are back..."

"If I say she'll make it, she will."

# CHAPTER FIVE

Eden woke up slowly and without any pain, which wasn't the norm for her. Any time she opened her eyes, she would mentally prepare for the pain to hit her. Yet this time, there was nothing. Hence, her instincts took over as soon as her eyes were open, and she sat up, checking her surroundings.

The place was completely unknown to her. Her heartbeat accelerated, extremely confused. Was she dreaming? Or in a simulation? This room was so big and luxurious, something felt wrong. Instead of a wall on her left, there was a large screen displaying a gorgeous panoramic view of Chicago, but Eden wouldn't be lured by such a thing. High-resolution screens were common in rich people's houses. This place could be anywhere, even in a basement. She looked around, but other than that, the room was pretty much bare. A single chair was strangely positioned in front of the bed and behind it, a shelf with only three books. On her right, only a wall with a lonely light bulb. That was it. Eden couldn't understand. Where was she?

She then looked down, wanting to check her legs. She was in a very large bed, although she couldn't see its framing. The mattress was so large it could have easily welcomed three people. She pulled on the gray silk sheet, revealing a large tiger embroidered on it.

The Tiger.

As her hazel eyes remained locked on that sight, it all came back to her. The bar, the attack. Visions of her dead colleagues came back in flashes. The chaos around her, glass and bullets flying in all directions. Eden couldn't calm down. Her mind was still there, in Jack's wrecked bar. She took a few seconds to calm herself down and try to think. She forced her memory to remember the last events.

The gunshots. She had been injured. She looked down, but her abdomen was... perfectly fine. Not just fine. There wasn't even a scar or injury. Eden grimaced and checked everywhere else she recalled getting shot. She knew that bastard Yang hadn't hit any of her vital points, but she still remembered very clearly she had taken at least five bullets. Yet, her body was as good as new... except for her legs. She glanced under the covers but found nothing she didn't already expect, other than the fact that her camouflage was down, revealing the two long leg-shaped pieces of metal.

"You're finally awake."

Eden grabbed the cover and pulled it back over her legs with a frown. She was only wearing panties, her breasts exposed, but for the moment, that was the least of her worries. She glared at the man who had just walked in.

Just like before, De Luca was wearing an impeccable suit ensemble, although he didn't have a jacket on this time. That new outfit had hints of green that highlighted his jet-black hair. Eden wasn't happy to see that man alive, far from it. She wasn't happy to see him at all. He came to sit down in the chair, perfectly calm, and slowly lit his cigarette.

"Did you have a good night's sleep?" he asked in a mocking tone.

Eden frowned. Was it morning? She glanced at the screen, which displayed something like a couple of hours after dawn. Although she didn't trust screens like these, it may have reflected the weather outside. Had she slept here? Why? From her wounds, she should have died there. Why had he bothered to take her and heal her?!

"...I take it you aren't a morning person," he chuckled.

"What am I doing here?" coldly retorted Eden. "What do you want?"

He squinted his eyes.

"A lot of things, little songbird. First, I want you."

Eden rolled her eyes.

"No thanks. Are you done now? Give me my clothes. I need to go back."

The Tiger chuckled and took a drag from his cigarette. Eden had just woken up, but she had that fire in her eyes of someone who couldn't be swayed easily. Everything in her body language said she loathed him and wanted to leave. She was sending daggers with those hazel eyes of hers. At that very moment, that little piece of a woman in his bed was the one acting like a fiery tiger... or a grumpy kitten.

"Aren't you going to thank me for saving you?" he asked.

"That's my line," she retorted, annoyed. "Let me go home. I didn't save you to become your fucking pet!"

She stood up, wrapping the bedsheets around her. Dante was very intrigued by Eden's attitude. She wanted to hide her lower body but didn't seem to care about her exposed breasts. She was considering her bionic legs as more important to hide than her feminine traits...

"...It's odd," he said. "When we scanned your SIN, there was no trace of you being a hacker at all. How did you do that?"

Eden froze. They had scanned her SIN? Her blood went cold, and she raised her hand to touch the little spot where her SIN was hidden. Indeed, it felt slightly bruised when her fingertips touched it. ...Was it deactivated? Probably so. Otherwise, Loir would have already located her and done something. At least, it looked like they hadn't found out the truth about her. Still, Eden knew she couldn't stay here. That guy was dangerous.

"I'm not a hacker."

"You're a poor liar," he said. "I saw you. You made the lights turn off and disabled some of their guns."

"It wasn't me. Maybe they had enemies on the outside."

"One who knew what was going on inside, precise enough to find which weapons to deactivate? Even if someone externally did this, they needed intel from inside."

Eden frowned. This guy wasn't an idiot, and that was a problem. How much did he really know? She looked around, staring at the door he had come from. She wasn't stupid enough to suddenly barge outside when she had no idea where that outside led. Moreover, with him here and her SIN deactivated, she couldn't call out to Loir either. She was literally trapped here.

"Why the hell did you bring me here? Wasn't it easier to let me die?"

He chuckled.

"I'm curious about you, Eden. Moreover, since you survived, I have decided to make you my new bodyguard."

"As much as I'd love working for a jackass, that's a no. I'm not a bodyguard, and neither am I for hire. Is it your custom to pick your bodyguard from people who nearly died because of you?"

"I saved you."

"Says the guy who intended to use me as a fucking shield."

"You did quite a good job as one, actually."

"Fuck you."

It had been a ten-second decision, but now, Eden was regretting shielding that man. If the Tiger wasn't worse than Yang, he certainly felt much more dangerous. She hated being trapped at a man's mercy, especially this one. Plus, she could tell this wasn't going to be an easy one to get out of, now that she was in his... bedroom. She glanced around.

"Where am I?"

"My bed. My bedroom."

"Where am I?" she insisted.

"My penthouse, in the Italian district. I thought you'd enjoy the view once you woke up."

Eden frowned. The view? So this was a real window? She glanced at it once again, but she couldn't trust that man's words anyway. This whole room

74

might be just a trap to lure in some idiotic women who found it appealing to wake up naked in a mafia lord's bed... She had never been to the Italian district before; she'd much rather stay away. What kind of trouble had she gotten herself into?

"I'll be going back now," she said. "Give me my clothes, and I'm getting out of there."

"No."

His tone was too firm for Eden to even try and bargain. She had made it this far because she had good conservative instincts, but now, this was the worst situation she could have faced. She had no idea how to get out of there. She pulled the bed sheets a bit closer to her body, trying to think fast, but she knew she'd have no choice but to negotiate. The only good point was that he looked disarmed. With his current outfit, she would probably have seen if he had a weapon on him. Yet, that wasn't enough for Eden. She took a deep breath.

"What do you want? Why me?" she asked.

"I told you, I'm very curious about you. I think you are hiding some secrets from me, like your hacking abilities."

"I'm not a hacker," she stubbornly repeated.

"I wonder why you're so obsessed with keeping it a secret and so good at hiding it," he said, ignoring her. "I think you have a friend outside, but he wouldn't have been able to help you if you weren't a hacker yourself. However, we couldn't find anything on your SIN, which means you are either not a hacker... or a very good one."

Eden remained silent. She was tired of repeating the same thing over and over again and just hoped he'd finally say what he really wanted from her. He stood up, putting his hands in his pockets, and came closer. Eden immediately stepped back.

"Are you going to remain so stubborn?" he asked.

"Probably."

He nodded, looking upset. Then, he turned his head toward the door, and a man walked in. He was a thin, tall guy with freckles, also dressed in a shirt and suit pants. Eden's eyes widened. That man had a gun, and he handed it to his boss right away. She backed away again, wary.

Dante raised his arm, pointing the weapon at her.

"Still a no?"

Eden clenched her teeth. This was probably just an act... or was it? She tried to think fast. She didn't want to die, that was a given. However, what other choice did she have? If the Italian found out she was Ghost, she'd get killed eventually. That bounty on her head was too high of a sum to make her think it was any good. She would only be buying some time. Maybe she could survive? Although Eden wasn't nearly optimistic enough to think a mafia lord would miss, not when she was that close. Maybe, if she dived right in time, rolled on the floor, and rushed toward the door, then...

"I'm waiting."

His cold voice made her look at him again, but this time, at his weapon. Could she kick it out of his hand? That was one really crazy bet... De Luca sighed.

"George."

The other guy nodded and left the room, making Eden even warier. Why would he ask one of his men to leave the room if he was about to shoot her? Her heartbeat went up a notch.

However, the freckled guy came back, and to her shock, he wasn't empty-handed. He had a gun in his hand, and in the other, a puppy that was whining and wriggling around.

Bullet.

Eden's heart sank. They had her dogs? Would they use it as leverage against her? Dante chuckled, seeing her baffled expression.

"We found two really cute pups in the bar's basement. I thought I had seen them somewhere before."

Seen them before? What was he talking about now? Eden's blood went cold, but before she could even understand what he was talking about, the window on her left suddenly changed.

It was now obviously a screen, but the clip displayed was of really poor quality. It kept jumping, and the image wasn't stable, as if filmed by someone whose hands were shaking. It even took Eden a couple of minutes to realize what she was looking at.

The back alley next to her building, the one with the dumpsters. She couldn't understand. Had someone from a nearby building filmed the scene? It looked as if it was taken from far away but with a zoom, which would explain the poor quality. Why? A wave of panic came over Eden. The scene began with the Mexican thugs fooling around and being loud. Was that why it had been filmed? Someone spying on the local mafiosos? Yet, Eden couldn't stop watching. Even though she knew very well what was coming next. The angle wasn't good, but her blonde hair and thin figure were too identifiable even from afar. Worse, she moved exactly as she did the previous night. Her fighting style was recognizable to anyone with a decent level of combat. There was no sound, so they remained strangely silent until the moment when Eden could be seen grabbing the pups and going back inside.

A cold shiver went down her spine. What if they had found the basement? Was that why she had no news from Loir? Had he been caught too? She didn't even dare ask. His sole existence was one of the biggest secrets she had sworn to keep. Loir was probably one of the only people in Chicago with a bounty higher than hers without being affiliated with a member of the Zodiac.

Although, that was about to change soon. Eden turned her head back to the man who was holding Bullet, glaring at him. Dante De Luca already had his eyes on her too.

"So?" he asked.

"Fine. What do you want exactly?"

"I said it, didn't I? For you to work for me, as a bodyguard and a hacker. I'll even pay you a decent salary, of course; I'll provide anything you need. A roof, food, and, uh... clothes."

He had said that while glancing down at Eden's body, which made her even madder. She was not in the mood to joke around.

"I want my dogs back. Both of them."

"Of course."

As his boss was saying those words, the man let go of Bullet. The pup had been moving around so frantically he almost dropped him on the ground. Yet, the pup was quickly back on his feet and ran to Eden, who crouched down to grab him immediately. He didn't look harmed, despite all his whining.

"I want the other one too," she said.

"I'll give him back once we sign a proper contract."

Eden squinted her eyes, pissed. If they signed a contract using their SINs, she would have no way to get out of it. She knew how the Zodiacs worked. There would probably be a death sentence hanging above her head if she refused. She took a deep breath, trying to think quickly.

"What of my friend? The people at the bar?"

"Those who made it through the fight are fine and went home, I suppose." He shrugged.

"The bartender?"

"He didn't like us taking you, but the bullet in his leg didn't really help."

Eden grimaced. So Jack had been shot too. At least if it was in his leg, it probably wasn't a mortal wound... She wanted to ask about her other colleagues, but the sight of Bella and June's dead bodies came back to her mind. Everything had happened so fast, Eden hadn't even had time to be sad. Plus, she wasn't sure who else had made it...

She took a deep breath. Too many things were uncertain right now, but she was clearly at this guy's mercy. She knew the Tiger wouldn't stop before he got what he wanted from her. After her pups, he'd find every friend, every person she cared for, and threaten their lives until she agreed.

In her arms, Bullet barked at the Italians, but Eden covered his eyes with a sigh.

"I want immunity. For all of them."

"All of them isn't really precise," said Dante, taking a pull on his cigarette again.

He was that confident to turn his back on her as he glanced back at the other man. Eden checked each of their movements, but it wasn't time for action. She knew when a fight couldn't be won; she had survived for too long in the streets to not know.

"I want all the workers of the bar immune against... against your people. You don't come near my people, and you fucking leave my dogs alone."

"...Aren't you going to ask what I want from you first?" he said, raising an eyebrow.

"You're the one who hired me thinking you know everything. Those are my terms," she retorted.

Dante chuckled, a snarky smile on his face.

"...Fine. But if you don't give me what I want, your agreement will be considered invalid."

"...What is it that you want? What do I need to hack?"

"Nothing in particular. However, I have one thing I ask all of my hackers. It's a succeed-or-die mission. Is that fine?"

Eden frowned. He was offering her a choice now? She tried to think, but no matter what, the one thing Eden was most confident about was her hacking abilities.

Even if she had to do without Loir, she was among the best Dive Hackers. She worked alone until she found the creepy guy in his basement, but was doing fine on her own. He had allowed her to improve all of her skills, but that wasn't all there was to Ghost's abilities. She'd rather keep him out of all this. Eden thought he might be able to contact her once she returned online.

Moreover, she would probably be given the best equipment, unlike all the other times... No, whatever the mission was, she knew she could probably succeed without any big issues. She glanced down at Bullet, who was curled up in her arms, still looking afraid. Did she even really have a choice?

"...Fine. What's your deal?"

The Italian smiled.

"It's simple. Win a hack against Ghost."

That was probably the last thing Eden had been expecting to hear. Beat Ghost? What was that even supposed to mean? How could she... How could she possibly be able to beat Ghost? Of all the things he could have asked, that was the only one she hadn't thought of and certainly couldn't do!

"Beat Ghost?" she repeated unconsciously, completely baffled.

Dante De Luca smiled, visibly very satisfied to see her so troubled. However, next to him, George had let his jaw drop, and he looked at his boss as if he had gone crazy. Then, he nervously chuckled.

"B-Boss, you can't be serious! No one can beat Ghost!"

He looked down at Eden, checking her out from head to toe with a smirk.

"That woman can't beat Ghost! We are talking about the best hacker in Chicago! You," he said, calling out Eden. "Do you even know who Ghost is?"

Eden rolled her eyes.

"Every hacker knows who Ghost is..." she grumbled, a bit annoyed at this situation.

"Exactly! Ghost, the legendary hacker," recited George, looking lost in his admiration. "Nothing is known about Ghost, nothing! The only thing is that he only connects on the Chicago server. That's it. No one has ever been able to get any clue about their identity. Even the hours they are online is unknown, if they work with a partner or not..."

"Every hacker needs a partner," retorted Eden.

Why was that kid pretending to know everything if he didn't even know the basics? She sighed and made sure she was covered and, more importantly, that Bullet was held tightly in her arms.

"The very reason one role is called 'the Dive Hacker' is that you can't ever dive alone," she said. "Every hacker needs a partner to pull them back, but also coordinate. Ghost can't be working alone..."

"Well, maybe he is good enough to not need one!" retorted George, a bit embarrassed. "No one has ever been able to find any trace of him communicating with anyone else! The only way to get in touch with Ghost is through a super encrypted script which, in itself, is even hard to find!"

That was one of Loir's ideas and probably a bit of his paranoia at play too. He had hidden the access to their contact in such a way that only people who already had half-decent hackers could find them, which meant they could avoid all the automated ones or any newbie that might have been tempted to fool around. Moreover, it allowed them to secretly get some first-hand info on their buyer, usually Loir's favorite part. He left himself little backdoors in the systems of anyone who were interested in working with them... and only God knew what he eventually did with them.

"Ghost is famous for so many brilliant hackings!" resumed George, getting excited all by himself. "He has the record of the top twenty-three hacks on the Chicago server! Twenty-three! He even beats his own records frequently. He demolished a Russian server three weeks ago, literally made it implode from the inside. He hacked the Chicago Online Exchange Market three times, five banks, and destroyed sixty different platforms last year. That guy appeared out of nowhere, and he never spends more than thirty minutes on each hack. Right on the clock!"

Dante glared at his subordinate, but Eden chuckled.

"Sounds like someone's a fan," she said.

However, George didn't appreciate that tone and glared back at her.

"Well, that's common knowledge for any proper hacker. Moreover, the boss is..."

As he said those words, his eyes unconsciously went to his boss, and the deadly glare of the Italian Tiger made those last few words stay stuck in his throat. The young man swallowed his saliva, looking down in a cold sweat. Eden wasn't really impressed, or at least, there wasn't anything she didn't already know. Those men killed other people daily, but no matter what, the head of the organization ought to be the most fearsome of all...

"...Why do you want to beat Ghost?" she asked. "Why not simply recruit him to work for you?"

"We've done that. However, it seems that Ghost won't take any master, only the highest offer on each run. I do not like to see some... opportunities leave my hands before I've played all my cards."

In other words, De Luca wanted Ghost all to himself and did not like the hacker winning for his opponents from time to time... How ironic, thought Eden. Many hackers were probably dying to work for one of the Zodiacs. It was the promise of protection and money, two of the most valued things around. Yet, it came at the high cost of being tied down to one master... and bearing the consequences of failure.

It also explained why De Luca needed a new hacker. Even if they didn't die during their dives, the others had probably paid for their failure with their lives. She frowned.

"...I am in no hurry to die. You heard your... that guy. No one has ever beaten Ghost. Why would I be different?"

"I didn't say you only had one try."

"You didn't say I wouldn't die if I failed either," she retorted. "Why don't you ask one of the hackers on the Black List?"

"I fear there are no more available at the moment."

Eden stayed silent, shocked.

There were no Black List hackers available? The Black List was supposedly a register of the best hackers for hire. Only the best were allowed in, and they were ready to commit even the worst cyber-crimes as long as one was willing to pay the price for it. In reality, this was no different than mercenaries, the worst and best of them. However, it seemed unthinkable that none of them would be available... unless someone had used the whole list.

"...I guess that means less competition," she whispered.

"There's only one win that matters. Against Ghost."

"You make no sense. Why don't you ask me for specific information instead of asking me to beat Ghost? No one knows what Ghost will be after next. It may be of no value to you. I've never heard of someone being more interested in the competition than the prize."

"Consider it a personal vendetta then. I do not like someone making me lose face, and Ghost has been an issue for quite some time. If he doesn't work for me, I need to find someone better and get rid of him."

Eden squinted her eyes.

"...You want to kill Ghost?"

"I want to kill anyone who ever dares to stand in my way. Ghost has done so about... sixteen times."

Eden bit her lower lip. Pissing off a Zodiac sixteen times wasn't just a lot, it was a death sentence. She had never thought there would be someone that petty, though. The Dark Web was a very, very big sea anyone could fish in. Ghost had never meant to stand in someone's way; like any hacker, Ghost did their job and disappeared as soon as it was done.

While she remained silent, Eden was trying to think fast. Would it even be doable? She could always ask for Loir's help, but would he be willing to do such a crazy thing? Well, Loir was always happy or crazy, but still... In her arms, Bullet suddenly barked, reminding her of his presence. The pups... She was worried about Beer, about Jack, and whoever else had survived the attack at the club. In any case, she was... trapped now. Could she even find a way to escape somehow?

"While we wait for Ghost to show up," said De Luca, "you will be welcomed here to work as my bodyguard. I have to say, the previous one met an unfortunate fate last night, and you've proven your worth already."

"Boss, we can't have that woman protect you!" said George, looking shocked. "You can't be serious! She's a wh... I mean, she's clearly not a bodyguard! Look at her!"

Eden glared at him. She was getting annoyed at all his interruptions and wondering how he still had a tongue.

"People who judge others by their appearance are idiots," she said.

"Don't you dare call me an idiot, you damn bitch! You're just a Part! All you did was take a few bullets for the boss! Do you know how much it cost us to repair and heal you?"

"I did not ask for it."

"Well, you should at least be grateful you're even alive!"

"Enough."

Although he wasn't loud, George went silent as soon as Dante glared at him again. However, just after a few seconds of silence, he regained his composure, even putting his hands back in his pockets with a little smile.

"...Since you're so curious, George, how about we test my new bodyguard?"

"What? But–"

"Take her to the training room."

Right after those words, Dante turned around after one last glance at Eden and left. She glared at his back. That was it? Was he already considering that their negotiations were done?

Left behind, George sighed and looked at her in disgust.

"You'd better be ready," he said. "There's no way we're going easy on you just because you're a woman!"

"Do you mind if I get dressed first?" retorted Eden, left untouched by his petty remarks.

The young man swore in Italian and left the room.

Eden sighed and finally let Bullet down. Although she was glad to see him fine, she was far from being relieved as his sibling and the fate of her coworkers remained uncertain.

Alone again, she glanced around the room. It was all made of some dark wood, except for that screen wall. She couldn't reactivate her SIN and call Loir; Eden was sure this place was rigged with cameras and hidden microphones.

She walked to the dressing room and surprisingly, there was brand new female clothes in there. It wasn't even one of those fancy print-on-demand systems like people had in the Core, but a regular, plain old wardrobe. She quickly found a black sports bra in her size and leggings to put on. She wondered what had happened to her dress... Barefoot, Eden walked toward the door and to her surprise, it opened. Bullet followed her, intrigued, but the puppy was still too wary of their surroundings to walk ahead of her.

Eden stepped into some corridor and wasn't surprised to find two men guarding it. One of them pointed an index down the hall to her left, and she proceeded in that direction without exchanging one word with them.

It was a strange atmosphere here. Like the bedroom, the hallway had a large window-like screen wall showing the other side of the city, and the floor under her feet was a cold white marble. She wasn't feeling well here... She didn't belong here. Eden kept walking until she reached a large square room. The floor was clearly meant for working out as it was made of some sort of braided rubber material.

Her arrival was welcomed with whistles and gross remarks in Italian. Not the gentlemen of the bunch... There were five men, all surprisingly young. Some looked younger than Eden, and she realized those were probably the youngest recruits. On the side, George was waiting, with a smile on his lips.

"Since you sounded so arrogant earlier, I thought it might be better to bring you a real challenge," he announced with a smile.

Eden didn't even bother wasting her time to answer. She was used to the petty ways men had to try and show who was the strongest and she wasn't interested in fueling that fire. Instead, she walked toward them on the red mat. Bullet was smart to stop before and lie down, looking a bit unsure but curious.

She walked until she was standing in the center, with all five men spread like a star formation around her.

"No blades allowed, guys," announced George. "Let's be nice to the lady since the boss still needs her..."

"I'd have some need for her too," chuckled one of the guys, the oldest looking of them.

Eden hit him first.

Right after he had finished his sentence, his jaw had been violently smashed by a rotating kick. He made a weird expression just as he realized he was hit and fell loudly on his shoulder, emitting some gruesome cracking sound.

Eden didn't even wait to see him hit the mat. She knew all too well that stopping is not an option when attacking multiple opponents. She flipped her body at an incredible speed and sent her fist to hit the next guy's stomach. She didn't have enough strength to actually make him fall from this hit, but it was the surprise she was looking for. She twisted her body again, and this time she sent her elbow to his jaw.

Those boys were trained, and she could tell. However, there was one flaw with training: it prepared for many things, but not the reckless fighting style of people who had learned the hard way. Only one of them managed to hit her twice, on the flank and her face. Another one had actually tried to swipe her legs, but his hand made a terrible crunching sound as it was met with Eden's bionic parts. His screams echoed throughout the training gym. The fight wasn't over but by then, those young men had already understood they couldn't win.

82

Eden was clearly scaring them as they began focusing on avoiding her hits rather than trying to hit her.

"...She's obviously toying with them."

One floor above, the tinted glass allowed Dante and his second-in-command to watch the whole scene without being noticed. The Italian Tiger was smoking again, with a complex expression on his face. He would squint his eyes from time to time as if to decipher Eden's movements.

The middle-aged man next to him nodded, looking at his tablet.

"...I think so too, sir. She clearly has the skill to have ended this fight around five minutes ago but... she's merely hitting them lightly, making sure they can still stand. Except for the first one, of course. I'm... I don't think he'll get back up, sir."

"Get rid of them as soon as this is over, except for the one who managed to hit her."

"Yes, sir."

Dante stayed silent for a few more seconds, staring again. His expression was stone-cold but if one was to look at him closely, they could detect the little wrinkles at the corners of his eyes, as if he was about to smile. His micro-expression showed that he was having fun watching the scene below them.

"Looks like someone needed to vent."

His second didn't say anything to that but he stared at the little screen in his hands. His eyes would go from Eden to the recorded scene, back and forth.

"...I think you were right, sir. Even with just an initial comparison, the fighting style of that woman is... very similar to the records we have of Ghost's fights. However, as Ghost's silhouette was blurred, I wouldn't be able to say for sure, sir. My apologies."

"Let's keep her here, under our watch. Give her the other dog but do not let her out of the building. Record all of her actions and... make sure she has no way to leave until we have confirmed it. If anyone tries to contact her, let me know. In any case, if Ghost doesn't show up in the next seventy-two hours, it will be further proof."

"I need to remind you there have been records of Ghost not showing up for over a week, sir."

"We can keep her longer than that."

"...What if Ghost shows up, sir?"

Dante smirked.

"Well then, it will be a lot more fun to watch."

# CHAPTER SIX

"Enough! Enough! Stop, please! I... I give up..."

Eden was panting, her fists still up as the young guy kept miserably retreating, crawling away from her. She let out a long breath and went to calm down, her heart still beating wildly in her chest. They were really too young. All of her opponents were on the floor whining and crying about their broken ribs. She hadn't gone easy on them, as expected. She wasn't in the mood to let anyone simply get away today. However, those guys were clearly not in fighting condition anymore. She wasn't so dumb as to kill a mafia's recruit in their own house.

She turned to George, who was grimacing on the side, looking pretty shocked with what had happened to his men. After staring at them, his eyes slowly went up to Eden. The young woman was standing alone in the middle of the ring. Her only injuries were a couple of bruises on her shoulders and a cut on her lower lip. She may even have done that one to herself because she couldn't remember any one of his men getting close enough to hit her face.

The only one visibly happy for Eden was Bullet. The little pup happily yapped now that Eden's opponents were down and trotted to her, his little tail wiggling around behind him. She smiled and lifted him up in her arms. She was a bit sweaty as expected but surely the little pup wouldn't mind. He even began licking her cheek as soon as she held him.

As George was still standing speechless on the side, she turned to him with a sigh.

"I take it we're done?" she asked.

"Y-yeah... Uh... Th-there are showers in the back if you want to... uh..."

"Thanks."

Eden didn't wait for him to finish stuttering and turned around to go take a shower.

It was one of those big communal showers with rows of large shower heads, but it was empty at the moment. Eden didn't expect her opponents to walk in there either. She had left them in quite a bad state already. Of course, she couldn't do anything if there were hidden cameras, but she didn't care about peeping Toms. She went to stand under the furthest one in the room and undressed, putting Bullet down to play with her abandoned clothes on the floor. As soon as the water was turned on, he left the clothes to splash in the small puddle of water, although he seemed afraid of the sprinkler.

Eden was surprised to have hot water for free and even shampoo and soap available right there. She made good use of those products. She was wearing her hair long, not really by choice but because both Jack and her mother liked it better this way, and she didn't care enough to cut it. Eden had gorgeous honey-blonde hair with hints of copper in it and natural curls. Although she couldn't compare to the other girls from the club, she definitely was a rather tame beauty herself. She had a heart-shaped face, a thin nose, strong lips, and a marked jaw. Her upturned hazel eyes were her favorite part about herself. It often made her look older than her twenty-three years. Eden didn't have any other specific traits about her body that she particularly loved. She was of average size with a body without many curves and wide shoulders she didn't like. She only took care of herself when her work called for it, and she didn't care enough to wear makeup or spend time on herself otherwise.

As soon as the room was filled with steam and the shower was running loudly above her, she took a deep breath and pretended to massage more shampoo into her hair as she turned her SIN back on.

"...Loir," she whispered.

"Eden, my blondie! Happy you're still alive. What's new? Did you have fun?"

"I'm at the Italian's."

She was doing her best to talk into the softest voice possible, and a bit impressed Loir could hear and understand her just fine. She hoped no one else was able to.

"Nice! Are you bringing back pizza? I'd like one with anchovies, pineapples, chili, and–"

"I'm really at the Italian Zodiac's place, Loir. The Tiger."

"Oh! Oh... Well, I hope you have me in your will."

"You're not funny," she grimaced. "The Tiger wants me."

She heard him hiccup.

"Is it... the thing about adult relations? The thing where human adults do naughty things I am not supposed to watch? You know I'm too young for that!"

85

Eden sighed. She couldn't exactly tell, but Loir was at least a few years older than she was.

"Why would you even... never mind. De Luca doesn't want me as a woman. He wants me as a hacker."

"Oh... Wait, Big Kitty wants *you* you? Or the other... you?"

"He wants Eden to beat Ghost."

A long silence followed, and just when she wondered if they had been cut off, Loir suddenly began laughing out loud. She rolled her eyes, annoyed at his antics, but then remembered to pretend to be washing her hair. Irritated by his little fun, she waited until he had toned down his stupid laughing.

"Seriously? Wait, do you think he knows?"

"I sure hope not, but I need to prove it to him."

"Well, now this is interesting. Big Kitty chasing the Little Kitty. I like a little bit of fun... What do you need, Kitty?"

"First, can you run a convincing clone program? A very convincing one, in a hack?"

"It could be fun! I mean, it wouldn't be a first, but I need to find records of you and work on them though. I haven't played with other little Ghosts in a while..."

"Find an old one so it seems like I can beat Ghost without making it too easy. I really need to win Loir, or they'll kill me. Just get a convincing one."

"Yes, yes... How will the big mean Tiger know, though?"

"I have no idea. He just said I needed to beat Ghost in a hack, any hack. I don't know... I guess he'll want me to wait for Ghost to show up."

"Playing cat and mouse again! That's one really mean kitty... Alright, alright, I can do that. For once, that might be a little bit of a challenge, anchoring you and playing around with our little Diggity-Ghost!"

"I'll also need new gear, as Eden. The one I have won't be convincing enough if I need to beat Ghost. Can you help me out?"

"A little upgrade? Of course, Baby Kitty Girl! I can find the best stuff on the market..."

"Nothing too much, Loir, I don't want them to know where it comes from..."

"Gotcha! Plus, I'll assume your wallet has a big mean hole as always?"

Eden sighed. It wasn't about money anymore, more about staying alive, if she could... which felt like one hell of a bet already.

"They are tracking me, Loir," she said, changing the subject. "I can't talk to you all the time, and I'll have to turn my SIN back off too."

"No problem! I'll have a lot to keep myself busy with anyway..."

"And... can you do me a favor and check if Jack and the others are okay?"

"Oh, yeah, about that..."

Eden felt a cold shiver go down her spine.

"Wait, what? Loir?"

"I kind of already did that when I heard there was a little party at the bar.

Hacked everyone's SINs... There is some bad news, Kitty; the Grim Reaper went mean."

Eden closed her eyes, letting that pain sink in her heart. She already knew. She had seen the bodies of June and Bella... She just wasn't sure she was ready to hear who else had been a victim. However, she ought to know. It might even fuel her anger against the Italians for later.

"Three women are dead, Kitty. June Oswald, Bella Garcia, and Yuri Li. But the others are fine."

"What about Jack?"

"Your friend Jack is fine, he went to the hospital and his records show only a broken arm and two gunshot wounds; he'll be good as new next week."

She let out a long sigh. She was a little bit relieved the death list hadn't gotten much worse without her knowledge... She felt sorry about Yuri. She had just joined the bar's staff a few weeks ago.

"Keep watching them, please. I need to cut off now, Loir. Just run the Ghost program once everything is ready, okay?"

"*Arrivederci*, Kitty!"

Eden cut off her SIN again, hoping the Italians wouldn't have been able to trace that short exchange between her and Loir. She knew the hacker was smart enough to blur it out of the radar for her...

When she finished her shower, smelling of a faint cedar and peppermint scent, she wondered if she should wear her gym clothes. It would have been a good option if Bullet hadn't chewed them.

Eden sighed and grabbed the pup with a towel wrapped around her body, but just then, she realized someone had left a new outfit for her. She frowned and walked over to the entrance, checking what was inside the little basket they had left. It was actually decent and the right size too. There was some new underwear, a sexy black set from a brand she didn't know, and a white lace top with a pair of black leather pants. Eden put it all on, surprised that they had gotten her size right. The only things she didn't have were socks or shoes, but she didn't need them inside that building; all of the floors she had seen so far were sparkling clean. Although her hair was still wet on her shoulders, she walked out as soon as she was ready, wondering what the Italian Tiger would want from her next.

There wasn't anyone in sight. Eden had taken a long time in the shower, and when she came back to the gym room, everyone was gone, only their blood left on the mat.

She frowned and turned around, trying to think of her options. Could she possibly leave? It couldn't be that easy. She doubted they would simply let her out like that. Moreover, she still hadn't retrieved Beer. She didn't want to escape at the cost of leaving one of her pups behind...

Hence, the young woman kept walking, checking the various corridors. All were made of this cold marble floor, sometimes white and sometimes black, and the walls were either a dark oak wood or one of those large screens displaying Chicago. It was already midday outside, and her stomach grumbled a little. Still, Eden felt worse, realizing Bullet and Beer were probably getting hungry too.

"Enjoyed the bathroom?"

She turned around, and the pup growled a bit before hiding behind her legs.

Dante De Luca was standing there with a tall white-haired man behind him. He stared at Eden from head to toe with a little satisfied smile.

"That will suffice," he said mysteriously.

Eden frowned, but she didn't want to ask, nor did she like how he had just stared at her as if she was already his property. Then he motioned to the tall man behind him with a little head movement. Eden would have noticed him even without that; the guy had the shape and size of a humongous wardrobe...

"Meet Rolf, my second."

Rolf was the sternest man one could imagine. Everything about him looked square: his head, his body, and his nose, even the way he was constantly frowning as if his eyebrows were stuck downwards. The man nodded, but Eden did not return the courtesy and crossed her arms instead. She wasn't sure why it was relevant for her to meet this guy, but she didn't like it. She didn't like being treated like some sort of guest or a new recruit. She wanted nothing to do with Dante De Luca or his people. She'd be out of here as soon as she had proven she was better than Ghost, and that was it.

However, that man suddenly stepped forward and revealed Beer, which he was holding by his nape. The little pup stayed very still, but his ears and tail perked up as soon as he recognized Eden. The tall guy dropped the pup in her arms as soon as she had opened them to receive the puppy. She checked him quickly, but Beer didn't look traumatized, just a bit sleepy. She let him down to reunite with his brother, and the pups, probably thinking things were safe, began playing at her feet.

None of the human adults glanced at them.

"Now what?" Eden said. "Do you intend to keep me locked in here until Ghost shows up? I am of no use to you trapped here, so why don't you just–"

"Oh, you're about to make yourself useful, Eden," retorted Dante, with that smile on his face. "We are going out."

"Where?"

"I never eat at home, and since you're here, I thought it would be a great occasion to take my new bodyguard for a little lunch outside."

Eden was speechless, and she couldn't help but stare at him as if he was crazy.

"Lunch together? Your bodyguard?"

"It was part of our deal, remember? I said I would hire you as both a bodyguard and a hacker. Well, if I was taking any other woman to dinner, she wouldn't be dressed like that."

Eden glanced down at her outfit, but it only made her even madder. She should be glad she wasn't treated like any of his whores, is that what he meant? Still, when she glared back at him, the man didn't even flinch. Actually, his smile grew even wider, making her think she should prepare for the worse...

"Plus, it would be a great occasion to discover the Chinese district, wouldn't it? Old Man Long always said I ought to try their cuisine sometime. Aren't you familiar enough with that place to show me around?"

Eden squinted her eyes.

She knew what he was doing. It wasn't about trying a restaurant at all. It was another one of his stupid tests. Ghost always appeared through one of the Chinese servers of Chicago, making everyone think the starting point was in the Dragon's district. It was a very vague clue, though. There were many reasons one could transit through a Chinese server, either because of their gear, their network use, or even their SIN's DNA reading. That man was just fishing blindly for answers, and she was that worm hanging at the end of his hook. Eden took a big breath in.

"Fine, I will show you around. However, I want my dogs fed first. I also want you to reactivate my SIN. I need it if we are leaving this building."

"They are both already fed," replied Rolf right away.

Eden was a bit relieved to hear that. Now that she was thinking about it, those two would have been a lot whinier and louder if it wasn't the case... Just as she was about to glance down at the pups, she caught Rolf's gaze on them too. For a second, he realized she had caught him observing them too and looked ahead. ...Was he embarrassed to have been caught? As she kept staring at his second, Dante cleared his throat.

"You won't need your SIN if we leave," he said.

"What? I can't walk around without a SIN. I won't be allowed anywhere!"

A SIN was a very little device implanted under their skin, but it was indispensable in most aspects of life. They used it to buy things, as I.D., but also to communicate with other people, access database information, or even be allowed inside some buildings. Not having a SIN was the equivalent of being homeless or an animal!

Of course, the Italian Tiger was well aware of all that. He smirked.

"You're my bodyguard, Eden. I'm one of the Zodiacs. You'll see that if I say you don't need a SIN, you don't need a SIN."

Eden glared at him. She had never signed up to be his slave!

Although she knew a Zodiac going out had to be somewhat of a big deal security-wise, Eden was shocked at how ceremonial it felt. Walking behind Dante, she was annoyed by how all his men bowed to him and avoided looking up in his presence yet still checked her out. She'd much rather have been invisible. She hated being under someone's scrutiny, even more so if they were all male.

At least she wasn't wearing anything revealing. If it was her, she would have never picked something so elegant, and instead, she would have gone for whatever covered her skin the most. She hated when men looked at her, and here, she felt too exposed. She wasn't sure if she could keep the pups with her, but no one told her anything as Bullet and Beer stayed stuck to her heels. Like her, the two young dogs looked rather uncomfortable and unsure about this new environment, so they quietly followed.

Still, Eden was shocked by how big the place was. It took a long time before they reached the elevator, and at the speed at which they got downstairs, she had calculated they had been at least thirty floors up. How could she get out of there if he kept her upstairs? Maybe there were some emergency exit stairwells?

The parking lot was filled with shiny brand new cars, all Italian brands, of course. Eden couldn't help but be envious; she loved cars. She sometimes even used her SIN to play some online races, and she was actually good enough to have won the prize money a few times.

"Want to drive?"

Dante's amused expression as he agitated the keys under her nose activated Eden's stubbornness instantly. She shook her head and sent a glare back. He smiled. That was probably the reaction he expected from her anyway.

A dozen people were apparently coming along with them. Eden wondered if this was too much or not enough. They were all wearing perfect Italian suits, but none looked as good or neat as the one on Dante De Luca. She would have never said it out loud, but he was very elegant under the blue lights of the parking lot. He was actually rather tall, regardless of the little heels on his soles.

Eden stopped staring, realizing she had her eyes fixed on his side for too long.

"Here."

He turned on a black Lamborghini, and Eden's heart jumped in her chest. She was going to sit in this thing? To her surprise, Dante went to the car alone while all of his men, Rolf included, scattered to take various cars, none half as luxurious as his. She hesitated, but he opened the passenger's door with a smile, waiting for her. Frowning, Eden carefully put her pups down on the passenger's side and got inside the car. She tried not to look impressed by the gorgeous leather or the widescreen.

"Do you have any preferences?" he asked, starting the engine.

"On what?"

"Food, of course. I'm taking you on a date. I might as well start to know your tastes."

Eden's brain stopped for a second, and she blinked, turning to him as if he was some idiot. Regardless of her feelings at the moment, the car had already begun driving itself out of the parking lot, a line of black cars preceding or following it.

After a few seconds, she realized he must have been making fun of her, so she sighed, thinking what an idiot she was, and leaned back against the seat, crossing her arms.

"It's not a date," she retorted. "Moreover, I'd advise you to take your whores out before trying to kill them."

"I didn't try to kill you."

"You used me as a human shield. Call it whatever you want. You tried to kill me."

"I did not. If I wanted to kill you, I would have done so on the first try."

"Lucky me."

Her bitter answer was given with a snarl as she was staring outside. She didn't want to trust one word he said or to even think he was somewhat innocent in anything. She hated him, and she had no problem showing it. After all, she had been forced into this situation, no more and no less.

De Luca remained silent for a little while. He had put the car in manual mode, so she wondered if he was only pretending to be absorbed in his driving. Eden truly didn't care. She kept staring outside at the Italian district she always avoided normally. It wasn't unpleasant, though. It was actually one of the safest neighborhoods for those who could afford to live there.

"How did you come to live on the Eagle's territory?"

"The neighborhood was cheap."

"But you weren't born there."

Eden glared at him. She was annoyed that he was suddenly prying into her private life. She shook her head.

"...I don't know where I was born."

"It's strange that your SIN couldn't give out that information either."

Of course, it couldn't. Eden's SIN had been carefully encrypted by Loir several times to hide as much information as possible. Although they said they had scanned it already, she knew her partner hacker was good enough to give them only the tip of the iceberg and keep the real information hidden.

"Your SIN didn't know your birth name, your birthplace, or even your exact birth date," continued Dante. "Isn't that strange?"

"What's strange is that you care so much," retorted Eden. "I thought you picked me up to be your bodyguard and hacker, not your conversation partner."

"I'm of a curious nature."

"Try being of a mind-your-own-business nature."

Their banter felt childish, but Eden just didn't want to give in to him. She would clam up and make sure not a single bit of information about herself came out of her lips. She had too many secrets to protect.

"...It's strange that your mother is registered as a Native."

Eden's blood suddenly went cold. This time she turned her head to glare at him, her hands gripping on to the leather seat.

"...Why the hell did you look into my mother?"

"I told you, curious nature," he retorted with a smirk.

"De Luca, I swear, if you get within an inch of my mother–"

"Oh, why would I do that?"

Eden didn't trust him. She was mad and annoyed at this half-threat. If they

91

had found her mother, they already knew too much. Eden's mother was her weak point. If Dante got to her, she might as well be his slave for her whole life.

Trying her best to keep a cool head, Eden's brain went into overdrive. Although he may have found out about her mother, Dante De Luca probably hadn't been able to find her physical location. Her mother's information had been as hidden as Eden's was, and she trusted the hacker to at least have done a decent job with that... No, De Luca was probably toying with her, acting like he knew everything to make her talk. Crossing her arms even tighter, Eden silently promised herself to keep her damn mouth shut from there on.

"...So, how did you become a Part?"

Eden rolled her eyes, looking back outside and staying silent.

"I doubt you needed that kind of enhancement from what I've seen of your skills. You actually rely on those legs a bit too much, in my opinion. No, I wouldn't think it was voluntary. Plus, not many people can afford that change, and with everything it implies... Were you in an accident? Although people rarely become Parts due to an accident; they usually want to make some dirty money..."

She remained silent.

"Do you know what they do with the human parts that are sold? Most of the time, they use them for experiments. If they are good, the people in the Core use them for their own bodies. They can buy thin, pretty, white legs whenever they want. Sometimes, they even use them for their androids. Can you imagine machines walking around with human parts...?"

"Have you considered selling your mouth?" asked Eden. "I don't think you'll get a good price if you keep using it so much."

De Luca chuckled.

"The funniest part is, they call us Parts, but they are Parts too as soon as they buy what we sell. They are just better at hiding it."

"...Us?" repeated Eden, intrigued.

De Luca turned to her, his golden eyes suddenly glowing.

"You didn't think these were natural, did you?"

This time, she really was surprised. ...This guy was a Part too?

There were two kinds of Parts.

First, for those in the Suburbs, Parts were people who had one of their limbs replaced by a bionic replica. If they really lost their limb in an accident, to a disease, or sold it, anyone could become a Part overnight. It wasn't expensive to get an artificial replacement unless it was a vital organ. Some shops were even entirely dedicated to this business, selling various models and offering to perform the surgery on site. Still, they weren't selling anything but artificial parts made of metal or plastic. At least in the Suburbs, that was what most people could afford. Eden's legs were among those that were enhanced for combat purposes, one of the most expensive models, and she should have never been able to afford those in her birth condition.

The other kind of Part, those that no one talked about, was the Parts who received those discarded body parts. It was the case for most people at the Core. If they had a limb missing, an accident, a failing organ, they could get it replaced within a day. Anything could be bought nowadays, even a lung or a hand. People in the Core could probably afford to lose a finger a day if they were wealthy. Replacements could be created within minutes with their genetic data and DNA records from their SINs. Human flesh could be produced by machines like one would print a file.

The reason Parts were so hated was because some people had actually begun selling their limbs willingly. The Core couldn't produce human flesh out of thin air, so they recycled it.

At first, it had come as a good way to use bodies instead of burning or burying them. Using mass-produced campaigns across the nation, companies had convinced people it was fine to sell their dead, as a good sum would come out of it, and they were reborn in a different way. After some reluctance, the green-washing had worked. So, for a few decades, the dead were sent. Nowadays, people didn't wait to be dead anymore. Living limbs were sold at a much higher price, and people in the Suburbs were highly conscious of that.

As that business had gone overboard, Parts had appeared. Those people who had sold themselves while still alive. It had caused a massive divergence of opinions in the population. They were considered half-humans, as if they had sold their pride for a shortcut to money. Even those who didn't become one willingly were treated in the same regard. The line between them and machines was blurred, and instead, they were considered filthy for selling their bodies to the people of the Core. The irony was, in that process, people had focused on hating the sellers instead of the buyers. The people in the Core had adapted to that new type of life, while in the Suburbs, the hatred for those who had sold their body parts, had only grown greater and greater.

People like Eden, who walked around with enhanced Parts, were considered the worst.

However, she never would have thought Dante De Luca was a Part too.

"...Only your eyes?" she asked.

"Only your legs?"

Eden rolled her eyes and went back to her silence. She wasn't going to let herself be beaten by that little game of half-truths.

# CHAPTER SEVEN

The car stopped, and she realized they were at their destination. As expected, they were at a very fancy Italian restaurant. A bit unsure, Eden got out of the car and grabbed her pups, keeping Beer and Bullet by her feet. De Luca didn't seem to mind at all. In fact, he barely glanced at the pups before walking inside the restaurant.

It was extremely uncomfortable to walk inside a building with so many people glued to them, but Eden quickly understood this was a ritual. Six men stayed outside guarding the entrance, while two walked ahead of them, their weapons visible. Rolf was one step behind De Luca, on his right, while Eden was on his left. Although she didn't like it, she hadn't forgotten she would also be acting as a bodyguard. Even just by habit, she had already spotted the exits and gotten a sense of the overall restaurant layout.

It didn't look like there would be an issue, though; there were no other customers, and Dante and the little group were immediately taken upstairs. It was obvious everyone here knew him and feared him. The servants were bowing low at a ninety-degree angle, some visibly sweating.

"Here."

To Eden's surprise, a unique table for two had been prepared in front of a superb view of Chicago. She wanted to roll her eyes, but instead, she glared at De Luca.

"Seriously?"

"I did mention it was a date and us having lunch together," he said with

94

a cunning smile. "Are you surprised?"

Eden crossed her arms once again. This was way too much, and what he intended was too obvious. The table had been prepared in the most cheesy, romantic way possible. There was a horrible amount of flower petals all over the place, the silverware was way too gaudy, the champagne was in a bucket filled with ice, and there were even candles lit. Candles, in the middle of the day? Eden could not even think of a word to describe this. It was ridiculous and cringeworthy. What kind of weird pervert was he? She grimaced.

"Are you insane?" she asked. "What is this?"

"A lunch table. On the fancier side, I'll admit it. Aren't you going to sit down?"

Just as he said that, he pulled out a chair, clearly to have her sit in it. Instead, Eden stepped back, seriously disturbed by what was going on. What was he playing at? He couldn't possibly think this kind of low strategy would work just because she was a woman? Or did he seriously have a death wish?

"Is something wrong?" he asked with a smile, seeing her still frozen there.

"Yes. How can I be your bodyguard when I want to kill you every time you open that damn mouth?" she hissed. "I'm not eating here."

De Luca sighed, but he was still waiting for her to sit.

Eden was perplexed. What was going on? This really looked like some fancy, romantic dinner, and she just didn't know how to react to the crap he was pulling. Moreover, his men were scattered all around them, adding to her torture. She really wanted to say no to all that shit and run away. Beer and Bullet had begun playing with some of the petals on the floor, and she wanted to call them back, but at that moment, Eden was frozen.

"Is there anything you don't like?" asked Dante.

The worst part was that he was probably having fun torturing her like this. Eden had been visibly pulling away as much as she could from the beginning, and this was just too much. The whole romantic thing was just too shocking of a situation for her. She had no idea how to handle this. Was he doing that thing, killing them with kindness? She would rather have had him take her straight to bed and fuck her rather than go through this kind of humiliation!

"I don't like this," she said. "I'm your bodyguard, no? I can have a sandwich and wait."

"I'm inviting you to have lunch with me," chuckled Dante. "Is that so scary?"

Yes, for Eden, it was. Still, she did not want to admit it.

However, she had to decide. The mafia lord was waiting for her.

"I can wait like this all day," he added, as if he'd read her thoughts.

Eden's feelings were mixed.

It didn't mean anything to sit at that table with him. Yet, she felt like if she gave in just a little, the Tiger would swallow her whole. She took a deep breath and reluctantly approached the chair with a defiant glare. De Luca smiled and stepped back to let her sit. Although Eden was his bodyguard, she felt a sense of relief when he moved away. They both took their seats, facing each other in that strange atmosphere.

Eden couldn't relax at all. She couldn't forget about the men posted all around them, the nervous waiters, and their strange, romantic setup in a big empty restaurant. She even grabbed her pups to put them on her lap, like a buffer between her and Dante. He didn't seem to mind, though. He quietly poured the champagne into their glasses, very casually, and put his napkin on his lap.

"To our new collaboration, then!" he said, toasting all by himself.

Eden barely looked at her glass. She watched him drink the fizzy liquid in silence, petting Beer and wondering what the hell he was trying to do with her.

Dante had impeccable manners. After only one sip, he put his glass down and wiped his lips carefully. His posture was very straight, showing off his square shoulders and body sculpted for action.

"For someone who works as a hostess, you don't seem very used to this."

"My clients are not Zodiacs," she retorted.

"Oh, I'm your first in at least one thing, then."

Eden frowned. She really couldn't understand this man.

The starters were brought by a young waitress who couldn't help but send a flirtatious glance toward Dante, despite her nervousness. He caught it and responded with a cold smile. Eden was even more annoyed. That bastard was just playing around with his arrogance laid out on the table.

"Why work as a hostess?" he asked.

"Why not?"

"How much were you paid?"

"Enough."

"I'll pay you triple of whatever 'enough' was, then."

The mention of money made Eden's lip twitch. Her mother. She had forgotten about that massive debt above her head, and it wasn't a matter that was going to wait just because her employer had suddenly changed.

"I want it up front," she suddenly said.

De Luca raised an eyebrow, actually surprised this time, and put his fork down.

"So you're in it for the money. It's funny; that was maybe the last thing I would have tried to get to you."

"You don't get to anything. It is just the same for anyone here. We all need money."

"Mh... What if I'm not willing to pay upfront? After all, you haven't proven anything yet."

"I can ask which other Zodiac wants to beat Ghost, then."

This time, he lost his smile.

Eden felt good about that. So he hated having competition. After all, it was known that most of the Zodiacs didn't get along at all. Of course, some had agreements so trades could continue, and one could avoid being completely isolated with a shortage of food or supplies, but the territories existed in the first place because they did not get along, and the communities had grown wary of one another. The difficulties that came from living outside the Core in the Suburbs reinforced the hatred between the various communities. Those born with a clear cultural background were luckier than the mixed ones or those whose people were not protected by one of the Zodiacs. Eden was one of those people. As a white woman with few clues about her own background, she had to go from one territory to another with extreme caution. She had gotten into fights before simply because she was mistaken as Italian or Russian.

"You're my property from now on," suddenly said Dante De Luca.

His cold voice surprised Eden. He wasn't just being serious; he was threatening her. She felt a chill go down her spine as his eyes glowed. She couldn't go to another territory without him suspecting that she'd betray him from now on.

This was exactly why she didn't want to work for a Zodiac. The bigger the employer, the bigger the target on her back. As a hire-for-money, she could at least pick whom she worked for and stop the next day... or at least that's how it should have been. She sighed and finally grabbed her fork to start eating as well. She may not like his methods, but at least, she should eat her fill of what she could. Actually, Eden couldn't even remember the last time she had eaten something. She started picking at her plate, eating the vegetables with delight but ignoring the brown square next to it.

"What is this...?" she mumbled, poking at it.

"A steak. Organic," said Dante, chuckling.

Eden frowned, a bit disgusted.

Buying real red meat wasn't possible in the Suburbs unless one had a lot of money. The only kind of meat she could afford was cheap chicken once in a while. She knew there were now too many laws about meat consumption, which made it only affordable for the wealthiest, and of course, the people of the Core. Even knowing it was organic, she didn't even want to try it. Eden had never had actual red meat before, although she knew what it was supposed to look like. Artificial meat was more common, but she knew the ones sometimes available in the Suburbs also had chances of being infected with some strange diseases. The labs tried to perfect the taste and properties of lab-grown food by experimenting with it on the people of the Suburbs. That belief kept her from trying this one, although Dante was eating his.

Instead, she cut it and put the plate down to let the pups chew on the little bits.

"What do you want the money for?" asked Dante.

"Why do you care?"

"It's my money."

"It won't be once you make the transfer. Triple my usual salary, right?"

"I'll make it five times if you tell me what you want it for."

Eden glared at him. She didn't like bargaining.

"...My legs cost a lot."

"I figured as much. However, you shouldn't need that much money if you're also a hacker. Plus the salary and tips from your work at the bar."

Eden grimaced. Why did he have to be smart too? She sighed. She just didn't like to talk about herself, but this guy was poking at her relentlessly.

"I have debts," she simply said, "a lot of debts I need to cover. For my legs, for my mother. Is that enough? Because I don't have receipts to show you if that's what you're asking for."

Dante squinted his eyes, not convinced. He knew Eden wasn't telling him everything. She was a poor liar, and her sullen attitude meant she was reluctant to say more. She was a mystery. For someone riddled with debts, living in a shitty neighborhood, and willing to work as a hostess to cover her debts, she still took in two dogs that would be a pain to take care of. She didn't seem like a good Samaritan, either. Or was it just because those were pets, as opposed to humans? Dante couldn't decipher this woman, and he was intrigued by the mystery.

"...Fine," he said. "I'll make the transfer as soon as your SIN is turned back on."

Eden was surprised. Was he actually going to keep his word? For some reason, she had expected him to come up with some lie to get out of it. Still, she was happy to have been wrong, although the money wasn't in her account yet.

"Let me go! Let me go, you criminals!"

A ruckus came from behind, and within a second, all of Dante's men present took out their guns. Eden frowned, but there was no need for her to react to this from what she could hear.

Two of his men walked in, dragging a young woman in a pitiful state. Her knees had been scratched so badly that her blood was spilling onto the wooden floor. Her clothes were completely torn apart, revealing her underwear, and she was covered in dirt. From the bruises on her face and arms, Eden could tell she had been abused. However, this ought to be fresh. She easily recognized the young woman who had been dropped the previous day by the Overcraft from the Core. An Exiled.

"Let me go!" she screamed, completely panicked.

"We found her hiding at the back of the restaurant, Boss. She was trying to sneak in, probably to steal food."

The woman kept trying to get them away from her with screams and threats, making everyone grimace. Eden's dogs began barking, excited by all the noise.

"Let me go! Let me go, you criminals! You're filthy! You're going to give me your diseases! You criminals! Let me go! Let me go, I swear I'll sue you! I'll have you killed! Don't touch me!"

One of Dante's men slapped her, and she finally stopped screaming. Either it was from the shock because she was scared or her jaw was hurt, but everyone seemed relieved that she finally shut up. She began sobbing, and Dante's men dropped her onto the floor, down on her knees.

Dante stood up with a smile that couldn't mean anything good.

"What do we have here..." he sighed.

"Y-you!" she said. "You have to take me back to the Core! That's an order!"

"You're a bit slow, aren't you?" he chuckled. "The Core exiled you, young lady. You don't have a SIN."

The girl opened her eyes wider in utter panic. The bloody hole on her neck was a disgusting and painful sight to see. Her fingers reached out for it, and she began crying louder as if reality had hit her just now.

"I-I can't..." she mumbled. "I'm a citizen of the Core; I'm not a criminal! I'm not a criminal!"

"Oh, for fuck's sake, shut up," hissed Eden, pissed.

She suddenly stood up, and Dante stepped aside with a smile.

"You should be glad you're even alive, you selfish bitch," Eden continued.

"Don't talk to me!" retorted the young woman, suddenly angry. "I know who you are. All of you! You're just criminals, all jealous of us in the Core! They tell us about you, what kind of criminals you are. I'm different from you; I'm pure! You should be glad you're even allowed outside. People like you only deserve scraps! If it wasn't for the Core, you'd all be dead! I'm not like you!"

"Oh? So you were exiled from the Core because you were a good girl, then?" sneered Eden.

She slowly crouched down, staring at the girl with an annoyed expression. "You think you know everything, don't you?"

"I don't think, I know," retorted the woman, acting haughty. "The people in the Suburbs are just criminals. You would have been allowed into the Core if you weren't criminals. You contribute nothing to society. You're just like vermin wasting air. You pollute, sell weapons and drugs. You're all junkies, thieves, prostitutes, and murderers!"

"You think that's it?" chuckled Eden.

Her laugh took the woman by surprise.

"Th-The Core only allows people with no criminal... records..." stuttered the woman.

Her confidence was failing because Eden seemed so sure of herself and wasn't flinching at all. Moreover, Eden didn't look like a criminal. She was white, like most privileged people living in the Core, and at that very moment, she was more beautiful, proud, and confident than that newly-exiled woman. She had no visible weapon, wore beautiful clothes, and her blonde hair was shining like a gold mane around her face. Compared to her, the Exiled was the one who looked like a bum...

"That's right," said Eden. "After the Great North American War, when it all ended, and the Cores were created, they wanted to design the perfect society. The Architect had designed the Cores to be beautiful, perfect places of harmony where humans could live under a smart computer's supervision while the Earth healed itself. However, the Cores were too small, and the society was just at the perfect stage to be shaped. So, the leaders of these Cores decided to only keep people with no criminal records inside because the Cores couldn't host the entire population."

Next to Eden, Dante smiled, crossing his arms and letting her continue to do the talking.

"However, do you know what happened when they checked the numbers?" she continued. "The Cores were still too small. So first, they decided to execute all the people who had committed capital crimes. Murderers. Child rapists. War criminals. Arms dealers. All of them were killed in a blink of an eye."

"N-no, they said they... exiled them..." muttered the woman. "They exiled them here, to the Suburbs."

"No," retorted Eden. "In 2089, the Chicago population was a little over 2 million people. How many people live in the Core right now?"

"F-five hundred thousand..."

"Do you think three-quarters of the population were criminals?"

The woman remained silent, lowering her head. Eden could see her mumbling, but soon enough, she raised her head.

"You're lying," she said. "The people in the Suburbs—"

"Are criminals? Oh, yes, they are. Once the prisons were empty and there were no more criminals to rule out of the Cores, your leaders began doing another kind of sorting. The small crimes were still crimes, after all. Building the perfect society came with ruling out every single convicted person. They let the SINs do all the work for them. They just encoded a few rules in the system, and the sorting was done in a mere fifty days. Any kind of criminal had to leave. People who committed a level 1 crime were killed on the spot. People who had committed more than one offense? Killed. Not enough? Let's get down to level 2. Did you steal a car? You're executed. Did you drive without a license? Executed. Offend a law representative? Executed."

Eden was doing all the talking, but around her, everyone had cold expressions. No one had forgotten that dark part of the Suburbs' history, and the young woman was telling that story in such a raw and blunt way, it felt both violent and beautiful to them. The Exiled woman had her mouth open as if reality was hitting her.

However, Eden wasn't done.

"When they couldn't kill any more people, because that would have been too much, they thought it would be enough to exile them. Branding them

100

as criminals, they drove more people out. The smallest offense was enough. The Core just couldn't fit everyone, so only the perfect, stainless citizens could stay. Even if you had stolen a single piece of candy, you were sent here, regardless of your age, gender, and race. You think we are criminals? Fuck yes, the ones your leaders decided on."

Eden scoffed.

"Criminals. Citizens who didn't pay a bill on time or couldn't afford to. The poorer people, all of them. Someone who came here with the wrong papers. The immigrants. People with no proof of address. The homeless. People with unregistered jobs. Prostitutes, minors, illegal workers who couldn't be employed anywhere. Even the very people who helped build the Core were kicked out as illegal workers. People who couldn't afford medicine from the Core? Yeah, the junkies."

The woman's lip kept twitching as if she was out of words. Eden's eyes were burning a hole through her, and she had no response. Not because she still didn't believe it, but because Eden's hazel eyes showed so much pain as if she had witnessed all this herself.

Eden stood back up and suddenly pointed at Dante.

"There are criminals like him. You kick out all the criminals, you say? No, you're just letting new and more dangerous ones grow right on your doorstep. The monsters the Core created because people here needed worse monsters to protect them. You just created a lower level of hell to blind yourself in that fucked up little paradise of yours."

The woman looked up at Dante, and suddenly, it was as if she was seeing him for the first time. Fear grew in her eyes. Maybe she had heard of the Zodiac, or she was frightened by Eden's words.

The blonde sighed and took one step back. The Exiled one finally turned her gaze toward Eden, shivering. All of her beliefs were crumbling. Eden didn't have the eyes of someone who was lying or spoke without knowing.

"W-what... what about you...?" she asked.

Eden frowned and glared back at that woman.

"I'm a hacker. The one thing your leaders fear the most. Someone who can cheat your system, wreck it, corrupt it. The one who digs up your dirt and exposes all the blood you shed. I don't play by the disgusting rules that they wrote."

A long silence followed Eden's words as she swept her blonde hair over her shoulder. She had spoken arrogantly, but everyone in the room knew she was completely in the right.

"A h-hacker...?" muttered the exiled woman. "What's that...?"

The people in the Core had no concept of what a hacker was.

They were never taught that the Core's rules and the System their society was based on were only numbers and codes, a digital structure so fragile it could be modified by humans. Eden knew enough about the Core. The Architect, the founding father of all the Cores, had created the perfect artificial intelligence to control them all; a completely automated system with hundreds of agents. Since it ruled itself, there was no need for human interventions. Any kind of job related to the System had completely disappeared in a matter of weeks. The humans had been sent back to their role as consumers, and the rulers of the Core had made sure no one could alter or interfere with the Core in any way. They had understood how it was dangerous to let free agents modify the System when the System offered complete automated control of their lives.

It also meant anyone with any knowledge on the matter had been hunted down, and gotten rid of. There were no more black or white hats. Anyone who had the knowledge and ability to get into the System was a high-level threat and target. Some may have been hired secretly, but according to the rumors, most had been killed. The Architect himself had disappeared before the rise of the twenty-second century.

However, all this was a history Eden had no intent to give a lecture on. That woman had been raised to believe in a System: a System that had allowed her to live a privileged life, and she had been kicked out by that same arbitrary System.

"Something you'll never know," suddenly said De Luca.

The next second, that woman was shot dead.

Eden closed her eyes. It was one precise and deadly shot, making a quick job of it. Things were over in a second. She didn't look, but she heard Dante's men act quickly to get rid of the body while she returned to her seat. Eden took a deep breath and sat down. She wasn't saddened by that death; death was so common in the districts, there was nothing about it that could surprise her anymore. Considering she had walked into a Zodiac's lair, that woman had already exceeded her life expectancy by a few minutes.

"My apologies for the interruption," said Dante, going back to his seat as well. "I fear my security has been rather... lacking, lately."

He had said that with an ice-cold gaze toward his men. Surely, there would be a few more paying with their lives later on...

Eden didn't reply and resumed eating, still hungry. It was amazing how her primal needs took over the stench of blood and death. The food was good, and she just couldn't leave any when she had a chance to eat something so good. Plus, she was in a hurry to get this ridiculous lunch over with and get out of there. Being next to a Zodiac was like standing in front of a gun. She knew that man had a lot more money on his head than she did. Too many people would be happy to see the Italian Tiger fall.

"...What were you doing on the Dragon's territory?" she asked, suddenly remembering the strange course of events.

"To piss off Yang. I already told you that."

"You must have bigger prey to play around with," hissed Eden. "Yang is... was annoying, but he's an idiot. Old Man Long wouldn't have picked him as his successor."

"Maybe, but he was at least useful to make a clear statement."

Eden stayed quiet this time. So that was his plan... not only to get rid of Yang but to intimidate all those who had eyes on the Chinese Dragon's territory: the other Zodiacs, but also all those waiting in the shadows for the old man to die.

Old Man Long was one of the oldest and most respected Zodiacs, even among the Zodiac itself. Rumor had it that he was the one who had created the Zodiac, to begin with, using the ancient Chinese zodiac to give all the mafia lords a title to be known and remembered by. Hence, each mafia and territory leader could change, but they inherited their predecessors' reputation and Zodiac title.

In a roundabout way, the Zodiacs respected their peers, sometimes even without ever meeting face-to-face. Even for the territory wars, they never went head-on against each other, and instead, they let their underlings fight for them. There was no open war, but dozens of little conflicts spread around the Suburbs. It wasn't much better, but at least it kept it relatively peaceful.

"...You want the Old Man's territory," said Eden. "Why? The Chinese won't accept someone of mixed race as their leader."

Dante raised his golden eyes toward her. She wasn't the type to judge people by their looks, but she had to say it. The communities were so cautious toward one another in those times they lived in; someone like him, someone biracial, couldn't get to the top... It was already surprising he was the Italian Boss.

"Times are changing," he said. "It's not about blood or territories anymore. It's about getting stronger."

"So what? You'll be at war with the Rat and the Snake to get a measly portion of Chicago?"

Dante smiled, but he did not answer. Instead, Eden watched him slowly cut his portion of steak, and bring it to his lips. She was nervous once again. Not because she feared him, but because she couldn't decipher his intentions.

"...It's not about the territory," he then said.

"Money, then?"

"No, power."

Eden frowned. Those enigmas. Again. She couldn't understand his train of thought.

"I want it all," he said.

"...All of the Dragon's territory?"

"All the territories."

Eden remained silent for a few seconds, rendered speechless. Then she chuckled nervously.

That man was crazy. She laughed uncontrollably, even if she knew he could kill her for that if he wanted to. This was just so unbelievable to hear. After a while, and since she was still alive, she grabbed her glass, shaking her head. She took a long sip, tasting the delicious champagne for the first time. The fizzy and sweet bubbles on her tongue somehow made her laugh even more until she put it down.

"You're crazy," she said. "You might be able to conquer one territory. But you can't have them all. People won't respect you, and the Core will hunt you down. They will send their agents to shoot you down. They are letting the Zodiacs be because you're powerful but not powerful enough to annoy them. The Core hunts down people who threaten them. It's not–"

"People like you?"

Dante's sentence made her lose her smile.

Eden regained her seriousness. He wasn't laughing at all. In fact, he didn't even have the beginning of a smirk on. Not only was he serious, but he believed in his own madness, which was even scarier. Eden took a deep breath.

"Yes, people like me. However, I'm not stupid to let people know my face and my name when I commit crimes against the Core. Hackers act undercover. Mafiosos don't. That's where the line between us is drawn. You keep the balance in the Suburbs and kill each other peacefully. The hackers attack the Core. If you start attacking the Core, you'll be dead in no time."

"Should I be scared, then?" asked Dante, a cunning smile appearing on his face.

"That, or crazy, and I think you're the latter."

He chuckled and cut another piece of steak. What was going on in his mind? And more importantly, how had she gotten herself into that mess with such a crazy bastard?

Eden wasn't hungry anymore. She was back to making plans to get out of there, out of his grasp, and as far as she could from him. She never wanted to be involved with the Italian again. She already hated him, but now she wondered if she shouldn't kill him. It felt like a lot less work.

"...Why did you become a hacker?"

Eden frowned, turning to him. They were back to personal questions now?

"...I had to survive, so I found a way."

"No one becomes a hacker by mere chance. It takes knowledge that someone your age doesn't get just like that."

"I did what every hacker does: I learned from someone else. Why are you interested in that too now?"

"I need the best hacker by my side for my plan. I need to know if you're the best."

Eden was speechless.

So that was why that man wanted Ghost. Not just for Ghost to work for him, but to help him with his crazy plans. She was too shocked to even speak. This was madness. Of all people, she had fallen into the hands of a crazy megalomaniac, some narcissist with crazy ambition in which she had become a part of.

"You're really crazy," she mumbled.

"Well, that's what it takes to shake the world. Or at least, a large city."

"No, you're seriously mad if you think you have a chance. You can't beat all nine of the other Zodiacs. Even if you do, so what? You're going to attack the Core with your little fists and your guns? Are you insane?"

"...Isn't that what you're doing yourself?"

He slowly crossed his arms, waiting for Eden to figure out what he was saying.

"...What?"

"You're a hacker, Eden. Shaking the Core is exactly what hackers do, isn't it? The Core's artificial intelligence hates isolated agents like you. Human agents. Each time you dive, you're risking your life not only because of your competitors but because the System wants to get rid of parasites like you. Compared to me, hackers are an even bigger threat to the Core."

"I'm not like you," hissed Eden. "I do it for the money. I dive, get what I came for, and get out before the System gets me. I am not trying to lead a whole rebellion. I'm merely a flea to the Core."

"A flea that risks a lot for something it doesn't even care about."

"I care about the money."

"What if now, you dived with a real reason?"

"Boosting your ego? Yeah, that's not a life plan, it's a pending suicide mission. Sorry you thought your pretty Part eyes were going to be enough to convince me."

"Careful how you talk to the Boss!" said one of Dante's men, suddenly pulling out a gun.

Eden glared at him, her eyes glancing less than a second to that gun. The man glared at her, but she wasn't scared. Instead, Eden slowly walked toward him, making all the others react. Half pulled their guns out, some only had a hand in their pocket. Still, no one would fire unless Dante ordered them to and Eden knew that. She smirked and grabbed the gun, disarming the man with ridiculous ease.

"You think you can scare me? I can't be scared of people like you," she said.

The man, feeling stupid, lowered his head and stole glances at their boss. Eden was now holding his weapon, but Dante hadn't said a word, still sitting at their table and slowly eating his vegetables. The situation was so tense, but the boss wasn't worried one bit.

"I am no hero trying to save the world from the Core. I am just a girl trying to survive the shithole she was born in. I am not going to put myself in danger just to fulfill your selfish ambition."

She lifted the gun, and this time, she directed it toward De Luca.

All the men present reacted. The sound of a dozen guns having their safety taken off was heard, and those who hadn't taken out their weapons before were ready to shoot. Eden's arm was shaking, but she held the gun at arm's length, her heart beating like crazy.

She had come to a conclusion, a conclusion that wasn't any good. That man was going to have her killed. If she proved she wasn't Ghost, she'd die. If she proved she was indeed Ghost, she'd die an even more horrible death trying to fight against the Core. It wasn't as simple as dying. Many hackers were captured by the Core and tortured. Regardless if their bodies were caught, Eden had heard of hackers being trapped in endless loops of nightmares, the Core forcing them to live their worst fears until they were completely broken. It was the beauty and the horror of an A.I. who could imprison your mind. Eden had already made her decision. She had enough nightmares haunting her already; she'd much rather have the painless death...

"Let go of the gun!" yelled one of the men.

Eden ignored him. She ignored all of them but Dante, who stood up after wiping his mouth once again. His slow and controlled moves were annoying and caused the tension to increase inch by inch in the room. With his smile on, he took off his jacket and put it on the back of his chair, leaning himself against the table. He was staring at her the whole time, and even put his hands in his pockets very calmly. Eden was intrigued by his change of position and how composed he was.

"Are you going to kill me?" he asked. "You won't get out of here alive."

"I'll die anyway if I follow you," she said. "I don't want to die becoming someone's expendable pawn."

"Fair enough."

He glanced around, and slowly, most of his men lowered their weapons. Eden couldn't understand. She wouldn't have been surprised if she had been shot a dozen times already, but she was still there and no gunshot had resonated yet. Or was he giving her the benefit of the doubt?

Dante took a deep breath.

"...I like an interesting woman."

Eden frowned. She didn't want to be swayed by compliments and sweet talk. She had heard enough from her job as a hostess to not believe them so easily. There was always a painful hook behind the bait.

Dante stood up, suddenly coming closer. Eden panicked and took one step back. Why had she come here, exactly? She should have run when she had the chance to. Eden's heartbeat went wild again, her fingers sweating on the gun.

"...Let me go," she said. "You find yourself another hacker, another Ghost, and we will be done."

"Why would I?"

"There are dozens of other hackers out there who'd be happy to work for your money. I can even find you one if you want, but I'm not interested. Find someone else."

Dante sighed, still staring at her with a mysterious expression.

"That's too bad," he said. "You're the one I want."

Eden felt cold chills going down her spine. Why? Why did that man have to be so bent on her? She couldn't understand. Was it because she had saved his life? His sense of duty or something? A man like Dante De Luca wouldn't be capable of something like that!

"...Find someone else," she repeated.

His smile grew larger.

"I don't want to. You seem pretty interesting, Eden. I don't like mindless puppets. Your survival instincts are quite admirable too. You have what it takes to take down a Zodiac."

"You'll be the first to go if you don't let me get away from here," hissed Eden, determined.

She didn't like this situation.

Although she was the one holding the gun, Eden felt at a disadvantage. Not because of the dozens of other weapons aimed at her, but because of that cunning grin of his. As if he was still in charge. As if he was on her end of the gun, holding the weapon, deciding on her survival or not. Eden was trying to think, and think fast. How? How could she get out of there without murdering a Zodiac and getting shot down right away?

She wanted to survive. No matter what, she wasn't stupid enough to just sacrifice herself. She had a weapon in her hand, and it felt like if she didn't leave now, she would never be able to.

"...Let's make another bet," he said.

"W-what?"

"I'll let you go if you survive this."

"Survive what?"

Suddenly, all the lights went out. Not just the lights, but the fake windows turned pitch black too. Eden heard the first gunshot somewhere over her shoulder, and someone grabbed her and threw her onto the floor. She rolled, her shoulder injured. She heard another gunshot, and one of the fake windows was blown, a downpour of glass falling over her head. Someone yelled an order in Italian, but she didn't catch it. She heard her pups whimpering and crawled toward them, trying to stay as low to the floor as she could. More gunshots echoed above her position.

The restaurant had been thrown into total chaos in a matter of seconds, and she could hear people running all around. Someone stepped over her legs, and she heard a body falling somewhere on her left. More gunshots echoed, and she realized the shooters were outside. Snipers shooting from a building opposite? Eden grimaced when more gunshots ricocheted. She could only hear one of the pups whimpering, and she grabbed him. She swung her arm around, trying to find his brother. Where had he gone?!

The gunshots kept firing, and she suddenly understood that this was her only window of opportunity. Eden's heartbeat slowed suddenly, as she realized. All his men were busy trying to keep him alive, if he still was alive. No one would care if she left. No one would shoot her. She looked around, trying to find the exit; it was already full of people, more guards who had run from the outside. Eden grimaced and turned around until she found another option. The kitchens. She had seen the woman come through there. There had to be another exit. She couldn't spend more time there, and she had no idea where the other pup was. She only had this one shot.

Staying as close as she could to the ground, Eden ran in the direction where she vaguely remembered the kitchens to be. Another raffle of bullets blew more of the windows, sending light inside again. Eden glanced behind her shoulder, but there was no sign of the other pup. No time left.

She dove behind a panel, rolled down, finally close enough to the exit. She ran toward the door.

"Boss!"

Eden stopped, her hand on the door, and after half a second, looked back.

Dante had been shot. She couldn't tell where, but two of his men were over him, and there was blood. Still, she met his eyes, and he stared right back at her. His lips moved, saying something.

Eden ran past the door as soon as she understood what he had said, and she kept running as if the devil himself was after her. She could hear the gunshots still resonating behind her. The only objective was to put as much distance as possible between herself and the restaurant. She finally found the emergency exit, and with all of her body strength, she pushed the door open and ran as fast as her legs could carry her. In her arms, she could feel Bullet's little heart beating like crazy, and the dog didn't dare emit a sound either.

Chunks of glass exploded somewhere above her. Eden had to cover her head so she wouldn't be injured. Where were they shooting from? She couldn't even locate the enemy! However, she didn't have time to pause and look. She knew those kinds of fights never lasted for more than a few minutes. And Dante's words were haunting her...

Her heart beating fast, Eden tried to remember where she was and where to go next. She wasn't familiar with the Italian territory, and for a good reason. She had never wanted to be here in the first place. If she was in the northern part of their territory, she would have to go southwest to get back to the Eagle's. However, what if Dante's men found her before she could get there? She had to cross all of the Italian territory to get to the border, and she wasn't even sure about where she was heading.

# CHAPTER EIGHT

Eden just kept running, only picking narrow streets that went in the same direction. She tried to see the signs around, seeing if she was on the right path. Perhaps she was heading more west than she thought.

Finally, she found an underground station, Polk. Although it was called an underground station, it was actually one floor above the ground, not under. Eden climbed up, feeling nervous; no trains were running this line since the explosion of 2098, and she wasn't sure what she was going to find upstairs. Many abandoned stations had become the lairs of dangerous people or hosted some very shady businesses. Thankfully, as Eden finished climbing she realized that was not the case with this station. Instead, rows of homeless people turned their heads to her, looking scared. However, Eden had no time for them. She remembered what outfit she was in, and she certainly couldn't stay here wearing name-brand clothing. She was too easy to spot and didn't fit in. So she got down onto the tracks and followed the direction to the south. It was easy from this height, as she could see the buildings in the distance. She put Bullet down, as he could follow once she started walking.

Only then did Eden feel a bit better, and took a deep breath.

Those rails and trains were no longer in service, but they were now hosting a lot more life than before. Hence, people were dotted all along the railroad tracks, their backs against the walls.

Moreover, there was no signal up here. Around the end of the twenty-first century, special fences had been put up to turn off any signal that wasn't part of the train's electrical functions to avoid potential hijackings and other hacking attempts. SINs didn't work; any type of tracking device was useless. Which was why the people coming up here were those without SINs or those who wanted to hide theirs. Eden sighed, massaging her neck. She would have to be quick once she got back; grab her things, pack a bag, and leave. If the Italians had scanned her SIN, it meant they would be able to find it again the minute it was reactivated... Would she have to spend her life SIN-less? Eden couldn't do that. A SIN was absolutely necessary to live with. Without it, it was the same as having no identity, no money, no rights. It was essential, and it was horribly expensive to get one. While people in the Core received one for free at birth, most people in the Suburbs had to work like crazy for ten or twenty years before they could afford one. Some even began saving ahead for their children before they were conceived.

"Woof!"

Eden looked down at Bullet, who was trotting ahead of her, getting excited about a couple of mice. She frowned. Beer had been left behind... She hoped the pup had survived the gunfight. She was surprised she had come out of it unscathed. It had felt like shots came from all sides, yet she had managed to get out of there just fine...

Something felt off about this whole situation, but she couldn't put her finger on the detail that felt wrong. It was too late to think about it now anyway. She had fled, and she would never go back. Eden kept walking and tried not to think about the words Dante whispered to her at the end. How could he say such things when he was shot down...

Finally, she arrived at the next station, the 18th. This one she was familiar with, as it was on the lower west side, right next to her place. She noted to herself that if she needed, the two closest stations were fine to use...

Carrying Bullet, she got down but didn't reactivate her SIN right away. She had to win as much time as she could. Eden hurried back to her apartment. Even there, she tried to be careful, checking over her shoulder at each intersection. She felt like those golden eyes were following her everywhere and it stressed her out. She wished she could shake off that sensation that something was wrong and tried to calm down her thumping heart.

Once she reached her building, nothing seemed strange or out of place. No one was guarding the entrance today, but that wasn't unusual. Eden hurried upstairs as Bullet became excited to be back in a familiar place. However, she didn't have time to play around with him. Eden grabbed the largest backpack she had and began throwing in the few belongings she owned. She was suddenly reminded of those lemon seeds Jack had given her... She would never get to try and grow those, she couldn't take any of her plants either. She could only focus on what was important. She changed into some of her own clothes, abandoned the previous ones on the floor, and gathered everything else into her backpack. She also took some of the pups' stuff that she had bought just days before. Bullet protested loudly when she took some of the toys and began chewing the

110

backpack angrily, but his little teeth were not doing much damage.

Only when she was ready did Eden grab her bag and the pup, then ran downstairs.

"Loir!" she yelled, banging against the door.

It opened right away and she ran into the darkness.

"Oh, Kitty is back, and... Oh, hi, puppy!" squealed Loir.

He was still the same, stuck to his desk chair and wearing the same dark clothes. Eden was out of breath and panicked, but he barely noticed.

"So, how is your stay at the Italians'?" he asked as if it was a mundane situation.

"Not good. I ran while they were caught in another fight... Loir, I have to get out of here. They scanned my SIN. They will look for me the second I reactivate it."

The hacker didn't seem worried at all. He shrugged and tilted his head, glancing at her backpack.

"Oh... Where are you going?"

"I-I don't know," confessed Eden. "I wanted to go and check on Jack first..."

Loir said nothing, which felt extremely awkward.

Then, he slowly widened his smile, making Eden step back, a bit disturbed. Loir smiling was like a shark showing all of his fangs. There was nothing happy to be felt about it. A shudder went down her spine.

"Eden is running away again..." He whistled. "Running away from the bigger kitty..."

"You know I don't have a choice," she retorted, frowning. "I'll never work for the Italian, never, Loir. After what they did to Adam... I can't forgive it."

"...You're curious," he suddenly said.

"What?"

Loir rested his chin on his knee, his pitch-black eyes staring at Eden.

"Eden is all alone," he sang in a slow and creepy tune. "Eden hates but Eden doesn't take revenge. She runs, and runs, and runs... who taught you to always run, Eden?"

"You're one to talk," she retorted. "You're the guy hiding in a basement!"

"I know who I'm running from. Do you?"

Eden sighed and looked away, avoiding that annoying smirk of his. She crossed her arms, feeling very lonely and cold all of a sudden.

"You know why I have to be on the run, Loir. I can't afford for them to find me. It was already dangerous that the Italians went as far as to scan my SIN. If they knew the truth..."

"Your secrets are very costly, little Eden," said Loir. "You can't run away forever... or stay alone."

"I'm fine being alone," she retorted.

"You left your mother..."

"I didn't abandon her!" she retorted, angry. "I did it to protect her. She can be happy wherever she is now."

"Is she, though?"

Eden glared at him.

"Mind your own business, Loir. You stay away from my mom."

"I'm just saying. Maybe Mama Kitty isn't so happy..."

Eden hated the thought of anything being wrong with her mother. She convinced herself her mother was safe and fine where she was. She shook her head.

"Stop it, Loir. I sent my mother away to protect her. She risks nothing where she is and she's getting the help she needs. What could I have done, take care of her by myself while working to feed us both? Where she is now, she doesn't need me, and she's stable."

"But the little Kitty misses her mommy..."

"I'm fine."

A silence followed Eden's words. She was feeling cold right now and upset at all of Loir's questions.

"Do you regret, Eden?"

"What?"

"Selling your legs to protect your mother."

She froze and glared at him. Eden then looked down at her fake legs that had carried her there.

"No," she retorted. "I regret telling you so much, though, that's for sure."

Loir laughed, a weird laugh that had a creepy ring to it. He sighed.

"Oh, curious little Eden... Are you sure you want to be on the run again? Weren't you looking for your master?"

Eden's heart sank. Master. She had stopped searching recently. No, the truth was she had reached a dead end and was scared to look for him again. She had run out of clues and had no idea where to look next. Her master had disappeared two years ago and it was as if all traces of his existence had been erased. Eden had dived again and again to try and find him, to find any clues, but there was... nothing left.

"...No. I think Master doesn't want me to find him," she said.

Loir tilted his head.

"So Kitty isn't just on the run. Kitty is abandoned too..."

"Are you done making fun of me?"

"Hm... maybe? So? Did you bring me anything interesting?"

"I wasn't on a fucking trip, Loir. The Italian wanted me to work for him and find Ghost, you already know everything! He took me to a restaurant, a fight happened, and I escaped. I just had enough time to run out of there. I even left Beer behind..."

Her eyes went to Bullet, who was lying down at her feet, looking tired from their journey.

"That's funny."

Eden glanced up at Loir, smiling again while staring at her, his head tilted to the side.

"What?"

"I didn't think the Italian would have let you go like that."

"He didn't! Didn't you listen? There was a gunfight and I ran away!"

"So easily?"

"Y-yeah..."

"Hm..."

Loir's smile made Eden uncomfortable. She had felt something was wrong with her escape too, but she just couldn't figure it out. The more the young woman thought about it, the more nervous she became. Her SIN was still deactivated and she was pretty sure she hadn't been followed here. So what was wrong?

"It can't be," she whispered. "De Luca said he'd let me... go..."

"He said that?"

Eden swallowed her saliva, her heart beating scary fast all of a sudden. That wasn't the only thing Dante had said. However, the second half of the sentence was too scary for her to say out loud. She kept thinking about it, feeling nervous. Was he hunting her? Was it all a game? Loir was right. It had been too easy and he had no reason to let her go in the first place!

Unless...

Eden suddenly glanced up at Loir.

"...He wanted me to get back to you," she whispered, "to my partner."

"Oh! Big Kitty wants me too?" suddenly exclaimed Loir, slapping his hands against his cheeks, pretending to be surprised. "Oh my, is it the start of something?"

"Loir, enough! How...? How could he find me?"

"Well, it's not just your SIN that can track you," chuckled the hacker, visibly not nearly as scared as she was.

Eden frowned trying to think. Then, she suddenly raised her top, glancing at her skin.

"The gunshots," she said. "They healed me from those stupid gunshots! What the fuck did they do to me?"

Loir rolled his chair over to a little pile of weird instruments on the left, technology of which half of it was completely unknown to Eden, although she had seen Loir work on it many times. Finally, he rolled back to her carrying what looked like a gun, with a screen instead of a barrel. After pushing some button on it, he pointed it at her body.

"Oh, found it! Little tracking device in your abdomen... Can you give it to me? I don't have one like these!"

"Loir, it means they know where we are, for fuck's sake!"

"Oopsie-doopsie!"

He turned to his screens and after pianoing on his keyboard, camera surveillance videos appeared from the streets nearby. Eden's blood went cold. They were almost here: the Italians' cars, three of them.

Loir cackled, looking at the cars coming toward them.

"Someone wants their pretty kitty back!"

"Loir, we have to go. They are going to find you too!"

"Really? It would be nice... Do you think they will feed me pizza? I love pizza with artichoke... and pineapples..."

"What the hell is wrong with you!" yelled Eden, grabbing Bullet. "If they find us, we will have to work for them!"

"...So?" asked Loir with a smile. "Are you going to run again, Eden?"

"What do you expect me to do? You know I hate them!"

"...Why don't we kill them, then?" asked Loir with another one of his creepy smiles.

"What are you saying? ...I can't kill a Zodiac like that..."

Eden took one step back. The mere thought was terrifying.

She wasn't scared to kill someone but she was terrified at the thought of going head-to-head against a man like Dante De Luca. If she had ever considered herself strong, she knew which fights not to start. Eden never wanted to start a fight that would put her life in someone else's hands.

Loir slowly rolled his chair closer to her.

"Think about it, Eden... Don't run away anymore. Just a tiny, cute little bullet and the Italian will be dead. No more issues... no more hatred."

"I won't stop hating him or the next Tiger just because this one is dead. It won't bring Adam back!"

Suddenly, they heard a ruckus upstairs. Loir chuckled.

"Sounds like the party has come to us," he said.

"Loir! You can't let them catch us!"

"Why not? They have money and pizza. I'm really hungry right now. That would be perfect!"

"They might kill you!"

"I'll ask for the pizza before they do, don't worry. Oh, and the pepperoni... and mushies... "

"Loir!"

Eden ran to his keyboards, trying to activate some defense of some sort, but nothing happened. She had never used Loir's computers before, and maybe they were even modified to only work for him because literally nothing happened no matter what she did.

"Loir!" she insisted.

"Oh, I need to pack my teddy bear..."

His chair rolled away from the desks as sudden bangs were heard on the door. Eden was totally speechless! They were banging against the main garage door, the one that was completely blocked. How long before they'd burst it open? Maybe five, ten minutes?

She had time to run. Completely ignoring Loir, she ran to the other door, which opened up onto the street. According to Loir's cameras, they weren't there yet. If only she could run fast enough to get out of there and make her

114

way to another territory...

The door opened wide just a second before Eden got to it. She froze there, holding on to her dog with her heart beating like crazy.

Dante was standing in the frame, a large smile on his face, his golden eyes glowing.

"Hi again, Eden. I missed you."

She stepped back. There was no sign of any injury on him, and that's when she understood. The way he had taken off his jacket and the sudden attack on his own territory. She should have known it was all fake. He probably had faked an injury to let her think she could run away too.

He was perfectly fine. Fine and holding a gun when he stepped inside.

"I told you, didn't I?"

"You said you'd leave me alone if I survived..." she hissed.

"Yes. I said that, but you heard the second part too, didn't you?"

Yes, Eden had heard it. Even if she hadn't heard it, Dante's lips had moved so clearly, she couldn't pretend. They moved again, repeating those words that had made her run away.

"If I catch you again... you'll be mine forever."

A chill went down Eden's spine. She took another step back, unsure of what to do. It was too late to run. Dante's men were already taking over the underground garage, appearing at the only two exits. Moreover, Dante was slowly approaching her. No matter how much Eden retreated, he just kept stepping forward with that cunning smile on his lips.

"What is it?" he asked in a deep voice. "You didn't think I would keep my promise?"

Eden glared at him. Oh, no, she knew he was going to pursue her and try to capture her again. She was even mad at herself for thinking it could really have been that easy. She had enjoyed not even two hours of freedom, and she was already back in his clutches. Eden wasn't so stupid as to try and fight her way out of this. She knew when a fight was over, and she had clearly lost this one.

"*Buongiorno!*" exclaimed Loir, absolutely not impressed by the men barging in.

He was waving at them as if he had organized a party here himself. Eden glared at him, annoyed by his attitude. Was there really nothing that could make him panic?!

"So this is your partner," said Dante. "A crazy anarchist, hidden in a basement."

"Leave him the fuck alone," hissed Eden.

However, Dante ignored her with a little chuckle and walked up to Loir's console. On the ground, Bullet was growling, but as soon as the mafia lord's eyes looked down at him, the pup stopped and ran back to Eden's feet. Eden grabbed him and turned to watch Dante approach Loir. She was restless about this confrontation. Loir was crazy, probably unreliable, and a ton of other

115

things, but he was still one of her only friends. Seeing him, the man who had been living alone in his basement for years, hidden from the world, approached by the Italian Tiger was enough to make her terribly nervous again. It was clear something was wrong about this whole scene that was happening. Still, Dante approached him calmly, and Loir had that stupid smile stuck on his face, his eyes not shying away from the Italian.

"So, you're Eden's mysterious partner," said Dante.

"So, you're the Big Kitty," retorted Loir, not impressed at all. "You're not as cute as I had imagined..."

Dante raised an eyebrow. With his completely black eyes, it was hard to decipher this alien. Loir tilted his head, smiling as if his hideout hadn't just been brutally invaded.

"...How long have you been working together?" asked Dante.

"A few years."

"Loir!" protested Eden, furious that he answered Dante's questions so calmly and promptly.

However, those two were completely ignoring her at the moment. Loir had his hands on his knees and was staring at Dante with a curious expression like one would have while observing some unknown creature. It was probably the same feeling for Dante, although the mafia lord acted very calm and composed.

"How did you get her to Dive for you?"

"I didn't," answered Loir with a creepy chuckle. "Her previous partner disappeared, I was there... and we like the same toys."

"I see... So, what is your motivation?"

Loir immediately beamed.

"Well, do you pay in pizza?" he asked, tilting his head, his mouth wide open.

Eden wanted to slam her head into a wall listening to Loir at the peak of his ridiculous attitude. Dante chuckled, simply amused by the hacker's crazy demand.

"We've got all the pizza you want if you'll work for us."

"Yay!"

"Loir, shut the fuck up!" retorted Eden, furious.

She walked up to the tattooed man, grabbing the arms of his chair and turning him to face her.

"Have you gone mad?! This is serious, Loir! Don't start making deals with these people!"

"Give up, Eden," said Dante, turning to her. "Your partner seems fine working with us. I already said I'd provide everything you would need, and now, we even have your Back Hacker."

Eden ignored him. She was just furious: furious to have been tricked so stupidly, furious to have led them to Loir, and furious at that idiot who was willing to become their slave just to get free food. This didn't make any sense! She knew Loir acted crazy half of the time, but he was smart, surprisingly

116

smart. He couldn't be stupid enough to agree to this without knowing what it all meant!

"Loir, stop your charade," she said. "This isn't funny anymore. If you refuse to work for them, they can't force you. You're a hacker; you're smarter than the idiot you're acting as. Why are you giving in to their crap?!"

Loir smiled and leaned toward her.

"Don't worry," he whispered, although obviously too loud, "I have a plan!"

Eden glared at him again. She hated that he was acting crazy like this; it wasn't the time for stupid jokes. She couldn't even understand why he had agreed to let himself be taken in the first place. This is his lair; there is probably much more protection in place. Moreover, didn't he have another hideout, a backup plan? Why stay here at all if he had known Eden was bringing the Italians back to him?!

"Alright, let's wrap all of this and go home," declared Dante, grabbing a cigarette from his pocket.

"Boss, are we taking all this... stuff?" asked one of the guys, baffled by the number of screens and random technology gathered there.

"Of course we are!" retorted Loir, as if he was now in charge. "Stuff? This isn't just stuff! You big noobies! Do you even know how to use a keyboard?! This isn't for playing Scrabble!"

The mafioso glared at him, visibly annoyed to be called names like this, but Dante just chuckled.

"Alright, grab all that stuff and the crazy one," he said, pointing at Loir with his cigarette.

Loir checked over his shoulder as if he was expecting to find someone else.

"Who's crazy?" he asked.

No one bothered to answer him. All the Italians moved to guard the area or gather the technology to carry it to the cars. Loir was yelling at them from time to time and complaining about the doofus carrying his cables and screens in a way in which he didn't approve. On the side, Eden was stubbornly staying put, her arms crossed, with Bullet growling at her feet. Strangely, no one seemed to approach her or force her to go with them. Instead, Dante was calmly smoking his cigarette, letting his men work while he stood there.

"...Why are you so fixated on me?" she finally asked.

They were standing a few steps away from each other and there was also a ruckus going on in front of them, but she knew he'd heard her just fine. Indeed, he took a long drag and slowly exhaled his smoke.

"...I wonder," he whispered. "All my instincts are telling me I must have you, and I must not let you go..."

Eden froze as his golden eyes looked at her. There was something about the way they shone that made her... shiver. She felt her heartbeat accelerate and her cheeks flush red. Why? Why was he so bent on having her? They had only met once in that bar. They had nothing in common, and he wasn't even sure she was the one hacker he was looking for. So... why?

"My teddy bear!" exclaimed Loir. "My teddy—"

"You're so annoying!" yelled one of the men, brutally pushing Loir's chair. "Go get it yourself!"

The man had pushed the rolling chair so brutally that it tipped over, sending Loir to crash on his flank. The chair broke, and the sound echoed in the garage.

"You asshole!" yelled Eden, running to them.

She pushed the man away from Loir with a threatening glare. She didn't have as much strength in her arms as she did in her legs, but she wasn't defenseless. The man glared back but still stepped away with an annoyed expression. Ignoring him, Eden's focus immediately switched to Loir, who was still lying on the floor, not getting up.

"Loir, are you okay?" she asked, grabbing his skinny arm to try and help him up.

To her surprise, the hacker sighed but did not try to get back up. He only tipped over to sit, ignoring Eden's efforts to pull.

"Ha..." he mumbled. "I really liked that chair, though..."

"Come on, Loir, get up," insisted Eden, tired from trying to pull him up by herself.

"I can't, Kitty."

"What? What do you mean you can't?"

Eden tried again, but it was no use. Unless Loir made an effort himself, he could not be moved. Annoyed, the other guy rolled his eyes and walked to the other side of the hacker to help him up.

"Enough of this circus," he groaned. "Get up, now!"

He grabbed Loir's arm before Eden could protest, but just as he tried to pull him up, a bit of Loir's shirt was pulled up as well, and they saw it. The little bit of skin exposed was covered in scars. The man, surprised, suddenly let go, but Eden was already frowning.

"Loir, what the..."

She went directly to his legs and pulled up the bottom of his pants to reveal his ankle.

She pulled it back down right away. Eden needed to take a deep breath. This was just... unbearable to see. Loir's legs didn't look like legs. She had thought he might refuse to move because he was ankylosed from staying in that chair for so long, but she was wrong. Loir simply wasn't able to walk at all. Whatever had happened to his legs wasn't natural. It wasn't an accident or a simple scar. What she had seen underneath wasn't even bearable to look at.

"You... you were t-tortured?" she whispered.

Loir smiled, tilting his head.

"I told you," he whispered back, "no running away for me, Kitty..."

That sentence sunk deeply into Eden's heart. Loir wasn't willing to be taken by the Italians; he simply had no choice. He couldn't run away, and Eden had literally brought them here. She knew nothing about his past, but she knew he had been hiding alone in this basement for as long as she knew him. Hiding from who or what, that was a mystery. But it probably had a lot to do with his body's state...

Eden tried to think fast; however, there was no satisfying solution, no matter how hard she tried to think about it. Loir's legs couldn't carry him anywhere, and dangerous people were probably looking for him. Even more dangerous than the Italian, most likely. She hated this, but... she had to admit, they really were cornered. It would be foolish to try and run away again. She wouldn't be able to do anything without a partner either and, obviously, Loir wasn't going anywhere.

"...Fine," she mumbled, standing back up.

No one had been waiting for her to agree, but as soon as she said that, the largest and biggest guy came forward to carry Loir in his arms. The hacker blushed and put his very skinny arms around the guy's neck.

"Oh, it's my first time being carried like a princess! What's your name, cutie pie?"

"I don't have to tell you!" protested the man, pissed.

"Really? Oh, that's too bad. I guess I'll call you Margherita, then."

"What the hell?!"

Eden smirked. Although he had no fighting skills, Loir was a mastermind at pissing people off. Whether he liked it or not, the newly-named Margherita had to carry him out of the garage. Quickly, that place was back to being completely empty again. Eden had never realized how small it actually was until all of Loir's mess was taken out and the Italians themselves left. To her surprise, only Dante stayed behind, still smoking his cigarette and clearly waiting for her.

A long silence followed as Eden was having a hard time making her decision. It was hard to take that step.

"...I still hate you," she hissed.

"For offering you this opportunity?" retorted Dante. "I see nothing but favorable conditions for you."

"I told you I don't work for anyone. Even if I had to, you're the last one on my list."

Dante crushed his cigarette under his shoe slowly.

"It's alright," he said. "I'll give you what you need. What you want. You may not like my vision or being tied down, but—"

"You think you can give me what I want?" retorted Eden.

The glare she sent back to him spoke volumes. Her hazel eyes were gorgeous, but at this very moment, she was using them to kill him with a deadly gaze. She finally grabbed her pup, swung her backpack onto her back, and walked up to him with that furious expression in her eyes.

"You don't have the slightest idea what I want," she hissed.

119

"I'm all ears."

"Really? Then give me my brother back."

"...Any information I need to know first?"

Eden chuckled bitterly.

"Yes. The previous Tiger killed him, eight years ago. Shot him dead in the streets, right in front of me. You think you can do anything about that?"

Without letting him answer, Eden stepped out of the garage. In the alley, the black Italian cars were all lined up and, as expected, some of Dante's henchmen were waiting, guns and rifles in hand and watching the perimeter. The most luxurious car was parked right in front of her, a door opening into a leather back seat. Eden wondered which car Loir had been taken to, but she knew he would have screamed or something if they had done anything to him. Almost happy she was wearing shabby clothes, Eden got into the car, with one last glare at the men outside. She had no intent to wait for Dante. She took a seat, letting Bullet settle on her lap and dropping her bag at her feet. Right away, she heard a happy dog's little bark.

"Beer!" she exclaimed as the little pup's head popped up from the front seat.

To her surprise, the pup was looking perfectly fine and happy. The two little pup siblings happily barked at each other, running on the little floor space of the car to reunite. The driver, who turned out to be Rolf, glanced at her through the car's rearview mirror.

"C-Cooper's been well-behaved," he simply said.

"His name is Beer," said Eden.

"Oh..."

Rolf didn't seem to agree with that choice, but he didn't add anything, staying focused on the street. Then, Dante got in the car, taking the seat next to Eden, and all his men simultaneously went to their cars. Dante briefly glanced at the pups playing at Eden's feet, and she grabbed them to put them on her lap. Somehow, the little dogs stopped brawling and settled down under Dante's stare. Eden decided to ignore him and looked out the window at her neighborhood. The cars all started and they quickly left the area, with no signs of the Mexican mafia showing up for action. It had only been a few minutes actually, but Eden was surprised. Were they too intimidated by the Italians?

"...The previous Tiger is already dead," said Dante suddenly. "I fear there's nothing left to do about that."

"I wish I had shot him myself," hissed Eden.

"...What if I saved you the pain?"

She frowned and finally turned to him. Dante was lighting up another cigarette, opening the window to let the smoke out. Just as the window opened slightly, Eden caught sight of a unique, very distinct reflection of metal from a rooftop two blocks away. She grimaced and jumped over him to press the button to close the window. A gunshot was fired one second later. It hit the car but was deflected by the bulletproof coating. Another one followed immediately afterward, hitting the side without making a single scratch on the car. They were still on Mexican territory, and not welcome. Eden's blood pressure rose right away as she saw more weapons aimed at them. However, there was something else going on that made her blood rush. She had jumped without thinking to close the window, but her hand had pressed on Dante's knee for support, and her upper body was above his legs, putting her face right in front of his. Hence, she was very close when he smiled.

"...What do you mean?" she asked.

"I killed the old man already," he said. "Myself. One single, clear shot, like your brother... So, where does that put your desire for revenge now, Eden?"

Eden glared at him.

He had killed the previous Tiger? Why? Was that even the truth? She kept staring at him, but there was no hint of truth or lie in those golden eyes, just overconfidence that made people want to kill or follow him.

Another bullet hit the car, making a metallic sound again. Eden clicked her tongue, annoyed.

"...You're lying," she hissed, defiant.

"Certainly not. You can ask any of my men. I made it quite clear to them. To everyone, in fact. I got rid of those who did not enjoy this and took over the spot of the Tiger. In one night."

Eden frowned. She wasn't close enough to the Italian territory to know these kinds of things. She usually restrained herself from straying too far away from the Zodiac territories she did know, which were the Rat, the Dragon, and the Eagle. The others, she avoided unless absolutely necessary. She wouldn't know something like a Zodiac changing unless there was a war between the two of them, which usually caused a lot of noise around the neighborhoods. But internal struggles? That was something else.

By now, the bullets were raining on the car. Rolf was driving faster to try and get them out of there. When one finally caused a crack on Eden's window, she squinted her eyes. The pups whined, hiding under the front seat with a scared expression. Dante smiled as if he was about to ride a rollercoaster.

"Aren't you going to do something about this, bodyguard?" he chuckled.

"I'm not your bodyguard," Eden immediately retorted.

She then turned her head toward Rolf.

"You have a weapon? A gun?"

"W-what for?" asked the man, surprised.

"To play golf!" Eden yelled, pissed.

However, before she could add anything else, Dante took out a gun. Eden frowned, surprised to see him hand her one so casually. It was a heavy model, with an automatic shoot system and no electronics in it, which wasn't surprising for someone who avoided the Core's control.

"...Aren't you afraid I'll kill you?" she asked, taking the weapon.

"Well, you're not the first woman to ask me that," he chuckled.

Eden rolled her eyes. Was he ever going to answer her seriously? He was a tiger indeed, a tiger only too happy to play with her nerves all the damn time... Upon hearing the next shot, Eden retreated back to her position and waited, stuck to the back of her seat for the next bullet to cause the window to break. Her hazel eyes were already spotting all of their opponents, and once the window did break, she stuck out her arm immediately, shooting one after the other. She was the first to respond to the fire from the Italians' side, which surprised her opponents. She was incredibly precise too, not wasting a single bullet as she shot one target after the other, quick and efficient. The shots stopped for a second. Their enemies all went into hiding or attempted to find who was shooting them like rabbits.

The weapon recharged automatically, but it wasn't made for long-range. Eden only got the closer ones and was glad none of them was an actual sniper. The Eagle's men often preferred heavy weapons like rifles without much precision. She bought them as much time as she could while Rolf and the other cars sped to get out of there. However, with this complicated angle, Eden's arm did get hit, and she had to take it back inside, her blood staining the leather. By then, they were out of there and relatively safe. She groaned, checking her injury.

"Efficient," said Dante, looking in the rearview mirror.

Still, Eden pointed the gun right to his head.

"Enough," she said, out of breath.

Dante didn't look surprised at all. He took out another cigarette and re-opened his window. He had barely glanced at the gun. He had a weapon pointed right to his head, yet he was quietly relaxing there, glancing at their surroundings and taking a drag of his cigarette. Eden was just furious.

"...So you don't mind if I shoot you?" she asked, baffled.

"When people want to kill, they don't ask for permission," Dante retorted.

Eden let out a frustrated grunt but lowered the gun. Dante didn't even try to take it back and instead let her cross her arms with the weapon still in hand, since she turned the safety back on.

"...Why did you kill him?"

"Why did he kill your brother?"

That question-for-question game wasn't to her taste, and Eden answered with a glare. However, it was clear Dante wasn't really curious. He was just saying there was no reason. People working for the Zodiac rarely needed one... Eden was too frustrated to ask or talk anymore. She was in pain from her injury and mad that each sentence she threw at Dante was coming back to her face like a stubborn boomerang. Hence, she simply stared outside, ignoring him with her arms crossed, her hand still solidly holding that weapon.

"Boss, the fourth car is calling... They are saying they want a break."

"A break?" said Dante, raising an eyebrow.

"Yes, uh... They want to put the hacker in another car..."

Eden smiled. That was probably Loir having fun driving them crazy... The hacker had a knack for making people mad while pretending to be crazy.

Although he probably was, Eden knew him enough to know that half of it was for show and to confuse people. Loir was a lot of things, but certainly not dumb. He was the best at what he was doing, and he wouldn't have been taken if he didn't want to. She still couldn't help but wonder if he had done this for her or if Loir had truly chosen to be taken by the Italians.

"...How did you meet the crazy one?" asked Dante.

"...I found him," Eden simply said. "I needed a new partner, and we ended up working together."

"What happened to your previous partner?"

"...Who knows."

Eden wished she knew that too. Her master had disappeared overnight. She had been desperate to find him for several months. It was the first time she was truly left alone. Her master had taught her absolutely everything about Diving and made her the best, and once she had reached the top, he had vanished. With no idea of his real identity, no clue, no lead, Eden had been desperate to find a single thing about her missing master. She had dived so deep into the Core's secrets, she had almost not come back. It wasn't like he was simply gone, but as if he had never existed at all... She had found Loir during one of her searches, following a lead that had guided her to the hacker's hideout. He was a single hacker who wasn't working with a fixed Diver at the time. That's when Eden had understood: her master wasn't related to Loir, he simply wanted to show her who her new partner should be. After that, Eden had stopped searching.

"...I see. Well, he was well-hidden too. What kind of hacker hides in a basement in reinforced concrete?"

"One who really doesn't want to be found," replied Eden. "Maybe you should start adding concrete to our golden cage."

"I had something funnier in mind," mysteriously said Dante.

Eden decided not to answer, once again, to his little game of words. She sighed and wished internally that Loir makes the trip a nightmare for his men. Unlike her escape on foot, it was only a matter of minutes before they returned to where she had woken up that same morning. Eden felt utterly defeated to be back so soon. She was like a runaway child who had been brought back home right away. Hence, she had a sullen face when they parked the car in front of the building. Rolf opened the door for her, a gesture that somewhat confused her until he held his hand out. With a bit of a sulk, Eden handed him the gun without a word exchanged. She was more focused on keeping pressure against her injury to slow the bleeding. The pups jumped out after her, both excited again for some reason. Unlike some of Dante's men who walked into the building right away, Eden waited for the car transporting Loir to stop. Dante waited with her, although it was most likely just to finish his cigarette.

The men who stepped out of the fourth car looked exhausted and some were red with anger.

"He never shuts up! For fuck's sake!" yelled one of the men before adding a long line of what ought to be Italian slurs.

"Well, it can't be helped that you guys are little uneducated monkeys! Seriously, you don't even know the twenty-third decimal of Pi or your classics! Oh, Eden!" exclaimed Loir, escorted out of the car.

They brought forward a wheelchair for him and helped him sit up, although all the men who had made the trip with him were carefully stepping away for some reason. Loir seemed perfectly fine, and as soon as he was in, he rolled his wheelchair to Eden as if it had always been his.

"Eden! Oh, hi, puppies!" he added, waving at them. "Eden, can you believe this? This bunch of uneducated monkeys has never heard of *The Return of the Jedi*, a Tamagotchi, or Pam! Ignorant primates!"

Eden ignored his rant, grabbing the handles of the wheelchair and pushing him in front of her, a little smile on. Maybe she had wished loud enough because half of the men were staring at Loir with an expression that was an interesting mix of disgust and anger.

"Kitty, do you realize? I'm a bald man in a wheelchair! Oh, gosh, this is a childhood dream of mine! Should you call me Professor L from now on?"

"You've always been in a chair with wheels, Loir," sighed Eden, "just not the right one."

"Oh, don't ruin my fun! Anyway! What games do we get to play today with Big Kitty?"

He had said that while clearly looking at Dante, who smiled. The mob boss had already understood that to handle Loir, there was no choice but to give in to the craziness.

"I got new toys for you," he answered.

"Oh..." said Loir, his eyes shining.

Eden was still very suspicious of him, but they walked inside the building and followed the man. Eden wasn't relaxed because they were back in the Italians' territory, but somehow, the fact that Loir was with her in this foreign environment was giving her an extra dose of courage.

Moreover, this time, she had more time to see and explore the building, following Dante and Rolf. While Loir didn't seem to care at all, only making strange noises and gestures to get the pups' attention, Eden kept looking around. Everything was a strange mix of modernity, yet not quite like the Core. Just like Jack's bar, there were some obvious inspirations from the thirties, like the golden table lamps, the rich green velvet couches, the ceiling mirrors that made the room seem impossibly big, and the patterned rug over the marble floor. It was as if one of those very fancy hotels from the Loop had been stuck in time, and only some small hints of technology were hidden here and there, like the android behind their welcome desk or the cameras hanging from the etched, lacquered walnut walls. Eden couldn't help but look down, annoyed by the cameras following them.

Quickly, Dante led the way to a hidden elevator, using a code to open the doors, and it slowly lifted them to the upper floors.

The doors opened back in the twenty-second century and Loir literally squealed. An impressive panel of new technology was laid out in front of them. The gray floor was so impeccable, there wasn't a single speck of dust. The pups ran ahead to play in the large room while Loir began rolling his chair as fast as he could toward the giant computers laid out in a semicircle, completely over-excited.

"Didn't I promise you?" said Dante, visibly satisfied by the hacker's reaction. "Brand new technology, all you need and want to work for me..."

Eden glared at the last part, but she had to admit, all this must have cost a fortune. Loir was beyond himself.

"Eden, Eden! Look at the processor! That baby is so new and shiny and powerful! Oh my goodness, and this! They don't even have one like that on the Chinese Market! Oh crap, Eden, I think I'm going to soil my diaper!"

Behind him, Rolf grimaced, and a couple of Dante's men quickly found an excuse to leave. Eden sighed. She had to admit, this was the best technology there was. Moreover, this was obviously brand new, as there were two men, probably technicians, still installing some of it.

"Hey, hey, what's he doing?!" exclaimed one of them.

Eden sighed. As always, Loir had decided to throw people off and was practically climbing on the desk to pull out the cables, tossing them and other pieces across the room. He began throwing them at the two technicians and screaming.

"You damn savages! You dare to pull out this kind of crappy model on my new princess? Savages! Do you want to have pig intestines instead of yours? I should hang you by your balls! Savages!"

"...A-aren't you going to stop him?" asked Rolf, looking a bit worried at all their hardware being thrown across the room.

"Oh no," retorted Eden, a smile on. "He's the one in charge of the equipment, and your guys really have no idea what they are doing. Plus, Loir can't aim for the life of—"

Just as she was about to end her sentence, Eden was proven wrong. A piece of some already-damaged hardware had just hit one of the men right in the face, who groaned loudly, his nose bleeding.

"What the fuck! You crazy piece of—"

"Out."

Dante's words resonated like a whiplash in the room. All his men immediately scampered like frightened rats, and soon, there were only the four of them left. Bullet and Beer played with the cables Loir had just thrown away in the corner, each pulling on one end.

"...We can get the parts you don't like replaced," said Rolf, stepping forward.

Loir's head popped out from behind one of the screens, as it seemed the hacker had somehow found a way to pull his body onto the desk, going through his new equipment. He had his arms wrapped around a large piece of hardware like he was protecting something precious and gave them a suspicious look.

"Don't let your monkeys play with my toys again," he hissed.

"Understood."

"And I want my equipment brought up. You guys really don't appreciate the art and can't just buy whatever is new! You big noobs! Doofuses!"

"We will bring it up right away," said Rolf, nodding.

He walked out of the room, but not without giving the pups another look; Beer and Bullet were having a lot of fun in the pile of rejected hardware. Eden crossed her arms and walked over to Loir's side. He was now under the desk, changing all the cables again and grumbling about the monkeys who had handled his new equipment. It was obvious he was having a lot of fun. He kept wriggling and would sometimes let out that creepy little laugh of his before crawling under another part of the desk.

"...What do you think?" asked Eden, a bit bitter.

"Well, this is my first time having a sugar daddy, Kitty. It is a bit overwhelming I'll admit, but so far I like it!"

Eden rolled her eyes. As if she could have expected a serious answer... She stepped back, letting him have his fun. It was clear Loir had found his new habitat and wouldn't move out of there. She heard Dante approach and tried not to react to it, her arms still wrapped around herself.

"...If I promise no gunfights this time, will you dine with me tonight?" he asked with his deep voice that gave her chills. "After we are done treating your injury."

Eden glanced at her arm. The bleeding had stopped, but it was still probably looking rather ugly under her red-tainted fingers.

"You mean even staged ones?"

"Nothing but maybe a pair of knives."

"...Fine," she mumbled.

Just then, Loir suddenly popped his head out from under the desk.

"I'll have a Margherita with extra anchovies, artichoke, and pineapples, please!"

# CHAPTER NINE

With this second invitation, Dante was probably trying to make up for the disastrous first.

Eden was a bit confused, staring at the outrageous piece of clothing in front of her with her arms crossed. This wasn't a dress but an overpriced piece of fabric. She could tell just from all the strass crystals on it. It was an old shade of pink and incredibly well-balanced between sexy and innocent. Even without putting it on, Eden knew this would be the perfect size for her. She sighed. Did she have to wear that? A part of her had wanted to keep her dirty clothes. Unfortunately, they were stained with blood and she smelled like trash after that walk outside. Not only that, but while she had given in to the strong appeal of a nice hot shower, fancy soap, and fragrant shampoo, once again, her clothes had vanished. She didn't regret that hot shower. Hot and clean water raining on her was such a luxury to Eden, and this time, she had taken it in a very, very fancy bathroom. Eden's eyes circled the room once again.

A suite. This time, he had given her a suite, which was much bigger than the previous room she had slept in. It was the real thing, with a view, marble floors, wooden walls, a king-size bed with silk bed sheets, and a private bathroom. This place alone was three times bigger than Eden's apartment. Her dogs could run around and chase each other as much as they wanted without anything in their way.

Still, Eden didn't like this display of how wealthy he was. She didn't like people flaunting their money in her face and she didn't like standing alone in there either. She had been told dinner would be served half an hour later, and since then, she had been staying in her room. No one had come in and the door wasn't locked. Eden sighed and brushed her blonde hair out of her face. There was no use in staying in the room in her underwear. Even that was fancy and new, a black ensemble that certainly would have suited a rich lady from the Core. Not a poor girl from the Suburbs.

A bit annoyed, she grabbed the dress to put on. The sexy silk slid down her curves so fluidly, yet Eden was shocked at the weight. Those strasses... they couldn't be real diamonds or jewels, right? Eden had worn a dress full of strass before, but none had ever felt that heavy. She sighed and shook her head, trying to push her thoughts to the back of her mind.

A few steps away from her was a full-length mirror, and Eden approached it. Her reflection sent an image that wasn't so new to her: Eden wearing a dress, Eden pretending to be a rich woman. To her, this felt wrong. How her curves were enhanced, how she was suddenly prettier. The way her blonde honey curls feel now that they were clean and shiny, her skin clear of any dirt, even her face. So relaxed. No frowning, no sullen expression. Had she softened up a little to the Italian now? She should have been a bit mad at herself, but Eden didn't care much anymore. She was getting tired of running away from him. This tiger was playing with her like a cat with its mouse. She just wanted to know his goals, and if she could survive being around him.

Eden found the pair of heels they had picked for her. Once again, they were shiny and looked expensive. She frowned and threw them to her pups to chew. She should have brought their toys up here. Maybe that was why Rolf had offered to keep them? Eden sighed. Somehow, she knew she couldn't fully hate someone who liked her pets. No bad man likes animals, they said. Eden loved animals, but she didn't like men much... Aside from the shoes, she didn't care for the makeup or jewelry either. She didn't want to become some kind of trophy yet. That dress was nothing but a piece of clothing, and it wouldn't be enough to sway her heart.

Eden decided to stop caring. She had served men before. She had sold her body for their pleasure, she had poured them drinks until they were nothing but drunkards, and no man until now had managed to make her think any better of the other gender. In her mind, men just couldn't be trusted. They either patronized her or used her. Eden had decided long ago she could only survive on her own.

Feeling a bit better after reminding herself of all this, she got down on her knees, pulled the skirt up, and began playing with the pups, not wanting to think until it was time for dinner. Seeing Beer and Bullet so excited and happy to play, completely not caring about her events, made her regret she hadn't been born as an animal too. Eden wished she was a bird, so she could fly away. Away from Chicago's Suburbs and their violence. Away from people's manipulative and selfish ways. Away from the filthy air, the rough asphalt, and the muddy waters. Just a bird, ready to go anywhere she wanted.

The door opened, and to her surprise, Rolf appeared. Both the pups immediately ran to him, excited. The man didn't walk in, though. Obviously restraining himself from focusing on the pups, he simply nodded politely her way.

"He is waiting for you."

Eden stood up and walked to the door without a word. Rolf simply stepped aside to let her out. She hesitated about leaving the pups with him, or inside the room, but somehow, their presence had become extremely necessary to her. They were like two little comfort buddies, ready to cheer her up anytime. Eden only hoped she wouldn't need them too soon...

She followed Rolf inside the elevator and they went up. So they were staying inside this time. That was fine with her. She wasn't ready for another fight anytime soon. The door opened up into a smaller room than she had imagined. Eden still had the devastated restaurant in mind from before, but this was obviously a normal dining room. Moreover, even more surprisingly, Dante was behind a kitchen counter, with his sleeves rolled up, and a large kitchen knife in hand. Eden had to blink a couple of times. Was he seriously... cooking?

"...Have a nice dinner," whispered Rolf, closing the door behind her.

Eden just had time to see his second-in-command disappear, and realized that this time, she was truly alone with Dante. She felt a little knot appearing in her throat. What was he planning this time? This place was his headquarters, surely he wouldn't have a bomb explode or something, right?

"Good evening," he suddenly said, not lifting his head from whatever he was cutting.

She could hear the knife cutting through the veggies at an expert speed on the chopping board, making her a little curious. He wasn't putting on an act, then? Eden approached cautiously. For once, Beer and Bullet were behaving and simply following her with their little noses up.

"...The shoes were not the right size?"

Eden froze, but then, she realized he had probably been expecting to hear her heels on the marble floor... She snorted.

"More like not the right price tag..."

"Mh... I'll tell them to take it out next time."

She knew he was just joking around. He knew exactly what she had meant, he probably just didn't care...

Eden cautiously approached some more. She didn't want to, but her stomach was desperately hungry after smelling whatever was going on in his pans. Moreover, she was curious to see him really cooking... and so focused. There were a lot of things laid out on the kitchen counter, even some utensils she had never seen before. Cautiously, Eden sat on the little stool against the kitchen counter.

"Will you drink rosé wine?" he asked.

"...Sure."

He smiled and pushed a wine glass in front of her, already half-full with a pink fizzy drink. Eden recognized the smell of Prosecco. It was strange that she knew more about alcohol than actual food. Dante's glass was by his side, but from what she could tell, he had been waiting for her to drink.

Strangely, he didn't add anything else, and, for a little while, she watched him crush and mince garlic, stir-fry shrimp, and cut some herbs in silence. Only after a few seconds did she realize the herbs had come from a tiny greenhouse behind him.

"...You grow it?"

"Only a few, for cooking. Basil, thyme, chives, and—"

"Rosemary."

Eden was a bit jealous. No matter how hard she had tried, none of her plants had grown enough to survive more than a week in the polluted outdoors of her neighborhood. Each little piece of green had been a victory for her, but he was growing full little bushes in that mini greenhouse so easily. His whole apartment probably had a filtration system just as good as those in the Core.

"So?" she sighed. "What are you... cooking?"

"I felt like having some Shrimp Fettuccine Alfredo," he said. "I usually have lighter dinners, but my new bodyguard looks like she could use a fuller meal."

"Those I get to finish."

Dante chuckled.

"...Your hacker friend is enjoying his pizza, by the way."

"I'm not worried about him."

"Really?"

"Mh... I'd be more worried about leaving him without surveillance. He could blow up the whole place if his pizza didn't have enough anchovies."

Dante chuckled, but his smile disappeared as he raised his head to finally look at her. Eden wasn't joking, and from the way she raised both eyebrows, she wasn't suggesting this simply out of the blue... He eventually nodded.

"Noted, then. I'm glad the first delivery was to his liking."

Eden slowly nodded and grabbed her glass. Dante grabbed his too, and before she could take a sip, directed it to her so they could clink glasses. Eden frowned, making him chuckle.

"Surely, you must have done this with your customers, right?"

"You're not a customer."

"I'm your employer cooking food for you right now. Isn't that enough to get a little toast?"

To both their surprise, his sentence made Eden blush out of the blue. Dante was so surprised he lowered his glass and chuckled, but Eden had to look over her shoulder to completely avoid him. It had caught her completely off guard! She took a deep breath, mad at her cheeks for blushing without her

130

consent. Why? Why now?!

"Now, that was unexpected," said Dante, his tiger smile coming back. "What was it? The fact that I wanted to toast with you? Was I so wrong? Is it a first?"

"N-no," she mumbled. "I... I can't remember anyone cooking... especially for me... before."

Dante's smile fell a little bit. He was going from one surprise to the next with Eden, yet strangely, he couldn't get enough of it, although he normally hated surprises.

"Well, that deserves a toast all the more, then?"

Trying to hide her embarrassment, Eden finally clinked her glass, a bit too violently, and took it to her lips, drinking the wine like water. Dante was much more refined when he took a sip, but his golden eyes weren't leaving Eden at all. It was as if blinking would have him miss some extraordinary reaction from her. Moreover, that dress suited her very well, he was enjoying the effect of the vintage pink silk on her skin. He put down his glass, grabbed the bottle to refill Eden's, and picked up his spatula again to stir the shrimp.

"...Not even your parents?" he suddenly asked.

"No."

Once again, a quick, cold answer to shut him down. Eden could feel the alcohol warming up her body. At least it would give an excuse for her pink cheeks...

"...I take it you don't want to talk about it," he simply said.

Eden frowned a little. He wasn't pushing for an answer or saying this out of mockery this time. It was like he was simply acknowledging her choice, which was quite a first. However, she didn't want to stay here and answer more of his questions. Plus, her stomach was starting to grumble, and she wasn't willing to embarrass herself again. Eden got down from her stool to explore the place. It really was his place... probably. At least, it felt like someone was living there. There were a few more plants than she would have expected, and even an aquarium with colorful fish. Eden stared at it for a long moment, wondering if this was a screen, hologram, or real... If this was a fake, it was a very realistic digital illusion. She wouldn't have known what species those fishes were, and she even doubted such colorful ones with blue, orange, and red shades could even exist.

She moved on, and to her surprise, there was a little speaker on one shelf. Eden grabbed it and turned it on.

"You can play whatever you want."

Eden glanced over her shoulder. Dante was still focused on his cooking, but he knew exactly what she was doing. It was a bit annoying... but she didn't care. She put the speaker back after choosing a quiet, calm piano tune, which began playing. Somehow, she had the whole world of music open to her, but she only felt like hearing this at the moment. She was scared anything else would have set a mood, but, after a full minute, she realized the piano piece made them feel even more... like they were alone in this world.

Ignoring that, she moved to the little table set for two and sat. As promised, only two knives... except for the sharp, big one he was holding. Eden sighed and stared, once again, at the superb window view.

"...Is it real?" she asked.

"The window? Yes."

She had somewhat guessed so. The fake screens didn't show the pollution over their Suburbs, or use filters to tone it down. From where she stood, though, she could easily recognize the neighborhoods she lived in and that horrible cloud of dust, filth, and other unknown elements that hovered over them. Has the air pollution gotten worse again? If Eden turned her head further left, she could see the Core. The clouds never got over the Core. Their huge air filters not only took the air to filter and release the clean air inside, but they disposed of all the harmful particles back on the Suburbs' side. She could almost see the barrier between the two worlds.

"Have you ever dreamed of living there?" asked Dante.

He walked over, carrying his glass and the two plates like a professional would have. Eden watched him put down the plates, even with a little bowl of grated cheese, and then sit. Like the perfect gentleman part he liked to play, he put his towel on his lap and handed Eden hers. She grabbed it, but now that she was looking at the table, she didn't like it: neither the small space between them nor that stupid rose on the table...

Suddenly remembering the pups, she looked around for Beer and Bullet, but the two of them had settled in one corner, sleeping quietly. Eden felt a bit anxious now that her sidekicks were down...

"The Core is appealing to anyone," he said when she didn't reply. "However, if you go there, their society is so controlled, no one is really free anymore. Each movement is controlled, each decision is judged. It is so systematic, even their identities are settled at their birth. For each of them, there is a precise position waiting. They are raised like ants, programmed for one line of work, one partner. The Architect built a system so perfect, it decides everything for humans without them even knowing."

Eden grabbed her fork, poking at the shrimp, a bit curious. She had never eaten pink shrimp... but it sure smelled a lot better than what she knew. She carefully took one to her mouth, eating a piece. It was good. Not just that, but the intense taste of garlic, cream, and white wine that came with it too. As if her stomach had opened wider to the amazing flavor, she was already craving more. How could he be so skilled at cooking? Wouldn't it have been better if he could just remain a mythic jerk with crazy intentions...

"When one goes out of control," continued Dante, still staring at the window, "they expel them here. They don't realize how much they've been controlled their whole life. The Core makes them see what they want to see, on each screen, wherever their eyes go. The more they conform to their society, the more points they get. The more they obey the system, the more

132

the system rewards them. You're giving up your freedom for wealth, eternal life, and safety..."

He sighed, and brought his glass to his lips, drinking more of the wine. Then, his eyes went down on Eden. She was eating her pasta so well and so fast, it made him chuckle. He knew he would never get thanks or praise from her, so that was already plenty enough. Dante finally picked up his fork.

"So? What do you think of the Core, Eden?"

"...I hate them."

"Wouldn't you be interested, if you had the chance to live there? Wouldn't you want to try? Never risk being hungry, afraid, in danger?"

Eden chuckled.

"I think we don't have the same version of the Core..." she finally said, with a bitter smile.

"There's only one version of the Core. Anyone who doesn't conform–"

"Shall be expelled. I know."

Eden put down her fork, her plate still half-full, but she needed a break from eating so fast. She had some sauce around her lips, contrasting the seriousness with which she was staring at him.

"...I was born there," she suddenly said.

Dante almost dropped his fork out of sheer surprise. His fingers tightened around the silver at the last second, but he was still shocked. However, he could read the truth in Eden's eyes. As hard as it was to believe, she wasn't lying. He took a silent breath in to try and process that information. It was... strange. Something didn't add up. Eden had revealed many surprises up until then, but this was definitely the biggest one to date.

"You were... born there?" he repeated.

Eden nodded.

"Yes... Just like all those other ants," she whispered.

Dante frowned. Someone expelled from the Core should have had their SIN removed and a large, visible scar on their neck. Eden clearly didn't. Not only that, but she had proven she was used to the Suburbs and didn't think like someone from the Core... How would she have been able to make such a turn-around, even in a few years' time? While a hundred thoughts were flooding his mind, Dante grabbed his napkin and directed it toward Eden's mouth to wipe the sauce off her lips. As one would have expected, she moved to back away and grabbed his towel to do it herself.

"Were you expelled then? When?" he asked, still intrigued.

"I wasn't expelled," she retorted. "I fled the Core. I don't remember how old I was. But I was very young."

"With your mother?"

"Stop asking about my mother," she suddenly glared at him.

It didn't put an end to all the questions Dante had. How could she have fled the Core alone? She ought to have had an adult, someone helping her...

"No one runs away from the Core," he said. "It doesn't make sense."

"Some things... some people don't make sense."

Her words didn't either. The people from the Core were raised with three principles: they wouldn't need anything as long as they served the Core, loved the Core, and loathed the Suburbs. Since they were raised from their very birth to hate anything outside the Core, why would one want to leave? The hundreds of lies and myths presented to them were precisely there so they wouldn't. That was why anyone sent to the Suburbs from the Core never lasted a day. They naturally feared everyone and everything. It was simply tattooed in their brains their whole life. They didn't want to leave the Core, so they never did. So who would have taken little Eden out and why?

Still, Dante purposely fought himself to hold his questions back. Eden had grabbed her glass of wine and was sipping it, her eyes set on the window again. More precisely, her hazel eyes were directed at the Core.

"...I don't even remember most of it," she said. "Only... the vague memories of a child who had no idea what was going on. I was dragged, told to flee. My mother and Master's voices kept saying this. Run, Eden, run. I remember running, fleeing those white walls and something that was chasing me. I remember hiding where I could and obeying everything they told me. I was too young to understand, but I was scared. I knew we weren't safe, and something or someone was chasing us. My mother... guided me outside, and that was it."

"Your mother was the one who made you leave the Core? And that master you mentioned?"

Eden slowly nodded.

"They made me promise never to go back... and I didn't. I hid in the Suburbs without knowing what I had fled. Master helped me for over ten years, to work as a Dive Hacker and get just enough money to survive on my own."

"Your mother didn't come with you?"

Eden slowly lowered her head, avoiding his eyes, and finished her drink in one go.

"She did. She didn't stay."

Dante remained silent, and Eden turned to finish her plate. The pasta was just so good, and she decided to stuff her mouth instead of wasting it unnecessarily. Why had she ended up telling him so much? Maybe the wine, or the atmosphere. She hadn't intended to reveal that part of her past, but... Oh, whatever. It didn't really matter. He couldn't get to her mother or Master from where they were, anyway.

"...How come they never found you? The Core?" he asked. "Since you were born there, you should have had one of their SINs. It should have been like a tracker right on your neck..."

"Master did something to my SIN," she said, "to hide it, wipe everything on it."

Dante nodded and grabbed the bottle to refill her glass. It made sense. The only way would have been to turn her SIN into a corrupted one... which was what most hackers were capable of and did. So her master was definitely the one who had taught Eden to be... what she had become. It was somewhat strange to witness how her actions did not match her appearance. She was pretty, even more so when she was wearing this dress. However, she wasn't acting like a dignified lady. Instead, she was like a cautious animal, ready to leave and run at any given moment. How had she survived in the Suburbs with such an unusual background? That was one more mystery to add to his list.

"So... you want to find your master?"

Eden nodded and grabbed her glass to wash down what was stuck in her throat.

"Any leads?" Dante asked, tilting his head.

"No."

"No?"

"I don't have any to give you," she retorted. "I spent years looking for Master, and I never found him because I had no clue where to look."

"What about his appearance? His habits?"

"I don't know what Master looks like. When I was a child, whenever I was Diving, he'd just be there."

"So you mean, that master of yours is another hacker, but you've never met him outside the...?"

Eden remained quiet, visibly annoyed by his question. Dante was impressed. So there was another hacker on the list of very hard people to find. For even someone like Eden, who he did believe to be Ghost, to struggle to find her own mentor, that master ought to be quite something.

"What about his partner?"

"His what?" Eden frowned.

"His Back Hacker. Like the crazy one for you. Do you have any idea who his Back Hacker was?"

"I don't know... I don't think he had one," she sighed, suddenly standing up.

Eden walked to the window, ignoring his stare. She knew there were too many mysteries. More surrounding her master than herself. Eden wrapped her arms around herself, feeling a bit cold. The view was a bit too high from where she stood, and the edge was too close. It felt like she could just take one step and take off. The glass was so clean, it was almost invisible. It didn't even show her reflection. The only way she knew it was there was because of the clean air she breathed and the lack of wind. Chicago certainly wasn't so tame on those higher floors...

# CHAPTER TEN

"Are you cold?"

Eden froze when she heard him stepping behind her. Strangely, her heartbeat accelerated a little, and a hot chill spread on her skin. Dante was coming toward her, but she didn't move. She didn't know how to react. Why? She had kept hundreds of men company before him, and yet... feeling him so close glued her feet to the ground. This time, Eden regretted she hadn't put on those damn heels. She would have felt less small compared to him...

She thought he'd come to her side, but instead, she felt his presence right behind her, like a large shadow looming over her, so close she could almost feel the fabric of his shirt against her exposed back. Eden tried to take regular breaths, but it was hard to control her blushing. She was just glad he couldn't see it.

"...Are you cold?" he asked again.

Eden didn't know how to respond. What would he do if she said yes? He was close... too close for comfort. She wanted to look back, see what kind of face he was making. She could feel her chest going up and down exaggeratedly, barely containing her conflicted emotions. She felt like a little bird, trapped in front of a tiger. Quiet and immobile, not making noise before trying to eat her...

Suddenly, she felt him move, and Eden unfroze to glance over her shoulder to see what he was doing. To her surprise, a piece of fabric fell on her shoulders... his jacket? She touched the piece of clothing, but it was indeed the jacket he was wearing earlier. Had it been on his chair? She hadn't noticed.

136

Eden blushed, feeling a bit embarrassed for thinking too much.

"...Aren't you a little tense?" he suddenly whispered in her ear.

As if to confirm his words, Eden jumped away from him, surprised. She brushed her cheek and ear, where his breath had touched her. Dante chuckled and took one step back, almost acting innocent.

"Still not trusting me, are you?" he said.

He walked back to the table, pouring himself another glass, but Eden was mad.

"Stop playing around with me. What do you want?!"

"Mh... Many things," he answered, sitting back down.

He gently swirled the wine in his glass, staring at the pink color. Eden was annoyed. Mad at him and mad at herself too. She clenched her fists, trying hard to contain her emotions. She wasn't acting like herself around him and she couldn't figure out why. He was just fooling around with her, obviously.

"...Would you sing for me?"

His sudden question took her by surprise once again. Eden unclenched her fists, unsure. Sing? Was that a new game of his?

"Why?" she asked.

Dante chuckled.

"Just because I like your voice. It was quite pretty when you sang at that bar to entertain me."

"I wasn't entertaining you," she retorted, a bit annoyed.

"I thought you were. I was entertained."

She stopped replying, feeling like this would be nothing but stones thrown at a wall. He had decided she was entertaining him in particular at the time, and she wouldn't fight that.

"...I don't feel like singing," she said, shrugging.

For a few seconds, he didn't add anything and took another sip of his Prosecco.

"...Why are you mad all of a sudden?"

"I'm not mad."

"You obviously are."

"You annoy me with all your questions," she retorted. "You keep making me talk."

"That's what people usually do on a date. They eat nice food, enjoy wine, and chat..."

"This isn't a date, and you're just fishing for information."

"Well, at least you thought the food was good. Thanks for the compliment. I wish you liked the conversation with me just as much."

Eden let out a long sigh, completely exhausted by that discussion with him. She knew she was acting more wary than necessary, but... he was always looking for a way to pull her strings, and she didn't like that. Eden hated opening herself to anyone. She clung to her secrets as if they were her lifeline, and they probably were. Yet, Dante De Luca was slowly sneaking his way in, making her lower her defenses and talk before she could think.

She uncrossed her arms and shrugged.

"Fine, then. I'll sing. What do you want me to sing?"

"Anything you want," said Dante. "I like your voice, I don't care much about the song itself."

Another compliment. Eden blushed. She took a deep breath and tried to think of a song that wouldn't be too... sensual. After thinking for a few seconds, she thought she had the perfect song in mind, and opened her lips to sing.

It was a slow and deep song. Dante took a few seconds to enjoy her voice, how she put each emotion just in the right place without overdoing it. He didn't pay much attention to the lyrics of the song, at first. It matched the piano in the background, although it wasn't made for it. It was a song she could have sung without any accompaniment. He didn't recognize it, but then again, he didn't listen to music that had lyrics, usually. Eden's voice was unique. It could be surprisingly deep at times, and yet she hit each high note easily. It was clear and mesmerizing. He didn't even touch his wine while he was listening. He could only see Eden, hear Eden. It took him a few more seconds to understand the meaning of the song she had chosen very purposefully, it seemed. A song about a little songbird who wanted to leave her cage. He quickly understood there were two voices in that song, one that wasn't the songbird, but someone offering the songbird a deal... probably the devil. It was a sad song, where the songbird was tricked, but still clung to hope. Dante thought this song didn't match Eden. She didn't seem the type to have hope at all, or certainly not one to make a deal with the devil...

When she finished, he smiled. He could tell Eden liked to sing. It seemed like she had completely forgotten his existence while she sang and only returned to the room after the last note. He took her glass and poured some more wine. Dante stood and slowly walked up to her, bringing her the cup. Eden was flustered by his approach, but she did not back away. Her cheeks, a bit pink, were cute. She tried to endure his stare, but her hazel eyes soon went down to the cup, unable to hold his gaze any longer.

"Thank you for the song," he said softly.

Eden nodded. Maybe it was from the singing, but her throat was strangely tight again. She took the glass and turned her head to drink. She tried not to drink too fast, but she really was thirsty. She could feel the alcohol rush in, leaving a sweet taste on her tongue. That glass was emptied quickly and soon, she had nothing else with which to keep her eyes busy.

Moreover, Dante was... close, dangerously close, and facing her this time. It was even harder to breathe, and she could barely glance away.

"D-do you want another," she asked, more softly than she had intended, "or..."

"No," he said. "I think that was enough for tonight."

"Okay. Th-then..."

Then what? Eden couldn't properly think of what to say next. He was close... his musky scent was getting to her, making her dizzier than that rosé. She tried to control her senses, but Dante's heat was just there, an inch away from her, and hard to ignore. She couldn't move, she wasn't sure her body was ready to. Eden had no idea what to do from then on. He was just there, so close, a smile on his lips and his hands in his pockets. What did he want? Why was he standing so close to her? She just couldn't think straight.

When that silence went on for a bit too long, she slowly turned to him, ready to cross his stare again. She thought she was prepared, but his golden irises caught her. She was mesmerized by the majestic glow, and couldn't look away. She felt her heart miss a beat, and start again, too fast; her stomach filled with a mix of ice and fire. Her skin reacting, her hair standing up, all of her body on edge. Dante smiled, and it made something melt inside.

Suddenly, his hand wasn't in his pocket anymore; his fingers were gently grabbing her chin, and Eden didn't think of pushing them away. She didn't think of anything, but those lips that were coming close, so close, too close... Very softly, Dante's lips pressed against hers, ever so gently. Eden felt it through her whole body. She opened her mouth slightly without thinking, and his lips pressed again. Another kiss. Eden's heart went wild, and finally, something in her snapped. When he kissed her again, she reacted. She closed her eyes, wrapped her hands around his neck, and gave in.

Eden had been kissed before, but never like that. There was some wild, untamed passion in that kiss that she couldn't part with. It was a kiss full of desire, without any shame or restraint. Their experimenting lips were touching for the first time, and it was just incredibly good. Like a match made in heaven... or the lower depths of hell. Eden couldn't process what was going on, and truth be told, she didn't want to. Her desire kicked in, took over, and guided her movements. Her fingertips brushed on his hairline, discovering the lines of his neck and the touch of his skin. She just couldn't stop. Neither of them could bear to. Where did all this passion come from? It was as if a long-built desire had suddenly been crystalized in that one kiss. Both of them were completely at a loss as to why this was so good. Why did it feel like that kiss had been waiting forever to happen? It was a spark of passion that had been ignited from the first time their eyes met. And now, the fire was rapidly growing out of control. From her chin, his fingers quickly went down to her back, wrapping her in his arms, trapping her in his embrace. They could hear the sounds of their kiss, their confused breathing, their lips missing each second they parted. It was a kiss only a few have experienced, and neither wanted it to stop. The alcohol wasn't guilty for their drunkenness, nor the heat that solely came from their bodies.

The sound of shattering glass stopped them. Out of breath, their lips separated, and they finally looked at each other, a bit confused. Even Dante was frowning a bit, looking bewildered. Eden blushed, realizing what had just happened. She hadn't just given in, she had literally jumped in feet first! Several emotions flashed in her mind, but she couldn't decide on one to focus

139

on. Anger, frustration, confusion, happiness, desire, angst, fear... There was just too much, and her heart was beating too fast. The only rational decision she could make was to take her hand off his neck as if it could erase her previous gestures. She was about to step back, but he grabbed her wrist firmly.

"Don't move!" he said. "The glass..."

She finally glanced down at the shattered glass under her feet and immediately answered him with a glare.

"I have metal feet," she hissed. "It's fine."

"Not if you damage it."

"Hey!"

Before Eden could protest more, Dante suddenly grabbed her by her hips and lifted her, taking her across the room.

"Put me down!" she protested.

"Sure..."

Before she could add one line of complaint, he threw her on the large sofa in the room.

"Well, you are a little heavier than you look," he sighed, "I'll give you that..."

Eden answered with a glare, the best self-defense reaction she could come up with at the moment. Of course she was heavy, half her body was made of metal! She was even slightly impressed he had been able to carry her and walk at all. She was a lot heavier than she looked, not just a little. Still, she was even more confused when, as she was laid down on that sofa, Dante put one knee down between her legs, bending over her.

"W-... What are you doing?" she asked.

"Finishing what we started," he answered with a smile.

His answer sent her heart racing. She gasped, but he already had a hand on his shirt, undoing the top buttons with a naughty smile on. Eden was baffled.

"We are done!" she shouted.

"Are we? I don't think I've had enough."

"I had enough," she retorted.

Dante chuckled but didn't stop undressing. Eden was panicking a bit now. He wasn't serious, was he? She couldn't tell if he was playing or not, but he was already half-naked. She wanted to shout back at him again, but the large tiger tattoo on his torso fascinated her before she could. It really was a large tattoo... She had only seen a glimpse of it before, but it was even bigger and more impressive than whatever she had imagined. She had to focus on the actual man, though.

"How much?" he asked.

"Excuse me?"

"How much to sleep with me?"

She slapped him. Eden was furious, but Dante, far from angry, moved his jaw as if to check if it was alright, and smiled.

"Thank God your hands aren't metal too," he sighed. "I felt that one."

"I'm not having sex with you," Eden hissed. "Certainly not for money."

"Would you do it for free, then?" he chuckled.

"Fuck you, De Luca."

"...I'll take that as a no. However, I didn't ask for sex."

Eden blinked, utterly confused. He was already half-naked and leaning over her on a green sofa. What could he possibly mean other than sex? She tried to look away as she realized that under that tiger was a very fine and remarkable male body.

"I don't understand what you mean," she mumbled, trying not to look at him despite his imposing presence.

"I meant I want to sleep with you. No sex involved."

She rolled her eyes, and suddenly decided she had enough. Eden pushed him away and awkwardly tried to sit up on the opposite side of the couch. Very confident and arrogant, with his cunning smile on, Dante sat comfortably on the other side. He extended one arm on the back of the couch and had his foot perched on his knee. He was still very much half-naked, to Eden's annoyance. She had a hard time looking him in the eye, or his way at all, without her cheeks flashing an embarrassing dash of red.

"...I don't sleep well alone," he added.

"Well, call someone else."

"I don't want anyone else."

Eden rolled her eyes again. He really had an answer for everything, didn't he? Especially for things that weren't going his way in the first place.

"Well, that's too bad," she retorted. "I don't sleep with anybody."

"I'm not anybody."

"I meant I don't sleep with anyone!"

This time, her angry answer had him raise an eyebrow. Eden wasn't just annoyed by him; it was obvious talking about this made her angry. She was even more bent on avoiding eye contact and wore a sullen expression. Dante tilted his head, his smile even more of a smirk now.

"...Why is that?"

Eden let out a long sigh.

"I just can't sleep with anyone, alright? That's just how it is."

"Why?"

"I told you, there is no why!" she yelled, suddenly jumping up and backing away. "I just can't! I can't sleep with someone else in the room, let alone in the same bed! Try sleeping in the streets when you're a girl, you'll know why!"

This time, Dante lost his smile, changing to an unhappy expression. Eden noticed, but somehow, it made her even more embarrassed, and she hated that. Yes, she had slept in the streets and it hadn't been the best experience. It had shaped her into an overly cautious woman. She didn't trust anyone that was a man, and she couldn't sleep with anyone either. It didn't matter if they had sex or not, the level of intimacy was completely different in her mind. If she felt someone close in her sleep, she'd wake up instantly. Her survival instincts took over, and fear would crawl into her mind and keep her awake. Realizing she may have overreacted without knowing, Eden took another step back, crossed her arms, and sighed.

"Anyway, I... I won't sleep with you."

"...I won't force you," he suddenly said.

For a second, she wondered if he was mocking her again, or if this was another one of his cunning remarks. Yet, there wasn't a shadow of a smile on his face. His expression was the most serious too, and it even took her by surprise. Eden was the one to be mocking him this time.

"You aren't talking seriously, are you?" she said. "Coming from the man who already kidnapped me twice?"

"I don't think I forced you. The first time, you passed out while protecting me. I brought you here, healed you, and you left."

"I left during a gunfight you had staged to have me lead you to Loir and capture the two of us this time. Isn't that the same?"

"I captured you? I thought this was an open invitation. Your partner seems satisfied."

"Can you please stop judging Loir with normal criteria only when it suits you?"

"You didn't have to follow him either."

"You made a fair point of having me come."

He opened his arms.

"I don't think you've been at a disadvantage at any point, have you?"

"I did state I didn't want anything to do with you."

"And still there you were, kissing me not ten minutes ago."

This time, Eden had nothing to respond with. She blushed again, embarrassed to death by that kiss. Yes, she had kissed him, and even worse, she had fully taken part in that kiss, and liked every second of it. What was wrong with her? Her instincts and her actions didn't match. It didn't make sense for her to have given in, but... it was good.

"...You slept with those two," he suddenly said.

Eden frowned and looked behind her, suddenly remembering the pups. Her mouth was left open in shock.

"...Seriously? You're going to be jealous of my dogs now? They are dogs!"

"They are puppies and noisy and brawly."

"Leave my dogs the fuck alone," she frowned.

Dante chuckled.

"I meant that they are noisy, Eden. They sleep in the same room as you, but it doesn't wake you up, does it? Because you trust these pups. You know they are harmless and hence, your subconscious does too. Since you don't see them as a danger, you can sleep with them in the room."

He suddenly stood, putting his hands in his pockets and coming forward.

"You could learn to trust me too," he said, approaching her.

Eden wondered if it was too late to run away. Not because she was scared

142

of him, but because she was starting to genuinely fear what Dante De Luca was awakening in her. She had never been kissed like that, and she had never let a kiss affect her like that. She had never lost control. She had never blushed so much in her whole existence as she had done in the two or three days she had known that man. It just... didn't make sense to her. It was as if all the survival instincts she had relied on until now were all suddenly failing her, in Dante's favor. Eden wasn't sure what she wanted anymore and she didn't trust her own judgment either.

"Unlike my dogs, I wouldn't call you harmless," she said.

"Fair point. But I'm not a danger to you."

"How many bullets did I have in my body again?"

"I didn't shoot any of those."

"You tried to use me as a fucking shield."

"You acted as one. And I healed you."

"You put in a fucking tracking device instead."

"It didn't harm you."

"I wouldn't be here either if it wasn't for it!"

Dante tilted his head.

"...And what's so bad about being here? I gave you a suite, clean clothes, hot water, and a bed with fresh sheets. Food for your dogs too. I even cooked you a nice dinner and kissed you... a kiss we both enjoyed."

"Maybe it will work with your next mistress, then," Eden shrugged.

"I don't have another woman waiting in line," he chuckled.

She rolled her eyes. She wasn't blind. Dante was handsome, dangerous, rich, and powerful. A deadly combo for any member of the female population. There was no way a man like him didn't attract women like moths attracted to a flame. Even smart women like Rose were literally at his feet.

"Didn't you pretend you can't sleep alone? Who was your cuddle buddy then? I don't see Rolf fitting in your bed. I doubt George is your type either."

"Indeed, I don't sleep well alone," he said, "and sex somewhat helps."

"Then call one of your whores!"

"I don't want any of them anymore," he said. "I want you, or no one."

"Asshole..."

Eden was getting tired of this. He had her dancing in his palm while playing with her feelings. She didn't want to give in. She knew she was just so stubborn, but she couldn't. She was afraid of how deep she'd fall if she made just one wrong step. She crossed her arms and turned her back on him. Each of his movements was like a honey trap she wanted to glue herself onto. Her lips were still hot from that kiss, and every time his body moved closer, her whole body was reacting to it like a junkie needing her fix. It was horrible. She couldn't even tell why she was resisting him, what she was holding onto, but she felt it was important.

"...I've never cooked for anyone before."

She turned to him, taken by surprise. Dante shrugged, his golden eyes

143

going around the room.

"I've never let a woman in here either," he said.

He took one step closer, and Eden didn't step back.

"I've never opened a bottle of my favorite wine for anyone else."

He took another step. Eden felt goosebumps, and that wave of heat went down her stomach without any warning.

"I've never gone outside my territory for a woman... twice."

Eden frowned. Twice? She could understand the time when he had come to get her and Loir in the basement after that fake gunfight, but... twice? Did he mean the first time, he had also come for her? It didn't make sense. He was there to get Yang... Dante took another step. He was getting close, too close, but Eden wasn't sure she wanted to move. She still had that kiss in her mind, and his golden eyes on her were the most efficient trap.

"I've never offered a woman to sleep with me... especially with no sex involved."

Now she was getting annoyed again. She didn't want to hear him brag about his other women, probably lined up by the dozen outside to throw themselves at him. Eden didn't want to be one of those women, she didn't want to throw herself, or her dignity, away. She was stubbornly holding on to it and trying to kill her desire despite its growth. Dante took another step, and this time, they were almost toe-to-toe, him right in front of her. Eden was still, but that fire in her eyes spoke volumes. She wanted to cry, or scream, that frustration out of her mind. Her conflicted emotions were at war with her survival instincts. She couldn't decide, she couldn't tell. She was no damsel in distress. She could have kicked him out of the way, ran out of the door. Maybe she would have made it outside and disappeared into the Italian district. However, this was all too... good. The sweet taste of rosé wine. The lemon cream, the pasta that filled her empty stomach. The amazing view most could only dream of. The music. And Dante. Dante De Luca, cooking for her, focusing only on her, spending an evening with her, and giving her few choices. Eden knew she was lucky right now. Most men wouldn't have asked her anything before jumping on her. She had seen monsters in human clothing. This man was a monster that owned a tenth of the Suburbs, probably more. And yet, there he was, pretending to act like a tame cat in front of her. He was peeling off her layers one by one, going at such a slow pace that she was almost the one begging him to hurry. Eden's heart was in bad shape.

He smiled.

"...And for sure, I've never been slapped before," he whispered.

"Well, m-maybe you didn't have enough," she said in a breath, unsure.

Dante chuckled and turned his head.

"Want to try slapping the other one?" he said. "That could be a thing."

Eden glared at him again. He was making her feel like a child.

"...I'll save it for another time," she finally said.

"Mh... how about another kiss, then?"

Eden's cheeks flushed with red.

What about another kiss? Eden didn't even know how to respond. One minute he was joking, and the next, he was looking dead serious and sexy as hell. Even now, his golden eyes were completely subjugating her. He was dangerously close, so close Eden wanted to run away, or... run to him. Her heart and her head were at war right now, while she was frozen there, unable to utter a word. She should have said no, told him to fuck off or something, stood her ground. But... she couldn't. She had no words to answer back to him, nothing that came to mind. Not when he was so dangerously close; Dante and his confidence were like a high wall she couldn't get past.

"...Can't decide?" he whispered.

His fingers came to gently lift her chin, and Eden opened her lips slightly without thinking. She didn't want to say yes, but she didn't want to say no. It was this horrible thing. She couldn't think straight, her survival instincts had suddenly been tamed by those of the woman inside her. Dante brought his face closer to hers, so close she couldn't see or smell anything but him. He was hovering over her like a tiger over its prey, with that cunning smile on his face.

"Cat got your tongue?" he chuckled.

Eden blushed, but she had never been so vulnerable. He was mocking her, and she was mad at herself for not saying anything back to him. Dante was just too dangerous for her. She couldn't even understand why. She had always been able to refuse any man. From an early age, she had understood her survival wouldn't rely on how she could give men what they wanted, but on how hard she was willing to fight to resist them. Eden never froze out of fear. She had done so once, and it had cost her brother's life. Adam's life. She had sworn not to make that mistake again. She would fight with everything she had, she wouldn't ever give up on her own survival.

In front of Dante, however, it wasn't fear that made her immobile. It was a thought. One single, dangerous doubt that made her hesitate. A voice she had kept silent for years was making itself heard right now, dangerously. Very dangerously. The thought that maybe, maybe, she could finally rely on someone. Trust someone else. Trust Dante De Luca, trust that he'd really do what he was promising. That maybe there was a light of truth in those golden, playful eyes of his. Not only that but in his heart too. That maybe there was something real about this, in the way he looked at her, in the way he talked to her. Everything that had happened tonight was nothing like she had experienced before. Eden knew it was dangerous to give in, to be lured by that sweet trap the Tiger had laid out for her. Yet, it was so hard to resist a trap that promised everything she had ever hoped for...

"...One night," she whispered.

Dante slowly pulled his face away. They had been as close as a kiss, but now, he was carefully looking at her, reading her face. Eden swallowed her saliva, trying to make up her mind as she spoke.

"...I'll sleep with you just one night," she said.

145

"And then?" he asked. "What will happen if I'm a good boy?"

"I don't know."

Eden honestly had no idea. She couldn't even imagine anything past the next minute, let alone after a full night of sleeping in the same bed as him. Even now, a part of her was screaming that this was a bad idea. That the Tiger was going to betray her, devour her. Still, it was too late. Too late to take back her words, or that satisfied smile on his lips. She just didn't want to promise him anything. It would have given him more room for demands, and she just wasn't sure she could afford to take anything else right now.

Dante smiled and, to her surprise, still leaned closer.

"One night, then," he whispered.

If Eden thought that was it, she was proven wrong right away. She felt his mouth on hers before she could react. This time, there was something a bit more ferocious than before. As if she had let him in, as if he suddenly had gotten some tacit permission. Eden took in his kiss with a little moan of surprise. She had trouble keeping up, but she still found herself trying. It was just too good to refuse. His lips on hers already felt strangely familiar, and it was so easy to just give in. She knew the more they kissed, the more she'd get used to this, and how dangerous it was, but it was too late. Eden didn't feel like stopping. She wasn't a child anymore, she was a young woman with desires too. Moreover, this was just a... kiss. A kiss to quench her thirst, or maybe to seal the deal. It wasn't leading to more, but it was fulfilling in itself. Without moving, Eden let him kiss her, or maybe she was the one kissing him back, she couldn't tell. Neither of them was in control, they were simply both enjoying this. Dante wasn't even acting forcefully or dominating her. She could have pulled back and stopped this at any moment. She knew it. She just didn't want to.

This was good, so good. Eden felt like her whole body was about to melt under this. She could already foresee how easily she could give in to this, get addicted to it. She had to be careful not to dive in too deep...

Suddenly, something in the room rang. They separated, their lips still a bit open and hesitant, but Dante immediately glanced at something behind her. Eden turned her head to see, but it was a simple clock on the wall. She frowned. Was it that late already? When she turned back to him, only then did she realize her hands were on Dante's chest. Eden immediately blushed, and she was about to take them off, but Dante took her hand without warning.

"Come," he said.

She frowned, and he pulled her toward the window wall. Eden couldn't understand what was going on, but any hint of playfulness was gone from his eyes; instead, the Zodiac was back. His eyes were looking as scary and dangerous as before and extremely serious. She came to her senses right away too. They both walked together toward the glass, Dante still holding onto her hand. That stupid, silly detail was disturbing Eden. He was holding her hand gently, guiding her, but without any intention of letting go, it seemed. She said

146

nothing and kept that little knot in her throat. Dante was already staring outside at something happening in the streets below. Eden frowned and, standing by his side, tried to see what he was staring at with such a dark expression.

It took her a little while to see it. A black Overcraft, landing in the middle of the Suburbs. Eden frowned; she had never seen one of the Core's Overcrafts with such a dark color before... Was this meant to be some sort of camouflage? Moreover, the arrival of that engine didn't seem to alarm anyone; no nearby lights were lit on, no one seemed to be at their windows to see what was going on.

"...What are they doing here?" she whispered.

It made no sense for an Overcraft of the Core to be there in the middle of the night. They even had laws for the Core citizens to be back at a certain hour, and they could only come to the Suburbs on certain days too. Eden was sure it wasn't one of those days, as it was usually the days she would have worked at Jack's bar. They couldn't be bringing exiled people either, not at such an hour. Dante remained silent, so she continued to observe. She didn't like this at all either. The Overcraft had landed, but no one was coming out. Nothing was happening. However, after a few seconds more, and squinting her eyes to try and understand, Eden finally saw it. A slight red ray, going over the building. It was just a red line that went up and down horizontally on a building, but it disappeared. Then, it appeared again, on the next building. She didn't like this at all.

"...They are scanning the buildings?"

Dante nodded.

"They do this almost every night, each time on different blocks. We first noticed it two weeks ago."

"...Which territory is this?" she asked.

"Tonight, it's the Hare's. Four days ago, they were at the Zebra's."

"No one else noticed?"

"If they did, they didn't share it with me..."

It wasn't surprising. None of the Zodiacs were on good enough terms that they'd willingly share information on something so important. What the hell was the Core doing? Why would they scan all the buildings in different areas? She kept staring, but no one came out of the Overcraft. Maybe there wasn't even a pilot or a passenger at all. However, if this was simply about scanning, wouldn't they have sent drones? Although the drones were often destroyed as soon as they came inside the Suburbs... Eden knew those things were costly, and a lot of people were happy to shoot at them if it meant whoever took it down could get their hands on the parts... Overcrafts were left alone because no one was crazy enough to risk injuring a member of the Core. There was a certain level of retribution no one wanted to handle. The Core had the money, the weapons, and the means to hurt people in the Suburbs.

"...So they just come and scan the buildings every night at the same hour?"

"Basically, yes. Strangely, it's just one Overcraft, though, and very, very careful not to be noticed..."

Indeed. If this had been a regular operation, the Core would have had no issues sending it during the day and giving some excuse as to why it was there... Eden had an odd feeling about this.

"It's not just that," said Dante.

This time, he let go of her hand and walked to one of the shelves to grab a remote, turning on the flat screen on the wall. Eden wasn't surprised to see him use old technology from the twentieth century. It was the best way to not get hacked, having technology that was too old for that. For a few seconds, she stared at the TV, looking at what seemed like the Core's regular channel of information. Very few people in the Suburbs could afford a TV, let alone get the kind of network that would give them access to the Core's news. It was because everything was so white and perfect on that show that Eden immediately knew it was one of the Core's TV channels. A woman with platinum blonde hair cut in a perfect bob, perfect skin, straight nose, symmetrical purple eyes, and a bright golden dress was talking. Definitely some sort of news anchor. The sound wasn't on, but the images spoke for themselves.

They were showing images of the Suburbs, but only... violent images. Eden began frowning the more she saw. It was only short sequences, showing nothing but gunfights, violence, and young people brawling. Bottles of alcohol shattered on the sidewalk, a car burning, graffiti on a wall, and... bodies. Eden was shocked. They weren't blurring images, but showed dozens of bodies, together in a pile, on the street.

"Where is... What the heck is that..." she whispered, taken by surprise.

She read the sentences at the bottom of the screen. "Violence escalating in the Suburbs. Non-Pure population getting out of control."

"They are trying to show people in the Core that the Suburbs are... out of control? What the hell...?"

Although the violence wasn't faked, Eden quickly recognized some of the streets in those videos; this was also a very narrow vision of the Suburbs she knew. The Suburbs were violent, it was true, but not out of control. There were no actual killings in this video, and Eden knew some of those young people shooting were probably just aiming at walls for fun like the young people sometimes did in her neighborhood. She liked the graffiti on the walls; it was on every street and, in a way, part of their culture. As long as the Zodiacs were there, nothing would go out of control. There were ten Zodiacs, ten territories, and as many different types of ambiances in the streets. Eden lived in one of the most dangerous ones, and even she couldn't recognize her daily life in those videos.

"...What the hell are they trying to do?" she asked.

"We aren't sure yet," said Dante, his golden eyes still on the screen, "but it doesn't look good..."

It didn't, indeed. The Core generally didn't care about what happened in the Suburbs. They were fine with the mess going on outside as long as it didn't

148

get inside. And it never did. The Overcrafts dropped exiles outside, but they never ever came in with more people than they had kicked out. It was hard... no, almost impossible for someone from the Suburbs to even set foot in the Core. Eden knew how hard it had been to get out when she was years younger. She couldn't even fathom how she'd get inside. The Core was too happy to kick anything that bothered them out to the Suburbs and let it be as it was. ...So why would they have a problem with the Suburbs now? There wasn't anything bad happening now that hadn't happened before. Even Dante attacking inside the Chinese territory was anecdotic, to be fair. How many times had the Zebra and the Hare's people gone against each other? And the Eagle, the Mexican mafiosos? They were the ones making the most noise.

"...You said 'we'?" she repeated.

"Since we noticed, I've had men watching in a lot of districts or from where we could. The territory they go to the most is the Dragon's. The south, in general."

Eden frowned. She was familiar with the south, where she worked and hung out the most. That area has Chinatown and most of the Asian population: the Rat's, the Dragon's, and the Snake's. Why would the Core's Overcraft go there the most often?

"What about the other territories?"

"It went to all of them, at least twice. My territory is the one it came to the most after the three Asian ones, it seems."

Eden frowned. What does it mean...? She had a bad feeling about this, but she knew there was no way the nine other Zodiacs hadn't noticed too. They were all watching their territories for external attacks; it would have been crazy for no one to notice a strange Overcraft flying over their heads in the middle of the night. The only thing they had in common was that they couldn't attack. Even the Zodiacs weren't crazy enough to risk killing a citizen of the Core and facing retribution. Not only for them, but each Zodiac had thousands of lives under their responsibility. It would have been too risky...

In silence, Dante and Eden watched the Overcraft do a few more stops, each time in a different block, and leave. It quietly went back to the Core, and Dante turned the TV off too. Everything went back to silence in the room. Eden turned to him.

"...Is that why you need me? You wanted a hacker to investigate what the Core is... doing here?"

Dante tilted his head, his cunning smile coming back.

"That's one of the reasons I wanted you, yes. I do have a lot of work for you as a Dive Hacker."

Eden slowly nodded. She was curious now too. She knew Loir would find it strange and help her investigate. It wasn't as if she hadn't tickled the Core before. The System hated her, as she was a big threat, but Eden had visited that System a few times before. It was no easy trip, but if Loir could get her deep enough into it, then she could... Dante gently grabbed her chin again, taking

149

her out of her reflections. The bubble of thoughts in Eden's head popped as she was suddenly faced with those dangerous golden eyes of his... again.

"...Someone's already thinking too much," he chuckled. "My new Dive Hacker needs a night of rest if she wants to be at her best for the jobs I have for her tomorrow... For you. Now it's late, and time for you to go to sleep, Eden... with me."

# CHAPTER ELEVEN

Locked up in the bathroom, Eden kept glaring at her reflection, mad at herself.

Why had she said yes to this? Now that she was by herself, it really felt like she had been crazy. Bewitched, drugged, or something. Why? Why in the world would she have agreed to this? What was wrong with her? She let out a long sigh, probably the tenth one in the past few minutes. Eden knew she hadn't been drugged, and she knew she was under no spell, except maybe for Dante's charms. Those cursed golden eyes of his... so alluring. She took several deep breaths.

She could hear one of her pups whining outside the door, waiting for her. The other one was perhaps asleep already. The past few minutes had happened like a dream. To her surprise, she and Dante had gone back to the very same room she had been given, the large suite. Was he fine changing rooms like that? She had thought the place he had been cooking in was his private apartment. Maybe there wasn't a bedroom there? Or was he unwilling to bring her there? Or maybe he simply didn't care where he slept. Eden brushed her hair with her fingers and scratched her head, too many questions popping up annoyingly in her mind.

She was annoyed that she just couldn't read his intentions clearly; she could not predict his next move. Was it ever going to be clear at all? What did he really mean by just... sleeping with her? Maybe it would have been easier if he had just asked for sex. At least she could have put her feelings aside and done it mechanically... perhaps. No, even then, she wasn't sure she could control her feelings. What feelings? Eden wasn't sure herself. Dante was waking up things in her she couldn't remember feeling in... a very long time.

Angrily, she brushed her teeth and washed her face, using every single piece of luxury that was offered to her. She brushed her long, blonde curls for a while too, although it was just to win herself some time to think. Her heart was beating like crazy just from thinking about going back there and sleeping in the same bed as him...

However, Eden knew she couldn't stay locked up in the bathroom forever, no matter how luxurious it was. She had cleaned and cut her nails, and taken some of the brand-new and expensive skin products left there for her. She wondered who had prepared this room. Maybe it was custom for all of his "partners" to get this? Maybe it was like in those fancy hotels: they had stocks of beauty products ready to be changed when the boss' new mistress came in... Eden tried to chase all those dark thoughts from her mind. She should just enjoy this while it lasts before he gets her killed or throws her back in the streets.

At least the pajamas she was in didn't feel too sexy or anything. It was a gray ensemble in silk and the bottoms were shorts, but she certainly didn't care about showing off her prosthetic legs...

After taking a deep breath, she finally came out of the bathroom. Bullet immediately jumped on her feet, whining again, but with his tail wagging. With the perfect excuse given by the pup to take it slow again, Eden crouched down to play with him. Her hazel eyes glanced sideways to see what Dante was doing.

He was already in bed, not paying attention to her. Well, that was what it looked like from a quick glance. He was reading something on a tablet, frowning, his hand behind his head. Eden wanted to roll her eyes. He wasn't wearing anything on top, once again showing off his muscles and that tiger tattoo... That posture was even flexing all his abs. She wondered if he was doing this on purpose.

"If I had known you liked being in the bathroom so much, I would have gotten you a spa..."

Eden glared his way. She didn't stay inside because of the products... After that sentence, Dante didn't add a word, still deeply absorbed in whatever he was reading. Eden had a hard time walking to the bed, though. She tried playing with Bullet a bit longer but even the pup was getting tired. Hadn't those two slept enough earlier? She looked around for Beer and to her surprise the pup was already on the bed, lying on his back and sleeping without a care in the world. Had Dante put him there? The bed was definitely too high for the pups to climb up.

After a while, when it was clear Bullet was too tired to play anymore, she hugged the pup and walked to the bed, trying to ignore Dante with all her might. Maybe he was pretending to read, but he didn't move when she climbed on the bed and put Bullet down. Eden sat on the edge of the bed with her back turned to him, but she immediately realized it was almost worse to not see him. It was too late for regrets; she took a deep breath and looked down at her legs.

"SIN, camouflage off."

Her fake skin disappeared, revealing the dark metal. Eden frowned and inspected her legs. They had been through quite a lot recently... but aside from a few superficial scratches, they didn't seem too damaged.

"We can have them checked for you if you need."

Eden was about to refuse, but she hesitated; having Parts revised was usually extremely expensive. Even while saving up all she could, Eden could only afford to have them revised once in a while. Which wasn't nearly enough considering how much she used them, especially for fighting. She constantly feared they'd break down or something...

"...Or get you new ones."

"I like this model," she immediately answered.

She had picked this model out of all the others because it wasn't too expensive. It was suited for fighting and most importantly, it couldn't be hacked without hacking her SIN first. The newest models were defaulted to have their own systems, which could be hacked themselves. This one only worked in symbiosis with her SIN and nothing else.

"But... a check-up would be nice," she muttered, a bit ashamed.

"Okay."

He didn't add anything after that and Eden felt a bit relieved. Her legs were an annoying topic to her. She finished checking them but she wasn't sure she wanted to take them off.

Sleeping with her legs on was extremely uncomfortable but Eden was worried something would happen while she was sleeping and that she wouldn't be able to put them back on in time. Would she? This was probably a very secure place but nothing could guarantee an assassin wouldn't come for the Tiger. Maybe a fight would break out.

"...What is it?" asked Dante, having noticed she was too still.

"I... How secure is this place?"

She heard him chuckle.

"Secure enough that no one uninvited has ever made it past the first floor alive. Each floor has its own security, including this one. This apartment has been secured, so no one under the level of lieutenant can walk in. No one but you and I can walk in without the password."

"What's the password?" frowned Eden, remembering she hadn't noticed any panel.

"I don't want to tell you."

Eden glared at him over her shoulder. Seriously? He kept ignoring her, although he was smiling as he read. Eden rolled her eyes and went back to her legs; she could probably walk out without it anyway since she had managed to do it before. Maybe he was just making that password thing up to mess with her.

Still, there was another thing bugging her about taking her legs off. If she experienced phantom pains again, there would be nothing to calm her. She had left her pills at her place. She certainly didn't want to ask Dante but she was scared of what could happen without them.

"...What is it?"

Dante was probably wondering why she was still so hesitant. Eden shook her head and unlocked her legs, slowly taking them off. She was making a bet right now, but her phantom pains only came once in a while. Maybe she'd be lucky for tonight.

"Nothing," she replied, putting them down alongside the bed.

The feeling of relief that came with taking her prosthetics off was incredible. It was like taking off a helmet after she'd had it on for hours. The skin on her legs could finally breathe a little, although Eden was glad to have that silk covering them. For some reason, she didn't like people looking at her cut ends. She laid herself in bed, grabbing the cover to pull over herself, hiding them more. The temperature didn't really call for it but that blanket was thin anyway and she couldn't sleep without something on top. Beer and Bullet felt movement on the bed and moved closer to curl up against her. Eden wrapped one of her arms around the closest pup, glad those two were there. At least she wasn't alone with just Dante in bed; moreover, that bed was large enough that she wasn't stuck right next to him.

"...Good night."

The way he said it, Eden knew he was smiling. She frowned and didn't answer, ignoring him. She just needed to fall asleep quickly... She forced herself to not move and simply listen but there wasn't anything to listen to. Unlike her place, this apartment didn't have any sounds but her breathing, the pups snoring softly next to her and Dante De Luca reading somewhere on the other side of the bed. He was immobile and Eden wondered if he was simply fine reading while she fell asleep. She hadn't expected anything else but she was surprised he kept his word in the first place...

Suddenly, the lights went dim and Eden wondered if he had used some remote or if this was scheduled. She could now see the city lights shimmering through the large windows. This view somehow helped her calm down a bit, along with Beer's cute snoring sounds.

Eden fell asleep after a long while.

Dante heard her breathing slow down and her shoulder was now moving very slowly. He put down the report he was reading, staring at her silhouette perfectly cut by the lighting. She was skinny with barely any curves. Her sun-kissed skin had little scars here and there, faint memories of her life in the streets.

He had read all the reports his men had gathered on her, yet something still bothered him every time he looked at her. He just couldn't pinpoint what and that was even more annoying. Rolf too had been questioning his strange obsession with her. It was going beyond the fact that he believed her to be Ghost. Dante was never so nice as to let someone talk back to him like that. Some of his men had taken a bullet for a lot less than that; it didn't matter that she was a woman. Eden didn't even belong to his clan. She was a stranger, a rogue pawn that couldn't be controlled so simply. Yet, his desire for control was getting extremely hard to hold back. She was just pushing each limit she could, constantly answering back, smart and quick-witted. Why was he letting her set her own limits like that? Dante hated what he couldn't control, but he didn't hate Eden. Instead, he felt like he was playing a new game, too focused and amused to be annoyed by it.

There was no game going on, though.

His fingers gently grabbed a strand of her blonde hair lying on the mattress. He played with it between his fingers, wondering if that'd wake her up. It looked like it wouldn't; Eden didn't even react. What was that whole thing about her not being able to sleep with someone in the room? Another lie to try and keep him at bay?

He kept stroking her hair and staring at her sleeping figure. He didn't like being in the dark about anything and he was almost blind when it came to Eden. Still, for some reason, there was something about her that kept him strangely calm. Even his headaches were nothing but a quiet buzz whenever she was around. He had wondered if that would even happen when he couldn't look at those hazel eyes of hers and it did. Something was happening, not in his head but in his chest...Why? How? What was it with this woman? Could he keep her by his side indefinitely? It would be hard, considering his plan. Eden was a Dive Hacker, perhaps an even more dangerous position than his. If only...

"Adam..."

He frowned.

She was mumbling in her sleep, almost crying. Adam? Was she dreaming about her brother? She began breathing louder and more erratically. A nightmare? Next to her, one of the pups opened his eyes and raised his head, half-asleep, but curious about his mistress' disturbed sleep.

Dante hesitated but Eden was still mumbling that name over and over. It sounded almost as if she was crying. Her body started getting agitated until her hair slipped through his fingers. He frowned, unhappy and unsure.

"Adam... no... no..."

"Eden."

He called out her name twice but she didn't seem to wake up. Dante sighed and put his hand on the mattress to stand over her, grabbing her shoulder.

"Eden, wake up."

"No... Adam... don't..."

As he rolled her toward him, he realized she was crying for real. Her lips were twitching and her forehead was sweating. Something was really wrong.

"Eden!"

She finally opened her eyes, still in a confused daze.

"A-Adam...?"

"No. Wake up, now."

Eden opened her eyes a bit more. Her crying calmed down, although tears were still rolling down to her temples. Suddenly, she grimaced and curled her body to the side.

"No, no, no, not now..." he heard her wailing.

He frowned and looked down. Her hands were tensed on the sheets covering her legs, and her lower body kept wriggling. He immediately understood.

"Phantom pain?"

She nodded, although her eyes were closed and she was biting on the pillow. The pups, now awake, began barking, worried, but Dante quickly pushed them out of the way.

"How do you usually treat it?"

"I... have... pills..." she groaned.

Dante didn't like that answer at all. No way he was going to let her become a damn junkie. He grabbed her arms, forcing her to sit up and face him with her back against the bed's headboard.

"Eden, look at me."

"No... No, I... need my..."

"I'm not giving you any narcotics, so look at me. Now."

She opened her eyes to glare at him but that was enough. Dante pulled the sheets and put his hands on each leg, suddenly massaging them while holding her gaze.

"Eden, look. You're fine."

"I'm not... fine!" she groaned.

He could see the pain in her grimace but he was set on not giving her any drugs. Instead, he reached out for a gun under his pillow. Eden's eyes reacted to the weapon and for a second he had her full attention. A glimpse of fear crossed her eyes. He suddenly pointed at her legs.

"Look."

He shot twice, right where her knees should have been. Her breathing accelerated and she gasped but the holes in the mattress were right in front of her. Eden stared at the feathers flying, out of breath.

"See?"

She glared at him but he put the gun down. His hands went back to her legs and started massaging them again.

"Look at me."

She obeyed only out of reflex and Dante suddenly kissed her.

It was easy. Her lips were right there, so close, so desirable. Eden answered that kiss weakly, her breathing still not stable, Dante wasn't giving her any room to think. He kissed her again and again until she let go of the bedsheets and grabbed his shoulder to push him away.

"W-what are you doing..." she mumbled.

"Distracting you."

Eden blushed. She was tired, still a bit lost and dizzy, but she couldn't tell if it was from the nightmare or the kiss. As soon as she put enough strength into pushing him and keeping him at bay, Dante stopped. He had one hand on the headboard next to her head and the other on the mattress, still dangerously close.

"...Feeling better?" he asked.

Eden swallowed her saliva, her heart still beating like crazy, and nodded weakly. Yes, the pain was mostly gone. Indeed, he had succeeded in distracting her... She still felt like she was dreaming, though. A bit out of breath, she wiped the tears off, embarrassed to have cried in front of him.

"...Want to talk about it?" he asked.

"No."

That was a clear and definitive answer, but to her surprise, he simply sighed and retreated. He looked... angry. Silent, but angry. Eden didn't know what to expect but she watched him get up and walk to get a glass of water, half-naked again. She glanced to the side. He had left the gun there, at arm's length. She kept staring at it for a long time until she opened her mouth.

"I always dream about it... of the night Adam died."

Dante's hand froze on the pitcher but he didn't say anything. He didn't seem very surprised either. Eden wasn't sure though because she had never seen him surprised before... Instead, he calmly walked over and handed her the glass of water. Eden took it without saying a word and slowly drank it. The room was so quiet; she felt like the sounds of her own throat were embarrassingly loud. The icy water felt like a much-needed breath of fresh air, chasing the fever from that nightmare away. It took her a few long seconds to finish it and cool herself down. With trembling fingers, she put the glass down on the bedside table. Meanwhile, Dante sat down next to her, dangerously close.

Beer, who had been woken up too, crawled onto her lap, half-asleep, so Eden grabbed the pup to hug him. The dogs were becoming more of an emotional support to her than she could've imagined... Beer yawned but let himself be handled like a plushie, too tired to struggle. Eden took several deep breaths, trying to bring her mind back to reality. She was finally calming down, except her heart was still thumping like crazy in her chest, which she hated. She hated it even more because she couldn't tell if it was from the nightmare or how close Dante was to her...

"Aren't you going to ask?" she asked with a hoarse voice.

"Not really."

Either he didn't care enough to ask, or he didn't want to pry into her memories. Eden sighed. It wasn't something she wanted to relive again anyway. The memory was already painful enough and he already knew enough. His predecessor had killed Adam. Eden could see the scene play over and over when she closed her eyes.

The wet asphalt. The sound of the downpour covering everything. All the men in dark suits standing in a circle. A flash in the night. The gunshot. Adam's body, just lying there. The young Eden, hidden around the corner, her body curled up by fear against the concrete. She had felt sick like never before when they dragged his body away. She had no choice but to run so she could puke without being found. When she had gone back, only a few minutes later, they were gone and they had taken Adam's body with them. There was nothing left of her brother.

Sometimes, Eden was scared to close her eyes, it was as if that scene was printed with dark ink behind her eyelids. She couldn't escape it or the darkness that troubled her every time. Eden sighed, still holding Beer against her chest, and let herself slowly fall backward on the bed.

She kept her eyes open, staring at the ceiling. With Dante laying down next to her, Eden knew he was staring at her. It was even more embarrassing that he wasn't saying a word or asking anything. Hence, she rolled on her flank, showing her back to him and staring at the large bay window. How late was it? She had no idea. It didn't really matter; what she feared the most was the moment she'd struggle to fall asleep again...

To her surprise, Dante moved closer and a few seconds later she felt him hugging her from behind. His large arm wrapped around her waist and she felt his torso against her back. Eden froze, too shocked to move. What was he doing? He was hugging her almost the same way she was holding Beer and she hadn't asked for that! The bed was super large too; did he really have to stick to her like that? She was nobody's pillow...

Yet, Eden strangely kept her protestations to herself. Something in the warmth she felt all over her back kept her mute. It was... somewhat soothing, having so much warmth against her. She swallowed her saliva, wondering if he could hear her fluttering heartbeat. In this instance, some long-forgotten feelings came from deep inside and she couldn't recognize them. Was it comfort? A sense of security? Protection? Eden just couldn't decide. She tried to sort out her feelings but no matter what, she just knew she didn't feel like moving away. Dante was hugging her from behind and it wasn't as annoying as she thought it would be. He must've been close enough that she could hear his breathing but she wasn't able to say exactly how close. She allowed herself to deeply breathe in but he didn't seem to pick up on it. She could tolerate this, but she probably wouldn't be able to fall back asleep like this...

This situation was too close for comfort. Eden knew she wasn't going to go back to sleep. Instead, she stared emptily at the large bay window. Chicago was strangely quiet at night. A light was lit or extinguished in a building from time to time, but that was it. There were no cars outside, no music; there was not one soul moving. It was strangely calm and peaceful...

Eden hadn't realized she had fallen asleep. She woke up very slowly from one of those very long and restful nights that rarely come. It took her a few seconds to realize and remember where she was and with whom. As it hit her, she opened her eyes but didn't move. Mostly because she could feel a man's body under her. She frowned and waited for a second as she heard his slow breathing. He was asleep, right? She slowly got on her elbows. Dante was lying there; she had been sleeping with her cheek and half her upper body on his torso! Eden blushed and retreated as fast and as quietly as she could.

How did that even happen? She had fallen asleep with him hugging her, so when had they changed positions?! Eden looked around, confirming they were still alone in the room as her eyes went back to Dante. For now, his eyes were still closed. Either he was good at pretending to sleep or this was her chance to run away from this situation. Eden got to the other side of the bed, praying silently he wouldn't hear her. Judging by the lights outside, it was still early... Eden leaned over the bed, trying to grab her legs. To her surprise, there was only one. She frowned. Had the other one rolled under the bed?

"Good morning."

Eden froze at the deep and husky voice coming from Dante, who had just woken up. She didn't want to look over her shoulder at Dante's half-naked figure. She had a pretty good idea of the look in his golden eyes already...

"M-morning," she mumbled.

Her throat was a bit dry again. And why was her heart beating so fast, so early, anyway? Moreover, he had to wake up when she was in such a stupid position, supporting her upper half with her arms, on the edge of the bed...

"Woof!"

Eden glanced to the side.

Her pups were guilty for her missing leg. She couldn't tell if the two of them had managed to pull it away from the bed or if it had fallen. In any case, Beer was biting into the metal as if it was a toy, while Bullet was wagging his tail trying to get underneath it. Eden grumbled.

"You two..."

She hesitated to get down on her elbows and crawl there or hop with one leg. Neither option was very gracious and she knew the Tiger was definitely staring at her.

"Need help?" he chuckled.

Eden rolled her eyes. Of course, he had to make fun of her.

"I'm fine," she mumbled.

"Eden."

She looked back, wondering why he was calling her, but just as she did Dante's lips greeted her.

It was so sudden. Eden's strength left her arms, almost falling over, until Dante grabbed her confidently. He hadn't even noticed but he was holding her arm and keeping her from falling, doing all that while still kissing her. Eden was still so confused, she could only take it and blush.

That kiss was short but Dante pulled back slowly with that horrible smirk on his face. That man was a devil... Eden ignored him and quickly got out of his grip to grab her leg. It was only one or two hops away and she didn't want to spend more time thinking. Thinking wasn't doing her any good in this situation.

"Do you like coffee?"

Eden frowned in his direction. Dante had already left the bed and was walking away. He really was half-naked and casually walking around... She swallowed her saliva once more and prayed that he wouldn't look back while she threw herself onto her other leg. Eden quickly took it back from the excited pups and put her leg back on, stretching right away with a grimace. Putting them back on was always a bit of a weird conflict between discomfort and relief.

Now that she was up, Eden felt a bit awkward. She entertained the pups for a little while, glancing Dante's way every so often. The suite they had given her didn't have a full kitchen but there was a little corner with a kettle, some mugs, and apparently a little cupboard that contained coffee. Ignoring the fact that she hadn't answered, Dante poured two cups and walked back to her.

"Thanks..."

Sipping a hot drink in the morning, with a view of the Chicago sunrise, was a unique experience she hadn't encountered before.

However, it didn't look like Dante had time to spare. He walked to the bathroom without saying a word. Maybe he wasn't a morning person, thought Eden. She was, though. Eden walked up to the window and played on the control panel until she was able to open a portion of it to let some air in. She was surprised. Even if she had expected the air to be better in the morning and at this height, she didn't think it would be that good. She leaned on the window, letting her arms and face enjoy the breeze. There probably wasn't any wind on the ground because she could barely feel it where she was. Beer and Bullet kept barking at her feet and trying to bite her metallic toes, curious, but Eden just ignored them. She needed five minutes of quiet before resuming her crazy new life.

Dante took his time in the bathroom. She heard the shower running for quite some time before he finally came out. Now clean-shaven and dressed in another Italian suit, he passed through the doorway and put on a different expensive watch. Eden felt a bit silly now that she was the only one left in pajamas.

"I have to go," he simply said. "I'll see you later."

"...Aren't I supposed to accompany you?" asked Eden, frowning.

"Already can't bear to be without me?" he smirked, doing his cufflinks.

"I meant as your bodyguard," she retorted.

"No. Not in here."

She suddenly remembered him bragging about his building's security while Dante left without adding a word. Eden was so surprised but what was she expecting? Breakfast together in bed? She'd gone crazy for sure... Silently mad at herself, she sipped her coffee and spent a bit more time at the window.

All of a sudden, she realized that since she was in Dante's building anyway, she could put her SIN back online.

"Jack?" she called.

"Holy shit, Eden! You're alive, you little swine! I was so sure those crazy Italian bastards had thrown you into the dang river!"

"Yeah, no... uh... things happened. Are you alright?"

"Alright? I ain't alright at all but I'm alive! Dang it... Oh, I swear, I'm glad you're alive, but babe, it's been a mother fu–... Ugh. I shouldn't complain but dang... Anyway, where are ya? You could have brought your butt back around if you were alive!"

"Not really, I had... uh..."

Eden frowned. She didn't know how much she could tell him. She didn't really care about Dante's opinion but she also didn't want to put Jack or one of the girls at risk by saying too much.

"I'm... in the Tiger's territory," she finally said.

Which was the truth, aside from the fact that Eden didn't mention how deep in it she really was...

"You wha–? Eden, hun, have you gone cray-cray? The Italians? You hate the Tiger! I know they took you but I figured if you were alive you would've gotten the heck away by now!"

"The Tiger... offered me a contract. A job."

"What? Eden! This is an effin' Zodiac we are talking about! ...Wait, is it your... other job?"

"Sort of. I can't tell you everything now, Jack, but don't worry, I'm okay."

"Oh, God... Oh, whatever. At least you're probably safer than here."

"What? What are you talking about?"

She knew there was something wrong from his tone of voice. Eden closed the window and went to put her cup down and then headed to the bathroom. She went in and closed the door behind her, ignoring the whiny pups.

"Jack?"

"It's a mess here, babe. There's weird stuff going on and I ain't liking it. Since the shooting, things are going really bad here, as expected. The Old Man must really be living out his last days because all the crazy punks are making a mess everywhere. Plus, there were no customers last night."

"W-what? What do you mean, no customers? You didn't open the bar anyway, did you?"

"With the state it was in? Girl, I spent the damn night picking up freakin' bullets! I'm just glad I had enough savings to afford the hospital... No, I didn't mean me. No one came from the Core last night, Eden. There were no customers that weren't locals, our locals."

Eden frowned. She didn't like that. There had been no one from the Core coming to the Suburbs? There were always people coming! They always used the Suburbs like some adult amusement park. Because there were almost no laws here, all the young people liked to come and have fun and enjoy everything that would have been unlawful inside the Core: adult shows, sex, gambling, drugs, and everything that made the Suburbs both dangerous and thrilling to them.

"No one...?"

"No one, hun. It's super odd; it freaked out half the territories from what I've heard. The Core hasn't released a statement but I heard from the hag next door that they've been showing some nasty stuff on TV. I don't like it, hun."

Eden didn't like it either. What was the Core planning? The only times they didn't allow their people to go to the Suburbs was when there were some big political events or something had happened in the Suburbs that would have put their citizens in danger. However, this was usually followed by them sending a few drones to "reinforce security". A few dropped bodies later, the situation was settled... It never took more than a few hours, either. Now there had been no one since the previous night?

"Did you hear something from... the other side?" asked Jack.

"No, I haven't gone since," admitted Eden.

Maybe it was time she Dived again. Quickly washing her face, Eden opened a wardrobe to find some clothes for herself. They had prepared a few simple outfits of her size, so she settled for the fitted top that covered the most skin, and shorts she could comfortably walk around in. While she rushed, Jack told her what she already knew, about the girls who had died, those who had made it, and his own situation after the battle.

"No one else showed up?" asked Eden.

"After that mess? Girl, no. Everyone stayed away, thank God. Rose and I went to the hospital and as soon as they patched us up, we left to hide at my place for the night. I don't think I would have had the balls to go back if it wasn't for her being there too. My poor bar... Oh, damn it..."

Eden grimaced. She knew how much Jack had invested in that place and she felt sorry for him, too.

"I'm sorry, Jack."

"Babe, don't be sorry, be glad you're alive! I can't take any more sorrys today. Just stay wherever you are if it's safe. Thank God you've got good survival instincts..."

Eden wasn't so sure. If that was the case, she wondered how she'd gotten herself in the Tiger's lair...

"Okay. You stay safe too, Jack. I... I'll see you when I can."

"Don't worry about me, hun, I can handle myself. Just let me know you're alive from time to time, a'right? It's nice to have some good news in these crazy times..."

Eden was left with a bittersweet feeling after that call. At least she had confirmed Jack was alive and well, Rose too. As for the others... She was just trying not to think about it for now. She closed her eyes, brushing her hair with her fingers. She walked back inside the room, glancing at the pups. They both ran to her as soon as she stepped out of the bathroom. She picked up Bullet, the whinier of the two, and stroked him gently while staring outside the window.

...What was she supposed to do now? She didn't want to go and find Dante. She was already so unsure about whatever was going on with him...

A gentle knock at the door answered her question. Rolf appeared, nodding politely.

"Good morning," he said. "I... wondered if the puppies needed a walk..."

Eden looked down. Right... She had forgotten because they were relatively well-behaved, but they probably needed to take a walk. It was impressive they hadn't soiled the room yet. Unless they had and she just didn't see... Well, with a bit of luck, maybe they had soiled somewhere that would annoy Dante.

"Thanks," she said, walking up to him.

Rolf curved his lips in an attempt at a smile, but he looked like the kind of man who just didn't know how to. Instead, his eyes were on Beer, who had run to bite his shoelaces, excited.

No words were exchanged between them while they left the room. Rolf was actually the one man around that Eden was most likely to trust... He had this kind of demeanor of someone straightforward without a hint of malice. She wouldn't say it out loud but Eden was feeling okay with this man. Moreover, the way he looked at Beer or stole glances at Bullet in her arms spoke volumes. He was just interested in the pair of pups, not her.

They walked together in silence, Rolf a step ahead to guide her. Beer was having no trouble chasing behind, amused even, while Bullet was quiet in Eden's arms. The middle-aged man took her to an elevator and after ascending a few floors, it suddenly opened onto a large terrace. Eden was surprised. This wasn't just a large terrace; it had some grass growing in square patches. Even more incredible, there were trees! She let Bullet down for him to go and play with his brother while she went to one of the trees.

"...Is it a real one?" she asked.

"Yes. It's genetically modified, though. All of these are."

Eden nodded. There wasn't anything surprising about that. An organic tree couldn't simply grow like that in a place like the Suburbs. That would have been too hard. Still, she loved being able to see a large full-grown tree. Hundreds were growing in the farms and greenhouses of the Core, but in the Suburbs, the pollution in the air and the ground had made it almost impossible for anything to grow from their soil. Those trees must have cost a fortune... both to buy and to keep.

A few steps behind, Rolf got down on his knees and actually took out a bag of food and some treats, immediately getting the pups' attention. Beer and Bullet began barking and jumping around, both excited and visibly hungry. Eden watched the stern man gently indulge the pups' whims, playing around with them, making them run after a treat or bark for more. It was cute to see such a big and cold guy totally smitten by a pair of puppies...

"...How long have you been with the boss?" she asked, putting her hands on the bark of the tree, pretending not to care much.

"Since just before he took over."

163

"You don't mind... what he did?"

Eden couldn't understand how a man who had killed the previous leader himself could be so... respected by his men. She didn't care, as she loathed the last Tiger, but it was quite a mystery how those men could simply change their allegiance after a murder. Moreover, it wasn't just respect; she could tell Dante's men would follow any order he gave without blinking. If he moved, they moved. If he said anything, took a breath, or stayed quiet, they obeyed every command. Rolf also seemed like a very strong and determined guy, but she knew by his demeanor that his boss came first before anything.

"No," he simply answered.

Eden frowned. Was he unwilling to expand on the matter or was it some sort of taboo? She hated half-answers but she could tell he wouldn't say more. She had to find another angle.

"...What about his plans to attack the other territories?"

"If the boss decides to, we will."

Eden frowned. What was wrong with them? They were fine with being sent to their deaths just because Dante De Luca had decided so? She wanted to roll her eyes. Instead, she glanced down. Beer was still playing with the big guy, hoping to get some more treats. Bullet met her eyes and hopped back toward her, yapping cutely at her. Eden let the time the pup took to get back to her pass in silence before she tried asking a question again.

"Why did he kill the previous boss?"

"...It was his decision."

"That's it?" Eden raised an eyebrow.

"...He was one of the possible successors anyway. The boss got rid of the other candidates and his predecessor and that settled it. There was nothing else that needed to be discussed."

Eden just couldn't understand this strange world they lived in. It wasn't just about killing or getting killed; they didn't even seem to hold any regrets or resentment toward a man who had murdered their previous leader... If someone came to replace Dante, would none of his men try to avenge him? Was that so simple?

"...I don't understand," she muttered.

"It doesn't matter much if you do," said Rolf, surprising her. "Most people in the clan will follow blindly regardless of who the boss is. It just happens that Dante De Luca is probably the one we are the most willing to follow."

Eden frowned, confused once again. She had valued her freedom her whole life. The concept of being willing to follow someone regardless of their own aspirations wasn't something she could ever agree to. Her own reasons for staying around were still unclear too. She had understood running was pointless and, for now, that was her best excuse.

Instead of adding another question she probably wouldn't get a proper answer to, she decided to turn to the trees and wander between them. She liked to touch them and feel that strange warmth under her fingers, wondering what

164

was happening inside. She had heard trees were alive, just like humans. How similar were they? Just like humans, trees were struggling to survive but it wasn't their own doing... Sometimes, Eden hated her own species for putting the rest of the living beings through such hardships. She had seen pictures of wild, gigantic forests before and wished she had lived in those times when she could have simply stepped out and taken a breath of fresh air or grabbed a fruit from a tree like this. This was a dream only the people of the Core were allowed to live now.

Beyond the edge of the terrace, she stared at the Core. Just like the previous nights, no Overcrafts were coming to the Suburbs. Normally, there would have been at least a couple flying in or out every hour. Even if they weren't going to the Suburbs, they could travel from one Core to another just like that. What could possibly forbid those journeys, even temporarily? Eden just couldn't think of anything good... and she didn't like doing nothing about it either.

"Watch the dogs," she suddenly said, walking back to the elevator.

"I'm supposed to watch you," said Rolf, immediately jumping back to his feet.

Eden answered with a glare. She had understood that much but his stating it so openly annoyed her even more. She really didn't need a babysitter. She could already guess that most of the cameras on this floor were probably watching her every move for their master. Eden shuddered, remembering her night and being close to Dante for some reason. Way too close... She shouldn't have let herself go like that. Why was she so weak when it came to him? If it had been anyone else, they couldn't have taken a step closer without her jumping away and she certainly would never have slept with any man either...

Trying to ignore her own blushing, she pushed the buttons of the elevator. Beer and Bullet immediately ran to her, ignoring the treats they hadn't collected yet, to get to their mistress' side with little barks. Rolf followed the pups and stood next to her in the elevator. Eden crossed her arms but she didn't protest, it probably wouldn't have mattered...

Instead, she now wanted some action. She had been way too still for someone who was not fine about all this. Her best remedy for anxiousness was to keep herself busy with something else. Preferably something dangerous or thrilling at least. Of course, it involved going to see Loir.

Despite the change of environment, she wasn't surprised at all that her partner hadn't dropped any of his bad habits by coming here. She walked into his new lair and no Italian had any intention to stay around; no surprise there. They had probably decided that watching him from behind a screen would be much more bearable. Moreover, Loir had his music horribly loud over the speakers and she grimaced while walking in. Had he been unable to do this when he was living and hiding in that basement? He seemed to be enjoying himself fully while listening to some absolutely stupid song with some loud techno beat, making the whole place jump.

*"Ring, ding, ding-ding-ding, ring! Ring, bam, bam..."*

Loir was singing and moving way too much, even for someone who couldn't use their lower half. His singing made absolutely no sense; it was high-pitched and annoyed Eden the minute she entered. Plus, he was following every high note with a jump at each beat. It was like watching a meerkat hopping in every direction while also moving his head like a dingbat.

"Loir! LOIR, damn it! "

He didn't even hear her yelling. He just kept jumping in his chair, his eyes fixated on the screens, his shoulders moving left and right, opposite to his head. He had even illuminated the whole room with purple lighting as if this was a nightclub or something. Eden sighed, while the pups barked behind her, annoyed by all the noise and unwilling to approach. She walked up to him and tapped his shoulder.

"Kitty!" he yelled, as loud as the music. "Look! *Ding-ding-diiiiing! Riggi-ding!!*"

He kept making some dance moves that weren't even matching the rhythm. Eden ignored him, pissed, and went to his keyboard to find out how to cut off that stupid music.

When it finally stopped, she let out a long sigh. How could he even stand this?

"Kitty! But that was so fun, I didn't even get to hear the second part..."

"Loir, you've had enough, I think... What the fuck, they gave you caffeine?" she gasped, seeing the rows of cups on the side of his desk.

She sighed. As if Loir wasn't crazy enough, they had actually come up with the stupid idea to give him caffeine, of all things? Moreover, there weren't only one or two cups! She grabbed them and threw them across the room, annoyed. Beer and Bullet immediately ran to play with them, Rolf jumping after them to make sure the pups didn't get any. Meanwhile, Eden glared at the camera in a corner.

"If I find out who gave him coffee, they're dead!"

No response came but she hoped that was enough. Loir pouted.

"But I like coffee... They have really good coffee!"

"Yeah, it works wonders on you, apparently. Did you even sleep at all?"

The dark circles under his eyes were worse than usual, giving him an even more skeletal appearance with those pitch-black eyes of his. He shrugged.

"Sleep? I don't know. Wait, what time is it? Is it midnight already?"

"It's morning, Loir. I already told you to keep a damn clock on your computer, you crazy owl... Anyway, I need you to check something... about the Core."

He tilted his head.

"Can't I have breakfast first? I asked for carbonara and they said they'd kill me..."

"Kill you? Why would they kill you for..."

Eden rolled her eyes. She couldn't even blame the Italians; she knew how Loir could be absolutely insufferable at times.

"Loir, what did you do?"

"I simply said there was no cream in their carbonara!"

"And?"

"I asked for anchovies..."

"Loir, enough, you're just making fun of them. I don't care about you annoying them but they are the ones who feed you, so you behave if you want breakfast next time."

Loir smiled, showing all his multi-colored teeth, and turned to the cameras, waving.

"My sweeties! Can I get some pizza? I want Calzone to bring it, he's my cutie pie!"

Eden grimaced. It was going to be a miracle if he survived until the end of the week without one of them pulling a gun on him with that kind of attitude... She grabbed the arm of his chair and pulled him back toward her to get his attention.

"Loir, focus," she sighed. "The Core. Did you find or see anything unusual?"

He tilted his head.

"Unusual, like some drones popping up all over the place?"

"Drones?" she repeated, surprised.

"Yep..."

He turned to his keyboard, finally serious. He typed for a little while and a map of their area appeared, with little red spots appearing at random blocks in between buildings. One was bigger than the others and Eden guessed this was where she and Dante had seen the black Overcraft the previous night. She hadn't seen any drones, though...

Loir extended one of his black-painted nails, showing the little dots.

"All those are cute little drones that appeared throughout the night..."

"Appeared? You mean they came and left?"

"Nope, Kitty. They came, but they didn't leave..."

"Wait, what? Those things are still there?"

Eden frowned. Why would the drones stay in the same spots? They were bound to be destroyed by the locals; it was nothing but a waste of money for the Core!

"Anything else you found?"

"Those are new little toys!" exclaimed Loir, a playful smile on his lips. "I actually want one to play with, but it would be a bit dangerous to get it from... the physical world."

Eden knew exactly where he was going with that. She crossed her arms.

"You think we can deactivate it from the inside?"

"Of course! The Core wouldn't send their little toys on their own, would they? Now, if a cute little kitty could go in and switch off the right buttons, then our cute little Calzone and Margherita could go to retrieve it..."

"You're not fooling anyone, Loir, this isn't an easy Dive. Those things are a part of the Core's System. It means I need to get into the Core's System, not just close to it but literally inside, and find my way to those drones to disconnect them!"

Loir smiled and took out one of the cables with a naughty smile.

"I just want one to play with, Kitty, I promise. Moreover, aren't you curious to know what our naughty friends from the Core are doing in the area? We gotta play with them a bit, don't we?"

Eden hesitated. Surely, Diving now would be the perfect opportunity to get a ton of information, but she hated going into the Core's System. The Core was constantly chasing her, trying to trap her. These weren't exactly the perfect conditions...

"Don't worry," he said, showing an even creepier smile, "I got it aaaaall ready so we don't have to use the big stuff!"

Eden sighed. So he did have another profile ready to hide that she was Ghost... Still, from the way he smiled, she wasn't too eager to know what he had prepared for her.

"It better not be some dumb crap, Loir?"

"Me, doing crap? Kitty, I'm a virtuoso; I only do art!"

Eden rolled her eyes. She'd better be prepared for the craziest Dive ever.

# CHAPTER TWELVE

"Loir, I am so going to kill you!"

"Kitty, don't yell; I'm literally right next to you... Plus, I found you some super upgraded gear! Do you know how hard it was for me to get all this? You're just too mean!"

If she hadn't been in the middle of a Dive right now, Eden would have kicked him without any hesitation. However, right now, her body was probably lying unconscious next to Loir while her brain was Diving into the Core's System. Still, not being able to beat up Loir or make him regret this in some way was terribly frustrating.

This had to be the most ridiculous gear he could have ever come up with. Eden couldn't believe he had dared to do that, knowing that she'd get out of there sooner or later. She was going to kill him.

"You're so dead," she hissed again.

She was dressed... in pink. Not just in pink but in a horrible cat outfit that gave her giant paws, a long fluffy tail, and even more annoyingly, long pink hair and pointy ears. If she moved, all her fingers and toes reacted. It was like wearing large boots and gloves with retractable claws at the end, but this was just horribly... geeky. She didn't even want to see what her face looked like; what she could see already annoyed her to no end. Her outfit would have been sufficient if Loir had left it as the gray sportswear ensemble she was wearing, a simple bra and leggings, but he had to add that ridiculous cat gear to it.

"Loir!" she shouted.

"Oh my pasta, stop yelling! I have headphones on! Moreover, I really don't understand what you're mad about; you're adorable in this!"

"Loir!"

"Try purring? I added this as an extra. I'm positive you can–"

"Loir, you're so dead!"

"Meow, meow..."

She just wanted to disconnect herself and kill him. She could withstand a lot of humiliation, but just knowing that there was a chance for Dante De Luca to actually see her in such a ridiculous outfit was a nightmare.

"Oh, you're so fussy, Eden... bad Kitty! So ungrateful; it took me some extra effort to come up with all that gear! This is really top-notch stuff and you're not even the slightest bit thankful!"

"I'd be grateful if it wasn't for this stupid design!"

"There she goes complaining again," he sighed. "You'll thank me later, then. For now, our pissed-off Kitty should really get to work; I'm transferring you into the Core in three... two..."

Eden braced herself. Being transferred from one system to another was like switching worlds. She had been in the Core's servers before but was in no hurry to get back into that scary maze.

The transfer was less than a second but it was enough to make her dizzy. It was like she was sent through a hurricane, thrown left and right by an overwhelming force. When it stopped, Eden grimaced, a headache kicking in. However, she knew she had reached her destination. The Core's first defense system was right in front of her.

"You hangin' in there, Kitty?"

"Yeah..."

Eden faced the large wall in front of her and pushed against it without thinking. The illusion broke just as quickly, the granite evaporating like dust in front of her. She moved again and ran into the wall, which let her through without much resistance.

"Welcome back into Hell..." muttered Loir.

His voice didn't have an ounce of humor in it this time. They both knew that being in the Core's System was serious and possibly deadly. It was much easier to get in than to get out. Eden waited a couple of seconds but her new identity didn't attract any attention. So, she kept walking as the world around her changed again. The maze she had been preparing herself for slowly appeared.

It wasn't an actual maze, but large black blocks, with several little lights on them. They were beginning to rise like buildings emerging from the ground around her in all sizes. Despite those black-colored walls, the floor and ceiling were an impeccable white. Eden hurried inside, glancing around, carefully trying to spot any sign of movement. Most of those block buildings were tall enough that she couldn't touch the ceiling above her, yet narrow enough that she could touch both sides simultaneously. She was careful not to touch any, though.

"Loir?"

"Let's try the second one on your left."

She nodded and quickly walked between the columns, extremely careful. Eden knew she only had a few minutes; this one was merely the server's antechamber. She ought to pick a point of entry quickly or the System will be alerted of an intruder. However, she had to run along the walls until she spotted the first screen. Eden didn't even glance at the images and kept running, waiting for the next one.

"Loir?" she asked.

"You're almost there."

He was right. Eden finally spotted the second one just a few seconds later and accelerated; because of the strange appearance of that maze, distances were blurred. Something that looked small and close could actually be huge but pretty far away. Eden knew that all too well to even consider slowing down.

Suddenly, a beeping sound was heard.

"Loir?"

"...They aren't here for you, but don't slow down."

Eden nodded, not wasting her breath on words. The sentinels must have spotted another intruder. There were always one or two hackers who tried to enter the Core at the first real border. If not backed up properly, they were usually spotted within a few seconds. For Eden to run this long and Dive this deep meant that Loir was doing a great job of shielding her presence.

The stressful beeping quickened, meaning the sentinel was closer, but so was the screen that Eden wanted. She wasn't even worried when she finally reached it.

"Loir, I'm there."

"I know, I know..." he sang. "Paw on the screen, purr-etty please!"

She rolled her eyes but obeyed. Immediately, the screen read her cat-like hands with an obviously-fake identification. Eden briefly read the information the System received about her.

"'Pink Kitty Cat'? Seriously, Loir?" she hissed.

"You are so unappreciative."

She didn't have time to curse him. The screen validated her arrival and Eden was once again blown into the server, the real one this time.

She fell down on her knees while the world around her changed.

This time, it was much more precise and somewhat... scary.

"What the..."

Gigantic cubes appeared all around her, in so many vivid-colored blocks. Eden had never seen that type of defense before and she kept looking in all directions, nervous. This place was creepy. The cubes of different sizes moved, going up and down, left and right, moving in any one of their six faces' directions. It was like being in the middle of a toy box, but in a large space that would have its own laws of gravity.

"Loir, where am I?"

"Hm, they have funny programmers," he chuckled. "This has been one of the entry points for the Core's main security archive for the last month or two."

"Here? Are you kidding?"

"Yup. This is only the first level. From what I can see, there are probably one or two more to cross before they give you the information. I think they might have been inspired by a kid's game. Anyway, business as usual. You gotta find the key to access the next level."

Eden kept looking, but with so many cubes moving in different directions, she would get thrown to the other end of the room within seconds. The giant blue cube she had landed on was simply moving up and down, and like all the others, it changed direction if it met another one.

"Any clue?" she grimaced, trying to look around her.

"It's like a pointer game. You have to find the one spot that looks a bit different."

Eden kept looking around nervously. There were so many different blocks of color everywhere; how could she spot something different? She jumped to another cube that was flying laterally instead, looking around.

"There's some sort of timer hidden in the code, Kitty. Hold on."

That was basically all that she was doing while looking around frantically. Every different color meant another cube. Even the walls were covered in various-sized squares and they were coming out at any moment to start gravitating in the room. Some were bouncing off the walls but some stuck to it and joined the rest of the wall. This room had already changed a hundred different times in size and shape since she had gotten there.

These were typically the kind of tricks programmers of the Core would put in place to chase intruders. A real battle of nerves, where one had to keep calm no matter what chaos was going on around. Eden tried to control her breathing but so many cubes were moving all around her, she was scared she would miss the clue she needed. As the platform she was on joined the wall, she had to jump to another one. Every time she looked down to see where she'd fall if she were to, she couldn't see the floor. It seemed as if it was a bottomless pit with no ceiling either. No matter how long she looked, there was nothing but moving cubes, which meant her clue could be much higher or much lower, and she couldn't decide which way to go.

"Loir, I need a clue!" she insisted while jumping again.

"I'm digging, Kitty, I'm digging. This thing is a loop, which is good news..."

"Meaning?"

"Well, if you fall, you're not going to fall anywhere. The ceiling is the bottom, the bottom is the ceiling. Upside down! So fun, isn't it? I need to beat the genius who conceived this..."

"Can you modify it from the outside?"

172

"Nope. Already tried. It just keeps going, doesn't give two olives about me."

"What can you do?"

"Nothing! The only thing I see moving is my favorite Kitty Cat girl! This code is just a damn loop and it won't let me squeeze in!"

"A loop..."

Suddenly, Eden had an idea.

"Do you see a gravity code?"

"Gravity? Uh... Oh, good question, Kitty. That's funny... The gravity code seems to be modified too."

Eden nodded. She had found her clue. She took a deep breath, jumped onto another cube, and grabbed the edges of it, lying on her stomach. Then, she took a deep breath and pulled herself to get underneath it, only holding on to the edges. She had picked a smaller cube on purpose so that she could grab the opposite edges. Using all her strength, she kept going until she was under the cube and holding on to both sides with her arms. She then pivoted her body to lift her legs and put her feet against its surface. Now, she was literally upside-down, her feet on the bottom of the cube. She tried to take deep breaths, ignoring the blood that wanted to rush to her head. This wasn't real. Her body wasn't really upside down...

"Oh... Oh! Oh! My Kitty babe is a genius!"

She heard Loir frantically typing while singing some new stupid song.

*"Kitty-kitty pong! Kitty-kitty pong-pong! Chabada-bada,* my Kitty kit-kat girl is a genius!"

Suddenly, things changed around Eden. All of the cubes stopped moving and turned black. She felt a strange movement and suddenly, she didn't feel like she was upside down anymore. Nothing had actually moved but the space above her was now the ceiling and that feeling of being pulled down was gone. She let out a long breath of relief.

"Prepare to run, baby; your delivery man's almost there!" chuckled Loir.

Eden rolled her eyes but when a cube suddenly vanished on her left and opened a door into a new, dark corridor, she jumped in, ready. This one was even more narrow than before and Eden had to be on all fours, in the dark, to keep going.

"You couldn't have opened that bigger..." she groaned while squeezing her body through.

"Well, I don't think that even this super duper cute kitty is welcome where you're going... Oh, there comes the second fence, Kitty, get ready... Oh, my god, I'm hungry again. Do you think I can order another pizza for breakfast? Have you tried them? They are just so amazing! I just can't believe they won't put anchovies or pineapples on it! They call me crazy!"

"I hate to be the one to break it to you, but you are crazy, Loir..." grimaced Eden, still struggling in the narrow corridor, "...and do something about this space, I'm running out of air!"

"Nah, you're fine and almost at the end. Hey, can this be called a kitty hole? A kitty tube?"

"I'm going to kill you."

"Oh, I wish there was a way to take some screenshots of this, my little Kitty. You're so cute! Did you see I even put some details on your tail? It changes according to your movements and moods, just like a real cat! Oh, I'm just too talented for this world. I'm a genius."

"Loir, you actually spent time on stupid shit like that? Are you kidding me?!"

"Don't yell, it's the inner artist in me. I can do anything. Plus, I hesitated with the Valkyrie outfit too, so I also lost a lot of time on that. Oh, you would have been so cute in a nice little helmet with wings..."

Eden would have slammed her head into one of those walls if they hadn't been so close. Thankfully, she was almost there; she could literally see the end of the tunnel.

"Are you sure the next one is the last security?"

"Yep, the last border before we get to the secret land they don't want us to get in, with all their naughty-bitty secrets. I bet there will be some nasty traps there too, though... Damn, I should have added more fur."

"Loir, focus, for goodness sake..."

"I am focusing! I was torn between a marvelous lilac E39FFC or a more risky taffy pink like FA86C4."

Eden could see the colors of her cat hands shifting between several shades of pink as he was talking. She rolled her eyes and kept going, ignoring Loir, who was having fun changing her fur color. She was almost at the end of that tunnel but it was strangely quiet on the other side. Not completely quiet; more like the kind of quiet one could hear in a large open space...

She finally arrived at the end. There, the tunnel was strangely shifting from a square shape to a round one and it was going down. Eden frowned but kept going, even when she noticed that the tunnel was descending... more and more. At least it was getting larger but also more slippery. A toboggan slide...? She let herself slip and was suddenly engulfed into a spiral, following this weird tube without any idea where she was going to land. She didn't like that.

"What do you think? Too pink?"

Eden wanted to yell at him, but she arrived at her destination too fast. She landed on all fours, not elegantly at all. She grimaced and struggled to get back up. Where was she...? She had landed on some dark gray asphalt, a bit humid too. If it wasn't for the horrible furry paws at the end of her arms, she would have thought she was back in the real world.

However, it was nighttime where she was... and at a deserted location. Eden glanced over her shoulder. As she had suspected, she had come out from a toboggan slide. The previous programmer was a damned childish one. It was common for programmers to let their tastes shape their security borders or use their favorite games or movies for reference. However, the more she looked around, the less Eden felt okay about this new one... She was in what looked like a deserted amusement park. It was out in the open. There were sounds of leaves from the trees and sounds of screeching metal from nearby attractions. A flat ride was the closest one to her but she could see a rollercoaster from afar. There were probably more if she continued down the various paths ahead of her...

"I like that pink better too," chuckled Loir.

Eden rolled her eyes.

"I don't give a shit about my fur, Loir!"

"Oh, I'm not talking to you, Kitty! I'm talking to Big Kitty!"

Eden went completely red in a split second. No way. Dante was watching this...?

"Nice pink, Eden. It suits you..."

If Eden could find a small hole and hide there for the next few weeks or months, she would jump at the opportunity without any hesitation. However, right now, she was Diving into a digital world while Dante De Luca was watching her from behind a screen. Eden was as red as a tomato and completely ashamed. She felt like she was naked in the middle of a crowd or on a large movie screen for everyone to see.

Of all people, why did he have to be watching her? Why now? Had he seen her inelegantly land on all fours just a minute ago too? Eden had to take deep breaths to calm herself down. Once she got out of there, Loir was really going to—

"Easy, Kitty, your heartbeat is going cray-cray."

"Fuck you, Loir," she hissed.

"See? She can even hiss!"

"Really cute, indeed..."

Eden rolled her eyes. Dante was enjoying this way too much and he wasn't bothering to hide it. She crossed her arms, upset, and imagined that she was only showing them her back. It was probably more like Loir had some external view gravitating around her as if he was remotely controlling her character. Most of the Diving systems had been created using remnants of old role-playing games, except that now, the character was also a player, with a teammate on the other side of the screen.

"Loir, when you're done playing, would you mind telling me where the hell I'm supposed to go?"

"Mm... I don't know, Kitty. That's an interesting one... Ugh, what a lazy job. This one is definitely copied straight out of some horror game, no doubt. Oh, my Kitty, I hope it's just you in there... Maybe a couple booby traps but I think you should be fine if we don't trigger more security. I don't think you've been noticed yet, so time to explore."

Eden nodded. At least she had something that would keep her busy, rather than thinking about her shameful appearance. She looked around. Loir was right about the horror game concept; this place was definitely creepy. It was night time and there was no light except from the moon. She walked in a bit farther. The paths confirmed her idea that this was some sort of amusement park. There were a lot of rides she had never seen before which she made sure to stay away from. They were definitely the kind that a good programmer could have placed a trap or two on...

"What is she looking for?" suddenly asked Dante's voice.

"Anything," answered Loir. "There are usually some sorts of clues about how to get through. Because it is too complicated for programmers of the Core to do a complete check of anyone who comes in, they create these kinds of funny little levels that all visitors of the server have to go through. If you are supposed to be there, you know exactly what to do. If you're not supposed to, like our Kitty Cat Eden, you have to find out how authorized visitors get in and do it too, and before it kicks you out..."

"How do they know whether she's supposed to be there or not?"

"Well, the Core is a bit vicious. Best case scenario, there is some sort of time countdown and once it's up, she gets kicked out. However, if the Core is in a nasty mood, then it may try to keep our Kitty Eden and play with her..."

The latter was the worst scenario. Eden had almost been caught by the Core more than once, and she had no intention to risk it again. There were too many stories of Dive Hackers who had gone absolutely insane because of the mental torture the Core had inflicted on them. Many were trapped in their worst fears that played on a loop, while others had to experience a completely different life, inside the Core, unaware that they were actually unconscious and in a deep coma somewhere in the real world. As she wasn't sure what her fears or phobias could be, Eden feared the latter most. Either way, she just didn't want to risk her mental health. She had to be quick and efficient.

She followed the paths inside the park, quickly realizing there wasn't a living soul anywhere. They hadn't tried to mimic animals or even other park visitors. There wasn't even a bird. This only made the world much creepier than it already was.

Eden walked silently thanks to her cat paws, careful to not make any noise. There was the wind, slithering through the tree branches and its leaves, leaving some howling whispers behind her. She knew this level was made to scare people away; hence, she wasn't surprised to hear many of the rides making some rattling and creaking sounds. The one thing that worried her the most was the darkness. She felt like there were things lurking in the shadows. Eden glanced over her shoulder many times as she progressed through. Like the second room, she thought maybe this one could change at any moment as well, and she wanted to be prepared.

"That's a really interesting one," whispered Loir. "The code seems to be evolving according to Eden's stats..."

"What does that mean?"

"Uh... Kitty, could you act more scared?"

"More scared?" frowned Eden, approaching one of the rides. "Why?"

"Because you're not scared enough and I think this level isn't going to like that..."

Eden sighed and decided to ignore him. There probably wasn't going to be a change from her acting scared or not. If the System was trying to scare her out of there, they were probably going to make it worse until she seemed panicked enough, but she wasn't at that stage yet. She still had a portion of the park to explore. The System could try to scare her more until she was done, but she didn't like playing along.

"Do you see anything worth checking on the rides?"

"Let me check... No... Uh... Do you see anything when you get close, my Kitty? This seems a bit too easy-peasy to me, it might need a trigger or something..."

A trigger? Eden wasn't sure what he was hoping for, but she could always try since she hadn't seen anything else. These types of worlds often reacted to particular actions, like pushing a button or her accessing some code she could give to Loir. Maybe the visitors were supposed to stand at one particular spot or get on one of the rides. However, unlike a simple visit to this place, actually getting on something that could have its own separate code and be triggered, like one of the rides, could mean there is a trap behind it...

Like one would expect to see in some abandoned theme parks, Eden had noticed some graffiti on the rides. It could be there for no particular reason, but it could also have been there as a clue... or an access point. Eden tried to look closer, but as she had just noticed, not all the rides were accessible while staying on the path. There was a lot of vegetation around, as if the park had been built in some national park but she didn't feel safe going off the path. Those kinds of levels were usually made to be relatively safe. They didn't want to attack people who were regular citizens or guests coming in, hence it was quite literally safe to play by the rules. Eden wasn't sure what would happen if she decided to go against what would have been considered as reckless behavior by the System... like going off the stone path.

"Oh, found it!"

"Loir?" whispered Eden.

"Sorry, I was checking to find where the programmer had taken his inspiration... and see if I can get some clue for our Kitty Cat! Well, I got good news and bad news!"

"I'm listening," she sighed.

"The good news is, you're in Atlantic Island Park, a charming abandoned theme park fictionally located in Maine, on the East Coast."

"Fictionally?" repeated Eden, frowning.

"Yup. That place is completely fake, invented. It's from a series of video games from the twenty-first century... Damn, I love those geniuses from the previous century. I have to say, the programmer worked nicely on the decor, though, we got better quality. The bad news is, our fellow programmer friend also made sure to insert some new rides for fun..."

177

"To confuse intruders," sighed Eden.

Although Loir was talented, anyone could have probably found where this level had been copied from. The genius of the programmers was usually more on how they hid secrets inside these worlds...

"Rule number one, Kitty, stay away from the boogeyman."

"Okay..."

Eden hadn't seen a soul since she had come in here, let alone a boogeyman. It felt like this place had absolutely no one inside it and she didn't like that at all.

"So, what's my best shot?"

"We should probably stick to the real rides from the original game. The others are probably traps. The closest to you is... the House of Horrors."

"Nice..."

Of course, it had to be a creepy one with a name like that. Eden kept walking, following Loir's instructions, as he now had a detailed map of the game. As she had suspected, the rides off the path were all the fake ones, probably traps. Eden didn't have to take one step off the path to get to the House of Horrors. However, the closer she got, the more she could feel that something was observing her. She had previously blamed it on her own reflexes because there were so many blind spots, but now she really felt like she was being followed.

She didn't say it out loud, but she resolutely kept walking. She would glance over her shoulder from time to time unsure, but then the sounds she had mistaken for steps would disappear.

"Oh crap... Is that...?" she heard Loir mumble.

"What's that thing?" asked Dante.

"A cleaner," immediately whined Loir. "It's an added program that cleans the System. If something is there that is not supposed to be, the cleaner takes care of it. Eden, keep going girl and do not look back!"

Eden nodded and kept walking, as if she was a hundred percent sure where she was going.

"Can't you do something?"

"Nope, no, no... Those things are trained to recognize human behavior. If Eden looks scared or hesitates, it will attack... Oh, it's too scary, I can't watch!"

Eden grimaced. How was she supposed to know what to do if Loir wasn't guiding her! Trying to ignore that fact, she kept walking until she finally got to the entrance of the... house. It didn't deserve the name of a house, it was just a giant open mouth of a scary figure.

"...Loir?" she whispered, unsure.

"Sorry, Kitty, I can't look, that thing is too scary for me!"

Eden rolled her eyes. Did he really have to play the chicken now? Moreover, the steps behind her were getting closer and louder. From the rhythm, she could tell it wasn't human. She had no idea what the cleaner looked like, maybe the boogeyman, but she was set on not looking and not showing any fear either.

This was part of her experience and training from years and years of Diving into the Core's System illegally. However, as she was almost at the... mouth, Eden hesitated. Was it really fine to go in there? It was pitch black, and she couldn't see what was behind...

"Walk inside," suddenly said a much calmer, deeper voice.

Eden blushed a little but nodded and entered. Everything was completely dark. However, to her surprise, Dante's voice kept guiding her without an ounce of hesitation.

"On your left, a bit... Walk about a dozen steps, then take a right. There... Stop. You'll feel steps. Try going down slowly."

Eden nodded.

The room was completely dark and she could no longer hear the boogeyman behind her. Only Dante's voice cut through, guiding her very precisely. Eden didn't even have to think, she just took step after step, focusing only on his voice, her confidence in him unwavering.

"Now, stop there. Turn to your right and you should be able to take five steps... Alright. You're doing great. Now, there are steps right in front of you, very narrow, and they're going up. No, no ramp, so go very slowly."

Eden could almost feel the emptiness next to her but she simply listened to his voice and climbed those stairs slowly. She was glad the room was dark, because once again, she found herself blushing uncontrollably. She could control her fear but why was there no switch for the emotions Dante gave her...?

"Alright, two more and stop. Now, if you extend your arm, you've got a door right in front of you."

Eden nodded and with her hands, quickly found said door and its handle. She tried to open it, but it wouldn't budge.

"It's not opening! Is there a key I missed or something? Loir!"

"Oh, you know I'm still here? Sorry, I didn't want to interrupt the naughty whispery moment between you two..."

"Loir!" she roared, annoyed.

"You two Kitties are just so cute together!"

"Loir!"

"There's a switch, by the way, for the lights."

Eden opened her mouth and just then, the lights went on, letting her see where she was. She closed her eyes, annoyed. She should have known there was no way all the allowed visitors had to do that much walking in the dark... Loir probably had the switch on his side of the code all along, and he had just...

She crossed her arms.

"Loir, open the fucking door. Now."

"Coming right up, my purriest Kitty!"

Indeed, she heard several clicks behind the door, and it finally opened.

The change in lighting blinded Eden for a second. She squinted her eyes

179

and stepped in. This looked like the inside of a very, very big building. A square one but with a hole in its center. Eden approached that hole in the middle, the balcony letting her see all the way down to the lower floors. She looked up and in the same way, there were dozens of floors above with all the same mapping.

"Congratulations, Kitty, we made it! Damn, that was easier than I thought. Oh well, not going to complain. Plus, we're not done yet."

"What now?" asked Dante.

"Now, our favorite Kitty has to find the tasty information... Wait, what are we looking for again?"

"Anything the Core wants to hide from us," retorted Eden, beginning to walk.

"Damn, I should have ordered popcorn... or another pizza," sighed Loir. "Anyway, you can get upstairs, Kitty."

"Isn't she going to stand out?"

Indeed, the people Eden crossed paths with were all clones: white men with glasses in striped suits and colored neckties, walking with the same mannerisms. Eden was careful to step out of their paths.

"Those? Nah, they are not real people, merely automated little minions. The character design shows terrible taste, by the way. It has depressed corporate rat written all over it. Bruh."

Eden kept walking, unsure where to look. There were no real walls and aside from the balcony rail to her left, everything on her right was merely large glass walls, with a door from time to time. From experience, she knew those doors were probably controlled too so she couldn't get in like that. She ought to find an open one...

# CHAPTER THIRTEEN

She had to check two floors before she spotted one. Eden squeezed herself inside. It was an office, just an ordinary office with nothing that could have made anyone think a human with actual emotions lived in it. There were black boxes everywhere, with a code on each one and a unique desk with a white computer on it. Nothing else. No pen, no sticky notes; not an ounce of warmth could be felt in the room. Eden walked inside, glancing at the boxes on the shelves.

"Loir, where do I start?"

"Tell me the codes you see."

Eden began spelling them out as fast as she could read them. Most were names without much meaning to her or a series of numbers. On one, though, she stopped.

"...Kitty?"

Eden ignored him and walked up to the box, tilting her head. It was a box that looked somewhat older than the others. Instead of being a simple black box, it was an old cardboard one, and it looked strangely full. Eden raised her hand and without thinking, slid her fingers over the three letters.

"Crazy one to Kitty, do you copy?"

"Loir, there's... a box with the code PAN on it."

"PAN? Like a frying pan?"

"What about it?" asked Dante.

Eden hesitated, then grabbed the box and took it out of its spot. Her heartbeat increased again on the monitor. She breathed louder and, with shaky hands, placed the box on the desk.

"Eden, what is it?"

"Pan was... one of my master's code names. ...Whenever we were in the Core, he called himself Pan..."

"Pan, like the Greek God?"

Eden chuckled nervously.

"No... Pan, like Peter Pan."

In the real world, Loir and Dante exchanged a glance. The crazy hacker looked rather serious for once, and he adjusted the mic on his helmet.

"You never mentioned this, Kitty. Your mentor was... Peter Pan?"

"Yes..."

On the screen, Eden looked like she could barely hear him. She was obviously fascinated by the box, her purple, cat-like fingers gliding over it, probably dying to open that thing. Loir sighed, scratching his bald head.

"Well that's... intriguing."

"Eden mentioned she's looking for her former mentor," said Dante, turning back to Loir.

"Well, Kitty isn't the only one!" scoffed Loir. "Peter Pan is among the pantheon of hacking legends. He was there even before we were born, and he holds the record of oldest hacker known to still be working against the Core... It's been a while since he's been spotted though. Now he's getting closer to being something of an urban legend."

"Is he in hiding?"

"Yes, probably from the whole world too! He is the only known hacker who actually managed to hack the entire Chicago Core. Not just Dive inside, but to actually shake the system so much that it had to restart."

"I... I have never heard of him," said Dante, frowning and now genuinely interested.

Loir sighed.

"Well, some of the greatest heroes are anonymous. The hack actually lasted some mere five to six seconds too, so it probably never made it into the records... or they didn't want it to be known that something had happened. But in our world, Peter Pan is a legend!"

"So you've... never met him?"

Loir looked at Dante as if he was crazy.

"Of course not! Do you know how shocked I was when Kitty showed up at my door? I hadn't seen a living human being in years! That pretty Kitty found me and showed up just like that, it was such a scary experience! I soiled my diaper, mind you! And guess who sent her to me? None other than the legendary Pan! I mean, this guy is a living god! Damn, I would share my cheese with him without thinking."

Dante turned back to the screen. Eden was still staring at the box, completely lost in her thoughts. Now he was curious about that master of hers... Was she missing him? Was he working against their interests? More importantly, what file did the Core have on that strange Pan character, and was it a possible threat?

"Kitty, I wouldn't open that thing if I were you."

Eden suddenly raised her eyes from the box, as if Loir's voice had woken her up. She sighed, but her hands were still on the cardboard box. She just couldn't let it go. It was her master's name, right there, on a different box, older than the others. Why was this even here? Eden tried to slow her breathing, and the strange adrenaline rush in her veins, but she just had the hardest time trying to calm down. This was her first clue in... almost forever.

"Loir, it might be my only clue to Master."

"Yes, Kitty, but it might also be a mean trick-or-treat box with a huge tricky mean bug inside. I want to find that old schmuck as much as you do, but this sounds fishy. Like fishier than the fisherman's shop next to the old sewers."

Eden rolled her eyes.

"You've never been out to actually smell that. Also, my master isn't old."

"He's been in the system since before even I ever touched a keyboard, Kitty. That's very, very old."

Still, Eden didn't want to let go of that box. Of course, she wasn't so foolish as to completely ignore that this might indeed be a trap; yet, she just couldn't abandon her first potential clue like that. She glanced behind the glass walls. Aside from those automated men in suits, it looked like she was pretty much alone, and nothing had been triggered yet. Eden took a deep breath.

"...Alright. I'll check the computer; meanwhile, can you try and see that box from... the outside?"

"Kitty, I don't have my full safety-check kit on me. I know I'm a genius, but that's—"

"Loir, I'm not going to leave without having opened that box. So either you check what you can now or we're all in for a surprise in a few minutes when I open it."

She heard him groan.

"Oh good Lord, this is why they say curiosity kills... Alright, fine, I'll try to work my magic somehow. Check the other boxes in the room, though, you never know. There might be one with Candyman written on it..."

"...Who is Candyman?" asked Dante.

Eden chuckled, shaking her head while going to inspect the other boxes.

"My other favorite sugar daddy," chuckled Loir.

He was obviously making fun of the Italian which, in Eden's opinion, was a nice change. She went to the other boxes. There were other names, but nothing she nor Loir took any interest in. It was all about that PAN box... Eden couldn't believe it was so full either. What did the Core possibly have on her master for them to have such a large box about him? She knew there was also a possibility for it to be on a different person, or just a codename used for something else, but somehow, she doubted that. Pan was a rather specific three-letter name...

"That's it," she said after reading the last box.

She turned around, making sure she hadn't missed one, but all the boxes were lined up in such a symmetrical and precise order that she couldn't have possibly overlooked any. She heard Loir still busy typing, so she walked back to the desk. The only things left on the table were the PAN box and the computer. Unlike those boxes, it was probably going to be much more difficult to get into the computer. They were usually used as an internal form of protection for the most sensitive data. Eden could get through most programmers' levels just fine, but those were another thing. This time around, Loir was going to have to do his share, the bigger of the two.

Hence, she couldn't act without his go-ahead. Eden simply decided to sit down behind the desk, staring at the box as if some clue would suddenly come out of it. It was torture to have to watch that stupid box when she was just so close to opening it...

"Loir," she called again after a while, tired of waiting.

"Yes, yes... I mean, I haven't found anything... The code looks old, actually, just... very basic. I don't want to say it, but this just doesn't look like something the Core would create."

"What does that mean?"

"That means whoever put that box in there, Kitty, they were not playing on the Core's team. This is... artisanal work. Beautiful work, if I may say so myself. It looks like whoever did this knew... their thing."

Eden's breathing got a bit tenser, and she stood back up again, her fingers shaking, grabbing the top of the box.

"Loir, it's him, isn't it? It's my master's work?"

"Easy, Kitty. It does look like it, but we're very deep in the Core's system. You think Pan would walk around and just leave bombs like that? ...Wait, what if that's an actual bomb?"

"With his name on it?" Eden sighed, rolling her eyes.

"Hm... Alright, you got a fair point."

"Loir, please tell me I can open it."

"Oh boy, looks like Kitty wants to open her Christmas present. Fine, open it. If you blow up, I'll just hold a pity party..."

Eden chuckled, but now that she could, she was oddly a bit reluctant to actually open the box. What if there was no clue inside, just some random information that didn't involve her master or some stupid trap? Well, it was high time she found out anyway. After another deep breath, Eden lifted it.

Just as she had suspected, the box was full. There were some documents inside, and she grabbed them, quickly scanning what she saw with her eyes.

"Loir, what does that look like to you?" she asked with a frown.

"Oh... nice bedtime reading. Those are documents about the Core's System... I mean, the origins of it. The Core was one of the first successful attempts at creating Artificial Intelligence, and that looks a lot like some of the papers that the Architect had presented..."

"Right? But I've never seen those."

"Eden, Kitty, I think you're looking at all of his research that was supposedly lost... Why in the world is that here... It's like finding some very fine cheese on a microwave pizza!"

Eden rolled her eyes. How did he still have enough time to blurt out some of his stupid jokes to the Italian? Ignoring him, she kept reading all those documents.

"Can you copy these?"

"Baby, as long as you see it, I can even make a billboard poster with that and save it to three different chests. Just check them all quickly, Kitty. You've been in there for a while now and soon they are going to smell the Kitty inside the sushi shop."

"...Is it really dangerous if she stays in there too long?" asked Dante.

"...You really don't know much about hacking, do you?"

"I'm a better shooter in real life."

"Ah... Well, she probably isn't at much risk unless I decide to play a game of beer pong. Still, Kitty, let's not stay there too long."

"Wait, there are more."

Eden kept looking through the documents, but the more she looked, the less she actually understood what some of them were about.

"Loir, there are some in... Is that Russian?"

"Oh, yeah... *Интересно.*"

"Okay, I guess you can look at these later..."

Just as she thought she had reached the bottom of the pile, Eden's eyes fell on an object that had been pushed to the corner. She frowned and grabbed it.

"Kitty, I already told you not to take the toys Mommy doesn't want to pay for..."

"What is this?" she asked, ignoring his antics once again.

She could sense from his tone of voice that Loir was intrigued too. From behind his desk, Loir was squinting at the screen, visibly confused as well. Eden turned the object several times in her hands, checking it from all angles.

It was big enough to fit in her two hands and had a strange star-shaped form. It reminded her of one of those wood puzzles she had seen at a craftsman's shop before. However, it wasn't made of wood, but of several metals: gold, silver, and multiple copper-colored ones. The metals were spread into various shapes and sizes that constituted that strange contraption. Eden could see dozens of little gears and mechanisms, some she could probably spin or move...

"I have no idea," said Loir, as intrigued as she was. "That one didn't come out of the toy factory... Don't start playing around with it just yet, Kitty. Let's finish our business here first."

"Right."

Quickly, Eden put all the documents back in the box, only keeping the strange star with her. She wasn't sure if she should put that box back or destroy it, though. It would be like putting a file back where it was after she had made a copy... Maybe it would be better to just destroy it. For now, she left it on the desk and turned to the computer. It wasn't like real-life computers. It had a square screen, and instead of a keyboard, there was just one large mat.

"Ready, Loir?"

"Let's play, Kitty."

Eden nodded and pushed the single button below the screen. The computer lit up instantly and lines of codes began appearing. This part was completely Loir's domain of expertise. Despite her own knowledge, Eden could only understand half of what she could read, and most of it was way too fast for her to grab anything. She only noticed that the code defiling was some sort of loop, with only a few lines changing each time.

"Oh, nice, nice, typical Core style this time... Oh, I like a little fun. They've done twenty-three upgrades since our last visit? Really? Damn, their builders have been busy..."

"Builders?" repeated Dante.

"The ones who keep building the Core," explained Eden, letting Loir focus on his part. "Although the AI should be able to develop by itself and adapt, it often needs some human help to check on some breaches in the code, help put in new defenses, or simply do routine maintenance. They are like the human part of the Core, even if it could function without."

"They are no better than bees working for the Queen," sighed Loir. "A builder is like a hacker who never grew out of the sandbox... Poor little ones, so young and already being chewed up..."

Eden could witness it too. She smiled when a black-and-white Pac-Man character suddenly appeared among the lines of the code and began eating it. Loir just couldn't help himself... She waited for a while as he dug through the code, breaching the security more and more. Eden was ready to go, though. This was the most complex and risky part of their little excursion, and where she was the most at risk of being found out. While Loir could never have gotten inside this deep if it wasn't for his Dive partner, Eden was the one that was most vulnerable.

She kept glancing around to check if anything unusual moved. Her eyes were frequently going to the star too. She wanted to try it out. Just like those documents they had found, this was so typical of her master's work...

"Kitty, get ready!"

Eden refocused on the screen, putting her fingers on the flat mat. She quickly found Pac-Man, who had changed appearance, still fighting against the Core's code.

"Is that a... white orangutan?"

"It's a yeti!" protested Loir. "I actually spent time on that, Kitty, I'm really offended now."

Eden rolled her eyes. He really had too much free time on his hands... Still,

186

she didn't have time to scold him. Soon, the lines of codes began disappearing, and the normal access appeared. It was like looking at a different folder with black boxes and dozens of files with name codes. Eden used the mat like a keyboard, hacking her way inside each file. She only had to open them, glance at the document, and close it. Loir could access and view it again from her SIN... as long as she came out. It was like a direct transfer from that computer to her brain, her eyes going in all directions on the screen like a scanning machine. If she couldn't open a file and didn't manage to hack it, Eden left it aside for Loir to try his luck with it. The yeti was still jumping from one file to another, working his way through those that had refused to open for her.

"How much?"

"We're about 30% through."

She kept opening and closing them fast. She had to make sure not to leave any open for too long or it could trigger some sort of security breach. However, the number of files Loir had forced to open was growing, and this would definitely grab some unwanted attention sooner or later...

Suddenly, an alarm rang above her head.

"Oops, time to run, Kitty!"

Eden nodded, but she was already typing fast to finish closing everything. She knew that from then on, she didn't have a single second to lose. The yeti disappeared, and she turned the computer off quickly, getting up. She grabbed the star but was hesitant about the Pan box.

"Loir, destroy it," she finally declared.

"Are you sure? I don't mind but it's going to have your location light up like a Christmas tree on their radars, Kitty!"

"Just do it!"

She ran out of the room, holding her star and letting Loir destroy the box she had left behind. Now that she was back on the square balcony, she could see all the bots in suits from earlier had suddenly changed their directions, heading toward her. They weren't walking anymore, and the closest one was barely two rooms away.

Eden glanced around, but there was another one coming behind her, and she knew trying her luck with any one of the rooms would be pointless.

"Lower floor?"

"Second one," said Loir in a breath, his typing furiously buzzing in Eden's ears.

She nodded and ran to the end of the balcony. Eden quickly pushed the star into her sports bra, the only available pocket she had, and grabbed the rail of the balcony, jumping over with perfect form. Her body did a 270-degrees flip into the air, and she used the strength of her spin to launch herself onto the balcony right under that one. As Loir had said, this floor also had bots waiting for her. Instead of climbing up, Eden let go of the guardrail for a second, and let herself fall so she could catch the one on the floor below that. This time, she used the strength in her arms to pull herself over and back onto a solid floor.

"On your left. Emergency exit."

Eden ran, following Loir's instructions. Although this wasn't a real building, the system always had an emergency exit, in case any actual human employees had an issue that prevented them from leaving. The Core would never let one of its working citizens be trapped inside the system. Luckily for Eden, that emergency exit was made to let all humans through, regardless of their right to be there or not.

"Now?" asked Dante.

"Now, Kitty had better run, really, really fast back home, or we lose both her and the information she got... Run, Kitty, run, run!"

Just as he had said that, Loir played some techno music that matched her heartbeat. Eden rolled her eyes. He really could have fun anytime, anywhere... Although, that musical beat was actually somewhat welcoming. It gave Eden an extra adrenaline rush, while not letting herself panic over the fact that about two or three dozen Core bots were on her tail. She ran toward the emergency door, and just as she put her hand on the handle, a huge explosion happened behind her.

Eden closed her eyes and was thrown against the door by the blast. She grimaced, feeling her shoulder hit it, as more emergency alarms resonated within the building.

"Loir?" she asked, coughing from the smoke that was coming from upstairs.

"That was your master's file going up in an incredible firework explosion. Ha, I'm really too talented for this... Don't miss your stop, Kitty!"

Eden nodded and got back up, barely glancing at all the unconscious bots that were close to her. Like puppets, many had been thrown across the place by the blast and were now lying in unnatural positions. One even had a leg hanging off the balcony rail, while the rest of its body was a few steps away, and not a drop of blood in sight. They were like figures made of silicone, or toys. More importantly, they were already twisting their bodies back into their original shapes and trying to get back up to chase after her again.

Eden glared at them and pushed against the emergency exit door. She fell onto a set of stairs as she had pushed too hard. Ignoring the pain, Eden got back up and ran down the stairs. She was going extremely fast, almost flying down them. She had to. She could hear them coming from upstairs, their steps resonating with a scarily synchronic rhythm. Eden was almost glad for the techno music Loir was playing; it made the situation a bit less stressful and a bit more game-like. She kept running as fast as she could, but they were fast too. The stairs even began trembling from so many bots stepping on them. Eden was getting out of breath; she began jumping down over the rails whenever she could to get to the next row of stairs faster.

"You're almost there, Kitty," said Loir.

"Are they close?" she asked, out of breath.

"You don't want to know!"

188

She frowned but didn't ask again. That kind of response was more than she needed to know already... Eden kept going, but she was starting to get out of breath. She hoped her real body could endure the mental stress...

Still, she was incredibly fast, and soon enough, she saw the stairs turn into a tunnel instead.

"The toboggan slide?"

"Get ready for a new ride, Kitty!"

Eden nodded and jumped in feet first. More often than not, she had to exit through the same place she had entered from. Sometimes, Loir would find another back door for her if something happened to the first point of entry, but it was still simpler to sneak out using the same door she had already used previously.

"Can't she just unlock it?" asked Dante.

"This isn't a shopping mall, darling," sighed Loir. "If they make it hard to get in, it ought to be hard to get out... especially for sneaky little intruders like us. They are too attracted to the possibility of trapping us to not leave a few traps here and there... and no highway out."

Eden was still amazed that Loir could talk to one of the Zodiacs like that, but she certainly didn't have time to discuss it. She was sliding down the tube, keeping her arms crossed in front of her chest, and trying hard to ignore the sounds she heard from above. Instead, she was focusing on the music and trying to take deep breaths to keep herself calm. She knew her condition during a Dive was directly linked to her body's condition in real life. It wasn't by accident that two hackers out of three died of a heart attack during a Dive; although her body was perfectly fine, just like her mind, it was entirely focused on this Dive. Anything Eden experienced, the SIN transmitted to her brain, and thus her whole body took this as reality, even though she knew it wasn't. If anything happened, she'd feel it. She felt pain because the SIN transmits the shock to her brain, which triggers all of her pain receptors. There would be no blood or bruises, but if her brain believed she was dying, she would. There wasn't anything complicated about it.

"Loir, play my music."

"So selfish..." he chuckled.

Still, he obeyed. A powerful piece of rock music resonated in her head and Eden focused on that as if she had headphones on. It was easier for her. She could focus on each instrument, each sentence of the lyrics, and refocus for a few seconds. The slide was still going down and she leaned back to accelerate.

"Prepare for delivery of the package..." said Loir.

Eden lifted her knees and prepared herself for the landing. She knew the speed at which she was going down was dangerous, but she shouldn't slow down from what she could hear farther up in the tube.

As expected, after a few more seconds, light started to appear, and right after that, the end of the tunnel. Eden braced herself and rolled outside on the ground. Her feet hit the ground hard, but she was already trying to stand before she had even finished falling through the tube. Pushing her paws against the ground, Eden began running.

"Where to now?!" she yelled.

She was back inside the abandoned park, except this time, the park was open. The rides were running, the twinkling lights were up, and she could hear movement in all directions. There was some creepy music too, but she was more focused on hers. When she glanced over her shoulder, she saw more silhouettes coming out of the tunnel in such large amounts that they were falling on top of each other, their bodies piling up. The bots weren't pretending to look human anymore. Their body parts had begun to grow out of proportion and weren't as defined either. The jelly-like humanoid characters were chasing after her. They didn't even have faces anymore. She could only see their black suits and all their ties that had turned red.

"Loir!"

"Try the one on your left."

Eden followed his instructions, although she wasn't pleased that Loir really didn't sound sure at all. She was heading toward some sort of carousel. Like all the others, the attraction was playing and spinning at a normal pace. However, Eden had another issue as she approached.

There were barriers in front of the ride, and in front of those barriers were large silhouettes.

"Oh, crap..."

"What's that?" whined Loir. "...A boogeyman and his twin?"

Eden turned her feet in the other direction, immediately running away.

"Clowns!" she yelled.

She could tell from the red noses, white faces with big, creepy smiles, strange outfits, and orange hair. But those weren't funny clowns; they were the type that belonged in a horror film. Eden just knew she had to get out of there, as they were probably on the bots' team.

"Loir, I really need an exit now!" Eden shouted again, as she spotted more enemies coming from the direction she had taken.

She was now running erratically through the park, unable to pick a destination, yet she couldn't stop. This space was extremely large, but Eden could feel her enemies getting back on their feet to chase after her, and their steps gaining more and more on her tail. She accelerated again, trying to control her breathing.

"Her speed..."

"Yeah, she's the fastest Dive Hacker I've ever seen. ...Eden, next one on your right, Kitty. Jump over the fence."

Eden nodded, but she had no breath to spare on actual words. The fence Loir had mentioned was about two meters tall, standing between her and a roller coaster... Would she be fine once she got past that thing? As she got closer, Eden accelerated, focusing on the obstacle she had to jump over. It was tall, but she could do it...

"Now!"

She bent her knees, and built up as much strength as she could before jumping. Defying the physical laws of gravity, Eden jumped over that fence, but landed brutally on the other side.

She felt the shock throughout her entire body and winced.

"...You okay, Kitty?"

"Yeah..." she groaned, holding her arm.

"Good job. I'd say you bought yourself three... or two minutes' break."

"Awesome," Eden grimaced.

Once again, she had to ignore the pain and pick herself back up. On all fours, she glanced to the side. As expected, her pursuers were already running toward the fence, but those automated bots didn't have any superhuman abilities. They were resistant, but as dumb as nails. They literally had no brains to think with, so to speak, and couldn't begin to process the most simple obstacles. Once the first one reached the fence, it just ran into it and bounced back, falling on its rear. Eden watched the bot get back up again and run into the fence just to fall back down again. She let out a long sigh. It would indeed take a minute or two for them to process the issue, send the information to whichever master system they belonged to, and get a solution...

Eden got back up and looked around, holding her injured arm. Although the roller coaster was actually running, the fence around it was completely closed for some reason.

"What is this?" Eden asked, watching the ride go.

"...Hm, looks like an abandoned project. One of their programmers probably left it to trick the intruders... I see remnants of a code, poorly done, but doesn't have a 'Don't jump over the fence' sign, so I guess we're good. They didn't think a jumpy kitty cat could just get inside, so there's literally no security."

"Can you do something with it?" asked Eden.

She walked up to the little cabin, probably where all those buttons and switches were to control the ride... None seemed to actually work, though. There were no lights on, and a thin layer of dust covered it for the effect. She heard Loir sigh.

"You have a genius by your side and you want me to play with toys for three-year-old hackers?"

"I need time," groaned Eden.

Through the cabin's little rear window, she could see more and more bots gathering against the fence. They were still bouncing stupidly against it, but the number of them was still worrying. By now, she could count about three dozen at least, plus one of the clowns... Eden walked over to close the door of the cabin.

"Hm... That code is full of errors, there are more holes than on my piece of Gruyère..."

"Should be a piece of cake for you to grab, no?"

191

She could already hear Loir furiously typing on his keyboard.

"Yes, yes... What do you want? I can't just build a back door, Kitty."

"Did you actually find the door I came through? I guess it wasn't the toboggan slide..."

"Still looking, but you may have closed it without knowing. I think the Core's builders may have come up with one-way entries and different exits now. Do you think they get offended when we get in and out so quickly?"

"Probably. Still, it doesn't change the problem. You're going to have to find me an exit... but I need you to win me time first. I need a break."

"Kitty's tired, Kitty needs a nap... Kitty's going to purr when she gets back on your lap..."

"Loir, shut up."

Eden sighed and let herself slide down against the wall of the cabin to take a break.

"...Are you alright?"

Dante's voice took her by surprise. Eden hesitated, but she slowly nodded, a dash of pink covering her cheeks and ears again. At least, she hoped the darkness of the cabin hid her enough...

"Y-yeah," she mumbled.

"Kitty's the best Dive Hacker around," chuckled Loir. "I mean... aside from Ghost."

"...Really?"

From the tone of his voice, Eden could tell Dante definitely didn't buy that. Loir was just having too much fun...

"...Is it because of her legs?"

"Ooooh, you're smarter than you look, Sugar Daddy! I mean, smart is the new sexy, but you look too sexy to... Oh, well, you got me."

"Thanks."

Eden couldn't help but roll her eyes. She was trapped in a cabin during a Dive, with fifty or so bots waiting outside the fence to kill her, and they were just... flirting? She added that to the things she'd have to kick Loir for, along with the pink cat attire and his not-so-subtle remarks about Ghost.

"Technically, Kitty's SIN sends information about her legs to the brain, but since the brain has no legs to transmit the info to, no problem! Isn't it great? No legs, no pain. Our Kitty has god-like legs... or cute, pink, furry paws. No pain, no fatigue, not even the smallest ankle twist! Oh, I should make you a centaur next time–a unicorn! Damn, I should have been a character designer. I bet I would have become a billionaire..."

"Loir..." grimaced Eden, tired already.

"Yeah, yeah... Oh, look! There we go."

Eden frowned and got back up to look out the window. Loir was indeed working to win her some time. Now, the fence was electrified. Each time one of those stupid bots bounced off it, they were fried a bit, and some were actually too burnt to get back up... They were literally melting on the ground.

"Gross," she said.

"A 'thanks' would have been nice," retorted Loir. "Now, now, about our next issue... Do you have a favorite car?"

Eden rolled her eyes, and instead of answering, grabbed the chair to slam it violently against the ride's panel. The machine made a horrible sound, as smoke started coming out of it.

"Oh, thanks, Kitty. That makes it a lot easier..."

Eden finished destroying the control console and left the cabin. Now that Loir was efficiently keeping her pursuers out, the only issue was that Eden was trapped inside. She looked around.

"Where's that car, Loir?"

"Coming, coming! You know I like to make precise work out of it..."

Eden sighed and put her hands on her hips, getting ready to see a car appear at any moment.

However, what appeared wasn't quite what she had prepared herself for. Instead of an actual car, a buggy appeared on the rails of the ride. Eden blinked several times, but the lights of the buggy car suddenly lit up, and its engine made a sound like the roar of a tiger, matching the cringey pink and black stripes of its paint.

"...You've got to be kidding me."

"Introducing, for your kitties and gentlemen, the Kitty O' Ride! A unique piece created by the best designer hacker in the world, subbed me!"

Eden rolled her eyes, but she didn't have much of a choice... She ran to get inside the strange vehicle. This looked like a mix between a kart and a bumper car, with only one seat, one wheel, and two pedals. As soon as Eden sat down, the car roared again and a belt appeared around her waist.

"What now?"

"Get ready for the riiiiiide!"

The creepy laugh that Loir made after that had Eden wondering if he had finally lost it. The car began moving, and followed the ride's rails, slightly increasing in speed. It was following the track lines, and Eden realized the original train she had seen was gone, probably deleted by Loir. Meanwhile, hers quickly reached the higher parts of the roller coaster, giving her a view of her surroundings. Since she was safe inside anyway, the car didn't need to go fast, so Eden could look all around, trying to see her way out.

"There! Loir!"

There was a giant head, like the one she had walked inside on her way in. This was a different one, though. Chances were high that one was the new exit.

"I see it, Kitty. Prepare for the ride!"

"What?"

Eden had just enough time to grab the wheel before the car suddenly accelerated violently on the ride. With a furious roar, the car took the next loop at full speed, making Eden close her eyes, then it did a U-turn, another spin, and suddenly, she felt like the car had gone... off-rail.

"Because tigers can fly!" suddenly yelled Loir.

"Tigers can't fly!" Eden shouted back.

It was a bit too late, though. The car was already off the rails and diving fast toward the ground below.

# CHAPTER FOURTEEN

She wasn't one to be easily scared, but inside a pink tiger-themed buggy car made in just a few minutes by a crazy hacker, she couldn't help but close her eyes and scowl. Her vehicle had left the rail in one sudden movement, making her stomach somersault. She seriously hoped her body wasn't throwing up or something in the real world...

It stayed suspended mid-air, and for a few seconds, Eden was sure it was going to be sent to crash itself into the ground or something. The speed, the height, every ingredient was there for a violent crash...

"Kitties and gentlemen, as we start our descent, please make sure your seat is back in its full upright position. Make sure your seat belt is securely fastened, and your tail and paws are inside the vehicle. We are happy to have you in the Kitty O'Ride today. The local time is probably something like very late and a creepy hour in the night, and the temperature is something around twenty or so. For your safety and comfort, please remain seated with your seat belt fastened until your favorite hacker advises you to jump out of the vehicle."

Eden let out a long sigh and opened her eyes. Her crazy buggy seemed now to be quietly floating in the air, and upon closer inspection, she found out why: two little wings had appeared on the sides and a parachute above her head, with another cringey cat face on it; it even included ears...

After the fight just before, it was a very strange change of pace to simply glide in the air while it took her to her destination: the giant face she had spotted from the rollercoaster ride. At least, she hoped it was the place she was supposed to go. Underneath her, most of the bots had noticed her leaving the area of the abandoned ride and they had begun trying to follow the flying buggy. Thankfully, Eden still had a little bit of time. That crazy launch off the roller coaster had sent the buggy high in the air and she was still high enough that she didn't have to worry about those bots for now. Moreover, they were following her by foot, and while Eden was flying in a straight line toward her goal, they had obstacles in their way that would slow them down. Those stupid bots were even bumping and stumbling into one another in the areas where their group was crowded.

"Loir, did you have time to check out that thing? The giant head?"

"Well, Kitty is keeping me busy! I was playing in the sandbox, and now you want me to check this out too? Oh, I'm not paid enough pizza for this..."

"I can raise your salary if that's all it will take," chuckled Dante.

"Oh, I really like this Sugar Daddy, Eden, you better be a good Kitty with him. I ain't going back to the basement. I'm going to stay here and be a pepperoni hoe."

Eden rolled her eyes. She really needed to teach Loir a thing or two once she got back there...

"I think you're right, Kitty... This might be your exit ticket."

"Might be?"

"The door is locked for me, Kitty. Can't guarantee anything! You might be out in two minutes, or you might be eaten by giant piranhas. How's your swimming?"

"Not great..." grimaced Eden.

"Oh well, at least I prepared you a cute bikini and a cute duck buoy... Alright, get ready to jump. I'll buy you some more time."

Eden stood carefully and got on the edge of the tiger buggy. She was now much closer to the ground already and unfortunately, she still had some pursuers. The smartest among those bots had made their way under the tiger car, and were just waiting for her. However, as crazy as he was, if Loir said he'd buy her time, he would. She took a deep breath.

"Alright... now!"

Eden jumped and, as one would expect of Loir's creations, she was able to land on all fours perfectly this time, just like a cat. She raised an eyebrow, agreeably surprised, and stood back up.

"Run... now!"

Eden took a deep breath and turned on her heels, running toward the giant head. She'd had plenty of time to rest and now was the time to go full speed. She didn't even glance back to check how many of the bots were after her. She had to get to that giant head as fast as possible, get inside, and pray there would be nothing involving swimming in a stupid bikini waiting for her...

"Goodbye, my darling," suddenly sighed Loir.

When Eden was about to ask what he was talking about, she suddenly heard and felt a big explosion behind her. The tiger buggy! Loir had probably

196

programmed it last minute to reconfigure as a bomb and send it against her pursuers... Still, even if she felt the heat of the explosion on her back and smelled the smoke, Eden had no time to watch it. She kept running toward the head. She had underestimated its size from afar. She didn't know if this was meant to be a trick to the eye, but this thing was obviously farther and bigger than she had anticipated.

Whilst she had thought she'd reach it quickly, Eden was still running, trying to flee her pursuers.

"Uh-oh..." suddenly said Loir.

"What? What uh-oh? Loir?" she asked, worried.

"You might want to accelerate, Kitty. We've been spotted for real this time. The Core's System is going to come after you..."

Eden's blood went cold. This was the last thing she wanted.

So far, everything they had triggered were automatic systems. The bots spotted an intruder, they would chase it as a reflex. They weren't smart; they were merely little tools inside the Core, programmed just to chase intruders and do the simplest task. Just like when they'd rebounded against the fence, they weren't capable of making any big or smart decision.

Loir mentioning the Core's System meant something much smarter was going to join this little game of chase, and Eden was sure this would not be so easy... The System was artificial intelligence. It was smart, and unlike the bots, it could make decisions even faster than a human being. If it knew she was there, it was going to chase her relentlessly and, even worse, try to keep her there.

Eden accelerated again, feeling the devil behind her. She had to get out before the System got there. It could generate much scarier things than stupid bots...

She heard them just as she was only a few steps away from the door. Dogs.

Not cute puppies, but real, big, ferocious dogs! Eden heard them growling furiously and running behind her.

"Oh, crap, crap, crap..." said Loir. "Mean doggies! Mean!"

She could hear him typing frantically, probably trying to do something, but it wasn't like Loir could reconfigure something generated by the Core, or create a wall between two moving targets. Eden was on her own. She accelerated, but clearly, the dogs were almost on her already. Damn things...

"Eden, Kitty, no...!"

She did it anyway. Eden stopped all of a sudden and, trusting her hearing, she instantly rotated her body. She sent her leg flying mid-air, trying to figure out where she thought the dogs were. She hit one and the horrible beast, which was actually half-dog and half-robot, was sent flying. A second one, though, growled and immediately jumped on her leg. Eden used the claws on her paw and scratched it off. Like a real one, the dog whimpered and retreated. The Core was probably confused that she hadn't felt the pain on her leg. With the two dogs down, and no more in sight yet, Eden turned back and finally ran into the dark hole.

"Oh, damn it, Kitty, I really thought you were going to lose one of your nine lives there," sighed Loir.

"Where am I?"

"We're about to find out..."

Indeed, she was back in the darkness. Eden was walking carefully this time, but she could still feel the ground under her feet, something completely flat, so smooth like a mirror or something. This had to be another level from the cubes earlier, but she didn't know what to expect. Could she make it outside? She patted her chest, checking the star was still there. In fact, she realized that not only was it there, but that it was glowing for some reason...

Eden took it out and used it as a dim light to help her.

"Ooh... Shiny..."

She ignored Loir's comment and kept walking. She just wanted to make it out of the System safely so she could study what that star was. Eden was dying with curiosity, but for now, her survival instincts were speaking first.

The room changed all of a sudden.

The lights lit up so fast, Eden was blinded and had to cover her eyes.

"Oh... same architect."

Loir was probably right. This room had similar features to the colored cubes one, strikingly familiar features. Eden had to move right away; a small cube was coming at her. However, this time, the cubes were all black and white, and the ones moving were much smaller. She couldn't stand on any, and instead, she was stuck on what was the ground floor of the room. She put her star away and began walking.

This was a completely square room, but just like the previous one, chunks of it would come out of the blue and go to another part. Another thing was that wherever she walked, the cubes would change from black to white without warning. Eden took a step, but just then, she was hit by a cube in the flank, and thrown to the side.

"Ouchie... You okay, Kitty? Sorry. Didn't see that one coming. Oh, and I wouldn't..."

Too late. Eden was hit in the head again just as she tried to stand back up.

"...get up yet if I were you. Damn, this really isn't your day, my poor Kitty."

Eden grumbled for a while, and only sat up when she was sure nothing was going to come at her. This room was more dangerous; the cubes were flying faster from one point to another and worse, some were actually changing direction and color halfway without warning.

"Loir, anything for me?"

"Well, the good news is, the Core has yet to make its way here. The bad news is, this code is extremely... strange."

"Strange how?" asked Eden, while diving to the side to ignore another hit.

"I don't know. It's full of holes, and it actually changed into black and

198

white for me too! Moreover, it keeps moving around, and if I try to change it, it ignores me like a flea! So rude. I think I can solve a part though. Tell me what you see."

Eden could only see those cubes moving from one place to another, but the more she looked and was careful, the more she began to notice things.

"They all change direction or color at the same spots. When it gets to the middle of the room, the color of the cube changes, and then it goes to a random spot in the wall in a straight direction. But... If the room is a cube, then it's cut into two big screens, and the screen is the thing that probably needs some... damn fixing!"

Even if she had understood, Eden still had to watch out for the cubes flying at her. She couldn't find a spot in which to stay clear. She tried to use her claws to climb, but this wasn't good.

"It probably means something, all this black and white," said Loir. "There's always a solution."

"I can't redo the same thing. There's nothing for me to get on," retorted Eden, still climbing up.

She tried to get to the ceiling of the room, and just as she reached it, she heard a horrible sound.

"What the..."

She spotted it right away. A corner of the room suddenly went gray and flickered like a screen with something that shouldn't be happening on it.

"...Loir, tell me you're the one doing that."

"Uh, no, I think the Core is trying to win this hide-and-seek, Kitty..."

Eden felt another chill go down her spine. She couldn't think of a worse scenario than the Core trapping her there in a square room. She already felt like a mouse in a cage!

"Loir, find a solution, fast!"

"We got about ninety seconds before it traps you completely," he groaned. "I'm searching, Kitty, I'm searching. It has to have some logic to it. It's not piano keys. It's not some partition or a domino... It could be a chessboard, but there are way too many spaces then... The black and white ought out to be a clue. ...A Dalmatian?"

"Loir, for fuck's sake!"

"Those holes in the code, can you fill them?" asked Dante.

"Not with anything, Sexy. It rejects me every time I try to enter a word. ...See?"

"Here. Try putting white."

"White...?"

Eden heard Loir typing, and suddenly, one of the cubes that were about to go inside the wall, stopped mid-air and ran to the middle of the room, where it had just changed color, but it stayed white.

"Loir, it worked!" exclaimed Eden.

"Here, put black. This one, white."

"What are we playing at?"

While he asked, two more cubes stopped flying and went to their spots. Eden breathed a bit better. It looked like Dante had found the solution...

"It's a game of Go. It's an old game, played on a nineteen by nineteen grid, containing three hundred sixty-one points for the players to put their white or black stones."

"They put such a complicated thing for their people to pass through?" frowned Eden.

"The rules of Go are actually extremely simple. The game is much more complex than chess because of all the possible combinations, but as long as you know the basics, any idiot can play, and this code is already filled, I just need to look at the area you're in to know what to put. Here, white, and this one too. This one, black."

"Oh my gosh, he's smart and rich, and he knows some super weird Asian chess game that's about to save my Kitty's eighth life. Oh, I can't have two white ones after the other. Alright, one player after the other, I get it..."

Quickly, Eden saw the board filled in front of her. She saw the grid, and those cubes were probably meant to be those stones... Still, she couldn't see her exit, and the corner in which the Core was attacking was growing rapidly.

"Guys... faster..." she said.

Dante was still continuously saying where to put what to Loir, and the hacker was typing fast to finish filling the code. Eden could see the grid rapidly filling itself. This probably wasn't like chess, as she saw large areas filled with white, and some with black. She suddenly understood; once the game was over, one of those zones was probably going to be the exit. Eden grabbed one of the cubes and, following the logic of what she could understand as the basic rules Dante had mentioned, she threw it against the grid, in a suitable spot.

The grid reacted, and all the cubes stopped moving. Instead, the white area opened, and all the white cubes turned into a strange sort of void. Eden let out a sigh of relief and jumped inside.

She heard the Core behind her, and it prompted her to start running immediately in the tunnel she was in. The Core was going to chase her until the very end!

She accelerated. Why was that tunnel so long again! Eden was almost out of breath, but she could see the end of it. She could hear the Core, screeching behind her like a machine overspinning. It was trying to scare her, but Eden knew she ought to run, just keep running!

"Good job, Eden."

That voice.

Eden almost stopped as she glanced over her shoulder. She only caught a very brief image. A smile, blonde hair, and an index finger against thin lips. Suddenly, a hand pushed her forward and Eden fell.

She fell on her knees in Loir's new room.

"Welcome back to Pizzaland!"

"Pizzaland?" sighed Eden.

She was still on all fours, trying to recuperate. For her brain, everything that had just happened was perfectly real. Hence, she was still tired from all the running around, sore from the strenuous movements, and worse, still dizzy from everything that had just happened in a mere few minutes.

A large hand suddenly appeared in front of her; she knew whose it was without even checking for black nail polish. Eden tried to control her blushing and took it, helped up by Dante.

"Welcome back," he said.

His low and deep voice made Eden blush even more as she tried to avoid his gaze. He helped her sit down in the closest chair while Loir was still on his keyboard.

"Good job, Kitty," he chuckled. "We have a lot of pretty, shiny data to recover, but I got it all here–"

"Loir, I saw Master."

His fingers froze above the keyboard as he turned his creepy, black eyes to her.

"Huh? You saw who?"

"Pan," she elaborated. "I saw him. He was there. I... I just caught a glimpse of him before I crossed back. It was definitely my master."

"Are you sure?" asked Loir, looking back at his screens. "I don't see anything, Kitty..."

"I'm sure it was him," she nodded. "Just... right before I came back. Check again. It was definitely Master."

Loir kept double-checking, his fingers running across his keyboards, but he was definitely frowning a lot, even for someone without eyebrows... Eden also frowned and came to his side to check too. The memory was still freshly engraved in her mind, but there was no sign of it on the screens. It was as if she had dreamed it.

"...He was definitely there," she muttered.

"What did you see?" asked Dante.

"It was very brief, he came right before I crossed over. He just... He pushed me out, and said I had done a good job."

"You saw him right before you came back?" asked Loir, stopping the frantic typing.

"A second before I opened my eyes," nodded Eden.

"Damn it," grumbled Loir.

Eden sighed and walked a few steps away to lean against the wall and let herself slide down slowly until she was seated on the floor. Rolf was standing still by the door, an indecipherable expression as usual. To her surprise, Beer and Bullet appeared, running to her with a great deal of yapping and their short little tails wagging; however, she didn't feel like playing with the pups. She was exhausted and confused. Each Dive strained her body, and she was definitely going to be sore soon. She massaged her neck, her SIN still hot

201

under her blonde hair.

Meanwhile, Loir was still glaring at his screen, reading Eden's last images over and over.

"...You can't find him?" asked Dante, visibly curious as well.

"No..." grumbled Loir. "Kitty's Master is that good... I can't believe it. He used the Ether."

"What's the Ether?"

Loir made a strange gesture with his head, and from the way he moved, Eden imagined he was probably trying to roll his eyes. They stayed completely black, though, so it was hard to tell.

"It's like the space for all hackers," she explained. "The Ether is like a thin layer we all go through the moment we travel between reality and the System. It was there before the Core and before any other system. It's like the larger space in which all the SINs are in, although no one is connected."

"Like an asteroid field," added Loir. "Everybody's there, but no one's partying..."

"The Ether is like an outlaw zone. It's so chaotic, no one can control it. No one even knew it existed before we found a way to connect it to our minds. However, everyone has to travel through the Ether before we are connected to anyone. It's... like being in a coma. We don't know where we are, it's not physical or tangible, but we're neither awake nor dead."

"I can't understand how your master got to you through the Ether," said Loir. "Even the Core can't go there..."

"Why?"

"It's human-only," said Loir. "It's out of the Core's web. It can't follow a human mind going back to their body once they reach the Ether. But no one should be able to follow anyone at all... Maybe Master just played a nasty trick and came right before you got into the Ether, Kitty. Everything else would be too crazy."

"Maybe..."

Eden felt a bit sad. She couldn't believe there would be a day where a theory would be too crazy even for Loir... She let out a long sigh. Still, she was sure of what she had seen. It was definitely her master. How he had found her, she couldn't tell. Had he seen what she had done inside the Core? She blushed, a bit proud. She hoped he had seen everything, how good she had gotten...

"Argh, I can't believe I missed an occasion to see Pan!" whined Loir. "How was he, Kitty?"

"He didn't change at all, from the little bit I saw. His blonde hair, still looking so young."

"Ugh. I hope he's very old and smelly in real life," grumbled Loir.

Eden smiled. She knew he was just upset he hadn't been able to catch the legendary Pan. She let out a long sigh. She was upset too, but having been able to catch a glimpse of him, no matter how brief, made her very happy anyway.

"...Are you alright?"

She raised her head. She had almost forgotten Dante De Luca's presence... He was standing very still, expressionless, his arms crossed and staring at her. She must have looked tired. She nodded slowly.

"That Dive was a bit intense, but I'm fine."

She suddenly remembered... he had actually watched everything! Eden grumbled, and grabbed one of the pups to hug him, hiding her face behind him and her long hair with that excuse. She was so embarrassed. That stupid pink cat outfit! Loir ought to be glad Dante was standing between them at the moment, because Eden had some very clear ideas on how she planned to get revenge.

"It was intense for sure," moaned Loir. "I'm starving. Staaaaaaaarving."

"We can have food ordered," said Rolf.

Dante was still staring right at Eden, and clearly not listening to Loir's long list of desired dishes. Eden kept trying to look down, but she couldn't keep strangling a wriggling pup to hide herself. Instead, she just scratched his belly and tried to think of something else.

"...Do you want something too?" asked Rolf, walking past her and toward the door.

"I'll share with Loir."

"Understood."

Eden was a bit surprised at how polite and obedient Rolf was to her, but the man simply walked out to go and probably gather the crazy amount of food Loir had requested.

Eden glanced to the side. This time, Dante had turned his feet, and she could see the leather Italian shoes pointed toward Loir's screens. She looked up, and indeed, Dante was staring at the screens with his arms crossed, looking interested.

"So that's your online identity... Miss... Pink Sexy Jelly Paws?"

Eden tried really, really hard not to roll her eyes. Loir was clearly doing this on purpose. There was no way Dante was going to believe this was really her identity! Still, she took a deep breath and nodded, deeply ashamed. She couldn't even believe she agreed to that...

"Interesting," chuckled Dante with his deep voice. "Interesting name, and... outfit. Not quite what I had imagined. However..."

Eden froze.

He couldn't have found out, right? This was her online identity. Loir had made a decent job of preparing something in such a short time; he couldn't think there was anything else. No matter how insane her online appearance was, he ought to know an online identity couldn't be forged. Even if Loir had very likely gathered all of the gear last minute, Eden was clinging on to the one thing Dante ought to know.

Every person had only one identity online. If she was Miss Pink Sexy Jelly Paws, she couldn't also be Ghost. It didn't make sense. Her SIN couldn't lie. There was the Eden in real life, and the Eden her SIN was using each time she went online. Dante had been there all along too. He had seen Eden use her SIN to get online and come back. She couldn't fake that. Would he let it go then?

Obviously not. He was leaning over, one hand on Loir's chair, his golden eyes fixated on one of the screens. Eden wished she could tell what was happening in that brain of his. Dante was simply smiling, smiling like a tiger about to eat his share of fresh meat...

"How long will it take for you to decipher all of the data?" he asked Loir.

"About three hours," said Loir with a large satisfied smile. "Our Kitty worked well... The Core must be crazy unhappy right now! Alarms ringing on all floors, everybody out, ladies and babies first!"

"...What do you usually do with the extra data you get?" asked Dante, grabbing his pack of cigarettes.

Loir rubbed his fingers together.

"Money, Sugar Daddy. Information is the one thing people are willing to pay a lot of pretty numbers for... Once we get what we came for, Kitty and I just wait until we catch more fish, and sell what they want..."

"Don't you ever get caught selling that information?" smiled Dante.

"Only if you're trying to sell a carpet to a monkey!" exclaimed Loir. "No, no, no, Big Kitty. I prepare the yummiest little fishies, and then I hook the biggest shark..."

"Loir, shut up," groaned Eden.

She wasn't sure it was safe to let Dante know their way of working. Not just because Loir usually sold most of the data they got on the Black Market, but because some of those sharks he happily hooked were probably enemies of the Italian Tiger... other Zodiacs.

Dante turned to her with a little smile.

"Keep it all for me, then," he said. "I'll buy everything you got."

"Are you sure, Big Kitty?" asked Loir, smiling from ear to ear. "That's going to be a lot of *kaching-kaching*..."

Dante smiled, cigarette in hand, and turned to Eden.

"I'll buy everything," he declared.

Just with that, he simply walked out, leaving the two of them alone with the pups. Eden was baffled. ...What had he meant by that? He wasn't talking about her, was he? She wasn't fine with being treated like some stupid merchandise!

She took a deep breath and stood up, walking to Loir. She slapped his shoulder, making him whine loudly. The pups barked after him.

"You're so mean!" protested Loir, making a fake sad expression. "After everything I did, you beat me? Bad Kitty, bad Kitty!"

"This bad Kitty is going to take your damn eyes out if you pull something like that again! Seriously, Loir, a pink outfit? He didn't buy it for one second!"

Loir sighed.

"I did what I could, Kitty. Moreover, even if he thinks he knows, he can't know your secret just like that. He has no proof of who you really are... You

204

know, inside the box. Even I had a hard time believing it when I learned the truth..."

"Shut it," she groaned.

"Hehehe..."

Loir kept smiling like a hyena and got back to his screens. The computers were working fine without his help, though. Eden could see all the files being encrypted and decrypted one after another, pages and pages of information lined up in front of them. This wasn't something that would excite her at all; she was used to this. The Core was nothing but a huge bundle of data on every Core citizen, everywhere, anytime. It was a bit scary, and it made her truly glad she was out of that System. This was the price of living in the Core: no liberty and absolutely no privacy, either. Eden thought it was frightening. The slightest mistake was immediately penalized unless the Core wanted to test them out, see how far it could go, and the price would get even heavier...

"So boring," yawned Loir. "Do you think the Core ever wonders why humans are such boring little creatures? Or does it just secretly rewatch good films like we do?"

"I'm not sure the Core has any interest in human movies, Loir. ...Hey, did I bring the star back with me?"

"The... Oooooh, it was a star? I thought it was just a shiny thingy. Let me see. Oh, yes, there it is, with your files! Still warm from your cute little bra too, hehe..."

"Stop being gross. See if you can let me open it."

Eden walked past the screens and computer installations to stand in a large, blue hexagon just behind it. As soon as she walked on it, the blue tiles lit up and Loir squealed.

"Oh, I've been dying to try all my new babies," he said.

Eden couldn't help but feel a bit excited too.

Although screens and computers were mostly for Loir to play with, the augmented reality area was her playfield as well. Like her SIN recreated her body and her movements inside the System, this simple zone, which was like a very, very fancy mat, was there to take objects from the System into reality. The pups walked over to see what their mistress was doing, curious, but neither of them dared to step on it.

It was completely harmless, though. Loir controlled everything there. He spent a short minute transferring the file over and, just a second later, a very similar image of the strange star appeared in front of Eden. This version was made like a hologram, with hundreds of little lights secretly activated. It used the properties of light reflection to recreate the image for the human eye. To Eden, this object looked very real. She lightly tapped her SIN, and now, the mat's system was reading her hands' movements. She was able to manipulate the star as if it were in the real world, grabbing and moving it however she pleased.

Loir kept jumping back and forth to compare what was going on for Eden and on his screens.

"So exciting!" he squealed. "So exciting! Can you imagine everything we can do with such good stuff? Oh my, I can even rewatch all nine of *The Lord of the Rings* movies as if I was there..."

"Loir, work first. I need to open this file."

The hacker sulked.

"You party-pooper... Alright, I'll let you play with the toys that my Sugar Daddy bought for me. You don't know how to share, anyway. And you're not getting any pizza!"

Eden didn't care. She was fed up just hearing him talk about pizza all the time... She was more curious about what she could see in her hands.

This was a rather unique object. She wondered how she was supposed to use it. It really looked like those wooden puzzles she used to play with when she was younger. This was clearly made of different pieces or something that could move. Eden sat down, crossing her legs. She could spin some of the ends and turn some parts, but it wouldn't open. She kept trying. She knew Loir was probably studying it on his side, from the way he was frowning.

"...That code is so rude," he said after a while. "It won't even let me touch it! So arrogant!"

He began sulking, but when Rolf came in carrying five boxes of pizza, he completely seemed to forget about it. Beer and Bullet happily ran to get their lunch too.

Eden didn't even seem to notice Rolf was there. She was still in the middle of the augmented reality mat, trying to figure out her puzzle. Rolf brought a plate to her before everything was eaten by the three gluttons behind her, but he was very curious. That woman was curious... He was surprised by how fascinated the boss was with her too. He had seen the boss around women before, but none as peculiar as Eden. She always behaved like one of those street cats, hungry but also extremely cautious and ready to run away at any moment. She was feisty and always somewhat angry. However, she also looked extremely pretty and exceptionally gentle when she played with the puppies.

"She'll figure it out."

Rolf turned around to see Loir, a slice of pizza in each hand. His eyes were focused on Eden too, although he looked extremely calm, engulfing his pizza.

"What is she doing?"

"Her master left her a toy. So, Kitty wants to play..."

# CHAPTER FIFTEEN

For several long minutes, Eden really tried her best to open the puzzle. This was nothing she hadn't seen before. It looked like so many of the toys she had played with, back when she was still a little girl from the Core.

Eden only had very vague memories of it, but she knew her room and her life, even back then, weren't like others. She couldn't remember going to school with other children or even living in those modern apartments. What she had preciously stored in some faraway memory was the smell of wood, the imperfect fabric of a handmade toy, the light of a candle, and the smell of fruit juice. Eden had spent hours trying to remember more. Sadly, everything before she had to leave the Core was a blur. Her mother was the one she remembered the best because she had been such an important part of her life. No, she had been her only point of focus during Eden's first years of life.

Eden was getting impatient at this star-shaped puzzle. She couldn't figure it out, even after she felt she had pressed, spun, and shaken every one of its corners.

"Pizza?"

She glanced up, only now realizing someone was standing next to her. Rolf was handing her a small plate with a few slices he'd managed to save from Loir's ferocious appetite... Eden sighed and nodded, taking a slice. She hadn't realized how hungry she was until now. The pizza was good too; she could somewhat see why Loir was always so crazy about it... Not his level of crazy, though. She put the star down in front of her, slowly eating her pizza.

Beer and Bullet quickly ran to those who were probably their favorite humans. One began pulling on Rolf's shoestring, while his brother was climbing on Eden's lap, hoping to get a little bite of that nice-smelling pizza.

"What is this thing?"

"A puzzle," she sighed. "My master left it for me... I have no idea how to open it though, and it sucks."

"Why did he leave you that?"

"I wish I knew. I had tons of toys like these when I was younger, I think... I wonder why my master left me something similar. I even wonder how he ever knew so much about my childhood."

"You've never met him?"

Eden shook her head.

"Not in the flesh. But I do know his avatar's appearance by heart, he's never changed it. I know it was definitely him I saw during my Dive earlier. It was his voice, and the way he called to me..."

Eden's voice died, and a wave of nostalgia hit her. She really missed her master. The man who had almost raised her after she had been left alone in the Suburbs. Pan was an enigma, and yet, she had felt like he was her best friend for the longest time. It was as if she had always known him, although she really knew nothing about him...

Her master had been her everything for a long time, and Eden had never realized how close and emotionally attached she was to him. She knew one thing for sure: she would have never survived this long in the Suburbs if it wasn't for him. He always knew how to find her, where to guide her for safety. Eden had no idea if he lived in the Core or in the Suburbs. Maybe he was another weirdo living in an underground basement like Loir... He had a strangely young voice for someone who had been in her life for over fifteen years. His youthful appearance was also disturbing. She had always thought he was using his real physique, but now, his avatar looked younger than Eden, which he couldn't possibly be.

Eden was still a bit bitter about their short encounter. Her master had always been able to find her anytime, anywhere. She suspected he had done something with her SIN, because he had always popped up when she needed him, until that time he abandoned her. Because that was how she felt at that time. Abandoned.

He hadn't left her clueless and defenseless, but it was just not enough for Eden. Since she was a child, Pan had always been there, even for moral support. Whenever she felt lonely, she could Dive and find him. Now, she couldn't even do that anymore and Eden hated it. She still didn't know why he had gone into hiding and cut ties with her, leaving her with Loir instead.

"Is it something he'd do?"

Rolf's question took her by surprise.

No, the fact that he was sitting there with her and getting curious was already surprising in itself. Wasn't he supposed to... simply accompany Dante, his boss? However, now that Eden thought about it, there really wasn't anyone hanging around Dante all day, from what she had seen. Or more like, there was no one hanging around at all on those upper floors. Was he mostly relying on their heavy security then? It would explain why he was always so comfortable, and why Rolf himself didn't seem to have anything special to do either. If he was the boss' second-in-command, then this place ought to be a safe one for him too. Maybe that was why he could freely play with the pups and hang with her and Loir like this...

Eden realized she had remained silent for too long, and Rolf was still waiting for her answer. She nodded.

"Yes... My master is the one who taught me how to Dive and everything. I learned when I was much younger... so he'd often do it in the form of games like this. He never put me in any dangerous situation, but he liked to leave keys for me to find and solve, even when he wasn't there..."

That was right.

Eden wasn't just calling him Master because of how he had taught her everything, but also because of how talented Pan was. It wasn't just a pupil's admiration for her teacher. Pan was the best Dive Hacker she had ever seen, and she was the only one who could even dare to touch his level. This guy was like a shadow and an annoying parasite to the Core. She had seen him flee from the direst and most dangerous situations, and escape the Core like it was nothing. When he was backing her up too, he was like a magician. He found the most hidden openings and could get Eden out of any situation. He was the main reason she had survived for so long and been so successful as a hacker.

"How come you never met him?" frowned Rolf.

For a second, his question put Eden on guard. Was he inquisitive on Dante's orders? Were they trying to find her master and pretending to be friendly to ask such questions?

She wasn't sure. Yet, seeing how Rolf was calmly pulling at his shoestring and playing along with the pup, she figured... he might be asking out of sheer curiosity. It didn't sound or seem like he was fishing for information. He hadn't asked a thing about Ghost, and moreover, they really had no business with her master either. Plus, even Eden didn't know enough. She couldn't even find a clue about her master herself; how would the Italians find him before she did?

"I don't know," she shrugged. "Master always said it was too dangerous... no matter how many times I asked."

Eden had never stopped asking, though. Somehow, she wanted to know the real Pan. The master whom she was so close with; she wanted to feel him for real, see the human behind the screen, the man behind the SIN. She had those strange feelings toward him, like a child looking for a parent or a sibling. She had felt as close as one could be to another human, and yet she had never even seen him in real life...

"I'm sure Master is the one who left this for me," she said, staring at the star. "He knew I was there, and he felt me..."

What was her master doing so deep in the Core? Did he really follow her, or did he have another objective? It was like back in the day. He was never afraid to Dive so deep, and he appeared in the most unexpected places... even the Ether. Or had he done this on purpose so Eden wouldn't be able to find him? There was absolutely no way to find someone she had barely seen in the Ether. Even Loir had no trace of him. It was like trying to find someone stuck inside a time and space portal; it made no sense.

She finished her slice, licked her fingers quickly, and after wiping them, Eden manipulated the star, annoyed. There ought to be a solution.

"Loir! You still haven't found anything?" she asked.

His mouth full, the hacker appeared to be rolling his black eyeballs.

"So pushy! Leave me and my pepperoni alone! Your master is a nasty one, there are no clues in that code..."

Eden glared back, making Loir shrink in his seat, although he stayed resolutely away from his keyboard. For him to not try and solve that code again, his dignity as a hacker must have been hurt, thought Eden.

What had her master planned...?

Eden heard the doors opening again as Dante walked back in, followed by George. This one glared at Eden, clearly still bitter about last time... but she just ignored him.

"We are not the only ones who noticed the black Overcraft and the lack of customers from the Core," said Dante. "Three other Zodiacs suggested a meeting."

"Three?" repeated Eden and Rolf at the same time, baffled.

It was rare for even two of the Zodiacs to meet, so for three of them to suggest they all gather was... unprecedented.

However, this situation might call for it. Regardless of everything else, the people from the Core were the ones with money, and that could spend it in the Suburbs. This was the one and only way to make the Suburbs survive: finding ways for people from the Core to spend as much money as possible so that money would transfer to the people in the Suburbs. That was why almost all the territories were principally trying to attract their attention with entertainment, leisure, illicit pleasures, and other things they couldn't find in the Core. As soon as they stepped out into the Suburbs, the Core citizens were like small fish in a big pond, with people from all sides ready to prey on them. There was no way for the Suburbs to produce money; they didn't produce any resources they could sell themselves. All the money came from trade and patrons from the Core.

If the Core citizens stopped coming every night, the Suburbs would soon turn into a large, chaotic mess. Those like Eden who worked to entertain others would lose their income. The restaurants, the bars, the nightclubs, the shows, everything would suffer from the lack of customers. Aside from a handful of wealthy people like the Zodiacs, everyone else was barely surviving...

"Who was it?" asked Eden, getting up.

"The Hare, the Dog, and the Rat."

Eden nodded. It made sense... Those three usually relied a lot on the trade. No, it was fair to say all of the Zodiacs should be alerted about this. However, next to them, Loir made a sudden strange noise with his throat, and began to cough loudly, getting their attention.

"Loir...?" called Eden.

"N-nothing!"

If it was nothing, why was he literally trying to crawl under his desk...? They all hesitated for a second, but seeing how he wasn't coming out of his strange hideout and he wasn't making a sound either, they silently decided to ignore his crazy behavior, once again. Dante too had an eyebrow raised, but he didn't seem to care much, his hands in his pockets. Beer and Bullet, however, must have thought this was some funny game, because both pups ran to go and try to find Loir under his desk. Eden sighed.

"Are you going to go...?" she asked Dante.

He chuckled.

"Block party. How could I miss that..."

In other words, he knew perfectly well how dangerous this little meeting would be and didn't care...

"Has your toy given you anything yet?"

Eden glared at him, a bit pissed. How dare he call something made by her master a toy... If it was a mere toy, she wouldn't have been so obsessed with opening that thing in the first place!

"It's not a toy," she couldn't help but growl. "It's..."

What was this thing anyway? It annoyed her even more that she couldn't figure it out. Was this even really a star...? She had been trying to open it, but maybe the solution wasn't the inside, it was the outside. Suddenly, it was as if something had clicked. Eden moved it slowly, turning each edge and corner into a different position. She had been trying to make sense of it, unlock something and open it, but this couldn't be as simple as that. Although she had pushed it into a different formation, maybe she hadn't been precise enough on what she wanted to shape it into. Eden tried to make a sphere first, but it just didn't work as something completely round. No matter how she tried, there were some hills and bumps, nothing that would take a completely spherical shape, maybe a pyramid then? Eden tried it. A square, a diamond, anything with edges didn't work either. This thing didn't want to have sharp edges, but it still had little bumps and corners...

Since she was so focused on it, Dante and Rolf were simply staring, curious to see if she could figure it out. Meanwhile, Beer and Bullet were still barking and happily playing under the mountain of computers Loir had hidden himself in. Who knew when he'd finally come out...

"What could he have done with that..." grumbled Eden.

Dante came down to the mat, stepping next to her. Eden tried to ignore him, but it was hard to ignore a presence like Dante De Luca's. She could feel a faint wave of heat come over her... Still, she stubbornly stayed focused on the fake star instead, trying to figure it out. She had games like these when she was young, she knew there ought to be some shape or something she hadn't tried yet, some sort of key only she had. Her master wouldn't have made something so simple that anyone could figure it out. Pan was good at games. He had definitely picked something that would work only for Eden, something she'd have to be the one to figure out.

"Are you sure your master did it?"

"Yes. I recognize his work. The fact that he appeared too and said..." Eden paused.

What Pan had said. "*Good job, Eden.*" He had called her by her real name. The name she rarely used in Dives, a name only her closest ones knew. Before, he always had a gentle nickname for her. Baby, Little One, Girl, or Ghost. Loir calls her Kitty when she Dives. It was a precaution. They never knew who could be listening to their Dives. It was very unlikely with Loir or her master's skills, but it was still something they ought to be careful about. Using real names was often a dangerous key to their SINs. The Core was constantly looking for their real identities, which was why Eden didn't even know Loir's real name. She didn't know Pan's. Even the name Eden may not have been the one she was registered as in the Core. It was something intimate... The name Eden was something only a handful of people knew.

There was no way someone like Pan would have made such a mistake... It was definitely not a mistake. Plus, he had appeared while Eden was in the Ether. Why there? Was it to be sure no one but her could hear him? Eden chuckled, and quickly moved her fingers. It was hard, as it wasn't something as simple or precise as a square or a sphere, but... she was excited. She knew she had the answer.

Dante understood she had figured something out, because he carefully stepped back, staring at the shape Eden was quickly working on. Maybe he thought that it might explode, but it was unlikely. Not while Eden had that smile on her face... Loir too carefully popped his head up from behind his desk with a suspicious expression. His hand grabbed a new slice, and he chewed his pizza silently, too focused on Eden.

The last click resonated in the room, and in Eden's hand, the shape was done. It was perfect, there was no doubt about it now. She smiled, her heart beating loud and fast in her chest.

"...An apple?" questioned Dante.

"Eden's apple," she chuckled. "That's definitely Master's idea..."

There was a little piece sticking out, probably meant to be a leaf. Eden grabbed it and slowly spun it.

The object in her hands began to shine brightly, and suddenly, it exploded into thousands of shiny pixels. Eden opened her mouth wide in wonderment, and stepped back to see what was going on. They all were in awe. The Apple had spread into dozens of shapes, high and low, squares and... buildings. Eden realized right away, they were looking at a three-dimensional map.

Moving her hand, Eden grabbed one of the buildings and zoomed in, making the building a lot bigger for everyone to see.

"Holy macaroni..." squealed Loir.

Eden slowly stepped back, still completely amazed by what she was seeing.

"Is that..."

"The Core," said Dante, with a terrific smile appearing on his lips. "An impressive and very precise map of the Chicago Core..."

None of them could believe what they were seeing.

The Core's geography wasn't so hard to find. Some old maps could be found in stores; those on paper were bound to last longer. For the Dark Reality, though, it was a little bit harder to find such a thing. The Core was protecting itself, and protecting itself meant keeping its configuration hidden where no eyes could scrutinize it. Research on precise parts of Chicago were possible, but recent, genuine maps were rare, and expensive. If not the Core itself, many owners of those buildings were extremely careful with who they allowed to look up their information, and why. This very building was probably heavily protected by hackers the Tiger would have hired to prevent intruders from accessing it easily. Accessing a building's systemic map meant having a front row seat to its functions, and for hackers, there wasn't a more solid base with which they could use to hack.

Loir too had come out of his hiding place, and was now leaning over his desk to look at the Map, his creepy smile stretching from ear to ear. The way Eden could completely zoom into a building, a street, or a park was absolutely amazing. Not only that, but if she moved her fingers, the Map would evolve to show different layers of Chicago. At first, there was only a basic three-dimensional configuration, like the premises of any building. However, if Eden moved her fingers, the shapes would change to show thousands of little lights, probably meant to be all the electrical conductors. If she moved again, there were now green and blue pixels, and those were moving like a very precise network, the web of a spider named Chicago. Eden was completely in shock. This Apple... no, this Map's knowledge had an unfathomable value. Eden was curious to know what more she could show them...

"Interesting..."

Eden turned to him. On the side, the Tiger's golden eyes were shining with a scary glow, like a cat ready to bite its prey. Of course he'd also know the value of such information. There was no way someone like him, who probably had both hands in the Black Market, wouldn't know...

"Bloody Mary, Kitty! The Master is a living god!" squealed Loir.

He moved too fast and ended up falling somewhere behind the screens, making Eden frown. She walked over, but Rolf was closer, and faster, to pick the hacker up and put him back in his chair. As soon as he got in there, though, Loir literally jumped on his keyboard and began typing fast, his eyes stuck on

213

the screen. Curious as to what was going on, Eden came to look at the screens, but things were happening back on the Map.

Loir had now gotten full access to the Apple's control panel; hence, he was toying with it, making the Map change to show more and more new layers. Eden was in awe. She couldn't even understand half of what she was looking at, but this was clearly classified information. Not only that, this wasn't information that anyone should have been able to access at all. There was just too much in there. The data center's position. The electrical, air, and gas conduits. The air filtration systems, and their layers of particles. All the roads, the electric vehicles, and the real-time movements of those vehicles, hundreds of little lights shining and moving on the Map. The government's Overcrafts and their hidden parking spots. Even the top secret location of the magnetic field of the train that railed Chicago to the other Cores!

"...How did he get access to this?" she whispered.

Eden couldn't understand. This wasn't something she would have ever dreamed of getting her hands on, and she was one of the very best in her field. Still, this was exactly the kind of thing the Core would retain in its very center, keep secret, and do anything to protect. Eden knew better than anyone how the Core could act to protect its System.

"I have to find Master."

Loir turned to her.

"I-I need to find Master," Eden said, a bit louder this time.

"Kitty, calm down..."

"Loir, you don't understand! How did he get his hands on this? Master can't have something like this!"

"I know, but..."

"Can you imagine how deep he had to Dive to get this? Not even the Core builders could do something like that!"

Eden was in sheer panic, and not even Loir could calm her down.

This thing was an incredible tool, but it was way too much. She couldn't even understand how her master had managed to steal something like this, then hide and store it away for her to grab. Wherever he had stolen it from, it was impossible for the Core to have simply let him get away with this. Even if this thing was just a copy, it was still some of the Core's most precious information. Loir's reaction spoke volumes too. As someone who traded daily in the Black Market, he knew how valuable this Apple was.

Still, he grabbed Eden's wrist, and let out a long sigh.

"Kitty, cool down; you're going to overheat like a pizza oven... Do you want some pizza?"

"I don't give a fuck about pizza, Loir! I want to find my master, now! I need to ask him!"

Eden's shout resonated within the walls. The pups whined, stepping back. They were scared by their mistress' sudden expression of anger and pain. They weren't the only ones. Loir was frozen like a deer caught in headlights on

214

his seat, his eyes wide open. After a couple of seconds, though, he was still holding Eden's wrist, and he sighed.

"Kitty... The Master doesn't want you to find him."

The truth hit Eden hard.

She glared at Loir, but didn't retort. She knew he was right... Eden had searched every corner of the System for days and days with Loir to find Pan. It was like the most thrilling treasure hunt at first, but after a while of finding absolutely nothing, it had become tiring. Loir was acting as crazy as usual, but even he knew Eden's quest was never going to be rewarded. He had only agreed to keep searching because of how obsessed she was, and because he was curious too. When Eden had lost patience, he hadn't asked her to look again, and when she wanted to give it another shot, he was fine with it. However, even the craziest hacker knew what was going on.

Pan didn't want to be found. The best proof was, as he had just proven, he could find Eden anytime. He could give her the Core's biggest secret, but he couldn't reveal himself to her. It was as if nothing mattered as much as hiding his identity to her. It made her sad just to think about it. Someone who had played such a huge role in her life was... a complete stranger. Sometimes, Eden even wondered if Pan existed at all. Just like her father, he was nothing but a name and a vague silhouette. Still, she was bitter about it. Bitter, frustrated, and angry. Right now, she was glaring at Loir, but he wasn't the one Eden was truly mad at. She freed her wrist without any difficulty, and turned around to leave the room angrily.

As soon as Eden had stepped out, Loir sighed, and the Map suddenly disappeared. He frowned.

"Oh... It reacts to Kitty's SIN. It really won't work without her? Master, you're really picking favorites..." he muttered, staring at his screens.

Dante was still staring at the door, a complex expression on.

"She likes to go to high and open spaces when she's angry," Loir said suddenly.

They didn't look at each other, but Dante left the room without a word.

He stepped inside the elevator, touched the screen, and put his hands in his pockets while it was going up. A vivid pain in his head made him frown... again. He should have followed Eden right away, but she would probably have hated it. He let out a long sigh, and massaged his forehead. That spot got so painful at completely random times... He hated it. Moreover, he couldn't understand why it never happened when she was near.

It was a mystery that made him truly wonder. The pain was always unpredictable, sharp, and violent. The epicenter was the worst, but it spread throughout his whole skull nevertheless. A bit annoyed, he cracked his neck, left and right, then exhaled. It was really something he couldn't explain. It never happened when Eden was around. Was it a coincidence? Their night together had been the first one where the pain never woke him up. He couldn't explain it, but he liked the idea. A smile appeared on his lips. Eden... His Eden.

215

The doors finally opened on the highest floor.

It wasn't a garden like the terrace Eden had visited; it was a former helipad, now just a large, open space. Still, this was the highest point of the building. This building was one of the tallest ones in the Suburbs itself. They were high enough to see the Core from afar and get a glimpse of almost all of the Suburbs.

Dante glanced over and immediately found Eden. She was sitting, facing east toward the Core and beyond Lake Michigan. She was visibly upset, her eyes red and lips in a pout. With her arms wrapped around her knees, she looked as if she was mad at the whole world, the Core being the first in her line of vision. Dante approached her carefully. For someone keeping so many secrets, Eden was surprisingly easy to read at times...

He came close, and stood a few steps away, just staring at her. Was she going to tell him to go away?

"...I hate this," she suddenly said. "I hate it."

Dante stayed silent. Eden took a breath in, but the anger was visible, boiling beneath the surface.

"Everyone," she continued. "My father, my mom, my master... They all left me. Even Adam. They all leave and they don't care about me, about what I feel inside. My feelings... How it feels to be abandoned."

She gasped, only to fail in holding back her tears. Dante watched them roll down, caressing her cheeks beautifully. Eden shook her head, upset.

"I've had enough," she said. "Why is everyone, always..."

She suddenly stood up to shout at the world beneath.

"I never asked to be alone! I never asked to be saved! And I never asked them to do what they did for me! I would have been fine, if they had just... stayed with me."

Eden broke into more tears, and this time, Dante stepped forward, walking up to her calmly. He managed to come within arm's length before Eden noticed, and stepped back.

"You too!" she yelled at him. "You're just another selfish bastard! You're going to leave me as soon as you're done using me, aren't you? All you want is Ghost, the hacker! Why do you even bother with something you're going to throw away eventually?! I don't want your dinners, your gentleness, your stupid dates! I don't want you to be so confusing! I hate that you're so nice to me, trying to get in my head! I hate it! I hate you!"

"...I'm not going to throw you away."

Dante's calm words took Eden by surprise. She glared at him, still crying, but she remained quiet, and didn't move when he took another step closer.

"I won't leave you," he said.

Another step. Eden's shoulders kept moving, and her feet looked as if they were about to retreat at any moment. Still, they remained stuck on the ground, and she was staring at him, conflicted. Her mind was split in two, a part of her

216

wanting to run to him, the other part wanting to run away.

"You're a liar," she said.

"I'm not."

"You're a liar," she repeated, "and you're going to leave me. Everybody makes promises and breaks them. There's no such thing as staying together, not in this world, and not with me. You more than anyone else. I can't trust you and your sweet lies. Bastards like you crush hearts."

"Not yours."

Eden remained quiet, still staring at him with a mix of anger and pain in her eyes. She was hurt; not by him, but by all those that had left her before. He could tell. Eden was good at keeping those walls erect around her heart, but that didn't mean it hadn't been badly hurt already...

Dante took another step forward, and she retreated, but he kept going.

"I won't leave you," he said. "I don't care nearly as much about Ghost as I care about Eden. I want Eden. Not Ghost, but Eden. Only Eden, no one but Eden. I've wanted you since I saw you at the bar. Once I want something, I take it and I don't let go. I won't leave, and you won't be able to escape from me."

Eden gasped as she kept retreating. She was now almost scared of this man, and that hint of madness in his eyes. His possessiveness and the way he looked right at her. Still, Dante did exactly as he promised. Eden couldn't escape him. The more she retreated, the faster he stepped forward, until her heels reached the edge of the building. Eden felt the wind from behind, and for a second, it felt like her body might tip over. She wondered if that would be a better option.

Dante grabbed her and pulled her back to face him. Eden was breathless, but he didn't leave her any room to breathe. With his hands holding her shoulders, he suddenly kissed her.

It was one furious, hungry kiss. One full of possessiveness, passion, and danger. Still, it melted all her senses. Eden moaned under his aggressiveness, and her lips began moving too. Dante's kiss was difficult to withstand. His lips and tongue were recklessly attacking her, without an ounce of restraint. It was savage. Her lips didn't get a second of rest, and instead, had to keep up with the furious rhythm of his relentless kissing. Eden moaned helplessly, feeling the temperature rising despite the cold wind around them. She was hot. That kiss was hot, and getting hotter fast.

Dante's hands were not letting her back away or run. He was all over her, keeping her close and caressing her body. She felt his warm, large hands sneaking under her top, pressed against her skin, rushing up and down restlessly. He was driving her crazy. Crazy for wanting more of this. This was the kind of passion she wanted, what she needed. She held onto his shirt, holding him close and tight. Their kiss was salty from her tears, but it felt so good. Eden didn't want this to stop. She needed warmth, someone's warmth, even if it was just for a fleeting moment. Someone to chase the loneliness away.

"Dante," she gasped between their kisses.

There was something thrilling and dangerously intimate in calling his name. Had she ever called him by that name before? Eden wasn't sure, but she probably would have remembered if that were the case, no? It was too late to think. She didn't have time for questions, just for his kisses.

Chicago's cold winds couldn't help her cool down this heat. Eden was so hot, just too hot, and now things were getting worse. They were slowly retreating toward the elevator. His fingers on her neck, grabbing the base of her hair and keeping her against him, were driving her crazy. Eden wanted more. She wanted him to keep caressing her, making her body even hotter. She could feel all her senses burning with the color of passion. It was as if she didn't need air, and all her needs were now focused on one man only. She just needed someone, and that someone had to be him. The Tiger, Dante De Luca. If he was lying, she just wanted to live in this lie for a short moment.

At least, this moment...

They reached the back of the elevator without stopping their kisses, even for a second. The elevator started to move, but Dante suddenly lifted her up and Eden wrapped her legs around his waist, putting her hand on the mirror behind him. Eden didn't even glance up to look at their reflection. The elevator reached whichever destination it was headed for fast, and Dante stepped forward, taking the two of them out. Eden already had her hands on his shirt, and she was moving to get it out of the way as fast as possible.

The black tiger appeared on his skin and she couldn't help but glance at it, intrigued. Noticing Eden was less focused on their kissing but more on his tattoo, Dante smiled, and instead, began attacking her neck furiously. He kissed, sucked, and licked it, making Eden's senses run wild again. The young woman gasped and closed her eyes, forgetting all about the tattoo. How long has it been since she was kissed and seduced by a man like this? Dante wasn't letting her think or breathe. He was the one half-naked, but Eden felt completely exposed under the Italian's hungry hands, his fingers running all across her skin, above and under her clothes. His fingertips were following her back, making delicious chills crawl under her skin.

After a while, he finally let her down, and Eden decided to take command. She was as hungry as he was, and had no intention to let him lead the way. With both hands on his torso, she pushed him until the mafia boss tipped over onto the bed. She had just now realized they were back in the room they had slept in... but she didn't care much. Truth is, bed or not, it didn't change a thing. Eden just wanted him. They could have done this anywhere, as long as it was now. Absolutely nothing else mattered.

Now she was on top of him, on the edge of the bed, with the Tiger on his back. Eden stood back up, just to quickly get rid of her top and her bra. Dante smiled and tried to sit up, but Eden wasn't having it. She pushed him back aggressively and kissed him, pinning him down to the bed. He didn't seem to hate it, though. Instead, he groaned against her lips, as his hands held her waist, his fingers sneaking inside her pants... Eden kept kissing him but at a slower pace this time. She was hot, even with half her outfit gone. Desire was crawling in, and some knot in her stomach was slowly torturing her. Moreover, from where she was seated, she could feel the bump in Dante's pants, slowly rubbing between her legs... Even with the layers of fabrics, she could feel the heat of excitement, making her crazy. She began slowly undulating her body without thinking, and he was moving too. Although she was on top, his hands on her waist were in control, and making sure their bodies didn't part... It felt as if they were making love already. Their position was too enticing, and their uninterrupted kiss wasn't innocent at all.

As Eden lowered her body against his, Dante's hands climbed higher, grabbing her breasts, making her a bit flustered. He smiled again and played with them, making Eden react unexpectedly. His fingers got a bit playful, until Eden blushed and stopped their kiss, breathing harder.

"Interesting..." he chuckled.

She sent him a glare, a bit annoyed and confused.

"It's... the first time I'm so..."

She didn't finish her sentence, breathing harder than expected. She had never found her breasts to be so sensitive before, and the fact that her body was reacting so much to Dante's hands was confusing. Eden was no virgin, and she had been with many men before. She had learned to put a thick barrier between sex and her feelings.

Dante was completely wrecking that barrier with ease. Everything was so good with him, it was disturbing. She kept trying to be in control, to stay strong, but her body was winning over her rationality. It felt good, and it was hard not to give in. His large hands on her skin, on her back, on her waist, and his lips not giving her any rest. Eden caressed his hair. She liked how short it was on the sides, and how silky it was on top... She didn't care about messing it up at all. No, she was actually having fun making a mess of him. But she needed more than all that playful exchange. Eden's hands quickly moved to unbuckle his pants, freeing him. This time, Dante was the one to groan while she caressed him. Now Eden could use some of her experience to tease him; any chance she could get to have the upper hand, she'd surely take. He shivered as her fingers tortured him, the heat growing in his lower half. The proximity of her own body, the warmth between them, and the mere thought of Eden riding him were exciting enough already. He couldn't tell how much longer he'd last, but the excitement was reaching a dangerous peak...

The truth was, Eden was just as excited from what she could caress of him. Dante had an alluring body, with strong and defined muscles, slightly golden skin, and that impressive, sexy tattoo that covered half his body. With one hand on his manhood, the other on his shoulder to keep him down, Eden was staring at the large, Asian-style drawing on his torso and thinking how incredibly sexy the detailed feline was. The ink was so black and so dark, it looked incredibly fresh, and the tiger was ready to jump on its prey. The eyes

219

were strikingly similar to the golden irises a few inches above. His golden eyes were fixated on her, with so much heat in them Eden found herself blushing again. She wanted to drive him as crazy as she felt, but his gaze was the ice-cold stare of a dangerous individual. Still, Dante was breathing heavily, and his hands were acting possessive on her skin. She could feel the strength of his fingers on her waist, preventing her from moving even an inch away from him. Eden was on top, but she might as well have been a mouse caught in a trap...

"Eden," he finally gasped with a faint groan.

She smiled, and increased the movements of her hands on his end, hoping to drive him even more crazy. She wanted to see him surrender to her, to confirm her victory.

Yet, Dante was not one to give in so easily. Instead, he grabbed the fabric of her pants, and began opening them and pulling down, hoping to get rid of them. Eden didn't think twice before helping him get her pants out of the way. She was too hot to endure them, anyway. Her inner walls were throbbing, excited by the earlier rubbing and the enticing scene of his lower member standing tall and firm... Still, she moaned when Dante's hand ventured between her legs. He smiled, as she was already excited enough and kept melting more under his fingers. Eden grimaced, and wriggled her body unwillingly. She wasn't ashamed to be so wet already, but by how fast she was reacting. She was so hot and excited already, she wasn't sure she could endure this much longer... She wanted him. She wanted him bad. Eden leaned forward to resume their kissing, more savagely than before, letting go of him to grab his nape instead, while positioning herself back in the most dangerous position. She knew exactly what she was doing, and when their bodies began rubbing against each other again, with no fabric in between this time, she moaned against his lips. How could mere foreplay be so good? She shivered in pleasure, while Dante's hand moved to her butt, caressing up and down her thighs. Eden was growing impatient. She was on edge, all extremities of her body begging to be released from this torture. Dante too seemed restless. He was moving his lower body under her, accentuating the rubbing, and his hands were getting more and more possessive, the other one firmly grabbing her blonde hair to pull her close.

"Eden..."

Her name in his mouth sounded like a sacred word, something so holy one could only whisper it. He repeated it against her ear, before kissing her jaw, her neck, sucking her pale skin, and biting it like the hungry Tiger he was. Eden moaned again, and bit her lip right after, a bit annoyed. Why did she even think she could take control? There was no control whatsoever, just the guidance of desire and pleasure, driving her crazy and forcing her body to become a slave to all that passion burning between them.

"Ride me," he whispered.

Those two words were dangerous, but so tempting. Eden took a big breath in, and moved her body, slowly falling onto him. She moaned out loud, not bothering to hold back her voice anymore. She had intended to go slow, but

Dante betrayed her, grabbing her hips and pushing the last of it in. Eden gasped at the stranger inside. She was out of breath already, and he hadn't even moved yet, thankfully. Just having their bodies united was enough of a challenge already. Eden had her legs in a dangerous position, open wide around his hips, and Dante could move as he pleased while he held her waist. She took deep breaths, her lower body already in a turmoil of sensations. She was well aware of the intense stare coming from those two golden eyes below... Her blonde hair falling over her shoulder, her skin and exposed breasts in front of him, and blurry blue eyes, Dante was given absolutely everything, a front row seat to her expression, so easy to read. Eden was panting a bit, her cheeks flushed with red, and her lips open to catch her breath. Dante didn't move to kiss her, he just stared at her, relishing in how vulnerably beautiful and enticing she was...

Eden decided to move before he did, her hips slowly undulating. She stared right back at him, as if to prove she could excite him too. Not that she needed proof, though. The Tiger was obviously very, very excited. His hands on her hips were firm as if he needed something to hold onto while he held back his wild desire. Eden was left alone in charge, and she liked that. She rubbed their bodies slowly, like their foreplay earlier, except that now, all of him was rubbing her insides. The sensations were reaching all the way out to her lower abdomen. She could move her body above his, and Dante was quietly lying still, although his eyes weren't quiet at all. She could see those golden rings glowing with passion and excitement, and she could guess the raging battle between his passion and his desire to keep it tamed. Eden loved that; she loved that he was battling his own instincts to let her lead. She accelerated, breathing harder and making the mattress bounce under them. Dante grimaced, his breathing becoming more intense as well. Now he wasn't so still anymore. Everytime she came down, he'd move his waist to collide with her, reaching deeper and making Eden moan louder each time. It was as if each time their bodies got farther away, it would be even more savage when they collided again.

"Harder..." she gasped. "Do me harder..."

Dante didn't wait to comply. Holding her waist, he moved faster, helping Eden bounce on his lap. She wanted to feel him, feel him more until she went insane. The fierce rubbing of their bodies together felt so good, so hot, and yet so savage. She couldn't believe she had waited this long to give in to him, but she didn't regret it. It was just... too good. All of Eden's senses felt electrified, and she didn't want it to stop. When she was tired of moving back and forth so fast and so hard, Dante took over, his hips moving fiercely under her, lifting her from below and making her legs go weak. Eden felt hot, and her own voice resonated loud and clear.

Dante loved that voice. He wanted her voice raspier and more worn-out from their love-making. The Tiger's pounding under her had gotten merciless, and he wasn't getting tired of it. Eden moaned, and he groaned, their voices making it all so real and indecent. Their wild sex was nothing short of passionate, something so hot and fierce, it was almost animalistic. There were no sweet words needed, no gentle caressing, just the furious expertise of two adults, excited and needing relief in each other's bodies. She wanted it hard, and he was giving it to her. Eden had closed her eyes now, but her hot body bouncing in front of him was even more enticing. From the delicious sounds of her voice and how her body trembled, he could tell exactly what she wanted. Her hands were holding onto his shoulders to keep herself steady, but she had lost all reason already. Eden's only focus was on their wild sex, the sensations, and how her inner regions flowed with pleasure.

It was indecent how much she liked such fierce sex, but Eden had forgotten all about the reason why a while ago. She just wanted this, she wanted him so bad she'd forget everything else. She just needed to be taken hard right now, and he sure was giving it to her.

"Eden... Eden... Oh, you're... good..."

Eden heard his groans under her, and it was driving her even more crazy to hear his deep voice. He kept repeating her name, as his pleasure wasn't stopping either. She opened her teary eyes to see what was going on below. She hadn't realized how sweaty they both were from all this... exercise. She leaned forward to make him shut up, and his lips had a bit of a salty taste. Even his sweat tasted good... She was definitely going insane. Still, Eden cried out again when he grasped her hips and suddenly shoved himself in deeper. Her lower stomach was a hurricane of hot sensation, begging to be released. She tried to clench and hold it in a bit longer, but his voice... As soon as she released his lips, unable to focus on any decent kiss right now, she'd hear his manly groan of pleasure, and it was driving her crazy. How could he sound so sexy? His voice was so deep and captivating... She moaned again, and leaned forward to bite his lip. Dante smiled, but he dared to slow down to focus on their kiss... Eden enjoyed the tongue play, but he shouldn't have stopped. She kissed him even more fiercely, and once their lips parted, she gagged him with her hand, her hazel eyes glowing with the fierceness of a goddess.

"Move," she ordered.

She felt him smile under her fingers, and without pushing her hand away, he moved. Eden resumed moaning and trembling right away, his pounding more relentless than ever. She could feel herself getting so wet it was indecent, and her pleasure was about to reach its peak like a waterfall begging to flow. She moaned, while he was condemned to breathe through his nose under her. She enjoyed this little victory, although she knew he was willingly giving in to her.

Eden tried to hold it in as long as she could; still, it was too tempting. She wanted it. She wanted it bad... She held it until the last possible minute. When she finally let go, she cried out loud as a firework exploded in her lower stomach, making her whole body feel like lightning. The waves hit one after the other, making her inner walls throb and relish for a long while. Eden felt the tingling under each inch of her skin, and shivered for a long while as her body relaxed. She had barely felt Dante coming too, but he was breathing heavily, and then grabbed her wrist to free his mouth.

"...Kiss me," he said, still panting.

Eden chuckled. She was satisfied to see him exhausted too, and the tiger on his chest moving up and down with his breathing... Her fingertip followed the line of black ink, and his abdomen reacted. She smiled. One of his hands was caressing her thigh, the other still on her wrist.

"...Eden, kiss me," he insisted.

She was still staring at him but not moving.

"Say please."

He raised an eyebrow under her imperious tone. Eden was still trying to catch her breath, but her hazel eyes were glowing with confidence, and something a bit defiant too. They were still in the same position, bodies united, but now they were staring at each other, both tired and panting but still very awake. Dante didn't move, still lying under her, a drop of sweat running down his shoulder.

"Say please," she repeated, a hint of excitement in her eye.

"...Please."

Eden smiled.

"Good Kitty..."

She caressed his cheek and finally leaned over to give him that long, slow, and sexy kiss.

# CHAPTER SIXTEEN

Eden rolled on her side, exhausted. How late was it now...? She didn't remember falling asleep. She still felt a bit sweaty, but... content. At least the wild sex with Dante had somewhat managed to make her forget all about her earlier troubles. As if he would have stopped at one round only; she should have known better with that hungry Tiger. Not satisfied enough after doing it once, he had turned the tables for a second round, and a third one... Eden had passed out at some point. She was already tired from the Dive, so this really wasn't a smart thing to do.

She just had sex with Dante De Luca, the Italian Mafia Boss. Eden felt a bit foolish, but she didn't regret a thing. First, because the sex was good. And second, because it was obvious this sexual tension between them would have needed some release sooner or later... Grabbing the sheet, she sat up, looking around for Dante. The room was empty, though. The only thing that had changed from earlier was the orange light of the sunset outside and the temperature, a bit colder. Eden frowned and got up, using the silk sheet to cover herself. She grimaced as she felt her insides react. They really had done it raw... That bastard. She sighed. She really hadn't bothered either, to be fair... When had Dante left the room? She was so tired, she hadn't even noticed.

Eden sighed and walked around, trying to find her clothes before going to the bathroom. They had been thrown all across the room, quite literally. She was surprised to find Dante's shirt among them. Had he gone half-naked...? Eden took it as well and walked with the bundle of clothes to the bathroom.

To her surprise, Dante was there.

Not just that, but he was sitting on the floor with his head in his hands, grimacing. Eden completely forgot about the clothes, letting them fall at the doorstep, and walked up to him.

"Dante?"

She grabbed his wrist, but he barely seemed to acknowledge her presence. The frown between his eyebrows was making her worried. Eden knew the face of pain all too well.

"Dante, what is it? Talk to me."

He finally opened his eyes, and strangely, they were now black. Not gold, but as black as coal; the irises had completely changed colors. Eden gasped. She hadn't expected that. He was staring at her blankly, as if he couldn't see her through the pain. Eden sat a bit closer. She didn't dare touch him more than her fingers on his wrist, so she was just waiting to see how he'd respond to her, her heart beating fast. What was going on?

"...Is it your head?"

Eden wasn't sure if she could touch his head or not. She had noticed he'd strangely frown sometimes. She had guessed early on he was putting up a front all the time, in front of her and his subordinates. She had no idea what that was about, though, and she wouldn't have guessed it was that bad either. Eden was more flustered to find Dante so vulnerable than to learn there was something wrong with him. He was usually so good at keeping his emotions in check, so this was taking her by surprise. Still, she couldn't ignore this and walk away. Not now that they had gotten a lot more intimate...

"Talk to me," she said, trying a more authoritative tone. "Dante."

"My head... hurts," he groaned.

She had figured this much, but Eden was glad to have managed to make him talk at least. She knew how hard it was for herself when her phantom pain kicked in.

"Do you need me to fetch you something? Water? Do you have meds?"

She couldn't imagine for someone as wealthy as a Zodiac not to have at least some headache medicine. Drugs and medicine were among the most expensive items in the Suburbs, but it wasn't completely out of reach. Not for someone who owned a whole building and probably many more. Eden glanced at the little cupboards, but she couldn't remember seeing medicine in those she had opened before, only clothes and bathroom products.... She was about to get up to search again, but Dante suddenly grabbed her arm, keeping her right where she was.

"Dante..."

"Stay."

His voice was more hoarse and lower than usual, but even without that, Eden wouldn't have moved. She was unsure of what to do, but she wouldn't leave him alone. Not after what he had done for her before... She changed positions, sitting down on her knees to get a little closer to him. Eden kept her hand on his wrist. She wouldn't have been able to move it anyway as Dante was firmly holding onto it.

"Talk to me," she said, swallowing her saliva.

He took a deep breath. She could tell he was fighting the pain and trying to win over it.

"...I should have stayed in bed with you," he whispered between his teeth.

Eden glanced around and the fact that he only had his underwear on, he was probably about to take a shower when... this happened. How long had it been? His skin felt cold to the touch, and their bed was definitely still warm...

"Yeah, you should have," she said. "Can I do something?"

"Just... stay with me."

Eden nodded. Dante was taking deep breaths, obviously trying to wait until it passed. With her free hand, Eden gently began to stroke his hair, very slowly and softly. Dante let out a long sigh of relief, and his shoulders relaxed a little. He closed his eyes and leaned his head down. Eden felt strangely happy by that sight. An almost-naked Dante, looking so vulnerable, and tame for once too... This strangely felt a lot closer and more intimate, seated together on the cold tiled floor of the bathroom, than when she was riding him a few hours ago.

Feeling a bit daring, Eden silently leaned in closer and kissed his forehead very, very gently. To her surprise, that was enough to lessen that frowning of his a bit. Dante's breathing seemed a bit calmer too, and his grip on her wrist loosened. She waited for him to say something, or feel better. Eden wondered how long it usually lasted and how many times it happened. Considering how a usually cool-headed and calm man was entirely overtaken by the pain, Eden didn't even want to imagine what he was going through right now. She could only sit by his side, and be as patient as he needed her to be.

After a while, Dante moved her hand, still holding her wrist, to place it against his cheek. Eden naturally opened it to caress his skin. She brushed the little spikes of his growing beard under her fingers very gently.

"I can't... stay away from you."

She hadn't expected to hear him talk, and he had spoken so faintly, Eden wasn't sure what she had heard. She tried to calm her heart and smiled.

"I noticed."

He found the strength to smile back, although it was more of a tense, edgy grin.

"I don't know why," he resumed. "Just... the nearness of you makes everything else so faint. I want you... I need you."

The possessiveness in that last sentence was a lot more like Dante De Luca, and it made Eden smile. She gently kissed the corner of his lips, but backed away as soon as he tried to kiss her lips.

"Come on, let's get in the bathtub," she said. "I'm getting cold, and I'm all sticky too. You could use that shower as well."

"I don't smell good?" he chuckled.

"You smell like a musky tiger. You still have a meeting to attend with the other Zodiacs too, don't you?"

Dante sighed. He didn't try to move, though, so Eden had to pull him up until he stood, and they walked together to get into the bathtub. Dante stood against the wall, while Eden had the shower running with hot water from above. She'd never get tired of that luxury... She could go without food, but a hot shower a day was her definition of heaven.

Leaving him alone for a while, Eden freed her hands from his grip to take her shower, grimacing when she got to cleaning her tender parts...

"You animal," she groaned.

She heard him chuckle behind her.

"You're the one who jumped on me."

"That's not..."

"Rode me."

"Stop it."

"...and gagged me."

"Will you shut up?!"

He laughed again, but at least, he didn't insist. Now Eden was blushing, and began furiously washing her hair with generous amounts of citrus-smelling shampoo. Her long hair was a pain to take care of, and some days, she was on the verge of shaving it off or something. Now, she was happy she had kept it until the day she could give it proper and decent care...

To her surprise, larger fingers suddenly came from behind to help her massage her scalp gently. Eden lowered her hands and closed her eyes, enjoying the impromptu massage.

"Feeling better...?"

"I should be the one asking you that," she retorted.

"I'm fine."

Eden wanted to insist he didn't look fine earlier, but that might have been too soon, and she wasn't one to prey on someone's weaknesses. That looked like a significant weakness, though, so she really wanted to ask. Instead, she stood silent, and waited until he was done. Dante took a long time, though. He was obviously enjoying this. His fingers made soft circles in her hair, washed the soap off, and then applied some other fancy product on each strand. If it wasn't for the hot water running, Eden might have been a bit embarrassed at their position, the two of them standing in the bathtub and sharing this intimate moment together.

"Dante..."

"Hm?"

"It's poking me."

"I know."

Eden rolled her eyes. He was obviously doing this on purpose and having fun. She liked it better when he couldn't do stuff like this because of his headache... She decided not to insist, though. It would be too easy for him to keep annoying her. Instead, she smiled and discreetly turned the tap to cold water...

"Ah!"

He stepped back and Eden chuckled, finally turning around and washing the conditioner out of her hair. Dante was now standing away from the cold water with a sullen expression.

"What is it?" she smiled. "Mr. Rich Tiger isn't used to cold showers...?"

"We could have had some fun."

"We had enough, and I just finished washing. So keep the tiger in check. We need to talk too."

The smile disappeared from his lips. Dante sighed and sat back on the edge of the bathtub, staring at her under the cold stream. They both knew what Eden was talking about, he just didn't look in a hurry to get there.

"It's nothing interesting."

"I'm your bodyguard," she retorted. "I need to know what I need to know."

Dante raised an eyebrow. When Eden was finally admitting she was his bodyguard, it was only to have the upper hand. He grabbed the shampoo to start washing his own hair, and Eden slowly turned the hot water back on. Oh, it was even better after a cold one... She slowly raised the temperature, to the point where her skin got all red, and it was one degree away from unbearable. Next time, she'd definitely take a proper bath in here...

"Your eyes were black too," she said.

That was one thing she was the most surprised about. Eden knew there were many different kinds of Parts available, some made of actual human bodies but genetically modified to have some extra properties. Those were the rarest and most expensive, of course... accessible only to the very wealthy.

"You didn't think they were naturally gold, did you?" he said with a smirk.

Eden frowned. Of course not... Dante sighed, and put his hand between his eyes. For a few seconds, she couldn't see what he was doing. He seemed to be moving his fingers and wriggling something around... until his skin came off. Not just a thin layer, but a large chunk. It began halfway up his nose, spanning the area between his eyebrows, and ending a bit higher on his forehead. Eden gasped.

Underneath that area, a large, blood-red scar was now exposed. It was one ugly scar, but what struck Eden the most was the visible hole in the middle. It was an obvious gunshot wound.

"...Who?"

"Enemies of my father," said Dante. "I was kidnapped, and they asked my father to pay ransom while I was being tortured to make him comply. He didn't give the money. He only sent Rolf to retrieve my body... Only to find out that I was still alive. So he sent me to surgery. In my father's book, surviving a gunshot wound was more worth his while than letting me be kidnapped. I woke up with new eyes to replace those that had been burned by the blast, the crushed bones replaced by Parts, and a synthetic skin to cover it, as a Zodiac

228

shall never show his weaknesses..."

Eden believed that easily. Actually, she never would have found out about that horrible scar if it wasn't for his headache, and Dante removing the synthetic skin covering it.

However, now that she could see this apparent gunshot wound on his head, there was serious doubt hovering in her mind. It couldn't be... right? The very precise spot of his gunshot wound was disturbing her. No, maybe it was merely a coincidence. It had to be. The Tiger and many of the other mafiosos always shot someone right in the head when they meant it to be a clear, clean execution. Moreover, Dante was of half-Asian descent. He had black hair and was tall... A chill went down Eden's spine.

"...How... How old were you? I mean, when you were shot?"

"Nineteen."

She let out a very faint sigh of relief. The timing didn't match. Adam had been shot when he was fifteen or sixteen, about ten years before. He would have been twenty-five today. Dante was shot at nineteen years old. Eden didn't know how old the Zodiac was, but it didn't match. For a few seconds, she felt stupid.

"...What is it?"

Eden blushed, realizing Dante had noticed her trouble.

"It's just... My brother Adam was shot in the same place."

Dante slowly nodded, putting back his fake skin. It was impressive how easily it got back into its spot and how unnoticeable it was once it was there...

"It was my father's favorite... spot to shoot at. Apparently there's an extremely slim chance of surviving this with the current weapons if the bullet hits right on the bone. Sometimes I wonder if he didn't shoot me himself."

"What do you mean? Didn't you see who shot you?"

"I probably did, but I don't remember it," he shrugged. "On top of the wound, I was bedridden for three months, and forgot almost everything about the previous eighteen years of my life. I only remember fragments. My father's harsh mental and physical training, growing up in his house among the other possible heirs... I remember some things so precisely it's striking, and some parts are completely blank."

Eden was shocked. She wouldn't want to lose her memories, no matter how hard it was. She would still cry sometimes, thinking about how she had been separated from her mother, about her happy childhood in the Core, but those were things Eden wanted to remember. She used the pain to grow stronger...

"So that's why you have those... headaches?"

Dante slowly nodded.

"Ever since then, I get them from time to time... There's nothing that can be done about it, medically. That's the thing about having a Part in your head, replacing your eyes, skull, and a part of your frontal lobe... The original body doesn't like strangers."

Eden grimaced. Given how much she had suffered after she had lost her legs, she couldn't even begin to imagine the nightmare of it being in his head... At least he had gotten a much better device than what was usually found on the market. Even the surgery itself ought to have cost millions. In her eyes, the previous Tiger was an idiot. He could have saved his money and his son, but instead, he had left it up to fate and ended up losing tons of money and feeding a filial grudge...

"Can I rinse my head now?" Dante asked with a little smile. "I'm not taking a cold shower."

Eden let Dante finish his shower alone, just in case he'd get any more ideas from the proximity of their naked bodies together... She escaped the bathtub and grabbed one of those fancy bathrobes he had. This place really felt more like a hotel than a home. It was too clean, too neat, and everything was like it was on display. It was pretty but cold, just like the marble floor under her feet. Eden walked up to the wardrobe, knowing she'd find some women's clothing like last time. She tried not to think about why Dante had them in there... Did they get this prepared for her? Was it for any of his women? Or was it perhaps just some weird instruction given to whomever prepared this room? Eden couldn't tell, and she didn't want to waste her time thinking about it. She was just glad most of it was her size.

She was actually more concerned with how she should dress herself for a meeting between the Zodiacs... She ignored all the flashy and sexy dresses to look through the piles of more casual clothes. She ought to find something she could easily move in or get rid of to use her legs... Eventually, Eden picked a black jacket to pair with a pale gray shirt, and some flared black pants. After finding some brand-new black underwear, she slowly dressed until Dante walked in, drying his hair with a towel. As soon as the Tiger's eyes gazed upon her choice of clothes, he frowned.

"...What's that?"

"You've never seen pants before?" responded Eden, buttoning her pants.

"I like you in a dress better."

"I'm going as your bodyguard, Dante. Not your hoe," she retorted.

"You can be a sexy bodyguard. That shirt is horrible."

He walked to the wardrobe and took out some backless top with pink strass that immediately reminded Eden of her outfits at the bar.

"This is more what I like," he said with a sardonic smile.

"You can wear it, then."

"I'd like it better on you."

Eden decided not to answer to his whim. Still, was the shirt really that bad? She glanced in the mirror, and the fitting really was worse than she imagined. It made her look somewhat sick, with her complexion. She sighed and took off her jacket and shirt. Walking up to Dante, she went to grab the top he was insisting on, but he suddenly lifted it out of her reach. She glared at him.

"Are you done playing yet?"

"...How about you go like this?" he asked with a smile.

Eden looked down. She was only wearing the pants and the black bra... Dante had his eyes on her exposed skin. She rolled her eyes and snatched the pink top out of his hands.

"Get ready, or you'll be the one to go in your underwear."

Although she wanted to look mad, Eden had a little smile when she turned around to put on the pink top. Dante's eyes on her and his bantering were merely a game, and after what they'd experienced earlier, she couldn't help but find it sexy. It was far from what she had imagined. Somehow, Eden would have thought, like most men, he'd have gotten bored and back to his serious self once they were done with the sex. She was completely wrong. Because they had actually done it now, and with quite an enjoyable memory of it too, their chemistry had increased. Not only did his little game excite her, but Eden found that she didn't just want to give in, she was actually craving more. She was just glad she had enough sense left to be more reasonable...

Ignoring Dante, who was now rummaging through the wardrobe to find his own outfit, she turned to the tall mirror on the wall. To her surprise, that strass pink top didn't make her look much sexier or anything. It was an old, vintage shade of pink that was rather discreet, and the strass wasn't too flashy either. She actually looked like a bodyguard, just a female one with a top that's a tad sexy... Deciding this was good enough, Eden walked back inside the bathroom to dry her hair, but instead, her eyes fell on a mysterious velvet box on the side of the sink... She frowned, as her name was engraved on it in golden letters.

"What is this...?"

She grabbed the box and opened it.

She was almost blinded by the dazzling set of jewelry inside. Eden had rarely gotten a chance to spot some real gems like these... and a chill went down her spine just thinking how much these cost. There were two long earrings, two smaller gold hoop earrings, a bracelet, a necklace, and a ring. The ring was too big for her to dare stare at. The necklace had a thinner design, like little pink petals and a flower on a golden line, but Eden still felt this was too feminine for her to wear... Even the bracelet was simple, just several lines of gold, but this was just too much. She took a deep breath and closed the box. Eden knew this was for her; all the jewelry was beautiful and exquisite. She just felt like she only deserved to wear that fake zircon ensemble in the dressing room of Jack's bar...

"You don't like it?"

Eden turned her head to see Dante, who was now looking superb in a black Italian suit, leaning against the door frame and staring with his hands in his pockets. From his confident smile, he could already guess some of her thoughts. Eden sighed and grabbed the hair dryer.

"...Not really."

She hated sounding like an ungrateful person, but this was just a lot to

231

process right now. She turned on the hairdryer to try to mute her thinking, but it wasn't working.

Why was he gifting her jewelry now? Right after they had sex? No, it couldn't be linked. They had sex just a few hours ago, it had probably taken longer to prepare all that, and a box with her name... Unless he predicted this was going to happen sooner or later? And even if it wasn't related to the sex, was it alright for her to accept something? She wasn't a whore. Why would she get presents from Dante? No, the real question was... what was she to him now? His people probably knew they were sleeping together, but what were his real intentions? She kept thinking about their discussion earlier, in the bathroom. It felt like the absolute truth.

From the start, Dante had acted... obsessed with her. It wasn't really about Ghost anymore, was it? Or was it because he thought he had Ghost, so it was the same? Eden just couldn't find an end to her looping thoughts. She tried to focus solely on drying her blonde hair, taming a couple of natural curls here and there. She was staring at her reflection, almost not recognizing this stranger. In just a matter of days, so much had changed, both on the inside and outside. She was now wearing some fancy clothes and perfume. She smelled good, she felt clean, and her blonde hair was shining too. There were no remnants of her dark circles from before, her tired shoulders, or the fear in her eyes... Did she really feel so safe now?

As Eden got lost in her thoughts, and her hair was now dry, she suddenly felt a hand on hers and jumped. Dante had come in silent as a cat, and was now staring at her from the side, with his mysterious smile on.

"...Why are you always so stubborn?"

His deep voice seized Eden's voice, leaving her without anything to answer to that. Instead, she watched him take the hair dryer from her hands and grab the little velvet box. He opened it, staring at its contents for a little while as if he wasn't certain what he wanted.

Then, his long fingers took out the bracelet. Slowly and without a word, he carefully put it around her thin wrist. Eden found it to be heavier than it looked, but it was really pretty... Before she could react, Dante was already moving to put the necklace around her neck. The movement of his fingers sent terrific hot and cold waves down her nape. Eden froze, making sure not to move an inch. She couldn't help but realize how well that piece of jewelry matched her complexion... and even her outfit. It worked together, but instead of a bodyguard, she now looked like some powerful woman boss... or a sexy office lady. When Dante grabbed the earrings, she took a step back.

"I... I won't wear it."

"But your ears are pierced?"

"I meant, all of that jewelry. I'm going to see the Zodiacs, not to work..."

Dante suddenly frowned. Something about that last line had upset him, but she couldn't figure out why. Still, he opened his hand, presenting her with the earrings.

"It's a demonstration of power like any other," he said. "I will look powerful if the woman by my side wears these..."

"Pretty rocks?"

"Expensive rocks. ...Also, I really want to see you wearing them."

Eden hesitated. The truth was, those earrings were really pretty... She liked them the most out of all the pieces. She sighed, and took them from his hand.

"Fine, but not the ring."

"Alright."

Dante agreed to her not wearing the ring so easily, Eden was a bit surprised. She silently put the earrings in, only to notice, once again, how great they looked on her... They made her neck stand even taller and thinner, showing off her jawline. Then, with her senses coming back to her, she turned to Dante, shaking her head.

"No, I can't, that's—"

He shut her up with a kiss. Eden couldn't react before his lips were on hers, but it was like an automatic reaction inside. Her stomach twisted, her skin shivered, and her extremities twirled... She answered the kiss a bit too late, but Dante was leading this one. She had been so careful not to kiss him, or at least, not when she feared she might lose control, but now... She was clearly losing it. Dante's possessiveness was transcribed in this savage kiss of his. His hand was on her neck, holding her head and grabbing her hair, as if he needed to hold on to all of her. Eden grabbed his shoulders, but she had a hard time focusing when his other hand was already on her waistline, playing with the edges of her top. He could easily slide his playful fingers under the fabric... She realized this was perhaps the reason he'd wanted her to wear this thing. Eden blushed, but with all the strength she could gather, she pushed him away.

She had to insist a bit, but Dante finally stepped back. They stared at each other, out of breath and excited by this tension between them. The remnants of their savage sex from earlier was still floating in the air, threatening to induce them into another round. Still, Eden kept her hands up, keeping the beast at bay. Dante smiled.

"...Wear it," he simply said.

"Fuck you."

"You're very welcome to, anytime."

He left, leaving a red Eden behind in the bathroom. She sighed and ran her fingers through her hair, mad, and a bit ashamed too. She had given in to his whim... again. Had she ever won against him? No wonder it felt so good to ride him and dominate... She sighed and turned to look at herself in the mirror, promising herself she'd get back at him somehow.

Eden finished styling her hair and, a bit curious, opened the cabinet. Perfectly displayed as always, there were many male beauty products, including cologne, everything one needed to shave, and even some things she didn't know how to use. Yet, in a little pouch, there were a few feminine products, all brand new. Eden took them out, having already understood she was free to use anything. She was so used to going big, like she had been trained at the bar, or doing nothing at all, but when it came to makeup, she struggled to do something natural. Still, she managed to pull it off, and once she was done with only her lips left, she looked her usual self, just a bit prettier and sexier.

She grabbed the lipstick, and began applying it on her lips. It was a darker color than she'd initially thought, something like a raspberry pink. Obviously, each layer would make it darker too, so Eden only applied it on the inside of her lips before spreading it around with her finger until she got an idea. She stared at her reflection in the mirror, and a naughty smile, a bit like that of a certain man she knew, appeared on her lips. A spark of craziness shining in her eyes, Eden applied a couple more thick layers of lipstick on her lips, with a smile.

"Dante!" she called, her heart beating a bit fast.

She didn't look so bad with that dark lipstick on, but it wasn't the best, and stood out way too much. Still, she needed to wear this a bit longer if she wanted to carry out her revenge…

Dante walked in, absorbed in his new tie. Eden pretended she was absorbed in the pouch's content to keep her head down and her hair covering her face, until he was close enough.

"What is it? I–"

Before he could finish his sentence, Eden grabbed his tie and pressed her lips against his. The Tiger stood there stunned, surprised by the sudden attack. He could probably tell something was off by the strange way she was aggressively kissing him, but Dante didn't push her off until Eden was done.

When she retreated, she got to witness first hand the horrible mess on his lips, and all around. Eden smiled, very pleased with herself. It now looked like Dante had been savagely attacked by purple lipstick… She chuckled while he touched his lips, visibly at a loss.

"What was that…?"

"Wear it," she ordered, using the same imperious tone as his.

Dante was stunned for a second, both eyebrows raised. He then turned to the mirror, only to see the mess. It wasn't really that bad, but it was obvious he'd been savagely kissed… He smiled.

"Alright."

Eden's smile fell.

"What?"

Dante gave her a quick wink and walked out, still busy with his tie. Eden was the one left shocked. He was kidding, wasn't he? He wasn't going like that to meet the other Zodiacs!

She hesitated several seconds, turning to her reflection again. That kiss had considerably lessened the layers of lipstick on her lips, but it was also a mess. Trying to focus on something else, she grabbed a tissue and used some water to fix it, but the gears of her brain were spinning at a scary pace. Dante couldn't be serious. He was probably just toying with her again. He'd take it off later and enjoy seeing her panic until then... Convinced of that, Eden finished preparing. She walked out, thoughtlessly picked a pair of shoes and ignored the smiling man in the corner of the room.

"Ready to go?" asked Dante.

Eden nodded, glancing his way. He still had that stupid smudge of lipstick on his lips... She crossed her arms and decided to ignore it. She didn't want to give in to his game this time. It was her plan to make fun of him, not the other way around. Eden was sure he'd take it off soon, even as they walked side by side into the elevator. Still, she wanted to erase that stupid grin off his face. Dante was visibly having fun, with his hands in his pockets and that wry smile of his, as he stared at the lights of the elevator while it descended slowly...

# CHAPTER SEVENTEEN

They arrived on the floor of Loir's playground, and as soon as she stepped out, Eden was greeted by a lot of barking and happy yapping. She lowered herself to grab Beer and hug the excited puppy.

"Kitty and Big Kitty!"

Apparently, Rolf hadn't left Loir's side this whole time. The bodyguard was sitting behind the hacker, and stood up, straight as an arrow, as soon as he spotted them. The only things that had changed here were that puppy toys and snacks were brought in, and Loir's empty pizza boxes had been replaced by a unique plate of half-eaten pasta.

"Boss, you have some–"

"I know."

Eden tried hard not to roll her eyes once again or look back to see his expression, and instead, she walked up to Loir.

"Did you find anything else?" she asked, trying to hide her embarrassment.

The hacker raised an eyebrow and shrugged with a pout.

"Find what? This stupid Map disappeared as soon as you left the room! The Master encoded it so it can only be used if you're around... and yes, this genius sitting in front of you tried to crack it! So vexing!"

Eden frowned. The Map was still there, though. Did that mean it had been reactivated when she entered the room? She approached it again, curious. Why would her master have given her such a thing? He must have gone to a lot of trouble to get it... What about this Map was worth it? Eden knew how valuable this thing was, but she couldn't understand why her master had decided to reappear now to give her this. What was he expecting of her? Eden knew her master well enough. He never left anything to fate. Every time he had done something or given her a mission, there was a point behind it. It wasn't always clear what, though, and she hated being left in the dark.

The events of the other night with that dark Overcraft came to mind. ...Could it be related? Because the old Dragon wasn't well, there was a lot of unrest already between the territories, but now this... Eden took a deep breath. Perhaps she was getting some hints ahead of time, but they weren't enough.

"What about the other things we found? The files?" she asked, turning back to Loir.

This time, the hacker put down the fork he had in his mouth and finally looked at his screens. He tilted his head, but with his completely dark eyeballs, Eden couldn't even tell which screen he was really staring at. Chewing slowly, he began running his hands across the keyboard.

"Well, the itsy-bitsy meanie Core has tons of useless information on his little ants. The Queen Bee runs her hive like usual... Ah, there was some data about their new regulations on aging... Oh, well, who cares? Come on, talk to Daddy, my pretties... Numbers, numbers, numbers..."

Losing patience, Eden walked to stand by his side and read the columns of data as well. Like Loir had said, a lot of it was just the regular type of data the Core always gathered about its inhabitants. Every single one of their movements was tracked by the Core's System: when they slept, what they ate, what they bought, wherever they went, who they interacted with, what they did... Eden shivered just thinking about how much it was controlling people's lives. The Core knew absolutely everything. Data was collected day and night relentlessly from people's SIN; each SIN was like a little cell, a part of the System, and implanted into each citizen's nape. It was invisible, yet omnipresent in their lives. Eden was glad she had left the Core; the System didn't care much about the SINs outside its walls. Although it was a one-way ticket to what most inhabitants of the Suburbs would call a peaceful life, Eden saw those things as a poison that slowly took their sanity away. She felt disgusted just thinking that all of her actions had once been watched and analyzed like some guinea pig in a laboratory.

"...Do you see anything about the Suburbs, Loir? Something in those files might help us understand why that Overcraft was in the neighborhood and wanted to be discreet about it...?"

"Here."

He zoomed in on some of the files, opening them to display rows and rows of data. It may have looked like numbers and figures to those who couldn't read code in the programming language, but Eden quickly understood the content as well.

"...What is it?" asked Dante behind them.

Eden showed the columns one by one.

"Those numbers are the codes of SINs from people in the Suburbs. According to the first numbers, these are reused SINs. An original SIN will always start with a 1, but these all have a 2 or a 3 at the start... They ought to be SINs that have been reconfigured for a new use like we do here. The following numbers represent data about their carriers: gender, age, district of birth, employment status, everything... I can't read the last ones, though, I don't know what those numbers are about. What the hell did they extract? SIN readings aren't usually that long. Loir?"

The hacker was already running the numbers to find out their secrets, frowning and making strange movements with his lips. Eden too was frowning and staring at the numbers, trying to make sense of them. What other kind of information was the System looking up about people from the Suburbs? Those numbers shouldn't even have been there in the first place! Each SIN was produced when a Core member was born and followed them throughout their whole life. It was only deactivated if they were expelled or if there was an issue with it, but it was rare even in those cases. Like they'd witness weekly, people banished from the Core rarely got to keep their SINs... mostly because the Core was afraid the people from the Suburbs would get a hold of them.

Over the years, everyone had understood that having a SIN was the first step into the Core's System. It was the major difference between them and those people: while on one side of the wall, they were given a brand new one right away, people in the Suburbs struggled their whole lives hoping to get one. They could do without, but there were a lot of issues. SINs were used to record employment, make money transfers, and have access to minimal health care. Otherwise, the old bank bills were still in use in the Suburbs, but their value couldn't be compared to the real money of the Core. That was the dilemma of the System: either they were fully in or fully out, and each side came with its own issues.

People like Eden, who had a SIN but lived outside of the Core, shouldn't have been on that list at all. Reconfigured SINs weren't part of the System; they were simply borrowing its most basic functions. It was as if the machine had been rebooted outside the network. It worked like a single, lone cell, not a part of the System... So how the hell were they looking at lines and lines of data on reconfigured SINs?

"Wait, did those just change?" asked Eden, staring closer.

"What?"

"Those lines, just there," she pointed out. "About five lines or so just changed their end numbers... Look! The ones below just did the same!"

"Funny funny..." whistled Loir, a grin on his face. "Why are you changing, little numbers... So interesting..."

"...Those are locations."

They all turned to Rolf, surprised. The bodyguard looked very sure of himself, though. He nodded as if to confirm his words, and pointed at the screen again.

"All of those are location coordinates. The first and fourth pairs of numbers are always so similar because they are in the Chicago area. This one should be somewhere near our position."

"Oh... You're so much smarter than you look, Cutie Pie!" Loir jolted.

"...Cutie Pie?" sighed Eden, putting a hand on her hip.

She really couldn't associate that nickname with the tall, stern man with gray hair standing next to them. Loir ignored her question, though, and Rolf didn't seem to mind, either. Eden rolled her eyes, but Loir was already entering the coordinates into a precise map of their surroundings, and the most precise one he had was that of the Apple they had acquired earlier...

Slowly, dozens of little red dots appeared all over the Map. Eden frowned and walked to get closer to the Map, staring at the areas where they had appeared. It was soon clear they were, indeed, people of the Suburbs exclusively. The Map's coordinates didn't specify an actual height, so all of them were like they were on the ground level, but gathering in large numbers. The more that appeared, the more Eden felt uneasy about this. Loir zoomed in on the closest territories. Because the Map was so precise, Eden could easily recognize which streets and buildings they were. Her eyes naturally went to her own building, where half a dozen dots had appeared... and Jack's bar. There were two there. She shivered, staring at those two dots.

"...SIN, call Jack."

She waited a few seconds, feeling very uneasy.

"Eden? Are you alright, honey? I thought you wouldn't call for..."

"Jack, where are you?"

"Me? At the bar, why? Are you coming?"

"...Who's with you?"

Jack paused. He probably had felt the tension in Eden's voice. She heard him breathe a bit louder.

"...With Rose. Just Rose. Why?"

Eden didn't answer, she just stared right at Dante, on the other side of the room, his arms crossed with a dark expression. This wasn't good at all. The System didn't just have information about the people of the Suburbs, it was also aware of where they were right now!

"Jack, deactivate your SIN after this, you hear me?"

"What? Eden, what the hell! What's wrong, hun?"

"Jack, I'm serious. There's something odd, the Core is fucking tracing our SINs. All of them. It knows where you are, right now. I have eyes on a Map with your exact location as we speak. So please, deactivate it, and you and Rose hide, okay? I'll come to get you."

"Wha–... Eden, what the heck... Honey, where are you?"

"I... Jack, I'll explain later, okay? Just trust me, please. I promise I'll come and... get you out of there, somehow."

For a little while, Jack didn't answer, making her even more nervous if that was possible. Finally, she heard him sigh.

239

"Fine, honey. If you say so. I'll... just stay with Rose in the basement for now, okay? Don't worry about us, we got everything we need down there, just don't be too long, alright?"

"I promise." Eden nodded. "Just stay there, I'll try to come soon."

With that, she hung up and turned to Loir, her eyes sending daggers.

"Why the hell are they tracking people from the Suburbs?"

"I don't have the slightest idea about that, Kitty," said Loir, looking serious for once. "I've got eyes on their list, and... they managed to locate and trace all those SINs, but they didn't finish the job. Look."

Eden had noticed even before he'd said it. As she looked at the full Map of the Suburbs, it was obvious some areas were completely clear of any red dots. Some only had one or two... which was nothing compared to the crowded areas around several blocks.

The pieces were starting to align. She turned to Dante.

"You think this is what that dark Overcraft was doing?"

"...It could be."

She nodded, but they had no way to be sure. The only certain fact was that the Core's System had somehow found a way to observe and trace thousands of people outside the Core and access their SINs, or at least their locations. Eden was more afraid of why they'd want that information and what they could do with it. Their anonymity was the people's best defense against the Core's arbitrary System.

"We are probably not the only ones who noticed..." said Dante, very calmly.

Eden frowned and turned her eyes to the Map once again, checking the locations where the SINs were being traced. Dante was right. Eden didn't know the exact borders of each territory, but everyone could at least tell the main areas apart. The more she stared, the more she could make out. The Rat, the Eagle, and the Zebra had hundreds of those red dots on their territories. So did the Arabian Hare and Dante's territory. The area where Eden lived probably wasn't fully scanned, and the Goat's too had a lot less than the others. The only territories with just a handful of dots were the Snake's, the Ox's,... and the Dragon's. Which meant only three out of the ten territories had been spared so far.

"Loir, can you find out how to undo this?"

The hacker chuckled and moved his skinny shoulders, massaging himself and making his nape bones crack.

"I can try, but only because it's you asking, Kitty. And also because I have my stomach full of delicious pizza... Can I get some coffee?" he asked with a high-pitched voice, opening his eyes wide.

"No," Eden and Dante answered together.

His attempt at trying to look cute only made him look weirder and creepier. The bald hacker sighed and turned to his screens again, actively looking around for an answer.

"See, Cutie Pie? You're the only one that understands me. Those two cold-hearted cats never care about poor, lonely Loir. They go away to play naughty stuff that's only for adults and they leave me all alone here with just work and work and... yummy pizza. I'm so glad I have my Cutie Pie here. Otherwise, I would be so, so lonely..."

"We're going," declared Dante, ignoring his rant.

"You can't leave me alone here!" cried Loir.

"Do you want to come, then?"

Just as he said that, Loir's expression fell. He slowly rolled away from them, shrinking in his chair as if he was trying to be engulfed in the leather.

"Uh... I'll stay here and keep an eye on the puppies..."

"Lock the room, without my dogs in it," Eden said immediately.

"If Kitty goes, the Apple stops working!" protested Loir.

"You don't need the Map, just the data. I'm not sure I want that thing for you to play with anyway. Just be ready in case I need to Dive."

"So mean... You bad, bad Kitties!"

She ignored him and walked out, grabbing Beer and Bullet one after the other. After glancing Loir's way, both Dante and Rolf did the same, making sure to lock the room behind them.

Meanwhile, Loir turned back to his screens and sighed.

"Agh, they are really too mean. How can they leave poor Loir alone here? So heartless! Now I'm all alone to play here and I don't have any toys left... Oh, well. I can always find some."

Suddenly starting to wiggle in his chair, Loir ran his fingers on the keyboard with a wry smile. He turned on his techno music very, very loudly in the room, so loud that the floor beneath him began vibrating. Yet, Loir didn't seem to care at all. He was dancing around in his chair, moving his arms in random directions, and making circles with the little wheels of his chair. It wasn't long before someone showed up.

"Finally!" exclaimed Loir, raising his arms in the air and visibly overjoyed to see the mafioso that had just walked in.

"You crazy bastard!" yelled the Italian. "Cut that out right away!"

He went to the keyboard, pushing Loir out of the way and turning off the music.

"Don't you fucking do this again, or I swear you'll regret it!"

His ears were still ringing from the crazy loud music. Everyone had heard the techno beat several floors above and below. It was unbelievable that the hacker had been able to stay in that room for even a couple of minutes without going insane or deaf.

"Oh, you're Margherita!" exclaimed Loir, completely ignoring the warning. "Can you believe they left me all alone? I'm so bored!"

"Don't call me that! The boss said to leave you locked up. If you take one step outside we will shoot you down!"

"Ooooooh..."

241

Loir tilted his head.

"You know, your games are not very fun," he said. "If you're going to play Shoot the Loir, you should at least give me a place to hide! Or some rollers... It's really not fun if you're just waiting for me to step outside!"

"Yeah, yeah, shut up, you crazy... and don't turn the music on again."

"Oh, no, you're not leaving, are you?"

"What now?" said the one named Margherita, rolling his eyes.

"What about my order?" asked Loir, looking shocked.

"Your order?"

"Of course! I'm hungry, and you came without a single pizza! I want... three Margheritas with pepperoni, a mountain of pepperoni, some pickles, and some peanut butter on it! It has to be organic peanuts, though!"

The Italian sighed.

He shouldn't have opened that door like the blonde chick had warned them...

# CHAPTER EIGHTEEN

The car had been moving for a while. Rolf, who was their driver again, touched his neck and looked up in the rearview mirror.

"Boss, it's Headquarters again. They're saying the hacker is being... troublesome."

Eden chuckled. Of course, he was. Loir's favorite game was testing people's patience, and from what she'd seen, Dante's men didn't have much. She was only surprised they hadn't given in sooner to his whims. He could get really, really annoying when he wanted to.

Dante glanced coldly at Rolf but didn't say anything. It probably meant they had to deal with this on their own. The news of Loir being burdensome was certainly not what he cared about at the moment... Eden crossed her arms. She missed the pups already. Rolf had entrusted them to one of their men, but she wished she had brought them in the car so she could cuddle and play with them, rather than suffer this tense situation here... Dante hadn't said a thing since they got inside the car, and it was annoying her a little. He even had his eyes closed, but she could tell he wasn't sleeping; his upper half was sitting upright and his breathing didn't match that of someone dozing off. It felt more like he was focusing...

"...Have you ever met another Zodiac?" he asked out of the blue.

"I've only seen the Rat and the Eagle... both from afar. Old Dragon Long never comes out of his place, from what I know... What about you?"

He chuckled.

"This isn't my first school reunion."

Eden frowned. Although he made it sound like a fun gathering, it was probably very far from it... It was no secret that all the Zodiacs were at odds with each other. Their only interactions were power struggles, and sometimes, direct fighting. It was rare for a Zodiac to show up rather than letting their underlings do the job, but it did happen a few times.

Eden tried to think of what she knew about all the Zodiacs, but it really wasn't much... Even if she had worked for some of them, she'd never met them directly. Loir usually handled their requests and he seldom let her know who they came from. It wasn't like Eden cared much until now, either. She usually handled the job and did her best to forget about it soon after. She didn't care who she worked with; the money that came in didn't have their name on it. As long as she could pay for her mother's bills...

"Which one is the crazy one scared of?"

"Probably the Dog," said Eden. "The only contracts he's ever avoided were the ones that came from the Russians or anyone under the Russian Watchdog's protection..."

Not every ethnic group outside the Core was strong enough, so a lot had rallied under a Zodiac they could align themselves with. In that aspect, the Eagle and the Zebra were among the Zodiacs with the most population in their territories. Hence, the Eagle also protected and oversaw people whose families originated from now-disappeared or ruined countries of Eastern Europe... people who had literally nowhere to go, even if they made it back to the other side of the Atlantic.

"...Aren't you afraid the Rat's only going to be there to kill you?" she asked. "You made your statement clear by going onto the Dragon's territory... and killing Yang."

"I'll just make sure that she doesn't kill me first."

Eden sighed. The Rat was known for her short temper, though. Eden had seen her kill people who had merely trespassed on her territory... Such a small community like hers wouldn't have survived if it wasn't for her peculiar character. Compared to the Chinese Dragon or the Japanese Snake, the Rat's population was more like a congregation of different ethnicities from South-East Asia. In a way, she was the protector of all those who didn't fit in those first two groups, nor with the Indian Ox. Despite her character, Eden respected her for being one of only two female Zodiacs...

"Have you met them all already?" asked Eden.

"They'd be dead if we had."

"I meant the three we're about to see."

"Yes."

She was surprised. From his earlier speeches, she thought Dante was out for blood with all of the Zodiacs, but now, it sounded more like he actually had some sort of half-decent relationship with them.

"...Do you think it will end badly?"

244

"No."

He had said that with a smile; he even grabbed a cigarette to smoke, opening the window. Eden grimaced. How could he be so reckless? Even if they were on his territory... Still, she kept her arms crossed, trying to suppress her urge to light it for him. She had done that gesture so many times at the bar that it had become an annoying reflex. She took a deep breath and looked the other way, watching out the window for enemies. Like before, they were traveling with two more cars, but she thought it was rather useless. If people were to attack them in those narrow streets, they'd most likely come from above... Dante was only lucky because the Mexican mafiosos liked to brawl in the open, but on the other territories, the other groups wouldn't be so direct. Unlike her expectations, though, nothing happened until they reached what seemed to be their destination. Seeing how Dante looked very relaxed, Eden thought it might not be the first time he came here to meet these people, either... Still, it didn't mean there was no danger. She waited in the car with him while his men moved around to check the perimeter for potential assassins. Eden tried to go back into her bodyguard mode, adjusting her jacket, when her eyes fell on Dante's lips.

He still had that lipstick on. He couldn't be serious about going in like that? His golden eyes caught hold of her stare quite quickly, and a wry smile appeared on the Tiger's lips.

"What is it? Should I have worn red instead?"

"...Enough, take it off," she said.

"You told me to wear it."

"I know what I said. I didn't think you'd be an idiot and actually do it..."

He chuckled, but clearly, he showed no intention of taking the stupid lipstick off. Eden was conflicted. Should she leave it like that? He was about to meet the Zodiacs like this and pass for an absolute idiot! Even worse, she was wearing the matching color on her own lips. She was going as his bodyguard; she didn't want them to know that they were sharing a bed! Yet, Dante, perfectly calm, was taking another drag from his cigarette and visibly enjoying her annoyed expression. Eden took a deep breath, trying to calm down. She couldn't believe this was now turning against her.

"Take it off," she insisted.

"You take it off."

She frowned. What was she supposed to take it off with? She didn't have a tissue or anything... She glanced toward the front seat but upon meeting her gaze, Rolf avoided her and quickly got out of the vehicle. Eden internally grumbled.

"Fine," she said.

She could always use her sleeve, it was black after all... Yet, when she tried to approach Dante's lips with her wrist to wipe them off, he avoided her.

"Not like that," he said.

"How, then? We don't have time for your little games!"

245

"Well, you started it."

"No, you started it when you decided what I had to wear. Now, can you stop acting like a jerk for five seconds?"

"...I want a kiss first."

Eden rolled her eyes. He really was going to be childish and whimsical until the end, wasn't he? Still, she decided to end this push-and-pull game with him. With a sigh and a silent prayer that she'd be able to keep her emotions in check, she leaned forward to kiss Dante. She saw him smile right before they both closed their eyes.

Their kiss had a faint taste of cigarettes. Still, Eden found herself quickly absorbed in it. Of course Dante wouldn't have settled for a mere peck on the lips... Soon, she felt his tongue on hers and his fingers in her hair, grabbing it and keeping her close. Eden tried her best to stay calm, but she could feel her heart pounding, and her blood heating up from the mere feeling of that long, passionate kiss. She tried not to give in, but it was hard to ignore those sensations tingling in her stomach... After a couple more seconds, Eden finally pulled away.

"Happy now?" she muttered with a sullen look.

"Very," chuckled Dante.

In front of her shocked eyes, he suddenly pulled out a handkerchief from his jacket and offered it to her. Eden glared, before snatching it and wiping off his lips in a couple of seconds. He was now a bit red, but clear of makeup and she angrily erased hers as well. She couldn't believe she'd been led on again... Angry, she exited the vehicle without waiting for him. He could get shot, but she wouldn't save his ass this time.

"The area looks clear, Boss," said one of the men as Dante finally appeared.

Once he stood up, Dante's attitude did a complete U-turn. Even Eden was slightly surprised by the cold mask that donned his face and brought all his men who weren't watching their surroundings to look down like obedient dogs.

The Italian Tiger had arrived. That realization seized in her chest, making Eden remember she had a role to play as well. Dante calmly walked around the car, no trace left of his playfulness from before. She placed herself right by his side, the only person allowed to stand so close to him. Everyone else was following from afar, like the legs of a spider keeping at an invisible distance. Eden was the only one close enough to see the details of his Italian designer suit. She brushed her blonde hair back, acting as professionally as she could. No one could see it, but she still felt the heat on her lips...

They walked inside a large and ancient-looking building Eden did not recognize. There was a great hall... Perhaps a school? It felt like the trip by car had taken a long time, so Eden couldn't tell where exactly they were now. She only knew they were somewhere up north, from the route Rolf had taken...

The place was full of the Zodiac's people, though. The minute they walked in, she could feel the pressure of dozens of stares on them. Each Zodiac's men were covering all exits, and staring at the newly-arrived group with distrustful eyes. Eden made sure to stay close to Dante and find a handful of possible emergency exits. She wasn't sure they'd get out as quietly as they'd gone inside... They walked up some large stairs, which split left and right, but Dante clearly knew exactly where to go. People were also letting them through without questions, despite the suspicious stares. One glance from the golden eyes was enough to persuade anyone...

Finally, two men opened the doors for them to another room. It was a former conference room, although it was now full of empty seats and everyone present was standing.

Eden felt the tension double as they walked into the room. The three groups present all turned their eyes to them. Eden tried to look composed, but internally, she had trouble calming down. Most people would never meet a Zodiac in their lifetime, thankfully for them. Now, she was facing three at once, all potential enemies. Although she was used to fighting, meeting three of the most powerful people in the area was still very impressive. Each of them had a very different aura from the people surrounding them, so much so that even without any introduction or distinctive features, she could tell which ones were Zodiacs.

"De Luca!" exclaimed one of the women, with a smile. "Finally, the Tiger makes his entrance..."

That was the only one Eden already knew. Thao, the Rat. Despite being surrounded by angry and hunky men, she looked very calm, even smiling at them, and playing around with one of her knives. Aside from the weapon she was playing with, she looked like any woman one would see in the streets. She was wearing a fitted black dress with black boots and leather, fingerless gloves. She wore her hair in two buns, but the loose strands of her black hair were dyed blue and burgundy, matching her unique makeup. She also had a few piercings on her ears, mouth, and eyebrows. Eden had no idea how old that woman really was. She looked young, but she has also been the Rat for longer than Dante has been the Tiger...

"We were wondering if someone had finally gotten rid of you," added the Dog. "Your bounty is attractive."

Unlike her smiling peer, the woman known as the Russian Watchdog was completely stone-faced. Eden couldn't understand why Loir was so scared of that woman... She wore a red suit that matched her lipstick and looked like she could have been some famous movie star with her short, platinum-blonde haircut, colored glasses, and jewelry.

"Thao, Tanya," said Dante, greeting them with a simple nod, "A."

Surprised, Eden glanced toward the only one who hadn't spoken yet. His name was simply A.? The Arabian Hare was younger than she had imagined but as mysterious as she'd heard. He had a very square face, a long nose, very short hair, and wore a long gray jacket with a black shawl and leather gloves. He looked strangely singular, with his apathetic expression and wide eyes.

Unlike the two women, he seemed like a nobody, yet he had that strange aura about him... He barely nodded when Dante acknowledged him. Had he been dragged there or something?

"I wondered if you'd come at all," said Thao, waving around her long black nails. "Since you never bother to answer messages..."

"I'm a busy man."

"We all are."

The hostilities had started already on a very hot-and-cold tune. Standing next to Dante, Eden could feel herself being dissected too. Standing around each Zodiac was a group of four to ten people, all immobile but ready for action. On their side, only four men had followed them inside. There was probably some silent agreement between the Zodiacs about not bringing a full army in...

"So you noticed them too?" asked the Russian Watchdog.

"Indeed."

"Damn Core," hissed Thao. "We should have shot down those Overcrafts when they showed up the first time. I'm sure the Dragon knows too."

"What of the others?" asked Dante.

"King and Sanyam confirmed they saw them on their territories too..."

"So did Lecky," nodded the blonde woman. "He'd be here if he wasn't so worried about that mad Пиаф Pasquale... When are you going to take care of him, De Luca?"

"Soon."

"We will take care of him some other time, Tanya," retorted Thao. "We should deal with the Core first. I don't like seeing those bastards sneak their machines in like that. What are they preparing?"

"They were scanning our territories."

They all suddenly turned their eyes to Dante, who was lighting up another cigarette. The two women looked baffled.

"Scanning them? Why?"

"And how do you know?"

Dante suddenly glanced toward Eden. She was surprised for a second, before quickly grabbing the lighter in his pocket, and lighting the cigarette for him. He faintly smiled, but she may have been the only one to see it... Yet, this small interaction between them had caught some attention in the room. Although she moved back to her original position, Eden felt A.'s eyes on her, very briefly.

"They were turning on some sort of tracking system," he said.

"Wait, tracking?"

"They were tracking everyone in the Suburbs who has a SIN implanted. The System checks their location every five minutes or so."

Eden was shocked. Was it really alright to lay everything down already, just like that? How much did he trust those people, exactly? Moreover, this was too big. The two women exchanged a look, both visibly doubtful. Tanya crossed her arms.

"You're not making this up, are you?"

"The reconditioned SINs cannot be tracked by the Core, De Luca," added Thao, shaking her head. "They are out of the System, out of its reach. Moreover, why would they bother locating our people? What does that information do for them?"

Dante remained quiet while the two women kept arguing about how impossible it was. However, they were suddenly interrupted. Although his voice was very low and so faint it was akin to a whisper, A. immediately got everyone's attention as he turned his eyes to Dante.

"...How did you get that information?"

Dante smirked behind his cigarette.

"From a Ghost."

Eden froze upon hearing Dante's words. She glanced at him, wondering what he was playing at. It couldn't be; he was planning to blow her cover now? He was insane! For a minute, she wondered if she should run or deny it. He hadn't mentioned her, though, just... Ghost. The message was clearly for her, yet the Tiger wasn't looking at her at all. He confidently faced his peers; the two women of the Zodiac looked baffled, and even A., who had remained stoic from the beginning, tilted his head slowly.

"...From Ghost?" he repeated.

"Last time I checked, Ghost refused to work for you," said Thao with a smirk. "I don't know what you did to them, but that was the rumor."

"We recently came to an agreement."

Dante was so confident that neither of them dared to ask again. It was obvious they still doubted him, but they just wouldn't question him anymore. Eden relaxed a little. He had no intention to reveal her identity... It was just for the others to trust the source of his information.

She slowly realized just how powerful of a being he was, even to other Zodiacs. Although the conversation sounded amiable, she had no doubt they'd all shoot at each other without blinking if the situation called for a fight. They were only conversing like normal people and politely keeping appearances for the sake of exchanging information. No one had checked how many weapons the other side had brought, or discussed how many men were allowed in. There were simply no such rules in the Suburbs. The Zodiacs had to impose their strength, and that was it. The four of them were standing, but visibly ready to run or move at any moment. Eden too thought she had to be ready at any moment, just in case things went wrong all of a sudden...

"So?" asked the blonde Russian. "What else did Ghost find? Is that tracking story true?"

"It is," nodded Dante. "I saw it with my own eyes. Using a map, we were able to figure out and confirm the positions of random people in the Suburbs using a part of the Core's System. It seems to update every five minutes or so."

"I don't like that," said Tanya, a strong accent surfacing with her anger.

"Yeah, me neither," hissed Thao. "If the Core found a way to track reconditioned SINs, they can track about sixty percent of the Suburbs' population."

"...What else did Ghost find?" asked A. with his low and slow voice.

Dante slowly took a drag on his cigarette.

"How about you tell me what you found first?" he retorted.

"As arrogant as ever..." hissed Thao.

"The black Overcrafts come about three times a week and only carry two passengers," immediately said Tanya. "A pilot and a co-pilot. They don't land either; I think they try to stay out of our weapons' range."

"You've studied them," said Dante, raising an eyebrow.

"I do not like those *придурки* on my territory," she groaned. "My men have been watching them ever since we first noticed them."

"...So have we," said A. "The Core is preparing something for the Suburbs."

He suddenly took a little object out of his pocket, making everyone alert. Eden moved to place herself in front of Dante, and most men in the room took out their weapons, pointing them at him.

The only ones who did not react at all to the threat were the Zodiacs. Dante took another drag on his cigarette and, very discreetly, put his hand on Eden's waist to gently pull her closer to him. She blushed, but no one else seemed to have noticed. The other bodyguards all had eyes on A., but the man didn't even look like he had noticed. Each of his movements was so slow; Eden even wondered why she had reacted to someone who looked so harmless... unless her instincts felt something past his apparently apathetic behavior. She glanced around, ignoring Dante's hand. She obviously wasn't the only one who had reacted... No, there was definitely something more dangerous than meets the eye about that guy.

Still, the little device he had pulled out was inoffensive. Everyone lowered their weapons, as if nothing had happened, while he fiddled with it.

"Ah... There we go," he said with his raspy voice.

A little beeping resonated in the quiet room, and a hologram appeared. It was another map of Chicago; it certainly was not as detailed as the Apple Pan had given Eden, since it was only 2D. Still, the map was very easy to recognize, with a clear line separating the Suburbs from the Core. A. pushed a button, and several colored areas appeared. Eden realized those were, more or less, all the different neighborhoods of the Suburbs, while the Core appeared in blue.

"...Where did you get this?" asked Thao.

"The Tiger isn't the only one who knows talented hackers..."

"Ghost?" asked Tanya.

Dante and Eden exchanged a quick glance. However, A. slowly shook his head.

"No... Courtesy of the Edge."

Eden gasped.

"You know how to contact the Edge?" she asked.

All eyes turned to her, probably surprised to hear her talk. Thao and Tanya's eyes went to Dante as if to silently ask if he was allowing this young woman to speak, but Eden didn't care about those two. Her eyes were fixated on A. The male Zodiac too had slowly raised his eyes to meet hers. They were still expressing nothing, but he stared at her for a while, before slowly nodding.

"I knew too," said Tanya, with a pissed expression, "before that stupid hacker of mine flew..."

Eden's expression fell. Why did she have a feeling that this hacker the Dog was mentioning was no stranger at all? Next to her, Thao chuckled.

"Didn't you say he had been captured by your enemies? So what now, you scared him off?"

Tanya glared at the Rat, but that didn't wipe the smile off of Thao's face. It was clear that that woman loved to get on others' nerves, but the Russian woman, as angry as she was, didn't give in, and ignored her instead.

Meanwhile, Eden felt a cold chill down her spine. If the hacker who had fled was Loir... did that mean he could really contact the Edge? He had never mentioned anything before... No, he had pretended not to know a thing each time the subject had been brought up. Eden had never asked openly, but still... Once again, she felt like Loir's past was a mix of lies and mysteries he had no intention to unveil. She glanced at the Dog... Was that woman responsible for Loir's state? Despite her appearance, Eden knew she shouldn't be deceived. No Zodiac had ever reached their position by mere luck...

"...Who's the blondie?" suddenly asked Thao, her tone colder than before.

"My new bodyguard," retorted Dante.

His tone was even colder than the Rat's. He glared at Thao with his golden eyes, warning her not to ask anymore. There was no trace of the smile he normally used to pacify Eden... The young woman didn't care for the Rat's curiosity, though. She was more intrigued by the enigmatic A...

"Can we get back to business?" sighed Tanya. "A. Explain."

The man finally stopped staring at Eden, slowly going back to his map.

"...The Edge got this last week."

"'Got this'?" repeated Tanya, raising an eyebrow.

"You mean they stole it from the Core," smirked Thao.

Ignoring the two of them, A. pressed a button on his device. This time, the blue area expanded considerably. Eden frowned. What did that mean? It was now going all the way into the Suburbs... about halfway in. Everyone in the room froze, visibly disturbed.

"A... What the hell is that supposed to mean?" hissed the South-East Asian woman, not smiling anymore.

"...The Core's expansion plan."

A few seconds of silence followed, everyone speechless. Tanya said something that sounded a lot like a slur in Russian, and Thao looked absolutely disgusted. Eden felt Dante's hand stiffen too. She was in the same state. This couldn't be good...

"It can't be," said Thao. "That thing is at least five times the size of the actual Core!"

"Their population is growing," calmly said A. "The Edge found this during a ride inside the Core's System... These plans are to be implemented next year."

"This is ridiculous. They can't expand that much in just one year! What of the Suburbs?"

"Something tells me they had no intention of sharing this with us," groaned Tanya. "So that's why you called us, A."

The man slowly nodded. He raised his finger, following the border of the blue area. Eden felt her head spin just looking at the line. This was huge, and not good at all. If the Core had decided to expand, they wouldn't care one bit about the locals already there. If the Edge hadn't found this and given it to the local Zodiac, what would have happened? Would the Core have marched on them, gotten rid of all the people living there without a second thought, overnight...?

"They plan to expand all the way to Oak Lawn, Cicero, and Wicker Park."

"This is almost all of Chicago from the twenty-first century," said Dante. "It looks like they are tired of the Loop..."

"We didn't move when they got past the river and built the wall on 90th fifteen years ago," hissed Tanya. "Now this? They already treat us like vermin, now they want to take our land too?"

"I feel like they had no plan to ask for permission anyway," said Thao. "If this is for next year, they probably just put the first step of their plan into action with those Overcrafts they are sending to the Suburbs... I don't care about them scanning the buildings, but with what the Tiger said, it is clear they plan to use the reconditioned SINs against the population."

"...They are preparing some sort of attack," nodded Dante, very calmly.

"What else did the Edge get?" asked Tanya, turning to A.

The man sighed.

"Nothing. They said this was all they could get us... They are busy with another Core. We are on our own..."

"What?! They can't leave us like this, those bastards!" said Tanya, adding a lot of angry words in a foreign tongue after that.

"...This is plenty enough."

The Tiger had his golden eyes on the map, and Eden was sure he was thinking about the one they had back at the headquarters too... The three other Zodiacs had all their eyes on him.

"We know what the Core is after," he said, a wry smile appearing on his face. "Now we can act."

"We know nothing, De Luca!" retorted Tanya. "This isn't enough!"

"We have our own hackers," suddenly muttered Thao, strangely calm.

"We can dig for more information on our own, now that we know what to look for. If De Luca has Ghost, we can investigate for ourselves. Who else has hackers?"

"Mine are not good," said Tanya, clicking her tongue, "ever since that rat fled..."

"...Let's ask everyone."

A. took his map back, slowly nodding for some reason.

"What do you mean, everyone?" hissed Thao.

"...Lecky has a decent hacker," said Tanya.

"...So does the Snake."

"Fuck you, A.!" roared Thao. "If you think I'm going to ask for help from that bastard Snake–"

"I'll ask Yasumoto," said Dante.

"...You?" snorted Thao. "We all know you're after Old Man Long's territory too, De Luca. Stay out of there."

"Stop me."

All the bodyguards from the Rat's side reacted this time, pointing their weapons right at Dante. Eden moved immediately, putting herself in front of him. So did the Italian mafiosos, all whipping out their weapons. Thao glared at the young woman.

"What's the matter with you?" she hissed.

"He told you. I'm the bodyguard," retorted Eden.

She was feeling strangely calm and composed, for someone with half a dozen weapons pointed her way. Still, she was in business mode right now and focused. She was collected and cool-headed enough to keep facing the Zodiac woman without blinking. Thao seemed to hesitate, facing a woman who wouldn't get out of her path. She glanced up at Dante, who was still taller than his partner.

"...You wry bastard..."

Dante answered with a chuckle, taking another drag of his cigarette. For a while, they kept glaring at each other, both sides tense. The only two to not care were Tanya and A. The Russian sighed.

"I'll contact King and Lecky. A., if those two kill each other, you contact the others."

A. nodded, his eyes shortly going to Eden again.

"...If he can contact Ghost, we need him," he said to Thao.

"Ghost can work for us too," she retorted.

"Not anymore," smirked Dante.

This only aggravated the woman, who looked even more pissed.

"Yasumoto is mine, De Luca. Don't touch him."

"Then you two kill each other quickly. I want the Old Man's territory soon."

"Enough, you two," grumbled Tanya, crossing her arms. "You can sort this out later. Unless you haven't noticed, we have other priorities now. Either

253

you convince Yasumoto to help or you get rid of him and take his territory. The rest can wait."

"...It's a race, then," chuckled Dante.

"Just you wait," hissed Thao.

Eden could barely believe her ears. Did they both just agree to try and kill the Snake? This was like her hearing a conversation out of this world. They were bantering about this like two children bragging about some brand-new toy they wanted to get their hands on... They were dangerous, all of them. No matter how slim and elegant that woman looked, Eden could recognize the face of a cold-blooded killer. The four of them were no children. They were no ordinary humans either. They were the Zodiacs, four of the people who controlled a whole city with fear and violence.

Suddenly, Dante tightened his grip around Eden a little, pulling her closer to him and taking her out of her thoughts.

"...Are we done here?" he asked the other two.

"I don't care how, but make sure you contact Ghost and get them to work for us," said Tanya. "We're going to need all the best hackers in Chicago if we're going up against the Core..."

A. simply nodded, not adding anything.

"Oh, I will," said Dante, confident as ever. "See you later, Rat."

Thao glared, but before anyone could add anything, Dante pulled Eden toward the exit, with his men following behind them. She heard another group following them out, probably everyone going back to their territories. Eden was still stunned by everything that had just happened, and in such a short time too. She had no idea how much time had really passed since they walked into the building, but she could tell it hadn't been long at all. They had come, listened to and exchanged information, and left. She had thought things would be... not so smooth. Eden couldn't even tell what she'd been expecting, but she was just glad they walked out alive. The Zodiacs were surprisingly... reasonable people. Or perhaps they were more careful of their actions in front of their peers. She had felt the danger surrounding each of them. Even the mysterious A... She was most curious about that man as he could contact the Edge. How? Was he a hacker as well?

"Eden."

She looked around, realizing they were outside. Dante chuckled, his arm still around her waist, keeping Eden close to him. She felt a bit annoyed that she had let herself be engulfed in her thoughts without paying any attention to their surroundings, especially when they weren't in their own territory. She quickly followed him into the car, only letting out a long sigh of relief once she was inside. Rolf started the car right away, finally taking them out of there.

"...What did you think?" asked Dante.

"I think the threat is real... Do you trust that guy? A.?"

"I trust none of them. But A. rarely comes out of hiding... so it means the emergency is real."

"...He seemed a bit strange. ...Is he a hacker too?"

"What makes you think so?"

"The Edge. They only work through other hackers, from the little I know... I doubt they'd just hand the information to anyone, especially a Zodiac."

Dante chuckled, finishing his cigarette. He opened a hidden drawer between them, which, to Eden's surprise, contained a crystal bottle of whiskey and two glasses. Dante swiftly poured himself a glass despite the movement of the car.

"You're right," he said. "A. is a hacker... Although we don't know his codename either. We only know him as A. We don't know much at all about him... not even his main residence. The previous Hare was a crazy bastard, a bit too trigger-happy... A. appeared during a meeting one day to claim he was the new Hare."

"That was it?"

Dante nodded and put the glass against his lips to sip some whiskey. Eden was shocked. So not even the other Zodiacs knew what had happened to the previous Arabian Hare... It was shocking. She sighed.

"That Thao too. What's your story with her?"

Dante shrugged.

"Another crazy one... Her thing is poison and drugs. Her older sister was the previous Rat, but she didn't last long... I guess their family wasn't a happy one."

"Do you think she'll really attack the Snake?"

"Not if we get there first."

Eden froze.

"...You were serious?"

"Of course I was," chuckled Dante. "You heard it. It's a race... That's why we're attacking tonight."

"Dante!" Eden exclaimed.

"Prepare yourself, Eden. You're going to help me wipe them out... or should I say, Ghost?"

Eden glared at him, unhappy with his smirk.

"...I never agreed to do this for you, and I never said I was Ghost, either."

"Oh, come on, we're past that now. I don't care about your name."

"What's your obsession with Ghost, then?" she retorted.

Dante suddenly paused, seemingly lost in his thoughts. That complex expression in his eyes intrigued Eden. He waited a few seconds and eventually sighed.

"I wish I could explain too..."

Eden glared again, unhappy with his answer. Yet, Dante remained silent and instead, took another drag from his cigarette. Annoyed, Eden took it from his lips.

"Stop smoking inside the car," she said. "It stinks and I hate it."

Rolf glanced at his boss from the rear mirror. Many would have gotten mad at that gesture, regardless of their position, and the boss was not known for his patience. Yet, to his surprise, Dante simply smiled, as if that cigarette being taken away by Eden was just funny. He brought his hand in front of his face to hide it, but he was definitely smiling... Rolf glanced to the other side after a quick check on the road.

# CHAPTER NINETEEN

The car ride continued silently, but it was clear the young blonde was upset by the boss' attitude. Arms crossed, frowning, she resolutely looked out the window, making sure not to glance in his direction. Eden was truly annoyed, and she could almost sense his annoying grin anyway. Done smiling, Dante slowly poured himself another drink.

"...You can't attack Yasumoto," she said after a while.

"Why not."

"He's crazy and, from the little I know, he lives in a fortress."

"I thought we were used to crazy by now. Moreover, his fortress is a technological one. Which is why I need you to help me get through."

"You want me to hack his house?!" she exclaimed.

"Who else?"

Eden rolled her eyes. He was insane, and she didn't sign up for this. Hacking the house of a Zodiac was completely different than infiltrating the Core with a quick trip in and out! Eden tried to remember as much as she could about the Snake, but nothing was good from what she recalled. Yasumoto was known to be temperamental, unforgiving, and violent. She had worked for the Japanese Snake once or twice before, and things had gone well only because she had done the job exactly as asked. Eden had heard about their ways, though; a mistake meant a bullet in the head. Loir had warned her before they took the jobs that other hackers had been killed for making a mistake or not fulfilling the task... Death threats were common in their world, so Eden had never backed down from a job, but... a frontal attack was very different.

Moreover, she had no idea what their server was like. She had never gone inside the Yakuza's stronghold, so she would be going in blind with dozens of lives on the line. Even if they were mafiosos, Eden couldn't fathom the responsibility of Dante's men all weighing on her.

"...Why do you have to kill that guy?" she asked. "Let the Rat do it."

"I like winning."

"You're just going to do this to satisfy your freaking ego?!" she shouted.

"I have a reputation to live up to."

"You're going to get yourself killed!"

"Not if you help me out."

Eden was shocked. Exactly how much did that insane man trust her skills? It was true she was good, but... she had no idea what she was getting herself into this time, and the Zodiacs weren't playing as nice or by the rules as per the Core's System. She may even have to face other hackers, which was another kind of problem she'd rather stay away from. Additionally, Eden felt even worse as he had turned this into a "you-and-I" situation. She felt like she was going to be his lifeline in this mad plan of his, and it wasn't sitting well with her at all.

"Listen," she sighed, "even if I somehow manage to hack into that fortress his place is said to be, I might get caught up with his hackers. I know for a fact the Japanese employ some, and I don't think any will let me in nicely, and even if I manage to gain control, they won't leave me be. This means that you can't rely on me to help you there! Also, with both you and the Rat going, it will become a real battlefield!"

"It wouldn't be my first one," chuckled Dante, sipping his whiskey.

"Well, then it's surprising you've made it this far. Zodiacs don't go after each other, you leave the small fry to try and do that!"

"Eden, if we have to go up against the Core, we need Old Man Long's power," he declared, very serious.

"...What do you mean?"

Eden had an odd feeling about all this. Earlier, it was clear all four Zodiacs were determined to end the Core's plan, but they weren't even fully sure of that plan yet. Still, it felt as if everyone was already gearing up for some kind of battle, and with the way Dante talked about taking the Dragon's territory, Eden was slowly starting to realize just how big everything was threatening to become. She wasn't sure she was ready for that.

As a lone hacker, it was easy to make intrusions into the Core's System, get in and out in a matter of minutes, and put it behind her. There were no real consequences on the line aside from her own life, like a nameless thief on their own committing a small robbery: easily done, and alone to bear the guilt and consequences if caught. But this... this was different. Eden could feel something big about to happen. She already hated the idea of Dante fighting another Zodiac, although he made it sound like a mere school trip. Now, she was starting to envision what would come after... what Tanya and A. were really thinking about when they said they'd warn everyone. The Zodiacs were truly about to fight. Not through their people this time, and not against each other.

They were prepared to fight back against the Core.

She felt her chest tighten. Eden was used to running, running away. She couldn't see herself on the frontlines of a large-scale fight against the Core. She shook her head and crossed her arms. Gently, Dante put his hand on her knee.

"Eden."

She turned to him.

"I don't care much about Ghost," he said. "The hacker I need and want is you, just you. Regardless of if you're really Ghost or... a girl in a pink catsuit."

Eden rolled her eyes. She'd make Loir pay for that one...

"I mean it," he resumed with a chuckle. "I saw what you are capable of. You're an average bodyguard, but the best hacker I've seen. If I'm going to take down the Snake tonight, I can't do it without you."

"...What if I refuse, then?"

Dante shrugged.

"Then, maybe we'll have more casualties. Or I'll let Thao's people die first..."

Eden shook her head, helpless. He was the definition of ruthless. Eden already could tell that once Dante had decided to do something, he'd do it regardless of the consequences. He was the kind of man who'd get his way no matter what. Even worse, his men would surely follow him into this madness. She couldn't understand why or how they had become so blindly devoted to him, but it was the truth.

She sighed, and leaned her head back, ignoring his thumb caressing her leg... Could she really do this? Eden knew nothing of the Yakuza's defenses. It would probably need to be checked by Loir first to assess the risks, but even so, there would be no saying how dangerous it would be. Her only positive point was that she'd very likely be away from the main action, away from the gunfights... and gunfights would definitely happen. Not only were they going to attack the Yakuza, but they might even have some altercations with Thao's men. Unless the Rat didn't attack tonight and waited for the next day or later? Eden had no idea, but she felt like that woman was probably just as ruthless as Dante. Moreover, he seemed sure they'd run into her... Eden let out a long sigh.

"...I hate you," she grumbled.

"I'll take that as a yes," he said, a smile on his lips.

She shook her head but didn't tell him otherwise. She wasn't sure, and she didn't feel like saying a definitive yes. She could always discuss it with Loir later... She had no idea how her crazy partner would react to it, but at least she knew he'd back her up if they decided to go...

"What about—"

Before Eden could finish her sentence, a massive explosion was heard behind them. All the cars around began honking, and Eden turned around to look out of the window.

The building they had left just minutes ago was on fire, large clouds of black smoke coming out of it. A bomb? Someone had planted a bomb at their meeting spot? Eden was shocked. They were inside that building not even a few minutes ago! She turned to Dante to see his reaction, but he had barely glanced. Even Rolf was only accelerating a bit, not looking concerned, as if they were already expecting this.

"What happened?" asked Eden, still shocked.

"I guess someone else heard about our little reunion."

"Who?"

"How would I know? We all have enemies, and we are each other's enemies as well. It doesn't matter who."

Eden felt a cold chill running down her spine. She glanced at the hand on her leg. This was the world of a Zodiac... a world even more ruthless, cold, and cruel than the one she knew. She had always thought she ought to be careful and look out for herself, but now, she was getting a glimpse of a world with even more dangers. One where the place they had stood minutes ago could be blasted, and he wouldn't even bat an eye at it. It was so scary, but it was a daily thing for Dante. Eden suddenly realized how sheltered and protected she had been, living in his headquarters, in his apartment. Perhaps she was in more danger than ever now, solely based on the place she had agreed to take by his side. It was frightening to stand so high and only now realize how close she was to the edge...

"Eden."

Him calling her name shook Eden like an electric shock. She turned to him, a bit lost, but Dante had that very serious expression on.

"Don't be afraid."

"I'm not afraid," she replied.

Eden couldn't explain the emotion that was boiling up inside her at that moment. It probably wasn't fear, but something much more complex. A feeling that couldn't be described with normal words, something she had yet to fully understand and embrace. A bundle of so many things, Eden couldn't detach her heart from it. She was stuck in that leather seat, with a narrow view of her future, and many, many questions unanswered.

Who had blown up the building, and why? It felt odd they would have missed the Zodiacs if they were trying to kill them. Or had someone stayed behind and been injured, or worse? Strangely, Eden couldn't imagine either Tanya or A. being killed so simply...

"What kind of woman is she? Tanya?" she asked Dante.

"...Why are you asking that now?"

"If we are to work with the Zodiacs against the Core, I ought to know."

"Not all of them."

260

"But Tanya you do get along with, don't you?" Eden insisted.

Dante sighed.

"More like we don't have much to fight about. Her territory is farther up north, so we have several neighborhoods in between us. It's not like I particularly dislike her, either... We need the Watchdog to oversee the northern border, hence her nickname. That woman is level-headed, smart, useful, and she doesn't annoy me. That's pretty much it."

"Anything else?"

"...She's former military."

"Military?" repeated Eden, shocked.

"I guess she has that in common with you... She was from the Core, until something happened, and she got kicked out. She had to start over from scratch and took over after the previous Dog passed. She extended her territory by making alliances with the once-enemies of her predecessor... Now she has a lot of the North, which she shares with Lecky."

"Lecky... That's the Goat then?"

"Aleksander Lecky," nodded Dante. "That one I've never met."

Eden had only heard about the Goat... It was the one Zodiac that didn't care much about its people's real ethnicity, race, or background, which also made it one of the most chaotic. The history itself wasn't very clear. Some said the Goat was initially a group of gypsies. Others said it was the forgotten religions assembled or a former West-European civilization that hadn't made it to the Core... Nothing was really clear, and no one really cared. The Goat was said to be the Zodiac of those who didn't belong to any of the other Zodiacs, and that was probably the one truth everyone could agree on. It also made it one of the most dangerous... There was reportedly a lot of infighting, and the Zodiac spent a lot of time trying to pacify his population.

Eden tried to mentally recapitulate what had been said that day, and, from the looks of it, only two of the Zodiacs wouldn't be involved: the Mexican Eagle and the Japanese Snake... which meant the other Zodiacs would be ready to work together against the Core? Eden was surprised. She wouldn't even have fathomed a meeting like the one she had witnessed was possible, so imagining this many Zodiacs working together was still unreal to her.

"...Do you really think we can stop whatever the Core's preparing?" she asked with a sigh.

"Yes."

"How?"

"That, we have yet to determine... Although, I think Ghost might help us, don't you think?"

Eden rolled her eyes. How could he still tease her in such a situation? She was already tired just thinking about it.

However, she did understand they had to do something. Everyone knew the Core wouldn't mind stepping over thousands of people, as long as they were the Suburbs' citizens, to get what they wanted. This was a daily thing for them: living with the impression of being the lesser people, those who didn't deserve fresh air, real plants, organic food, or hot water. Eden felt bitter each time she remembered her childhood in the Core.

She had very faint memories, but she knew that, even then, she was different from the other children in the Core. Her family lived in a large, beautiful house with a huge garden and a high fence. They didn't receive visitors, and Eden had no memories of playing with other children... only her mother. It was as if... they were living in a bubble, away from the rest of the Core, but with all the luxuries it could offer. It was strange. She didn't like to think about those times, but she sometimes wondered. Why had she been forced to suddenly leave? Why had her mother made her run to the Suburbs, as if... as if they were chased? She remembered that scary night. Her mother's panicked whispers, in the cover of darkness. Them running in the streets, hiding in the shadows, aiming toward the wall. The tears, the fear. The pain of her bare feet, and the soft touch of that plushie she had held against her the whole time.

"Eden?"

Dante's voice took her out of her train of memories. She turned, and he was staring at her, looking curious and concerned. Eden cleared her throat.

"...Can you drop me at the border of the Eagle's territory?"

"No. Why?"

"I want to stop by Jack's bar."

"I thought it was in the Dragon's territory."

"It is, and not on your way."

...And it isn't your territory either, she wanted to add. Eden knew how dangerous it was for Dante to go on the Dragon's territory at the moment. With Yang dead, probably even more so. Yet, the Tiger chuckled, sipping more of his whiskey.

"Rolf. Drop us off at the bar."

"Yes, sir."

As soon as they had crossed the Tiger's territory to get to the Dragon's, Eden had been extremely tense. She couldn't believe Dante was crazy enough to venture there again after what had happened the last time. Yet, the three black cars were indeed making their way through the Chinese neighborhood, dozens of eyes following them. The cars' windows were probably tinted so people outside couldn't see them, but Eden could feel the glares nonetheless. Perhaps she would have glared too if she had been outside of that car. The people had a way of knowing when someone dangerous was passing by, someone like one of the Zodiacs. Moreover, the situation in that area was dire.

Old Man Long's state left his whole territory vulnerable, and the first effects could already be seen. To Eden's surprise, a few stores had been closed and barricaded, and she was seeing more Caucasian and Hispanic people than before. The other population groups were already trying to stake a claim on the territory even before the Old Dragon passed for real... She didn't like this at all. They were like hungry dogs looking for bones to pick. Eden liked the Dragon's territory too much not to care. Although it was obviously a predominantly Asian population, White people like her were tolerated, and no one would mess with her, unlike in some other territories. There was a deep respect for each individual, instead of a constant nerve-wracking climate of fear and anger. Because the Dragons were long-lasting leaders, they had plenty of time to make their people feel at ease and strengthen their borders too. Hence, even people like Jack and the girls who would have been rejected or killed in half of the other territories could work in the blurred margins of the Dragon's property.

She turned to Dante.

"...Have you ever met Old Man Long?"

"No. Only his lieutenants," Dante answered honestly.

Eden wasn't surprised. Long was known to keep to himself, and his men respected him too much to let their leader be put at risk... They probably wouldn't have allowed him to meet any of the other Zodiacs face-to-face.

Despite Eden's worries, the cars finally arrived without any issue in front of Jack's bar, or what was left of it... While the cars parked, she had a chance to see how badly that poor establishment had been treated during the gunfight. The entrance was a wreck, and only the security roller shutter didn't have any bullet markings on it, since it wasn't down at the time of the fight... Eden let out a long sigh and got out of the car. Dante followed right after her, grabbing a cigarette right away to light up. Trying to act the part of his bodyguard, Eden looked all around for potential threats, but aside from some curious stares, they were only grabbing attention so far, not real danger...

Dante's men surrounded them, the drivers staying in the car in case they had to leave in a hurry, so their group really stood out. Eden found it annoying, but it was probably inevitable. She walked up to the door and put in the passcode for the roller shutter to lift it. The thing slowly moved up, revealing the door, once again in a poor state from all the bullet impacts on it... Eden grimaced, and opened the door's lock with another passcode.

Inside, a frightening silence reigned. The whole room, previously so lively and joyful, was dark with a dreadful atmosphere. Eden took another step inside, the wood creaking under her feet. She could still smell the gunpowder, the alcohol, and the blood that had left large stains on the floor... There were no bodies, but it didn't make a difference. A stench of death was still floating around, marking the bar forever. She slowly walked in, following the trails of blood. Her eyes fell on the sofa, and she remembered the sight of her colleagues' bodies: Bella's twisted leg and June's body that hung like a broken doll. Eden took a deep breath, running her hand through her hair, trying to calm down.

She could feel Dante behind her, but he didn't say a word. The smell of his cigarette was almost welcome at this moment. Eden didn't even glance back to see how many of his men had followed them inside. Less than a handful, from what she could hear... She walked down the stairs behind the counter and knocked on the closed door.

"Jack, it's me! Are you there? Are you okay?"

"State your name!" yelled a voice from the other side.

"It's Eden, Jack," she replied, her shoulders relaxing a little. "Open up."

"Wait! Tell me somethin' only Eden would know!"

"Seriously?" she rolled her eyes. "Jack, open!"

"How did we meet?" he asked, ignoring her.

Eden frowned.

"You saw me kicking two guys' asses, and you offered me a job to work for you as a bodyguard... It was late one afternoon, and you were on your way to open the bar. I got into a fight with two guys who were following me and you offered to help me out... I beat them up by myself. You offered me a drink here afterward, Jack... Come on, open up."

The door finally opened. Jack was there, frowning and holding his shotgun with one hand. He looked tired and was wearing some old gray sweatshirt and joggers. Once he saw Eden, he visibly relaxed, put down his weapon, and opened his arms to hug her.

"Eden, thank God! Come here, ya babe!"

The young woman chuckled and happily walked into his embrace. Jack's strong arms around her lifted some weight off her back. Eden had been worried about him all this time and felt guilty she couldn't come in person sooner... Still, there was nothing of that in Jack's hug, just a brotherly relief to see her. He gently pulled away, checking her out from head to toe, concerned.

"Oh, you crazy chick... Sorry about all that, you know how they imitate people's voices and all nowadays... Oh, thank God it's really ya... Are you a'right?"

"Yeah, yeah... How are you?"

"Getting bored in here," said a voice behind him.

"Rose!"

Indeed, standing a few steps behind Jack was Rose. Arms crossed, she let out a long sigh upon seeing Eden. She wasn't the type that would hug her, but she did seem relieved to see the blonde. Unlike her usual sexy dresses, Rose was wearing a crop top and some simple jeans, her hair up in a high ponytail of red curls. The two of them did look like they had a rough time, and from the dirty stains on their clothing, they had probably been trying to clean the place too...

"...How are you two?"

"Lucky to be alive, I tell ya!" said Jack.

"We sent Bella and June's bodies to their families before you called..." explained Rose with a grimace.

"What about the others?" asked Eden, looking at Jack, worried. "Do you have any news?"

"With everything going on, Xixi's probably trying to find herself another patron before it's too late," scoffed Rose. "Minnie said she was going to disappear for a while, but she's fine."

"Aside from the twins, I warned the other chicks not to come for a while, babe. Lula said the Eagle's goin' fucking crazy with everythin' going on... The only one we ain't heard from is Dalilah..."

"Yeah, she probably found some rich guy's place to hide at... or she got herself killed."

Eden nodded. With everything going on in the area, it felt rather fair that each of her colleagues was trying to survive on their own... She hoped they would be fine, but she couldn't afford to look after them too. Plus, they all had their own backgrounds, connections, and resources they could rely on. No one could make it far without some wits to ensure their survival...

"...Eden, who did you come with?" suddenly asked Rose, her eyes pointed toward the ceiling.

Eden had almost forgotten about Dante and his men. They hadn't followed her downstairs, but they could hear them upstairs walking all around.

"Are you still with him?" squealed Jack, opening his eyes wide.

"Who? Who are you talking about?" asked Rose, frowning.

Eden and Jack exchanged a glance. He hadn't told her? Eden was sure Rose would have known by now, but Jack helplessly shook his head. Rose caught on to that.

"What are you hiding, you two? Who is up there? You said Eden was hiding with her hacking partner."

"You told her about that?!" exclaimed Eden, shocked.

"You chicks are driving me crazy with all your secrets!" whimpered Jack. "You know how Rose is when she wants to know somethin', don't ya glare at me!"

It didn't stop Eden, but Rose ignored both of them to walk upstairs before they could try and stop her.

"Rose!"

She arrived on the ground floor right before Eden, who sighed, finding her facing Dante. Rose was visibly shocked, but still didn't lose that haughty attitude of hers, with her arms crossed in front of the Italian. Amused, Dante smiled and dragged on his cigarette, his eyes going to Eden as she arrived next to Rose.

"Seriously? You were with him all this time?" said Rose, raising an eyebrow as she turned to Eden.

"Yes, and don't give me that look."

"I'll give you whatever look I want. I can't believe it... You, with a Zodiac...? What the hell?"

She glanced at Eden, scrutinizing her from head to toe as if she was re-evaluating her or trying to find a detail she missed before. That attitude annoyed the blonde even more, and when Jack finally popped upstairs as well, he found the two women glaring at each other in front of an amused Italian.

"...Are you sleeping together?" Rose asked Dante.

"Don't answer that," growled the blonde.

"Yes."

"Dante, shut the fuck up!"

"...I can't believe you," scoffed Rose. "After all your speeches about how you hated the Zodiac... And it had to be the Tiger, of all people."

"Can you pack up your damn ego for a minute and mind your own business?" retorted Eden, pissed.

"What do you like about her?" Rose asked, ignoring her.

"She's my bodyguard."

"Dante, I said shut it!"

He chuckled and brought his cigarette back to his lips, very amused by the banter between the two women. Meanwhile, Jack, looking desperate over the situation, kept glancing with worried eyes toward the open door and Dante's men standing there. Rose sighed, annoyed by Dante's evasive answer.

"Damn it... You're hot but you have weird tastes."

Eden shook her head, mad at Rose. She hated when the redhead's overinflated ego got the best of her. Rose hated to lose, in terms of beauty and seduction, to any of her colleagues. She was even worse over handsome, powerful, or rich men, and Dante happened to be all of those.

"Are you done?" she said, glaring at Rose.

The redhead shrugged, but she was still glancing Dante's way with curious looks Eden didn't appreciate.

"...Babe, did you learn more about that tracking stuff?" asked Jack, frowning. "Is it over?"

"No, it's far from over, and there's more. The Zodiacs think the Core is about to take more of the territories."

"Wait, what?" said Rose, finally shifting her eyes from Dante to Eden. "More territories?"

"Yeah. It has yet to be confirmed, but plans for an expansion were found, all the way to the former I-90 Express."

"Are you kidding? That's this area too!" shouted Jack.

"Sounds like the kind of shit the Core would pull, though," scoffed Rose. "What are you guys going to do?"

Eden glanced at Dante, who hadn't said a word since she had asked—rather, ordered him to shut up. She sighed.

"I'm not sure. We have—"

Before she could end that sentence, gunshots resonated, and they all lowered their bodies as a reflex. After a second, it was clear the gunshots weren't coming from their location, though. The echoes were most likely from a few streets away, but it was enough for all of Dante's men to have pulled out an impressive arsenal of weapons. Those who were inside closed the door, and Eden was sure all those outside got in position, ready to protect their boss if the fighting approached.

They were almost completely in the dark, the only sources of light were from the basement they had come out of and the burning tip of Dante's cigarette reflected in his golden eyes.

The three of them waited for a bit, but the gunshots died as quickly as they had started. After a few more seconds of silence, Jack let out a long sigh.

"My God..."

"What was that?" asked Eden, frowning.

"Babe, this neighborhood has been fuckin' cut-throat since the rumor about the Dragon has been goin' around! The Snake's people keep tryna attack the area now; they've been terrorizin' the locals. The Dragon's lieutenants are tryna keep 'em out, but there are also some internal struggles going on..."

"They all got much more agitated after Yang's death," added Rose, glancing Dante's way again. "They know they have to act fast if they want to claim the territory and have a chance to defend it. The Rat made sure everyone knows she wants a piece of it too."

Dante glanced toward Eden as if this was another reason to justify his new crazy idea. Eden ignored him, turning to Jack.

"Are you going to be alright?"

"Alright? Babe, I just spent three days in this place! I still have my head on my neck, but a'right, I don't know! I'm Black, gay, and a drag queen. What do you think they are going to do to me once the next head's in charge?"

"They will want to get this place back too," said Rose, glancing around the bar. "The whole street is an entry point to Chinatown and a hot place for all the customers from the Core... but I guess it won't matter much if the Core wants to claim back this area anyway. It might not be worth fighting for a place that's going to be destroyed soon, Jack."

"I ain't leaving my bar! Do you know how hard I worked my ass off to pay for it? And yes, I mean that literally!"

Eden and Rose exchanged a glance. Of course, Jack would never leave his bar... Neither of them wanted to abandon it either. Both women were very different in many things, but they both valued this place as one of the only places that would welcome them when they had nowhere else to go. They had both slept here a few times, out of money to have a place to go to or walk through Chicago with fresh oxygen. All the girls Jack had employed had a special relationship with this bar, and although none of the others were there, Eden was sure there would be no other place the girls would like to work more than here...

"...I'll buy it."

All their eyes turned to Dante, who was calmly lighting another cigarette.

"...W-what do you mean?" asked Jack, a bit hesitant.

"I'll buy it. I will own the territory soon, and buy this bar with it. You can keep running it once I'm in charge."

"You want to take the Dragon's territory?" said Rose, raising an eyebrow.

"Dante, can I talk to you for a second?" Eden said, annoyed.

Rose and Jack exchanged a glance, wondering if they were supposed to go back to the basement, but Dante chuckled.

"Sure... You two go and wait in the car."

If they were surprised by his order, neither of them dared to ask or refuse. They walked silently past the Italian, his men opening the door for them, leaving the pair alone.

With only the two of them left in the room, Eden crossed her arms, upset.

"Can you stop making decisions so rashly for once? You're not going to take the Dragon's territory overnight, and Jack doesn't need false hope like that."

"Tonight I'm raiding the Snake's territory," he said. "The Dragon is next."

"Dante!"

"My decision is made, Eden, and I'll do it with or without you, although I'd rather it be with you. I'm not letting you go either way, and I'm keeping your friends in my protection to make sure you're not tempted to run away again."

"So you didn't have enough hostages before?" she grumbled.

"Your pets don't really count."

"I'm talking about Loir!"

"Me too."

Eden rolled her eyes. It was truly impossible to negotiate with that man; he was just living in a different world from her.

"...Alright, fine," she said. "I'll help you. But you have to promise nothing will happen to Jack, Loir, and Rose."

Dante simply nodded, as a little cloud of smoke escaped his lips. Eden let out a long sigh. She was tired of fighting with him about every single crazy decision of his... At least she had secured Jack and Rose's safety, for now. She looked around, but there was nothing here she needed to take. All her outfits downstairs were Jack's anyway.

"Let's just go," she grumbled, walking back to the entrance.

"Can I get a kiss first?"

"Fuck you," she retorted, walking past him.

"Are you sure? I'm sure Rose would say yes..."

"Kiss her and I'll really kill you."

She heard him chuckle behind her. That jerk...

# CHAPTER TWENTY

A headache was added to Eden's bad mood on the ride back. Perhaps it was actually a consequence of everything piling up from earlier, but she felt like her head was about to explode. She remained silent, staring out the window, and ignoring Dante the whole time they were in the car. Once again, they were alone with Rolf; Rose and Jack were in one of the other cars. The Italian cars crossed the Dragon's and the Eagle's territories without another incident, which amazed Eden. Either everything was too quiet, or there was something going on elsewhere. Regardless, she was relieved when they finally got back to the more familiar streets of Little Italy. Strange how the once-hated area had now become the safest one for her...

Still, Eden relaxed once she could get out of the stuffy, closed space she had been trapped in with Dante. She didn't like their argument earlier, and she didn't like being backed into a corner because of his reckless decision. Eden felt like she was walking on a fine line, like the edge of a cliff that would soon make her plunge to her death... It was as if that man had no fear at all. For a survivor like her who had been constantly aware of her weaknesses to survive, she couldn't understand Dante's unwavering calm and assurance...

Once the cars finally stopped in front of his building, Eden was the first to step out. She let out a long sigh and glanced above at the sky. It was turning dark gray, not a good sign. She could tell it was probably going to rain, perhaps a storm too. The wind was picking up.

"Wha..." said Jack, looking up at the building. "I can't believe places like this are inhabited by actual people!"

Eden felt a bit embarrassed, as she knew how small Jack's studio was; it was even tinier than her place. She didn't say a word and followed Dante and his men inside. Only Rose looked unfazed, as she was probably used to such places from her most prominent customers.

"What now?" she asked, glancing around as if she was going to put up an offer for the place, or live there permanently.

"Now, we get ready for tonight," replied Dante with a chuckle.

Eden glared his way, but she wouldn't have been able to tell what angered her the most: his crazy idea to attack the Snake as a competition with Thao, or the smile he exchanged with an interested Rose. She walked ahead, ignoring him.

George came out of the elevator, almost running into them, and went white as soon as his eyes met Dante's.

"B-Boss!"

"What's going on?" asked Rolf, frowning.

George glanced at his boss' second-in-command, visibly unsure, and the duo of strangers behind them. The other mafiosos had scattered as soon as they had stepped in, leaving the poor young man to face the five of them.

"A... We, uh... The hacker..."

"What about Loir?" groaned Eden, suddenly worried.

Dante was slowly taking another drag on his cigarette, but the glare in his golden eyes was clear: whatever George was about to say, he'd better say it quickly and be careful with his words. The man swallowed his saliva, looking down as if he was putting the sentence together in his head.

"W-w-we lost him, Boss."

"What do you mean, you 'lost him'?" repeated Eden, furious. "He can't even walk!"

"I-I know, but... he complained about the pizza we brought, and... for a while, he was very noisy too, so we were just trying to watch from outside... but then, the cameras went down, and... when we got inside the room, he was gone..."

Dante and Eden exchanged a look. How could Loir be gone when he was obviously in no condition to walk? Eden rolled her eyes. She couldn't decide if she was mad at Loir for escaping his room, or mad at the mafiosos for losing him.

"What about my dogs?" she hissed. "Where are my dogs?"

George nervously glanced his boss' way, but from the way Dante remained calm and quiet, Eden was in charge of asking questions and fully entitled to be the one yelling at him. He looked back at the young blonde.

"I-I'm not sure... There was only one when we got in..."

"Oh, for fuck's sake!" she yelled, running down the hall.

Eden was worried. Where the hell would Loir have gone and why? He looked fine where he was before she left! He had been the one to let the Italians take him; how could he pull an escape stunt now? Moreover, why the hell would he take one of her dogs?!

She rushed to the elevator, furiously slamming the button as Dante, Jack, Rose, and Rolf followed her inside. Somehow, her colleagues had decided whatever was going on with her was their concern too. As the elevator went up, Jack couldn't help himself from whispering, although they could all hear him.

"The hacker, does he mean your partner...?"

"Yeah."

"And the dogs..."

"The pups I had with me the other day."

Jack grimaced but didn't ask more. To their surprise, Dante pushed the button to a lower floor than the one Eden was going to, and once the door opened, he leaned against the elevator wall, letting them through.

"Wait for us here," he said.

Jack and Rose walked out without complaining, going into what looked like some sort of very luxurious waiting room or perhaps a bar's salon. Eden couldn't tell, and she was too bothered to check. In any case, she knew Dante wouldn't do anything to them as long as she stayed with him. George glanced at the room too, dying to escape his boss and follow them. His eyes lingered on Rose's figure, but he quickly looked back down. The doors closed, and Eden glared at the elevator's screen as if it would have gone faster this way.

She ran out as the doors opened to the control room. Right away, a whimpering met her ears as Beer was trying to get out of one of Dante's men's grasp upon seeing his owner. The man, surprised to see his boss, let go of the pup and nervously assumed a stand-by position with the other mafiosos. Beer ran to Eden, who grabbed him right away, but she was already glancing around the room for a hint. Not only were Loir and Bullet gone, but so was his desk chair...

"How the hell did you manage to lose him?!" shouted Eden.

The men didn't look scared of her, but Dante's presence alone was obviously what made them terrified. She ran her hand through her hair, trying to think where he could have gone...

"...Our men are already looking throughout the whole building for them," suddenly announced Rolf, a finger on his neck. "They are not on the upper floors or near the entrances. They didn't leave."

Eden frowned. She did believe it was very unlikely Loir could have actually left the building without Dante's men catching him. She could understand he had hacked their system and hidden himself from the cameras, but there was actual human surveillance at each entrance, and that was something even Loir couldn't evade. That was why he had never physically left their previous building, and instead...

"...Do you have a basement?"

"A basement?" repeated Dante, amused. "...We do have an underground garage."

"If he's still in the building, he's definitely there..." she sighed.

"...What would he do in a garage?" asked George, who couldn't help it.

"Don't ask."

They ran back into the elevator, this time hitting the button for the lowest floor. According to the panel, there were three underground levels, but they stopped at the first one.

It opened into a wide garage, with dozens of black cars lined up. The closest ones, though, were much more colorful and luxurious; probably Dante's personal collection. Eden tried not to look too long at any of them, even the gorgeous bikes. She had always dreamt of having one...

"Did he possibly steal a vehicle?" asked Rolf.

"How the hell would he drive?" scoffed Eden. "He's too scared to even step on the sidewalk by himself... No, he's probably just hiding in here... Loir!"

As her voice echoed in the parking lot, no one responded. Eden sighed and put down her pup.

"Go get him!" she said.

The pup happily barked and began running across the large parking lot. Eden couldn't tell if Beer was only having fun with all that space just for him or if he was actually running to his twin, but she followed him nonetheless. After a while and some more barking, another pup's bark answered, making her feel relieved. At least Bullet wasn't lost... The pup appeared from under a car and ran to her, not looking upset in any way.

"Now, where is that idiot..." she sighed.

As the pups began playing together, Eden kept walking between the vehicles, unsure where to look. Rolf and George both arrived to help her look, although they seemed unsure about what was going on.

"Why would the hacker come here?" whispered George, probably worried about his boss hearing him.

Dante, who was leaning against one of his cars near the elevator, was smoking another cigarette and watching them, with clearly no intent to help.

"Loir!" Eden roared.

Where the hell was he? She kept checking inside the cars one after another, around the area Bullet had come from, as he probably had hacked his way inside one of them... With the tinted windows, it was taking a long while, though. Moreover, she wondered why Bullet was out if Loir had gone into one of them. Worried, she glanced toward the exit of the garage... He couldn't have gotten out for real?

"Here!" suddenly exclaimed George.

He pushed Loir's desk chair from between two cars, making Eden roll her eyes and join him.

"Where the hell... Loir!"

Suddenly, she froze, after she heard something. From his shocked expression, George had heard it too.

"...Was that snoring?"

Eden rolled her eyes and held her hand out.

"Give me your gun."

"What? I'm not giving you my gun, you crazy wom–"

Before he finished his sentence, George glanced toward his boss and, with lightning speed, changed his mind and handed her his weapon with a grimace. Eden sighed and lifted the weapon. She fired two shots in the air, the detonations resonating in the empty parking lot.

A high-pitched yelp came from two cars away, with the loud bang of something hitting metal. Eden gave the gun back to George and walked over to where the sound had come from.

"What the fuck, Loir?!"

She got on all fours, and finally found the hacker, lying under a vehicle, grimacing and massaging his head.

"You scared me..." he whined. "I thought we were under attack..."

"Your ass is going to be under attack if you don't crawl your way out of there before I come and get you!"

The hacker whimpered, but he obeyed, using his arms to get himself out of there. Beer and Bullet came along to bark and happily play with him, thinking there was some strange, fun game going on. As soon as Loir was out from under the vehicle, George pushed the chair forward, but the hacker ignored him, sitting against the car and grimacing again at Eden.

"Why are you so mad at me..."

"Why the hell are you here with my dog?!"

"What? I only came here for a nap and Bullet wanted to come along..." yawned the hacker, rubbing his neck.

"A nap?" repeated George, baffled. "In here?!"

"So what? I love the smell of rubber and gasoline. It's very soothing."

"Loir, you can't disappear out of the blue like that!" yelled Eden. "You don't take my dogs anywhere and you don't leave without telling someone where the hell you are! Do you know how many people could be trying to kill you right now!"

"I do have a dozen names at the top of my mind. Do you want alphabetical order or–"

"Loir!"

He grimaced.

"So much yelling... I get it... It can't be helped. Those crazy people locked me up without any food or a nice place to sleep, so I had no choice but to get out and find a very comfy place..."

"Oh, so now we are the crazy ones?" scoffed George.

"Your name is Pesto, how is that crazy?"

"You're the one who calls me that, you damn—!"

"Stop giving in to his nonsense," sighed Eden, raising her hand to have him shut up. "It only makes him want to continue... Loir, get on your chair, we're going back upstairs."

"So bossy... Are you the one in charge now that you've laid down with the Big Kitty?" asked Loir with a pout.

"W-what? How the hell do you..."

Loir suddenly noticed Eden's angry expression, and that what he had said probably shouldn't have been said out loud. With a confused expression, he tapped his index fingers together, visibly unsure.

"Well... You know, it can't be helped. There are cameras everywhere in this place. They don't have any security, either, so I—"

"Loir, shut the fuck up and get back in that chair before I permanently imprint your inked face onto this damn floor."

He squeaked and obeyed quickly, pulling himself up with some effort. With a long sigh, trying to calm his blushing, George pushed him back toward the elevator, not daring to add a word. After what he had just heard, which confirmed everything he and his peers had already been suspecting, he just didn't dare to utter a sound. This hacker truly was asking for a beating... Perhaps that woman was just not daring enough to beat a disabled man. She only angrily walked back to the elevator, her pups struggling to follow her until Rolf picked them up.

Their strange group arrived at the elevator, Dante waiting with a grin.

"Welcome back," he said to Loir.

"Why is she always so grumpy?" Loir whispered back, unable to realize he was still too loud for anyone not to hear him. "You must be bad at massages if she's still so—"

"Loir, I said shut the fuck up."

The doors to the elevator closed and no one added a word; only Dante's amused chuckle could be heard, and Eden's glares were alternating between him and the hacker, unable to decide which one she was the maddest at.

It finally opened again into the control room Loir was staying in, and he rolled his desk chair alone back to the desk as if nothing had happened. Eden followed him, deciding not to let the hacker out of her sight this time. Meanwhile, Rolf put down the pups and leaned toward George to whisper.

"Get rid of our Chief of Security."

"But..."

"Trust me, it's either you or him."

The young mafioso glanced toward his boss' treacherous smile and ran back inside the elevator.

"Now what?" asked Loir, massaging his shoulders. "I hope you brought back some fun for me!"

"I did, but I have some questions first," said Eden, crossing her arms. "You didn't happen to work for the Dog, did you?"

Loir froze in the middle of his stretching movement and his pale face got even whiter under all the ink.

"I d-don't know who you're t-t-talking about..."

"Are you sure?" said Dante with a smile. "I could call Tanya right now and ask her. Tanya Raha, the Dog. Sure you're not familiar?"

Loir shrunk in his chair and turned to Eden with a very uncomfortable expression. This time, he looked really upset, his hands on his knees and almost trying to hide himself behind them.

"I may have... worked with her... a bit..." he whimpered.

"So you're the hacker she supposedly lost?" said Eden.

"Perhaps...? I mean, I may have fled after she threatened to freeze my toes and make rolled sausages with them..."

"She said you were captured."

"Please don't tell her I'm alive," begged Loir. "Do you know she puts you in a freezer and makes you into ice cubes for her gin if you make her unhappy?!"

Eden sighed. She didn't really care if Tanya's threats were real or fake, but Loir genuinely looked scared.

"I promise I won't; however, she said you can contact the Edge. When I mentioned them, you always said you couldn't, so which one is it?"

Loir grimaced.

"I might be fine with her making sausages out of my toes after all..."

"Loir, answer me."

"I don't want to contact the Edge!" he grumbled. "They are even naggier than you are. They probably still hate me since last time; they won't talk to me after they kicked me out..."

"Wait... You don't just know them, but you were actually part of the Edge?" Eden gasped.

Loir shrugged and scratched his inked head with his black nails.

"Yes, yes... I was."

"How? For how long? Who are they?"

The hacker grimaced.

"That's a lot of questions, Kitty..."

"Answer her."

Loir glanced at Dante, surprised by his authoritative tone. With a frown, he slowly grabbed the huge cup on his desk and took a loud and long slurp with the metallic straw before he put it down.

"You two are so pushy... It's really not that interesting... Hm... I was kicked out about two years ago, I think?"

"Two years ago?" gasped Eden, getting excited. "So you know about the attack on the Miami Core?"

She couldn't believe she was talking to someone who had once been part of the Edge and committed one of the most rebellious acts ever against the Cores. Moreover, he had been right there, acting like a lunatic all this time and working as her partner! Eden had always known Loir was a brilliant hacker, way better than most, but with all of his paranoia and insanity, never would she have suspected this crazy guy in his basement was ever part of the most

275

significant hacktivist organization in the world!

"Oh, that one and many others: we hacked Miami twice, and New York," he counted on his fingers, "Houston, Atlanta, Charleston, Charlotte... all the Cores that were bigger than a hotdog stand, we tried to bugger them!"

"How...?" whispered Eden, completely shocked.

"The Cores all have the same architecture, Kitty!" He suddenly waved his arms. "Once you got the key to one, you have the key to all! The Architect did a good job initially, but all the dumbbells who tried to duplicate his work are no smarter than waffle toasters! And trying to make thief baboons protect something they don't understand? They wouldn't be able to increase the Cores' securities even if their butts depended on it! Those guys wouldn't even be able to do a three-piece puzzle!"

Eden sighed.

From what she knew, it was true. The Core was actually doing a great job of defending itself... by itself. The builders were only able to add security rooms around it to prevent intruders like herself from just jumping in without any sort of security first, but fundamentally, the Chicago Core was the only one to be able to modify itself, and it had been evolving since its creation around thirty years ago.

"So... You and the Edge know how to hack the Core itself?"

"Yes, ma'am. I mean, most of them."

"What do you mean by most of them?"

Loir tilted his head left and right like a pendulum.

"Well... You know how the first Core was built here, in Chicago? It's the oldest and meanest one. The Big Boss of Cores. The Bowser of all Cores! The others are mini Bowsers, so easy to kill, but here? Nope!"

"You said you guys could hack all the Cores!"

"All the Cores but one! This one, Kitty. The Big Bad Boy of the bunch, the Chicago Core. The Joker to this Gotham, the Chucky to this House, the Al Capone to this—"

"Yeah, yeah, I get the picture. Why this one, though? If the others are copies?"

"Because it's the Architect's best work before the old man disappeared, Kitty! God's masterpiece! He wouldn't let his epic creation get as stupid as it could become in the hands of some annoying little handless peanuts..."

"Loir," sighed Eden, tired of his antics.

"He made it smarter!" exclaimed the hacker, visibly delighted by this information. "The Architect worked for years on the Chicago Core to make it smarter, and he succeeded! It's like a newer version, one we don't have access to!"

"...So the other Cores are merely a copy of the first version of the Chicago Core, but because the Chicago Core was upgraded into some sort of... 2.0 version, the Edge couldn't hack it?"

"Yep," nodded Loir, grabbing his cup again.

Eden frowned. It did explain a lot of things... She had always wondered why Chicago seemed like such an important city to the other Cores. Historically, the Northern States Republic Union regarded New York City and Washington as its important cities, while the Southern Confederation was centered around Houston... Yet, Chicago was the one city all the other Cores seemed to turn toward; people from the other Cores were reportedly trying to migrate there, and this city was privileged by having a big Congress between the States' Senators.

"If he managed to make the Chicago A.I. smarter, why didn't he do it to the other Cores?" asked Dante.

"...Because he disappeared," whispered Eden.

"Bingo! Ten points for the little Kitty! Exactly. The Saint Padre of the Cores went missing around twenty years ago, right after he completed his masterpiece, but just before he could duplicate his latest Chef d'oeuvre to the other Cores. No one knows what happened to the old grandpa, but most likely? He's dead."

Eden remained silent.

The story about the Architect disappearing was one of the most known among the Cores, even though the government had tried hard to conceal it. It was just too big. For several decades, the man called the Architect had been considered a living hero of the modern world, one who had literally forged the twenty-second century. Originally, the Cores were simply meant to be isolated cities that remained independent of each other and the humans' main habitations while the rest of the land tried to return to its once prosperous state. Without the Architect, they would have been nothing more than bubbles of cities where the humans gathered.

The Core was now a fully autonomous system, capable of self-regulating its food productivity, energy use, and ensuring the livelihood of each inhabitant. Like the queen bee that controlled everything in its hive, the Core's newfound intelligence had been both the salvation of humanity and its jailer. It was no secret, among hackers, that the Core controlled the government just as much as the government thought it controlled the Core. The superior intelligence of that thing allowed it to overrule human decisions if it came to think its own were better, and most of the time, that was precisely the case.

As a result, the Architect had been seen as both a savior to humankind and a genius that made sure the future generations would survive, but the man had also received heavy criticism for allowing a machine to rule over humanity. Not only that, but after it had first been put into place, the government had used the Core to justify every time they had chosen to murder a citizen or send them to the other side of the wall, banished here to the Suburbs. The Core calculated how many people could survive inside its walls, and the closer the humans were to that number, the more comfortable they could live. At first, everyone had thought this system would be fairer, allowing all to receive the same as their neighbor, abolishing the differences between the rich and the poor.

Things hadn't turned out that way.

After just a few years of experimenting with the Core's System, anger had grown within the population. Some were against sharing and wanted more, always more, than the little rations of food, small spaces to live in, and constant monitoring of all their expenses. The solution had been easy: the fewer people the Core had to take into account, the more those who were left would have to share between themselves. Hence, the government had begun its mass trials, recorded in history books as the "Great Legal Purge". Under the cover of deep reformation of its society, the government had simply killed or kicked out the people who couldn't afford to stay, the ones who were easy to kick out, and the ones they could justify expelling. With mass propaganda ensuring the population that only "criminals" were expelled, Eden had seen, through her eyes as a child, the extensive list of people who were asked to leave the Core. She had seen on TV the long lines of citizens being kicked out, officially "voluntarily leaving". There had even been fake testimonies of people pretending to leave because they didn't deserve their spot in the Core and wanted to atone for their crimes by being outside the walls...

That reality had only been revealed to Eden much later, once she was on the other side of the wall, with her abilities as a hacker allowing her to see what the government didn't want the people to know.

"So how... how did the Edge crack the Core's code? Who are they, and why did you leave?"

"So curious, my Kitty!" giggled Loir. "Well first, it's not like the Architect was the first hacker ever... You're a bit too young for that my Kitty, but for a lot of people in our world, hacking the smartest hacker's work had become the most exciting game ever! Back a decade or two ago, the entire cyber-underground world was filled with cute little innocent hackers like me, dreaming to beat the Grand Master!"

Eden frowned. She had always thought Loir couldn't have been older than her by more than ten years, but perhaps she was wrong... It was hard to tell how old this alien was.

"The Edge emerged from a congregation of innocent, cute, hungry little hackers like me! The oddest thing was we were united by none other than the Grand Master himself in an international, clandestine competition! Oh, those were the good days..."

"Wait... The Architect was the one who created the Edge?" muttered Eden, shocked once again. "I thought... I thought the Edge is the Core's nemesis!"

"Oh, thank you for the compliment, darling! ...Sure, we are, but it doesn't change the fact that someone claiming to be the Architect himself threw the bait!"

"So what, you believed it? That it was really... the Architect's idea?"

Eden couldn't understand this whole ordeal. Why would the Architect have created something like the Edge? He already had his own students, and although none were nearly as talented as he was, there were definitely a lot of promising young people, and many had tried to take over his work after his disappearance...

However, creating something like the Edge just didn't make sense for him. If Loir was telling the truth, a man working for the Core had gone to look for underground, illegal hackers! The cyber-underground was openly trying to fight the Core's System at the very end of the twenty-first century; Eden couldn't understand why the Architect himself would have wanted anything to do with them...

"No? I mean, I don't know, I didn't really care," shrugged Loir.

"What was it? A competition, you said?"

"Yup. The Architect promised a huuuuuuge prize for everyone who managed to beat him! This was a funny man!"

"Beat him? How?"

"Oh, there were a lot of fun little games involved, and a lot of rules! My favorite was the preliminary one: we had to hack into the Congress President's Office and take pictures! You don't know how many weird passwords those people have..."

Eden and Dante exchanged a glance, both at a loss for words. This was going beyond what they could have ever thought. Actually, it sounded more like some TV show since Eden thought this was incredibly insane and unbelievable. Yet, Loir was saying all of this as if... as if it had been true!

"...What did he want?"

"Well, he had those twin secretaries, an amazing duo of very pretty blonde ladies, Veronica and Arabella, and they–"

"Not the Congress President, Loir; the Architect!"

"Oooooh, the grandpa? Well, I told you, he wanted us to beat him. Or, more exactly, to defeat the Core. Yes, if we could manage to hack the thingy, the whole prize was ours! Not easy, I'll admit, but what a challenge! Everyone in the chat rooms was jumping on their little unicorns!"

"What prize?" insisted Dante.

"Well, the Core itself, of course. There was also a lot of money and hardware involved. Oh, I still dream of that magnificent, sexy holo-luminescent keyboard..."

"...The Architect had promised the Core?" repeated Eden, with a smirk. "Loir, it can't be. The Architect wouldn't have given the Core to anyone... I don't even think he owned it himself. The Core went independent from the Architect as soon as it was launched!"

"Of course," shrugged Loir. "Why else would he ask us to try and retrieve it? The Architect just wanted us to overpower the thing, to beat that little monster he had created. I must say, it was very fun, but not so easy! I mean, the first levels of his little game were relatively easy, so we pocketed some nice money, *kaching-kaching*! But then, when we got to the annoying part, everyone started dropping like worn-out fleas! Dumb-dumbs! A lot of people fled; I mean, we did get a bit naughty and may have caught the attention of a few governments by then..."

"Like the Russian Government?" said Eden, raising an eyebrow.

"Oh, don't go there," grimaced Loir, shivering. "Do you know what the Imperials did to us...? Well, I don't wanna fry my brain processor thinking about it again, so let's just skip that unpleasant part... Anyway, we got to the part where we could hack the old Cores, per se."

"We?" repeated Dante.

"The group, of course! Come on, I'm a marvelous genius as we all know, but I can't do this much by myself! We needed Dive Hackers, Back Hackers... The whole shebang! I think there were about... thirteen people left, at that stage?"

"That's more than the members of the Chicago Zodiac," Eden scoffed.

"Oh, don't worry, half of those cute little chickens left before we got to the next stage..."

"Why?"

Loir chuckled.

"Well, we may have been burning our cheese a bit too close to all those governments... It began to smell bad for everyone! I mean, I'm a bit offended my bounty went down since they think I am dead, but..."

"...So what happened?"

"We all came here to Chicago to try and get the thingy done... and things went aaaaall the way south. I don't mean south like a nice spot in Louisiana, I mean south like underground prisons, toasting your toes until they fry and all that smelly crap!"

"You were arrested then?"

"Yes, as soon as I landed a toe in Chicago! Oh, I miss my poor little toes... They were really cute, you know!"

Eden grimaced.

So that was Loir's story... A hacker baited by the Architect to come and beat his own creation... Was that what the Cores had planned all along, to trap rebellious hackers? It was plausible, and actually, Eden herself knew she would probably have gotten cold feet when half of the Edge did. Who wanted to risk getting captured by the Core? Moreover, if the Architect had invited them himself, why did things go wrong? Unless something had happened to him...

"Wait... So that's when the Architect disappeared?" she asked. "You guys were arrested... when the Architect vanished from Chicago, right?"

Loir made a sad expression, putting his chin on his knee.

"Maybe? The authorities got us right when we arrived! So disappointing... I really wanted to meet the old man... I can't believe I missed the opportunity of a lifetime to meet one of the few geniuses smarter than myself! And my prize..."

"What would you even do if you had control of the Core?" chuckled Dante, visibly amused.

"Oh, a ton of things! I would make Taco Tuesday mandatory, banish yellow shirts, and add another season to all my favorite shows!"

"Of course," sighed Eden.

With Loir as its head, the Core would definitely end up like some very strange amusement park, being the weird character he was... She couldn't even imagine it.

"My holo-luminescent keyboard..." he whined. "I could never get my hands on one, even when I tried to sell my kidney!"

"Don't sell your kidney," retorted Eden without even thinking twice. "Now, where is the Edge, Loir? Can we contact them or something? Someone warned A., I mean the Hare, about the Core expanding, expanding physically beyond the current wall. We need to know what else they know."

"Oh, no, no, no," said the hacker, shaking his head. "I told you they are still mad at me! Why would they talk to me..."

"Why are they even mad at you, what did you do? If it's been two years, perhaps they have let it go by now."

"You think?" asked Loir, his eyes suddenly shining with excitement.

"...Loir, seriously, what did you do?"

He scratched his head with his black nails.

"I only asked a friend if he knew a nice place we could stay at when we arrived?" he said in a small voice.

"Who was that friend?"

"Well, the President, of course!"

"Oh Loir, you crazy piece of sh–!"

# CHAPTER TWENTY-ONE

Eden was pacing back and forth in her room after she had finally changed into something more comfortable. She had thrown the pink strass top across the room and instead, put on a black turtleneck and some comfortable denim pants with black leather boots. She definitely liked this outfit a lot better than the one from before.

As usual, Dante was watching her from afar, leaning on the kitchen counter and following her movements with a complex, indecipherable expression.

"It doesn't make sense," she muttered. "The Architect died years ago, way before two years ago. I get that Loir has no concept of time and he was already hiding in a basement before I met him, so he's probably got it all mixed up... but even if that was four, five, or even six years ago, way before I met him, the Architect was already long gone. How could he have given instructions to the Edge? Moreover, why would he have instructed them to attack his own creations, the other Cores?"

"...Unless it wasn't the Architect," said Dante.

Eden stopped. She had thought the same, but it didn't make sense either. Who else but the Architect would have been able to pull off such a thing? No one had ever come close to attacking one of the Cores before that, but once this strange contest from someone posing as the Architect surfaced, and some keys were handed to young hackers like the Edge, several Cores almost fell or were without power in the span of only a few years... According to Loir, at least. If they believed the crazy hacker and considered all the major attacks against the

Cores as the Edge's work or part of that competition, the challenges had lasted over several years. A lot of the most impressive hackings must have been kept under wraps by the victim Cores...

"The only other explanation is that the Architect didn't die when the Core said he did," said Dante.

"I know..." Eden grumbled, biting her nail. "There were a lot of speculations, but most think he did die. A lot of Dive Hackers like me tried to look for him... The most plausible leads that surfaced were that he was tortured for several months, then killed by the government."

"Why would the people of the Core torture the Architect?"

Eden didn't answer. She wasn't surprised at the Core's Masters trying to destroy the Architect; they hated anything they couldn't fully control. She was more surprised that his creation had been used against him, the most impressive code builder of all time... Eden felt very strange the more she thought about it. Did it make any sense that the Architect would have let himself die at the hands of his own creation?

She sighed. Perhaps she shouldn't have interrogated Loir... That crazy guy had left her with more questions than answers. On top of that, it was now clear that the Edge would most likely not help them if they knew they were working with him. He had basically sold them out to the Chicago Core because of his crazy-filled stupidity and inability to understand a situation. The Congress President had probably collected all of them the second they had set foot in the Core... The one mystery that remained, though, is how they were still alive and active after that! Eden thought that once captured, the Edge would have been tortured and killed, but their recent contact with A. proved otherwise. So how had they survived?

"Eden."

She turned to him, a bit bemused. Eden was at a comfortable distance, where he couldn't reach her, and Dante didn't move either, but she still felt a bit on edge. He was simply staring with his curious golden eyes.

"...What do you know about the Architect?"

She remained silent for a short while. His question felt deeper than what he was letting on... Eden took a deep breath and turned away from him, staring out the window instead.

"He was the best of his generation, the first man to achieve the creation of a perfectly autonomous Artificial Intelligence in 2094. After that, he imagined his creation on a larger scale and created the first Cores five years later for the sake of the government. Several decades later, he had created Cores in every major city in the world or sold the plans to other countries... who paid handsomely for his work. Rumor had it that he was kidnapped thirteen years ago in 2117 by an unknown enemy of the government."

"I bet a Core history book would have been able to tell me exactly the same thing," he scoffed.

"You asked."

"No. I asked what do you know about the Architect, Eden."

She stayed silent. She knew exactly what Dante was digging for, but she didn't like it. As he suddenly began walking closer, she froze. She didn't want to look back, and she didn't need to; Eden could hear his steps behind her, slowly but surely shortening the distance between them until he stood right behind her. Once again, he didn't touch her, although he stood just a step away.

"...Why do you think I'd know anything?"

"You were born in the Core. You have been close to Pan, a legendary hacker, for most of your life."

"If you have a point, Dante, just say it."

"I think the Architect's disappearance in 2117 was the exact reason you fled to the Suburbs as a child, Eden."

She turned around, glaring at him.

"...The Architect had a family," he continued. "He had a daughter, didn't he?"

Eden's chest grew heavy, and her breathing was getting more erratic as her eyes teared up. Still, Dante's golden gaze didn't change at all. He was staring right at her, perfectly calm and composed.

"...What pushes a ten-year-old little girl to flee the Core and hide in the Suburbs?" he whispered.

Eden could feel her throat tighten, an alarm ringing in her head. She had tried so hard to seal away and bury her secret all this time, to the point she had almost forced herself to forget.

"...I was nine," she muttered in a whisper.

Dante's lips parted faintly, but he didn't say anything. The two of them stared at each other for a long time, without saying a word. Eden was very disturbed. Having her secret revealed and feeling her heart opening to Dante after remaining firmly sealed all these years made her panic. Facing her, the Tiger was an absolute wall, showing no emotions. Dante didn't look surprised, glad, or interested. He was simply staring at her, just like before, his golden eyes so deep she could have gotten lost in them. After a while, he blinked and slightly lifted his eyes, his gaze going beyond her to stare outside.

"...Do you know why?" he whispered.

"I have no idea. I barely remember... One night, my mother just said we had to run, so I ran. We escaped, and I... I had no idea what happened to him... I still don't."

"What of Pan?"

"No, Pan is different from... my family," Eden said, shaking her head. "He came to me when I connected myself to the Core's System for the first time as a child. He said it was a secret between us... My father had no idea. When... everything was over, and I ended up alone in the Suburbs, he found me again and helped me survive by teaching me how to use the Dark Reality and conceal my real identity... He disappeared again after he sent me to Loir."

Dante frowned a little this time. Of course, her story was very unique...

Eden was well aware of that. She had tried hard to conceal her identity, and reinvent herself as a lone hacker in the Suburbs, someone with no identity at all. It wasn't very hard to do, as most people there were either desperate to become someone else or hide who they were... Although, the first years had been hard; a child who had been brutally forced to leave her world and the comfort of her home to come here...

"...What happened to... the rest of your family?"

"I don't... remember well," she muttered. "I was too young; aside from blurry memories of my childhood, I'm not really sure I remember anything right. It all happened so suddenly, it's all too... confusing. I just... have vague memories of me and my mother running, for a long time. I think she tried to come with me, but she was probably too easy to find because of her SIN. She told me to keep running, and we parted ways... but she was right. When I tried to look for her, I... They had found her, and killed her on the spot... She didn't know anything about my dad's work."

Dante slowly nodded, but his eyes were still looking outside, and Eden couldn't make out what he was thinking. She took a deep breath, and stepped forward, to the point where their shoes touched.

"Dante, no one must know," she said. "If they ever found–"

"I know," he suddenly answered, putting his arm around her waist. "You think I would reveal your secret?"

This time, he had a little smirk on, but it wasn't making Eden feel any better. She still wasn't sure she could trust him after she had seen him act like a cunning bastard way too many times. So, she didn't answer and just stared at him suspiciously. Why in the world would he keep her secret? He had guessed most of it, so she didn't have a choice, but what could he even do with it anyway? It wasn't like he could sell her out to the Core, or be able to gain anything from it. At best, Eden was merely a tool he could use to his advantage. At worst, she would be his best weapon against the Core...

She looked away from him, trying to avoid his cold, golden stare, but just as she did, Dante gently grabbed her chin and pulled her in for a kiss. Immediately, she felt herself falling for this. Her mind was still cautious, and her cheeks were still a bit wet from the tears that had rolled down earlier, but she couldn't resist giving in to the sweet and salty taste of this kiss. She liked it too much. Dante's hungry lips, his possessiveness as if he was going to hold on to her and never let go, like a dangerous and silent promise between them, something that she secretly wanted to believe, imbued in that kiss. Perhaps it was just a kiss, but Eden didn't want to think about it. Even if she was deceived, it was her own mistake for wanting to trust that madman. It didn't matter much anymore...

Although their kiss lasted a little while, Eden and Dante slowly separated, their erratic breathing the only sound in that big room. Dante smiled.

"I had been waiting for that kiss..."

"We should go," mumbled Eden, embarrassed for some reason. "Didn't you want to attack the Snake tonight..."

"Sure."

She tried to rush past him to get to the elevator first, and possibly avoid his gaze, but Dante held her back easily, his arm still wrapped around her waist. Before she was able to take more than one step away, Eden was drawn back into his arms, making the young blonde blush even more.

As if it was perfectly normal to keep his arm around her waist, Dante smiled and escorted her to the elevator. Eden was red and desperate to avoid his eyes, which was even harder to do in a mirror-filled elevator...

"...Are you alright with attacking them?" he suddenly asked as they were going back down. "The Core?"

Eden knew why he was asking that. Although she barely held any memories of it, the Chicago Core was still her birthplace. Perhaps she should have felt something about going up against an entity her own father had built, but there wasn't anything. As a hacker, Eden knew better than most that the Core was nothing more than a system, a system that had failed the people it should have been serving, fallen into the wrong hands only to broaden the gap between people. She slowly nodded with a bitter expression.

"Yes. I think... I think there's some truth behind Loir's story. If my father was really aiming to eventually destroy the Core, then that's even better. I hate what he had created and what it became. I want to think he hated it too..."

"...Don't you want to know what happened to him?"

Eden was surprised by that question. Did she? The truth was, she had locked her past away and tried so hard to forget about it, she had never really questioned the truth about that night, thirteen years ago. What nine-year-old child could have understood and tried to look for answers? She only ran when she was told to, hid when she had to. She was living at twenty-three years old as she has been for the past decade, just trying to hide and survive... Eden suddenly wondered if she should have tried to look for more answers, but... the truth was she probably already knew what had happened. She didn't believe some invisible, unknown enemy had attacked her father. She knew enough about the Core and the people behind it to be able to figure out the truth behind her father's disappearance...

"...I want to know who gave the Edge all that data," she finally answered. "I want to meet the Edge and find out who was acting as my father. If it turns out it was indeed my father, I want to know what actually happened, how he survived all this time, and why he..."

Her throat suddenly tightened, and Eden herself was shocked by the wave of sadness that suddenly overcame her. She was... sad? She was about to say why her father had never looked for her as if she was truly... abandoned. Perhaps this was what she had felt all this time. Abandoned. She took a deep breath, trying to hold back those tears, and stared at herself in the mirror. Nothing showed that she was on the verge of crying and had cried before; her eyes didn't easily get red. She took another deep breath and tucked her hair behind her ears on both sides. Dante was still holding her waist, but his eyes were on the elevator's screen rather than on her. Perhaps he was actually being tactful, for once...

"So you agree."

"Agree to what?" she asked, frowning.

"Attacking the Snake."

Eden let out a long sigh.

"It's not like you are going to back down from it... Moreover, I'm interested in who is going to take over Old Man Long's territory. I'm afraid it will lead to more infighting between the groups if the new Dragon is some crazy guy like Yang..."

"Great," smiled Dante, visibly satisfied. "Then–"

"I don't want to do this in your style, though," retorted Eden.

"My style?"

"Bringing in the big guns and using innocents as shields?"

"...Do you have another idea, then?"

"Not all territories need to be conquered with fights. We can do it another way and even avoid bloodshed."

"And beat the Rat to it?" he insisted, raising an eyebrow.

"Yes... But if we are going with my plan, I have some conditions."

"I am all ears."

"I will need Rose and Jack's help. And Loir's, of course."

"Nothing too difficult so far."

"Also... your eyes, you can change their color, right?" Eden asked, finally looking at him in the mirror.

Dante blinked, and his eyes turned a striking blue color.

"Anything you'd like..."

Eden smiled. She wasn't sure the color was going to make a real difference in what she was feeling inside, but a blue-eyed Dante was quite... new and interesting.

"Come on," she said as the doors opened, quickly stepping out to avoid his new and mesmerizing blue gaze. "Call your men, I'll detail my plan."

Dante nodded and quickly, something like a war meeting was organized in just a matter of minutes.

The Italian Tiger called out to his men and all the mafiosos quickly assembled in Loir's computer room, the hacker's black eyes opening wide from all the Italians amassing in there. As Dante had promised, Rose and Jack were brought in too, escorted by George. Although the young Italian stepped away as soon as he could, Eden noticed his blushing as Rose wagged her fingers at him with the expression of a female cat staring at her prey... She was really as terrible as ever and wearing a devilishly sexy red dress too. At least the two of them looked fine and better than earlier. They were wearing new clothes, and Jack had a bit more color to his face; they were probably given food as well... While waiting for everyone to get there, the two of them quickly walked up to her, staying away from the Italian men. The puppies apparently recognized the duo and both trotted up to them, yapping excitedly. Jack smiled and bent down to grab Beer. As he stood back up, he was suddenly facing Loir, and almost dropped the pup. The hacker had rolled his chair over to them, a large creepy grin on.

"Hi, friends!" he said, excited.

"This... is your partner?" muttered Jack, shocked.

"Yes, this is Loir. Loir, these are my colleagues, Jack and Rose."

"Nice to meet you!" said Loir, smiling wide with the few teeth he actually had left.

"Hi..." grimaced Jack, obviously uneasy in front of the strange specimen. "Your... head is..."

"Oh, you're a baldie too!" squealed Loir, excited. "We're bald twins! Did you eat a candy?"

"A candy?" repeated Jack, visibly lost.

"Yup! I ate a candy one day, and everything fell... All of my hair! Poof! Look, even my eyebrows! Isn't it funny?"

"Yeah... Dang, looks like ya ate all the damn candies in the box, honey... Eden, where the hell did ya find this guy? Half those tattoos on his head could get him shot or put in jail!"

Eden chuckled. She had never imagined the day Jack would meet Loir... Those two had only one thing in common: the fact that they were complete outsiders. The four of them waited to the side with the puppies and watched the rest of Dante's men arrive. The Italians were all lined up with the same dark Italian suits and postures, like soldiers trained to act this way in the presence of their boss. Indeed, the atmosphere was incredibly tense with Dante in the room, although he was doing nothing in particular. The Italian Tiger was imposing his presence as if he was a head taller than everyone else in the room, gathering all eyes on him. He was actually still "wearing" his blue eyes which, of course, seemed to intrigue a lot of his men.

Eden glared at Rose who was sending him glances and biting her red-tinted lower lip.

"Are you done yet?" she hissed.

"Well, you should learn to mark your territory better then, hun," retorted the redhead, her eyes hungrily following the Italian.

"Stop it, you two," mumbled Jack, nervous. "Eden, what's going on, why did they bring us here?"

Before she could answer, Rolf stepped forward, facing their men. He was going to be the one to give the orders and act as Dante's spokesperson for now. The Italian Boss was calmly standing behind him with no visible intention to do the talking, his hands in his pockets.

"Everyone, tonight we are launching an attack on the Snake's territory," he declared.

"Wha–" muttered Jack, turning to Eden.

She covered his mouth before he could really shout. Unlike her friend, all of Dante's men were extremely calm and composed. Perhaps they were used to receiving such orders because none of them seemed surprised. At best, a couple of them glanced toward the strange quartet very discreetly.

While Rolf began explaining what information they had on the Snake so far, Eden was only half-listening. She already knew all of this, but she was more curious to know if Dante would actually go along with her idea rather than his. Rolf's explanation wasn't anything they wouldn't have been able to figure out themselves, either. The Tiger's and the Snake's territories were far enough from each other that the two didn't have much to fight over usually; however, tonight, it was more about gaining an advantage to get to the Dragon...

"...Is this about your money issue?" whispered Jack, leaning toward her.

Eden glared back. She didn't want Jack to start speaking now. He was the only one there who knew what her issues were truly about, and she hoped he would realize they were probably not in a safe enough place to talk. Who knew which of Dante's men could hear them, or where they had put secret mics and the likes...

"This isn't about money," she whispered, a bit annoyed.

"Wait, you're sleeping with him and not getting anything?" scoffed Rose. "Wow, I thought he was an idiot with poor taste, but now I think I might have mistaken who the real idiot was..."

Eden rolled her eyes. Did those two ever keep their tongues properly tied... Eden tried to reassure herself, affirming that she hadn't asked Dante for money because she didn't want to owe him anything, but... she knew this would have been nothing but lies. She still needed that money, desperately. The reason she hadn't asked was that she had actually managed to forget about it for the last couple of crazy days they had just spent together...

"...What are ya really here for then, Eden?" whispered Jack.

Eden stared daggers back, annoyed. Couldn't he at least wait until Dante and his men weren't here to ask? Jack was legitimately lost about her current situation, but a little discretion would have been great... Eden still considered herself to be in a very awkward position, and having three of her friends within Dante's reach wasn't helping at all. She was almost certain he wouldn't do anything to them, but she was also sure he would use them against her without any hesitation if he felt the need to.

She stared at his men, and their attitudes contrasted with the aloof, composed Dante. Eden was no child; she had enough experience to tell when men were actually intimidated. All the Italians lined up there were not just playing mafia; they were genuinely lowering their heads out of fear or respect for their boss. Dante could pretend with her, but she knew his men's attitudes were a dead giveaway about his true nature. Regardless of their newfound closeness, she didn't want to be hung out to dry.

While listening to Rolf exposing the known details about the Snake's residence, its defenses, and their forces, she stared at Dante. She usually avoided his gaze, but now she could watch him from afar. She was aware of Jack sending her worried glances, but Eden ignored him and focused on one of her rare opportunities to watch the Tiger instead... It was strange how she could feel the boss of the Italian Mafia, even as they were standing apart like this; he had a deeper connection to her than anyone else in the room. Eden couldn't describe it, but she felt like she had to constantly resist a magnetic force that pulled her toward him. She took a deep breath and forced herself to look elsewhere, pretending to be interested in Bullet as the pup was playing with Loir's fingers at her feet. The hacker was strangely crouched down at the edge of his seat while making weird noises and faces to excite the baby dog, his long black painted nails serving as bait.

"Cute little puppy... Chew-chew and nib-nib... That's right... Catchy! Catchy!"

"Loir, what do you think about attacking the Snake?" she asked him in a low voice.

"We're attacking the Snake?" he asked as if he had only understood now. "Oh my, does that mean we're having dim sum for dinner?"

"Dim sum is Chinese," she sighed.

"Are you sure? ...I think she's lying to have it all for herself," he whispered to the pup.

"...What do you think about Yasumoto?"

"He's stingy with money, very whiny, and he doesn't like kitties... He has a big ego too. Huuuuuge ego. Probably his Slytherin side... Do you think it's because he's got a tiny snakey, Bullet-chan?"

Eden frowned. Indeed, she didn't have one good memory from the times she had worked for the Japanese Yakuza. She knew she had only survived her two missions because she had done exactly what he had asked of Ghost, and gotten out of there before he could ask for more or kill her. However, Loir had declined the missions when he could, and there was probably a good reason for that.

Suddenly, a silence fell upon the room as Rolf had just finished exposing the bits of information they had. Dante turned his head toward Eden.

"You had a plan?" he said with a faint smile.

Immediately, all eyes went to her, and Eden sighed. She nodded and stepped forward, putting the pup down.

"Loir, show us a map of his residence."

"Right away, Kitty Boss!"

Eden crossed her arms and Loir immediately activated the Apple gifted by Pan. Several men in the room couldn't contain their awe and made sounds of surprise. Eden heard Jack gasp behind her, but she didn't have time to explain. Loir quickly zoomed in on the large residence, showing how incredibly precise the Map was in its three-dimensional representation of the area.

"This is the Snake's main residence, called the Red Temple. The Yakuza bought this land after the Second American Civil War bombs had destroyed it, as Rolf explained, and built their headquarters there, after settling the Japanese into most of the neighborhood. A few decades ago, there were only a few families, but many fled from the South Confederation to come here, making the Japanese population of Chicago almost as big as the Vietnamese one. However, they are not all fond of the Snake. The current leader, Yasumoto, drifted away from the core principles observed by the previous Yakuza heads and is not much different from a bandit playing around with his swords. Not only does he reign by fear over his people, he has actually been selling weapons to the Core, and made his clan rich this way."

"Wait, this bastard actually works with the Core?" repeated George, surprised.

"Exactly. He had me work for him once, as a hacker; that's when my partner and I got a look at those transactions. Under the Temple, the previous Japanese leaders, wanting to learn from the bombs, built several underground bunkers, now mainly used to manufacture weapons. Yasumoto buys plastic waste and metal from the outside or the local recycling centers, transforms them, and sells the weapons to the Chicago Core at a high price."

Dante smiled. This partially explained why Eden had eventually agreed to attack another Zodiac. She knew that if they could beat the Snake, they would also be inflicting a major blow to the Core, destroying one of their weapon providers.

Eden stepped closer to the Map, showing the gardens around the main building.

"Yasumoto loves technology. He has all the latest high tech to protect his residence, and pretty much everything is controlled by the residence's main system. If we take control of the main computer, we have control over everything in the Temple: the cameras, the doors, the entire security system."

"Sounds like a nice new toy for Loir to play with!" squealed the hacker, excited.

"So your plan is to hack the residence instead of attacking it?" asked Dante, raising an eyebrow.

"We will have to do both simultaneously," sighed Eden, focusing on the Map to avoid his gaze. "Their system is a closed circuit; we can't hack it remotely, no matter how good we are. I will need to be physically inside to control it."

"Now I'm not fond of your plan," whispered Jack behind her.

"So you're saying if we barge in from the front..."

"He's going to put his whole residence into a full lockdown," nodded Eden. "Everyone will be killed as soon as they take one step into the garden."

"And that's a big garden," nodded Loir.

He zoomed out on the Map, showing the whole area around the main residence. Similar to the traditional concept of many Asian-inspired architectures, the Red Temple was a tall building surrounded by a square garden, with several smaller residences scattered around, and the entire residence was enclosed by a large wall with a similar design. Upon seeing this, many of the Italians exchanged glances, suddenly worried.

"...Anything else you know about their security?" asked Rolf, who had crossed his arms and had his usual serious expression on.

Unlike the rest of Dante's men, Eden could tell his second-in-command was already trying to pinpoint the weaknesses in the Japanese defenses. However, the response came from Loir, who suddenly let out a very strange screech, making half the room jump.

"Thiiiiiiiis baby!!"

He quickly typed something on his keyboard, and suddenly, the Map of the residence was replaced by a large image of what looked like a gigantic Chinese dragon, with a long body like a snake, long whiskers, and four clawed legs.

"...What is that thing?"

"It's called Seiryū," said Eden, walking closer to it. "In Asian folklore, Seiryū is a mythical Azure Dragon akin to a protective deity. This thing is Yasumoto's favorite toy and the equivalent of his guard dog. According to the rumors, he specifically requested a dragon to try and piss off Old Man Long, meaning he thought he deserved the spot as the Zodiac's Dragon, but of course, it had no effect at all. However, that thing is still in his garden, acting as the main opponent to its intruders."

"But what is it? ...Some sort of robot?"

"According to the rumors, it's one of the latest versions of animatronics," said Eden. "An entirely tech-engineered creature. It was one of the side results of the creation of the first Artificial Intelligence. Rivals of the Architect came up with poor results at trying to reproduce human intelligence in a machine, so instead, they sold it as what could be used to power up intelligent electronic pets. However, it turned into a contest of who could do the craziest or more dangerous thing, and eventually, we ended up with results like this thing. It is crazy expensive, but it does work as an intruder-killer."

"...How are we supposed to get past that thing?" whispered George. "Animatronics are fast and almost as smart as humans!"

"From what I know, Seiryū works under one rule: it doesn't kill the guests that come into the residence through the main door," said Eden. "Anyone who tries to come in any other way gets killed on the spot."

"So no matter what, we have to go through that main door," nodded Rolf.

"Exactly. Unfortunately, the main door only opens under Yasumoto's command, and all the guests are strictly approved and monitored beforehand."

"So even if we want to try and sneak in a small group of our people first to take control of the residence, we need an excuse for him to let us in..."

"Exactly."

A few seconds passed in silence, everyone frowning about the situation. Loir suddenly slammed his desk, making them all jump again.

"I have an idea!"

"Loir..." sighed Eden.

"Let him speak," whispered Jack. "Ya never know, the craziest ideas are sometimes the best ones..."

"We could try knocking! We tell them we are selling girl scout cookies!"

"...Nevermind," sighed Jack.

However, after hearing Loir's idea, Rose and Eden's eyes met. The two women had reached the same conclusion long before any of the men in the room did, making the redhead chuckle.

"Oh, he is not the craziest one..."

"What do you think?" insisted Eden.

"I think we might need to call the girls to ask if they want to work an extra shift tonight."

Jack, who had just understood what they were talking about, suddenly went white.

"...You bitches can't be serious!"

"Why not?" smiled Rose, already biting her index finger. "I love that idea, darling. We're going to sell him some nice, yummy cookies...."

"See?" smiled Loir, very proud. "I knew I had a good idea."

Meanwhile, Eden's eyes went to Dante, who had lost his smile. This was one crazy idea indeed... and Eden was going to be the main bait.

# CHAPTER TWENTY-TWO

"I hate it."

Eden looked up from the belt of the outfit she was struggling to put on. Dante was standing there, arms crossed, with a sullen look. She shrugged and looked down again to try and figure out how to secure the leather belt around her kimono-inspired dress. It was very flashy indeed.

Still, Eden had to admit Rose had done an impressive job; a few minutes and a dozen calls later, she found out the Yakuza's tastes and secured entries for them as escorts for some of his lieutenants. Sure enough, her extensive repertoire had been quite useful for this plan... Now, Eden only had to put on this nightmarish outfit Jack had given to her. By itself, the red and yellow dress was quite pretty, and easy to move around in, but she had never worn anything like it; she was used to more vintage dresses...

"You don't have to go," Dante insisted.

Eden let out a long sigh this time. He had voiced that he was against this plan only because she was part of it, but now, she was more annoyed by his possessive attitude than anything.

"You're the one who wanted to take down the Snake and said you'd go along with my plan."

"You hadn't told me your plan would include you opening your legs to the Japanese."

"For now, I'm only going to open their doors. Stop whining."

Although he finally stopped complaining, Dante didn't get rid of that sullen look of his. They had gone back upstairs, just the two of them, for Eden to change, but she knew he hadn't ordered for them to be left alone only for him to complain. Rose had stayed downstairs and changed right there, to the pleasure of the handful of Italian men who had stayed behind to "guard" the room. Eden knew there was no need to worry or feel sorry for the redhead; she just loved the attention and had a very limited sense of decency too.

The one Dante wanted no other man to see was Eden. So, she had gone back upstairs to redo her makeup into a bolder, more feminine look, arranged her blond hair into a high ponytail with some Asian-inspired accessories, and put on that nightmarish dress. Secretly, Eden actually enjoyed this sort of dressing up, as if she was putting on a costume. She wasn't forgetting the primary goal of all of this, but she liked picking out which accessories to wear, customizing her makeup, and putting on a completely new kind of outfit. What annoyed her, though, was Dante's eyes on her throughout the whole process. The Tiger wasn't letting go, not even for one second. He didn't even blink, as if he was prepared for her to run away at any moment.

"...Stop staring," she finally said, as she was getting annoyed at the belt again.

"Why?"

"Because it makes me uncomfortable," she retorted.

"I make you uncomfortable?"

Eden raised her eyes, and sure enough, he had that grin again. He was visibly amused and pleased to know he was annoying her... He stepped forward, and Eden frowned. Slowly, he began walking in her direction, as a feline would silently approach its prey. She didn't move, but she glared at him as if warning him to stay away.

Of course, Dante ignored that. He walked up to her, slowly raising that tension between them, a wry smile on his lips. His eyes, back to their golden color, were almost glowing. Eden tried to stay calm and not step back. She wasn't scared, but she knew she had a very limited ability to resist that pull toward him... Sure enough, the Tiger soon found himself dangerously close to her, and the young woman's heart skipped a beat. Eden was a bit mad at herself. Why couldn't she resist him? Why did all her defenses suddenly vanish with one glance, one touch of his? How could he have so much power over her when she never let anyone get any?

As if to blow all of her worries away, Dante gently put his hand on her cheek and closed the distance between them for a kiss. Eden didn't even think twice before letting him do as he wished. Their kiss was incredibly slow, gentle, and chaste. As if he was deliberately torturing her... The pressure of his hand was so faint, she could have backed away, pushed him away anytime she wanted. But Eden didn't want to. She just wanted to feel her heart beating excitedly, fluttering irrationally, at Dante's gentle kiss, and get lost in his tenderness. As if she could say no to this, to him. She couldn't. Something in her heart and her mind had just given up a while ago, and she was holding on to the last strings of resistance to not give in completely, to not let all her secrets be exposed. Eden just wanted to dip into that pleasure a little and tell herself not everything was lost if she could at least keep that mental barrier between them since the physical one had disappeared long ago... The way he was kissing her was so gentle, so smooth, and so pleasurable that it was easy to give in and let herself float away. At times, Dante could be an animal, but he could also be painfully sweet.

"...Do I still make you uncomfortable?" he whispered with a smile against her lips.

This time, Eden frowned and pushed him away. Or she tried. Of course, Dante had decided not to budge and instead captured her hands, interlocking her fingers with his. Eden shivered. She didn't like this... She didn't like it when he was so dangerously gentle like this. Dante's eyes on her had more than their usual naughtiness to them. At times, he looked at her with something, something much deeper and more complicated. Eden took a deep breath, avoiding the eyes she could feel on her.

"...Won't you let me finish getting ready?" she muttered.

"Look at me."

She didn't want to. Her heart was already going crazy from their proximity, just the two of them in this room, while he was holding her hands. Eden felt like something was going to fall apart if she gave in.

"Eden."

The way he said her name echoed something painful in her. There was so much expressed in just that one word. Eden stubbornly looked to the side, toward the kitchen, feeling her cheeks and ears burn red, and the shivers going down her spine from his intense stare.

Suddenly, he moved, and as he released her hand, she thought he was going to let her go, but she was very wrong. Instead, Dante embraced her waist, and, without warning, put his lips on her neck. The shivers immediately came back, and Eden felt her whole body tremble at that kiss. Yet, the Tiger wasn't done. He kissed her exposed neck, again and again, torturing her until she could barely breathe. Eden closed her eyes, but it worsened the sensations. She could feel so much pleasure from just those kisses, her breathing getting louder. She was tense in his arms, stuck deciding if she wanted to push him away, or if it would be too dangerous to touch him now.

"Dante..." she sighed.

Those kisses were in a dangerous place between sensuality and tenderness, making that poison even sweeter.

"Dante, stop, please."

He obeyed and pulled away slowly. His arms were still around her, but now, Eden actually had room to catch her breath. She looked down, a bit ashamed of her blushing, erratic breathing, and shy eyes. She heard Dante slowly sigh, his chest movements following his breathing.

"...Why are you always so scared of me?"

"I'm not scared of you," she retorted with a low voice.

"You're scared of giving in. You're scared of your feelings for me."

"Shut up," she protested, now mad. "You don't know anything..."

"You're a poor liar, Eden."

She answered with a glare, this time directed at his golden irises.

"Can we just go, please?"

He smiled and put a quick kiss on her lips again, but he finally freed her, taking a step back. Eden couldn't help but let out a silent sigh of relief, although Dante took her hand again. They walked together to the elevator, neither of them saying a word. Eden was just silently praying that her cheeks would stop burning so much... Once they stepped inside and the doors closed, however, Dante let go of her hand and instead, moved his fingers to her belt to finish fastening it where Eden had failed before. There was something a bit embarrassing again about having this man tighten that large belt around her waist, and Eden looked away.

Her eyes fell on their reflection in the mirror. She could see Dante's large back, his clean-cut hairline above his shirt collar. In comparison, her head was barely popping up an inch higher than his shoulder, and she looked trapped in front of this man... She did feel a bit trapped, her back against the wall of the elevator.

Somehow, Dante got her belt secured and settled much faster than she could have and soon stepped back with a satisfied nod. Eden was now wearing the dress properly. The fabric was exposing her shoulders but dipped lower at her cleavage; below the belt, the two slits of the skirt started mid-hip. Although it showed a lot of skin, Eden had chosen that dress because it would allow her to move easily, although it was a bit too sexy for her taste...

Thankfully, the elevator reached the floor with Loir's computer room soon enough. Eden gladly stepped out, but just as she did, Rose walked inside, giving a sexy smile to Dante. The Zodiac barely glanced down at the redhead, but she didn't take her eyes off him for one second.

"Hey, handsome," she whispered.

Dante's eyes went to Eden. She had seen everything, but she only shrugged.

"...I'll catch you downstairs," she said.

The elevator doors closed, and Dante and Rose disappeared. Eden let out a long sigh, more upset than she wanted to admit. Ignoring this, she walked up to Loir. The hacker was slurping from an enormous cup, perched on his chair like an owl as always.

"Kitty!" he said joyfully.

Next to him, Jack grimaced. He also had put on an Asian-inspired outfit and was already wearing heels, makeup, and a new wig. Although it surprised Eden a bit, she thought he was simply wanting to wear it to match Rose and her, as he had brought too many of those outfits and loved an occasion to dress up.

"Loir, are you done with it?" she asked.

"Yup, yup!"

He handed her a little device with a glittery unicorn sticker on it. Eden quickly inspected it before hiding it in one of the pockets of her dress cautiously.

"Eden, this all sounds very dangerous to me," said Jack. "Are ya sure, hun?"

"Don't worry. I just need to get inside the Red Temple, find somewhere to plug this thing in, and Loir will have full control of the place. Then, Dante and his men can intervene. If Rose did her part as she said, it will be easy."

"None of that sounds easy, hun! Plus, trusting a Zodiac and this crazy guy?"

Loir suddenly slurped loudly again, making Jack jump and glare at him. The hacker smiled right back at him, but as his smile was more creepy than friendly, Jack shuddered and looked back at Eden, playing with his long, black wig and trying to act as if the hacker wasn't there.

"He's only half as crazy as he looks," chuckled Eden. "He is a very good hacker too. Don't worry, Jack, please?"

"Don't worry? Eden, he is just hella nuts! I saw him lick his keyboard. He licked it!"

"Jack, relax. It's going to be alright. I know what I'm doing. This is my other job, remember?"

"The little I knew about your job did not include ya pairing up with a Zodiac to kill another, hun! This is fuckin' war, and you're going to be in the middle of that mess!"

"I'll come back as soon as I can. I–"

"Oh, no, no, honey," he said, wagging his index finger. "Uh-uh. You ain't goin' nowhere without me. I'm comin' with ya."

Eden was speechless. So he had actually put on the full outfit thinking he'd come with them?

"...No offense, but that's a really bad idea. I don't think... I mean, it's not really like you're going to be the Japanese's type, Jack."

"Oh, offense taken, babe," he scoffed. "Don't underestimate a professional. You'd be surprised how many dudes secretly dig this piece of fine meat, honey. And, I don't effin' care. You ain't leavin' me here with that crazy monkey. No way. Jacquie is comin' with ya, Eden."

"Jack!"

"It's Jacquie, and we ain't discussin' it no mo'. You got yo' stuff, I got mine, so let's just wiggle these fine booties outta here and get ourselves into that nasty mess. Come on. I ain't stayin' here with that cray-cray..."

Before she could protest again, Eden was pushed toward the elevator, while Jacquie was visibly relieved to get away from Loir, who waved happily and shouted something about sushi as the door closed behind them. Even inside the elevator, Jack didn't let her say another word, making sounds with his mouth and holding up his index finger each time Eden tried. She still felt very uncomfortable about Jack coming along. Eden was already feeling guilty about Rose being involved, but the redhead was very used to mingling with dangerous, powerful men. Jack usually had more of a behind-the-scenes role at the bar, and he was one of her closest friends too. Eden was worried sick with the idea that something might happen to him.

"...Alright," she whispered as the elevator opened into the underground parking lot, "but you get out of there as soon as you can, and you let Dante's men protect you, okay?"

"Oh, I know exactly which cutie is goin' to be my white knight..."

Eden raised an eyebrow, surprised to see Jack sending a playful glance toward... Rolf?

Dante's second-in-command was standing right behind his boss, with all their men assembled as a group in the parking lot, while Eden and Jack made a detour around the little army to get to the head. She felt her friend close behind her, a hint of excitement in his steps.

"...Seriously?" she whispered, a bit amused.

"What? I like the strong, serious type. Plus, how can ya not fall for a man who likes puppies?"

Eden had to bite her lower lip not to smile, but as soon as her eyes landed on Rose, standing way too close to Dante, her smile disappeared. The redhead was flaunting her sexy figure and clearly trying to get the Tiger's attention while his men scattered toward the cars. They were talking, but Eden couldn't hear, what with all the cars' engines starting. She let out a long sigh as they approached them, but Dante had that suspicious smile of his on, while his eyes were still on Rose.

As George opened the door for Jack to get inside a car, blushing at the wink the tall drag queen sent him, Eden decided at the last second to follow him inside.

"Uh..." muttered George, visibly uneasy. "...Aren't you going to ride with the boss...?"

Eden crossed her arms, still sending glares toward the duo a few steps away. She was mad at herself for even being mad about this, and not knowing who, between Dante and Rose, she wanted to resent more. Meanwhile, George, obviously uncomfortable, didn't even dare close the car's door, sending worried glances toward his boss. Hence, when the Tiger looked over and finally noticed, he saw Eden already seated in a different car. Dante frowned, and while Rolf went to the driver's seat, he walked over.

"...What are you doing?" he asked. "Our car is there."

"Your car. You can ride with Rose. I'll stay with Jack and George."

Before he could add another word, Eden grabbed the door handle and slammed it. Dante had no choice but to step back or he would have lost some fingers. Eden locked the door, crossed her arms, and resolutely looked ahead.

"Oh, hun, you two really are–"

"Jack, shut up please."

"A'right, I ain't sayin' it... But damn, hun, you're in hella trouble."

As the cars left the parking lot, Eden was still sulking. She was well aware she had probably managed to piss Dante off for real, but she didn't really care. She was tired of playing his game, and if jealousy could help her take a stance this time, she would. He was suggesting things about the two of them, but then he was giving in to Rose's eyelashes and her attitude? Eden was new to these feelings, but she could recognize her own jealousy.

At least now that they were separated and riding in different cars, she felt like she could take a breather, with only Jack and George sharing the space. Eden hadn't realized how on edge she was from being in the same room as Dante... or even the same building. It felt almost like there was an alarm ringing inside, telling her to resist the pull, resist, resist... and making it harder just by trying. She sighed, about to brush her hair back as usual when she remembered her hairstyle shouldn't be messed with.

"You are all riled up, aren't you, hun?" said Jack next to her.

"Just... He gets on my nerves, and Rose is not helping."

"Oh, honey, you should know Rose by now. She'll jump on anythin' that's got some cash, and everyone knows the Zodiacs are loaded... Moreover, he already refused her once, and in Rose's book, that puts the guy higher on her hit list."

"It's not Rose I care about," pouted Eden. "It's about Dante playing along..."

"Oh... So it really is jealousy, then."

Eden rolled her eyes. Sure, it was, but she just hated to be reminded of it. She shrugged and decided not to pursue the matter anymore. She should enjoy these few minutes of quiet before they dive into trouble again.

"Babe... Did he really not give ya any money?"

"No."

"But... you kinda need it, hun. I thought that was why you are... I mean, you were still with him."

"He didn't give me much of a choice," said Eden.

"Well, then Rose is bloody right! You should be sucking the guy dry, honey! You know the drill!"

Eden bit her lower lip. She knew Jack was right... about some of it. She could have asked Dante for money; he obviously had tons of it and didn't want for anything. Perhaps he would have cleared her debt in a blink... except that Eden hated the idea of being indebted to him of all people. Moreover, she knew he would have asked why she needed the money and looked into it if she refused to talk. She wasn't scared of him revealing her lies; what was much more terrifying was the idea of letting the Tiger get an even tighter grasp on her. Eden didn't like the idea of finally clearing her debt by adding another chain around her neck. She wasn't sure of the consequences that would come of it... She couldn't figure out what would have been the logical choice either way.

Her eyes caught George staring at them in the rearview mirror but, as soon

300

as he noticed she was staring back, his eyes went back to the road. They ought to be careful with what was said here...

"I just... I'm not sure I want to be indebted to a Zodiac, Jack. This is almost like asking him to buy me outright."

"Oh, looks to me like his fine piece of ass got plenty of you already!"

Eden rolled her eyes again. Thanks to Rose, everybody knew or had confirmed that she and Dante had sex already... She didn't care about Jack knowing who she slept with, but she was annoyed about being reminded who that "with" was...

"It's... different."

"Honey, if you're not sleeping with him for the cash... I mean, I get that you two obviously have something going on, but..."

"We don't. Jack, don't–"

"Oh, spare me the cold-hearted crap, Eden. I know ya. I know your business expressions, and that back there ain't your business face; it was the real Eden that gets pissed and sulky and all that... and I don't know that guy, but he's devouring all of ya with his eyes, like, for real. He'd even suck the damn crumbs!"

To her surprise, hearing Jack say that made Eden blush... Was Dante really looking at her in such a way that others could see his desire for her? It had always felt like she was the one who was trapped in his golden eyes, but at least now she knew it was blatant to others...

"Eden... You're runnin' out of time, honey."

She turned to him, suddenly worried.

"...What?"

Jack glanced toward George, but the young man seemed to be focused on the road as they passed another building block. He sighed and spoke a little bit quieter.

"...They called me, honey. Since they couldn't reach you... You have to clear it soon. Or else..."

"You can't be serious," muttered Eden, in shock. "I paid enough for at least one more month!"

"I know, I know, babe, but they said... there's a lot of demand, and they need to look at... profiles with a better pay rate. I'm sorry, honey. Those people are sharks."

"Damn it," hissed Eden, slapping the seat between them in frustration. "Bunch of bloody bastards... Jack, what else did they say?"

"Just that, honey. They want at least a full year's payment within the next two days..."

"Two days!"

She was furious. How was she going to be able to find that much money? Now? Eden could feel her anger rising. This was a nightmare. Even if she did as many Dives as she could for a full month, she would never be able to gather as much money as they wanted, let alone in two days!

301

"You should have told me earlier!" she exclaimed.

"When? When I was locked up in the basement or when we were surrounded by Italian mafiosos? Ya got yourself quite busy surrounded by ears, Miss Don't-tell-anyone-ma'-stuff!"

Eden closed her mouth this time, beaten by Jack's logic. It's true, she had been quite... unavailable to be updated on the matter. Still, she couldn't help but have a hard time enduring this new pressure.

Two days. Two days was way too short... It would never be enough. It's not like she had never tried settling that debt before, or begged Loir to find her the highest paying jobs. Eden had tried everything, almost everything, legal and illegal, dangerous and life-threatening, without blinking, to get her head above the surface. It was never enough. Each time she tried to pay a little, her debt would come back with the same sentence hanging above her head. She closed her eyes, silently praying it would just all go away.

"Babe, you should just let it go," sighed Jack. "I know this is hard, but–"

"How do I let go, Jack?" scoffed Eden. "If I..."

She glanced at George. Even if he was focused on driving, or pretending to be, she couldn't underestimate Dante. Perhaps that car was rigged with mics, and the Zodiac was listening to her every word. She silently closed her fist and shook her head.

"Jack, I can't. This... is all I got left. I can't just say no or stop. I'll do what I can, until... until I can't anymore."

"Oh, honey, you're too good for your own sake; I get your feelings, babe, I really do, but... Damn, this is a shitty world, after all. Ain't fair to ya, it ain't."

Eden turned her eyes back to the window; she couldn't continue this conversation, and there was simply nothing more to add. Her decision wouldn't change... She had been fighting the same battle for years. She couldn't give up now, even if the chain around her neck got tighter and tighter every time... She couldn't let go of what was hanging at the other end of that chain.

Thankfully for her, while they talked, the cars had reached their destination. Or, more accurately, as far as they could go in the Italian cars. The border for the Asian territories was made clear by the different red gates sprawled across the next blocks of buildings. George parked the car and almost ran out to open the doors. Eden used the short interval to turn to Jack.

"Not a word," she said, right before her door was opened.

Jack didn't answer, but let out a long sigh instead. He liked Eden a lot, but he wished he didn't have to worry so much about that little piece of stubborn woman.

Only a handful of people actually stepped out of the cars, including Rose, Rolf, and Dante. Eden tried to put her angst from earlier somewhere at the back of her mind and focus on the job waiting for them instead. They walked over to rally together, Dante's men sending worried glances all around.

"This is where we split up, darlings," said Rose, confident as ever. "My contact will pick us up at the next block, and as discussed, we will be taken along with another group of escorts to the Red Temple. There, we each have our missions. The girls, Jack, and I will distract the Yakuza, while Eden sneaks out to find whatever she needs to find in there."

"I will send a signal as soon as I do," nodded Eden. "Loir will be in contact with me at all times, anyway."

She had noticed Dante's intense stare on her but was doing her best to ignore the two golden rings shining at her.

"It might take a few hours for us to entertain and distract them and for Eden to have a chance to sneak out, so... I hope you brought sandwiches and popcorn, my darlings," chuckled Rose.

Unlike half of his men who blushed at the escort's flirtatious glances, Dante's eyes only darkened. Eden smirked. He had been taunting her with Rose, now he had to face the realization that, as much as he hated it, she would have to entertain other men too...

"Be quick," he said in an ice-cold tone. "We will barge in as soon as we get your signal, or if we feel your approach might... fail."

"What if the Rat's men are ahead, or attack too?" asked Jack with a grimace. "Ain't against some action, boys, but I'd rather not be caught in the crossfire... again."

"Then we will attack too," retorted Dante. "This way the job will be done faster..."

"Alright," said Rose. "Let's get going, ladies..."

Flaunting her sexy blue dress and cleavage, she sent another wink to the Italians, and the redhead was the first to leave, looking perfectly confident despite walking in the streets with such eye-catching and vibrant attire. Eden glanced at Dante for one second before walking after Rose.

However, to her surprise, Dante suddenly grabbed her wrist. Everyone around either scattered back into the cars or stared in shock at the boss holding the young woman's arm.

"Let go," she groaned.

"...Don't take stupid risks."

Eden paused, a bit surprised. This wasn't what she was expecting to hear right then...

"A bit late for that, isn't it?" she scoffed. "Let go of my arm. I hate the grab-and-pull move, it's for dicks."

Dante let go, but slowly, his eyes still on her. Eden couldn't take one more second of his intense stare, and walked out of there as fast as she could, despite her heels. She felt Jack right behind her and forced herself not to look back as she quickened her pace to catch up to Rose.

"...Tell me again how there's nothing between you two?" whispered Jack.

She decided not to answer. Her heart was a cage of nervousness and angst, and that was already too much.

Rose walked in the streets without an ounce of fear or doubt. She had the assurance of those who knew the area perfectly. Technically, they were in one of those streets between two territories, with no owner and, as a consequence, the most dangerous. There were only two reasons for a woman to walk there alone: either she knew how to defend herself perfectly, or she had no choice but to put herself at risk. Although there were three of them, including Jack and his hunky figure, it was still dangerous. Hence, despite her apparent calm, Eden suspected Rose was speeding up to get to safety faster. The redhead's best defense was often her acting and the mask she wore at all times...

After a few more streets, Eden saw Rose put a hand under her nape, where her SIN was. She turned around, moving her hands to her hips.

"So?" she suddenly asked. "Are we really going there?"

"...Yes," sighed Eden.

Rose shrugged.

"I was just checking you hadn't changed your mind..."

"How about ya?" asked Jack, tilting his head. "That's a dangerous thing to do, Rosie."

"Oh please, danger is sexy and right up my alley. Moreover, this might be an opportunity to get into another Zodiac's good graces... No offense to your Tiger, Eden, but a girl's gotta eat. Things are pretty much going to turn into an all-out war between those crazy people as soon as the Dragon is gone anyway... This may not be my first gunfight, but I hope to make it out of there, and I'll go with whoever survives the murder party."

She finished with a smile, and turned around, resuming her walk. Jack and Eden exchanged a surprised glance. In a way, this was so typically Rose... Jack sighed.

"She ain't wrong, ya know. Can't beat bein' taken care of by a mighty man and not having to care about the price of oxygen for the rest of yo' short life... By the way, she knows the Rat is a woman, right?"

Eden shrugged. In a way, it couldn't be helped that her colleague was going to look for her own way out of this... This was why it was so hard to be true friends with anyone. Each individual had to look out for their own safety first. Friendship could sadly turn very expensive if one didn't look out for themselves first...

At least she was glad to find out Rose had been true to her word; another car was parked two streets down, with two people waiting for them on the side. One was a tall and very sexy Asian woman, with heavy makeup, long bleached hair, two piercings on her lips, and very flashy clothes. She was wearing a cyan, cropped fur coat over a long purple kimono dress, in a surprising contrast between modern looks and tradition.

"Hi, Rosie," she smiled as the redhead approached. "You got the money?"

Rose smiled and took a little card out of her sleeve. Eden had eyes on the guy next to her: a tall guy, also Asian, bald with a large, colored flower tattoo on the side of his head. His eyes were hidden by sunglasses, but he was obviously staring at them, from the way his head went up and down.

"Let's see..." The blonde grabbed the card and began checking the contents.

"Jack, Eden, this is Ayame, a... longtime rival of mine."

"Only the best deserve to be my rival, Rose," chuckled the blonde, "and you're almost as good as me... Well, the money is real. I am surprised you managed to get this amount... What's so important that you want to work in the Red Temple?"

"It's just a trial," shrugged Rose. "You know things aren't going too well on the Dragon's side lately. We're just looking for new opportunities..."

"Well, my client loves when I bring new faces, and the last girls got themselves killed, so... lucky you!"

Although she was smiling a lot, Eden had already decided not to trust that woman. Firstly, she was a bit too enthusiastic for an escort who was about to introduce her client to some potential rivals who could take her place. Secondly, no escort could afford a bodyguard unless they were really favored, and if so, she was way too accepting to bring new people into her sponsor's home... Finally, the car next to them was big, and full of young women already: all dressed in kimonos, none of them smiling or looking at all happy to be there.

# CHAPTER TWENTY-THREE

The car began moving as soon as the doors were locked.

The inside wasn't like a usual car, more like a van, with the seats in a U-shape so that all the young women could actually see each other. Ayame's bodyguard had gone to the front of the car and was perhaps the one driving it. There was a strange silence in the space. It may have been an awkward silence, but Ayame and Rose were a little too... excited for it to be awkward. The young woman with her bleached hair was looking at herself in a little pocket mirror, adjusting her cat eye with kohl and an expert hand, considering the little bumps on the road. Sitting opposite her, Rose was checking her nails in a similar fashion, visibly relaxed. Eden looked around. There were eight other girls inside, all Asian. Most were hiding their hands or had them on their knees, obviously nervous. Like Ayame and them, they were all wearing very fashionable yet traditional Asian clothes in bright, flashy colors. Ayame stood out the most, though, with her cyan fur coat and bleached hair. None of the other girls had their hair dyed.

After a short while, the car stopped again, but Eden knew it was too soon. She had a rough idea of the journey to the Red Temple, and they were still a few streets away. Ayame smiled at them.

"One last stop on the way," she said.

The door was opened, and she stepped out. Eden heard an exchange similar to theirs; other girls were paying to get inside the car and work for the Red Temple. The whole exchange was most likely in Japanese, but Eden's translator was working for her. Jack and Rose could understand too; to work on the Dragon's territory, translation software was a must... Rose let out a very faint sigh.

"...Ayame is basically a pimp for the Yakuza," she whispered. "She gathers girls and lets them try out with the Japanese. If they like them, they keep them. If they don't, they kill them."

"They kill them?" repeated Jack in a squeaky voice. "Couldn't you have mentioned that before we got on the ride to hell?"

"How is that relevant? It's not like we plan to get killed, right? Moreover, I'm rather confident in my skills... Aren't you?"

She had said that while smirking Eden's way. The young woman sighed. Rose wasn't wrong. In a way, they had come with a do-or-die mission in mind to begin with. This meant the Japanese would be harder and crueler than they had anticipated, but it wasn't like they had actually planned to stay anyway. She gently tapped Jack's leg and took a deep breath to stay calm. She would reactivate her SIN once they were inside the Red Temple, so her connection to Loir would be their eyes inside. Eden didn't have synthetic eyes, but Loir would be able to follow her position and vitals very precisely through her SIN, so it would be about the same. This way, they would know immediately if anything went wrong, and if she was killed, they would be notified in real-time too...

The new girls entered the vehicle, and everyone had to scoot over a little, as there wasn't much space left. Actually, once the five of them had been seated, it was clear there was no spot left for Ayame. She appeared in the doorframe and gave them a bright smile.

"Alright, that was our last stop, ladies. Get ready for the show!"

She gave them a wink and closed the door right after that. They heard her giggle from the outside until the car started.

"What a show, indeed..."

Eden frowned, and turned to the woman who had spoken. She was visibly different from the other girls. While the scared, mute, young girls were all very reserved and obviously nervous, this one was clearly standing out with her amused smile, haughty attitude, and relaxed pose. Her outfit was slightly different too. She was only wearing dark colors on her kimono. It was luxurious, in black, purple, and silver. Actually, her hair and lips were both purple too. She had a straight fringe above her eyes and a complex hairdo with many hairpins. She actually looked like a goth version of Rose or Ayame... More intriguing were the freckles Eden noticed under the concealer, and the silver hoops in her ears. This woman visibly had Asian-inspired makeup, but something felt off about her.

She caught Eden staring and, to her surprise, gave her a bright smile.

"Hi," she said, extending her hand. "I'm C."

Eden shook her hand after a slight hesitation. She could see the tip of a tattoo on her wrist, hidden under the fabric.

"Eden..."

"Just C.?" asked Jack, raising an eyebrow.

"Just C.," shrugged the woman. "And you are..."

"Call me Jacquie, honey. And girl, those earrings are bombastic!"

"Right?" smiled C. "A gift from a customer. I love them."

The two of them began to chat casually as if they were in a salon rather than on their way to a sex-inclusive and life-threatening situation. Rose and Eden exchanged a glance, both equally suspicious. C. was a bit too enthusiastic and relaxed, in a strange contrast with the rest of the girls present. From what Eden could see, she was probably not much older than them, and on her own too. Eden began wondering what a young woman like her, with no shortage of customers from what she was chatting with Jack about, was even doing here. Even more intriguing were the tattoos she had tried to cover. Not only with her clothes, but Eden could notice something like concealer coming off in her cleavage... Who was she really? It could have been as simple as an escort girl trying to change camps and her former alliance, but the way she spoke of several customers from different backgrounds meant something entirely different...

Eden forced herself not to stare too much, and watch elsewhere instead. For now, C. was probably the least of her worries, and at the bottom of the list of people to worry about. There were more than a dozen girls lined up at the rear of this vehicle, and they were all on the way to the Red Temple. Eden knew that Ayame's visibly joyful attitude couldn't be trusted either; anyone who worked close to the Zodiacs was potentially dangerous...

She remained quiet for the rest of the trip, trying to mentally think about each step of the plan. She'd have to leave as soon as the men were distracted enough, or find an excuse to leave, and search throughout the Red Temple for an access point. From there, Loir would be able to take control, and Dante's men would attack from the outside as soon as the door was open... There were many unknown parameters in the plan, but Eden had something else in mind. If they managed to take control of the Japanese territory, perhaps she could find some money stacked. Where else would a Yakuza boss hide his money but in his most secure house? Yes, perhaps this was an opportunity. With the urgent need for a huge sum hovering over her mind, Eden couldn't pretend to chit-chat with Jack, C., and Rose who had now joined in the conversation. She simply locked her fingers together on her lap and tried to focus.

"We're almost there, bitches!" resonated Ayame's voice suddenly.

Eden tried to look out of the car's window, which was obviously reinforced glass. Was this car owned by the Japanese Mafia too? If Ayame was in charge of regularly bringing new girls, it wouldn't have been surprising.

She couldn't see much, however. Only a very tall, dark brown wall the car was driving toward. A wooden fence? She felt the car slow down until it wasn't going faster than a normal person's walking pace. Still, it kept going. Eden had a vague idea they might be passing some sort of scan, as they were about to enter the domain. Perhaps they were scanning with some sort of X-ray, thermal vision, or bug scanner... They would find nothing on them though. They wouldn't have been so foolish as to bring actual weapons inside.

Yet, the car suddenly stopped. Eden, a bit nervous, lessened her grip on her knee, and sat back, ready for action if needed. She glanced aside. Rose was frowning and, a couple of seats down, C. wasn't smiling anymore either. She probably wasn't as light-hearted as she pretended to be. From her tense posture, she was probably expecting something too... Was she a fighter of some sort? Eden could usually recognize people with some sort of ability, either from the way they moved, the muscles of their body, or their attitude. C. didn't seem to exactly fit the profile, but there was definitely something about her lean body and swift reactions.

The door opened without warning, and Ayame's bodyguard suddenly grabbed one of the girls in the same movement. It all happened very quickly. She was dragged out and the door was slammed closed behind her before they could even hear her scream. Everyone exchanged surprised glances until they heard it. One single, clear gunshot. The screaming stopped at the same time. A few seconds passed in awkward silence. Then, the door opened again to show Ayame this time, smiling.

"Alright. Can't make an omelet without breaking a couple of bad eggs, can we? Everything's alright, and we're almost there. So exciting! Get ready, ladies!"

She closed the door again, and next to Eden, Rose began breathing again, having completely lost her earlier composure. Eden, however, was still a bit stunned. Behind Ayame's arm, farther back on the grass, she had clearly seen a pool of blood...

The car began driving again, a bit faster this time. They were probably almost there, and indeed, it soon stopped again, probably parked. Ayame came to open the door and stepped aside. For a second, no one moved, until C. stepped outside first. Rose followed, then Eden, and everyone after them.

Eden was absolutely stunned by the view this time. This felt like they had traveled through time and space. Everything around them was... exactly like they were standing in the middle of an amazing Japanese garden. The grass was perfectly cut, the little pebbles were forming gorgeous rivers of stones, and the river water was crystal clear. Eden even spotted a big white and red fish swimming by. She looked up. The sky was blue, the sun setting slowly. There wasn't this thin, muddy gray mist of pollution she usually witnessed above Chicago. This didn't feel like Chicago at all. As far as her eyes could see, Eden was somewhere in faraway, traditional Japan. She looked back at the area they had come from, but it was just a big, bamboo fence, with none of the tops of buildings that should have been visible behind it. An engineered illusion.

"Alright, ladies, I know it's gorgeous, but let's get going! Chop chop!"

The girls all began walking one after another, and Eden noticed the Japanese bodyguard from before was following them, bringing up the rear of the group. She made sure to look ahead and not look suspicious, but it wasn't hard.

She was fascinated by the place. As far as she could see, it was stunningly beautiful. This place was larger than she had thought based on the Map. There were pavilions here and there, scattered around the area, and she wondered if they were all real or some other digital illusion to make the place seem bigger. She noticed several pagoda pillars too, which could have been a good hideout for several security devices... Despite trying to watch out for threats and analyze the place, Eden was constantly getting absorbed in the beauty of it. The girls were walking on a little bridge over a large river, and she saw more of those fish from earlier, with amazingly bright colors. The moss on the side of the river was just as perfectly kept as the little sand-filled spaces, with symbols written in them. There were also trees and bushes of various sizes, but all perfectly fit the area. The most striking ones had blood-red leaves, their branches hanging so low that the tips of their leaves touched the water. Eden could hear water fountains, the sounds of steps on wood, and the gentle whistling of invisible birds. No honking, no sounds of cars or city life whatsoever. The only sound she couldn't recognize was an instrument, being played from the large, red structure they were headed to.

It was a gigantic three-story pagoda with red roofs, like on the Map. Eden realized this was the only thing about this place she had ever actually seen with her own eyes. This was the only tall building in the place, the only one that could be seen from outside their gigantic bamboo fence... Perhaps also the only real thing. Eden knew all too well she couldn't rely on her senses to trust anything in this place. Like in the Dark Reality, everything here could be generated by projections, games of lighting, and other tricks. Even the round leaf and flower floating in the river beneath them were perhaps completely fake...

Trying to keep the reality of this beauty in mind, Eden kept following everyone. If the car had stopped right at the entrance, it was still a pretty long way from the large gate to the main residence... If Dante's men walked in without the security system taken over by Loir, this garden could turn out to be much, much more dangerous. Even now, all the women and Jacquie were walking in a line, following Ayame closely. Eden realized that this was for a very specific reason, and that Ayame was taking a precise path like she was supposed to. Who knew what would happen if someone tried to run and stepped where they shouldn't... This was truly impossible to beat from the outside. If one couldn't trust what their eyes saw, it would be just the same as being completely blind. Even in the Dark Reality, Eden knew there were some rules, and even if she didn't, Loir would be able to see what shape or form the code around her was taking. Here, it was another kind of arena. They couldn't rely on their SINs or hacking partners–her SIN! Eden realized she had forgotten to turn it on. With a faint movement, she quickly turned it back on in stealth mode, with the most minimal functions, which would give Loir the information he wanted, but make her invisible to any kind of scope in there. Once again, this was the kind of thing that would have been impossible if she wasn't a Dive Hacker.

"Alright, we're almost there!" sang Ayame, visibly joyful. "I hope you're in good shape; the gentlemen are probably dying to meet you! Oh... Shall we greet this big baby first!"

Just as she had said that, she stopped in the middle of the new bridge they were crossing, and turned to the side, toward the river. Eden suddenly felt something, like a hint of fear pushed by an instinct. She glanced down at the river, wondering what they were waiting for. Jacquie put his hands on her shoulders.

"Hun, what do you think is—"

Before he could finish his sentence, they all heard it. A loud movement, like a wave, from the pond a bit further. For a full second, a scaled body made an arch above the water and disappeared again. Eden felt her heartbeat accelerate a bit and tried to calm down, remembering Loir was monitoring it. Still, knowing what was about to show up wasn't helping, especially as a much, much bigger shape than she had expected began moving in the water, steps away from the bridge they were on. The river suddenly expanded itself out of the blue, growing several inches wider in a very strange way. Eden gasped, and the scaled body appeared again. It was strangely hard to follow, despite the clear water, but the trick was in the color of its body; it was blue, almost the same color as the water itself. At times, it felt like catching a glimmer under the surface, and then, she could clearly see the scales moving.

"What is...?"

The shape moved quickly underneath, and Ayame suddenly grabbed the first girl behind her by her nape. The girl screamed, panicked and confused, but before she could react, she was violently thrown over the bridge's balustrade. Everybody froze in utter terror. Her body brutally hit the water, although it felt like it was just a couple of inches below them. She seemed to float until she began struggling and paddling in a panicked manner, screaming. It was obvious she didn't know how to swim and was struggling to stay afloat with her heavy outfit.

All of a sudden, she was gone. It felt like Eden had just blinked, but the body was suddenly gone, and instead, a lonely, single head was floating on the surface. Jacquie silently squealed in horror behind her, and Eden was just as shocked. There was only... a head left, and a large blood pool.

"Sei-chan!" exclaimed Ayame, smiling happily. "I hope you enjoyed dinner!"

She then turned around and resumed walking. Jacquie had gone from holding her shoulders to holding Eden's hand, his shaking like a leaf.

"What the heck was that... That thing... ate that girl? Was it supposed to do that?"

No, it wasn't. There was no point in an animatronic eating anything, it

311

was a machine! Even if it had somehow sliced or crushed that body, it should have left most of the body parts there. Spit it out, somehow. Yet, the head soon disappeared too, clearly... eaten. Eden felt a wave of fear go down her spine, for real this time.

That thing wasn't animatronic. It was very much alive and able to eat humans. .....A Chimera. A scientifically-engineered, living monster.

Eden had only heard of them, but had never seen one of those things in real life. Chimeras were so rare they had almost become something like an urban legend, where many people knew it was possible, but too few had actually seen one in real life to be sure it was true. Well, she now had the proof before her very own eyes that... it was. And it was scary. How much did it cost to create one of those? Had the Snake ordered one, or had the Yakuza always had such a thing in their garden, like a pet attached to their territory? Either way, it wasn't just a threat, but also a huge problem for their plan.

Eden had thought things would be very easy once Loir had taken control of the whole place. All it took was for her to find where to plug the device in and let the hacker work his magic. Things should have gone smoothly, and she even heavily counted on the fact that this place was full of electronically-controlled defenses for Dante's invasion to be done in an easy and almost non-violent way. However, there was no way to electronically control a monster made of actual synthetic flesh!

"Oh, I think I'm going to be sick..." muttered a girl close to them.

Eden felt nauseous too, but for a very different reason. She had promised Dante an easy way in, but it was now clear she had been fooled by the rumors about the Snake. Perhaps his infatuation with technology was real, but so was the gigantic dragon swimming in those waters. This would be a very different problem to settle.

"Anyone else want to take a swim, be my guest!"

Eden raised her eyes to Ayame. The young woman was smiling, and it was a frightening smile from someone who had just fed a human being to that thing. She could kill and be perfectly fine about it, not an ounce of remorse showing on her face. Eden tried to regain her composure, but she was almost the only one. All the other girls in the group were clearly horrified, their eyes on the pool of blood below, or the spot that girl had stood just seconds ago. Rose was white as a sheet and took a very faint step back. There was nowhere else to go on that narrow bridge filled with young women, though. Eden's eyes went a bit farther and fell on C.

She was the only other person who didn't look or act scared. Instead, she had a serious expression on, but that was it. Neither her face nor the hand on her hip expressed anything else. It was as if nothing shocking had happened, nothing worth getting a reaction out of her. Either she was expecting this, or she wasn't scared at all. Or she didn't care, but Eden was starting to be more and more curious about that woman's reasons for being here...

"I know Sei-chan is very fascinating, but let's get going, ladies!"

As if Ayame's excited voice had suddenly turned into a violent whip, the entire group began moving right away, half of them now scared of her. The girls there probably understood they didn't risk being fed to Sei-chan as long as they didn't anger or upset that woman and whoever they were about to serve. Eden, however, was more worried about the dragon. It also meant it probably didn't hold to the rule that anything coming in from the main door was spared; that thing was most likely trained to attack enemies and defend a certain territory. If Ayame had been the one thrown overboard, would it have attacked right away too? The attack had been really fast... Perhaps she was behaving as if she was safe, but the bleached blonde wasn't much safer than the rest of them, just acting like it. That thought reassured Eden a little.

The group resumed walking toward the red pagoda. Eden had already seen it as a miniature on the Map, so she knew its scale, but the rest of the group were almost breaking their necks looking up. That building was impressive. It was as if the very traditional infrastructure had decided to become tall and rival all the skyscrapers around. The red roofs were misleading them into thinking there were only three floors, but they were obviously too high and too far apart to be only one floor each. More like five or six... Eden tried to calm her nerves, remembering that Loir was monitoring her heart rate, but this was still quite a challenge waiting for her. This place was huge... It could mean good hiding places, but also a long time before she'd find what she had infiltrated this group for.

They arrived at the doors, and Eden realized they had seen absolutely no one guarding the place until now. Two men were standing on the terrace of the pagoda's entrance, with heavy weapons in their hands. Like the huge bodyguard following them, those guys were massive, covered in tattoos, and wearing sunglasses. They barely nodded when Ayame waved her fingers at them with a playful look. For a second, Eden even wondered if they weren't statues or holograms, as they were completely still and silent... Only when she followed the group inside and walked between those mountains did she confirm that they were indeed breathing.

They walked into a sort of entrance hall, with bamboo walls, mats under their feet, and, surprisingly, a row of shoes on the side. There were at least forty pairs lined up in perfect rows. Eden even noticed some had names on them...

"Shoes off," ordered Ayame, as she was taking her own off. "Heels are sexy but no need to ruin the mats with them!"

Jacquie and Eden exchanged a look, a bit surprised. That was surprising... It didn't feel like Yasumoto was concerned about customs or such a thing as preserving the mats. Still, everyone obeyed, and soon a line of high heels appeared in a row. Eden noticed how Ayame was staring at all those heels... Perhaps she was wondering if they had hidden weapons? A high heel shoe could definitely be a weapon in itself too... Eden had already seen one or two of her colleagues use it against some undesired or pushy customers.

Still, aside from the two gorillas outside, this entrance hall was strangely bare and unguarded. It felt like a museum entrance, with only a couple of Japanese art pieces hung on the wall or on little tables for display. Once all the girls had their toes exposed, Ayame turned around to face them. This time, the bleached blonde had a serious look on.

"Listen, ladies. You're now in the House of the Snake. I don't need to remind you he is a Zodiac, but his men are as impatient, merciless, and cruel as you all can imagine. If you make a mistake, no one here will think twice before killing you. So, business smiles on. You perk up those butts, do what you're told, and if you're asked anything, the answer is yes and a polite one. I warn you, you're not allowed anywhere above the fifth floor. For those who were wondering, the bathrooms are..."

Eden glanced at the stairs behind Ayame, probably leading to the higher floors. Just like Dante's building, this place most likely had the same configuration; the higher they went, the closer they would get to the Zodiac's private quarters, to what he was hiding there and did not want others to see. Despite the warnings, Eden was getting a bit more excited to be able to sneak around this place. If the Snake was as fond of technology as the rumors said, the place could be rigged with more tech she could steal once this whole ordeal was over. Perhaps Dante wouldn't care about her and Loir getting their hands on some precious pieces of equipment...

Eden glanced down at some of the items displayed, probably expensive art. Would those bring in a lot of money if they were sold? She didn't care much about what plans Dante had for this place, but she hoped to find some nice treasures before he could seize everything and get curious about what she grabbed for herself...

"...only some lieutenants today. So no need to freak out about broken glass, alright? Those guys are just a bit... ungentlemanly, but they are good guys. Right?"

Ayame finished her sentence with a little smile. So they weren't going to "serve" any higher-ups, only entertain the small-fry Yakuza... Eden had only half-listened to this crap, but from Jack's somewhat passive expression, nothing very thrilling or worrying had been said that she would have missed. She was more worried about where they were being taken to, and how to get out of there fast. Unlike Rose or Ayame, Eden wasn't really standing out amongst all the young women; they were mostly taller than her and wearing even more colorful clothes. Would they notice a missing person among the group...? They began moving again and Eden suddenly realized: they were already missing someone.

C. wasn't among them anymore. Eden discreetly looked around, but the goth was really gone.

"...What are you looking for?" asked Jacquie.

"C. She's gone," whispered Eden.

"Oh, she asked if she could make a stop by the bathroom. Ayame said yes, and the goril—the guy that was behind us went with her..."

Eden was surprised. The two of them had left so smoothly in her couple minutes of inattention that she completely missed them. The room was large and there were several girls around, but Eden didn't think one could really vanish before they realized! She already had an ominous feeling about it... Was C. looking to be isolated as well? Eden worried a bit and checked that she had really turned her SIN back on. If that woman was by any chance working for the Rat, their opponents were taking the lead already...

She didn't have time to pretend to go to the bathroom too, even in the unlikely event it would have worked. The group resumed moving. There were more guards standing inside on each side of the door.

Ayame was visibly very used to the place. While the little group behind her stayed close to each other and would look around to try and take in their surroundings, she moved easily from one room to another, greeting the Yakuza that walked by with a large smile, flirtatious glances, and calling some by their names. Eden noticed they hadn't gotten higher than the first floor. Yet, it would be scarily easy to get lost in there. Perhaps on purpose, every single corridor was exactly the same as the previous one. Same wooden floors, same dark red bamboo walls. The only thing that changed was the art pieces on the walls, sometimes ancient paintings, sometimes mere scrolls with calligraphy on it. The few rooms they walked by, though, were different. They all had mats, but they had different settings, some obviously to receive people, some for training. It wasn't often they passed by doors that were left open, however, so Eden had only been able to glance at a few before Ayame took them where she wanted.

"We're here," she finally said as they arrived in front of a large red door. "Showtime!"

She suddenly opened the door, and a wave of sound hit the little group. Because the doors were so thick and heavy, Eden hadn't even noticed there was music playing on the other side, and loud too. Not only that, but the room was filled with about thirty men and about as many young women already, everyone laughing and chatting loudly. The room had mats on the floor and dark red walls like the others, but that was the only similarity. Dozens of little tables were put on the floor, every inch of them crowded with glasses, bottles of alcohol, and food. The lights were dim and changing colors from red to a bright orange or purple, in a small spectrum of colors that made the whole place feel even hotter than it was. And it was already pretty hot. After the sounds, Eden realized the inside of that place felt terribly hot and humid and was... quite smelly too. A lot of the men there were half-naked, showing off their tattoos, but for some reason also sweating profusely. The masses of skin and sweat made Eden feel very uncomfortable, even as they all walked in. This felt like arriving in the middle of a party that had gotten too wild already. Even the girls already inside were obviously too drunk, laughing loudly and making wobbly movements.

Their group was probably there to serve as "refreshments". As soon as they arrived, a few of the ones already there stood up and left through the doors behind Ayame. Eden looked around, but she already knew it would be hard to escape from there, quite literally so. The room was big, and there were doors at both ends, but there was no way those doors could be opened without someone noticing. They were too large, there were too many people, and the lighting in this room was too different.

"New ladies! Come here, my pretties!" shouted one of the men.

If they had been terrified before, Eden had to admit that her new colleagues were very professional now. The girls had all changed from the scared expressions they had earlier to wide smiles, confident attitudes, and sexy moves, each picking her target already. Of course, they knew they would probably be paid handsomely for this if they acted well, and perhaps, the threat of what would happen if things went wrong convinced them to work harder too.

Another thing bothered Eden as the group scattered around: everyone there was sitting down on the mats on the floor. Hence, those standing up were all very visible and... standing out from the Yakuzas and their entertainers. She quietly sat down with Rose and Jack, as luckily, all Yakuzas were already taken care of by two or three ladies already. Eden had noticed that some women weren't busy servicing the men, but instead, were just bringing the bottles around and pouring them, or clearing the dishes off the tables for new ones to arrive. Hence, just a few minutes after they had come in, the doors were opened again, some women walking out while some walked back inside. Perhaps the ones that were most used to the place... In any case, it meant they weren't completely trapped.

"What now, honey?" whispered Jack. "What do we do?"

"Now, you two stay here," retorted Eden. "You already helped me get in, if they find you snooping around like me, they will kill you. You're safer here playing along than coming with me."

"I'm fine with that, but not with the small fries here," said Rose, her lips tight. "Those guys are obviously the lower ranks here... I don't see how I'll empty some pockets and fill mine. Even the alcohol they drink looks and smells cheap! I'll leave them to those bitches...."

"Rose, no! You wait here with Jacquie before you get yourself killed; we didn't come here to make money!"

"Perhaps you didn't, Eden, but I did! Don't worry about me, I'm a grown-ass girl. You do your business, I'll do mine. That's a... Wait, Jack, is that guy waving at you or me?"

Indeed, on the other side, one of the men seemed to be sending grins their way, and waving a bit strangely. Jack waved back, and the guy got excited all of a sudden, agitating the bottle in his hand until he almost hit one of the girls next to him.

"You're so pretty!" he shouted loudly. "Come here, my lovely lady!"

316

"Oh, dear," Jack muttered through his teeth, stuck into a fake smile. "Don't you guys dare leave me here..."

He moved toward the guy, trying to act polite and sexy, but Rose and Eden could see how awkward poor Jack was as the elated Japanese man grabbed his wrist and sat him on his lap, completely forgetting the other ladies next to him. Eden grimaced, while Rose was shaking her head.

"What an idiot," grumbled the redhead.

"He's in serious trouble... How do you think this guy will react once he realizes Jack is not a lady?"

"No idea. Don't worry though, I'll try to make sure he stays alive until you come back... Just go find your thing and we'll discuss my cash later."

"Thanks, Rose."

"Don't thank me, it makes it sound like we're friends..."

Eden chuckled, but she moved to the other side of the room. She wasn't too worried about Jack since Rose had promised to watch over him, but now she had to focus on her own mission. Her eyes were set on the door, so she moved to sit next to the Yakuza closest to it, and waited for an opportunity. She coughed faintly in her hand to cover her voice.

"...Loir, ready?"

"Ready when you are, my Kitty! ...Oh, did you get some sushi?!"

# CHAPTER
# TWENTY-FOUR

Eden tried hard not to roll her eyes at Loir's sentence. How did he always come up with the weirdest suggestions? ...Perhaps this wasn't his weirdest, though. There actually was sushi on a table not too far from her. Eden smiled at one of the Yakuzas across the room, trying to act the part. That guy was already surrounded by escorts and busy with them, though. She leaned toward the one closest to her, keeping the smile up, but her attention was still locked on the door. No one was paying attention to her, but Eden knew better than to trust what her eyes could see. Those men weren't allowed such favors just for the sake of it; they were probably valued men of the Snake. Hence, they probably weren't as dumb as they looked right now, and she couldn't trust their apparent inattention. Even Ayame, who was acting all coy with one of them, was sending glances left and right from time to time. Perhaps she was just looking to see which escorts deserve to be the most rewarded and work there again afterward, but Eden didn't trust that woman for one second.

"Sashimi! Sushi! Onigiri! Temaki! Nori! So many yummy things!" chanted Loir in her ear.

Strangely, being able to hear her crazy friend again made Eden feel a little bit more secure. It seemed like no one had picked up on her reactivating her SIN clandestinely, so she had high hopes she would manage to stay under their radars long enough to find what she had come for. This wouldn't have been possible for just anyone, so she was grateful her unique type of SIN made her undetectable, or almost...

318

"...Have you found it yet?"

Eden had a hard time concealing her surprise. How could she hear Dante too? Only Loir should have had a connection to her! She didn't answer, but Loir's hysterical laugh in her ear made her grimace.

"Big Kitty's in!"

"Why?" asked Eden, as quietly as she could.

"Because I was curious about your well-being," chuckled Dante in her ear. "It turns out I am quite a possessive man..."

No kidding, Eden wanted to say. However, she couldn't just keep talking out loud and making grimaces, not with so many people in the room; they'd end up noticing a woman talking to herself. Even the Yakuza closest to her probably wasn't drunk or dumb enough that he'd miss one of the escorts acting strange. She cleared her throat and with a bright smile, as all the girls had decided to take shots, she brought a little cup of something that reeked of alcohol against her lips. She recognized the characteristic taste of sake, which wasn't much of a surprise. Eden hoped she wouldn't have to drink too much...

"Kitty's in the fish tank!" joyfully announced Loir. "Cap'n, I repeat, we got the Kitty in the fish tank!"

"Can you tell her exact position?" asked Dante.

"Kitty's on the ground floor, with a lot of little fishies around! Woohoo, party time!"

It was frustrating not to be able to answer back. Eden glanced toward the door again. She ought to get out of there before she was too drunk, or deemed too useless. Most of the girls were trying to act coy to the Yakuza, and even Rose was actively seducing one of them, probably the one she had deemed most interesting. Jack was still on his too. The guy who had picked him had even gotten rid of all the other girls and was solely focused on the drag queen, looking completely smitten by Jacquie's chatting and gestures. Eden was a little bit worried. That guy was the biggest in the room, literally a little mountain by himself... Would Jack be okay if she left him here? She exchanged a glance with Rose, but the redhead gave her a wink. As she had promised, Rose would definitely watch him.

Eden looked at the door and stood up, acting determined. She should just act as if this was normal rather than trying to sneak out of a room crowded with over thirty people... She smiled at one of the girls bringing in more food, letting her in before she stepped out. Once in the corridor, Eden was immediately faced with a tall guy.

"What are you doing here?"

"Bathroom break?" said Eden, trying to act a bit embarrassed. "It's all that sake and raw fish, I'm not used to it..."

"Oh, yeah, European chicks all get that. Next door on the right, but not more than five minutes."

"Thanks!"

Eden turned to the right, going straight to the room that the guy had indicated. It was a small bathroom indeed, and she locked the door behind her as soon as she was in, letting out a long sigh.

"You should be careful with raw fish, Kitty. Have you heard of the Anisaki worm? It's super gross! It looks like a long, white worm and that thing can give you abdominal pain, nausea, and vomiting within hours, and–"

"Loir, shut up, I didn't eat any raw fish, and you're making me feel sick."

"Oh... Wait, you had premium-grade sushi right in front of you, and you didn't eat it? Are you crazy?!"

Eden rolled her eyes. Who was the crazy one? After telling her about that gross worm thing... She let out a long sigh and looked around the room. As expected, there were no windows, but she suspected there would be cameras, so she moved to face the mirror and turned the tap on all the way to have the water flow as loud as possible, pretending to wash her hands and rinse her mouth when she needed to talk.

"Loir, we have a problem."

"I know, I'm sure there was even red tuna, and yellowfish, and–"

"They have a Chimera, Loir. Seiryū isn't an animatronic. It's a Chimera."

"...Chimeras are real?" asked Dante.

"Of course, they are real!" exclaimed Loir, sounding offended. "Scientists have been working on Chimeras since the twentieth century! A single organism composed of cells with more than one distinct genotype exists naturally among all types of creatures with more than one cell. Like flowers with multiple colors or cats with two colors of fur! They're super cute, by the way!"

"Loir, focus," sighed Eden.

"I am focusing! There are tons of natural chimerisms in nature, but once they understood that, some crazy scientists also decided it would be fun to make mixes between animals and see what pops out of the hatter's hat!"

"Those experiments were forbidden," muttered Eden.

"Of course they were," sighed Loir. "For tons of reasons. Illegal testing on animals and humans, lack of protocols and total disrespect for nature, and, of course, the creation of potentially dangerous weapons for military purposes. I mean, I don't see why they never allowed the unicorn project. Unicorns are nice!"

"You're saying the dragon is one?"

Eden nodded.

"Yeah..."

"That's a bummer, Kitty, I can hack many things but not a dragon... Wait... The dragon is alive? Really? With the fangs and the mustache and all? The mustache is important! Oh my God, can we keep him?! Pretty please?"

"That thing is a mankiller," groaned Eden.

"I'm not asking you, bummer; I'm asking Sugar Daddy."

Eden couldn't help but roll her eyes again, especially since she could hear Dante chuckle.

"If Mommy says no, it's no, sweetheart."

"Can you not indulge in the craziness, please?" she groaned. "Loir, I got three minutes left in this bathroom before the guard realizes I didn't just come here to freshen myself up. This building is like the other Zodiac buildings we have seen or studied from what I saw. The higher I go, the more security there'll be."

"We could provide a distraction from the outside," said Dante.

Eden hesitated. She could use a bit of distraction so no one would have time to bother with one of the escorts missing, but she was a bit worried as to what kind of distraction the Italian would come up with... She knew the cars were located at the borders, and even if they entered the Snake's territory, it would take a few minutes until they got there. However, she wasn't sure she could find somewhere to plug in the device in as little as a few minutes, and she didn't want to have the death of several of Dante's men on her conscience.

"...No, I'll find a way to go upstairs," she finally retorted.

"I don't like this," said Dante with a cold voice. "The faster we get in, the faster you're out and we are done."

"You can't do anything unless I've unlocked the security, Dante. Getting impatient won't make things go any faster."

"Well then, make things go faster before I tear down that door and come get you myself."

Eden blushed and looked down, a bit taken by surprise at his angry tone. He really was serious about retrieving her... He definitely didn't like having her on the enemy's territory. She took a deep breath and splashed her face with some more cold water, trying to calm down. Having Dante's voice in her ear was already plenty enough to drive her crazy, but now, his possessiveness and guarding attitude toward her were definitely too sexy to handle. Eden hated to be considered a damsel in distress, and she had never been one to fall for possessive men, but...

"I don't like this," he grumbled.

"I'll be quick," she muttered, her face cold and her cheeks burning.

"Excuse me..." suddenly squeaked Loir's voice. "I can still hear you both... I don't wanna butt in Mommy and Daddy's conversation, but..."

Before Eden could listen to the rest of Loir's sentence, she heard someone loudly knock at the door.

"Miss?" the man said in Japanese. "I'm not supposed to let anyone out of the room for too long! Or, uh... in there!"

"Sorry, bad stomach!" she replied. "Just a couple more minutes, please!"

"O-okay, but... hurry up!"

Eden frowned, intrigued. That guy was a lousy guard, or perhaps shy around women.

"I'll go upstairs now," she muttered, taking several deep breaths. "Loir, get ready for when I plug that thing in."

"Always ready for the Kitty!"

"Anything else about the dragon we have to know?"

321

"I literally just walked in and had fifteen minutes inside that room, tops. I only saw about thirty Yakuza, probably small fry. Jack and Rose are with them. Two guards at the entrance, but I'm sure there's a lot more, on top of the security tech."

"Got it."

Eden raised her head, noticing how she had ruined her makeup. It looked like she had cried, or been through a rough time... It gave her an idea. She took a deep breath and, holding her stomach, she walked slowly to the door.

When she opened it, she noticed the guard, who had gone back to the other side, but his eyes went right to her, and he frowned. The young blonde woman was grimacing and holding her stomach with a poor expression.

"I'm sorry," she muttered. "I really feel sick... I think it's something that I ate, I... My stomach feels funny, and I threw up too... Do you think it's the raw fish?"

"I told you the Anisaki worm is dangerous!" Loir shrieked in her ear.

"She's faking," sighed Dante.

"Oh... Oh, our Kitty is a good actress, you know? Did you know once, she tried to make me think Santa isn't real?"

"No kidding..."

Eden tried hard to ignore those two and focus on her acting instead. The pearls of water on her forehead could easily pass for sweat, and thanks to the messed-up makeup, she probably did look bad. The guy grimaced and walked over, looking concerned.

"I'm sorry, miss, are you really sick?"

Eden nodded, and took a step back, leaning her body against the wall with a frown, opposite the bathroom door. The guy sighed and approached again, putting a hand on her shoulder.

"Okay, but I can't leave you here. I'll just get you back inside and ask Ayame-san to–"

Eden moved before he could end his sentence. She threw her left leg in the air with impressive speed, hitting the poor man right between his legs, and hard. His cheeks inflated like a balloon and he let out a faint sound, the pain showing on his face that had gone completely white. Eden didn't wait until he could breathe again; she stepped aside and rotated her lower body, using her other leg to hit the man's flank with enough strength that it sent him flying into the bathroom. His head hit the wall opposite, and he fell right there, unconscious. Eden stepped back and quickly closed the door.

She knew that it was going to be a matter of minutes before someone realized something was wrong; even if no one had caught the action on surveillance camera, they would notice the missing guard, or he could even wake up sooner than she hoped.

Eden began running across the halls, trying to stay far from the rooms, and find stairs to the upper floors; she was grateful for the mats that covered the sounds of her heavy legs, but each time she had to step on the wooden floors, it was a nightmare of squeaking and banging. She hoped she could make it to the room she was looking for... She finally found some stairs, and ran up, hoping not to find anyone yet. ...Why was no one coming, actually? This felt a bit too easy. She had only seen closed doors when the rooms weren't empty, and no one had come for her yet. Perhaps she was lucky, but her instincts were telling her otherwise. Something was going on...

"Loir, did you do something?"

"...How do you know?"

"What did you do?" she asked, surprised.

"I swear, I just opened the can to try, I haven't even tasted it yet!"

Eden rolled her eyes. So it wasn't Loir after all... She didn't even want to ask what disgusting thing he had been about to try, or where the hell he had gotten his hands on some cans. The only ones she had seen so far were the cans of dog food Rolf had gotten for the pups...

"There's something weird going on," she muttered as she reached another level. "How come I haven't seen anyone else yet? No other Yakuza guarding the rooms, and a lot of other rooms are closed too..."

She heard Loir type on his keyboard, but neither of them could explain what was going on, and Eden was getting very uneasy. Eden tried to count, but she had gone up at least four or five floors. It was strange she had seen literally no one, not even guarding the doors and corridors... She decided to stop in one of them and wait for a second, looking around. She might now be closer to one of the panels she was looking for. She walked up to one of the closed rooms, trying to listen. From what she had seen before, the doors were sound-proof, but...

As soon as she had put her ear close to the door, she took it back. She could hear men yelling in Japanese in there, and even more curious, banging against that door... as if they were trapped? Eden stepped back and resumed running.

"Loir, do you think someone else could have gotten to a control panel before us?"

"I doubt it, you didn't waste any time, and you didn't even have sushi! Plus, taking control of their whole security just from one control panel is the work of genius! I'm a genius! That device you have is expensive to buy or to make, there are only a handful of hackers who can do that!"

"The Rat may have come up with the same plan as us, then," sighed Eden. "There's clearly someone in control here, someone playing... against the Japanese. Dante, did you–"

"I did not send someone else ahead."

Eden grimaced. Then it was a high possibility they had been beaten at their own game. She reached a new floor, and this time, the decor changed. It was a lot less traditional, a lot more modern. This was her chance. Eden tried to find a crack in the wall, a little slit between two panels. She found it and, using her leg, kicked one of the panels until she deformed it enough to grab the edge and pull it off the wall. A portion of the wall as large as three doors came off with some more kicking, revealing what Eden was looking for. A very small square with an access port. She put Loir's device right in.

"Loir, you're up."

"Yay, come here, baby! Cutie cutie, come here show me your... sashimi..."

As she heard his excitement go down, Eden grimaced.

"Loir?"

"Oh. Uh-oh. Oh, *no bueno...*"

"Loir, tell me what's wrong."

"Kitty, you were right. Another hacker is on the case. Oh, this is not going to go well..."

"Can you beat them? Someone we know?"

"Yup... I recognize that kind of coding, very, very nasty... Oh, she's not gonna be happy... How badly do you want in, Kitty? Because this is trouble..."

"Her? You know that hacker? Is she working for the Rat?"

"I dunno, but... uh... She's an old friend from the Edge, so she's not going to be happy to see me... Oh, Circé, it's been a while, you old witchy lady..."

Eden let out a long sigh. Of course. Circé. C.

Eden stood still, hesitating. If that other hacker was ahead, it would be a lot of trouble to get control of the building, both from her side and Loir's. However, she had to do something. She had an ominous feeling about that woman from the start... She should have known she was no ordinary escort to begin with; if that woman was a hacker, perhaps she wasn't much of one... Could she go up against Circé? She knew nothing about that woman or her fighting abilities. She didn't even know who she was working for.

"Loir, what do you know about her?" whispered Eden, walking to the next corridor.

Now that she had to be less worried about the Yakuza, Eden moved freely, but she made sure to stay away from the doors and open rooms. If Circé was in charge of the place, she could easily trap her somewhere, and Eden would really be locked up without anyone to help...

"Uh... First, she really, really doesn't like me," whimpered Loir.

"Go figure..." muttered Eden.

If that woman was part of the Edge when Loir stupidly got them all arrested, she really couldn't be blamed for resenting her crazy ex-teammate.

"Circé is an alias, I have no idea about her real name, Kitty. I just met her while we were part of the Edge, and teamed up as partners..."

"Wait a second... She was your previous partner? She's a Dive Hacker?"

"Yup."

Eden gasped. She hadn't expected that. Seeing how Circé had been far ahead and taken control of the place already, she had thought that woman was a Back Hacker, not a Diver like her... moreover, Loir's former partner!

"...So she knows how to fight?"

"Oh yeah, she can kick butts!"

324

Eden leaned against a wall and let out a long sigh. This whole operation had taken a wrong turn way too fast. Now, she was trapped with an unknown enemy in full control of the area, no idea of her intentions, and separated from any possible backup except for Loir. Could she face Circé on her own? The fact that this woman was Loir's former partner made her wary. If she was part of the Edge, she couldn't be an ordinary hacker. What were her intentions anyway?

"What do you want to do?"

Dante's voice took Eden by surprise. She had almost forgotten he was listening in too... She let out a long sigh, making her decision.

"She beat us at this game; I need to know who she's working for at least. If it's the Rat, we can expect a full-on attack here at any moment. If it's anyone else, we'd better confirm who as fast as possible..."

"Can you and Loir regain control?"

"Loir?" Eden called out.

She could still hear him typing furiously on his keyboard and making strange noises with his mouth, which meant he was still fighting against Circé in his own world.

"It's not like I'm not trying, Kitty! But that old witch has a new partner, and they are not happy about me trying to kick them out of the system!"

"Perhaps she's working with another partner from the Edge."

"It does look familiar, but that old witch might as well be alone if she's got access to a control room!"

Eden nodded.

"Just help me find where that control room is, then I'll face her directly. With what you copied from Pan's Map, we should be able to get a rough idea. Moreover, she still hasn't tried to stop me, which is a bit strange."

"Got it, got it..."

"We're launching our attack," suddenly declared Dante.

"Not yet! I can perhaps regain control if I beat her..."

"Someone else is attacking the Red Temple, and I don't care who," he retorted. "I'm joining in."

Eden didn't know how to answer that. She had a strange feeling that Dante was launching his own attack prematurely because of her, but she didn't dare ask. If it had been anyone else, she would have been glad to get some reinforcements. For now, she felt like a mouse in a gigantic trap...

"Loir, keep trying to beat them," she whispered.

"I am!"

Then, Eden resumed walking, making sure she stayed close to a wall and watched her surroundings. She was really curious as to why Circé hadn't tried to capture her yet if she controlled the whole area. It didn't make sense. She ought to have understood Eden was no ordinary escort by now, and if she had come here alone, she should have been wary of any potential enemies. This all felt too easy, and the blonde woman didn't like this...

She kept progressing silently, trying to follow Loir's instructions. Although the Map couldn't show the inside of the building, Loir was using the various filters incorporated into it to roughly determine the location of the control room. The one showing the flow of electrical current was giving a pretty clear indication as to which room necessitated the most inflow of energy. Indeed, after climbing two more sets of stairs, Eden arrived in front of a large but locked door. This definitely looked like the entrance of a control room, with a digital code panel. Moreover, this was the only room on this floor, which meant the inside ought to be pretty huge.

Eden took a quick breath in and rose her leg, ready to force that lock by destroying it.

However, just as she was about to smash the panel, the door suddenly opened. She was stunned, to the point she left her leg hanging mid-air while staring around the room.

It was not as large as she had predicted but still pretty impressive, in a round shape. There was nothing left of the traditional wooden walls, mat floors, and Asian decorations. This was just like Loir's new playroom. Everything was metal: screens, computers, keyboards, hundreds of little consoles, and panels with video surveillance displaying several rooms of the building. Most were showing angry men locked behind doors, banging against the walls, or yelling at the camera, although it was muted. The keyboards were arranged in a circle, as if twenty people could have sat there to monitor them. There was a round central console in the middle, like a large tactile table. There were indeed about twenty people in the room, but most were dead on the floor.

The only person standing was Circé. She was smiling at Eden, from the other side of the room. She looked exactly like before except with her hair down. Eden could see why; most of her hair pins had turned into deadly weapons, some still deeply stuck in the dead men's heads or throats.

"Hi again," said the goth woman with a smile. "So you're my rival, I suppose?"

"You're... impressive," muttered Eden.

She realized Circé had let her in, which probably didn't mean anything good. Either the hacker didn't fear her, or she actually wanted Eden to come here from the beginning. It was disturbing how calm and composed that woman was. She had her fingers running on one of the keyboards at an impressive speed, considering the scary length of her black nails. It was clear she also knew her way around technology...

"So?" asked Circé, her eyes on one of the screens. "Which of the Zodiacs are you working for, sweetie?"

"...The Tiger."

"Ah, the Italian... I'm a bit surprised the Italian bothered with this territory. To be honest, as soon as I understood you were also a hacker, I expected you to be with the Rat."

Eden frowned. So Circé wasn't working for Thao? Then who was she with?

326

Eden had a very bad feeling about this. That woman was way too comfortable, even for someone with a head start like this. If she knew Eden was working for the Tiger, she ought to know this building was about to become a battlefield. Yet, she was there, still playing on the keyboard like a musician on a piano. Eden glanced toward the screens again, wondering if one could let her know when the Italians would arrive. She couldn't see the room she had left Rose and Jack in, either. She hoped they were alright...

"I have an annoying little bug playing against me right now, so I really don't have time for you," sighed Circé. "You looked like a smart girl earlier; you recognized a Chimera right away. How much does the Italian pay you?"

Eden felt a bit bitter, realizing Dante didn't need to pay her at all... although she certainly should have asked him to, thinking back. She shrugged, trying to act composed. Since she couldn't tell which camp Circé was in, she was unsure how much of a threat she'd pose. She was clearly a very good fighter, seeing how she had gotten rid of all those men. Not only a Dive Hacker but also an assassin.

"...A lot," Eden finally said. "Could I ask who you are working for?"

Circé chuckled.

"I'm a private contractor, like you... and my employer probably pays a lot more than yours. Why? Looking for a new master?"

Eden frowned, a bit more cautious. Circé was trying to outsmart her, but the fact that she still hadn't revealed her employer was getting on her nerves. She needed to sort out the situation as fast as possible.

"How did you–"

Before she could end her sentence, several alarms began ringing throughout the control room. Circé glanced at one of the screens, and Eden followed her eyes. The visual had changed, and it was now displaying the entrance of the compound, the same door Eden had entered through just a while ago. The door was closed, but a lot was going on there. It took her several seconds to realize the screen wasn't blurry, but there was actually a smokescreen covering the area. Men could be seen running out of the Red Temple, coming out of nowhere to the edge of the screen, all heavily armed and ready to defend the gate.

"Looks like someone decided to bring the party to us..." said Circé. "Your friends?"

Eden frowned, but it felt a tad too soon to be the Italians... There was obviously something pounding against the main door, seeing how they trembled on the screen. It was going to break open any second now. Circé chuckled.

"Shall we have a bit of fun then?"

She touched a few more things, and suddenly, the doors opened wide on the screen. The fight began right away, multiple gunshots were exchanged. There was no sound, but Eden could see all the vivid sparks on the screen, people running, and some falling to the ground, not moving anymore. It was an absolute war scene. If Dante's men walked into this, it would be even worse!

"Dante, hold on," she said out loud, not caring about Circé hearing her anymore. "The Rat's men are already here, fighting the Japanese!"

"I hear them. We're waiting a couple streets away for when to intervene. Where are you?"

"...I made it to the control room," said Eden, her eyes turning to Circé.

"I'm coming to you."

Dante's words and deep voice gave her a chill, making Eden feel even colder. She knew she was in a more dangerous situation than him, for now. The goth woman wasn't smiling anymore. Instead, she had turned her body toward her and was staring at Eden with a doubtful expression.

"You... were just talking to a Dante, like the Dante De Luca?"

"...I told you I was working for the Tiger," muttered Eden.

"You didn't mention you were on a first-name basis with him."

Suddenly, the door behind Eden closed. She felt her heart skip a beat. Circé was staring at her with suspicious eyes, and now she had imprisoned Eden in this room with her.

"...Who are you? I don't think I heard your name," said Circé. "Who is your partner?"

"I'm still waiting to hear your employer's name," retorted Eden.

"I'm almost done, Kitty!" shouted Loir in her ear. "Just give me two more minutes..."

Even without him saying that, another loud beeping resonated in the room, and Circé suddenly turned her eyes to the panel she was previously working on, looking upset.

"No!" she protested, her fingers furiously typing fast. "That wretched bastard..."

As she was busy fighting back for control of the room, Eden slowly moved to stand farther away from her, getting close to one of the panels. She still had Loir's device hidden in her hand... If she could plug it in here, it could give him a decisive advantage in controlling the room.

"Who are you working for?" Eden asked again, her heartbeat accelerating.

She couldn't help but send glances toward the screen displaying the fight outside, hoping to recognize Dante amidst the chaos. She could see a third group had arrived, but there was so much smoke and firepower, she couldn't tell who belonged to which one of the three opponents; however, it was clear the Red Temple was being invaded and the Japanese were losing ground quickly. The fight was moving toward the building Eden was in, which was a good sign despite the absolute chaos. She hadn't thought there would be that many people, yet the silhouettes kept pouring in through the gates. Eden closed her fist. She needed to take back control of the room, and soon.

She plugged the device into the first port she saw, and suddenly, all the screens flickered at once. Circé's expression fell.

"Damn it! How the hell did he..."

Her eyes suddenly went to Eden, glaring at her as she understood.

"You! You're that damn–"

A creepy laugh resonated around them without warning, even surprising Eden who knew that voice all too well. Loir had taken control and was obviously very happy about it.

"Hi, C.! It's been a while, my darling!"

"Fuck you, Warlock!" roared Circé, glaring all around her.

Eden frowned. Warlock? Was that Loir's alias when he was with the Edge? Groups of hackers usually shared a similar theme for their groups, so it made sense Loir had a different name when he was with them... Still, it felt strange to hear someone else interact so familiarly with him.

"Oh, that's some nasty language you've learned up there. What's up? It's been a while!"

"A while? You're the one who got us all fucking locked up by the Core! All of us, you damn psycho! I thought you were dead, but it sounds like I can still have you crawl out of the rat nest you're hiding in to kill you myself!"

"I know, I missed you too! Sounds like you're in good shape! Oh, by the way, have you met Kitty? I guess you have, since you're in the same room now!"

Circé eyes went down on Eden, who really wished he had forgotten about her for one more minute.

"I can't believe that crazy psychopath found someone else dumb enough to work with him!" roared Circé. "Do you have any idea what he fucking did?"

"I know... He was working with the Edge, and he had you all arrested..."

"I said I was sorry!" sighed Loir in the speakers. "You guys are just so sensitive..."

"I can't believe you're still fucking alive, you dirty rat! I thought the Core had killed you!"

"Oh, they did try," sighed Loir, "but sounds like you made it out of there too! Good for you, C.! Hey, how's Merlin?"

"You're still the same," Circé shook her head. "Nothing but a selfish, insane, and crazy bastard. Merlin is dead, thanks to you! They killed those of us who didn't escape or made a deal with them to survive!"

An explosion suddenly shook the room's floor. It had probably happened several floors below, on the ground floor, but it was big enough to shake the whole building up to their position. Eden was worried about Jack, but she had no time for that now. She silently prayed he had found somewhere to hide...

"Loir, the Italians are here," said Eden. "Make sure we work on their side."

"Okey-dokey, my Kitty!"

"You," said Circé, glaring at Eden. "How can you work with that maniac? Don't you know he murdered half his previous partners?!"

"I can take care of myself," retorted Eden, a bit annoyed. "Loir is my partner now, and as you can see, he took control of the building. So now, tell your group to leave, or they will be caught in the crossfire with a huge disadvantage."

Circé scoffed, her hands leaving the keyboard to stare at Eden with a dismissive look.

"Who the heck do you think you are?" she said. "You chose the wrong side by working with that psycho, little girl. You're going to get yourself killed too."

"Looks like you made it out, though."

Circé tilted her head.

"You think I escaped the Core, like him? ...Who do you think I am working for?"

Eden suddenly understood. Circé had never escaped the Core. She was working for them.


"Dante! Dante, the Core's involved in this!" Eden's voice shouted in his ear.

The Tiger fired two more shots, each finding their target's head. The bodies were falling one after another, and the Italians were progressing smoothly through the area. Since they had entered the gates, the gunshots hadn't stopped, resonating in the air like a concerto of death. The Japanese were pouring out of the building and yelling, but the Italians were slowly winning ground. With Loir controlling what was going on in the area, they were at a clear advantage.

Dante rarely voiced his admiration out loud, but the hacker was indeed impressive. The once peaceful Asian-inspired garden had turned into a deadly maze, full of traps and ready to swallow their enemies any minute. It was as if Eden's partner had become a god, shaping and bending their reality to his will. For every ten Japanese that ran out of the building, half of them were set to perish or be trapped before they even made it within shooting range of their attackers. Gaps were opening unexpectedly under their feet, gigantic walls pulled from the ground in a timely manner so they'd run into it and violently get hit, and the automatic weapons located in secret hideouts around them would only shoot at the Yakuza. It was as if Loir was controlling this like a video game at the hardest level. Yet, he somehow managed not to harm a single Italian in the process.

They were rushing toward the Red Temple, but not fast enough for Dante's taste. He was ahead of his men, and his lieutenants were shouting orders for them to advance, but it wasn't enough. They had to get inside the Red Temple, take control of it by eliminating the Yakuza and the Snake at its head, and then defend their position. This was merely the first part of the operation, and they weren't progressing as fast as he wanted.

Moreover, there was another nuisance: Thao's men. They were ahead of them in the race to the building, simultaneously helping the Yakuza defend their ground while trying to get in themselves. The garden had become a battlefield, with dozens of bodies scattered on the ground. The grass and river were soiled with blood. Shots were fired from all sides, each man trying to take cover behind a tree, a rock, or a wall while hoping not to trigger another trap.

In the midst of all this, Dante De Luca was still standing tall, impressively unscathed and unaffected by the chaos around him. The smoke didn't even make him frown, and his golden eyes were riveted on the tall Red Temple. More precisely, he kept trying to look up at wherever Eden was located right now. He was getting impatient and listening to her wasn't enough. She wasn't talking anymore; from her erratic breathing and grunts, he could tell she had begun fighting Circé, and that woman was not letting her win easily.

"Eden?" he called out.

"I'm... busy!" she grunted back. "Just. You. Hurry. Up!"

"Our Kitty is holding up for now," said Loir, "but that old witch knows how to fight, Big Kitty. They are both in the control room, so I can't help Kitty! What do we do now? I'm having a lot of fun over here!"

"Keep going," said Dante calmly.

He was looking around, ignoring the gunshots fired all around him as if they were a mere nuisance, looking for their enemy. The Rat's men and the Yakuza were nothing compared to the real enemy. If the Core was involved, this was about to go from a mere gang fight to an all-out war. He didn't believe they would have only sent in one agent. The Core had never used this kind of dirty move before, but they probably had no choice, like them. Hence, they most likely had a similar objective...

"The Core wants the weapons."

"To steal them?" exclaimed Loir.

"Whether they get them or not doesn't matter; they probably don't want us to use the weapons against them. Their goal is to empty our hands so we can't fight them later."

"Then they know that we know what they want to do to the Suburbs!" squealed Loir. "...Oh, those villains! Now that they know that we know that they know that we know, it's going to be so complicated!"

Dante didn't care much for the crazy hacker's nonsense, but he grew nervous as the parameters of the operation had changed. He didn't care about wiping out the Rat or the Snake, but now, they had to beat the Core first and foremost. And Eden was still inside that building while they had more enemies than planned.

"Rolf, I'm going in," he calmly announced.

"Sir, we haven't cleared the way yet! Our men are almost there, but the Rat's people are getting in our way!"

Dante looked around. Indeed, there were way too many people between him and the entrance. This place was too big to begin with. Now that the three groups were fighting, things had gotten out of control. Even if he killed everyone on his way, he would empty his magazines and lose too much time just to take one step inside.

"...That Chimera Eden mentioned. Will it attack if provoked?"

"Oh, our Big Kitty wants to bring havoc!" chuckled Loir. "Well, those things are trained as guard dogs, so even if it hasn't come out from the lack of orders to attack... it's still a dog! It should attack when injured!"

"...Then let's make a mad dog out of the guard dog," announced Dante, a wry smile on his lips.

Immediately, a dozen Italians changed their aim without a second of doubt and began shooting at the river from before. It was so sudden, many of their enemies stopped firing, trying to see what their firepower was now aimed at. The only man to move was Dante De Luca.

He moved like a shadow amidst the smoke, gunshots, and shouting. There wasn't a single second of hesitation in any of his movements. He didn't even flinch when a monstrous, furious growl resonated in the area. The furious Chinese dragon had just gone rampant behind him, the giant creature attacking each human moving without distinction. All the shots were now being fired at the blood-thirsty Chimera, but a small group of Italians followed Dante De Luca inside the red building, the doors opening almost magically for them.

"Do we need to take hostages, Boss?"

"No."

Just one word and no more questions were asked.

One after the other, the doors were opened, and the Italians walked into the room, fired, and it was over. They were progressing smoothly, but not fast enough. Dante had even gotten rid of one of his guns, out of ammunition, and taken one of the long Japanese swords off the wall to continue spreading blood. The Tiger was impatient and left long cuts in his enemies' skin like a feline drawing blood with its sharp claws. He was silent, precise, and deadly. He was the first one in a room to kill, the blade hissing before the Yakuza could even understand. Even his own men were secretly impressed to see the boss manipulating such different weapons in perfect tandem without breaking a sweat. Dante De Luca was rarely one to do the dirty work himself, yet this time, not only was their boss on the field, but he was leading them like a god of death, not making a single mistake. That man wasn't just enhanced; he was inhuman.

The Red Temple was being soiled with the color of its name, one room at a time. Loir controlled both the inside and outside with precision, letting out little amused giggles and regularly updating Dante on Eden's status.

"Oh, that one's gotta hurt... Well, our favorite Kitty is fighting like a lioness, Kitty Boss! But that witch is not giving her a good time... Oh, we could make a show out of this. Two ladies fighting in an arena! Should I broadcast this? We could be rich if we make the viewers pay!"

"Loir... Fuck... you!" roared Eden in their ears.

While the crazy hacker laughed, Dante's lips spread in a vicious smile. If she still had the time and energy to get mad at him, she wasn't doing so badly. Most likely, the confined space she was in wasn't practical to fight an opponent...

Suddenly, Rolf barged into the room from the other entrance, with more of their men, all of them looking tired or injured. It was clear they had barely made it inside, some bearing visible marks of their fight against the Chimera. Still, they didn't say a word and joined the rest of their group as they made their way to the next room. Dante grabbed an abandoned piece of clothing lying on the ground, and slowly wiped the blood off his weapon.

"Boss. Another group just took down one of the east walls. They are not the Rat's or the Snake's, they began shooting at everyone in the Red Temple without hesitating. All of these men were dressed in black, but they are clearly mercenaries armed by the Core. They have begun firing at all groups, and now all are making progress toward the building. The Chimera just fell."

"But I wanted it!" whined Loir.

"...What of Thao's men?"

"They found another way in, but they haven't caught up to us yet. We'll most likely run into them soon. Right now, our men are getting rid of the Yakuza first and trying to get to the weapons rooms downstairs."

"Oh, they won't!" protested Loir. "I'm saving the toy room for Kitty Boss!"

Despite the hacker's playful tone, Rolf knew how to read his boss. Despite the huge progress made inside the Red Temple and their men gaining more ground each minute, it still wasn't enough. His stone-cold expression wasn't good. Was it the Core's involvement or Eden's situation making the boss upset like this? He wasn't sure yet, perhaps a mix of the two.

Without saying a word, Dante turned his feet, taking a different direction than his men. Rolf decided to follow him, a bit unsure of his boss' new plan. He was clearly headed toward a different area, not looking to go upstairs or downstairs even as they walked past several stairs. When they reached a room, Dante walked in without any hesitation and, before anyone inside could move, began slicing one man after the other without blinking. Rolf took out his own weapon, a medium to long-range gun, and began shooting each one that could have hindered his boss. Only once everything was silent did Dante step over the bodies and move on to the next room.

"Eden, don't move from where you are. I'm coming," he suddenly said.

"Wha-whatever!" grunted the young woman, probably having a hard time as well.

Suddenly, a gunshot resonated in their ears, and Dante froze.

"...Kitty?" called out Loir with a tiny voice.

"...You damn bitch, my leg!" furiously shouted Eden after a second.

"Oh. She's fine!" announced Loir, as if Dante hadn't heard too. "She's grumpy, but she's fine! Damn, Kitty, you scared me for a second! You can't do that to people, I'm on my last pair of underwear!"

Rolf frowned, confused. That hacker really was a strange creature... However, once Eden's status had been confirmed, the boss resumed walking, visibly determined.

Suddenly, that woman appeared in a corridor. Not Eden, but Rose, the red-haired woman who had been all over the boss. As soon as she spotted them, her eyes lit up, and she ran to them, looking like a mess. Her previously beautiful hairdo was completely undone, and her clothes were a mess. She even had blood on her leg, as she had visibly walked over some bodies with her bare feet...

"Please!" she called out. "Save me! Those people began fighting in the room we were in, so I ran!"

"Which room?" coldly asked Dante.

"Th-the one over there!" she answered, her trembling finger pointing out somewhere further down the corridor they were in.

Dante was about to resume walking, but she suddenly grabbed his arm. Rolf noticed how she was purposely pressing her breasts against him, and probably acting more afraid than she really was too. The Tiger looked down at her with eyes as cold as ice.

"S-save me," she whispered. "I can be your woman like she can never–"

He shot her before she ended that sentence.

One clean, neat shot in the head, so quick she hadn't seen his hand move before the end of the barrel was on her forehead. The woman fell backward with that shocked expression still on her face, her body loudly hitting the floor. Rolf took one step to the side without saying a thing.

"D-Dante! Was that Rose?" asked Eden, still grunting and probably fighting meanwhile. "...Is she a–Agh!–alright?"

"...No. She was just shot down. ...I'm coming to you."

Rolf didn't say a word, but he was impressed by his boss' ability to lie without a hint of guilt. Although, he didn't lie. Only the way he answered, it sounded like the woman was shot by enemy fire, not his... Dante's golden eyes on him convinced him to stay silent, and forget about that scene quickly. He had learned long ago not to ask too many questions or say anything he shouldn't. The Tiger resumed walking, and so did Rolf, not adding a word, the two of them leaving one more body behind.

Dante finally reached the room Rose had indicated, but this time, he stayed outside. Rolf recognized Thao's voice as she was yelling at her men from inside that room.

"Lock this room," he said.

"*Okie-dokie*, Boss!" sung Loir.

They didn't see a thing but clearly heard metal clattering from the inside. Thao screamed in frustration.

"Dante, you Italian bastard! Open this damn room before I fill your body with bullets!"

"I want to make an alliance," he said. "I'll let you leave if you and your men agree to get rid of the Core's people with us."

"What? You want to collaborate against the Core? Have you gone mad? We're about to win! My men are almost at the Snake's hideout underneath. He and his men are hiding inside with their damn weapons!"

"That's true," said Loir. "I see a little snakey with about fifty men inside."

"The Core will be there soon," said Dante. "My hacker controls the room. Either you and I get rid of the Snake and the Core or I get rid of you all."

"The Core? They are one step behind! We saw and fought some of those idiots, but they don't know a thing! The few we didn't kill fled to the upper floors, not downstairs! They don't even know where the weapons are, they kept mentioning their target and ran the wrong way!"

Dante froze and took a step back.

Something felt wrong. It made no sense that the Core's men would go upstairs. They wouldn't have sent someone without knowing what they were coming for, or where to go.

And Eden shouldn't have taken so long to fight that woman off, nor escape from the control room. Circé herself had no reason to remain there to fight Eden, either. Both of them could leave that room anytime, Loir wasn't keeping them locked.

The only reason they were still in there fighting was that one of them actually had no intention of getting out.

"Loir, can you open the control room?" asked Dante, a wave of cold anger rising in his voice.

"What? Uh sure, but Kitty—"

"The Core isn't going for the weapons, they changed their target. They are going upstairs for her. Eden is their target!"

335

# CHAPTER TWENTY-FIVE

Eden only had a vague idea of what was happening on the lower floors. She could hear the gunshots and turmoil. She could also feel it from the loud ruckus that made the floor below her tremble, but it was too chaotic to even try and follow. Even the screens were blocked by all the smoke, rendered useless. Still, she couldn't afford to care more than that. Presently, she was too busy trying to survive this fight to even bother.

Just like Loir had mentioned, his ex-partner was a good fighter. Very good, even. Eden had rarely fought for this long without sending her opponent flying or being beaten herself. Circé was swift and deadly, using her hair pins like weapons, and as Eden had quickly understood, a mere stab could be enough to kill her because they were poisoned. She had the typical assassin fighter technique, launching quick and unpredictable attacks. She lacked in strength but tried to compensate with her speed, while Eden was somewhat the opposite; her legs were a real advantage, but in this enclosed space, they were very impractical to sweep around. In fact, she had already destroyed many of the computers with her violent kicks, rendering a lot of them useless. Loir would cry each time she hit one critically.

"You savage!" he squealed in her ears. "I was hoping you'd bring me back some of that masterpiece... Do you have any idea how much that kind of processor costs on the Black Market? Two kidneys! And I should know, I tried to buy one!"

Eden really didn't have time for his craziness right now. Circé wasn't getting anywhere close to killing her, but she was trying for real. Hence, when she heard the gunshots from Dante's side, Eden grimaced without being able to stop her dance. She just had to stay alive a while longer and get rid of this witch to get full control of the room...

"Eden, get out of there!" he yelled again in her ears.

"I... would if I... could!" she grunted, annoyed by his orders.

Despite Loir's best efforts and a lot of hitting his keyboards, the doors were still closed tight around her. She could hear Dante breathing loudly, shooting and slashing enemies, but he was obviously still too far below. Eden really was trapped here, but she couldn't understand why. It made no sense that the Core would be here for her!

"Why aren't they going for the weapons?" she asked quickly as she and Circé finally took a break.

The goth woman was out of breath and wiped some of the blood dripping from her lips. Eden didn't manage to beat her, but she had still hit her pretty badly a couple of times. Her cheekbone donned a massive bruise making a strange angle, and Circé was stepping back, leaning her back against one of the walls, panting.

"They heard something more precious was here, I imagine," she said.

"It makes no sense," Eden grunted. "They couldn't have known I would be here, and how would they know who I am?!"

This time, she wasn't talking to her opponent, but to Loir and Dante. While the Italian sounded busy with another fight, a lot of shouting and shooting going on around him, Loir let out a dramatic sigh.

"I have no idea, my Kitty! I followed the usual protocols, you know I'm as invisible as a dumpster rat! I'm looking, I'm looking... Damn, those bad boys don't have control but they are trying to fight back!"

"I thought you already had full control...?" sighed Eden, glaring at Circé.

"Well, you know, this kind of system doesn't exactly work like a five-star restaurant! It's a first-come-first-serve basis, and even if we are served junk food, it cares about the first customer first..."

"What the hell do you mean?!"

"Circé got there first, she still has a foot in the system, and so does the Core! I'm like the queen bee trying to fight off the rebel soldiers before they destroy the hive, Kitty! Although I'd make one sexy queen..."

"Loir, we can't let them get to the weapons," grunted Eden, "...or me."

"I know, my Kitty, I'm thinking, I'm thinking... Take a seat, I'll let you know when I got a ride ready for ya!"

"I can't go anywhere anyway!"

Just as she said that, Circé sent another deadly needle her way, and their fight resumed. Both women were tired and desperate to get rid of the other. Eden hadn't planned on fighting in here, and her outfit was so inconvenient too! She had already ripped and thrown aside what was hindering her, but there was still a lot of fabric in her way, floating around with each movement. She

337

regretted not being able to get into the Dark Reality, where it wouldn't have mattered much.

"Kitty, I have good news!"

"Good... news?" she grunted, sending another kick into Circé's stomach and throwing her against one of the walls.

"Yes, they are here to capture you!"

Eden rolled her eyes.

"Loir, one day we're going to discuss your notion of good news..."

"No, no, seriously! They don't want to kill you! This genius bald ball here managed to trace the signal back to the Core's own epicenter; you know, the kind of genius move only I can do. Anyways! You can clap later."

"I won't clap," Eden groaned for herself, dodging another dart.

Circé kept throwing more and more of them, it was impressive she was carrying that many weapons in her hair alone. Not just that, but Circé managed to pick up the hairpins she had used to kill the people in the room before and threw them at Eden as she was dodging them. It was hard to fight someone who was a long-range fighter when Eden was obviously a close-range fighter. Circé was trying to keep her at bay while attacking, and Eden had nothing to send back. She didn't have that woman's dexterity for throwing her weapons back, and since she had realized they were poisoned, she'd rather not touch them at all!

At least each blow Eden threw at her was a big win. Whether she hit her with her fists or her legs, Circé was not good at guarding herself and didn't have much endurance either. She was already trying to hold her stomach as she had received two kicks there and grimaced at each movement.

"My little pipsqueak was their gaslighter! I mean, I know I am quite a master in the art of coding, but I didn't think they would recognize my inimitable signature style! Either way, they duplicated my type of hacking and probably put some firewalls in all the systems. I bet some of that tech was the Core's..."

"What is he saying?" grumbled Dante.

"Basically, they recognized Loir's hacking signature and since that bitch had already opened a door here for the Core, they picked up on it. Some of the Japanese tech was stolen from the Core, so they probably managed to trigger something that would recognize him... to find me."

"They are after..."

"Ghost," Eden dropped, annoyed.

Facing her, Circé, who was catching her breath, frowning, visibly shocked.

"You're... Ghost?"

Eden glared back, annoyed with that woman for even thinking she'd answer. She had been very discreet, but after Diving so many times with the same Back Hacker, and exposing herself a bit more on each mission, it was still irritating that they had managed to find her. The Core probably had no idea who Ghost was, they only knew Ghost was trapped behind those doors. She was a huge thorn in their System, and the Core got rid of the tiniest bug they could find in their machine without thinking twice...

"They don't know," she quickly said to Dante. "They just want to kill Ghost while they're at it; they don't know."

Even if the Core thought they could trap Ghost upstairs, their main goal was still probably the weapons a few floors below. Yet, with Circé here and two gangs fighting downstairs, the Core had probably weighed their chances of success and thought they should get rid of their long-declared enemy first, take back the control room, and only after, get to the weapons. Eden couldn't let them succeed in any of these missions.

More motivated than before, she threw another fist Circé's way, hoping to get rid of that woman this time.

"Loir, will you open these damn doors already?" grumbled Eden.

"Coming up, darling, but with two ladies destroying half the tech in there, I'm not braiding my hair over here! Damn, if I had thought one day my Kitty partner would find my ex-partner... Is that what they call a *ménage à trois*? Oh my, so thrilling! No wonder they make TV shows out of this!"

"One day, I'm going to kill you..." grumbled Eden.

That was if said ex-partner didn't kill her first. She could easily imagine Circé and Warlock's relationship: work-based only, cold, and arguing all the time...

"Thao," said Dante's voice. "Last chance. More of the Core's people are coming in, and you won't be able to hold on long enough. I have control of their weaponry, you're locked in here. I don't care about killing you, so don't waste my time. Yes or no?"

Eden rolled to the side and hid behind a console in the middle of the room, catching a break. She was getting really tired of this fight, running around in an enclosed space and making impossible moves to avoid those darts... She looked down at her legs, pretty damaged by all this. From banging them against the computers to taking a few gunshots, she hadn't spared them today. Perhaps she'd take Dante's offer to have them changed, after all...

"Fine!" grunted Thao. "It's an alliance, but just this once. After that, I'm killing your tiger ass!"

"A very fine ass, one might add," chuckled Loir.

Eden blushed, trying to forget that she had thought the exact same thing just a second ago...

At least, two Zodiacs pairing up to fight the Core back was better than a tripartite fight. There was still something strange: where was the Snake? So far, they had been fighting the Yakuza, but there had been no sighting of Yasumoto, which made no sense when the whole building was under siege...

"Loir, any sign of the Snake?" she asked.

"A Japanese guy, a Japanese guy, or a Japanese guy?" sighed Loir. "There are tons of little men with tattoos, mean faces, and monolids in there! How am I supposed to know which is which?!"

"Yasumoto has red hair, tattoos that mimic scales all over his body, and two scars on his face," said Dante, in between several gunshot sounds.

He and Thao had probably come together to fight against the Core's men and the Japanese, as Eden could hear the woman's voice somewhere not far from Dante.

"Oh, we're looking for a punky snakey then... Let me see... Snakey, snakey, snakey... Damn, I'm going to want a steak with all this. ...Or need a new handbag."

"Loir, shut up and find him..." sighed Eden.

"Gotcha! I found him! Our Chucky-Godzilla mix is in the... Oh... Are those shiny dark stuffs around him all guns? I mean, they could be toys, right? But just in case, there are a lot. Someone went shopping in Bulletland!"

"He locked himself up in the armory," grumbled Eden. "Of course. With three different enemies, he's probably waiting for you all to kill each other..."

"Or for me to open the door!" said Loir. "Don't forget this cutie pie here controls everything! Should I kick them out and direct them where we want them? Oh, I feel like I'm playing Pac-Man... Let's play Pac-Sushi!"

"...Bring them out," said Dante.

Eden could almost hear the ice-cold smile in his voice. There was about to be a blood bath downstairs... She let out a long sigh, still tired despite her little break.

"Circé, I don't want to fight you!"

"You're doing the opposite so far... You damn bitch, you broke my finger!"

"Well, I'm not even sorry. But, I can stop if you fucking leave me be. You walk the fuck out of this room and disappear. I promise we won't kill you."

"You think you can promise me safety?" scoffed the other woman. "You're one delusional chick, aren't you? If not the Zodiacs, the Core will kill me the second I run away!"

"True that," sighed Loir. "I wondered how that old witch survived... Wait, how did she survive?"

"You made a deal with them?" asked Eden.

"A deal? Those bastards attached a bomb to my SIN! If I do or say one thing they don't like, I'll die."

"Oh, someone's gone past their life expectancy... Poor witchy..."

Eden sighed, and let her head rest against the wall behind her.

"Circé, if I could deactivate that bomb, would you give up?"

"...What?"

Eden felt genuinely bad about fighting Loir's former partner. She now understood why she had felt somewhat familiar with Circé: they were the same. Dive Hackers and survivors. They both hated the Core and had tried not to play by its rules, but Circé had been caught in the wrong trap and was now caged by a system she obviously hated.

If she kept fighting back until one of them died, even if she won, Eden would have felt like she was trapped in that cage too, murdering another tool for the Core. Circé wasn't her enemy, she was wearing invisible chains. Whatever deal she had made with the Core, if they could get her on their side, it would be even better...

"If I deactivate the bomb," she continued, "Dante can get you a new SIN, put you back in the System with a clean slate."

"You're insane, little one," hissed Circé. "You don't know what the Core is capable of. You don't know how much control they have. I won't risk my head for the sake of..."

Eden slowly stood up before she could end her sentence, making it clear she had no intention to attack.

"I can help you," she muttered. "I really can. I... am Ghost."

"Even if you're Ghost," said Circé, "there's no way."

Eden took a deep breath.

"Loir," she muttered, "get ready to deactivate it."

"You sure, Kitty? I mean, it's your business, but it's also a lot of trouble coming right up with it. Not that you aren't already in a lot of trouble with Tiger Sugar Daddy and the Pipsqueak Lady fighting the Punk Snakey and Men in Black downstairs, and also my once charming but deadly angry ex-partner lady facing you..."

"Loir, just do it. Quick."

"Alright, alright..."

Eden grimaced, as she felt a sharp pain in her neck. She was out of the system, her SIN deactivated. Now, no one else could contact her aside from Circé, who was physically in the room. She was completely offline.

The hacker frowned and tilted her head, confused.

"What are you playing at..."

Eden reached for her neck and touched her SIN to reactivate it.

Her appearance suddenly changed. Her long blonde hair turned a lighter color, a very pale shade between platinum and white, with shades of rosy pink, and shortened itself by several inches, as if it was growing back in. Not only that, but Eden's eye color changed to a darker shade, and her face changed slightly, showing fuller lips, skinnier cheeks. Even her body seemed to change slightly, as she grew an extra inch with another grimace. Circé was dumbfounded.

"Genetic re-writing... I thought it was a myth..."

"It's not a myth," said Eden, walking toward her.

She put her hand on the woman's neck, and Circé didn't dare move. After a second, she felt a sharp pain, like a small burn, but she could tell her SIN and the bomb had been destroyed. Or more like overrun from the outside. She couldn't hear the voices in her ears anymore, and she could smell her own burnt flesh...

Eden took a step back, staring at that woman very seriously.

"I'm not just Ghost because it's a hacking nickname. It's because I don't exist. I have a completely blank SIN; my real birth SIN was never entered into the System, nor was my birth name or genetic coding. There's literally nothing for them, I'm as untouchable as a ghost virtually, and I can destroy all their coding. I'm the only Ghost in the Core's System."

"That can't be," muttered Circé. "Every single child is entered into the System, the parents have no choice..."

"My dad had it. And he took it away from *them*."

Eden stepped back and turned off her Ghost SIN, turning the usual one back on again. She was always careful never to activate the other one for more than a few seconds, and rarely in public like this... The number of people who had seen her with that appearance could be counted on one hand, including deceased ones.

"You're... the Architect's daughter?" gasped Circé.

"You knew?" frowned Eden, surprised.

The goth woman sighed, brushing her purple hair back. She grabbed her hairpins and rearranged them, showing she had no intention to fight anymore. With her hair up, Eden could see the new burn on her neck, where she had just fried her SIN and the bomb to free her.

"We knew he had a child... When he was trying to recruit us, he did mention a couple of times he had a family. Moreover, when they caught us, the Core's people tried to have us spill all of his secrets. They were bitter about the old man dumping them, so they wanted to attack him wherever they could... including his family."

She massaged her neck with a sour expression, still staring at Eden with a doubtful look. After a few seconds, she sighed.

"...Alright," Circé said. "I guess that means we're even. But I'm still going to punch that damn Warlock once I get a hold of the bastard."

"Anything you want," chuckled Eden.

"Kitty, I heard that..." whined Loir in her ears. "Well, at least with our witchy friend out, I'm back in control! Woohoo!"

Yet, Circé walked up to one of the consoles, and began typing on the keyboards again, at a familiar speed only Back Hackers could have. Eden raised her eyebrows, surprised.

"You can do Back Hacking too?" she muttered, surprised.

Circé smirked.

"Trust me, it's better never to let men know how good we are at multitasking... Warlock may be one of the best, but I wasn't born yesterday either. ...Here we go."

The doors suddenly opened again, to Eden's relief. She wasn't claustrophobic, but she sure was getting tired of that room.

"What now?" Circé sighed. "Since I've betrayed the Core, there will be a bounty on my head soon. Yours are already sky-high, but with me knowing what I know, those guys downstairs will try to come for me too..."

"We came here for the Snake's weapons in the first place," said Eden. "Let's get them and push the Core back."

"I like the idea, but do you realize how many of those bastards are downstairs and trying to get to me and you? You're a decent fighter, but we're talking about dozens of guys armed with the latest technology."

"We have control of this place," retorted Eden. "It was conceived exactly for this: to be turned into a fortress against enemies. If we can keep controlling it like we have been, while the Zodiacs downstairs get to the armory, we can win this. There's no way the Core sent that many people; this is outer Chicago. Even if they don't care about the casualties on our side, they do care about their own people being killed. They aren't stupid enough to start a war outside their territory."

"...You sure know how the Core works," scoffed Circé.

"You have no idea."

Eden had been raised there and had observed them long enough to know. The Core usually took care of the most annoying targets first. She, Circé, and the Zodiacs ought to be at the top currently, and she was not willing to die today. She lifted her leg, and suddenly slammed the keyboard Circé had used just a second ago. The goth grimaced.

"Seriously?"

"I'm destroying external control in case they make it to this room. Loir can control the network since he's already in."

"Hm... Good point."

"Alright, let's go."

Circé nodded and the two women, now allies, ran out of the room, looking for the closest escape route. Eden had a vague memory about how she had gotten here, but they both ought to be extremely careful not to run into the Core's people already headed their way. Loir was their best shot, as he was controlling all the rooms and floors, and guiding them through this maze.

"Next door on the left... Then keep going... Oh, ignore this one, unless you have time to argue with a bunch of angry Yakuza... Yes, keep going! Second door on the right, and then the stairs! No Men in Black on the horizon, ladies! Oh my, should you call me Charlie? Loir's angels! How does that sound?"

As usual, Eden ignored his continuous chatting, filtering out the information she actually needed. Circé was also cautious, sometimes stopping Eden when she thought she had heard a noise, or entering a room only after she had double-checked it was empty.

"So you and L–Warlock were partners?" whispered Eden as they were waiting for the go-ahead next to a corridor.

Circé rolled her eyes.

"Not by choice... We were among the best your father had selected to form the Edge. I just happened to be the only one able to handle a guy that crazy. Although to be fair, I can't blame him... He was already damaged before he got to us."

"...What do you mean?"

"The Prussian Empire," muttered Circé. "An extremist group was secretly trying to raise a militia of super hackers... They kidnapped children and taught them everything known about hacking through an extreme program. It was actually one of the first attacks my mentor had launched, to free some of those teens. Most had died in the process, but Warlock was one of the survivors... He still can't walk, can he?"

Eden slowly shook her head.

"They did that too. Back Hackers only need their hands... After we were captured by the Core, Warlock alone managed to escape. But I heard he was captured again, by some Russian loyalists on the outside."

Eden suddenly remembered her partner's fright when the Dog had been mentioned. Could it be he wasn't scared of the Zodiac herself, but of her people in general...? It made sense. If anyone was still loyal to the Prussian Empire in this area, they ought to be on the Dog's territory. No wonder Loir had tried to hide far from them.

"I don't know much of his history, what's true or what he lied about," sighed Circé. "There were rumors that some new tech, allowing one to erase or modify someone's memories, had been released on the Black Market a few years ago, and it had been tested on young people by the cruelest Zodiacs... I wouldn't be surprised if Warlock had gone through that shit too."

Eden couldn't help but feel disgusted. She had always been wary of the Zodiacs, all of them. Now that she had an insight into Loir's history, she could understand why some people would hide in a basement for life rather than risk crossing paths with the wrong kind of people...

"This is so sad... Wait, I need a tissue... Oh, and a pizza!"

Eden chuckled. At least Loir was alive and more or less still optimistic in his own world... She and Circé moved to get to a new set of stairs, going down, hopefully back to the ground floor, at last. She had only heard gunshots and orders shouted on Dante's side for a while, and didn't dare disturb him or ask where he was. She was afraid she'd disturb him at a critical moment, or seem too concerned.

Circé suddenly took out two of her deadly hair pins to hold in each hand and Eden nodded. She had heard it too. Footsteps on the other side of the wall... From the way they moved, they were highly trained. Both women waited, not even daring to ask Loir what was going on... Eden rolled her eyes as she could hear him loudly chew and slurp.

Suddenly, gunshots resonated on the other side. Circé and Eden were about to walk in, but they jumped down to take cover instead, one second before several dents appeared on the wall they had stood against. Now, there was clearly a fight happening on the other side. The gunshots weren't stopping, men were shouting, and even explosions followed. The two women were both lying on their stomachs and covering their heads, waiting for the next opportunity to do something. Circé glanced over at Eden.

"Any ideas?" she muttered on her lips.

Before Eden could come up with anything favorable, the lights suddenly went out.

Everything became dark and Eden remembered there weren't any windows around to begin with. They were in complete darkness.

"Loir...?"

"Stay down, Kitty! The fireworks are about to start! Woohoo!"

Indeed, another huge explosion resonated and more gunfire resumed. This time, several of the bullets actually pierced the wall, falling around them with a loud metallic clatter. There was no way to know who was shooting at who, which was one of Eden's worst nightmares. Being caught in the gunfire, with nowhere to retreat. She could only wait for it to pass and hope no one would notice the two women hidden on the other side of that wall...

While she raised her head, she noticed Circé trying to crawl away, toward the stairs. Eden wanted to tell her to stop and stay next to the wall, but she couldn't. It was way too dark, and she couldn't risk speaking in case she spoke at the wrong moment and someone else heard. Hence, Circé disappeared from her very limited field of vision, with one last glimmer of her hairpins. Eden grimaced and had to wait a bit longer as the gunshots were still going. It was much more scattered, which meant most of the battle was over already. Whoever was left was shooting the remaining enemies, or making sure they were really dead... She tried to slowly get back on all fours, as no more bullets were coming through the wall. She had rarely been this scared. She was a very good hacker and fighter, but she was in the dark and unbearably vulnerable right now.

Then, someone slowly opened the door. Eden froze. There was no light on the other side either, meaning if she didn't move, the enemy might not notice her or Circé... She ought to act at the right moment. She was in the worst position, but she could still somehow move and hopefully place a kick at the right time. The main issue was that whoever had come through the door was very silent, and she could barely hear their steps. Moreover, she didn't want to risk killing one of Dante's men...

Suddenly, she felt a hand grab her wrist and lift her up without warning, banging her against the wall. Eden grimaced, but her first reflex was to launch her fist in front of her. However, without seeing anything, she inevitably missed, while whoever was still holding her wrist suddenly pressed their body against hers. Eden tried to fight it, but a second later, she recognized that musky smell, that tall stature, and more importantly, the pair of golden irises shining in the dark.

"...I missed you too," he muttered in a deep voice.

Eden let a faint breath of relief escape her lips, right before they got sealed by his.

Dante's kiss was sudden, forceful, and desperate. Eden felt all of his strength in this kiss and lost her own. She could feel his body, pressed against her, not letting her escape. He wouldn't even let go of her wrist. His other hand was already hooked around her neck, his fingers in her hair, so warm against

345

her skin. He was kissing her relentlessly, and she couldn't help but give in. It was too hot, too good, too necessary at that moment. All the stress and tension from before melted under his lips, making her weak in the knees. It was as if she had brutally gone from ice cold to flaming hot, and it was unbearably good. An alarm ringing in her head was telling her this was neither the time nor the place, but it was nothing compared to her body's sensations.

It was Dante. Dante, holding her close, pressing her against a wall full of bullet holes, confirming he was there in every way possible. The Tiger was acting wild even in the face of danger. He didn't care about the smell of gunpowder, death, and blood. He just wanted her, Eden. His hands were touching her body, as if to confirm she was alive, in his arms, and unharmed. He didn't have a scratch on him either. Only the faint smell of his sweat under his shirt, which was driving her insane...

"D-Dante," she gasped. "Stop..."

Her voice wasn't very convincing, especially as she had to talk in between his kisses on her neck. His hand was now on her leg, in the slit of her dress, making her shiver with something that was definitely not cold. He couldn't possibly be thinking about sex right now! Eden knew how insane it was, how crazy they were acting in the given situation, yet she could definitely feel him getting excited against her. They were against one another, in the dark, in a life-or-death situation, with probably a ton of dead people on the other side of that wall. This was definitely insane.

She grunted and pushed him back with both her hands on his torso, putting all of her strength into it. She was out of breath, her lips a bit sore, her body and mind were a mess, but she was resolutely keeping him at a distance.

"Stop... doing that," she gasped. "We need to get out of here... to the... armory."

"We already opened it," he immediately replied. "Yasumoto is dead. Our people are seizing the weapons. We're on the ground floor, and have locked the front doors; there are more people from the Core ready to ambush us outside."

"O-okay," nodded Eden, trying to absorb all that information. "Then... w-what about those who were still inside?"

"Thao convinced the remaining Yakuza to join us and we were getting rid of the Core's people still inside."

Eden suddenly understood. The battle on the other side was Dante's men against the Core's people. She slowly nodded, trying to think of the next step to take. It wasn't easy, considering Dante was holding her hands tightly and pushing to get closer to her, while she was still trying to keep him at a safe distance.

"Now that we've got the weapons and they didn't get any of their targets, they will try to take this place down," she muttered. "We can't stay. We have to get out somehow. As fast as possible."

"I know. Thao suggested we split the weapons, bomb this place, and run back to our territories."

"You left her with the weapons?" scoffed Eden.

"Technically, Loir left her with them."

"Yep, Kitty! This Warlock is launching Black Friday early! Grab one weapon, get two, hehe~ I'm still controlling the area and now that there's a massive blackout on this floor, everyone is waiting for the show to go on!"

"They can't see where to shoot," gasped Eden, suddenly understanding.

This was very smart indeed. This way, Thao had no choice but to wait for Dante to come back since, unlike everyone else right now, his eyes allowed him to see in the dark... Otherwise, she'd end up shooting her own men if she tried to force her way out. This place was way too big and too complex to know where to go while blind.

Eden nodded, only then realizing she had gone from pushing Dante's chest to holding his shirt... She blushed and let go, only for him to grab her hand and use this chance to step closer again.

"A-alright," she muttered. "What now?"

"Uh... You might want to hurry and get out, my Kitties," suddenly said Loir. "I don't want to be a party pooper, but... I think the Core might have had the same idea as you guys."

"What?" they both asked at the same time.

"Rocket. I have a... flying thingy looking like a rocket coming right to your location! This is not a drill! Time for Kitties to run, run, run!"

Dante and Eden exchanged a glance. They could face many things, but even for them, a rocket or a bomb coming their way was a bit much...

"Loir, how much time do we have?"

"Not much at all... If I'm being nice, I'd say three minutes... I'm always too nice, though!"

Eden grimaced. Even if they somehow found their way out in such a short time, there were a whole bunch of the Core's people ready to shoot at them outside! She couldn't remember seeing any sort of vehicle that could have shielded them as they ran out either. Going back to the upper floors was definitely a bad idea if the lower ones were wiped out, and the very top could even be the first target to begin with...

"Three minutes," she groaned. "There's nothing we can do in three minutes! Loir, tell me you have a secret way out of here. There's got to be some sort of escape route!"

"Uh... Nope, not in my plans, Kitty, and you know that stubborn little Apple from your master can't be used while you're busy eating sushi, so... no way to check if I did miss something!"

"Look at the ones you had unlocked while I was there, you must have some copy left in our computers' memory or something. Check if there's anything helpful!"

"Oh, I love when the Kitty gets bossy... On it!"

Letting Loir furiously type on his keyboards to try and find a way out, she turned to Dante, panicked. She hadn't even realized they were still holding hands, nor how strangely calm the Italian Tiger still looked next to her. He had clearly heard the same thing she heard, but Dante just looked as if they were about to walk out of there and perhaps go dine somewhere. Eden clearly was the only one showing any signs of panic.

"I was with Circé just before," she quickly explained. "We need to find her. She was one of Loir's allies, and one of my father's apprentices..."

"You need her dead?"

"Can you stop trying to casually murder everyone?!" protested Eden. "I saved her life, I actually need her alive. She can be a great ally; she's been to the Core recently and definitely knows a lot about them. She'll be helpful if we want to stop their plans, and I could use someone to help me inside the Dark Reality..."

"Fine."

Dante turned his head, now clearly talking to his men through his SIN.

"Find the other woman. Don't kill her."

Eden frowned as he had said not to kill her instead of not to harm her, but she really didn't have time to discuss the details with him right now while a rocket or something was coming their way. She had already begun a mental countdown of the time they had left, as Loir was usually very precise in his calculations.

Suddenly, she turned to Dante again.

"I need to find Jack! I left him in the other room we were in before, and–"

"He's probably dead."

"Don't say that!" Eden shouted back, pissed. "Rose died, but we don't know about Jack yet. ...Loir, can you find him?"

"Excuse me, I'm trying to save you from becoming red, flying, glittery pudding right now! I don't have time to look for... Oh, never mind, I got him. Same room as before, Kitty, I see a cute six-foot-tall lady with pink hair crawling under a... a... Oh, my ponies, is that a real sumo wrestler? I want one!"

Eden rolled her eyes but turned around to go and run to get Jack.

She had forgotten that Dante was still holding her hand, and as soon as she pulled, he refused to move, the difference in strength almost making her fall back with a vivid pain in her arm. She glanced back and glared at him.

"Let me go!"

"You don't need to save him."

Eden pulled on his hand, but as he refused to move, she slapped him.

"You don't get to decide for me, Dante. Let me fucking go," she hissed.

Dante barely seemed surprised by the slap. His expression didn't change at all, even if his head had slightly pivoted. Eden's hand was probably more hurt than his cheek, but he still glanced down at her again, and after a second, he finally let go. She glared one last time and ran off, leaving him behind.

"Oh... Is that what they call a catfight...?"

"Loir, shut up."

"Okay..."

She ignored him and kept running, trying to find her way back. She had a very vague memory of the rooms' positions, and she hit a wall a couple of times or stumbled upon what was probably a dead body, trying not to think about it too much. Thankfully, Loir lit up a couple of lights ahead to guide her, allowing Eden to quickly find where she was going and stop tripping or hurting herself. The fight was mostly over on this floor; there were a lot more people down and dead than up and running, although she tried to avoid both, and hid against a wall each time she heard footsteps. She wanted to ask Loir if Rose was really dead, but she didn't dare, knowing Dante could still hear her. He would probably have said something if the Tiger had lied, anyway...

"...Next one on your left, Kitty!"

"Got it," she hissed between her teeth, still a bit pissed.

Because everything was so quiet on the other side, Eden kicked the door open without hesitation. With Rose dead, there were high chances something had happened in here already, and the action was already long over. It was miraculous Jack had survived, but she quickly spotted why and how.

Just like Loir had described, Jack was stuck under a massive, half-naked guy, and trying to get out from under the dead body, grunting. As soon as he saw her, his eyes opened wide.

"Eden! Thank God you're alive, hun! Those bastards barged in, and everyone began shooting on all sides! That guy knocked me over, and then..."

"It's okay, Jack," she grunted, immediately running to help him out. "Jack, we don't have time, we need to get out of here. A rocket is coming right toward us from the Core, if we don't get out of here quick–"

"What?" he exclaimed as he finally crawled out. "Are you kidding?! I didn't live underground for two days and survive a mass shooting for–"

"Holy shit, that's it!" shouted Eden, reacting to his sentence. "Loir! Loir, what about a bunker? Isn't there some reinforced room to hide in instead of a way out? Something underground?"

"Ooooh, good idea, Kitty! Give me a second, I think... Holy unicorn! The armory is reinforced with massive steel or whatever that thing is, but it's a fortress. I don't really wanna thank your stingy master, but I'm glad I had that Map on my server... I guess they wanted to avoid one bomb going off by mistake and blowing up the whole building. A nice little fish tank to keep the sushi fresh!"

"What?" asked Jack, as he couldn't hear Loir but could see Eden's expressions changing.

"We're going underground," she quickly said, grabbing his arm and pulling him out. "...Dante, you heard that?"

"See you there."

She was a little bit glad she didn't have to explain, as she was still a bit mad at him for suggesting they abandon Jack. At least they had found a solution for now... She only hoped the armory was large enough to contain everyone. In fact, she didn't even have to ask where it was: all the remaining Italians were running there, and she and Jack only had to follow the group, running through some corridors with minimal lights.

Jack kept complaining about going back downstairs and locking themselves up with mafiosos as they were running, but according to Eden's clock in her head, they really had no time for other solutions. In fact, they arrived with the last group of Italians running inside the armory, and the very heavy door was closed behind them as Dante, appearing behind Eden, was the last one allowed in. Eden didn't know if he had left any more men behind, and she didn't want to risk asking...

"Did you find Circé?" she immediately asked.

The armory wasn't the small room she had imagined. In fact, it was the largest one she had seen so far, and it was crowded with people, Italian and Vietnamese thugs lined up against rows and rows of weapons. This place wasn't exactly storage only; this was also some sort of clandestine factory, as she could see desks meant for illegal workers, several boxes of unknown materials, and plans on how to assemble weapons stuck everywhere on the walls. No wonder the Snake's nest had become the prey of choice for anyone who wanted to wage war against the Core...

"Damn, you guys look like mackerels stuck in a can!" giggled Loir. "Say hi to the camera, Kitty! I see you! And you! And you! And..."

She ignored Loir and all the cameras above them following her movements. In fact, there was an astonishing number of them lined up on the walls, explaining Loir's latest little game of zooming in on people's faces. He was probably having a lot of fun right now, but those were definitely meant to watch the workers here... The mafiosos had them all lined up against a wall, some on their knees, heads down and their hands behind their backs.

"She's over there," simply said Dante.

He was pointing toward the end of the room, and before she saw Circé, Eden saw Thao, leaning against one of the tables with a sullen look.

"You bastard Tiger," she groaned as they approached. "You guys said you'd let us out, not lock us in!"

"There's a rocket coming to exterminate all the upper floors," retorted Eden, annoyed. "You're welcome to go back up if you want to pulverize all your men in the process."

A very strange noise that sounded like Loir mimicking a fart with his mouth suddenly resonated all around the room. Eden glanced around and noticed the speakers above.

"Oh, damn it..." she grimaced, as his creepy giggle echoed around.

"Boom! Boom!" he kept squealing.

All the guys present sent glares at the cameras, annoyed by his childish behavior and not doing anything about it. Eden, who already had him in her ears all day long, ignored it and put her hands on her hips, only now noticing how painful it was on her flank. Her fight with Circé had left some bruises...

"Anyway, it's a matter of seconds now," she sighed. "After that, we should probably leave as soon as we can."

"No one wants to stay, I guarantee you," scoffed Thao. "That bastard had kidnapped a lot of our people to have them do his dirty work... Now we can bring them home."

Eden nodded, but as she walked past Thao, she finally spotted Circé, leaning over what looked like a large box full of files. She frowned as she approached her, quickly glancing behind to notice Dante was still following her. She ignored him and stood next to the goth woman. Circé was reading a file in Japanese and frowning.

"So this is why I couldn't find it..." she muttered.

"What is it?" asked Eden, frowning.

"Remember that memory tech I mentioned earlier? The Core wants it bad, it was a side target for me. They promised a bonus if I could find any information about it. I mean, there were many things they wanted to find out and get their hands on around here, but the memory-control tech was kind of on the top of their list, reward-wise... Since it was a myth until recently, I was a bit surprised when I found information about it in the main control room, but thanks to our crazy friend up there, I couldn't get to the end of it."

The song "Sorry Not Sorry" suddenly began on the speakers, making both women exchange a glance and roll their eyes.

"...Anyways," sighed Circé, "I knew there was something about it, as I know the Architect had definitely mentioned it a while ago. The Edge was also looking for it, so... from what we had found up until now, our first hunch was that this crazy, tech-obsessed Yasumoto had made it somehow, but this is the proof he actually had it once, and purchased the original tech from someone else..."

"Who would want that?" frowned Eden. "And what for?"

"Oh, you can do a whole lot of scary things if you can manipulate someone's memories... I guess the Core isn't satisfied with controlling their people's present and future anymore; they want to manipulate their past. What I'm more surprised about is that a Zodiac actually had the means to create that technology. And over a decade ago, too... Look at the dates on the files. This is old. They didn't keep physical traces of it because they wanted to, they had it because they found some forbidden, twenty-first-century tech..."

Eden took some of the files, frowning. Circé had found this among the many other documents hidden in this bunker. As the safest room in the Red Temple, it made sense they were hidden there instead of anywhere else. In fact, having traces on paper sometimes could be proven to be much better for keeping secrets than hiding them in the Dark Reality, where all the hackers could find a way to things.

"That's all... This is insane," gasped Eden. "They really did experiment with this shit on kids!"

"It's not the worst," sighed Circé, handing her another file. "Here, look at the amounts. There's no way the Snake could have financed all of this. They had someone transfer the money to finance this shit, from afar. Someone who wanted to use Yasumoto to hide it, but it worked against them. The Japanese kept the money and sold this technology to someone else to shift the Core's attention temporarily. Help me look. You can read Japanese, right? We need to find if there's any trace of whom they sold it to..."

"Ten seconds before impact, people!" squealed Loir. "Ten... Nine... Eight..."

Eden and Circé quickly rummaged through the papers, trying to find an answer, a name, a clue, anything. Eden's heart was beating fast. Not only because of the rocket about to hit them but because she was scared of who was really behind the funding of that horrible technology. This way of doing things was all too familiar. Someone who had a lot of money, who knew a lot about tech, and who had to act behind the Core's back. If this turned out to be either her father or Pan linked to those horrible things, she couldn't...

"Six... Five... Four..."

"Eden."

Dante suddenly put a document in front of her eyes. Eden was speechless. There was no need to know Japanese to understand the answer. It was all too clear.

"Three... Two..."

She grasped it, in shock. The document wasn't in Japanese.

It was written in Italian.

"...One! Kaboom!!"

# CHAPTER TWENTY-SIX

That explosion felt like it lasted forever. At first, there was a huge detonation, and the floor below them began shaking terribly. Those who weren't thrown to the floor by the first blast couldn't keep standing without holding on to something or someone. Eden was suddenly grabbed and pushed against the floor, her already injured body painful again, with Dante's body covering her. The vibrations suddenly got a lot worse, and another boom resonated somewhere above. She understood that either it wasn't just one missile or it had triggered some sort of chain reaction in the floor above.

The ruckus didn't seem like it'd stop anytime soon. It was deafening, and she could hear some of the men shout or panic all around them. She tried to turn her head, noticing Circé who was also on the floor and covering her head. There was debris falling from above, but shielded by Dante, Eden hadn't even realized until now. Some white smoke was spreading across the room, making her cough. One of the walls had probably been broken, making the concrete dust fly around and stinging her eyes.

Still, that meant the room had probably managed to remain intact; otherwise, they would have definitely been crushed by all the floors that had collapsed above. All she could do was wait, her body pressed between the floor and Dante. She could hear voices, a lot of ruckus all around them and above, and a high-pitched ringing in her ears, but there were two more sounds louder than everything else. Dante's breathing and her own heartbeat, loud in her ears. He wasn't just keeping her shielded; he weighed over her, one of his hands on her head. His body was larger than hers and covered her entirely. Eden wished she had some sensations left in her legs so that she could feel what was going on at the other end of her body, but for now, she was completely unable to tell. When she tried to move, he didn't even flinch. Eden had a hard time breathing in this position, but she probably wasn't the only one...

"Loir!" she coughed.

"Oh, my favorite Kitty is still alive! How is it? Did you lose a limb? Someone dead? Red pudding party?"

"Not that I know of... Ah... I can't see a thing. ...Are they still attacking? What's going on?"

"Well, they threw some very nice fireworks! I think the Core's getting into the landscape design business because the Red Temple got rebuilt into a corner sushi shop..."

"What's left?"

"A couple of kitties in a big metallic box, maybe a floor or two... I'm surprised, I thought everything would explode like in the movies, but it turns out a building actually collapses vertically! Can you believe that? Oh, those special effects. Well done, well done..."

Eden grunted into her arms; she was too tired from all this to take in any more of Loir's very bad jokes. She just wanted to get out of this place, and for this to be over. She wanted to go back and take a shower... She got even madder when she realized she wanted to go back to Dante's place. Since when had she become so used to his building, to his apartment, that she considered it her place to return to? Even worse, she was thinking about all that with the man literally lying on top of her. At least she was facing the ground, otherwise, it would have been truly unbearable...

Finally, it seemed to calm down above. Everyone remained silent in the room for a few more seconds, and then all got back up carefully. Some helped those who had been trapped under collapsed shelves, or injured by debris; Eden finally saw the bit of ceiling that had collapsed, spreading that white smoke and letting some things fall through. The Yakuza may have anticipated a lot of things, but not that they needed to actually secure things to the walls and floor... She felt Dante get up but heard him grunt, which was unusual. Eden frowned and turned around to see him, on top of her, looking around the room with his usual ice-cold expression. Strangely, the lights hadn't completely gone out, some red lights taking over from the white ones, giving a strange, apocalyptic feel to the area. In that red-filtered vision, Eden almost missed the shining stain on Dante's shirt.

"Dante..." she whispered, sitting up to grab his shirt.

He glanced down, looking a bit surprised to have her pull on his shirt, but Eden was already absorbed in his wound. A piece of metal broken off from one of the shelves had cut and pierced his upper right flank, and his shirt was wet with the dark red liquid.

"You're bleeding..." she muttered, trying to see the extent of the injury.

Because his shirt was black and the lights around were red, she could only try and guess the actual size of the wound from the wet piece of clothing. Dante grabbed her wrist, pulling her hand away from it.

"It's fine," he said before standing back up and placing Eden on her feet.

The wound didn't look fine, but Eden didn't get the chance to insist. Many of the mafiosos around them were getting back on their feet and grabbing weapons to prepare themselves. Eden glared at the hole in the ceiling on the opposite side of the room. It looked like a chunk had completely fallen off, covering all the people underneath and letting some actual sunlight in... meaning the surface was dangerously close.

"Loir, I need to know what's going on at the surface."

"Uh... The lawn's been mowed?"

"Loir!"

"Seriously, Kitty, there's just a little mountain of stuff, collapsed stuff, and broken down stuff! Most of the cameras were destroyed, and I can only see the itty-bitty window of what was just blasted! ...Oh, and a fire or two. I mean, either that or that tree just turned red..."

"The Core's people?"

"Uh... Not a black suit in sight; they all ran away as soon as the rocket was on the way, to be fair. Let me see the other streets... Oh, a good old hacking of the street cameras. It's funny how they watched all the streets around, but they got blasted like a birthday candle, hehe! ...Hm... nope, nothing going on... Oh, is that a real dumpling shop? Oh, Kitty, can you bring me back some *Xiaolongbao*? I haven't had some in forever! Pretty please?"

"Looks like we can go," sighed Eden.

She looked around, but no one seemed to have heard her except for Dante. All the mafiosos were still busy gearing up or packing all the weapons and leaving nothing on those shelves. Eden's eyes fell on Circé, on the other side, who was still reading the documents. She had a lot of dust ruining her makeup and some blood on her exposed shoulder, but she seemed fine.

"I'm packing all these," she explained as she grabbed several papers. "I'm coming with you guys anyway..."

Eden nodded. She wasn't really sure what the agreement was about bringing Circé back with them, but she had visibly made up her mind already... For now, she was more worried about Dante's wound, although he looked like the last person to care about it. In fact, she wished she could find a pack of ice or something for those ribs that were killing her on both sides... Her fight with Circé was definitely not going to be forgotten anytime soon.

"You're bringing witchy back here?" squealed Loir. "No, no, no! I'd rather move back to my garage!"

"It was not your garage, and it's now empty, remember? Your new toys?" sighed Eden, grabbing as many papers as she could.

"My pretties..." cried Loir in her ear.

"...Are we going to be okay to go?" whispered Eden to Dante, glancing toward all the armed people around.

In fact, it felt like a very dangerous place to be at the moment. Dozens of gangsters lined up, with plenty of weapons, as if they were just about to be unloaded in a war zone... Not to mention, both sides were temporary allies. Dante's men were all in their black suits, and Thao's men in more sporty, day-to-day, black streetwear, it was easy to tell who was on which side. The Rat's men all had visible tattoos, piercings, and silver jewelry too, while the Italians wore the same luxurious suits like various clones of one another. Eden didn't feel comfortable locked in a room with that many people. It was like a warehouse with a bloodbath waiting to happen...

"Thao!" she called out as soon as she spotted her, arguing with one of her men.

"We have to go, quick," retorted the Asian lady. "Our people already spotted more cars coming this way, probably ready for war. They won't risk blowing this place, but I bet they wouldn't mind shooting us like rabbits once we come out."

"So we go out now," nodded Eden.

"The truce will last until the border of my territory," said Thao, this time glaring at Dante. "If a single one of your men opens fire before that, I don't care if it's at a fly, we'll shoot."

Dante didn't answer, but his golden eyes went to his men, who all nodded right away. Eden spotted Rolf and his salt-and-pepper hair a few meters away, who gave them another little nod. He was closest to the door and probably ready to lead the Italians out of there.

"Let's scatter," said Dante, probably to Rolf. "Let's get the Zebra's and Dragon's people worked up on our way out so they lend us some fire to cover our exit."

Rolf nodded again and turned around to give orders, some men running to try and force the doors open right after that. Eden frowned.

"You want to make the other Zodiacs fight?"

"The Core is already here," he calmly said. "We might as well let them know they are not welcome."

"...He's right," muttered Circé. "I didn't actually believe they'd dare come and stay that long in a territory outside the Core, but now they are sending more people. They must be pissed we didn't let them get what they wanted..."

"Let's just get out of here," sighed Eden, exhausted. "We have what we came for..."

She felt Dante's hand slide on her back, but she didn't even want to waste energy protesting about that. She was just holding the documents they had found, her head full of questions but too tired to even want to think about them. They could all be discussed later. For now, they weren't safe here at all; they just really had to get out.

"Loir, make sure to cover our escape route. Let us know if something happens."

"*Black cars coming from the left,*" he sang. "*...black cars coming from the right. Everybody clap your hands, a little boogie to the side, and woo!*"

"He's exhausting, isn't he?" scoffed Circé, noticing Eden's expression. "Tell that crazy punk he should try and hack their cars. They are linked to the Core's System. He should have some fun while he's in..."

"Loir, you heard that?"

"Oh, my ponies! I get to play Mario Kart 12? Woohoo! Hold your unicorns, Super Loir is incoming!! Give me some mushrooms!"

Indeed, he was pretty exhausting.

In front of them, the doors were suddenly slammed open by the few mafiosos working on it. They all began flowing out of the room, weapons in hand and yelling all around.

"Jack!" she called out as the room was slowly getting emptier.

"Here! Oh, God, why did I wear these heels... Here, Eden!"

She ran to him, finding Jack hidden in a corner not too far from them, visibly terrified too, and still holding one shoe in each hand for some reason.

"We're leaving," she said quickly, bringing him some relief. "Jack, we're going to have to run. Leave the shoes and get a gun."

"I'm not leaving these babies! They cost a... Oh, fuck it, they're ruined anyway."

He threw them across the room and grabbed one of the nearby assault guns with a heavy sigh.

"That's one hell of a long day working for free," he grumbled.

Circé rolled her eyes as she appeared next to them, having somehow found a bag in the mess, and she and Eden stuffed the papers in it before grabbing some weapons. Dante also had a gun in each hand, but his golden eyes were darting around like a hawk. Everyone was leaving before them and, since she couldn't hear any shooting, Eden silently prayed it went on like this and they could all leave this hellish place without any further damage...

"Let's go," said Dante as soon as the path ahead was cleared.

Eden nodded, and their strange little group walked behind more mafiosos, some visibly acting like their bodyguards, in a kind of shield formation ahead of them. In fact, it wasn't a clear path once they had left the room, but the dozens of people who had gone before had cleared most of the way, and they only had to jump over the debris and avoid tripping over the remains of the Red Temple. Eden felt a little bit gutted that none of the beautiful garden from before was left. In fact, not only was what was real wiped out by the explosions and gathered in a pile of rubbish, but the projectors that maintained the illusions were out of service. In a faraway corner near the wall, only one little square remained, with the pretty grass perfectly layered and some stones next to a piece of the river. But the river had turned a mud red, and everything else around revealed the truth: dried-out soil and the scattered remains of the Japanese garden from before...

She looked back once, just to see the collapsed Red Temple , a single wall hanging on in a corner. Other than that, it was just a mountain of bricks, metal, wood, and bodies...

For a long while, as they ran away, they had to rush into the streets, stick their back against the walls of the Asian district, and watch cars pass. Or more like, drive in a completely chaotic manner until they crashed somewhere. She could hear Loir having a lot of fun jumping in control of one car, driving it until it went off the road and was completely wrecked, then hacking the next one... The Core would probably regret sending those cars for a hacker to literally toy with it in the middle of Chinatown, but she couldn't have cared less right now. In fact, she was following Dante and his men's lead without thinking much, listening for any sounds of gunshots that would have ended the truce. It felt like they had passed dozens and dozens of streets when they finally got to one of the Italian cars. Eden climbed in, just realizing then Dante had been holding her hand all along. His fingers were covered with blood, but he didn't let go for a single second, and she could feel his large, warm hand enveloping hers. It was as if they were stuck together, and she didn't think twice while squeezing herself next to him in the back seat, with Circé on the other side and Jack in front with Rolf.

Only when the car drove off did she let out a long sigh of relief, exhausted.

After everything that had happened, being able to simply drive off and watch the familiar streets of Chinatown fly past the window felt strangely unreal. Aside from Loir's strident voice in her ear, the whole car was quiet, everyone exhausted, mentally and physically. Eden could feel the pain echoing in her ribs each time they drove over a pothole, but the vibrations of the car otherwise were just... strangely soothing.

Without thinking, she leaned her head against Dante's shoulder, closing her eyes. She didn't care anymore. She could feel his fingers still tightly clasped with hers, not moving at all. That's all she needed until they could reach a safe place. Dante was her safe place for now. She had dozens of questions about why the Italians would have used the memory technology and everything, just not right now. For now, she just wanted to go back to that old building, leave the mess behind them, get stitched up, cleaned, and changed. Dante's wound definitely needed medical attention, but he showed none of it as if it wasn't on his body. His other hand was still on the gun, his golden eyes watching outside for a threat.

"Damn... I really liked those shoes," sighed Jack.

After so much had happened, it was no surprise that Eden had fallen asleep without noticing. Still, she was a bit mad at herself once she woke up and slowly remembered the past day's events. She sat up in a panic and realized where she was, alone and back in Dante's bedroom. It was as if they had simply laid her there and left...

She looked around, and her eyes caught the sun going down through the windows. How much time had passed? She looked down, noticing she was wearing the same clothes, in a horrible state at that. There was blood on her flank, but she couldn't remember having an open injury there, and after she checked, there was none indeed. Eden felt a sudden wave of panic rising inside, and her breathing accelerated. What had happened, and whose blood was it? She knew Dante was injured, badly.

Eden got up, a bit too fast as she began to see some black and white dots, but she didn't care. She needed to know what had happened after she fell asleep.

"Loir?" she called out, suddenly remembering her SIN was still active.

"Good evening, our sleeping Kitty! Had a good nap?"

"Where's Dante?" she asked right away.

"Oh, he's in surgery right now. Your favorite Tiger is getting all patched up! It should be over in about... fifteen minutes?"

"How is he?" Eden asked, the bundle of worry growing in her stomach.

She rushed to the wardrobe, grabbing any shirt without thinking. It turned out to be a men's white one, but she didn't care much. She looked for some women's underwear, which she found, brand new once again. Had Dante gathered this for her? She really didn't want to think too deeply about this at the moment. Instead, she rushed to the bathroom, taking a quick shower while listening to Loir.

"Oh, he's fine, he's fine. Our sugar daddy is tougher than a few bullets and a few holes in his body! Plus, he's got all the green kaching-kaching to get himself patched up in no time! If you had slept a bit more, I'm sure he would have brought you dinner in bed! And then you would have probably done something my innocent ears can't listen to. Although I'd still listen, of course. You naughty little kitties..."

"Pervert..." grumbled Eden, washing the ashes off her hair.

The color of the water going down the drain was an alarming mix of red and brown, but she really didn't want to spend more time than necessary on herself. She grimaced when the water went over her injuries, and carefully checked her bruises all over.

"What about everyone else? Jack, and Circé?"

"Oh, Jacquie is here with your puppies, and Circé is... here too. I mean, the old hag lady who shall not be named is presently standing behind me, very close to me, and literally staring at me. I swear, Kitty, I can feel her eyes on the back of my neck. Is that weird? Because it does feel weird. You know, like when you walk, and you can feel someone following you. Well, she's not following me, but she is behind me. And staring hard. Staring a lot. ...Can you come and help me? Please? She's scary. I am scared. Pretty please?"

Eden wasn't surprised, nor would she blame the woman. She ignored his rant while trying to wash quickly. After all, Circé had no SIN now, and she had just found the ex-partner who had sold her out to the Core before vanishing, basically... Even if he claimed it was involuntarily, with Loir, one could never really be sure... He was too crazy and unpredictable to keep track of.

As soon as she was clean enough, Eden walked out of the shower, quickly putting on the new underwear and drying her hair. That shirt was definitely meant for Dante, and too long for her, but it went down to her mid-thigh, enough to cover her, she thought. After all, even though they looked like it, those legs weren't real and nothing would change that, not even the fake skin camouflage . Eden didn't bother looking for pants or shorts, and rushed to the corridor, her hair still half-wet on her shoulders, in search of Dante and the others. She could now tell exactly where to go, which elevator to take to go back down to Loir's new lair. She met a few of Dante's men on the way, but all of them carefully looked away as soon as they spotted her almost naked legs. Eden didn't care and ignored them all the same.

As soon as the elevator doors opened, she rushed out, walking quickly with her bare feet on the white marble. Finally, Eden walked into Loir's room, a frown on.

"Kitty!" exclaimed Loir, raising his hands in the air with a big smile.

"...You do know you don't have any pants on, right?" said Circé, who was indeed standing behind him with her arms crossed.

Unlike her, the other hacker hadn't taken the time to change or clean herself up. Perhaps because she was now clean herself, Eden noticed how bad Circé looked, with her hair in a complete mess, the dark soot all over her face, and her clothes ripped or stained.

"Eden!" exclaimed Jack's voice from the other side.

He was seated at the edge of the area for Dive Hacking, both puppies quietly napping on his lap. He looked just as exhausted. Eden turned angry eyes toward Rolf. Dante's second-in-command was standing next to the door, his expression as empty as usual. Unlike them, he had taken off his dirty coat, rolled up his sleeves, and looked fine, although there were still visible bloodstains on his arms, hands, and neck.

"They didn't even get to shower or change?" she asked, a bit annoyed.

"The boss didn't give any orders."

Eden couldn't help but roll her eyes in exasperation. Of course, Dante wouldn't have cared about Jack or Circé. Still, Rolf's completely neutral tone was annoying. At times, he was so much like an android, it was scary. It was as if the building could explode, and Rolf would still wait right there until Dante gave him the order to leave... just like a perfectly trained dog. About half a dozen Italians, including George, were in the room, but Eden paid them no attention. Instead, she kept staring at Rolf, crossing her arms.

"Can you please give them a place to change or something?" she insisted.

"Sure."

She hadn't expected such an easy answer. Yet, Rolf did give orders right away for two of the men to prepare a guest room for Circé and Jack to have a place to shower and change into something else. She was in shock.

"Didn't you say Dante didn't tell you anything?" she asked, baffled.

"He said to do what you want."

Eden was rendered speechless once again. So Dante had put all his men at her service... which she didn't know how to feel about. Instead, Eden shook her head, trying to chase those thoughts away, and brushed her hair back.

"Fine, whatever. ...Where is he?"

Rolf pointed to one of the doors at the end of the room. Eden had never noticed that door before, but she followed him as he walked there, crossing paths with Jack.

"Hun..." he whispered, visibly a bit nervous.

"Just go, don't worry," she said. "I'll see you later."

"Okay..."

Jack was still holding the pups in his arms and tight against his chest, almost as if they were comfort plushies. Neither Beer nor Bullet even bothered to wake up, sleeping soundly in Jack's sturdy embrace. Eden pet the two of them quickly before she walked away to follow Rolf. Seeing the two puppies sleeping was a strange reminder of how her brutal world could also be peaceful. She couldn't help but envy them a little...

While Circé and Jack were escorted out on the other side of the room, Rolf entered a code on a panel to open the door, not hiding it at all from Eden. She really did have access to everything here. The door opened to a not so different room. Except, there was no one controlling the machines in this one, and instead of a Dive Hacking area, a large table was there, with Dante laying on it.

"Dante," she gasped, immediately rushing to it.

Eden had never seen a surgery monitor before. There was a robot on top of Dante, moving its several arms over his body, making all sorts of noise and moving quickly. She approached, a bit taken back by the strange machine, but it was clearly healing Dante. One arm was quickly stitching up a cut on the side, another was spraying something that smelled like disinfectant, two others were like small tongs removing little pieces of metal or glass from an open injury. There was one arm for everything, all of them linked to a bigger machine on the other side of that strange bed. It looked like a giant metallic spider moving on top of him. Eden could see his heartbeat and several numbers on the monitors, which finally allowed her to calm down a little. He was obviously fine, and in fact, almost done. She let out a little sigh and stood close. There were already scars all over, but one of the arms was trying to erase them with some sort of skin-colored tattoo thing. It was a good enough illusion for anyone that would have been a bit further away, but from where she stood, Eden could clearly see all the irregularities, bumps, and dents the machine couldn't erase. She had already felt most of them under her fingers when she caressed his torso, but under the bright light of the surgery machine, it was even more obvious.

Dante seemed almost asleep, with his eyes closed and his heavy breathing. Yet, as soon as she got close, he grabbed her hand gently without hesitation. Eden didn't push him away, her eyes only going down to their locked fingers. She let out a little sigh, and sat next to him on that table, against his hips.

"...Leave us."

Rolf nodded and walked away, closing the door behind him.

For a few long minutes, neither of them said anything. Eden watched the surgery machine work, not disgusted at all by his open injuries or the blood pumping in and out. Her own heartbeat quickly adjusted to the one on the monitor. She lifted her knee so she could rest her cheek on it, the other one still hanging down. She was still a bit tired but feeling a lot better now.

"How are you?" he asked softly.

His thumb was now caressing her other hand gently, while Eden had stuck the other one between her cheek and her knee.

"Better than you," she sighed. "...Did you know? About the memory tech?"

"No."

She didn't question his answer. Dante didn't look surprised when they found those documents, but she knew he could hardly be surprised by anything. Instead, she let out a faint sigh, her eyes on the spot between his eyebrows. She could remember his injury, and the headaches he chronically suffered from too... In fact, she was afraid to ask. Memory manipulation was taboo, even for experienced hackers. It violated several laws, natural and federal ones, not even talking about the most basic human rights... Eden let out another sigh, a bit tired. Why did she only feel calm now, by holding his hand and being with him? She hated how she had grown used to Dante, somewhat needy even. Yet, he wouldn't let go of her hand at all, even if he laid completely still. Several minutes passed like that, in complete silence, only rhythmed by the slow beeping of machines at work.

"What happened after that?"

"We split the weapons as agreed. The Core bombed the place again after we left."

"Damn savages..."

"That woman said they were probably after you."

Eden froze. Circé had already talked? Why? She rolled her eyes to herself. Perhaps she shouldn't have saved that woman, after all... Yet, to her surprise, Dante didn't add anything. She frowned.

"...Aren't you going to ask why they'd be after me?"

"I have a rough idea."

Of course. He already knew she was Ghost because he overheard her confirming it. He also knew of her relationship with the Architect, but it wasn't exactly a perfect explanation as to why the Core would be pursuing her. Still, Eden didn't push the matter any further. Judging from Dante's reaction, or lack thereof, she could already guess whatever the Core was after wouldn't change things for him. At least, not his strange obsession with her...

"We still need to talk to the other Zodiacs, Dante," she whispered. "With what happened, no one can stand to the side anymore. We have weapons and the Core sent men right here to the Suburbs. It won't be long before they send some sort of retaliation, and since the Snake already fell, the Dragon will..."

Before she could finish her sentence, the machine suddenly stopped and left Dante's side.

He moved immediately, pulling her hand to have her fall awkwardly on top of him. Eden grimaced and immediately tried to get away, worried she might reopen his injuries, but Dante was holding on firmly, a sneaky smile on his lips. He was not going to let go. She grumbled, and as she had been pulled in that strange position over him, she had to climb further onto the table, or she'd fall to either side soon from the struggling.

"Dante," she called him out, annoyed.

His eyes were still closed, but from that snarky smile, he clearly did all this on purpose and ignored her pissed-off tone. He wouldn't release her hand at all either, even as she angrily slapped his shoulder. In fact, his other hand moved to pull her hip until she was straddling him, her knees on both sides of his flank. Eden was even more annoyed that he had completely ignored her serious speech earlier to get her in this flirty situation instead. Now, while his hand was still stubbornly holding hers, he had the other one moving on her hip, sneaking under her shirt. She wanted to slap him until he dropped that smug smile from his lips, but she knew it would be useless, and she wasn't too keen on aggravating his freshly stitched-up injuries. Instead, she sighed and glanced toward the door, aware no one would dare bother them.

"Stop fooling around..." she muttered, not very convinced herself.

"I am not fooling around. Only with you."

Eden made a pout, a bit annoyed that she was blushing from those words. She really didn't know how to resist him. When she dared to look down again, his golden eyes were open, making his wry smile even harder to endure. She slapped him again, weakly this time.

"...Don't do that again."

"What?" she asked, well aware it couldn't be about her weak slaps.

"Running off where I can't see you. Stay with me."

His serious tone cooled the atmosphere around them a bit. Eden let out a faint sigh. Her hands were now on his stomach, one of Dante's still over hers. The other one was lazily caressing her hip, and playing with the lace of her panties.

"You know it couldn't be helped."

"Not next time."

She let out a faint sigh. No promises could be made. Instead, she simply glanced down at his damaged yet still superb body. Her finger slowly went up the line of his abs, making him suddenly tense under her. Eden smiled, while his eyes went noticeably darker. She liked to be the one doing the teasing... and see how he reacted to it. There were no words between them, but their gazes locked on each other; as she slowly moved up, his skin reacted with the hairs standing up, and his muscles grew even more defined with each breath he took. She could feel the heat slowly climbing in the cold room. Her body was warming up, especially the part sitting on top of Dante, and her palm caressing his torso.

Unable to endure anymore, Eden slowly leaned forward to kiss him. She had no idea why she wanted to do this, but she chose not to resist that push. She wanted his lips, and the way he hungrily kissed her, caressed her, and grabbed her. She liked the forcefulness in his movements, yet he was so respectful and wary of her reactions each time. It was as if Dante knew exactly where the limit was, where he could bring her to the edge without forcing her past it. Delicious shivers went down her spine and she kept leaning on top of him, her half-wet hair falling to the side while his hand fondled her butt cheek. Eden had begun slowly moving her lower body without thinking, rubbing back and forth against Dante's lower regions. She could feel him react, their bodies excited despite the layers of fabric in between. He was still wearing his suit too; although his top had been removed, Eden wouldn't complain about that.

They kept kissing, although the rest of their bodies were obviously eager for more. They were both moving unbearably slow as if taunting the other was their new favorite sensual game. A game they were both happy to lose, though. Eden slowly began opening her shirt, while both of Dante's hands were underneath it already, getting more playful with her skin. Their lips just couldn't bear to part long enough for them to undress any faster, though...

Suddenly, Eden sat up and glared at the room all around them. Dante raised an eyebrow, but before he could ask, she sighed.

"Loir. Cameras off, right now."

"I wasn't peeking!"

Dante shrugged and kept caressing Eden, leaning on one elbow to sit up and resume their kiss. However, Eden wasn't into it.

"...He's still peeking," she grumbled.

"I don't care."

"I do."

"I can kill him after we're done."

"Okay, I'll stop peeking! I'll stop! Cameras off, right now!"

Ignoring him, they resumed kissing, a bit wilder than before...

# CHAPTER TWENTY-SEVEN

Her hips a bit sore and her cheeks a bit red, Eden let out a faint sigh and focused on buttoning up her shirt again. She felt a bit embarrassed by the faint sensation between her legs but tried her best to ignore it, one button after another, crossing her ankles together.

His fingers came from behind to gently brush her blonde hair back, his hot breath sending a delicious wave of shivers down her back. Eden blushed some more as his lips faintly pressed against her skin.

"...Let's do it again," he whispered against her neck.

"Only my legs are made of steel, Dante," she groaned. "...Stop it."

She tried to push away his chin, but Dante ignored her, as always. In fact, he used that opportunity to grab her wrist and cup his chin in her hand, leaving faint kisses in her palm. He moved to sit right behind her, his legs wide open and his torso pressing against her back. She rolled her eyes and jumped down from the edge of the table to stand up, grateful her legs were made of metal indeed. Otherwise, they surely would have given out under her. Dante was still holding her wrist, so she turned around to face him, trying to forget the passionate sex they had just had.

"We have to go," she muttered. "I want to find out what that technology was used for. And why your–the previous Tiger, of all people, bought it. Dante, we really need to get moving."

He sighed, but eventually stood up as well, although he was unwilling to release her wrist. Eden frowned. He was up now, but his pants were still open, and so was the shirt that he'd put back on. Seeing the cheeky smile he gave her once their eyes met, he definitely wasn't thinking about buttoning that up anytime soon... She grimaced and stepped closer to do it for him. While she was close, of course his hands moved to grab her butt and play with her hair, but Eden ignored his flirty ways.

"Do you know how many weapons we got?"

"They are still counting them."

"What else did you get from the Yakuza? Only weapons?"

"We lost men, but we found a lot of money. The woman unlocked some accounts for us to prove her worth."

Eden took a second to understand which woman he was talking about. So he had made a deal with Circé while she was sleeping... No wonder the goth woman was allowed in there with Loir. Eden had already figured Dante only kept useful people or those Eden wanted around and alive. Luckily, Circé belonged to both categories. In fact, she was a bit more interested in the mention of money earlier. She kept buttoning, her fingers a bit clumsy as she was getting nervous.

"The money... H-how much?" she asked, trying to act detached.

"Something like seven or eight hundred million, I believe. Maybe more. Why?"

Eden shook her head and let go of his clothes, now properly arranged. In fact, Dante would probably change into clean ones soon, but at least, his skin or underwear wasn't exposed anymore when they walked out of this room. She tried to step back, but he effortlessly kept her in his embrace.

"Just... to ask."

"What do you need money for?" he insisted.

Eden glanced to the side, trying to think of something. However, nothing convincing would come at that moment, and Dante wasn't easily deceived either. In fact, she was tired of making up excuses and lying. She crossed her arms.

"I just... need some money for a personal matter."

"How much?"

"...Twenty-two million. That was the bounty you put on my head, right? I want it."

"...Okay."

Eden raised her eyes in shock. Dante's expression was neutral as usual, despite his fingers still playing with her hair, cupped around her neck.

"S-seriously?" she gasped, her heart beating faster.

"Yes. If you tell me what it's for. Don't tell me your legs."

Eden glared at him without thinking. She should have known Dante wasn't going to let it be that easy...

Now she was feeling like an idiot for trying to ask and get away with it. She took a deep breath. ...Was it worth telling him the truth? That this money was for her mother? She didn't like giving him another way to pressure her, but the truth was, he already had plenty. Not only were things going to get pretty dirty now, but she already had no way to go back to her former life. Loir had established himself here, the Core had found her, and soon, there would be a real war starting here. With their recent attack on the Red Temple, all the Zodiacs were probably going to be involved. There might not be ten of them anymore once all of this is over...

While she weighed the few options she had, Dante was surprisingly patient. He was still caressing her neck and waist, but this time, he was staring down at her, his cold golden eyes waiting for an answer. Eden had a gut feeling that he wasn't waiting to know; he was waiting for her decision to tell him the truth or not.

"...It's for my mother," she finally muttered. "She... She's in a special establishment, back in the Core. I... I lied. She didn't die, and she didn't make it to the Suburbs with me, either. The night we tried to escape, she... my mom was caught at... they shot her at the border."

Eden's throat tightened up as she spoke, choked by emotions. Dante's hands were strangely comforting her, with their warmth caressing her skin, her waist. She was fighting to get the words out, as it was something she was confessing for the first time in a very long time. It was painful, just to remember it all. Eden would still have nightmares of that precise memory from time to time, so she mostly avoided remembering it at all. Still, Dante was waiting for her explanation, so she bravely took another deep breath in.

"For a while, I could just... I just saw how they dragged her back in. She screamed for me to leave, so I ran, and I hid. The last time I... saw her for real, she was being dragged into one of those Overcrafts by a dozen men in black. She just... kept screaming, and then it stopped, and they took off. I was... alone with Adam in the Suburbs, in the beginning. Then, he was shot and killed, and I was alone again, until my master... until Pan appeared again, and led me to Loir. When I got better at hacking, I began thinking of my mom again. I knew she was alive, so I... looked into the place they had put her in, with Loir's help."

Eden took a faint pause to catch her breath, Dante's thumb gently rubbing her cheek.

"She... I'm not sure if my mom was... tortured, injured, or she just got psychological trauma from the shock, but... they put her in an establishment for patients with mental health issues. I don't think my father had told her much, and she had no idea about my whereabouts after we split up, so there wasn't any information to get from her. I think the Core... relaxed their attention on her, so when we saw an opportunity, Loir and I hacked their System. We made it so she'd be registered like any other patient, no trace left of her involvement with me or my dad."

"You changed the data?" he asked with a soft voice.

Eden nodded.

"Yeah. I just... It was an easy hack," she muttered. "Just changing the information on a file, a fake name, different data, new numbers... Surprisingly, it worked. Nothing else happened to her after that, and I get to call her from time to time. Anyway, I managed to hide her from those people, for now. But because she's back to being a normal person, a... regular patient, someone has to pay for her medical bills, and... it's a lot."

She let out a faint sigh but looked up for Dante's reaction. As per usual, it hadn't changed at all. He didn't look surprised or shocked, which made her wonder if he had any idea before. At least, she felt a bit better now that this secret was out. She had just opened up a bit more to Dante and, unlike her expectations, it felt strangely good. She waited for a bit, but seeing how he didn't respond with anything to that, Eden swept her tongue across her lips, a bit unsure.

"They asked me for a year's worth... or else they'll kick her out. That's all I want the money for."

"I understand."

"Then...?" Eden asked, a bit relieved.

However, Dante's cold expression made her realize something was wrong. Eden frowned, and pushed him, this time freeing herself from his embrace, although he didn't let her get away easily. Eden took a couple of steps back, staring at him in doubt.

"Dante, I swear that's all I need the money for," she insisted. "I am not trying to double-cross you or anything. I'll fight with you!"

"I know. But I won't give you the money for that. You can't give that money to them. Not anymore."

"Wha–Why?" she exclaimed, furious. "You just agreed to it!"

"I agreed to give you two million, but not for you to be cheated out of it."

"What the heck are you saying?! I swear I'm sending money for her medical bills, they just tell me what it goes toward, and then all of her expenses are taken care of! I'm not even asking to see her, I just want to make sure they take care of my mother! Dante!"

He let out a faint sigh, this time looking away from her; it was the first time Dante was intentionally avoiding her gaze, and she hated it.

"Dante, look at me!" she ordered, upset. "What are you talking about? What cheating?"

"Your mother is most likely dead."

Eden rolled her eyes at him. So that's what it was... She shook her head.

"No, no, she's alive. I know how it sounds, but she's alive. I've talked to her almost every week since I changed her data, Dante. It's my mom, it's her voice."

"It's not your mother," he retorted.

"I know it's her! You think I wouldn't be able to recognize my own mother's voice? I know that's her! I asked Loir to modify the data so she'd be transferred where she'd be safe and taken care of! You don't know what they did to her!"

"She has memory issues, doesn't she?"

His words stunned Eden, cutting her anger short. She hesitated, frowning. "H-how do you...?"

"You had already mentioned the money was for your mother when we met," he said, "so I had it looked into. Your mother is... supposedly kept in an establishment not for retired people of the Core, but for people with mental health issues."

"You investigated my mom?" she repeated, baffled.

"So she still has a SIN you can call," continued Dante, "but when you call her, she probably has issues remembering who you are, how old you are, or anything about your past, doesn't she?"

"I told you they tortured her! My dad was gone before I could even get to meet him or remember him, and she tried for so long to survive on her own, just with me! When they captured her, my mom was tortured, so it just couldn't be helped that she'd... end up with those issues. That's why I had her transferred to that establishment, to one she could be kept in and taken care of! A lot of people send their family members there, I had looked it up before Loir and I even tried to hack it!"

"Eden, the Core wouldn't let go of her so easily. They never release someone once they have captured them."

"You don't know that. ...Loir made it, didn't he?" scoffed Eden.

"With a lot of help from the inside. Hackers, most likely the rest of the Edge, and Tanya, a Zodiac. Maybe even your mentor, Pan. He didn't come out undamaged either. There are very few ways people can escape one of the Core's prisons, and the main one is with their feet first. The only way to really escape their watch is to go to the Suburbs and have the resources for that. One of the best hackers in the continent hid in a basement for years, but you think they would miss your mother being moved around under their nose?"

"The hack worked," retorted Eden, her fingers going numb. "It was–"

"Surprisingly easy, wasn't it? Don't you think hacking one of the Core's prisons would be a bit more complicated than that? I know you're good, and so is your partner, but this... doesn't add up."

"You don't know what you're talking about," insisted Eden, constantly shaking her head. "You have no proof."

"We both know there are precedents of people escaping the Core," said Dante. "When the Core lost interest in them, or they had the right resources, or were incredibly skilled at escaping. However, your mother doesn't fit any of those categories. She was related to at least two of the most researched criminals of Chicago, and she was one of their citizens to begin with, implanted with one of their SINs. You escaped because you're different, Eden; your father's skills saved you, but your mother didn't make it."

"You're just speculating, Dante. I know I talked to my mother..."

"Those mental health establishments don't exist."

Eden's jaw dropped. That was the last thing she was expecting.

369

"...What are you saying?"

"If you ask A., the Zodiac you met earlier, he will tell you. It was exposed a couple of years ago after his hackers tried a raid on the Core. They found a bunch of information, including how they scammed their own citizens."

"I-I don't understand."

"The retirement homes, mental health establishments, they don't exist, Eden. Those places are just scams the Core put in place to have fewer citizens to take care of while allowing those who place their loved ones there to keep paying for it. I will have A. send you all the data. The Core's System has evolved to believe that the... non-useful citizens need to be disposed of, so they get rid of the real people while uploading things like their voices or physical appearance into their data centers. This way, if their family calls, they listen to a computer using their voice, using the basic information and patterns of someone with memory issues to maintain the illusion. They actually use it as a way to draw pity from you and make you want to pay more. If they are asked for a video, they can make one with basic augmented reality software. People just keep paying and, if they become doubtful or get close to lacking the money, they learn their loved one just passed."

"No... No, no, no, you're lying," muttered Eden.

"I'm not. When you mentioned your mother, I tried to look it up. We found the same information. Since she was transferred to that establishment, she followed the same path as any of their patients. ...If you ask Loir to hack deeper, he will confirm it for you."

"No!"

Her scream echoed in the room. Eden didn't want to believe it. She wished she could rewind the past five minutes and forget about all that nonsense he had just uttered. Her mother couldn't be dead. She hadn't suffered through the last ten years of her existence just to pay a machine that had already murdered her mom, the last member of her family.

She felt the tears running down her cheeks, but she was much too furious to care. Instead, she tried to hold it in.

"Loir. Check what he said, now."

"Sure..."

She could feel herself getting light-headed just from the thought of all of that. In fact, it was much worse than she could have foreseen. That hack was too easy. Her mom was no one but linked to the one person the Core was dying to find. She couldn't escape prison with just... some changed data.

"Loir!" she shouted, unable to hold it in.

"A minute, Kitty! I'm checking, checking... Oh, wait a sec, crazy, creepy witchy here says she needs a word with you..."

"...Eden, what he said is true," suddenly said Circé, through the speakers. "I... came to learn the truth while working for them. I even helped operate some... It's horrible, but it's the truth. I'm sorry."

Eden felt her heart sink. She stumbled a couple of steps behind and didn't even have the strength to push Dante away when he grabbed her to keep her from falling.

"...How... How long have you known?" she muttered.

"...I didn't want to tell you like this."

"You should have told me," she cried. "You should have told me..."

"I know. ...I'm sorry."

She grabbed his shirt, and they both sank down to the floor, Eden's legs unable to hold her for real this time. She didn't care that they were metal. She just couldn't find her balance with the sadness overwhelming her. They both got down on the cold floor, and she finally broke down in tears, in Dante's arms, unable to hold it in anymore.

Eden kept crying for a long time. She couldn't stop herself sobbing real, big tears for the first time in a very long time. She just couldn't stand it all. How painful the truth was, and how foolish she felt.

Because this was the worst. To realize she had been completely played for so long. All the energy, all the efforts she had made to try and keep her mother safe had all been completely and utterly in vain. She couldn't help but feel terribly sorry for herself, and foolish that she had held on for this long to an illusion, a horrible trap. It was a nightmare, just to think about everything she had done, how much she had suffered all this time, for nothing. For a mother she would never ever see again, for a mother who had been dead for so long while her daughter was played at the hands of the Core. Everything she had gone through, reduced to a mere, bitter, and cruel laugh. She was a pawn, like everyone else. Just an idiot down to play their game because she had believed in a foolish dream.

Not only had she never felt so stupid, but Eden felt lonelier than ever. The only remaining member of her family was gone. The one person she had held on to all this time, the one she could call to forget her hardships, the mother whose embrace she had almost forgotten, was gone. She was an orphan now. She had always tried to keep up the appearance, to look like a tough independent girl with no ties, but now that it was real, it was unbearable. It was as if her entire childhood had been crushed, her memories shattered. Eden felt sick to her stomach, just thinking about how much she and her mother had sacrificed, in the hope of each other's survival. All of this for nothing.

Her legs. Eden cried even harder when she realized she had sold her legs, her own flesh and blood, to feed the same machine that had eaten her mom. She screamed against Dante's shoulder, unable to hold her frustrations in. She was just unbearably sad and angry at the same time. If it wasn't for Dante hugging her, she would have destroyed this room, probably harmed herself, or wreaked havoc in some way. However, the Tiger wasn't letting her go. As if he knew, Dante just held on to her tightly, caressing her hair while whispering calm words into her ear. His lips would press against her temple from time to time, her cheekbone, like how one would soothe a child.

"You should have told me..." she sobbed quietly against his torso.

She kept trying to throw her fists at him in anger, but they were no stronger than a little bump against his torso, not even making the Tiger flinch. Dante didn't care about Eden venting at him, he was ready to take it all as long as she could calm down. The frustration was even worse as he was the only person she could be mad at, and at the same time, the one gently holding her. His touch was almost too gentle for her broken heart. Eden felt helpless and just kept sobbing and muttering incoherently, her own cries echoing in the room. Dante's comforting embrace was the only thing keeping her sane right now. Otherwise, she knew she would have drowned in despair.

He was all she had left. The one person who could hold her like this, make her feel loved and cared about. This thought terrified Eden. She had always been scared to depend on someone else, and now, Dante was right there, making her feel like she could depend on him all she wanted. However, getting attached to someone meant she opened the door to more pain and loss, and right now, she wasn't sure she was ready for that.

"I'm here," he whispered against her ear.

It was as if he knew just the right words to mend her heart, and help it beat again. Eden's crying slowly subsided at his gentle words, his warm breath, and his deep voice. She could just rest in his embrace, the two of them sitting on the floor of this deserted and cold surgery room. This position ought to be uncomfortable for him as she was resting against his torso and leaning in, but Dante didn't show an ounce of that. He just held her for the longest time, relentlessly caressing her hair, numbing her pain with his gentle hands. As her sobbing calmed down, a pounding headache crept in instead, and Eden groaned against his shoulder.

"...Are you alright?"

"No."

Her grumble made him sigh a little, but as expected, there was nothing else she could have answered. Her throat was hoarse from all the crying, her eyes stung, her head kept pounding like a hammer, and she felt terrible overall. However, as Eden began shivering from the cold in the room, they both knew it was time to go. The rest of the world wasn't going to wait for her to feel better, especially not the Zodiacs, the Core, or the messed-up city they lived in.

Dante gently helped her up, and the throbbing pain that hit her thighs from the change of position made Eden hate her mechanical legs even more. She didn't even want to think about it, it made her sick. Without a word, she got back on her feet, massaging her thighs a bit so they would stop aching. Dante was about to put an arm behind her to lift her up and carry her, but she refused.

"I want to walk," she muttered.

"Okay."

He left another long, gentle kiss on her forehead, and Eden couldn't help but close her eyes. Now that the worst of the crying had passed, she realized how much she needed his warmth. Those lips pressed against her skin were enough to keep her going, for now. She just wanted to hold on to him, to have his arm around her, his torso she could lean on, and forget about the rest for a little while. That was all she needed.

The two of them got ready to go out again, pushing their hair back and straightening up their messy clothes for a second. Eden hoped no one would notice her red eyes; she hated crying, but hated it even more when people knew she had cried. She forced herself to take several deep breaths, wipe away the tears not yet dry, and clenched and unclenched her fists a couple of times to get the blood flowing again. No one on the other side of the door was expecting her to be fine anyway, and she had no intention of putting on a show. This was more like her own self-defense reflexes coming back on their own.

The door opened in front of them, but to her relief, only Loir was there, playing with the pups again. Beer and Bullet ran to her as soon as she appeared, their little legs taking a while to get to her. Eden let out a little sigh and bowed to lift them up in her arms, a bit grateful to have those two. The two puppies immediately began licking her cheeks, as if they could taste the salt of her tears. Eden grimaced as their breath smelled like tomato-flavored chicken... Their weight had definitely gone up since she had found them too.

"Stop feeding them crap, Loir," she groaned.

"It's not crap!" he protested. "Do you know how hard it is to find good pizza nowadays? Those little, four-legged burritos love it too!"

Eden frowned a bit, worried for the pups' stomachs, but both seemed fine, just a bit plump. She didn't want to stay mad either; she already had enough of a headache and didn't want to add some painful frowning to it.

Suddenly, her instincts noticed the stares coming from the side. Some of Dante's men, who were most likely there to guard the room, had their eyes on her exposed legs. Eden didn't think anything of it since about seventy percent of them were nothing but a piece of metal anyway, but to those men, it probably just looked like flawless legs... She was about to glare back, but decided to ignore them.

"Where are Circé and Jack?" she asked.

"Oh, the ladies went to change!" exclaimed Loir, already back to his keyboards. "Everyone followed what the Kitty said, so they gave them a room to shower and change... Ah, it must be nice! I haven't showered since... wait, since when again?"

"You know you can take a shower too," grimaced Eden.

"I only take lavender-scented baths, once a year!" protested Loir, making a horrified face. "Otherwise, I get all pruney and my hair falls out!"

Eden wondered if he actually knew he had no hair, or if he was making another one of his weird jokes... She was never really sure, but she knew not to feed his madness. She sighed and turned to Dante.

"You should take a shower too," she muttered, having noticed his poor state.

"Come take a bath with me," he suddenly offered, totally oblivious to the dozen people who could hear them.

"We don't have time for that. The Zodiacs and–"

"We've got all the time we want."

Before she could protest, Dante pulled her hand, and took her outside the room, glaring just once at his men who had kept staring at Eden. She didn't mind him holding her hand, despite the struggle to hold two pups with one arm. In the elevator, she sighed, still hugging those two. She didn't hold herself back from leaning against Dante anymore, and he wouldn't comment on it either. It was as if they had taken a new, invisible step together.

The time it took to go up felt a bit longer than usual, and Eden closed her eyes, her headache gaining the upper hand.

"...I'm surprised you didn't do anything," she muttered without thinking.

"What?"

"Your men, staring at me."

She heard him scoff.

"All they can do is stare. ...But I can do something about it if you want. Shall I gouge their eyes out? It's easy."

"You sociopathic sadist... If you were to blind all the men who had stared at me, half of Chicago would be blind... Too many dogs out there."

As if he had understood her, Bullet suddenly barked out of the blue, although it was probably due to the long time spent in that strange enclosed space.

"...Hyenas," she grumbled.

The door finally opened to their suite and Eden felt a bit strange, remembering how she had left this place in a hurry just about an hour ago to look for Dante. Her feelings then and now were completely different, but at least now he was by her side.

Letting the pups down to go play around the room, Eden and Dante walked together to the bathroom. Opposite the shower was a large tub, with enough space for two people to sit in it. Eden had never seen such a thing before, so she hadn't really paid much attention to it the previous times she had come in here. Yet, Dante turned it on, and hot water quickly filled it, along with a surprising amount of bubbles, triggering her curiosity. Not only that, but something was coloring the hot water pink, with a strong floral scent. Eden couldn't resist herself and leaned forward to touch the water, but it really was just normal water. Meanwhile, Dante undressed at record speed, but instead of diving in right away, he began unbuttoning her shirt from behind. Eden frowned and put her hands on his.

"What are you doing?"

"Undressing you."

"Thanks, Captain Obvious, but why?"

"You don't want to take a bath with me?" he asked, sounding almost pained.

"I'm already clean!"

"I know..."

Eden kept glaring and holding his hands away from her shirt until he gave up, and took a step back. She was grateful for that, as his naked body against her was extremely troubling, and making things harder... Stepping where she could see him, Dante put a foot in, naked as a worm, and sat down, his legs and butt quickly disappearing under the clouds of bubbles. Eden stared helplessly until he turned around, his golden eyes now riveted on her. She had mixed feelings about seeing him and his freshly stitched injuries in there, but she kept her arms crossed, unsure about the situation.

"...I won't do anything," Dante promised as if he had read her mind.

"I don't trust that for a single second."

"I mean it. Not if you don't want me to."

Eden sighed. She hated how he could look so sincere while spouting those lies. Not innocent, but sincere. She let out a long sigh and began undoing her shirt. She was tempted by the bath's nice scent anyway... and her face was probably a mess too after all the tears and snot. That gave her the perfect excuse to step in. Dante helped her in, holding her hand, but he didn't say anything when she chose to sit opposite him.

The warm water enveloped Eden as soon as she got in, a delicious sensation that made her shiver with bliss. She had rarely been able to enjoy such a luxury, but she loved it. There were definitely some advantages to being with a very rich guy in this world. She closed her eyes, letting the hot water wash away all the tiredness. She had never realized how good it could be to simply immerse herself in a body of hot, scented water. It was almost unbearably hot, but it was a blessing to her sore muscles.

For a few minutes, she just let herself be, enjoying the heat her body was adjusting to, and keeping her eyes closed to ignore Dante facing her. She could feel his fingers gently caressing her leg. The model of her legs was of such high quality that she could feel it, but all pain signals were blocked when she thought about it. Many would have thought this was a luxury, but Eden would much rather have had her real legs instead. Not because of all the crap she had gotten from being a Part, but just because she hated not feeling completely human. She hated having parts of herself that could be replaced like one would replace the tires on a car, and not being able to feel the pain. Pain made her feel alive. Even during her Dives into the Dark Reality, she never shied away from pain. She deeply believed that pain made her more human, and also more survival-driven, at all times. She didn't want to feel like one of those emotionless robots.

"...What is going to happen next?" she finally asked.

"We should have dinner together."

"You know what I'm talking about."

Eden finally opened her eyes. This time, Dante was simply staring at her legs underwater, still caressing them slowly. He looked so calm and composed, as if everything from earlier had never happened. Aside from the scars on his torso, still red after the surgery, everything about him looked exactly the same as this morning.

"Dante," she called out to him after he failed to answer quickly enough for her taste.

"The others will make their own move soon enough."

He was talking about the Zodiacs. Of course, the Snake's fall was going to stir some turmoil in the other territories. Eden didn't know the details of Dante's agreement with Thao, and she actually didn't care much. Right now, her anger was turned toward the Core and only the Core. The in-fighting between the Zodiacs that had almost driven each of her decisions before now felt like some minor issue. It felt like things were slowly piling up, guiding them toward some final fight that could not be pushed back any further.

"Come here," said Dante.

Eden frowned at his open embrace. As usual, she was distrustful of him, but Dante's large torso and skin were... very tempting. She sighed and moved to sit with her back against him. He wrapped his arms around her waist right away and leaned his head on her shoulder. Eden rolled her eyes as soon as she felt something poke her lower back, but decided to pretend she couldn't feel it. She really wasn't in the mood... and thankfully, he did stay true to his word, for once. She sighed and put her hands in the water, washing her face until she couldn't feel any more of that stickiness from her tears.

"Dante..."

"Hm?"

"I really want to do it. ...Let's beat the Core. For real."

# CHAPTER
# TWENTY-EIGHT

"...Are you sure?"

Dante's question took her by surprise. Was he hesitating now? Or maybe he thought she should? Eden took a deep breath. She knew the anger would come to pass, but not that knot in her stomach. Nor the pain she had gone through, nor the legs she loathed twice as much now. For the first time, perhaps, she was deeply glad she had met Dante De Luca. Whatever had put him in her path, it felt like fate. He probably didn't hate the Core as much as she did, but he was powerful, rich, and insane enough that he'd be willing to go against the strongest power standing. With a bitter smile, Eden thought the last few days had been life-defining for her. Looking back, things could have ended sooner for her, she could have ended up much, much worse. She could have died in Jack's bar that night, or Dante could have grown impatient and finished her off instead of healing her. She could have been unfortunate and died under the Mexican Mafia of her neighborhood or even caught in a street brawl when they erupted once or twice a week.

"I'm just thinking... We can't let them continue like this. Murdering people and getting away with it, like my parents, or sending innocents here to the Suburbs. A lot of the families living here did nothing to deserve that. Nothing should be like it is. Surviving on polluted air, starving, and living in this chaos. I don't... I can't face more of that. I can't go back to how I was, and... I'm too mad to let them get away with it. Not anymore. They can't just crush us under their feet all over again, Dante."

She heard him chuckle and turned around to face him.

"I'm serious, don't mock m–"

Before she could finish her sentence, he kissed her. Eden was half-angry, but half wanting that kiss. She decided not to slap him right away, and just enjoy this for a short while instead. Although he would have deserved it for sure... When he ended their kiss, she was glaring at him, upset.

"Can we be serious for ten minutes?" she groaned.

"I'm serious."

"I meant serious and not lascivious."

"I'm serious and listening."

"I still feel your dick poking me."

"I can't help that."

Eden glared some more, but she knew she wouldn't win this fight anyway. If he had decided to act like that, she simply had no idea how she could possibly stop him. Instead, she rolled her eyes.

"Please tell me you're at least seriously hearing what I'm saying."

"I'm listening. You're sexy when you're mad."

"So that's why you never take me seriously..."

She tried to roll her eyes and look away, but Dante suddenly grabbed her chin, having her look at him instead. This time, his expression was back to being very serious, and his golden eyes glowing like they were made of actual liquid gold.

"I always take you seriously."

Something about his words seized Eden deep down, and she struggled a bit to get out of his grip and face forward in time to hide her blushing. He was so dangerously honest at times... She pulled her chin close to her chest and hid her face, leaving him to stare at her back. And she could definitely feel him staring.

"...The Zebra also began to move," he suddenly said.

"Wait, what? How?"

"He probably heard the news too and didn't quite appreciate it... Some of his people went and destroyed one of the Core's entrances to the Suburbs. They bombed it, making part of that area collapse."

"What... When was that? And which part did they attack, exactly?"

"I just heard it twenty minutes ago. It was the entry past Western Avenue. The Dog apparently lent them support, and A. camouflaged the whole thing. It's probably as much to warn the Core as it was to bring it to the attention of the other Zodiacs."

Eden remained quiet, but the gears in her head were spinning fast. The Zebra was definitely one of the biggest Zodiacs, one of the most powerful, and the one known to hate the Core the most. She had never seen him, and she had never gone to the Black community's territories either, but it was another of the large ones. Something was definitely changing for the Zebra to take such an obvious and loud stand against the Core. Never had a Zodiac ever done

378

something physical against the Core. The risk of retribution was too high to even consider it. There had been many cases of people openly trying to attack the Core, or even citizens of the Core visiting the Suburbs. Each time, the repercussions had been horribly violent and quick. A punishment to set an example for others, dissuading people from ever attempting something like that again. Eden had seen it. People were dragged into the street and publicly shot down by men in black. An entire building was blown up for the one gang that was hiding inside, even if there were also innocent families on the other floors. Hackers like her could hide through the Dark Reality and had higher chances of not being found out, but she knew she was putting her life in danger each time she Dived. This was why all hackers always operated so secretly, hiding their real identities and finding the weirdest hiding spots, like a deserted, underground basement. Everything was done to lessen the chances of the Core finding them.

Yet, all of this seemed to be amounting to something now. Thao and Dante had already faced the Core's people at the Red Temple, and now, the Zebra and the Dog were directly attacking the Core. There were only eight entrances into the Suburbs from the Core, and one had just been blown up. It was definitely big... or a sign something even bigger was about to happen.

"...Did the Core relay that? On their channels?" she asked.

"I don't know..."

"Loir, search it for us!"

"H-h-how did you know I was tuned in!"

"Because you're a freaking pervert stalker. Just look it up."

"Oh, fine, fine... But you two are boring, you know. If I had known, I would have just watched the latest season of *The Young and the Restless*... Let's see... Not this one, not this... Oh, is that a cooking show? Oh, those burgers look amazing! Is that duck? Oh, I love those fancy people, eating nearly-extinct creatures in our faces..."

"Loir," groaned Eden.

She leaned back against Dante while waiting for the words she wanted to hear, and the Tiger groaned a bit in satisfaction, immediately wrapping his arms around her waist. Eden didn't even fight it, as long as she was comfortable against him...

"Coming, coming... Well, they only have three main news channels, and none are talking about our bad boy Zebra blowing up their landscape, not even the most boring one! Instead, they are just talking about how great the council is, as usual, and their favorite celebrities of the moment... Oh, my bunny, is that guy eating a live octopus? This is so interesting! ...Oh, something's coming out his nostrils. Guess what? Octopus-chan is making a comeback. That's kind of gross but in a fascinating way..."

"So they don't plan on saying anything," scoffed Eden. "As usual..."

"You seem to know plenty," muttered Dante.

"I've spent years spying on the Core. In fact, a lot of the things I think

379

I remember from my childhood might have been from all the times I hacked into their surveillance cameras. The difference with our lives, here... Honestly, sometimes I envied them, sometimes I hated them even more. Those people have no idea what it's like here, but they just don't want to know. They have fresh air every single day, fresh food growing in their gardens, perfectly cut green grass, they have running water that doesn't taste like crap, and things they can buy without thinking... Free transport, free schools, free healthcare, and even their houses are made to be exactly the right size for the job they do, so the government takes what they owe and they get some pocket money left. It's like... paradise in a schoolbook. They do what they're told, enjoy what everyone enjoys, and pretend to like everyone so everyone likes them... They never see the color of blood or a speck of dust in their perfect lives... Their polished, oblivious lives."

"...Do you envy them?"

"Sometimes," admitted Eden, "but it's hard to envy something you know you once had, and lost. Even if I went back now, pardoned and everything, I wouldn't have my mom, or get to see my father. I'd be leaving more behind than I want to admit, I believe..."

"What about here?"

"What do you mean?"

She heard Dante sigh, and he gently pressed his lips against her shoulders.

"You could continue to live here, with me. Without fighting the Core, just being by my side. You'd get all those things, without the Core's control. You could enjoy all you wanted, with me. Just... let go of this fight, and have a life here with me. We already have everything the others want. You wouldn't miss anything you mentioned."

Eden was rendered mute by Dante's offer.

No, in fact, she could barely process what she had just heard. It just sounded completely unreal. However, it was actually what she was living right then. Enjoying a scented bath with bubbles, her lover hugging her, with clean air in the room. Fresh and new clothes waiting for her, fine food, a bed with silk sheets, and even toys for her pups... Because she had been refusing all of the privileges that came with Dante until now, Eden had barely realized how free she was now. Except for her mother, she hadn't bothered about money at all. Not about her growling stomach, how much oxygen she had left, or how to sleep on a broken mattress at night. In fact, she had been thoughtlessly indulging in this newly found life, mostly because she hadn't realized how it happened...

Eden had been so used to living day to day, only hoping to make it to tomorrow, that she had been completely blind to how much her situation had changed these past few days. In fact, she suddenly got scared of how comfortable she was, and a wave of fear took her by surprise. She tried to sit back up, but before she could, Dante's hand suddenly covered her eyes, and he gently pulled her back in his embrace, although his other arm was holding her tightly against him.

"I'm just saying, this is a possibility too," he whispered against her ear. "We don't have to fight. You can decide."

Eden finally remembered to breathe, and although her heart was still beating at what seemed like a hundred miles an hour, she could still try to stay somewhat calm, and seriously think about his proposal.

It really was... tempting. This life, with Dante, forever. Locked up in this tower, with nothing but warm baths, silk sheets, and bubbly wine forever. Nothing else to worry about, just... living with him. She could see it. She'd simply wake up in his bed, fall asleep in his arms. Perhaps she would help him with his Zodiac affairs too as his hacker, just like he had wanted... She could forget all about problems with money and the Core. Perhaps she'd disappear from the Dark Reality for real, never stepping foot in the digital world again. She would have been lying if she said she wasn't tempted. That path was so easy and open, she almost already had a toe on it, but...

"...I can't," she finally muttered.

"Why not?"

"Because that'd be... doing the same thing I hate about those people. Doing nothing and turning... a blind eye."

She sighed and took Dante's hand off her eyes, blinking a couple of times until her eyes adjusted to the light again. She glanced to the side, where the window showed them the view of Chicago's buildings, somewhere farther east. Eden stared at those buildings for a while.

"I can't. I've already done too much, and if I don't finish this, I would... hate myself for it, Dante. Even if I'm fine, from now on, many people won't be. I've seen way too much of what they do to us, I've heard too many of their most... horrible secrets. ...You know, in my building, there's that couple. They were both born and raised in the Suburbs, like their parents, and they have survived this far being good people. But there aren't any jobs where we live, so the husband had to get a SIN implanted. With it, he can find a job, but the jobs you can get with a SIN... He's probably going to work in one of those horrible green energy factories. They get people like him to run or bike every day, for so many hours, to produce that green energy, and then, they sell it to the people in the Core, calling it green energy... The most organic electricity there is. Made of desperate people's sweat..."

Eden took a deep breath. She hoped that the family was alright. She felt sorry for those normal people, who had a hard time every day and had to think twice about absolutely everything they did. That husband would probably get into countless fights with his wife about it, and work himself to death trying to make enough money for them to survive. Eden knew she was lucky that Dive jobs paid so well, for the most part. Still, it was never enough. Not when the Core always played horrible tricks like what they had done with her mother...

"I want to get to the bottom of this," she finally declared. "For my mom. I want to know what really happened to my father too and why I had to run to the Suburbs that night. Something definitely happened, I was just too young. I can't pretend to only be a victim or an innocent anymore; I've already come this far. They'll never leave me alone, anyway. Living with you wouldn't be enough."

She turned to face him this time, putting her arms around his neck. Dante was always so calm, it was hard to even guess what he was thinking. Right now, he was simply staring back at her, ready to listen to every one of her words.

"...Are you upset?" she asked.

"No. I'll do what you decide to do."

"Why? I don't understand why you're always so... indulgent to me. Aren't you supposed to be some cold-blooded bastard?"

"I am."

"Your body doesn't seem cold-blooded right now."

He smirked, and his hand gently caressed her back.

"I don't really know," he muttered. "It's just how it is. I'll follow what you say. I don't really care if I die, as long as I get to stay with you."

Eden frowned. That was perhaps the biggest mystery of all... Why Dante De Luca, such a powerful man, the Italian Zodiac, was so obsessed with her. She never found herself more outstanding than any other woman, and in fact, she knew many prettier, smarter girls. However, Dante's golden eyes were clearly set on her, and her alone. Eden let out a faint sigh, and rather than trying to get more answers, she leaned forward to kiss him.

He'd never resist her. As soon as their lips met, he opened his for their tongues to touch and mingle, letting that delicious spark bloom into a vivid fire between them. It was impossible to ignore his hands all over her, just like it was impossible to ignore the heat between them. They were both naked, excited, and although neither would say it out loud, in love.

"Um... excuse me..."

Eden groaned and pulled away, with real murderous intent at that moment.

"Loir, what the hell is wrong with you?"

"Alright, for once, I'm very sorry to interrupt the Kitties doing nasties in the bath, but, uh... something pretty big just, uh... kind of popped up on my radar. I don't think you got time to play the yadada right now..."

"What?"

"You know, the old Dragon Zodiac big boss...?"

"Is he dead?" asked Eden, panicking.

"Uh... Not quite. I think the old guy decided to pull a Darth Sidious on us."

"What is that supposed to mean?!"

"The old Dragon doesn't seem to be dying at all, he's alive and kicking! Like, as in... really kicking butts, right now. He's on TV, and not too happy about what we did. He's not the nice old grandpa I thought... Oh, he's inviting all the Zodiacs to meet him at his palace. That's nice of him! ...Do you think we're invited? 'Cause I'm very bad with chopsticks. Just saying."

"...Are you sure it's real?" Eden asked again, frowning at the screen.

"Yup," Loir nodded. "I checked and double-checked. It's real, and it was broadcasted just half an hour ago on all the channels they don't have in the Core. I guess our Old Dragon Grandpa really wanted to be sure he got everyone's attention. ...He looks in shape for someone who's, what, just seventy years old? Eighty? How old is he again?"

"No one knows," muttered Eden.

She kept nervously rubbing her finger against her lips, completely absorbed in the screen. The Dragon. Old Man Long was alone on the screen addressing the camera. He was speaking in Chinese, but they had even put on some subtitles for everyone to understand him.

Eden could feel Dante's arm around her, and he was also tense. They had both rushed out of their bath to see this downstairs. In fact, she was only wearing a silk bathrobe, and her hair was still a bit wet. Dante had also merely put on pants, and he was half-naked behind her, his bare torso distracting Eden a bit. They were alone in Loir's room, except for Rolf, standing a few steps behind with his usual stern expression. It was their third time playing the video, but Eden kept wanting to see it again, worried she had missed something. However, there was no hidden message. The Old Man appeared with a very simple wooden background, and a large dragon statue behind him, most likely his headquarters. He was sitting and confidently talking to the camera with a calm expression, and certainly not with the appearance of a dying old man.

"I don't understand," muttered Eden. "If he's upset that we destroyed the Snake, why would he invite all the Zodiacs to the Dragon Palace? Everyone knows all of you don't get along, this is obviously some sort of trap..."

"I don't think so," muttered Dante. "He hated the Snake too. He's just upset we broke the harmony between the Zodiacs at such a critical time."

"Isn't he the one who... created it?"

"Sort of. The Mafia Lords existed long before the Core, but they never got along or respected each other. When the wall was built to keep the people of the Suburbs out, the Dragon held a meeting exactly like this to involve them all. There were no rules, only some tacit agreement they wouldn't murder each other. At the time, they didn't really have a need to, either. He came up with the Zodiac system so all would be able to know who the Mafia Lords were. They didn't need to know their names, just who was associated with each Zodiac. This way, it didn't matter if one of them was killed, they would be replaced and their... community would be safe."

"No wonder he didn't like us blowing up Punky Snakey like a firework on Chinese New Year..." muttered Loir.

Eden sighed, and turned to Dante, who already had his eyes on her.

"Has a meeting with all the Zodiacs ever happened again since the first time?" she asked.

"No. Not with all of them. The only ones who were in the first meeting were Long, Sanyam, who represents the Ox, and Lecky, the Goat. All the other Mafia Lords have died since, except for King's father, who somehow... retired."

"I wonder what the Zodiac's pension plan is like," chuckled Loir. "I guess you can't have them drink tea and play backgammon nicely with each other..."

Eden glared at him, a bit annoyed, and the hacker made a grimace before rolling his chair back to his keyboards, putting his Pac-Man game back on the screen. She sighed and turned to Dante once again.

"Do you think the others will come?"

He remained silent for a second, visibly thinking. Meanwhile, he brushed her wet hair with his fingers, untangling it slowly.

"Most likely... We all get along, except for a couple of them, and they won't want to be left out. Moreover, we all have respect for the Old Man, and with what happened these past few days, no one will want to miss this opportunity..."

Eden faintly nodded, but she was nervous just thinking about it. All the Zodiacs in one room... It felt like a terrifying thing to happen. Why now, of all times? Between their attack on the Snake's territory and the Zebra and the Dog bombing one of the Core's entrances, it felt like they had triggered a chain of events. What would come next? Most of the Zodiacs were aware of the Core's plan to wipe more of their territories out by now. Was that the beginning of their response? If they did gather as the Dragon wished, what would come out of it? Most Zodiacs didn't trust each other. In fact, it would be shocking if they could even gather without a murder or two happening...

"Eden."

Dante gently calling her name took Eden out of her deep thinking. She raised her eyes, realizing he was gently caressing her neck.

"Don't worry," he said.

"Are you going?"

"Yes."

Eden slowly nodded. She expected as much... The Dragon was very straightforward, asking all the Zodiacs to come to his palace the next day at midday. There wasn't much time left to send a refusal or even hesitate. After the long day they'd had, it felt like the world wasn't going to offer them much time to rest. She sighed, a little glad that Dante's large hand was supporting her neck a bit. Even if she had caught a short nap in the afternoon and taken a bath, Eden felt tired. Not just physically, but emotionally drained too. It had been a long day of sneaking into the Snake's territory, surviving the fight, and then finding out about her own mother's death...

"Loir, have you heard from the other Zodiacs?" she finally asked.

"Uh... I don't think we're friends on any social media...?"

"In the Dark Reality. Look it up, maybe another one made a move today. I'm surprised there would have been no notable hack after you and Circé fought all day, and destroyed the Japanese server too. It must have made some ripples."

Loir grimaced.

"I'm not sure I want to go and sniff that, Kitty. You know, now that I've been identified, I'm pretty sure there are a few people who didn't like Warlock who might be hanging around to slap my skinny butt..."

"I don't care. Even if they hate you, they probably hate the Core even more. It may be time to gather the Edge once again, so you and Circé might as well show that it's not completely dead yet."

Loir's jaw fell, and he stared at her with his black, creepy eyes wide open.

"I'm sorry, Kitty, but my earwax must be piling up. I thought you said something like me summoning the Edge...?"

"Because I did say that. If you and Circé survived, maybe there are more hackers out there in hiding. Even if they aren't part of the old Edge, we might need more people on our side when we go up against the Core."

"We're going up against the Core?!" screeched Loir. "Since when are we going against the Core? Who's 'we'? I'm not going against the Core! Did you forget what they did to my toes?!"

"I'm going to do something worse to your fingers if you don't listen to her," hissed Dante.

Loir's face grimaced, rolling his chair a bit farther away from them. He shivered, and turned back to his screen, mumbling as if they couldn't clearly hear him.

"Those two are just acting like mean Kitties now. So scary! My poor little toes, I already miss them so much... Nobody loves me or my toes, they are all bullying me! Master Pan, you raised a little monster, and now the Kitty is acting like a tiger! Damn tiger, I wish there was a whip around... All they do is purr together and bully poor me! And I don't even have any pizza left... Poor me, poor me... Not even the shadow of an anchovy..."

Despite his complaining, he was obviously working hard already, all his screens flickering and displaying new data one after another. If it was Loir, she knew he would be able to gather some hackers' attention. They always had. His unusual way of coding and her exceptional skills as a Dive Hacker had built them a reputation that gathered attention each time they made an appearance in the Dark Reality. Eden sighed and turned to Dante.

"No need to bully him, he's already crazy enough as it is... and he will do what we ask without threats. But I do believe we're going to need more hackers. If things keep going like this, we're really going to have a massive fight against the Core."

"The Hare will provide some."

"I don't trust anyone whose name is just an initial, Dante. Especially after today..."

"We don't need to trust any of them," he said. "The Dragon doesn't, either. The Old Man is gathering us because he's the only one with the power to do so. It's the first time in thirty years the Zodiacs will gather again."

"I guess you're not going for his oolong tea!" exclaimed Loir.

They both glared at him, and he made a grimace before turning back to his screens, muttering complaints again.

"...You don't have to come," Dante whispered. "You can stay here."

"Oh, no, Dante. I'm coming," she retorted. "Don't even think about leaving me here."

"...Alright."

He smiled, and she realized he didn't really want her to stay behind either. He had intended on bringing her all along. Whatever was going to happen next, it was clear they would stick together from now on. Dante slowly leaned his forehead against hers, acting as if it was just the two of them in the room. His skin was already dry and cold again. His touch helped Eden calm down a little. She still felt nervous, but for now, everything felt incredibly calm. The calm before the storm, perhaps. She took a deep breath in, while Dante left a quick kiss on her forehead.

"...Let's go back upstairs," he said softly. "I'll cook you dinner again."

"I'm hungry," she admitted, only paying attention to the familiar sensation now.

"I know. I'll fill you up... here and there too," he smiled.

Of course, his hand went down on her butt, and Eden groaned, grabbing his chin between her fingers.

"You never stop, do you?"

"You're the one making me do this. And I'm tired of just imagining you on my kitchen counter..."

"Uh... Excuse me," mumbled Loir, raising his hand. "I'm still here... and I'm hearing all your dirty talk... Please get a room..."

Ignoring him, Dante wrapped his hands around Eden, beginning to kiss her neck. She wondered if he wasn't doing this on purpose to discourage Loir from spying on them, or if he really didn't mind an audience... She also didn't want to know the answer. With a sigh, she put her hand on his shoulder, but turned her head to Loir, trying to ignore the relentless kisses she was attacked with.

"We're going upstairs. Loir, can you also send a message to my master?"

"I'm not your mailbox, Kitty!"

"Just try to leave something in the Dark Reality, something he'll recognize us by. If he's been watching us, he might hear we could use his help..."

"I don't want to be mean, Kitty, but if Pan was interested in what we're doing, don't you think he would have appeared by now? It sounds more like your master is enjoying the show from afar right now..."

"Just try, please."

"Okay... Oh my Cheetos, you two, please get a room now!"

Eden smiled, but grabbed Dante's shirt and quickly dragged him into the elevator. He really didn't mind Loir's presence... or Rolf's. He hadn't said a word, but Eden exchanged a look with Dante's number two before the doors of the elevator closed. She let out a faint moan she had been holding in.

"You savage," she let out. "You could wait until we're upstairs at least..."

No, he couldn't. Perhaps because she had already refused him earlier in the bath, Dante was visibly at his limit, and they were already both half-naked. Eden could barely catch a breath before their bodies united, the elevator reaching their floor barely in time. Just like in his fantasy, Dante took her to the kitchen counter, Eden sitting in front of him, and she had no time to think before they began pounding against each other. It had become so natural to her now, she couldn't stop moving, moaning, and smiling while kissing him. He knew her body, and she loved the way he moved to satisfy them both. It was reckless, relentless, and she loved it. Dante wasn't trying to treat her like a fragile doll, he knew she was a woman and wanted this as much as he did. He didn't have to hold back, and Eden was just as eager, her hips moving just as much as his. She caressed his skin, his neck, his torso, his arms, all of him belonged to her. Just for a while there, she needed him, she needed them to just be two humans, a couple like any other, having wild sex and enjoying each other's bodies.

When he finally stopped, they were both out of breath, their hair in a mess, naked and smiling. Eden chuckled and leaned back, lying on the kitchen counter. She felt Dante kiss her tummy, and she shivered.

"That was good," she gasped, caressing his hair.

"Told you."

"Next time, I pick the time and place."

"I'm listening."

"No, right now you should start cooking. I'm hungry, and you just depleted what little energy I had left..."

She heard him chuckle, and he gently pulled her wrists to help her sit up. Eden was still on the kitchen counter, but she had no intention to move. She watched as Dante walked to the fridge, completely naked, to take some things out.

"...Are you going to stay naked?" she asked, raising an eyebrow.

Right now, she had a clear line of sight on his back, butt, and bare legs. He turned around, glancing at her naked figure with a smirk.

"I don't know where I left my clothes," he said.

Eden frowned, her eyes going down on the floor. There was nothing on the apartment floor indeed... Did they leave everything in the elevator? She grimaced. His men were in for a surprise... She sighed and got down from the kitchen counter.

"...Where are you going?"

"To put something on," she retorted. "You might be fine naked, but I'm cold."

"I can turn the oven on."

"Nice try, Dante."

With a smile on her lips, Eden walked to the wardrobe, grabbing a night gown for herself, and some pants for Dante. Not that he really needed it, but she wouldn't be able to stay serious if she had to see him walking around naked all evening... When she came back, he was already absorbed in his cooking, and only stopped to obediently put on the pants when she asked.

"Good Kitty," she chuckled, imitating Loir. "...What are you making?"

"Pasta again. Bolognese..."

Eden put her finger in the tomato sauce, tasting it. Dante raised his golden eyes to her briefly.

"If I see you licking that finger again, I'm not promising I can wait until we're done..."

"Can you save some of your stamina for tomorrow? I'm really tired this time."

He chuckled. Eden glanced at the windows. Judging from the darkness outside, it had gotten pretty late already. The next day would come soon enough... She didn't want to think about it too much, so she turned to Dante again. She loved how serious he was about his cooking, she found him incredibly sexy with every single professional-like move he made. He even poured them some wine, and this time, they ate together at the kitchen counter, chatting about trivial things, anything but the Zodiacs, the Core, and everything that was coming their way.

Eden felt half-drowsy even before Dante carried her to bed. She felt completely satisfied, despite everything that had occurred during the day. She was full, clean, sexually satisfied, and ready to sleep without a hint of pain coming from her legs. Much to her surprise, he didn't try anything either, simply wrapping his arms around her and letting her curl up against his body.

"Sleep."

She wondered how he knew when he couldn't see her. She moved closer to him, burying her face against his shoulder.

"...Don't leave me," she whispered.

She heard him sigh faintly, and he kissed her temple, holding her a bit tighter.

"I won't. ...I want to hear you sing again."

# CHAPTER
# TWENTY-NINE

Eden slowly woke up to the feeling of being suffocated. She quickly realized why she had a hard time breathing: she was lying down on her stomach, her face against the pillow, and Dante's arms wrapping around her from behind, his body on top of her. She sighed and moved around to try and get him off of her, at least enough that she'd be able to breathe a bit better... How had they even come to be in this position? She vaguely remembered falling asleep in his arms. Now, she was still in his arms, but facing the window, away from him. From the looks of it, it was still quite early too. The sun was barely rising behind the buildings, the sky in different shades of purple, pink, and orange.

Eden sighed faintly. Today was the day they would meet the Dragon and all the other Zodiacs... Rather than fear, she had a numb feeling in her stomach. Something big was bound to happen, something that might change their lives, and life in the Suburbs and the Core, forever. Perhaps the next few mornings would be the same as this...

"Dante."

He didn't move or react. Eden smiled and tried to move a bit, but he was really covering most of her. Sometimes, she forgot how tall and muscular he was... until he pressed against her like this. Not only that, but a certain part of his body was poking against her leg.

"Dante, I know you're awake."

"I'm not," he grunted, tightening his arms around her.

The way his hips were faintly moving against her butt was saying otherwise. Eden rolled her eyes. She didn't even know what to say at this point... Moreover, she was getting a bit excited too. Dante's warm skin against her and his breath on her neck was slowly getting to her. With a little smile on her lips, she slowly rubbed her butt against him, taunting him. She heard Dante groan, much to her satisfaction. One of his arms freed her and moved down her body, caressing her hip, butt, and thigh while he positioned himself between her legs.

She felt him rub against her entrance, making her even more excited. Dante gently kissed the back of her neck and shoulder, deliberately teasing her too. It was getting too hot in there. There was something a bit exciting about him pinning her down from behind, torturing her neck, and deliberately making her wait...

"Come on," she complained. "Dante..."

She heard him faintly chuckle, and finally, he entered her, making her moan in pleasure. Perhaps because they were having sex in the morning after sleeping together, this felt more intimate than ever. She couldn't see him, only feel his movements, his kisses, and caresses on her body. Eden's free hand grabbed the pillow to clench it, relishing in those delicious sensations he was giving her. Dante moved unbearably slowly, going deep but taking his time to go in and out. She grunted. She wasn't used to this tenderness, and it was both delicious and frightening.

"Come on, faster," she begged.

"No."

She would have glared at him if she could. Instead, she grabbed onto his neck behind her, while he kept attacking each bit of her neck. Eden could feel him sucking, biting, and grazing her skin mercilessly, like a tiger playing with its prey... She liked it, but it didn't match his tenderness on their lower halves... She was getting impatient. It felt good, but it was unbearably gentle and slow, too slow. She could feel herself getting hotter each time he dove in, and her lower stomach missing him each time he pulled back. She kept moving her butt to try and get more of him, but Dante was on top and in control. There was little space for them to move anyways.

"Dante, please..."

"As much as I love you begging," he whispered in her ear, "I want to savor you this morning."

Eden grunted in frustration, burying her face in the pillow. She was not used to this, and he was doing this on purpose. Then, his hand moved again, and just when she thought he was going to position himself to accelerate, he suddenly began caressing her front, making her gasp in surprise.

"Dante!"

It was too late. He finally accelerated, matching the movement of his fingers on her front. Eden found herself moaning and crying out before she could realize it. He was driving her crazy on both sides, finally going faster, and bringing her pleasure fast, too fast. She didn't want to wait this time. She abandoned herself to his sudden pounding, enjoying it to the fullest, feeling her pleasure explode like a firework in her stomach. She had never experienced this much so fast. She felt her body tremble, as Dante wasn't done yet and kept rubbing for a bit after, until he suddenly stopped, still deep inside her, making her moan again.

When they finally calmed down, both a bit out of breath, Eden was too tired to protest anymore. She felt Dante's lips on her shoulder and his faint chuckle.

"Good morning, my little songbird."

"I'm mad at you," she grumbled, a bit vexed.

"For making you come?"

Eden rolled her eyes, but she didn't even know how to answer. Even worse, she knew Dante would find a way to turn it against her if she mentioned the sex right then. True, she had liked it, but she didn't like how he made fun of her. Her pride was getting the best of her. He didn't seem to mind, though. He finally rolled off of her, letting out a satisfied sigh.

"That was good," he said. "...I think I like it too when I'm on top. And you can't glare at me like I'm some insect... or boy toy."

"I never glared at you like that," she retorted. "You're the one who glares at people like they are insects..."

"Sure. Anyone but you."

He suddenly put another kiss on her back and moved to get up. Eden sighed and stretched a bit, now that he was off her back. She turned toward Dante, watching him move around. He grabbed the two pups and put them on the bed. Since when were Beer and Bullet there? Had someone brought them into the bedroom while they were sleeping? She hadn't realized...

The two pups happily walked up to her, both wide awake already. From what she could see, someone had already cleaned and fed them. Rolf? In any case, she was glad to hug them and play with them on the bed while Dante walked up to the kitchen counter. She soon smelled freshly brewed coffee. This wasn't a bad way to wake up...

A few minutes later, he walked over with two cups and a plate with two pastries on it. Eden raised her eyebrows at the croissants. They smelled like hot butter and looked freshly baked...

"Seriously?"

"The advantages of owning a freezer," chuckled Dante. "I have more if you want."

"I'm going to eat both," she immediately said.

"Fine by me."

Eden sighed, but quickly began eating breakfast, more because of the food than actually being hungry. Dante didn't seem to mind watching her eat the two pastries either; he quietly drank his coffee while ignoring the pups that were making a ruckus on the bed. For a while, they had breakfast in silence, a bit awkwardly.

"...Are you ready for today?" she finally asked.

"I'm ready for anything," he confidently replied.

Then, Dante got off the bed and went to the little stereo in one corner of the room. He put on some music, making Eden smile.

"You really do like jazz?" she asked, a bit surprised.

"I know you do. And you promised me you'd sing again."

Eden almost choked on her second croissant. She had forgotten about that! She didn't think he was really serious about it... However, right now, Dante was slowly coming back to the bed, with an expectant look and a wry smile on his face. When he put his two hands on the mattress, leaning his body forward, Eden blushed uncontrollably.

"Come on. I'm sure you know that one."

"I can't sing if you're... that close and making that face."

"What face?"

"Like you're about to screw someone over."

"That's my normal face."

"Well, do something about it."

Dante chuckled, but kept leaning forward. To her surprise, he only took their empty cups back. With a hint of disappointment in her heart, Eden watched him leave the room again with the dishes. She let out a faint sigh. It was true she knew that song. In fact, she loved that song. It was strangely fitting too. With Dante out of sight, she began singing without even thinking about it, her hands petting her dogs.

As always, when she sang, her voice got a bit lower and slower and began to fill the room. She closed her eyes, thinking about those nice lyrics of love... Then, she felt Dante's hands gently pulling her up. He put her arms around his neck, put his around her waist, and slowly, began to dance with her. Eden kept singing, a bit disturbed, but their slow dance was so effortless, she was more perturbed by Dante.

"*The nearness of you...*" she muttered, ending her song with a faint smile.

"Fitting," Dante said, putting a quick kiss on her forehead.

"Except for the moonlight."

"The sunlight is fine for me," he said.

His fingers brushed through her golden blonde hair that was illuminated by the streams of sunlight shining through the windows.

"It's a bit crazy," he muttered.

"What is?"

"How I love everything about you."

Eden blushed, completely surprised by the sudden declaration. She couldn't even keep looking him in the eye, glancing to the side. Dante had no hint of shame in his voice, though.

"From the moment I saw you. I was attracted to you... I knew I had to have you. It got worse each time I saw you. Now, I feel like I can't ever part with you again."

"...Sounds like that song inspired you," Eden muttered, a bit embarrassed.

"Eden."

She didn't want to look into his eyes, not when he was saying things like this, but Dante wasn't of the same opinion. Gently, he grabbed her chin, pulling her face toward his. He was dangerously close... and making Eden's heart go insanely fast. She knew she was probably red up to her ears, which made it so much worse. He opened his lips, to say something, and she kissed him without thinking. Something inside was making her a bit fearful of what he was about to say, and a kiss seemed like a good option.

Dante didn't push her away, of course; instead, he happily answered her kiss. His hands held her a bit tighter, and they opened their lips to prolong that kiss, to make it more real, and hotter. Eden loved the simple and effortless way they completed each other. Their kisses always felt so... perfect, and easy. As if they had been made for each other, as if they were the perfect counterpart for the other. Dante's hands on her body never failed to make her feel hotter, and safer too. Like a promise that as long as the two of them were together, nothing could possibly go wrong...

After a long while, their lips finally parted, both needing to breathe a bit. Eden was in a bit of a daze, feeling warm all over. It didn't feel like they were about to meet the eight most powerful mafiosos of Chicago in just a few hours...

She cleared her throat, and carefully stepped back, unable to look Dante in the eye. She had avoided it for now, but she wasn't sure she would be able to distract him a second time if he felt like saying it again. Something about her was a bit scared of whatever he was going to say, and she was ready to run away rather than hear those dangerous words... She brushed her hair back, trying to regain her composure.

"I... I will go take a shower," she muttered. "...Alone."

"Okay."

She let out a little sigh of relief, and quickly moved to the wardrobe, grabbing whatever clothes she could before running to the bathroom, locking the door behind her. Her reflection in the mirror made her even more ashamed. She was red, her neck covered in bites and kisses, and looked like she had just committed a crime! Eden pouted at that shameless girl in the mirror and jumped in the shower, trying not to remember what had happened in the bathtub on the other side.

A cold shower turned out to be the best remedy for cooling her down. She let the stream rinse her thoughts for a while until she felt confident enough to get out and too cold to stay. At least she was clean and ready to face whatever was waiting. She took her time drying her hair with a towel, cleaning her face again, getting dressed, and even using a bit of makeup. As much as she tried to convince herself this was to not look like a nobody in front of the Zodiacs, she was also stalling a bit for time... She could hear Dante moving on the other side of the door.

When she walked out, spotting Dante in front of the wardrobe, Eden carefully stepped aside.

"The bathroom is available," she blurted, walking to her dogs and avoiding looking in his direction.

"Got it," he said.

To her surprise, he went to the bathroom without adding anything. She let out a faint sigh. She was probably safe, for now... and still felt a bit mad at herself for feeling like this. Why was she such a coward when it came to those things? The sex was easy, even if it was anything but casual or meaningless when it was with Dante. She should have been used to him by now; well, to any man, for that matter. So why was she still acting like an inexperienced teenager? She grabbed Beer, trying to play with the puppies to distract herself. Those two had no idea about anything going on except for games, naps, and their next meal... She hadn't even gotten to walk them much. It felt like Rolf was their part-time dad now, and she was a poor owner.

"Sorry," she sighed. "I'll take you two on a proper walk next time."

Far from her concerns, the pups happily grunted and tried to chew her fingers. Eden was careful not to let them dirty her outfit, though. For once, she had closed her eyes to the exorbitant items and tried to think like someone who had to meet the Zodiacs. She had grabbed black pants and a somewhat elegant black backless top. Something that she could walk and run around in, but still looked pretty nice. She remembered the female Zodiacs both wore pants, as well. This should be fine, surely...

Finally, Dante walked out of the bathroom, looking devilishly handsome as usual. He had picked another one of his Italian suits, paired with shiny cufflinks and a dark red shirt. His hair was combed back too, making Eden think he had also taken some extra time for the meeting... His eyes went down to her, and he frowned.

"...What now? Not sexy enough again?"

"Your shoulders are too sexy."

Eden frowned. She was *too* sexy, this time...? Then, she realized. Dante never considered his men's eyes on her, but for the Zodiacs, it was probably different. Was he afraid she was going to attract some of the male Zodiacs or their subordinates? She rolled her eyes.

"You're the only one who thinks of me like that, Dante," she sighed, "and I'm not changing. We're probably late already, we should get going and meet the others."

"Mh."

Eden was a bit relieved he didn't really protest, this time. She pet her dogs for a little while and hugged each briefly. She had just realized she had no idea when they would be back, once again. What was going to happen at the Dragon's Palace? She sighed and rubbed Beer's belly a little bit more before finally standing up. Of course, the pups were already scampering behind her and following her to the elevator, but she'd have to leave them here with Loir...

394

A bit disheartened, she stepped into the elevator, crossing her arms and leaning against the wall, opposite Dante. Because of that, it took her a second to realize he was staring at her, a smile on his lips. Eden blushed immediately, his stare too hot to endure. It was even worse as he kept staring, with his golden eyes, not saying anything.

"W-what?"

"...I love you."

The elevator doors closed.

"Y-y-you...!" Eden grunted, blushing all the way up to her ears.

Dante smiled, but this time, it wasn't one of his annoying smirks. Instead, his eyes were showing deep affection, and a hint of pity for her helplessness. He had done it on purpose. Waiting until she was stuck in this enclosed space, between four walls, to drop this bomb on her. She couldn't even run anywhere!

She felt stuck against the elevator wall, forced to face the Tiger and his cunning ways. Dante stepped forward, making things even worse. Her heartbeat was going insanely fast and out of control. Couldn't they get to Loir's floor already? Why was it so slow today?

He approached her, and gently pulled her chin up with his fingers.

"I love you," he repeated.

"S-s-stop it!" she mumbled, blushing and horrified.

However, before she could protest more, Dante sealed her lips with a kiss. Eden felt like she was melting under him, her body torn between fire and ice. What was he doing to her? What was wrong with her? She loved it. She loved his kisses, the way his hands moved on her body, all of her body. She loved his deep voice, and the way his golden eyes made her feel like his prey every time he glanced her way. She loved the way he spoke, even his terrible habits of mocking her, and the way he lied, killed, and threatened with a straight face. Most of all, she loved how Dante was with her. He made her feel like she was the one special person in the universe of a man that cared for no one.

That's why she didn't push him away and didn't even think about doing so. She loved his kiss, enough to answer passionately and get lost in it. She grabbed the hair at his nape, tightening her grasp and unwilling to let go. She didn't give a damn about wrinkling his shirt or making a mess of her makeup. She just wanted him. For a while, it was just the two of them, kissing wildly, barely holding off from undressing each other again. Dante had a hand on her butt, and the other in a fist clenched against the elevator wall. It was as if each time they kissed, things got a bit hotter, yet also a bit more serious between them. She could feel that connection between them, a special bond so strong she could almost see it.

When the elevator finally stopped, and they both parted, Eden was still blushing, out of breath, and glaring at him. Dante chuckled, grabbing her chin.

"You're cute when you're flustered."

"You need to stop doing that..." she muttered.

"I don't know. You haven't answered me yet."

Eden got even redder if that was possible. Of course, he expected an answer to his blunt confession... She couldn't even bear to look into his singular golden eyes right now. She awkwardly tried to gulp down her saliva, her eyes going past his shoulders, glancing at the outside of the elevator. Unfortunately for her, Dante knew better. One of his hands on her cheek, the other against her butt, there was nowhere to run off to this time... Eden looked down, trying to breathe instead of hyperventilate.

"I, uh..."

He chuckled and leaned forward to kiss her cheek. Eden knew he was teasing her on purpose, but this was torture... Could she call out to Loir now, or could someone appear? Even the puppies freely ran out while she remained trapped there! She took another deep breath, staring at the ceiling while Dante's lips went down her jawline.

"I..."

Eden was fighting against ten years of self-control, fears, and antisocial mechanisms to get those words out of her throat. It was hard, probably the hardest thing she had ever tried to do. She could do a hundred hacks, get caught in a crossfire, and meet with hitmen, but she couldn't say a single sentence. She knew how ridiculous it was, but she just couldn't calm her poor heart enough to take off the thick armor around it... Dante seemed to be barely listening anymore, which annoyed her a little. He found kissing her skin more interesting than what she was struggling to say. She rolled her eyes.

"I l-love you... too."

He froze, which made Eden jump a bit. Dante suddenly pulled back, staring at her with a shocked expression.

"W-what?!"

"...I didn't think you'd say it."

Eden pouted, a bit annoyed. He really didn't believe she could say it? Admittedly, she didn't think she could either until seconds ago, but it still was a bit hurtful to hear that... Yet, to her surprise, his expression suddenly changed into a wide smile, making her ten times more shy. He quickly turned around, pressing a button, and the elevator made a ringing sound, the doors closing. Eden gasped in shock. Did he just lock the elevator on purpose?

"Dante!" she exclaimed.

"Just a minute."

His lips kissed her again, a bit greedier this time. Eden moaned without thinking, feeling her body press against the elevator wall... She tried to fight him a bit, but Dante's greed was overwhelming her. How could he trigger her senses so easily each time? She quickly stopped resisting to wrap her arms around his neck, answering his kiss with a fire growing in her lower stomach...

"Beep-beep! Hello, this is the Kitty Rescue Service!" Loir's voice suddenly resonated around them. "Excuse me, I have a red alert for two naughty kitties locked in an elevator! Beep-beep!"

"Dante..." Eden groaned.

"Ignore him."

Eden chuckled, and they resumed their kissing, but she had a feeling the hacker was not going to give up just like that...

"Beep-beep!" he shouted. "I heard that, you bad kitties! We're on code red, I repeat, this is a code red!"

Suddenly, the elevator was filled with loud meowing sounds. If it was possible to ignore it for a few seconds, it quickly got annoying enough to kill all the sexual tension in the elevator. Dante groaned, and laid his face on her shoulder, slapping the elevator wall angrily. Eden giggled, somehow a bit amused that the only person able to get on Dante's nerves and kill his sex drive was her crazy partner... She hugged him, leaving a quick kiss on his cheek.

"Sorry," she whispered against his ear. "I think we really have to go this time..."

"Are you sure we still need him?"

"Please don't kill him. ...I promise I'll do it myself if he really crosses the line."

"Kitty, I totally heard that, you know! You're so mean!"

Eden sighed, and they quickly left the elevator while Loir kept complaining and whining through the speakers. When they arrived in the control room, he was still going at it.

"You know what?" he said. "That's it. Mommy's putting her food down this time. I do not approve of this new boyfriend of yours, you need a better man!"

"It's foot down, Loir, not food..."

"Well, mine are pretty much gone anyway... and do not change the subject! You need to change boyfriends, Mommy doesn't approve anymore!"

"You're not my mom," Eden chuckled.

She bent over to grab Beer, the puppy rushing to her to ask for pets. Next to her, Dante put his hands in his pockets.

"I can be your daddy then! No, wait... Isn't it weird if I'm your daddy and you're with our sugar daddy...?"

"Loir, you're not my dad either..."

"What? What am I supposed to be then?! I can't just keep being the creep in the basement... I'm not in a basement anymore!"

Eden raised an eyebrow. So he did know he was somewhat creepy... The hacker made a theatrical grunt, before turning back to his screens.

"I can't wait to retire," he grumbled. "Just me, Margherita, my taxidermied toes, and my pizzas on a desert island. Or perhaps an underground basement, but a really cool one this time. With tons of locks and go-karts. Oh, yes, I would love a go-kart..."

"Loir, you'll retire when we come back alive from this," sighed Eden. "... Are you ready for today?"

"Can I have a cat?"

"...We already have two pups, why in the world would you want a cat?"

"I want to use my cool boss chair to turn around slowly, make a very deep voice, and say, 'The plan is ready,' while petting a cat. A black cat, if possible. Followed by a creepy laugh."

"Your laugh is creepy enough as it is."

"Thanks!"

Eden sighed, and turned to Dante.

"I think we're ready on this side..."

Rolf arrived in the room, followed by a few of Dante's men. He quickly glanced at Eden and the pups, as usual, and walked up to his boss to give him a printed document, probably with a lot of information. At the end of the little group that had walked in were Circé and Jack. The two of them had changed clothes, but Circé was still wearing a long kimono-like dress, while Jack had simply put on jeans and a shirt. The two of them quickly detached from the group of Italians to walk toward them.

"Hi, Jack," said Eden, hugging him.

"Hi, honey. How are ya?" he asked while taking the pup from her arms.

Eden felt like she hadn't been asked that in a long time. She sighed, and brushed her hair back a bit, taking a second to actually think about an honest answer.

"I'm fine, given... everything," she finally declared. "How about you, Jack?"

"Yeah, hun... Your creepy partner talks an awful lot, so I think we're pretty much up to date. I don't really know if I'm lucky to be alive, or in the eye of a motherf–I mean, safe until the next thing blows up..."

Eden felt a bit sorry for him. She knew Jack aspired to nothing more than a quiet, peaceful life without any trouble, but now, he was in it up to his neck. The bar owner sighed.

"Oh well, no one's going to really be safe anyway. We might as well wait and see what happens. Who knows."

"What do you mean?" Eden frowned. "...You're not thinking of tagging along to the meeting, are you?"

"He's staying here, I'm coming," said Circé, putting a hand on her waist. "Jack and I already talked about it."

"Looks like you became friends, even?" Eden frowned.

"You know I like smart chicks. But yeah, I assumed it would be better to stay back for once," said Jack.

"You want to stay here?"

"Girl, I might get killed when I cross the street to get out of here anyway, right? Technically speaking, sticking with the crazy punk might be the safest place around for now. Since the Tiger seems fine with me here, I'll just try and spare my butt another gunfight... although I wish I could spare ya one too."

"I'll be fine. You stay here with Loir and watch the pups. I'll be back."

"Yeah... but keeping an eye on the crazy one?" he chuckled. "No thanks, I ain't that patient."

"But..."

Jack sighed, and suddenly stepped forward to hug her. Eden was not expecting this at all, and she froze, completely stunned.

"Don't worry. ...I just want you to be careful. Girl, you're the bestest friend I've ever had. I care about your scrawny ass, so if you're running into freaking danger, please try and stay alive, will ya?"

Eden sighed but nodded weakly. As always, she just had no idea how to respond to this kind of physical contact... Plus, a part of her had hoped Jack would stay out of trouble at this critical moment. If he survived both the gunfire in his bar and the Red Temple attack, perhaps he wouldn't find himself so lucky a third time...

"Eden," Dante called her. "Let's go."

Eden nodded, and after reluctantly parting with Jack, she joined the group of mafiosos ready to leave, with a strong feeling of déjà vu.

"Bye-bye, everyone!" chanted Loir. "Bring me some souvenirs if you can!"

They left, leaving only the hacker and barman behind with the pups, both crying out after Eden.

She had a strange feeling while getting in the car. As usual, they had Rolf driving while she and Dante sat in the back, but the Tiger wasn't the reason for her nervousness this time.

"...Are you alright?" Dante asked, gently taking her hand.

Eden nodded.

"Yeah, I just... I have a weird feeling, probably because I'm going to meet all the Zodiacs at once... Are they all coming?"

"Yes. Don't worry. We have our trucks loaded with weapons if needed."

Eden chuckled. That was Dante's typical response to something like that. She held his hand and turned around to watch his building getting farther away. At least, she was glad Loir and Jack would be safely kept out of this...

"How many men are you bringing?" asked Eden, curious about the long line of Italian cars behind them.

"Fifty. The Dragon gave his limit..."

Fifty men were still an awful lot, Eden thought. If each Zodiac was allowed to bring this many, it would be a never-before-seen number of strangers on one Zodiac's territory... What was the Old Man planning? She got a bit more nervous, realizing how serious things ought to be. She pulled up her pants, checking the condition of her legs. Dante glanced too.

"...Are they fine?"

"As long as I can run, it will be fine, I guess," sighed Eden. "It's thanks to these that I can be that fast of a hacker anyway... I feel like I'm going to need them."

Dante shrugged.

"I doubt anything will happen at the Dragon's," he said.

"Why?"

"A feeling."

Eden frowned. She didn't know how much she relied on Dante's intuition, but the Tiger seemed rather relaxed... Moreover, she did notice no one tried to kill them on the way to Chicago's Chinatown. They crossed each street without the shadow of a mafioso or sniper showing up, which surprised her. The Tiger's cars were rather easily recognizable, but that day, the streets were unusually quiet, empty even.

She had been in that area several times, enough to know things were never that quiet. Was this really the Dragon's influence? If the Zodiacs had all agreed to that meeting, it made sense no one would cause a ruckus on the way there. Instead, it was more likely they would brawl while leaving... which meant this was probably the calm before the storm. She sighed and leaned against Dante, who put an arm around her shoulders.

"...Are you going to be alright?" she asked. "The Dragon is..."

"He hated my father," said Dante. "They could never see eye to eye on pretty much anything... but somehow, they both respected each other. They only wished they could overpower the other, although they never went against each other, and never met a second time after the Zodiac was created. They knew there was a need to keep the other alive. That's why Long gave him the title of Tiger..."

"The Tiger?"

"The Dragon and the Tiger are the most powerful creatures amongst the Zodiac, like the Italian and Chinese Mafia are. They are also the only two animals of the Zodiac that don't actually exist anymore... or never did. I guess the Old Man thought it was pretty ironic when he picked all the Zodiac's names."

Eden slowly nodded. She could easily see that happening. Indeed, it was known among the population of the Suburbs that the Chinese and Italian Mafias were the two longest-established organizations in a city that already had a long history with gangsters... Aside from the Yakuza perhaps, most of the others were small gangs who had emerged as a means to resist the Core's strict regulation that made their populations outcasts. At first, things had been chaotic. Hundreds, if not, thousands of people pushed out of Chicago's central area and labeled as criminals had caused restlessness and uncertainty among the population. Not only that, but the total lack of supervision from any form of authority, including the Core who simply rejected them, had left many people fearing for the future, leaving them to make extreme decisions. Hence, the Zodiac emerged. In the face of that reality, real criminals had become the rulers of those who were criminals in name only, and through fear, instated some sort of compromised system where everyone had to mind their own business and leave the others alone or be killed. A trial-free and expeditious system might have seemed extreme, but in the Suburbs, people had grown used to it. They hadn't had a choice either. The Zodiacs were both their protectors and their executioners.

The cars finally parked in front of the large red door, symbolic of the Dragon's Palace. Eden could already see the many, many cars gathered in front of the Dragon's Palace. She was on edge all the way until Rolf parked, and the Italians all began coming out of the cars, unarmed. There must have been some rules passed along because even if the other mafiosos present glared at those newly arrived, no one moved or said a word. She let out a faint sigh.

Next to her, Dante smiled, his usual wry and scary business smile.

"Ready?" he asked, holding out his hand.

"...Ready."

She took his hand, and they exited the car together.

# CHAPTER THIRTY

Just like his men, Dante gathered the attention of the Zodiacs' men already present. In fact, as soon as they stood outside of the car, pretty much all eyes were on them. With the bright sun above them and the large crowd of so many cars and people from different backgrounds gathered, the place looked like it was about to hold a festival of some sort. However, the action wasn't bound to happen in that parking lot.

Eden turned around, facing the Dragon's Palace. She had actually seen that place many times before, from afar, but never had she gotten so close. While she knew very little about Chinese architecture, this building was screaming Asian influence. It was a five-story building, the top three having been added in the last century. It had a yellow exterior with extra, decorative terracotta pieces, red clay roof tiles, and golden dragons guarding each large, red pillar. A completely different world from Dante's thirties-inspired glass and marble lair...

The Tiger didn't seem to have any intention to let go of her hand. After a quick glance around, he pulled her toward the building, Rolf walking ahead of them. Eden was trying to remind herself she was supposedly Dante's bodyguard, but it didn't seem like he cared much about that narrative anymore... Even Circé quickly followed along behind them, with a handful of Dante's men. It looked like the others had instructions to remain on standby in the parking lot. She could only imagine all those henchmen would be glaring at each other for as long as the meeting would last...

The Dragon's Palace had strangely very little modern security, and instead, several men were spread throughout the building. They were guided inside almost as if they had come to visit a museum or booked a table at a restaurant. Eden glanced around. This place felt completely different from the Red Temple. It was buzzing with people walking in and out freely, and she realized most of them weren't even part of the Chinese gang. They were regular citizens coming here for different businesses...

"This place used to be owned by the Chinese Trade Lords," explained Circé. "They established themselves almost two centuries ago and were mostly helping the new immigrants while protecting their local businesses here... Although, the Zodiac is the one who made it what it is today."

Eden was indeed a bit curious about the strange crowd around them. Although there were a few guards here and there, they were not many compared to the number of people freely walking around. Was that why the Dragon wasn't worried about the Zodiac bringing so many men in each? The place was already crowded, which meant this would easily become an all-out war in this building with such complex architecture already... She was at a bit of a loss but kept following Dante while looking around for threats.

They were definitely getting a lot of side glances, but nothing unusual for a Zodiac walking into another's territory... The response was even a bit flat compared to the tension she had witnessed in the previous meeting between just four of them. Now, all nine of the remaining Zodiacs were to show up, and it looked like they were just going to have a casual lunch together in the middle of a busy indoor market... A Chinese man wearing a dark changshan showed up among the crowd, with long, black hair, and introduced himself as their guide with a bow and a polite smile. He led them to the upper floor, where things were already much quieter. Eden was starting to understand: the first two floors were most likely open to the public, but the three above had a very different atmosphere and layout. Eden could guess those had indeed been added recently, as there were more hints of technology, such as cameras and automated doors that opened in front of them. She estimated they had been scanned at least three times before their guide stepped aside in front of large doors.

"Our master is waiting for you behind that door," he said with another bow.

Then, he opened the doors himself. At this point, Eden felt a lot more nervous. She had been tense ever since they had left the ground floor, and she couldn't believe how easily they had been let in, but now, they were really about to meet all of the other Zodiacs. All of them... She pulled her hand from Dante's grasp, not to hide their relationship, but to be prepared in case anything happened. The Tiger didn't seem to mind, either. Putting his hands in his pockets with a detached expression, he stepped into the large square room first.

"Ah, here he comes! The prodigal son!" exclaimed a loud male voice.

Eden had expected a lot of things, but not this.

A large round table was in the middle of the room, an antique with dark, varnished wood and superbly sculpted ends. Around the table, Eden counted eleven chairs, in a similar style, with dark green cushions and large backs. Half of those chairs were filled already. Eden immediately recognized A., who barely glanced at them upon their entrance, as apathetic as last time, and Tanya, who was twirling a long glass between her fingers. Thao was present too, visibly sulking with her arms crossed and her feet on the table. The other people present were complete strangers, but it wasn't hard to guess their respective positions and titles. First, the Ox. It was a man with a golden skin tone and a thin, black mustache, a lot of hair, middle-aged, and wearing a very casual outfit. If he hadn't been seated at the table with the others, Eden wouldn't have thought this man was possibly a Mafia Lord from the way he looked. The only possible clues were the pieces of gold jewelry around his neck and on his fingers, but she didn't have a good eye for those things; he was also the one who had spoken upon Dante's arrival and was smiling wide at them. Next to Tanya was another man, very slender and wearing a motley outfit that gave a somewhat religious feeling, with a rosary around his neck. He had his eyes closed and his chin on his joined hands, elbows on the table as if he was daydreaming. He was also bald and wore a simple earring, which briefly reminded her of Loir. Most likely Lecky, the Goat... since only the Zebra and the Eagle didn't seem to be there yet. Eden glanced at the emptiest side of the table. One of the chairs had a golden dragon sculpture on it, clearly stating who was supposed to sit there. Dante sighed, and silently took one of the seats, the one right in front of him. It made him sit opposite Thao, and right next to Sanyam.

"Long time no see, Tiger," chuckled the Rat with a snicker.

He ignored her, and Circé and Eden exchanged a look, stepping back. All of the Zodiacs' guards were standing against the wall behind their master, at least a few steps away from the table, so they naturally did the same, following Rolf. Although the room was surprisingly animated, Eden felt the tension in the air. Half the Zodiacs present were completely still and silent, the others were casually chatting and eating. Dante chose to act like the first category, his arms crossed and waiting. The Dragon had yet to make his entrance, and in fact, Eden noticed the two seats right next to his had been deliberately left empty. All of the Zodiacs had chosen to sit together elsewhere around the table, leaving two empty seats, one on either side of the Dragon's chair, and two more on the opposite side of the table. Even if the Zebra and Eagle came, it would leave two seats empty. She wondered if the Dragon had added more seats than necessary on purpose, to see who would dare sit next to him, or to judge their characters beforehand...

"So," said Tanya, grabbing a piece of meat between her chopsticks, "what do you think that old Dragon called us for?"

"We all know why," sighed Thao. "The question is what does he want us to do about it."

"I hear you've been quite busy already, Tanya!" exclaimed Sanyam. "Didn't you and Michael already decide to blow up a few walls? Good for you!"

"They pissed us off, we sent a warning," scoffed the woman with her strong Russian accent. "King and I do get along when times call for it..."

"That's cold, Tanya."

They turned their heads. Michael King had arrived, with his own party of two men and one woman. The Zebra was very different from what Eden had imagined, but she immediately realized where his name had come from. He had random patches of white skin all over his naturally brown skin color. She had never seen it before, and she realized she was staring a second too late. Michael King felt her stare and glanced at her. However, he simply smiled gently at her and turned to the rest of the Zodiacs with that same smile on. Eden was intrigued. If he was named the Zebra because of this, did his predecessor have the same characteristic? She vaguely remembered he had taken after his father... unless this was only a coincidence? Other than his unique skin, he looked like a very average young man, wearing his glasses, a blue shirt, and his hair and beard perfectly shaped. He was probably one of the youngest Zodiacs in the room, perhaps around Dante's age, unless she was mistaken by his appearance. Yet, he casually walked to the table and picked the chair next to the Dragon's, the one on his left.

"Good day, everyone," he said politely. "How have you been?"

"Try the wine!" exclaimed Sanyam with a large smile. "It's great!"

"Thank you, Sanyam, but I don't drink. I'll have a bit of that rice, though, thank you, I'm starving and I have never had the chance to eat here..."

Eden was a bit stunned. She had expected a room full of mafiosos ready to murder each other, not all of them politely chatting around a meal like some corporate business lunch... This was most likely a facade for them all, though. None of them wanted to be the one acting scared, or ready to pull out a gun. Instead, all the Zodiacs were cordial to each other, friendly even for some, while their bodyguards were left behind to all glare at each other. Eden could almost gauge their skills from the way they stood, how they showed their tension, and how much they glared. Each Zodiac had brought up to five people, most of them only three, but there was such a large space between the table they sat at and their respective bodyguards, it felt like they were just some mismatched crowd in the background.

"We're only missing Joaquin now!" exclaimed Sanyam with his loud laugh.

"No one is missing that crazy punk," grunted Tanya, before biting a large piece of meat.

"He's on his way," suddenly said A., his voice so low Eden barely heard him.

Tanya grimaced but didn't add anything.

405

Suddenly, a knock was heard, but from the opposite side of the room this time. All of the Zodiacs turned their heads and went completely silent. Double doors were opened, and a very old man stepped in. He walked with the help of a cane, and a young lady wearing a green cheongsam. The atmosphere of the room had changed in the blink of an eye, and Eden felt Rolf and Circé straighten up next to her. She could feel it too. The Dragon didn't own his name by chance. Despite looking very old, the leader of the Chinese triad couldn't be taken lightly. His small, dark eyes were circling the room, spending a second staring at each of his peers. They were all staring back, none of them shying away from it. It felt like they also considered him like the elder, and perhaps some sort of spiritual leader among them. The best proof was that they were all here and abiding by the rules he had set. Eden tried to breathe, but she felt like any sound could be heard right now, even the smallest movement.

"Welcome," he finally said, with a surprisingly clear voice.

No one answered, and he didn't seem to expect them to. His eyes lingered a second on the empty seats, and the young lady pulled out his chair for him, helping him to sit. All the Zodiacs seemed a bit tense, waiting for him to speak up. However, the Dragon was clearly in no hurry. He waited for the young woman to pour him a glass of wine, and took a sip before putting it down, then taking another look around the table.

"I see most of you came," he said.

His tone was like a classroom teacher giving a compliment to his most rebellious students. Eden glanced at Dante, but the Tiger was still in the exact same position, his expressionless golden eyes on the old Dragon.

"Wooo, sounds like a fun party in there," chuckled Loir's voice in her ear.

Eden tried to repress her rolling-eyes reflex and ignore the hacker, who wasn't missing a second of this. He couldn't see what was going on, but no doubt he was listening to all of it through her SIN. Eden was a bit glad to have him on board too, for she always felt a bit safer knowing Loir could help if needed. Even now, she could hear him playing around on his keyboards as if he was right next to her.

"This place is so old-fashioned, my poor Kitty," he grunted. "Their security tech isn't even fun enough for me to play around with! That old geezer... They literally have zero circuits available in the Dark Reality, what am I supposed to play around with?! Ah, so not fun... Please tell me you'll bring me back some food at least. I am starving and bored, it's the worst!"

She let out a faint sigh. She had expected this much from what she could see in the building... The old Dragon was smart. He had given up on modern technology and preferred the older methods, which were about as efficient in this day and age. At least, enough to keep hackers at bay.

"Everything is electric, the best I could do is a complete black-out," sighed Loir. "I don't want all of Chinatown on my scrawny butt!"

She hoped there really wouldn't be any need for that. Aside from Dante, a black-out would help no one here. Plus, with the room configuration, he would most likely be taken in the crossfire if there was one... which was probably one of the reasons the Dragon didn't mind gathering all of them around a round table without even checking for weapons. If one began to shoot, chances were high they would all die here.

"I see we are still missing a few guests," said the Dragon, his eyes going to the empty seats once again.

"Joaquin is downstairs," said A.

Eden realized he was probably tracking the Mexican Mafia Lord in real-time. She felt a bit more tense, imagining the Eagle on his way there... Among the Zodiac, he was probably the one she was most biased toward, mostly because he barely managed his territory and his men. Eden had only experienced a few territories, but the Eagle's was the most violent one she knew.

Following the news, a ruckus was heard outside, and loud voices. Aside from the Zodiacs, who didn't move nor react, all eyes went to the doors a second before they opened again.

"Good morning, friends!"

The Eagle wore a multi-colored shirt, black pants, and two very visible guns by his sides. The tension rose by a sensible inch in the room, and Eden moved her legs slightly to be ready for action.

The Dragon, like the other Zodiacs, didn't flinch at all, but instead, he glared at the latecomer.

"You are late," he calmly said. "Sit."

"What, not even a word of welcome, *viejo*? So cold!"

Still, he quickly went to pick a seat, one of the two opposite the Dragon. None of the Zodiacs sent even a glance in his direction, ignoring him like a cold wind in the room. Eden let out a faint sigh. It would be a miracle if things went calmly... Yet, the Dragon sighed, visibly very calm.

"Well, we are still missing two more people who should be sitting here."

A. suddenly turned to the side, and took a little device out of his pocket, to put it on one of the empty chairs, the one next to the Eagle. The thing blinked a couple of seconds, and the hologram of a person appeared. Eden froze, and her heart went crazy. The young man had blonde hair, a simple white outfit, and thin traits. He moved his head a couple of times, as if he was stretching his neck, and smiled at everyone.

"Hello, everyone. My name is Prometheus Angel Newman. ...You can call me Pan if you'd like."

"Who is that?" groaned Thao, frowning. "No one told us there would be strangers here!"

"I invited him," said the Dragon, as if it was the only necessary explanation. "Pan is necessary for our plan. Now, we're only missing one person, the owner of the Edge."

All the Zodiacs reacted, this time.

"The owner of the Edge is here?" exclaimed Tanya. "Are you kidding?

What does that even mean?!"

Circé and Eden exchanged a quick look, confused, but when she looked back at the group, Eden realized a lot of eyes were suddenly staring their way. She looked at the Dragon, and this time, the Old Man was very clearly staring her way. The young woman next to him pulled out the last empty chair.

"Ghost, would you join us please?"

A heavy silence followed in the room, all eyes on her. Eden was so shocked, she didn't even know how to react, only glaring at the cunning old Dragon.

"Oh, boy..." whined Loir.

Suddenly, Dante jumped to his feet, pulling out a gun and pointing it toward the Dragon. All the other Zodiacs and their people reacted the same, all of them pulling out weapons toward different targets. For a short moment, it was complete chaos in the room, everyone on edge and ready to murder the next person. Most weapons were aimed at Dante, but some also had their guns pointed at the Dragon or other targets among the Zodiac. In one split second, all the earlier politeness had been completely erased to show the rivalries between them.

The only ones who hadn't moved were the Dragon, Pan, A., and Eden. Even Circé had stepped to stand in front of her, in a defensive stance, but the Old Man seemed to be staring over her shoulder. The young woman was staring right back at the elder, completely stunned. The Dragon hadn't even reacted to all the weapons pointed his way, as if he hadn't noticed them, or they were completely irrelevant.

"It's okay, everyone," said Pan with a smile.

"...What is this?" hissed Dante.

"Put your weapon down, Tiger," Lecky warned him.

"You're going to get us all killed!" roared Tanya. "What the fuck is this about?!"

"That woman is his partner," calmly said A., as if that explained everything. "They didn't know we were aware of her real identity as Ghost, the hacker."

He glanced up at Dante, his eyes as dreary as usual.

"De Luca's side chick is... Ghost? You're joking?" chuckled Tanya.

All eyes were on her now, but Eden was paralyzed. She had no idea how to react, what to do, what this situation was. Not only was the Dragon aware of her identity, but he had called her the owner of the Edge? And was inviting her to sit with them, like another Zodiac? To top it all off, her master was there.

She glared at Pan, furious.

"...Pan, what's going on?" she asked.

"It's alright, Eden," he smiled. "You'll be safe."

She had a hard time believing this. She was suddenly stuck in a room full of the most dangerous mafiosos, all armed, and now, they all knew her identity on top of that? If she hadn't been so worried for Dante as well, perhaps Eden would have run out of the room already. This was her worst nightmare happening, and ironically, her master was confidently smiling at her from across the room.

"...And who the fuck is that guy?" Tanya insisted.

"Tanya, language," sighed Michael King, putting down his weapon first.

"Who cares?!"

However, after he had lowered his weapon, a few others did the same. Only the tenser ones kept their weapons up, visibly still unsure about the situation.

"Eden."

Dante's voice seemed to wake her up. She glanced at him. The Tiger's expression was dead serious, and he hadn't lowered the gun pointed at the Dragon by one inch. She knew he wouldn't hesitate to shoot. It was all down to her choice, now. Eden knew that if she wanted, they could both try to flee this room right now, Loir shutting down the lights, and Circé and Rolf trying to cover them, although they'd most definitely all lose their lives in the process. She could imagine it so clearly it was almost scary...

"How long have you... known?" she asked the Dragon, her throat a bit tight.

"For a while now, young lady," chuckled the Dragon. "I am very much aware this must come as a surprise, but Ghost is not much of a secret. At least, not anymore. Your own father tried his very best so his child could survive and live a life of her own, anonymously."

"My father...?" Eden gasped.

She didn't know her father herself. How could the Dragon, of all people, know about both her identity as Ghost and her biological father she had no memories of...?

"Come, sit."

The Dragon's voice sounded polite, but Eden could read the tension in the room. Her eyes went to Dante, who hadn't moved an inch, not even blinked. She let out a faint sigh. If it wasn't for Pan also being here, she might have seriously considered running away. However, she wasn't as crazy as Dante and was not ready to die without understanding what was going on here... Hence, she quietly stepped forward, putting a hand on Circé's shoulder to let her know she was fine. Eden stepped up to the table, a shiver going down her back. In truth, she had no desire to sit there, she just wanted to understand what was going on, why this felt like she was just the target of a big joke...

They all watched her take her designated seat at the table in awkward silence. The Zodiacs all seemed about as confused as her, except for the Dragon and the Hare.

"Dante."

Her voice was the only thing that got him to move. The Italian slowly lowered his gun, and sat down, but his glare wasn't leaving the old Dragon for one second. He was visibly furious and prepared to do anything if Eden changed her mind.

As he seemed calmer on the surface, the few people left who were still also pointing their weapons lowered them, although most didn't put them away, only leaving them on the table, or where they could be grabbed. It was as if the mention of Ghost and Dante's threat had completely shattered the perfect image from before, and no one could be bothered to pretend to play nice any longer.

"...I didn't know school reunions could be this intense," muttered Loir in her ear.

"Pan, what are you doing here?" Eden asked, her eyes still on the Dragon.

She was even more nervous because she had to be seated next to one of the most powerful Zodiacs, and the oldest. Adding the fact that all eyes were now on her, scrutinizing the woman revealed to be Ghost, the pressure was real. For someone who had spent most of her life trying to survive, Eden felt like this was the worst situation she could have possibly gotten herself into.

"He isn't technically here," said A. "This is a long-range hologram that allows him to be here. Prometheus is still in the Core."

"In the Core?" Eden repeated, stunned.

"He has never left it," said the Dragon, grabbing his cup of tea.

Eden was shocked once again. She had never met her master in real life, and so far, she had thought he was either really well hidden somewhere in the Suburbs, just like Loir had been in his basement, or he was located in a different city. She had never completely ruled out the Core because he seemed to be exclusively focused on the Chicago Core, but to think he was physically there was so hard to believe...

"Once again, who the heck is this?!" groaned Tanya, impatient.

"The hacker known as Pan is one of the most proficient hackers in the whole world," said A. "In Chicago, Ghost is the number one Dive Hacker, but on a global scale, Pan is the only hacker to have successfully hacked every single Core in the world at least once. His main base of operations is Chicago, though."

"Well, it is the first and main one," nodded Pan, as if he was trying to act humble. "Moreover, I had promised to take care of Eden and the Edge."

"The Edge is gone," groaned Eden, annoyed, "and you barely showed up at all!"

"I am sorry I disappointed you, Eden," said Pan, "but I did appear when you needed me. Unfortunately, being in the Core, I am not as free in my movements as I would hope to be. I also had to be careful not to reveal too much about you, which is why I purposely minimized our interactions."

This wasn't nearly enough of an explanation for Eden. She was still holding a grudge from years of surviving on her own in the Suburbs, and all the time she had lost looking for a master that didn't seem to care at all.

"The Edge still exists," declared the Dragon.

"...It can't be," said Circé, stepping forward with a hand on her hip. "I was part of the Edge. It was destroyed when that damn Warlock sold us out; most of us got arrested! Those who aren't dead are still behind bars!"

"That is true, but you were only the first generation of the Edge," explained Pan with a gentle smile. "After the failure of your group, the Edge endured, thanks to new hackers who joined the cause. Not only that but not all of those you thought had been arrested are still in prison. I managed to free some of them."

Circé's expression changed. It was clear the hacker was stunned, and she had visibly missed her former companions more than she had let on. Her eyes were now filled with hope, and a bit of tears too.

"What...?"

Pan smiled at her but turned his head to the Dragon as if he was waiting for Old Man Long to explain things first.

The older man sighed and drank a bit of green tea before resuming. After all, there were all the other Zodiacs who probably still didn't have much of a clue as to what was going on there, and they ought to have been called there for a reason.

"As most of you should know, the Core has decided to expand once again," he said. "They envision extending their territory as well as wiping away a portion of ours for their comfort. The plans have been made, and they apparently plan to do so by wiping out a portion of our population."

"The SINs," muttered Thao. "We established they are trying to hack the SINs of all of the Suburb's inhabitants for this... They are already tracking about sixty percent of our population's movements as we speak. They sent Overcrafts to scan most of our territories for this."

"What will they use that data for?" frowned Lecky.

"Most likely, this is their version of a census," said King. "They had never been interested in the reused SINs before, but they used the Dark Reality to put them onto their radars. My guess is they are trying to count how many people are in the Suburbs at the moment. If they want to extend the Core and reduce the Suburbs, they know they can't do so without considering the people who already live there. Population control might be their end goal."

"The locations are re-actualized every minute now," said A. "Maybe they want to know where we are and when we are there for a stealth operation. Something where they will have control over how many deaths they cause."

"They don't want to completely destroy the Suburbs," spat Thao, "so they will only keep a portion of it? What are we to those people? Damn cattle?!"

"Calm down, Thao," said Sanyam, frowning and scratching his beard. "All of this is speculation... Do we have any proof of that? We might be causing a big commotion for nothing! ...Not that I don't like a nice dinner, Dragon, my respect."

"We do have proof."

All eyes turned to Pan, who smiled politely.

"Since Ghost uncovered this, I went on to hack the Core's central System. Their plan is to suppress forty percent of the current population in the Suburbs and allocate the territory for new construction for the Core. The plan is that in ten years, the entire Chicago area will be under the Core's control, with no non-citizens remaining."

"They have no plans to let people in, of course..." hissed Tanya. "Those damn people just want us all dead and to extend their masquerade on a greater scale!"

She swore in a Slavic tongue after that, but Eden couldn't blame her. She was just about as shocked, even more so because she didn't doubt Pan's words. This was even worse than she thought. To think all of the Suburbs would be gone in ten years felt absolutely insane, but it didn't shock her. This was exactly the kind of thing the Core's people would come up with. Most likely, Chicago could be the very first Core to do this, and all the other Cores throughout the world would follow, trapping each citizen into this manufactured, calculated, and freedomless paradisiac society.

"This is why I called you all here," said the Dragon. "We need to take proper action to stop the Core."

"How?" scoffed Thao. "I doubt they'll agree to negotiate since King and Tanya already blew up their damn doors and kind of got them pissed at us enough already..."

"It is true," nodded Pan. "They were quite mad."

Some stared at him, confused about his strangely serious tone as if it needed to be said. Michael King sighed, rubbing his temples.

"What is the plan, Dragon? I do not mean to be defeatist, but we have an insanely poor record of going against the Core. The last rebellion attempt was sadly completely destroyed, and there is a reason we have been living next to the Core all this time, not going against it. I get the urgency, but this will be a first for absolutely everything. We ought to be cautious."

"Funny you mention that after you and Tanya decided to attack them," said Thao.

"Can you remind me who blew up the Red Temple again, Thao? You and De Luca got lost on a field trip, perhaps?"

"We got what we wanted," shrugged the woman. "What did you guys get from that? A firework show?"

"We crushed two of their entry points into the Suburbs," said Tanya with her strong accent appearing. "Now there are only six left for them, and we considered blowing those up too."

"They will come from the sky if they can't come by foot," sighed Lecky, "and it's not much better, we have nothing to fight them in the air."

"We have hacking."

All eyes turned to A. this time, and the Hare scratched his temple with a completely indifferent expression.

"Hacking is what prevents them from using any technology in the air," he continued. "We can hack any of their flying vehicles, including the Overcrafts. The very first hackings committed by the Edge were meant to stop aerial attacks or recode bombs to prevent them from wiping out the population. Since the Core is constantly open and imbued into the Dark Reality, nothing they can invent should be impossible to hack."

"I've done it before," added Eden, clearing her voice. "I confirm, it's doable."

"Then they will choose to fight on the ground if they can," said Lecky. "Those cowards know hacking is their Achilles' heel. They won't risk it..."

"Are we seriously about to go to war with the Core?" muttered Sanyam, as if he had just realized.

"Old Man, you're not serious!" groaned Joaquin. "A hologram bastard appears to tell us the Core wants to attack, and we're supposed to believe that? Leave it be, things are fine as they are!"

"Didn't you hear a thing that was said?" retorted Tanya. "The Core is going to wipe us all out, things won't be fine as they are in just a few days, you idiot!"

"Shut it, woman! You're not going to tell me what to do! I don't believe this! I don't believe that *maricón*!"

"Pan speaks the truth," said A., completely unphased. "The attack will happen even if we decide to ignore it. Not only Pan, but several of our hackers have found concrete proof during their latest hacks. They are preparing for a large-scale attack. It's only a matter of time, whether we react or not."

"They have an army," said Sanyam. "We're not ready to go up against the Core! Even if we have a few weapons, our people are mercenaries, mafiosos, hitmen, vandals! We can't go against the army..."

"We have an army of our own," suddenly said the Dragon.

All the Zodiacs glanced at each other. Each time the Dragon spoke, his charisma was such that he could overpower the room with his voice alone, and they had to listen. Eden felt her throat tighten a bit. She didn't doubt the hackers' report, she knew that world enough to know no one would ring the alarm if they weren't sure it was worth risking their presence being known... However, it may not be enough to convince all the Zodiacs. What the Ox had said wasn't completely wrong either; although the powerful Zodiacs' men were trained like militias, they still were no match for a proper army like the Core's.

The Dragon shifted his gaze from Eden to glance at Pan, and the male hologram smiled back with a little nod. Eden was still in shock about the relationship between those two, and she couldn't help but be mad at her so-called master. She watched him move his fingers over some invisible keyboard, and suddenly, the hologram expanded over the table, showing dozens of silhouettes of people. It was as if they saw hundreds of miniature holograms. All those people seemed to be floating in tiny versions in front of them, some sitting, some visibly busy in front of a computer, a lot of them simply standing. Eden couldn't even keep up with all those that appeared, hundreds of them.

"Those are..."

413

"That's right, Eden," said Pan with a smile. "This is the new Edge."

"The new Edge?" Circé repeated, confused. "All those people...?"

"The former Edge was part of an experiment much larger than they knew," said Pan, staring at Circé as if he knew exactly who she was already. "Since the former Edge collapsed, a new one was created, trained, and prepared for a situation like this one."

"It can't be," muttered Eden. "Those are... hundreds of people..."

"Hundreds of hackers," nodded Pan. "So many of them were ready to take their place as part of the Edge. We have created something global, something that goes beyond the geographic borders of each city. On their own, each of those people is a Dive or Back Hacker like any other, doing private contracts, and completely isolated. However, they are all part of the Edge. And when the owner of the Edge is ready to summon them..."

All eyes suddenly went to her, making Eden feel uneasy again. She gasped a bit, turning to the Dragon again.

"I don't understand," she muttered. "I never had any connection to the Edge before I met my Back Hacker, b-but–"

"The Edge was created for you, Eden," Pan suddenly said. "Your father knew there would be a day you would need more protection than before, and a chance to escape the Core. He had hoped you'd pick up what he left... A chance to destroy the Core from the inside."

Eden was completely speechless. That was too much information at once. Not only from Pan, but she was even more shocked that the Dragon, the oldest and probably the most powerful Zodiac, knew all about this? She opened and closed her mouth twice, unable to utter a single sound to ask.

"Wait a second," said Lecky, glancing her way. "Who's the chick's dad we've been talking about? I feel like we're missing something here?"

Eden and the Dragon exchanged a glance. She was still at a loss as to what was happening. How does the Dragon know so much about her, her father, and Pan? Was it Pan who had explained it all? Why was the elder staring at her so kindly, like a grandfather to his grandchild, while he was keeping the rest of the Zodiacs in check?

She took a deep breath. Perhaps this really meant something now. She glanced at Dante, who, of course, had his golden eyes riveted on her. Things were different now... She didn't have to be a runaway anymore, nor hide her past. This room had no technology, and there was little chance anyone here would sell her secret to the Core. Not only that, but her master was there, which, although she was still mad at him, made Eden feel safer than ever. She had Loir, Dante, and even the powerful Dragon Lord seemed to be backing her up. Her identity as Ghost had already been revealed, what else did she have to lose here?

"...My father was the Architect."

A silence followed her words. Tanya first frowned, then stared at Eden who was seated next to her.

"...The Architect?" she muttered. "The man who–"

"Who created the Core, Tanya, we all know who the Architect is. Since when did he have a daughter, though? This is nonsense!"

"We knew little about him, it wouldn't be impossible..."

"Impossible?" scoffed Sanyam. "That child is so young, the Architect was barely younger than the Dragon himself!"

"I don't believe we need a biology class now," said Michael King. "It is not entirely impossible for the Architect to have fathered a child around twenty years ago, considering when he was arrested... Plus, if he had a family, it would make sense that it was a well-kept secret."

"I never met my father," explained Eden. "My mother and I were kept a secret for as long as I lived in the Core. When my... dad supposedly betrayed the Core, Pan guided me and my mother to flee here, to the Suburbs."

"Did I miss something," sighed Thao, "or did you say the Architect... wanted to destroy the Core? We're talking about the guy who created them, right?"

"The Architect was behind that technology, yes," said Pan with a solemn expression, "however, he failed to control what it would become and be used for. Which is why he turned against the Core's rulers and tried to destroy it instead, by creating the organization of hackers called the Edge."

"That is also when the Architect shared his plan with me," explained the Dragon. "That man knew it would be difficult for him to fight back against the Core from where he was. Those people were already much too powerful... so he reached out to their other enemies."

"The Zodiac," scoffed Michael King.

"Exactly. Of course, not everyone was ready to cooperate with a man like the Architect. What I am talking about occurred twenty years ago, before the Architect himself disappeared. The man shared with us some of the Core's secrets, including the existence of the Edge, young and promising hackers to whom he taught how to use the Dark Reality to fight back. I doubt he knew his own child would end up a hacker herself, but he did bring up the fact that he had a daughter, and that her survival would be his condition for this plan to perdure."

"I... I don't understand," muttered Eden. "My father promised... what to the Zodiac?"

"In exchange for your survival in the Suburbs, we would be given access to the Edge," said A. "Pan only reached out to us because you're alive and under the Tiger's protection."

Eden and Dante exchanged a glance. It was their relationship that had convinced Pan to reveal himself to the Edge now and all of the Zodiacs too? If they hadn't been together, would the Zodiacs have been left to face the Core without the Edge's support?

"But I wasn't... with Dante until recently," she muttered.

"No," said the Dragon. "However, thanks to Prometheus, we knew you

415

were still alive, and hiding in the Suburbs like the rest of our citizens. That was all that was needed; as long as you were alive and well, our deal with the Architect was valid."

Eden was in shock.

So she had been monitored by Pan all this time, and the Dragon knew of her existence and real identity all thanks to him? She glanced at her master with furious eyes. She felt like she had been observed all of her life, like the center of an experiment, and she absolutely hated that. All this time, she had struggled to survive in this terrible place, yet she had no idea how important her own existence was. She had no idea the Edge she had admired was initiated by her father for her own protection, and she had no idea someone like the Dragon was aware of the existence of a nobody like her!

"...You're telling us everyone's future depends on that chick?" muttered Thao. "Are you kidding? Since when?!"

"Since the first Zodiac," calmly said A., the Hare. "Not every member of the original Zodiac was onboard with the Architect's plan either, but it didn't matter as long as Eden was alive. My predecessor was one of those who had agreed to it. We were in touch with the Edge all this time too, although Pan is the one with the means to reach out to all of them. He's the main holder of the Architect's will..."

All eyes went to Pan, who was smiling politely, although many of the Zodiacs were still doubtful. In fact, a lot of it made sense now. The Zodiacs had changed several times since the first members, and if their predecessors had refused the Architect's plan, there was no reason they would have passed it along to their successors either. Moreover, not all of those people had gotten to their current spot through a clean and bloodless succession... like Dante. Eden was still in shock. She had known her father being the Architect would always make her a target for the Core, but she had no idea her own existence was also that important for the Suburbs. She was shocked and completely at a loss. All of a sudden, she, who had tried to make herself so small in this world, felt like she was brutally being put in the spotlight, and in front of all the Mafia Lords, to boot.

This was really too much. If he hadn't been a hologram, maybe she would have thrown a fork at Pan or something. She was just furious that so much had been prepared behind her back. She was mad at both him and her father. She didn't care much for the Zodiac anymore, she just felt like some idiot who had been manipulated all along.

"We knew a day like this might arrive," calmly said the Dragon, looking at all of the Zodiacs present. "The Architect had created this plan so the Suburbs would survive even if the Core got stronger. ...No, the aim of this plan is to do what the Architect wanted: to destroy the Core's System from within."

"...This is insane," muttered Sanyam. "I was half onboard until we talked about attacking the Core! There is a huge difference between defending our territories and going head-to-head against the Core!"

416

"And what do you think will happen if we simply riposte?" sighed Michael King. "They will apologize and not do it again? Let's be real, Sanyam. The Core will not let an insult like this pass; they will retaliate. What we need isn't a mere riposte, we need to strike back and make sure they have no choice but to forget about attacking the Suburbs ever again. We do not want to lead a war that will have to be repeated every ten years. ...Dragon, count me in. The Zebra will participate in this plan of yours and agree to cooperate."

"Oh, so now we're already voting?" scoffed Tanya. "...Really?"

"The door is open for anyone to walk out," said the Dragon. "We will not hold back those who refuse to partake in the fight."

"Well, I—"

"But," the Dragon said, interrupting Sanyam, "know that if you walk out of this fight, there might not be another. Not only that, but we cannot guarantee what will happen after."

"...What do you mean by that?"

"He means we might all die, you stupid cow," scoffed Thao. "If there is no one else alive, guess who will be attacked by the Core next? You. It's either you stand up now, or you face the consequences later if we lose. Good luck explaining to your people why the Ox was the coward of the bunch!"

"Who are you calling a coward?! I am merely expressing concerns!"

"Yeah, sure. Coward cow."

"Oh, that's funny!" giggled Loir.

Eden was in no mood to laugh, though. One by one, all the Zodiacs were speaking up, ready to rally with the Dragon or not. After Thao's speech, none were willing to be called cowards, though. Under her stunned eyes, all of the Zodiacs were slowly agreeing to rally behind whatever her father's plan was. Eden couldn't even keep up with what was going on. She had come here as a bodyguard, yet now, she was suddenly mentioned as the key to the whole operation?

Her eyes went to the hundreds of small holograms still floating above the table. Those people were all part of the Edge and ready to follow her and Pan? All because of her father? Why? Why had a father she had never even met done so much? Why did he have to make it all revolve around his estranged daughter? She couldn't understand what was going on, and it was scaring her.

"Eden."

She turned her head to Dante, who was staring at her silently. Unlike the other Zodiacs, the Tiger hadn't said a word for or against the plan. All this time, he had been watching her, gauging her reactions and waiting to see. Eden took a deep breath. She ought to snap out of it. Regardless of her father's plan or Pan's involvement, this plan wasn't just all about her now, it was about the survival of thousands of people. It was about people living on her block, and people like Jack who only wanted to live peacefully. This would all be reduced to nothing if she didn't step up herself. She had to stop thinking like Eden, she had to act like Ghost.

"...I want to participate too," she suddenly said to the Dragon, gathering all of her courage. "I will lead the Edge, and the hackers, against the Core. I want to know what my father's plan was."

The old Dragon smiled at her, nodding with a satisfied expression.

"We were counting on your participation, Eden."

"We could use Ghost to lead us inside the Core," said A. "No hacker but you can go inside, so you might have to lead a group there."

"...So you really want to send a group inside the Core?" Thao raised an eyebrow. "How is that even possible? You know there is no entry possible for the Suburbs citizens... You need an original SIN to enter."

"I should be able to go in," said Eden. "My SIN is an original, and my father modified it. It's a completely blank slate that even the Core cannot process. I'm literally a ghost to them; even if I enter the System, they won't notice that it's me."

"If Ghost can get in," said A, "we should be able to hack the System from both sides and allow more people to barge in."

"You'll need a distraction or you will be kicked out right away by the army," said Tanya with a wry smile. "We can do that here. If they want a war, they will have it."

She exchanged a knowing look with Michael King, who nodded, visibly excited by the prospect of a battle too.

"We will need two groups," nodded A. "One that will infiltrate the Core and hide Ghost's hacking, and another one to fight the Core on the ground. The explosions already caught their attention, so they might launch their attack earlier if we do something similar a second time."

"I would love to participate in that!" exclaimed Joaquin. "I have a few pretty little dynamites I'd love to deliver to those bastardos!"

"I'm going with Eden," said Dante.

All eyes went to him, but as before, his eyes were set on the young woman. She smiled back, feeling a bit relieved. Thao grimaced.

"Ugh, you guys need a room... Fine, I'll accompany the lovebirds. De Luca and I agreed to share the leftovers from the Snake anyway, and I would love to try their toys."

Quickly, a plan was starting to be designed, and Eden felt like she was fully part of the Zodiac. Despite what she had initially thought, the Dragon and the Hare's backing made the other Zodiacs fully consider her opinions, and as Ghost, she had full authority when it came to the hacking and the Edge. Pan was also doing his part, warning them about the Core's probable tactics in terms of attacks.

"They will also try to attack from the sky," he said. "The Overcrafts they sent were a new model, harder to hack."

"There is nothing that cannot be hacked," said A. "The Edge will find a way to hack them as they come and turn it against them. We have enough hackers to work on it."

"It still means there will be weapons coming from the sky," grumbled Thao. "I have no intention to be shot down like a freaking rabbit..."

"This is our terrain," said Michael. "We can prepare hideouts and headquarters on the territories near the border, prepare places for our men to regroup, while the inhabitants should be hidden in safer places, away from the battle."

"I can take care of the evacuations," said Lecky. "I am the only one who can speak to all the communities... and those who aren't in any. If you all entrust me with some men, I can make sure all the non-fighters will be safe. I won't be of any help on the battlefield, anyway."

Indeed, this man didn't seem like much of a fighter at all. Eden was shocked to see the Zodiacs all cooperating already, making choices to protect their people and deciding who would be on the field. She sighed, going silent to let the Zodiacs make their choices; this had quickly turned into a war meeting...

However, she glared once more in Pan's direction. She still had a lot of questions for her master, and she was still mad at him for hiding all this time. When he noticed, her master smiled at her.

"I hate you," she mimicked with her lips.

He kept smiling and answered in the same fashion.

"It's alright, Eden. Come and find me in the Core. When we finally meet... you'll understand."

# CHAPTER THIRTY-ONE

Eden looked away from him, still very much upset. She had a hard time believing that. Pan was just another in the long line of betrayals she had experienced her whole life. Loir, giving up to work under Dante. Dante himself, tricking her one too many times. Her mother, or more accurately, the Core, who had conned her with her mother's voice... The only person she was madder at than Pan was her father. Eden was baffled to hear that the stranger she shared her blood with had prepared so much, unknown to her and yet everything revolved around her. She hadn't asked for all this.

She hadn't asked to be put in the middle of a large plan to take down the most powerful organization in this city. She had never asked to be involved with the Zodiac in any way, yet there she was, sitting at this table like she was the eleventh member or something. None of this felt real, but it was definitely happening in front of her eyes. It was no simulation of any kind and she probably wouldn't have been able to dream such a thing either. Her own brain was on some sort of auto-pilot, quickly answering the questions shot at her while the Zodiacs perfected their plan. Eden's only comfort was Dante's warm, gleaming eyes on her. No matter what, she could feel his support from across the table as if there was an invisible thread between them signaling their alliance. The Tiger was actively participating in the meeting, his ability to lead dominated over most Zodiacs present. If Eden had to rank them, Dante, Michael, and Tanya were probably one level above the others, and the Dragon above them all. The elder was clearly leading this, despite leaving a lot of the talking to the younger Zodiacs. Eden felt like the newcomer at the table and she also probably was the youngest, except for Pan who looked barely out of adolescence. The strangest part was, everyone around the table seemed to have acknowledged the two of them in the blink of an eye after their identities had been cleared up. Or, to be more precise, the Zodiacs cared more about their usefulness than their identity. Things were very clear: they trusted their expertise, not the person behind it. Eden noticed how none of the other Zodiacs called her by her name, either. It was "you", "Ghost", or "the Architect's daughter". The only ones who used her name were A., the Dragon, Pan, and Dante. The first two obviously had known about her from her father's instructions, while the other two were familiar with her. All the other Zodiacs probably couldn't have cared less about who she really was, right now.

"...You do realize that if we succeed, this will change the city entirely?" suddenly muttered Lecky, fidgeting with his rosary. "It will... Nothing will ever be the same again. If we destroy the Core, this might lead to anarchy. The situation in the Suburbs would be the same in the Core. Their people too... they will be our responsibility."

"Our responsibility?" scoffed Tanya. "What for? We might as well burn them all to the ground, or use them like they used our people!"

"...The Core's population isn't responsible for their leaders," said Sanyam, frowning.

"Aren't they, though?" Thao tilted her head. "They were part of a corrupt system, and it's not like they never knew about us! They saw us like rats living in sewers and they didn't mind any of it!"

"The System is a double-edged sword," retorted Michael, slowly crossing his arms. "Sometimes, it's harder to get out from the inside. Those people were raised there and shaped into what their leaders wanted them to be. They received their beliefs like believers receive a lecture, day after day without any other option shown to them. While they certainly are guilty of being an active part of it, there is a systemic side to it."

"The Architect rebelled, though, didn't he?"

"The Architect was a different citizen. In some ways, he was more aware of the System than anyone else since he built it. Or rather, he built its foundations, only to realize his mistake and see what those people had done with it. ...I don't blame the man. I blame the leaders who were aware of their crimes and ensured they'd perdure. It's been decades now."

"Life in the Core is much more controlled than here," added Eden. "I was there for most of my childhood, and I remember enough. Every movement is controlled, every decision is overseen by the government. There is only an illusion of freedom, and each citizen is pushed in the way they want. It's not that they don't care about the Suburbs, they simply see what the Core wants them to see. Why do you think they only let their citizens come to our leisure businesses? To the sex shops, the bars, the gambling salons? They want them to see the vices in our streets, but not the virtues, the innocent people. Most citizens of the Core have no idea what's going on. Just yesterday, I learned the Core sends the old and the disabled people into fake nursing homes and gets rid of them! Who the hell would accept their family being treated like that?"

A heavy silence followed her words. The Zodiac was aware enough of the Core's ways to know Eden's words were nothing but the truth. After a while, Michael sighed and turned to his peers.

"Alright. We will see what happens to the Core's population after we take down their leaders. We will listen to those who want to discuss it with us. Those who don't... Well, I doubt they would be able to do much, anyway."

That was also true. The Core had an army to defend them, highly trained soldiers, but apart from them, no citizen supposedly had any way to defend themselves if some mafiosos barged in. Weapons were strictly limited and, for most people, illegal to own. Only the higher-ranked citizens were given access to weapons, and most would never use one in their lives as there was no need for self-defense. Eden confirmed those facts with the Zodiac, and quickly, they finished the details of their plan. She had given most of the intel she had, but it looked like they also took her as the highest authority when it came to hacking, even Pan and A. It wasn't just about her ownership of the Edge, but her reputation as Ghost as well. The other Zodiacs each had their own skills, and that was showing in the plan's creation. Tanya, Michael, and Old Man Long were clearly leading as the strategists of the group. Thao and Joaquin were more in-action people, coming up with the weaponry, traps, and unconventional tactics. Despite their constant bickering, they had the best ideas on how to operate on the field. Meanwhile, Sanyam and Lecky were more about the precautions to be taken, the defense, and the protection of the populations. Dante sounded like an expert on everything, and often, his voice weighed heavily on their decisions. Because his territory would be at the heart of the attack, the others were even more willing to listen to him, although he would be with the group infiltrating the Core. However, this only made Eden realize all the more, he would be at the center of the action.

When the Dragon insisted everyone start eating, it almost felt like a real dinner, except for all the mentions of firearms, hacking, and the snarky remarks or insults thrown from one side to another from time to time. Eden could barely swallow anything, and it had nothing to do with the food, The Dragon had made sure to accommodate all diets. She felt nervous and couldn't keep up with this act. Despite being a highly skilled expert in her own field, she was different from the Zodiacs. She felt different, like a child in a conversation full of adults. She could keep up and understand everything, but there was a wall between her and them, a gap in their attitudes. The Zodiacs clearly lived those kinds of battles every day. This one would be bigger than any other, but it wasn't enough to intimidate them. Eden, on the other hand, felt scared. Not for herself but for everything she had to lose in this.

After a little while, she excused herself and quickly made her way to the nearby bathroom, to get some time alone. She only realized once she was out that being in a room full of the most dangerous criminals in the city felt almost normal now. If not, at least it was bearable. Her feeling of fear had moved from these people to the upcoming war. They were all kind of crazy in their own way, but just like she had already seen, none of them had become a Zodiac by mere luck. Those people weren't afraid to kill or die and they would put their lives on the line without blinking. Some were blood-thirsty even, while others were more selfless and doing this for the sake of others... Eden could almost clearly distinguish who belonged to either of those two groups.

She rinsed her face several times with cold water, staring at her wet reflection. She could barely recognize herself. It was as if she had grown a few years older, looking the part with cold eyes, but there was still a hint of fear in the hazel of her irises. Eden didn't even react to the sound of someone walking in. She could recognize his familiar steps so easily, it was almost shocking. Dante's tall figure appeared behind her and he put his arm around her shoulders, pulling her against his chest with his elbow against hers. The warmth of his embrace wasn't embarrassing anymore to Eden. She put her hands on his arm and looked up at him in the mirror. He left a gentle kiss on the top of her head.

"...You okay?"

"Yeah. I just needed... a minute."

Eden leaned her head against his shoulder, staring at the two of them in the mirror. She knew Dante could feel her heartbeat going wild and fast, but she could only blush a bit about it.

"...Shouldn't you be with the others?" she asked.

"I needed a break too."

"Bathroom break?"

"...No, a you break."

She chuckled, a bit amused.

"...You're a bit crazy too," she muttered.

Dante didn't bother to refute that. His other hand was on her arm, gently caressing her skin and waiting for her. She knew he would probably not move from there until she did.

"Do you think it can work?" she asked. "That plan?"

"Yes. It could work."

"Do you trust the other Zodiacs?"

"No. I trust their interests, though. Most of them are smart enough to know that losing against the Core will be the end of our way of life. Their position, territory, and people are more important to them than us betraying each other. Even if they do, we are the mafia. We will use each other for as long as we can before turning our guns."

"I guess that means this kind of reunion won't become a monthly kind of thing. ...Maybe it's for the best, though. Some of them do worry me a bit... They seem a bit too trigger-happy."

"I don't know what you're talking about, my Kitty! They all sound like a nice, happy, and merry bunch of killers!"

Eden rolled her eyes almost by reflex.

"I haven't heard from you in a while, Loir..."

"Well, it was boring to only listen... The Edge part got me excited, though! Oh, but then it also got me very nervous, then I had to roll my butt to the bathroom, and... Oh! Did you know that eating mushroom pizza actually makes your–"

"I. Don't. Want. To. Know."

"Oh... Well, let's just say my train exited the tunnel at a mighty speed!"

Eden put her hand on her head.

"My God, Loir, do you ever stop saying such gross stuff like that? Stop it. Nobody wants to know. Just... tell me if you've picked up anything new and then we'll go back upstairs so you can shut up."

"Well, there's definitely some action coming up for my favorite kitties," he sighed. "I have all my radars lightning up, it looks like Santa's village in December! The Core is planning some nice little show out there, probably not too happy about having two of their favorite cat doors blown open..."

Eden grimaced. So they were definitely preparing for strong action as well... most likely the consequence of the previous attack. Neither side could wait any longer before attacking.

"...How long do we have?"

"Uh... I'm not sure Kitty, but I don't think you should make a reservation for dinner tomorrow night..."

Eden sighed, but Dante put another kiss against her temple, gently.

"It will be alright," he muttered. "...I won't let anything happen to you."

"You should worry about yourself first," Eden retorted. "I need you, and a lot more people do too. Don't worry about me, I can–"

"Eden."

She stopped, meeting his cold eyes in the reflection. He had heard those words before, and she had said them a hundred times. Eden bit her tongue, swallowing them back. Her mental defenses were so well built that she would utter those words without even thinking. However, she knew she needed his support. Something she didn't need before, a need that had been built by their relationship. Something choked her up a little. They were both used to risking their lives daily and seeing death. The other's importance in their lives was the only new factor, and Eden wondered if that made her stronger or more dependent. She couldn't decide.

"...I trust you," she finally decided to say.

Dante smiled back. This wasn't an "I love you", but it was all she had to convey right then. He released his grip a little, so Eden managed to turn around and get on her toes to put a kiss on his lips.

"...Let's go back," she muttered before the Tiger was tempted to try and have more.

The brief disappointment in Dante's eyes didn't escape her, but there was no way she'd agree to anything more than a kiss in another Zodiac's lair. She already had enough to worry about as it was, and she didn't want to miss too much of the meeting either. She turned again, toward the door this time, and while Dante left his arm around her shoulders, they left the bathroom together without a word.

To their surprise, the Dragon himself was waiting for them outside. Eden stopped, surprised.

"...What about the meeting?"

"Oh, the meeting is still ongoing," nodded the Dragon, "but see, an old man also needs a bathroom break once in a while..."

He visibly had no intention to walk into the bathroom, though. Even as they stepped aside, his eyes followed them, but the Dragon didn't move an inch, making Eden very uneasy. He had been waiting for them to come out of there, hadn't he? She could feel Dante was tense too.

"...Is there anything you wanted to tell us?" she finally asked, a bit impatient.

The Old Man smiled cunningly and tilted his head with a sinister expression. Until then, he had looked like any gentle grandpa, but now he was as scary as an old snake... His eyes were on her too and Eden could almost feel Dante ready to jump at any moment. The relative peace between the Zodiacs really was barely hanging by a thread...

"I've watched you for a while, little Eden, but you have grown to be an even more surprising woman than your father thought, haven't you?"

"...Thanks."

"What became of that boy that was always stuck with you?"

Eden's body froze.

"...Adam?"

"Whatever his name was. I remember, the two of you always hiding like little mice around my territory... You remained under my surveillance for quite some time before you both disappeared out of the blue. I was expecting you to reappear with him..."

His eyes went to Dante, visibly curious.

"How strange."

"...Adam was killed," Eden muttered.

"He didn't escape the Core with you, did he?"

"No, he was born in the Suburbs. He... found me after my mother and I were separated. He taught me how to survive in the Suburbs before he was... killed."

"Killed?" The Dragon raised an eyebrow.

"The previous Tiger shot him," Eden muttered.

A strange light appeared in the Dragon's eyes, his sinister smile appearing.

"Ah... That wretched man did have a short temper after all. ...Murdering boys to create his perfect heir. What a monster..."

His eyes went to Dante this time, and Eden felt a shiver go down her spine.

425

"W-what did you say?"

"Did you ever retrieve that boy's body?"

"N-no, they took it..."

"Well, I will tell you. They took it, and they made that."

His index finger pointed right at Dante.

Eden's whole body froze. In a split second, she felt very sick to her stomach, a wave of nausea that came and went violently. Her eyes went to Dante, and back to the Dragon.

"I d-don't... I don't understand," she muttered.

The Dragon smiled, a smile with no teeth that was the creepiest she'd ever seen, including Loir's. The Old Man squinted his eyes, reducing them to a thin line, like a scary mask. Eden couldn't even tell if they were open anymore, but she could feel his stare on her regardless. Under the disguise of a simple old man, she could feel a scary monster.

"That ambitious Tiger... He always was obsessed with his own legacy. He failed to produce his own heir, so he tried to make one, quite literally. I remember him always hunting around. Hunting for promising young boys, and technology to perfect them... He was quite bent on making his perfect heir."

"You're not making any sense. ...Dante killed his father."

Eden didn't dare look in the Tiger's direction, but she could feel the tension in his body, very clearly. He was leaning forward as if to step in between her and the Dragon. Dante already didn't like the old Dragon, but now, he clearly liked what he was hearing even less, and his arm was holding her a bit tighter too. Eden tried to control her breathing the best she could, ready to confront the old Dragon. As much as she hated what she was hearing, she also wanted to know the truth about what had happened to Adam.

"So he did," chuckled the cunning old man. "A perfect assassin... I guess the Tiger got exactly the heir he wanted, after all. Or maybe not completely."

His eyes went back to Eden, clearly referencing their relationship. If it wasn't for Dante holding her, she may have backed away from the old reptile out of reflex. Eden wasn't sure how much she could trust his words. She was remembering Dante's attitude toward her from the beginning, and his headaches... There were arguments for this to be the truth, but also for it to be a lie. Perhaps this was just another mind game between Zodiacs. Regardless of the previous Tiger, Dante did not look like Adam, the boy she had known wasn't of mixed origins. The age didn't match what both Dante and Adam had told her either, and she couldn't see why they would have lied about their age. No matter how hard she thought about it, she couldn't figure it out.

Worse, the more she thought about it, the more nauseating it was. What could the Tiger possibly have done to Adam, to create... Dante? How much of the boy she had known was actually involved? If Dante was Adam, why would the age not match, why wouldn't he have recognized her? Eden was younger than Adam was back then, but she was confident she would have recognized him. But Dante never mentioned a single memory of her before their meeting, only his childhood as a boy trained to become the next Tiger, along with other boys. No mention of a lost, little girl in the Suburbs he had taught to survive in the streets...

"...Enough."

While Eden was still lost in her thoughts, Dante suddenly pulled her, walking away from the Dragon without a second glance. She was still too confused to react and didn't even really come back to her senses until they found themselves walking in a different area of the palace, a deserted corridor.

"D-Dante, wait. Wait."

She stopped walking and pulled back a bit in the opposite direction so he'd stop too. She watched his back as he stopped, and heard him sigh before he turned to her. His golden eyes briefly went somewhere behind her, as if he was checking the Dragon hadn't followed them.

"...Why did we walk away?" Eden muttered.

"We didn't have to listen to his nonsense."

"Is it really nonsense, though? Dante... There are some things that match."

"He might be lying."

"And he might be telling the truth."

The Tiger's golden eyes went down to her. It was hard to decipher his emotions, but he didn't seem angry, or upset. In fact, he was surprisingly calm, Eden thought. Calmer than she was, at least on the surface. She could see his clenched jaw and the very thin wrinkle between his eyebrows. Plus, his golden eyes would sometimes glance somewhere behind her with a scary expression.

"...Is it that important to you?" he asked.

Eden's eyes looked down at their joined hands. Dante's thumb was gently rubbing the back of her hand as if to soothe her. He was always so sweet with her... It helped her calm down a bit, and she grabbed his hand with her other hand as well, nodding slightly.

"...Adam was really important to me," she said. "He... saved my life, when I came to the Suburbs. He was an orphan and had grown up there, while I had just lost my mom and had no idea what to do, where to go. The Suburbs terrified me, but Adam took me under his wing like a big brother. He shared his hiding spots with me and taught me how to run away if I ever got in trouble. He showed me how... to steal food, how to find places to sleep. He even showed me how to fight back and endure hits if an adult tried to beat me."

The more she talked, the more memories and regret began flooding Eden's mind. If the Dragon had wanted to make her curious, he had succeeded. Now, she couldn't bear to not know what had truly happened to Adam, if any of it was true. The memory of the boy being shot down, and then taken away, was still vivid in her mind. What had the previous Tiger done to him? And to Dante? How much of what the Dragon had said was true? Was Adam really... a part of Dante? How was that even possible and if it was, how many other boys were killed to create the man before her?

Eden felt truly sick the more she thought about it.

427

"...I think I'm going to throw up," she admitted, covering her mouth.

"You can do it here."

"It's the middle of a corridor," she groaned.

"Yes."

He obviously didn't care, but Eden did. She didn't want to throw up in the middle of the Zodiac's place.

"Loir?"

"There's another bathroom two doors down, my Kitty. On the left! ...Is it the shrimp dumplings?"

Eden barely had time to free her hand from Dante's grasp and run there. To her own surprise, she really did throw up in the bathroom, although it was mostly liquid since she hadn't touched the food from the buffet. She gave herself the time to make sure nothing else was coming out, breathing loudly and crouching down in front of the toilet.

"...Those were the most disgusting sounds I had heard in a while," muttered Loir. "Feeling better, my Kitty?"

"Are you alright?" asked Dante, almost at the same time.

Eden nodded, feeling a bit dizzy but less nauseous. She got to the bathroom sink to rinse her mouth and then stepped back to sit on the toilet seat, putting her head in her hands. Dante handed her something to wipe her mouth with. She took it and used it until she recognized the fabric.

"...You could have handed me something other than your shirt," she grumbled.

He crouched down in front of her, half-naked and almost too big for the little stall. He obviously didn't care about showing his skin, but Eden did. In fact, she did her best to look elsewhere. What kind of a situation was this... Her and her lover secluded in a bathroom stall, after she had thrown up from discovering he might be made out of other human boys.

"Our Big Kitty likes to put on a good strip show for our little Kitty!" squealed Loir.

Eden rolled her eyes. Each time she almost forgot about the annoying hacker, he found a way to remind her of his presence in her ear...

"Do you feel better?" Dante asked again.

"...I don't know. What he said... Dante, it's just disgusting."

"You think I'm disgusting?"

"No! ...I think what they did is disgusting. To do that to... young boys, and you... I was always somewhat shocked that you had killed him, but now, I'm starting to understand what a sick, rotten bastard the previous Tiger was."

Dante gently caressed her forearm, waiting for her to calm down. Eden couldn't stand how emotionless he looked, again.

"...Aren't you shocked?" she muttered. "This is about you."

"The Dragon is good at trying to play mind games," he calmly said.

"You know there has to be a bit of truth, though. Your headaches, and that data about the memory technology we found..."

428

"Does it change everything?"

His blunt question took her by surprise.

Eden looked at his sincere, unwavering, golden eyes. Dante didn't hold an ounce of sadness, fear, or anger in them. He was staring right at her, as calm and composed as before, letting her decide how she handled the situation. Pretty badly, so far. Eden was still ashamed she had vomited. She tried to breathe in slowly.

Did it change everything for her? ...No, not really. Adam was still dead, and Dante was still Dante. Nothing would bring back the kind boy she had known, the one she had considered her older brother for so long. And Dante wouldn't change, either. He was still there, with her. She let out a long sigh, trying to rationalize what she could. She had always known Dante was unique and a Part. In a way, they were a bit similar, with their broken, modified, and unnatural bodies. However, Eden was having a hard time processing everything... Perhaps the real monsters of this city weren't on the other side of the wall but assembled in a room around a Chinese buffet.

"Eden."

She realized she had remained silent for too long. Eden lifted her eyes, meeting Dante's.

"We can talk about it," he said.

"I'm not having this conversation on a toilet seat."

"I won't change. I'm still Dante, regardless of what that man did to me. I haven't hidden anything from you."

"Oh, so I guess we are having this conversation on a toilet seat..." she grumbled, looking away.

"Eden."

She sighed, but Dante grabbed her hands.

"Eden, look at me."

She obeyed, and his golden eyes instantly captivated her.

"I'll do what you want."

"...Do you find it strange?"

"What?"

"Your... infatuation with me. You've never acted like this with anyone else before, have you? Why me? You're so... kind to me, and you treat everyone else like gum under your shoe. Well, except for maybe a couple of people. But you've always been too... strangely tolerant of me. And I did my best to piss you off a few times."

"...You don't like that I'm like that with you?"

"I like it. I'm just curious as to why. ...Don't you find it odd?"

"...I did use you as a human shield once."

"Seriously, now's the time you're going to admit that? ...For the record, that only happened once."

"And you're going to defend me?"

A smile appeared on Dante's lips, which Eden helplessly mimicked despite a hint of annoyance. She sighed and opened her arms to lean against him, wrapping them around his shoulders. To her surprise, Dante grabbed her hips and lifted her up without any hesitation, although he grunted a bit.

"You're going to break your back if you keep trying to lift a woman half-made of steel..."

"...I forgot," he confessed.

Eden chuckled against his shoulder. He had forgotten about her legs... She loved that too. He put a kiss on her head, and she moved her face away from his shoulder to kiss his lips next, while he put her down. They kissed for a little while, chuckling and hugging each other as if they had found one another again.

"...You know, Kitties, this is a really unsanitary place to get nasty, just for the record. I'm not stereotyping Chinese restaurant bathroom stalls in general, but toilets are unsanitary anyway. No offense to the Chinese buffets. I love buffets."

Eden sighed, and they parted reluctantly.

"There is no way to mute him?" sighed Dante.

"Not that I know of."

"And even if you did, I'd find a way to unmute myself! You bad, nasty Kitties! Come on! Unless someone needs to parachute a choco nugget, time to go!"

"Damn, Loir, you're seriously gross."

"I'm not taking lessons from someone who just kissed in a toilet!"

"Shut up!"

Annoyed by her partner, Eden led Dante out of the bathroom, only to remember once they stepped outside that he was still half-naked, and she had no idea where they were either. She walked aimlessly around for a little bit but wasn't sure she would find her way back. She wasn't in the mood to ask Loir for help either. She turned to Dante and noticed the man from earlier, who had guided them all to the dining room when they first arrived, stepping out of nowhere to politely smile at them.

"I will accompany you back," he simply said, before walking ahead.

Eden and Dante followed him, but she noted how quickly he had appeared. They were probably being followed since she had stepped out of the dining room... They followed the man in silence, holding hands. Eden was still a bit bothered that Dante's shirt was in her hand rather than covering him, but he didn't seem to care at all. When they returned to the dining room, Thao's eyes went right to the piece of clothing.

"Wow, you guys must have been busy... Done already?" she chuckled.

"Very classy, Thao," sighed Michael. "Don't worry, you guys, we're leaving anyway."

"Wait, we're done?" Sanyam asked.

"We have a plan, everyone knows what they're supposed to do," said Tanya, getting up from the table. "I don't know about you, but I had no intentions of staying with that old Dragon longer than necessary, and am probably not going to say goodbye either. I got a territory to watch."

Eden noticed that indeed, the old Dragon hadn't bothered to come back to this room after talking to them... Pan's hologram was gone too.

She watched as the Zodiacs agreed to leave one by one, each giving the other ten minutes to get out of the territory, probably to avoid murdering each other once they stepped out... Tanya and Michael, who were the ones with the farthest territories, left first, followed by Sanyam. However, Eden noticed A. hadn't moved from his chair at all and was chatting in a low voice with Lecky. They weren't hiding, but it didn't look like they were expecting anyone to listen either. Eden sat next to Dante at the table, waiting for their turn. Thao was still busy drinking and sending amused glances to the Tiger, who didn't care at all. It had turned into some weird staring contest between them, and Eden wanted no part in it. The rivalry between these two wasn't too alarming, more like a slow burn between rivals... Eden was more intrigued by the duo whispering at the other end of the table. From what she could grasp of their discussion, A. was giving Lecky information about a possible escape route, and a safe with vital information, which surprised her that he didn't seem to bother hiding their conversation at all.

Suddenly, both men turned to her at the same time, making her a bit embarrassed she had been caught eavesdropping.

"Eden," said A. with his usual low and slow voice. "Could you give us some of your time?"

"W-what for...?"

"You're going to lead the Edge tomorrow," said A. "There are a couple of people you need to meet."

She frowned, but nodded, a bit intrigued. So far, she had felt like A. was the most trustworthy of the Zodiacs, and the least likely to set up some sort of trap. She glanced at Dante, but even if he had heard the whole conversation, the Tiger hadn't shifted his eyes from Thao, meaning he would probably follow what she decided. However, Lecky caught her gaze.

"We'd appreciate it if you came alone," he muttered.

"No."

Dante's voice was firm and cold, and he hadn't even moved. Aleksander Lecky grimaced, probably expecting this much. He and A. exchanged another look.

"This isn't about you," A. said. "It's about... the security of the people we want to introduce you to."

Eden knew this kind of speech. In fact, she easily understood that involving the Tiger could be a deal-breaker. Lecky and A. were Zodiacs, but they were more experts in hiding and protecting than killers like the others...

"...Okay," she sighed. "I'll come alone."

She felt Dante's grasp tighten on her hand.

"...It won't be long," A. said, more for Dante than for her.

431

"It will also be safer if she leaves this place with us," added Lecky.

Eden took a second to realize what they meant. Despite the apparent truce, Dante would become a target again the second he stepped out of the Dragon's territory... no, perhaps even when he stepped out of this place. It was exceptional enough that the Zodiacs had stayed together in a room for about an hour without trying to kill one another. Guns and knives had been pulled once, and it felt like the real fight was only postponed... or perhaps the upcoming war against the Core would be enough to keep everyone's thirst for blood at bay.

Next to her, Dante didn't react to their words, so Eden sighed and turned to him.

"You're going to have to go home without your bodyguard," she said in a low voice.

"No can do."

"Dante. ...Please."

Her voice was a bit more insistent this time. Eden didn't want to undermine Dante's authority in front of his peers, which is why she was seemingly asking for his permission, but this was her decision, and she wasn't going to back down. She wanted to go, despite his opinion. Finally, Dante ended his staring contest with Thao to turn to the duo on their far left, glaring at them next.

"We'll watch after her," said A. "Eden will be back on your territory before sunset."

Seeing as he was still glaring at them without saying a word, Eden pulled his hand slightly under the table.

"...She'd better," he finally said.

He had said this with so much threat in his voice, Eden was suddenly reminded of his short temper with anyone but her...

"Thanks..." muttered Lecky, although he looked a bit bitter about Dante's attitude.

"Can I know where we're going or who it is I'm meeting?" Eden asked.

"No, sorry."

She expected as much, but she had at least tried to ask. When Lecky and A. stood up, Eden stood too, ready to follow them, but Dante held her hand back, making her almost fall on his lap. She saved herself by grabbing his shoulder with her free hand while glaring at him.

"Dante!" she muttered angrily.

However, the shameless man pulled on her hand a bit more to bring their faces closer, and kissed her. Eden immediately blushed, well aware of all the pairs of eyes on them. Not only the remaining Zodiacs, but their respective bodyguards were still standing there as well! She pulled back as soon as she could, annoyed at him, but Dante spoke before she could scold him.

"...Come back to me safe," he said.

"O-okay."

"Oh, for fuck's sake," Thao rolled her eyes. "She's going with two herbivores, why are you acting all cranky?!"

Eden felt even more embarrassed by Thao's words, so she turned around quickly, and walked out of the room with the two men. She silently prayed Dante wouldn't lose his cool and end up murdering that woman once she was gone...

She couldn't do anything about it, though. After all, Dante was a Zodiac and knew his position well enough without Eden needing to worry about him. If he had survived this long without her, he probably could get out of there alive, even if he got into a bit of a fight with the Rat. Meanwhile, Eden reminded herself that her situation was a bit more complex. She had already noticed most of the Zodiacs seemed to address her almost as if she was one of their own since her identity had been revealed. From the beginning, all Zodiacs always seemed to behave as if everyone else was below them, insects that could be gotten rid of without thinking twice. Even their own bodyguards weren't allowed to speak a word during the dinner, but Eden had been left to speak freely. Her new position was definitely singular. They knew of her relationship with Dante, but even the Zodiacs who held animosity toward the Tiger had seemed to show her some sort of respect. A lot of it probably had to do with the fact that even the Dragon himself acknowledged her... The two men she was following out right now were those who seemed to respect her the most. Eden could easily see why Thao had called them "herbivores", not just as a pun on their respective Zodiac titles. She had been around dangerous people long enough to spot those who were practically harmless, and these two did not have the aura of killers. Among the Zodiacs, A. and Lecky definitely stood out as the aloof and placid ones. They didn't even seem to have proper bodyguards. Lecky was accompanied by one tall woman and a skinny man, both wearing ordinary clothes and hoods over their heads, without any notable traits except for their tattoos. A.'s people were two men dressed the same as him, with Arabian traits and simple dark outfits. If she had crossed paths with those two sets of trios in the street, Eden would have never believed them to be Zodiacs and their second-in-commands...

Right before she walked out, she crossed paths with Circé, who gave her a little nod.

"Let's keep in touch," whispered the goth woman. "...Try not to get yourself killed."

"Right back at you."

"Ugh... I feel like it's going to be a long trip home, now that your man's unhappy. ...I think you should be fine with those two, though."

Eden felt the same and gave her a little nod before stepping out. The little group went down in silence, no one apparently minding their presence at all. Things were the same as when they had entered the Palace, with more and more going on as they went down the stairs, all the way to the ground floor.

"Have you ever ridden a bike before?" Lecky suddenly asked her.

"A bike?" Eden repeated, surprised. "Uh, yeah..."

To her surprise, just as she said this, three bikes showed up in the street in front of the palace. Their riders all wore dark helmets, so she couldn't see their faces until one of them stepped up and took theirs off to hand to Lecky. Meanwhile, his bodyguards took their places behind the other riders.

"You should put this on," he said, handing her the helmet. "I have a feeling the Tiger might get really savage if there's so much as a scratch on you..."

Eden couldn't say otherwise. She put on the helmet without discussion and realized the original rider was already walking away, hands in his pockets while Lecky got on the bike. They hadn't expected to leave with one more person... Eden glanced around and suddenly realized A. had vanished without her even noticing it. Was he in one of the cars passing by?

"...A. will join us there," said Lecky, who had perfectly guessed her thoughts.

Eden nodded and climbed on the bike. She had more questions in mind, but for now, she had to be mindful of their location, and Lecky was still a Zodiac on someone else's territory. Not only that, but he would have to cross another one to get to his territory if that was where they were headed... He started the engine, and all three bikes rode away loudly in the streets of Chinatown. Eden felt a bit strange leaving without Dante, but there were more important matters at hand right now...

The three bikes left Chinatown quickly, and to Eden's surprise, they split up on the highway, going at different speeds to put distance between one another, and all taking different exits. Was this a strategy to lose potential pursuers? She glanced back several times, but it was hard to see anything from the back seat of a bike, so all she could do was hold on.

"Kitty..." whined Loir. "Your Big Kitty is harassing me... Are you still alive?"

"I'm fine," she chuckled. "Tell him I'm still alive and well. I left on a bike with Lecky, but I have no idea where we're going."

She heard Loir relaying the information to Dante. They had been on the road for a while, was the Tiger back at his headquarters already?

"Oh... The Tiger is not happy you're on a ride with the Goat, Kitty. He says you're not allowed to hug him!"

"I'm holding on to the back handle, for fuck's sake! Tell him to keep his jealousy in check, just for a couple of hours. I'll be back as soon as this is over, whatever it is they have planned for me."

"...He wants to know what you want for dinner. Damn, I feel like a carrier pigeon! Do I get a salary for this?"

"What, tired of pizza already? ...Tell him whatever he makes. I want to eat his cooking..."

"Oh my Kitties, you two are real homemakers now! Are you going to make a kitten soon? Not that I would know about it, but you two have been working hard at getting all purry at each other..."

"Heck no."

Eden felt a shiver just thinking about it. She had never considered herself having children. Who would want to give birth to children in a world like this? It was hard enough to survive by herself that she had never allowed herself to imagine having to care for a baby on top of that.

"We have two dogs and a creepy rodent already, that's enough for now."

"Rodent? You call me a rodent! You mean Kitty! You bad, bad Kitty! I'm extremely cute, you know! You could at least call me a bunny!"

"Yes, yes... Speaking of bunnies, what do you know about the Hare?"

"What do I know? Why would I know anything?!"

"Loir, that guy was in touch with Pan and the Edge all this time. Don't pretend you didn't listen."

"Well, he was in touch with them, but may I remind you I'm not exactly on the Edge's birthday-cards-to-send reminder list! If I knew about this bunny guy, of course I would have told you! Your master is so mean, hiding little secrets away from us and conspiring with the old Dragon at that! This is so upsetting, I'm gonna need some gherkins!"

"What about Circé?"

"I don't know, Kitty, our favorite witch is still kind of mad at me. They didn't even bring me any food! Can you believe they were at a Chinese buffet and didn't even bring me the shadow of a sweet and sour chicken skewer? No fortune cookie! Not even a toothpick! *Nada, nichts!*"

"Tell me when she comes to see you. I might need a bit of backup..."

The more she recognized where they were headed, the more unsure Eden felt.

The slums. This was allegedly the absolute worst part of the Suburbs. The most devastated place, and also where no one ever went of their own volition. This place was cut-throat, a cemetery. If the Suburbs were hell, this place had to be considered the lowest level of it. Eden herself had heard enough that she'd never even tried to approach this area. In fact, there was no actual reason for anyone sane to go. There was nothing but death, sickness, and a horrible feeling of danger twice as bad as anywhere else in the Suburbs. Yet, they were definitely headed there. Lecky's bike was riding slowly amongst the empty houses turned into squats, and they were getting tons of stares from all sides. Eden could see men standing against walls with huge machetes in hand, and cannons coming out of windows pointed right at them. She was shocked they were even riding by without anyone trying to attack them. Those people were definitely not open to strangers, and Eden soon realized they wouldn't have let them in if it wasn't for Lecky riding the bike.

Where the hell were they going? This place was one of the farthest from the Core, almost at the border. There weren't even many buildings left; most remains of the twenty-first century were turned into a refuge, and tents were fitting more people than they were supposed to. A bit farther on their right, Eden recognized the airport, only used by the Core's people now. She was surprised a portion of the Suburbs was even this close to that place, given the security they usually put around their transportation stations...

435

Finally, Lecky stopped, and she got off first, removing her helmet with an uneasy feeling.

"...I don't understand," she muttered.

"It's alright," Lecky smiled. "You'll see soon."

They had stopped in front of a tall, red brick building, the biggest in the area, and a former hotel, from what Eden could see. Lecky walked in right away, greeted by armed men at the entrance.

Once in the bare lobby, they reunited with A., who had somehow gotten there faster than them. The Hare nodded quickly as if to acknowledge their presence.

"...Where are we?" Eden finally asked, a bit confused and nervous.

"This is more or less my headquarters," said Lecky, putting his hands behind his bald head. "It's probably not as impressive as the Tiger's, but it's as secure..."

He and A. exchanged a look, nodded, and both went for the stairs that were going down to some underground floor. Eden was surprised by how much they trusted her... She could have turned around and fled this place right now, but neither of them bothered to check if she was following them down. She sighed, and went down the stairs as well, a bit curious as to what she was going to find.

As she descended, she heard a very high-pitched sound coming from farther down, which made her frown. It was so high-pitched, she felt like it was one of those sounds she may not have heard at all if she wasn't young. She kept glancing around to find a speaker, but it came directly into her ear, troubling her.

"SIN neutralizer," explained A., noticing her glancing around. "It blocks the signals of any SIN in and out with a parasite wavelength, basically. It keeps the SINs off the Ether's length, so while we're in the basement, nothing can come in digitally, nor go out."

Eden was half-amazed and half-worried. This meant she was truly on her own if anything happened, no Loir to help and no Dante to come to her rescue... It also explained why they weren't too worried about showing her what was downstairs. She soon heard voices, though, coming from ahead. Someone had called A. by a name in a tongue she didn't understand at all, since her SIN's translating function was cut off as well. Eden had rarely felt this vulnerable, and yet, something inside her, her instincts perhaps, let her know she wasn't in danger here.

"Ah!"

She fell forward, and Lecky moved just in time to catch her.

"...Are you alright?" he asked, confused.

His eyes went to the stairs behind her, probably wondering if she'd missed one, but Eden shook her head, gripping his arm with an annoyed expression. She leaned against the wall next to her.

"I'm... a Part," she muttered. "My legs... I can't use them properly without my SIN."

"Oh. Oh, shit, sorry... Let me help you."

Her legs weren't completely useless, but they didn't respond as well as when her SIN was working. Eden had to drag and pull them to take another step, using the strength in her hips as if each was carrying a heavy load, one step after another. It was extremely annoying, and she hated having to lean on someone else to do something as simple as walk...

Because of that, she entered the basement at the same time as Lecky. It was probably the building's former basement, split into several rooms, each door with an old-fashioned but efficient lock on it. Lecky used a code to open the first room, and A. opened the next one for them on a pad. None of the technology Eden saw was familiar to her, probably too old, or foreign. They crossed three rooms like this, making her realize how heavily sealed this place was. Finally, they arrived at a large room, which immediately reminded her of Loir's basement; there were many screens scattered on each of the four walls and about as many keyboards across several tables. Not only that, but very old machines like a century-old printer or a hand typing machine were also there. Cables of all colors were scattered around, and large columns, which Eden recognized as data centers, were put against the walls.

"Welcome to my headquarters, Eden," said A.

The five people that were in the room were staring at her with defiance or fear. She could tell they hadn't seen the light of day in a very, very long while... A beautiful young woman wearing a white hijab came forward, with a gentle expression behind her brown glasses.

"Nice to meet you, Lady Eden. My husband briefed me about you. I'm Malieka."

Eden immediately realized she was referring to A. ...So he had a wife? She wouldn't have known at all. He looked young, and he didn't wear a ring... Seeing that she was staring at his hands, A. understood, and as if to answer, pulled a thin necklace from his outfit, showing the ring attached to it. So he was hiding it...

"Everyone," he said, "this woman is Ghost and the Architect's daughter. She will be on our side, and leading the Edge for the attack tomorrow."

Then, another woman stepped forward. Her appearance was surprising. She had white bandages all over her very dark skin, even on her face. Her hair was cut very short, and she only wore an old crop top with large jeans. She had piercings covering her ears and lip, though, and to Eden's surprise, a tattoo on her neck, with the word Anarkia. Just like Loir. The woman, who was chewing something, extended her hand.

"Nice to meet you, partner. I'm Pratiti and the current Edge leader. My codename is Nebty."

"...Nebty?" Eden repeated, surprised. "You're the hacker Nebty?"

"Yeah," chuckled Pratiti. "I guess that makes us partners instead of rivals now. Nice to meet you, Ghost."

# CHAPTER THIRTY-TWO

Eden was a bit stunned. She had expected to meet other hackers, but not such familiar ones. If she was the top hacker in Chicago, excluding Pan, Ghost also had a list of rivals that took the following spots on the list of top-performing and just as expensive hackers to hire. Among those, Nebty easily ranked in the top five. The two of them had been opponents more than once, and although Eden had won almost every time, she still considered the hacker a notable rival.

"In fact, A. already briefed us," Pratiti continued, tapping the little device in her ear with a finger, "but I wanted to meet you in person, just to be sure."

"Be sure?"

"What kind of person you are," she nodded. "If I am going to entrust the Edge to you, I wanted to meet you first… I was a bit relieved and proud to learn Ghost is a woman, to be honest. And is it true you are working with Warlock? And that old witch, Circé?"

"I just met Circé recently, but Warlock's been my Back Hacker for a while now…"

"Wow," muttered Pratiti, visibly impressed, "and here I thought that old rat was long dead…"

Eden didn't see the use in hiding Loir's existence, and she was more intrigued about Pratiti and her relationship with the Edge. She was starting to understand why Lecky and A. had brought her here. These people were all clearly hiding under heavy security here, and those behind Pratiti and Malieka

438

were still avoiding her gaze, looking afraid of her.

"…Sorry," said Pratiti, glancing their way. "The five of us have been hiding here for a while; meeting complete strangers is not what we're used to. Don't mind them."

Eden didn't mind their attitude. Those three people behind them were clearly terrified by her arrival, even though she couldn't even walk on her own without help. They kept their heads low, and just like Pratiti, had signs of bandages or injuries under their dark clothing, some so massive it couldn't even be hidden under their long sleeves. Eden wasn't even sure of their genders because of their short hair and how they turned their backs to her at any given moment, but she was sure of one thing: those people had been in the hands of the Core.

"You are all part of the Edge?" she muttered.

"Yeah. I am a survivor of the first generation, like Warlock and Circé. They are from the second and third generation."

"How many generations were there…?" asked Eden.

"The Edge grew progressively but exponentially," explained A., stepping forward. "After the failure of the first generation, the second one was created almost right away, within the next two years. Instead of trying another frontal attack, Pan taught them how to conduct long-distance attacks on the System, and had them teach the next generation in turn. Each hacker had to teach at least two younger hackers of the next generation. Some were still captured, sadly, but thanks to this system, the Edge is what it is today."

"One hundred and thirty-two people," proudly said Pratiti, "scattered around the globe. Some hide in the suburbs of large cities like us, some in completely secret locations off of the Cores' radars. Now, we even have a few in hiding inside the Cores too. At least one hacker for each city with a Core System, with partners in their suburbs."

All of this was so incredible and hard to believe at once, Eden felt dizzy for a second. The Edge she had thought to be only a handful of people, like when it began, was now such a big organization? This changed everything!

"One hundred and thirty-two," she repeated, both amazed and shocked, "and you're…"

"The leader," nodded Pratiti, "or something like that, at least for now. When it became clear we had too many people, we decided to subdivide into groups, so each group could have its own individuality and not too much information was exchanged between all the Edge hackers. A silo system, if you prefer. Everyone only knows what they need to and we only gather when the situation calls for it… which seems to be the case right now."

She exchanged a glance with A., who nodded, turning to Eden. Next to her, Malieka gently pushed a chair for her, so Eden could sit instead of relying on Lecky. She thanked her silently before turning to Malieka's husband.

"Pan didn't oversee all of the Edge's rebirth," explained A. "We did. First, he helped Pratiti escape and led her here to me. Then, we began to rebuild what was left of the Edge, making its system stronger and safer. We knew other hackers of the first generation had survived, but Pan couldn't contact them. Luckily, you found two."

Eden nodded, but it was clear Pan had deliberately hidden some things from them. She hadn't found Loir, Pan had led her to him. The same thing was probably also true for Circé if she considered the bigger picture. Somehow, it felt a bit too easy that the other surviving hacker of the Edge's first generation, who had been forced to work for the Core, had been lucky enough to cross paths with the only person who could deactivate her SIN and make her an ally... Had Pan made sure she would meet Circé on that mission, knowing the hacker would be likely to join Eden and take revenge on her employers? It felt overly complex, and at the same time, with everything she now knew, not so impossible. More and more, this all looked like a huge conspiracy against the Core, orchestrated by her father and Pan, with Eden as the cornerstone.

"...So, Nebty will be leading the Edge, but... what are you expecting of me?"

"To lead us all," said A. "You're the only one with an original but corrupted SIN. We need you as Ghost to bypass all the security. They know hackers like Pratiti won't be able to take one step into the Core without triggering some alarms. However, if we manage to sneak you in first, and you give us an entrance point..."

"Then all hackers will be able to access the Core's System and hack it from the inside," said Malieka.

"You need me to open a door from the inside," said Eden. "I need to be... physically inside the Core and hack their System so the other hackers can access it virtually."

"Exactly," smiled Pratiti. "We know their System enough, but their latest levels of security are not something we can access easily. But we don't plan to leave you alone. If you manage to sneak into the Core first and find a spot to hack it from the inside, then more of our hackers will be able to get inside, not only virtually but physically too."

"...How many? Isn't there anyone already inside...?"

"Not Chicago," muttered A. "It's the only Core none of our hackers have been able to infiltrate; even Pan has to be extremely careful."

"Their security is way too high in Chicago because they need to protect the original Core," added Lecky. "Whatever we do to it will affect all the others globally. The attacks on other Cores don't affect Chicago, but whatever happens in Chicago will damage all the other Cores; the Architect built it this way."

Eden already knew that, but being reminded of it by two Zodiacs did have quite the impact. If they didn't succeed, aside from all the casualties, the Edge would collapse for real. Who knew how long it would take to rebuild a proper form of resistance again...

"Which is why this attack will be so important," she muttered. "A lot will rely on whether… I can hack it from the inside or not."

"You're Ghost," said Pratiti, a serious expression on. "Even if you weren't the Architect's daughter, I wouldn't entrust anyone else with that mission. I've seen you do things no other hacker can do. You have the best Back Hacker possible, and now, you have the whole Edge ready to be your backup."

"Everyone was quite excited when we told them Ghost was going to be participating," added Malieka with a smile. "I'm part of the third generation, but even I know how much of a legend you are to everyone. Most of the hackers present admire you."

Despite her words, Eden felt ridiculously small in her chair.

Outside of her father's heritage, she was pretty much a young woman like any other. She had always hidden and done her best to survive one more day for the past ten years or so. Never had she hoped to lead anyone, not even the Edge. Dante was a leader, but Eden was fine remaining in his shadow. She was used to hiding and running away. Even as a hacker, her ability was tied to her unique SIN and Loir's support. The Eden outside of the Ether and Dark Reality wasn't special at all. She was just… a Part, and without her SIN, she was disabled.

As she kept fidgeting and getting more nervous, Pratiti noticed and sighed. "Having doubts, Ghost?"

"…Ghost is just a codename," muttered Eden. "I don't know if I… if I can handle this. It's a lot of responsibility, and I'm not sure I'm the right person to…"

"Look."

Slowly, Pratiti began to undo the bandages around her face, revealing terrible scars. Eden frowned, but this wasn't enough to shock her. It would have made most people shudder, though. It was clear nothing was natural. Pratiti's skin had been burnt to the third and fourth degree, leaving rosy, bloody-looking patches of flesh in unnatural ridges on her face. Eden didn't avert her gaze, but she did feel sorry just imagining the amount of pain that had come from this.

"They are still painful," said Pratiti, as if she'd guessed her thoughts. "You know who did this, don't you? …I bet Circé and Warlock went through the same shit. I'm not putting you in this position because I blindly trust you, Ghost. Not even because of the Architect. I'm asking you to do this because you're the only one who can. Nobody cares about who you are outside of the Dark Reality. To over a hundred hackers, you're Ghost, the most talented hacker of our generation. Your special skills and your knowledge are what we need, right now."

She began re-wrapping her bandages, slowly and meticulously.

"We are hackers, Eden. We do what we can with our set of skills, and we only take responsibility for ourselves. All of us know what is at risk every single time we Dive. If we fail, we die. If we succeed, we move on to the next mission. This is our life and our motto. Although they do look up to you,

441

none of the Edge hackers are doing this solely because they are blind with admiration for you. They know who you are and what you're capable of. We might be talking in generations, but even the younger ones are used to risking their lives daily. They will partake because they can take that responsibility. You don't have to take it for anyone but yourself. I will be the one to lead them because I've got what it takes to do this. You'll infiltrate first because that is what you do best and you're the best at what you do. You're Ghost, and that's all we're asking from you right now."

She stepped forward, offering her hand to Eden, in a solemn gesture.

"I'm asking you as Nebty of the Edge. ...It's like any other contract, Ghost. Forget the stakes, focus on the mission."

The two women looked into each other's eyes, understanding each other like equals, peers of the same background. This was a language Eden easily understood.

Ghost had become like a second skin to her. Ghost was strong, swift, and smart. Ghost had no gender. A nameless hacker with perfect skills and the best success rate. If she put it all back into that perspective, Eden had little to worry about, nothing else but succeeding. In fact, this wouldn't be very different from what she had done so far... It was all about survival. It always had been.

Eden took a deep breath and shook Pratiti's hand, who smiled.

"Good."

She then turned to Lecky and A., crossing her arms.

"I'll take it the Zodiacs agreed, then?"

"Everyone's in, surprisingly," nodded Lecky. "We'll prepare the evacuation soon..."

He went on to explain, in a few sentences, how the meeting with the Dragon had gone. It sounded like he and A. had been involved since the very beginning, just like Old Man Long and their predecessors, and referred to Pan as the orchestrator of all this. They went on, detailing everything they had about the security system of the Core to Eden, which they had apparently attempted to hack a few times, mostly to test it. They hadn't been able to find any weaknesses, except for the fact that Eden's blank SIN would indeed be the only way to go in. They had even tried to steal a blank SIN from one of the original providers, from a factory in the European Cores, but the hacker had been found and killed. Then, Pratiti quickly explained the current layout of the Edge to Eden, although it was quite easy to understand: the system of generations made it so that the latest hackers added were at the bottom of the chain, with short and quick missions and little information given, while the older ones like her or Malieka were handed the most important data, and organized the missions across the teams, with several third or fourth generation hackers acting as captains.

Eden liked that the generations were completely independent of the hackers' real identities and ages; each new group had formed the next generation of hackers to join the Edge, and so on, making it grow exponentially even if some hackers had been captured or killed. It was like a tree that had expanded branch after branch; even if a twig was found and cut, the Core could only go so far back up that branch, and the other members of the Edge were always safe. Each mentor kept their mentee's identity to themselves, so even Pratiti had no idea who most of those people were outside their aliases. Only the very best of each city were invited by more experienced hackers to join, and the Edge's common knowledge was so advanced that being invited to join the Edge already put the newer hacker a step ahead of any other... Pratiti was like a spider at the center of her web, gathering all the information.

Quickly, Eden understood that A. had only been getting information he had about the Edge from Pratiti. Unlike what she had initially thought, he wasn't an experienced hacker himself, barely average. He only knew what he needed to; perhaps he was even more of a Back Hacker, not a Diver. The Hare was clearly mostly doing the field tasks that were potentially dangerous, like transporting their equipment or relaying information physically when it was too dangerous to do it through the Dark Reality.

Lecky, on the other hand, was in charge of protecting and hiding them. The Goat's territory had been the perfect center of operations; the farthest from the Core, not involved in territory wars, and with a population diverse enough that no one would pay attention to people of different backgrounds moving around. The slums were the perfect hideout for hackers in need of secrecy...

"So, you two have been working together since the beginning?" Eden asked the two Zodiacs.

For a while now, she had been intrigued about the relationship between Lecky and A., which seemed quite unusual for two Zodiacs... She'd never seen Zodiacs acting like this toward each other, almost friendly. The two glanced at each other.

"When you're the weakest, you have to make allies to survive," said Lecky with a smile. "Like our predecessors before us, A. and I have been involved together by none other than your master. Every time Prometheus freed or found a hacker, it was up to me to hide them, until Pratiti could add them back into the Edge..."

"And I would make sure of their security," nodded A. "The Goat having no firepower, he needed my help to secure some necessary tasks in the Suburbs, or even help evacuate a hacker whose position was compromised..."

It meant they had been somewhat led to work together to preserve the Edge, and their predecessors' will to see her father's plan through. Seeing how Malieka acted familiarly and relaxed around both men, Eden suspected she had a similar backstory before she'd become the Hare's wife. Eden had only ever interacted with dangerous Zodiacs, but it made sense some of them would not be all blood and guns.

Suddenly, something rang in the room, and Lecky grimaced, taking out an antique model of a cell phone and reading a text.

"Oh, shit..."

"What is it?" asked Pratiti, everyone suddenly on edge in the room.

Lecky put his phone back in his pocket, his eyes going back to Eden.

"We'd better get you back very soon. The Tiger's growing impatient, and he apparently does not like being unable to reach you..."

Eden suddenly realized she had spent a while down there, chatting with them about the specifics of the Edge and upcoming hacking. She had completely forgotten about Loir and Dante being unable to reach her...

"Let's go," she nodded.

She didn't want to show it, but she also was well aware of how short Dante's patience could be. It was better not to risk the Italians busting into another territory right before the actual war... She tried to get up as a reflex, but almost immediately, remembered her legs would not have it. Lecky caught her right before she fell, but it didn't save her the embarrassment, and Eden blushed, holding herself on the chair.

"Th-thanks," she mumbled.

"Watch your step," Pratiti jokingly added. "...Are both your legs Parts?"

"Yeah."

"Damn... Who did this? The Core?"

"...In a way. They forced me to sell them to care for my... probably-already-dead mother's safety."

If it had been anyone else asking, Eden might have found it somewhat rude, but as a hacker, Pratiti was different. Parts weren't as uncommon and unpopular in the hacker world as they were in reality. In fact, so many of them had been physically wounded and damaged, most hackers had joined the Dark Reality to find an escape from their real bodies. Plus, Pratiti knew how corrupted and twisted the Core could be to people. She wouldn't make fun of her or get disgusted at how Eden had been forced to sell her legs... She nodded, her eyes going down to Eden's legs.

"Damn. It does sound like the kind of shit they'd do... No wonder you're so fast in the Dark Reality! Everything that is fake about us in the real world makes us stronger on the other side..."

"...You too?"

"Mostly my spine, yeah," Pratiti grumbled. "Those bastards tortured me so much, I had to replace a lot of the shit they broke... Luckily, it became my strong point. What doesn't kill us really makes us stronger, huh?"

Eden smiled. Nebty was known for her incredible agility in the Dark Reality, which made her able to get into the smallest spaces and wriggle her way out like a snake. Pratiti was completely right, and Eden realized it felt good to have another woman, both hacker and Part, who knew what it was like to hide and live for the next hack. Although they had never met before today, the two of them were similar in so many ways, she felt like they both could feel close and trust each other already. She smiled at her.

"See you on the other side, Nebty," she chuckled.

"See you there, Ghost. Don't get yourself killed."

444

With Lecky's help, Eden got back on her feet, without stumbling this time, and bid goodbye to all the people present, even those who shyly glanced her way. To her surprise, A. stayed down there, while Lecky was the only one to help her up.

"…Damn, no offense lady, but you're hella heavy," he grunted.

They were struggling to get her up the stairs, as going down had been much easier. Eden chuckled.

"Steel is heavier than flesh… even more so when they are two dead weights."

"…I see."

He didn't seem to look sorry for her. Considering who was hiding in this basement, it probably wasn't as much of a shock or sob story to him as it would have been to other people. Since he had asked this awkward question, Eden cleared her throat a bit, before asking the one that had been on her mind.

"So you… I mean, you don't really… look like a Zodiac."

Lecky chuckled.

"No, I don't. I don't know what a Zodiac is meant to be, but it's probably not someone like me… I was put in this position, but unlike most, I didn't choose to be. Did you know the Goat is the Zodiac that gets replaced the most often? Even without getting into fights… A lot of my predecessors simply gave up. We don't need to fight for the position, we just get elected, or are the last ones who can do this. I'm the leader of the outcasts, an outcast myself. Not belonging to any group, or to too many… All my people are those who don't belong elsewhere. We just want to survive. Not make waves, just hide and leave the bigger beasts to fight between themselves."

"Maybe I should have been one of your people when I left the Core, then…"

Lecky chuckled and shook his head.

"Oh, no. No, Eden. You might… not belong to one of the Zodiacs in terms of background or skin color, but you're no sheep either, love. We all know it. Didn't you notice you stood as an equal to the Zodiacs today?"

"Yes, but that's because my father, and Pan–"

"Nope. Forget your daddy issues, you're a headstrong woman. Most people would not have even been able to go into that room full of Zodiacs without shitting themselves. Especially with the Dragon or the Tiger… You just don't feel that fear from them, because you're familiar with death yourself. I see people like you, sometimes. Like Pratiti, or A. Not killers, but survivors. People who still feel fear, but they've conquered enough pain not to be crippled by it. You're not like most people, Eden, you're on a different scale. It might not be obvious to you, but it's true. You don't need a Zodiac. You've got the backbone to stand up for yourself, love."

Hearing this from another Zodiac made Eden a bit proud, although it was still hard to really believe. She knew Lecky had no reason to flatter her or be nice to her. He was probably the weakest Zodiac himself, but he didn't need to suck up to anyone.

After this though, neither of them talked anymore. Climbing up the last stairs required a lot of strength and focus. Finally, they reached the ground floor, making Lecky let out a long sigh. Eden felt her connection to her legs come back, and moved them around carefully, checking that all the digital nerves were back online and connected to her SIN. She maneuvered her hips, not enjoying the painful sensations that came after using her real muscles to drag them around.

"Damn it," she groaned.

"Sorry about the bunker. Security reasons..."

"It's fine. They can be a pain even without that anyway, I'm used to it."

"Good. We should get back to the border, your... Tiger is really not happy, and I'd like to not be killed before tomorrow at least."

Eden chuckled. She could easily imagine Dante glaring at whoever was guarding the border and resolving to terrorize everyone until she came back. They walked back, this time not using the bikes but headed to the east at a quick pace.

"There's something else I needed to tell you," suddenly declared Lecky, "about tomorrow's attack on the Core."

The streets around them were now more of a real city than a slum, and Eden could see the first rows of real houses, meaning they were almost at the border. It was just the two of them, which was quite unusual for a Zodiac... Lecky really didn't have much security around him. No wonder he had needed the help of another Zodiac to protect the hackers.

"I won't fail," nodded Eden.

"Perhaps, but it's not that. Eden, some of the people under my protection were originally Core citizens."

She stopped, turning to him, surprised. Lecky took out a little piece of paper from under his coat, handing it to her mysteriously.

"Some fled, just like you. Not everyone who lives there is as controlled, nor as blind. It's faint, but there is resistance on the other side too. People who will help us out."

"...You didn't mention that at the meeting," muttered Eden, a bit shocked.

"Because most of the Zodiacs won't care, and the others won't believe it. We see the Core as the enemy, but... we need to remember the Core we are fighting is the people at the top, not the citizens. People who were born into a corrupt system can't just open their eyes and see the truth one day. They believe the lies fed to them since childhood. You can't hold them responsible for their blindness."

"...I know," muttered Eden.

Lecky smiled.

"Yeah, I figured you'd understand. The people on this list are ones that can be trusted. Citizens of the Core who know what's really going on in the Suburbs and will help us. Some of their relatives are here now, but they managed to prove their loyalty to our side. Go to one of them once you get to the Core tomorrow. They will help you to find a place to hack safely from and do what they can."

Eden's eyes went down to the list, a bit surprised. So this was the other reason they had wanted to privately talk to her... Dante would probably not have cared much, but the other Zodiacs would have refused to trust people from the Core. She nodded and hid it in her pocket.

"Got it, thank you, uh... Lecky."

"Don't thank me just yet," he shook his head. "Thank me once this is all over tomorrow... I have a feeling it's not going to be an easy one."

Eden grimaced a bit. Although she felt the same, she really didn't need a reminder.

They finally reached the border where, indeed, Dante was shooting daggers at the men standing at what ought to be the invisible border of Lecky's territory. There were a few bikes lined up, some with people on them, while half a dozen Italian cars were running behind Dante. He had a half smoked cigarette in his mouth and was glaring at the man standing in front of him, who was talking.

"She's almost here," insisted the guy. "Can you wait a damn minute and not pull out threats like that?!"

Indeed, Eden noticed a few of the Italians had guns in their hands, ready to fire at Lecky's men in front. The man leading the group of Lecky's men was tall, with long, purple hair under a beanie, and wearing a dark, somewhat grungy outfit with silver chains hanging at his hip.

Finally, Dante's eyes shifted from him to Eden, and his expression subtly softened. Noticing this, the purple-haired man turned around, spotting them too. He had bandages around his neck and one of his arms, making Eden wonder if he was a hacker too... He sighed.

"Finally! Can you not invite the partner of a bloody murderer into our territory next time, please? That guy was literally threatening to kill us all if his chick didn't come back! What the fuck, Leks?!"

"Sorry," muttered Lecky, putting a quick kiss on his shoulder while walking by. "I got this. Everything's fine. Take everyone home."

"You sure?"

"Yeah. You guys go first, I'll be right behind you."

Doubtful, the purple-haired man glared once more at Dante, pointing at him with his index finger to threaten him.

"If you touch him, Zodiac or not, I'm killing you!"

"Try me," retorted Dante with an amused but dangerous smile.

They walked away, still visibly upset, and all the bikes left except for one, probably meant for Lecky. He sighed.

"Sorry about my husband. We are not used to strangers around here... and certainly not to Zodiacs coming all the way here personally."

Dante was obviously not listening to him at all, his eyes riveted on Eden.

447

He extended his hand for her to take, and pulled her into his embrace, wrapping his arm around her shoulders and scrutinizing her up and down as if he were doing a full check-up.

"…You alright?"

"I'm good," she smiled. "…Can you tell them to stand down? It's not very nice."

As soon as she had said that, all the Italians lowered their weapons, some even quietly going back inside the cars. She let out a faint sigh and turned to Lecky.

"Thank you," she said, "…for everything."

"…You're welcome. I hope things go well tomorrow... Take care, Eden."

She nodded, and after Dante glared at Lecky once more, Eden followed him inside one of the cars. To her surprise, Dante opened the door for her, and closed it once she was seated, almost as if making sure he had her for real. Eden chuckled, and sat in the back seat, quickly glancing at the slums behind the windows. Lecky was right. This wasn't her world either... Those people weren't as lucky as her, to be able to make money and survive on their own.

Dante sat on the seat next to her, and the car started already, Rolf driving as always.

"I'm tired," she sighed. "Did you make di–!"

Before she could finish her sentence, Dante grabbed her and pulled her to sit on his lap, kissing her ferociously. Eden felt her whole body melt under his passionate attack. His hands were already caressing every inch of her as if to remember each curve, capture all of her skin under his touch. She shivered with pleasure, moaning faintly. They had only been apart for less than a couple of hours, and yet her entire body was electrified by his touch as if she had lost all resistance against him.

Eden had missed him too. Playfully, she grabbed the neckline of his hair, possessively gripping and pulling on it, making him groan a little. She bit his lower lip, moving her waist a little to rub against his pants, feeling the bump under the fabric...

"Missed me much?" she chuckled against his lips. "…What about my dinner?"

"I want to start with dessert."

His words made her wet in a second. His deep, hungry voice was making her crazy with desire. She smiled and wrapped her arms around his neck, kissing him like crazy while his rough palms wandered under her clothes, caressing her tender skin, playing with her.

"Easy," she moaned, feeling his hand grab her breast.

"I want you now."

"We're inside a car, you beast!"

"I know."

"Rolf's driving, and hearing everything."

"He doesn't care."

"*I* do."

Dante really didn't, by the way his hands kept fondling her. Eden groaned a bit in protest, but really, she couldn't bear for their lips to part for more than a few seconds, not even to scold her lover. His rough, large palm felt good under her shirt, and she didn't resist when he took it off of her or messed with her dark lace bra. The windows were tinted, anyway... plus, she loved the contact of his warm skin against hers. To tease him while he struggled to undo it, Eden leaned over and bit his neck. He groaned a little, but she could tell he was amused, his hands going down to her butt.

"You naughty kitty," he muttered.

"That's what I always say!"

"Loir. Shut. The. Fuck. Up."

"Oh, you two are so..."

Eden didn't listen to him, only resuming her deep kiss with Dante. She caressed his spiky chin with her fingers, using her tongue to taste as much of him as she could. She didn't want to have sex in the car when Rolf was right in front driving, but she was terribly tempted, the last strings of her rationality about to snap.

"Just a quick one," Dante muttered against her ear, his hand in her pants.

"No..."

"Please."

"I said no..."

He wasn't giving up, not forcing it, only pushing for her to agree. And Eden could find herself slowly tempted to fuck him right then and there. They both wanted it. If it wasn't for Rolf driving and the risk of getting shot by an ambush of some sort in the street... She glanced out the window, recognizing the buildings right away.

"We're almost there," she muttered before resuming their kisses. "Keep it in your pants for just a couple more minutes..."

"...Parking lot?"

"Deal," she chuckled.

Their kissing resumed, even more intense than before. Knowing they were so close to Dante's building, they had even begun naturally undressing each other, Dante finally getting rid of her bra, and Eden taking off his shirt. It was the second time he was half-naked in front of her that day, but this time, she couldn't sit still. Eden kissed the tiger on his torso, making the man shudder. His own hands were restless, and soon enough, he was the one with his face between her breasts, kissing and sucking her rosy skin.

"...Sir, we have arrived."

"Get out."

Rolf obeyed in silence, and as soon as the car door was closed, Eden looked through the rear window behind Dante's head. All of his men were really leaving... Dante's hands suddenly grabbed her face, pulling her to kiss him again. That kiss made her forget everything. Eden's fingers dove into

449

his pants, unbuckling his belt and revealing everything underneath. She then groaned, frustrated by her own pants, moving quickly to get rid of it all with Dante's help.

"I missed you..." he groaned against her skin.

Eden nodded and sat back onto his lap, letting him finally plunge into her.

She helplessly moaned out loud, feeling him fill her completely. He was thick and hard, making her shudder in pleasure. It was as if her body had made sure to adjust to his shape perfectly, the familiar mix of pain and pleasure overwhelming her. As usual now, Dante didn't move just yet, kissing and sucking her neck instead, letting her get used to it. Eden could take a deep breath and enjoy the warmth between their bodies, especially hot where they were joined...

"I missed you too," she suddenly muttered, her cheeks a bit red.

Dante smiled and kissed her cheeks, combing her blonde hair away from her face to reveal that her blushing had gone all the way up to her ears. Slowly, he began moving his hips, listening to her moans. He was so used to Eden's voice, he could tell what she enjoyed the most just from the shakiness and changes in its huskiness. She was shy with her feelings, but not with her body. She would spread her legs to take him deeper and undulate her waist the way she liked it. Putting one hand on his knee to hold herself and one hooked on his neck, she began moving more, riding him with her head back, letting out long sighs of pleasure.

"Oh... Ah, yes, like this... Ah... Slow... Hm..."

While she kept her eyes closed, Dante couldn't help but stare at her naked body, and the sexy way she moved on him. Did she even realize how much of a temptress she was? The way she undulated her body against his was enough to keep him hard and going. He just couldn't stop craving her, wanting more and more until it bordered on madness. Dante accelerated, grabbing her hips and grunting in pleasure. He wanted her so much, he couldn't pull the brakes on his desire. Eden's voice filling the car was like a siren's call, exciting the beast in him. While a woman's moans could be annoying, when it was hers, he was just dying to make her cry out more in pleasure. It was the ringing of his successful love-making, knowing he was pleasuring her to the fullest. He couldn't stop. The more Eden moaned and cried, the more he wanted her. Soon enough, his body was moving on its own, and she had to grab his shoulders to hold on. The sounds of their damp and hot flesh were indecent and exciting.

He suddenly shifted their bodies, laying her down on the leather backseat, getting above her to keep thrusting. Eden breathed even louder, helplessly being pounded under him. Dante was going fast, so fast she couldn't keep up. She could feel the sweat going down their bodies, the heat in the car, and the car's suspension moving under them, everything in a blur under his quick pace. She liked it, she loved the way he was losing control inside her, the focused expression on his face and his tensed muscles.

"Yes, yes, yes..." she kept muttering between her lips. "Keep going!

...Dante! ...More... Hn!"

She couldn't think about anything else. The sensations of her body were taking her out of this world, sending throbbing waves through her lower stomach.

"Dante... Dante..."

He grunted too, feeling her tighten a bit. The rubbing of their bodies was driving him insane despite his attempts to last. He sighed and leaned down to kiss Eden, slowing down on purpose. She wrapped her arms around his neck again, and they deepened their kiss, using their tongues and caressing each other's hair. She could still feel him moving slowly inside, but it was a bit more manageable than the relentless pounding from earlier... Still, when he almost completely pulled out and thrust again, she gasped loudly, her lower abdomen throbbing.

"You damn...!"

Dante didn't stop there. Attacking her neck with his reckless lips and teeth, he kept hammering, slow but deep, sending delicious waves throughout her body. Eden moaned loudly at each thrust, spreading her legs a bit more. She loved it, and he knew it. His slow, deep thrusts were making her shudder in pleasure, feeling the loss of him before he filled her again without warning.

"Dante..." she pleaded, knowing what he was doing.

He smiled and kept going, gradually accelerating again. Eden grabbed the leather seat, holding on while his assaults were getting faster, and driving her crazy. She could tell he was going to finish soon, and her own body was reacting to it as well. Worse, his hand was now touching her front, making her cry in pleasure, so good it was hard to endure. Her voice was filling the car again, but the Tiger wouldn't stop.

"Eden... Eden... Eden..."

He kept grunting against her ear, losing control in her. Eden felt him go deep, hard, and fast, completely letting himself go, in a hectic rhythm that drove the two of them crazy.

Suddenly, he stopped brutally, and she felt him come inside, with a long groan of relief. Her own body had gone a bit numb, but his fingers suddenly resumed touching her.

"No, no..."

"Come," he muttered against her ear.

It was like he had pushed the right button. With him still inside, Eden's body suddenly joined him in a violent wave of pleasure, inflated by all the furious riding from earlier. Her body spasmed for the few seconds it lasted, making her voice go mute and breathless.

When she finally calmed down, Dante's body slowly fell on top of her. In a post-orgasmic daze, she felt him gently caress one cheek and kiss the other, his breathing still a bit uneven. Her body was still feeling a bit numb and tense, her extremities tingling and feeling funny. She tried to recover her senses, bit by bit, all hot and dazed, but her mind was very clear. She let out a long sigh, exhausted.

"...That was good," she finally chuckled.

He let out a faint groan in response, kissing her shoulder. Eden had underestimated his energy a bit, but she didn't regret this car sex one bit... despite how gross she felt right now, with the moist feeling between her legs, and the leather sticking against her sweaty butt. With a smile, her hand wandered to Dante's exposed butt, pinching it playfully. He groaned again.

"Tiger, are you only going to growl now?" she whispered against his ear.

"...I'll do worse than growl if you keep playing like that."

Eden smiled, but after a quick little slap on his butt cheek, she took her hand back. She would much rather save the next sessions for upstairs. Although sex in a luxury car was rather exciting, it wasn't as comfortable as a bed, nor very practical. She was a bit tired, and Dante's body on top of her made it even more stifling. She sighed and tried to push him a bit, but he wrapped his arms around her, groaning and hiding his face in her neck. He was still inside her too...

"Dante... Move, please."

He groaned in refusal and gently bit her neck, making Eden shiver.

"Let's get upstairs," she insisted. "Please... I'm hungry too. Have you cooked yet?"

"I got the ingredients."

Eden tried to imagine her lover grocery shopping, and the image of Dante in his Italian suit in the middle of an aisle made her chuckle. Her reaction sent funny sensations through her lower abdomen, though, and she grimaced, reminded of their very close position.

"Dante, come on. Pull out now... We can cuddle upstairs, but not in a bloody car."

No matter how luxurious the car is, Eden thought to herself. If they had done anything but sex, she would have probably enjoyed staying there, but for now, she was just dying to take a shower and rinse the stickiness off, and she was really starting to get hungry.

Luckily, with a bit more pushing, and perhaps her words to convince him, Dante finally moved after another kiss on her neck. With all the biting and sucking, Eden didn't even want to know what a mess she was... He pulled out, making her wince, and helped her exit the car, once they were both minimally covered again.

# CHAPTER THIRTY-THREE

To Eden's surprise, there were still a handful of bodyguards in the parking lot, and for a second, she panicked, dying of embarrassment. However, all the men had their backs turned to the car, and had barely realized they had come out until they saw Dante and Eden walking past them. Perhaps they were listening to something on purpose to give their boss some privacy...

Ignoring them, Dante pulled her into the elevator, and with one glare at his men, they didn't get in and left the couple alone in there. As soon as the doors were closed, he wrapped his arms around her, his hands finding her butt. He kissed her again, a bit more tame this time. Eden didn't refuse him. In fact, she was still a bit hot from earlier, and she wanted more of this physical contact between them. Not just in a sexual way, but to have Dante hold her, and feel his skin against hers. Plus, he was clearly not intending to jump her again just yet, and when they got upstairs, he sighed while ending their kiss. Eden smiled and was the one to head to the kitchen first, holding his hand and looking around.

"What did you get? Pasta again?"

"A risotto. Do you like it?"

"Never tried it, but it sounds good to me!"

"Save me a portion, Eden," whined Loir in her ear. "Those mean hackers are already overworking me and I'm so hungry I could eat a puppy!"

"Loir, if you touch one hair on my dogs, you're dead. Also, what are you guys working on?"

"Ugh, turns out I am a celebrity and I didn't even know it! So here I am,

453

pharaoh at the top of the pyramid, guiding all these cute, innocent, little kittens on the right path. Seriously, I feel like a celebrity right now, they are asking me questions left and right and I don't even have a buzzer!"

"I met Nebty," chuckled Eden, gloating a bit, "in the flesh."

She walked up to Dante, giving him a quick kiss before pointing her index finger toward the bathroom. He nodded, already busy taking the ingredients out of the fridge to cook. She was a bit excited to have him cook again and wished she could stay to watch, but she really needed a quick shower first. While rushing there, she listened to Loir's rant.

"Wait, you *met* met? Nebty, *the* Nebty? Our favorite little rival? Ha! Here I go, gloating about how I feel like Louis the Fourteenth in his palace while our Kitty is already meeting all the big names! I knew I shouldn't have canceled my Scrabble club! Now you're going to make friends that are actually three-dimensional and smell like a real human!"

"She was nice, though. Aren't you chatting with her?"

"I am, but I haven't gotten to shake paws with the... oh, Nebty is a woman? Damn, I've been calling her Cheesecake for over an hour, I think. Got to think of something else. What about Choco Pie? I like choco pies more than cheesecake... They have no manners, anyway!"

Eden let him go on with his nonsense for a little while, washing herself quickly. She was so conflicted between the pleasure of a hot shower and the appeal of seeing the Italian Tiger cooking... Eventually, she stepped out of the shower and grabbed a bathrobe while Loir was still talking non-stop in her ear, although she had stopped listening.

"I mean, you can never know these days. Some people are allergic to carrots! Can you imagine? No carrot cake! I like carrot cakes, they are orange! Can you think of something sweet that is orange but not an orange? Carrots! Carrots are great. We should eat more carrots, Eden. Maybe I should launch a carrot pizza. It would make people nicer. Did you know eating carrots makes you more well-mannered? Also, they make your butt orange and your poop pink. Or was it the other way around..."

"Loir, focus." Eden sighed, walking out with a towel to dry her hair. "How's the Edge?"

"They're so cute! I feel like the queen bee, shaking my fingers and making all those cute little ones work for our money, honey! Apparently, I'm the Gandalf of this group! They are asking me tons of questions and making me work on some pretty funny codes. Those newbies are quite good, my Kitty! Of course, they don't have my style, but some of them really know how to use their booger-pullers and marbles! Well, there are a few of them who are about as useless as a rotten piece of damn celery and try to suck the strawberry by the stem, but..."

"Can you stop with all the food jokes, I'm starving already."

"Me too! Can you believe they tried to feed me a salad tonight?! A salad! Do I look like a hamster to you?"

"I'd say a weasel, but..."

"Well, they should feed this weasel its pizza! I'm a pizza-eating weasel! I'll be very understanding and accept risotto as a second option, though, you know. Or even some leftover pasta..."

"The chef only cooks for me, sorry," smiled Eden, making eye contact with Dante in the kitchen.

"Oh, you bad Kitty! You're getting all naughty again, aren't you? I can almost hear you purring all the way from here! I won't have it! This pharaoh wants his pizza, now!"

"The diva is going to calm down or I'm going to turn you from pharaoh to mummy real quick and tell them to feed you only celery for the rest of your life."

"You're so mean to me! Nobody appreciates me! All those little pepperonis are running away as soon as they see me!"

"Start by stopping with your damn remarks and stupid names about their heritage, you creepy sociopath. Have you tried asking nicely, for a start?"

"I gave them cute nicknames! I didn't even get that personal with my last succulent!"

"Forget the nicknames," sighed Eden. "Just... ask Jack or Circé. They should still have a mild tolerance to your bullshit..."

"...Who's Jack?"

"The tall, dark-skinned guy, minus his heels and pink wig?"

"...Wait, what? Isn't that a lady? ...I complimented her nails three times!"

Eden sighed.

"Good night, Loir. SIN, mute him for four hours."

Enjoying the silence, Eden sighed in relief and sat on the kitchen counter. Dante wasn't done cooking, luckily for her, but he had some spare time to step aside and come put a quick kiss on her lips.

"How was the shower?"

"It felt good, but I could have done without the Loir stereo... He's exhausting when he starts. It's a miracle no one's shot him down yet."

"Even you," Dante nodded with a smirk, cutting some vegetables.

Eden grabbed a piece of cheese to nibble while waiting, and sighed.

"To be honest, I like his rambling more than I'd care to admit. He's never really serious, unlike me, and he can find the stupidest jokes in the worst situations too. He has... no care for his surroundings or any kind of social convention, but he's still mindful enough not to hurt people he actually cares about with his words. He helped me relax in situations I never thought I could. He was just... there too when I needed him but would never say it. Sometimes, it was nice to just listen to his crazy nonsense at night, when I couldn't sleep... or when I felt lonely. It was like a little radio in my head, to remind me I'm not alone. He's crazy on many levels, but he's... he's been there for a while."

Dante put a pan on the stove, stirred it a little, and put a towel over his shoulder. He was still half-naked, for some reason that Eden didn't care to know. The half-naked Italian cooking for her was like a fantasy come to life... He noticed her gaze on him, her mouth half-open, and walked up to her again, biting the piece of cheese she was holding.

"...Hungry?" he asked, with a tone that had nothing to do with actual hunger.

"...Starving," Eden muttered, her cheeks a bit red.

Dante smiled and leaned over to kiss her. Eden was a bit amused that their mouths tasted of cheese... and pulled back, licking her lips.

"Can I have some wine, chef?"

"Sure."

Dante quickly poured them two generous glasses of some fancy white wine. Eden had no knowledge of wine, but the dry, slightly sour, and fruity taste that quickly filled her mouth was completely to her liking. She enjoyed it in small sips, trying to savor it while Dante went back to watching his dish. Eden liked how absorbed he genuinely was in his task even more than having him cook for her. He was relaxed, but focused, watching everything and putting it together in a perfect, timely, and elegant manner. He could have easily passed for a real restaurant chef anywhere.

Even the way he prepared their plates was impeccable, and Eden felt a bit sorry Loir wouldn't even get to see this masterpiece, let alone taste it. Dante simply handed her plate to her. though, and it was clear they would eat right there in the kitchen, with Eden still sitting and Dante standing next to her, leaning against the counter.

"Buon appetito," Eden chuckled, before taking her first bite.

It was so good, still hot and almost melting in her mouth. She had barely witnessed what had actually gone into this dish, but she just loved all of the tidbits she could taste. Next to her though, Dante was silently staring at his plate, visibly lost in his thoughts. His quietness worried Eden.

"What is it?" she asked, before taking another mouthful.

It took him a couple of seconds to get out of his head and suddenly turn to her.

"Let's get married."

Eden choked on her rice.

She kept coughing, trying to catch her breath and wipe the food off her bathrobe. Dante hadn't moved at all, not even startled by her sudden spitting, just waiting for her answer.

"Wha-... What did you just say?"

"I'm serious."

"That's what scares me!" she exclaimed. "Why are you spouting such a thing now, out of nowhere? Marriage? Dante, what are you talking about?!"

"You don't want to?"

"No!"

Eden had blurted that out so clearly, most would have been hurt or upset. But of course, not Dante De Luca. Instead, he didn't seem to have even heard that and just turned to her, taking hold of her hand. Eden quickly grabbed her glass of wine with the other one.

"You'd become my wife," he said.

"I know what a marriage is..."

"You'd get half of my assets."

"You know I don't care about that! ...Okay, maybe for the baths and hot water, but everything else..."

"If I die, you'd get everything."

This time, she got mad and slapped his shoulder.

"Shut up!" She slapped him again. "Shut! The! Fuck! Up! You can't say shit like that now! I don't want to talk about it! Don't you start saying shit like that!"

He grabbed her wrist before she could slap him some more and looked down at her. Her lips were pouting, her eyes teary, and her cheeks red, meaning she was genuinely upset. Dante smiled, but she fought his grip and emptied her glass in one go before trying to push him away from her.

"Stop it," she mumbled angrily. "I hate it when you do things like that..."

"Proposing?"

"Cornering me," she groaned. "...I just want to eat my risotto. Please."

Seeing how sullen she was, the mafioso sighed and backed away a little, releasing her wrist. However, they both knew it was too late. The words had been dropped, and like a bomb, they couldn't be ignored or forgotten so easily. Eden poured herself another drink, making Dante raise an eyebrow, but he didn't comment. He knew she was used to drinking, but he was more worried about her trying to literally drown the conversation. He began eating his risotto, but the corny smile wouldn't come off his lips, no matter how many pouting glares Eden would send him. For a little while, they both ate in silence, all the sexual tension from earlier gone, and instead, an awkward silence reigned throughout the room.

Suddenly, music started playing, making them both look up. It was the wedding march.

"Fuck you, Loir!" Eden groaned.

He was muted, but he could still listen and clearly hack Dante's stereo as well. The music then changed to a less ceremonial one, a kind of waltz that Eden could somewhat tolerate better than the previous piece. She sighed and put her fork down. Dante's risotto was delicious, but now, she didn't have the heart for it. She hated the heavy atmosphere between them, and how this evening that should have been akin to a date had turned somewhat sour.

"...Come here."

To her surprise, Dante put his plate aside too, and gently took her hands to pull her down from the kitchen counter. While Eden was still doubtful, she didn't feel like refusing him again, especially if he was trying to close the distance between them. She let Dante smoothly guide her, but they stayed in the kitchen, only standing against each other. He wrapped his arms around her waist, and slowly began moving, swaying from left to right. Eden blushed a bit, but a shy smile appeared on her lips, and she put her hands on his shoulders, dancing along with him. Because the volume of the music was just loud enough, and they were so close in a heated kitchen, the tension gradually dissipated. Instead, Eden's smile widened as she enjoyed this moment. Dante was obviously trying to improve her mood, with Loir as his accomplice... Their dancing wasn't even as awkward as she would have thought. It was a slow, little dance, just moving in his kitchen, mostly their lower bodies casually swinging left and right while taking small steps. But because he was half-naked and Eden was in her bathrobe with her hair still half-wet, it was strangely cute yet sexy. They danced for a little while, listening to the music and just gently holding each other. Dante wasn't even trying to initiate anything; Eden barely felt his thumb caressing her lower back, but that was it. He was really trying to soothe her. She let out a long sigh and leaned in, her cheek against his torso. Dante hugged her a bit closer, and she heard him faintly chuckle next to her ear.

"...I'm still a bit mad at you," she grumbled.

"Don't be mad. I'm serious."

"I know... That's what scares me."

"You're always scared."

Eden wanted to roll her eyes at his comment. She knew he was referring to how she was always so afraid of any form of commitment, but he didn't actually need to state the obvious... She was taking baby steps already and had gotten so involved in this relationship, she still couldn't believe herself at times. Eden hated to show her vulnerable side, yet she was almost laid bare with Dante, emotionally. She tried to calm herself down and think of what would be a better, more mature way to approach what she still thought was a very blunt and unthinkable proposal...

"...Why are you asking such a thing now?" she muttered. "It really doesn't make sense..."

"We both know tomorrow is going to be... the most dangerous thing we've ever done, and for us, that's saying a lot. If... something happens to me, I don't want you to–"

"Don't say it like something is really going to happen!"

"I'm only saying if. ...Besides, it's not like I had never thought about it. I want to bind you to me with every form of commitment possible. This seems to be the most appropriate one."

"Do you even realize how unbearably possessive you are?"

"Yes."

As always, his shameless and blunt tone... Eden knew there was just no way to win against him. She nestled in his arms, feeling a bit restless, but also soothed by his warm and firm embrace. She had grown used to his possessiveness; worse, she loved it. Dante's best weapon against the walls around her heart was how he'd never let her go. For most, such obsession

458

would have been scary, but for someone like Eden whose worst fear was to be abandoned again, it was reassuring. They were both a bit broken inside, but their jagged pieces just happened to fit together, was how she saw it.

"...We're going to be together most of the time, according to the plan."

"Not all the time," he said. "Plus, we don't know what could happen."

Eden felt like sulking again. She knew he was right, and even if Dante was part of those who'd try to break into the Core with her, they'd be separated while she got inside first, and perhaps farther along too... She hated it. If possible, she would have avoided this war entirely. However, she wasn't so oblivious as to ignore what depended on their success or failure. Even if she wished for it, they both knew they wouldn't be able to resume life like before in the Suburbs. If they didn't do anything, the Core would wipe them out, and if they fought back, things would still never be the same.

"...Are you mad at me?"

"Don't ask that, sounding like you're enjoying it."

"Well, you're definitely sexier when you're mad."

"Just my luck."

Eden interrupted their dance, putting her two palms against his chest and pushing a bit to get some distance between them. She knows Dante's sex appeal was a serious threat to her decision-making.

"...I don't need your money. Nor your possessions."

"You don't know that yet. What if things don't turn out the way we want? We don't know what will happen. I'm not afraid to die, but I'm afraid you'll be left... alone again."

That sentence made Eden shudder. She couldn't even imagine such a thing. She thought she had become stronger, but now that she had tasted such happiness with Dante and all that safety... She shook her head and dove into his arms again.

"If you're scared I'll be left alone, don't leave me," she muttered. "You don't have the right to leave me after you've made me addicted to your cooking."

"Only my cooking?"

Eden didn't answer that, knowing all too well it would only give him grounds to tease her more. Instead, she heard him chuckle, and he hugged her back. She was surprised he didn't insist anymore.

"I never win you over in the first round anyway," he muttered as if he had read her thoughts.

"...Can I eat my risotto now? No more proposals. I just want to eat and drink in peace."

"Got it."

Dante grabbed their plates and actually took them to the living space. Because the living room was so large, they had barely hung out there compared to the bedroom, but the bottle-green, velvet sofa was still pretty attractive, with its golden frame and comfortable-looking leather cushions. Dante sat on it, gesturing for Eden to join him, and put the plates on the little table. He grabbed a remote, and to her surprise, after he pushed a few buttons, the decor changed. The lights turned off, the window was covered with a dark filter, and a large screen appeared on the opposite wall.

"Movie night?" he suggested with a smile.

"...You're trying to get me to give in, aren't you?"

He smirked, meaning she was right. It was a very convincing display, though. Eden could barely refrain from jumping on the sofa and stealing the remote from his hands to check out the movie catalog. She loved watching movies. The only ones she had ever seen were the few she remembered from when she still lived in the Core with her mother or the few she had seen on the very small vintage TV in Jack's bar. From what she could see on the widescreen, Dante had access to hundreds of movies, even those the Core had prohibited that could only be found illegally. Because hackers knew their value and sold them, Eden herself had only ever bought a handful of them.

"Eden."

Realizing she was still standing in the middle of the living room, she rushed without running to put her glass down on the table and sit next to him, her eyes wide open and riveted on the screen. Dante handed her the remote with a smile while standing again to go get his own glass and the bottle. For a while, Eden was overwhelmed with the selection of movies. There were so many, she had no idea where to begin. Some she had been curious about, dying to see, and some she'd never heard of. Amused, Dante simply sat next to her, eating his risotto while letting her admire the selection.

"*The Godfather*?" she chuckled, glancing at Dante. "It would be fitting for you."

"Of all movies, you'd pick such an old one?"

"I love old movies... It shows us how life was so different back then. Is there one you like?"

"Not really... I think this is my first time using this for entertainment."

"I should have known... Oh, Jack mentioned this one is one of his favorites, but we couldn't find it anywhere."

She selected the movie, which was actually named *Chicago* and in color, but still over a century old... Despite crossing her ankles on the couch and grabbing her plate, Eden ate very slowly, completely absorbed in the movie from the very first minute. Dante, who had finished eating long before her, simply watched it with her, an arm around her waist and regularly refilling their glasses. He paid much less attention to the movie than he did to Eden's reactions. She was fascinated like a young child, laughing at the jokes, getting angry for the characters, and commenting on the locations she recognized. The young woman didn't even notice her lover's stare for the length of the whole movie. When she was done, still with some food on her plate, she didn't even wait and excitedly picked another movie. Dante stood up, not bothered by how she had completely ignored him, and went to the kitchen to prepare

460

dessert. From behind the counter, he could see Eden, enjoying herself while watching the movie. The puppies, awakened from their nap in the bedroom by the movie's sounds, ran into the living room with excited little barks. Neither of them spotted their mistress on the couch at first but were more interested in the smells coming from the kitchen, and carefully approached Dante. They stood at a careful distance from the imposing man they weren't too familiar with, but he didn't mind them; in fact, he even fed them some of the leftover chicken on the floor, and let them play around him while he finished preparing the dessert.

When he brought the two new dishes to the table, Eden's attention finally shifted.

"What's this?" she asked, allured by the smell too.

"Panforte."

Intrigued, she quickly took a bite, without realizing how hot it was. She panicked, her tongue burning, and kept huffing and trying to fan her mouth. Dante chuckled, before suddenly diving in to kiss her, using his tongue to take the bite from her and eat it. A bit shocked, but still teary from the hot food, Eden grimaced.

"You didn't have to do that... It's a bit gross... and it was really hot too."

"It just came out of the oven," he chuckled, "and I'm fine. I don't get burned."

"Not burned? What do you mean?"

"I really don't feel pain. My pain receptors don't work," he said, "or more accurately, they were... turned off. Another gift from my father."

Eden opened her eyes wide, shocked.

He couldn't feel pain at all? She looked down, her eyes going to the place he had been injured and had surgery on just a while ago. She remembered his shocked expression when she found the injury. He really hadn't felt it at all. This explained how he could have such rowdy sex right after the surgery...

"You don't... feel anything?"

"No, I can feel normally. I just don't experience pain. It's a condition that existed before we learned how to manipulate DNA... and it was made illegal to use for genetic modification, but my father didn't care much for regulations. He made me like this to make me stronger."

Eden was at a loss for words. She couldn't imagine not being able to feel pain... What if he got shot? He wouldn't even notice it until he actually saw it? He had to feel something, right?

Since she looked so lost and shocked, Dante sighed and gently grabbed her hand to kiss it, with a smile on his lips.

"Don't worry. I feel exactly what I need to..."

Eden blushed, and took her hand back, grabbing her dessert as an excuse to keep it away from him. She knew he was only trying to distract her from his condition, but it was working. She ate her dessert, which was once again very good now that it had cooled... Once she finished her plate, full, she took a sip of wine; Dante had opened another bottle, something a bit more suitable to accompany the dessert. Eden leaned against him, and he put his arm around her shoulders. For a while, neither of them said anything. The pups came to cuddle with them on the couch, and Eden petted them while watching the movie, warmed up in Dante's embrace, thinking this must be her own definition of happiness...

She woke up to being gently laid down on the mattress. After a minute of trying to figure out where she was and what she had missed, she suddenly realized she had fallen asleep before the movie ended. Next to her, Dante was already lying down under the covers too.

"We didn't even... do a second round!" she exclaimed, getting up on her elbows.

"We need to get up before dawn. And we can have celebratory sex tomorrow night."

She looked out the window. It was very dark outside, and probably late indeed... She gave up and laid back down with a sigh. She felt regretful and sorry she had spent so much time watching movies, and they didn't spend enough time focusing on each other, even if they had cuddled. Yet, Dante didn't complain at all. He moved to pull her into his embrace, his breathing already slow. He had even taken off her bathrobe, leaving her with only her panties on. She was impressed by his self-control, for once. Perhaps he was tired too, or the alcohol had gotten to his sex drive first... Eden nestled a bit deeper into his embrace, her forehead resting against his shoulder. She loved his smell and the gentle rhythm of his breathing. In the end, he let her have a quiet, worry-free evening. She could still feel the delicious Italian dinner filling her stomach, and a faint taste of sweet wine on her lips. From the end of the bed came two little sets of snores; Beer and Bullet had probably been put up there too... She smiled and closed her eyes, letting herself give in to this quiet little span of bliss.

"Dante... Wake me up a bit earlier tomorrow morning."

"...What for?"

"That annoying thing you talked about. ...Let's do it."

# CHAPTER
# THIRTY-FOUR

Eden woke up to the strange sensation of something hot, rough, and damp against her face. She grimaced, opening her eyes to witness the little pink tongue that was actively licking her face. She groaned and pulled the puppy into her arms, hearing a chuckle above him.

"...Dante?" she mumbled.

"You need to get up."

She opened her eyes for real and witnessed him putting the other pup in her field of vision, a smile on his face. So he had acquired the fur babies' help to wake her up... Bullet ran to her, wide awake already, and just like his twin, began enthusiastically licking her face. Beer was struggling to get away from her embrace too, his little body wriggling around. Eden was awake in a matter of seconds thanks to those two. She groaned and sat up, pushing them both on her lap while she grasped the situation. It was still very early, the sun had just begun to rise outside. She was wondering why she needed to be up so early when the previous night's conversation with Dante all came back to her.

"...What's going on?" she asked, suddenly a bit panicked.

The man was standing at the foot of the bed with a faint smile on his lips, cautiously putting on his cufflinks, shiny little diamonds that looked as expensive as his outfit. His shirt was white under his dark silk jacket, and it was the first time she saw him wear something other than black...

"Our wedding is in half an hour," he calmly said. "I tried to let you sleep, but you should really get up."

"W-what...?"

Eden's heart beat like crazy. Why had she said yes again? Since when was she giving in to his whims, so easily too? She vaguely remembered even asking him herself to wake her up a bit sooner, but now that this was all real, a huge ball of stress appeared in her stomach. She took a deep breath and got out of bed, her steps quickly taking her to the bathroom, the pups right behind her. She closed the door behind them and faced the mirror.

"You crazy woman," she muttered. "What now?!"

She then began splashing her face with cold water just to wake herself up. In the meantime, she was trying to calm down and think rationally. She had been fine with this the previous night. Perhaps it was the alcohol, but there was no use lying to herself. Right now, she was just too nervous. Beer and Bullet, with no clue about her troubles, were playfully chasing her feet and were even more excited when Eden began pacing back and forth.

"Oh, my Kitty is making the wedding bells ring! And... so early too. It's almost time for my before-dawn gimbap!"

"Not now, Loir..." she sighed, brushing her blonde hair back nervously.

"Easy for you to say! The Big Kitty woke everybody up at 3:00 a.m. to get everything ready while you played Sleeping Beauty! Well, I am a bit happy since I haven't slept in over a decade, but... Oh, can I be the flower girl? I'm sure I can find confetti or something! ...Would shredded mozzarella work?"

"Don't waste food," Eden groaned.

Then, a knock was heard on the door; she froze.

"W-what?"

"It's Jack, hun. Open up."

She frowned but went to open the door. What was Jack doing in Dante's apartment?

To her surprise, it really was her friend who stepped into the bathroom, checking her from head to toe and carrying a little vanity case.

"Jack, what are you doing here?"

"A rescue mission, from what I can see! Girl, you drank last night, didn't ya? Look how puffy your baby cheeks are! Damn, you're lucky I managed to find or borrow some makeup for ya! I mean, I can't make a miracle happen but I can probably avoid you looking like you were just forced into this... You weren't, right?

As much as she was surprised to see Jack, Eden felt a bit better. The tall guy was such a down-to-earth and normal person compared to all the mafiosos and hackers, it felt like he was the last bit of normalcy in her very complex world. Eden chuckled nervously and sat on the toilet seat.

"No... I mean, yes, I agreed to it... Did Dante ask you to come?"

He rolled his eyes, and put the little vanity case on the bathroom counter, quickly taking the makeup to sort it out and checking her face.

"Oh, babe, you don't actually think I'd miss this, would ya?" he sighed. "I mean, it might be a small wedding ceremony or whatever, but it's still my

464

honey girl Eden's wedding! Here, put a bit of this on. Did you even wash your face yet?"

For the next ten minutes, she let Jack nag her about her skin and pick her makeup, letting him do pretty much all of it himself. Despite his usual extravagant tastes for himself, Jack was a real artist in his own right. Unlike Eden who had never mastered this art, he could apply any kind of makeup in no time as if he had spent hours doing it. When he was done a few minutes later, she could barely recognize her puffy, sleepy face from just before. Her skin looked very smooth and delicate now, flawless, and he had somehow enhanced the shape of her eyes and brows and added a simple, magenta-pink tint to her lips. It wasn't too much at all and looked very natural. Eden blushed a bit, feeling like she hadn't looked this pretty in a while; it made her a bit self-conscious about what Dante had been seeing all this time...

When he was done, Eden begged for a bit of privacy to pee, which she hadn't been able to do since getting up. Hence, Jack took the dogs with him, and she caught a couple of seconds alone. Her heart was still beating fast, but now, there was a hint of excitement to it. A wedding had never really been part of her plans. She had the faint memory of wanting someone to spend the rest of her life with, but over the years, it had become nothing but a strange desire that would never really go away despite how unrealistic she convinced herself it was. How ironic that now it was almost taking her by surprise...

When she left the bathroom, she was surprised to find not Dante, but Jack, and this time Circé too, both waiting for her in the room. There was a little pile of clothes on an armchair which they seemed to be arguing about until they noticed her.

"Finally!" said Jack. "Come on, honey, come over here. Get in front of the mirror."

"Good morning, Eden," said Circé.

Although she knew the witch-like hacker had been up for hours, she didn't have the smallest trace of fatigue on her face; Eden wondered if she was used to sleeping very little, like Loir...

"Alright, so we obviously had no time to find a decent dress since you guys are in such a rush and clearly have no consideration for traditions, but we dove through your wardrobe and made a selection. So now, you try it on!"

"...All of this?" Eden muttered, a bit shocked.

There were at least ten to twenty different outfits! Circé smiled.

"Jack and I just made a selection, but feel free to pick whichever you like most. It will be your wedding dress, after all."

"Pick yellow!" shouted Loir in her ear. "Yellow is like a lemon! It makes everybody happy!"

Ignoring him, Eden began looking through the pile. There wasn't even anything yellow; in fact, she could almost tell who had picked what between Jack and Circé. The first had chosen very feminine outfits, with pastel or cream colors, all close to what a white wedding dress would have been. The other

465

outfits were all much more intricate, a bit sexy even, and in darker colors. Eden began genuinely trying to look through the pile, eliminating a few things without thinking twice. Eden had never been very into dresses anyway, she felt like most of those would have been awkward on her. For some, Jack and Circé argued for her to try anyway, so she didn't resist. In the end, the pile had gone from the original sixteen outfits to a solid eight, which was already more manageable. She began trying them on, and four of them were ruled out because of a size issue, then two more because Jack put what he called his "bridesmaid veto" on it. Hence, Eden was soon left with a simple, sleeveless, fitted, dark pink bustier dress, and a pastel pink one that was very layered with a puffy skirt and an embroidered lace top. She tried both, not finding either of them to particularly stand out. The first dress was pretty but a bit too strict, and the second showed a lot of her skin and felt too bubbly. When she had given her opinion to Jack and Circé, the two exchanged a glance. She was once again surprised at how close they had gotten.

"...Can it work?" Circé asked.

Jack was pensively rubbing his index on his chin, frowning while staring very seriously at the dress on Eden and the other one on the side. He took a deep breath, but finally nodded confidently.

"Yeah, I'll manage. Just ten minutes and a decent sewing machine should be enough!"

"Alright then. Eden, come sit here."

Intrigued, Eden obeyed and sat on a stool facing the window while, to her surprise, Circé began combing her hair for her. She could feel the hacker's fingers playing with her strands of blonde hair, and hear Jack grunting and complaining in a low voice, busy ripping and stitching fabric somewhere behind them.

"I'll lend you some hairpins," said Circé. "It won't hold for long, but it will be fine for just the ceremony, alright?"

Eden nodded, a bit helpless. She was so clueless about what was needed for a wedding, she was happy to sit there and let those two work their magic. In fact, she really didn't care much about the ceremonial part of it. She probably would have been fine with just a signature on paper like they used to do in old times... however, right now, she felt like she was being transformed into someone else. A real young woman, who perhaps would have had a glimpse of a normal life, surrounded by friends before her wedding... Loir even kept playing annoying wedding-themed music in the room. It felt unbelievable that, in a few hours, they would be heading out for a real battle. Eden was feeling strange, as if it was all a bit unreal. Her wedding, being held in the first hours of the day.

"Done!"

She almost jumped when Circé let her go, and Jack appeared right after.

"Get into this!" he ordered, opening the dress for her to step in.

She obeyed, and he pulled it up, carefully closing it in the back. When

Circé changed the window's settings in front of her to turn into a mirror, Eden gasped in surprise. Jack had seamlessly meshed the two dresses together, and the result was even better than anticipated. It was still the dark pink dress underneath, but now, the long, flowy, thin layers of the softer pink dress were making it a bit more ceremonial without overdoing it. The thin lace was modestly covering her neckline and shoulders, but only her chest was actually covered. It even matched her makeup and the elegant, Asian-inspired hairstyle Circé had done with her hairpins for Eden's blonde hair. She looked like one of those princesses from a fantasy video game, with a surprisingly pure look and lipstick that matched the pink shades of her dress.

"Gorgeous," sighed Jack. "Ah, I should have been a makeup artist in a previous life."

"We should get moving," said Circé. "We don't have much time, unfortunately..."

Because the dress only reached down to her ankles, and she wore some dark boots, Eden didn't need any help moving next door.

To her surprise, the living room had been prepared. It wasn't much, but a few bouquets of flowers had been put up, petals on the floor, some candles here and there, and even more dazzling, Dante was waiting for her, the sunrise behind him. Eden smiled and suddenly, all of her worries flew away. She walked up to him without hesitation, Jack and Circé behind her. Rolf was apparently playing the role of ceremony officer, despite his usual suit. When Dante opened his hand, Eden took it with a little smile.

"Oh my puppies, I'm going to cry," wept Loir. "I need to take so many screenshots of this scene! I'll make a poster! A billboard of my Kitties tying the knot!"

"Shut it," groaned Circé.

Eden could barely hear him. She was just a bit impressed at how elegant Dante was when she thought he couldn't get any more handsome than usual. She had seen him naked and in different suits, but he took her breath away in this husband-to-be look. He smiled, noticing her insisting stare.

"Loving the view?"

"A lot," she said. "You?"

"I prefer you naked, I think. Or with only the bed sheets around you..."

Next to them, Rolf loudly cleared his voice, the best way to remind everyone where they were. He had prepared a little speech that was most likely taken from somewhere, about the sacred vow of marriage and everything, but both Eden and Dante listened to very little of it, staring and teasing each other with their eyes along the way.

"Gosh, looking at them, you'd not believe for a second they're virgins," chuckled Jack.

"Oh, I can assure you they're not!" proudly said Loir.

"That was rhetorical, you idiot," hissed Circé.

They heard him chuckle, but after that, everyone went silent to respectfully

467

listen to the rest of Rolf's speech. It was unexpectedly long, and Eden glanced to the side, wondering if the usually-stern bodyguard hadn't paid a bit too much attention to the text...

"The sacred promise of marriage is to be a lifelong one, for the partners to respect, trust, and support each other through the good, the bad, and the unexpected. This union will represent the commitment to your partner despite the dangers ahead of us. Together or apart, you will be bonded, committed to one another forever. This morning, your partner becomes your confidante, your defender, and your weapon through all the trials to come. Everything from then on will be celebrated, mourned, or faced together. Love, trust, and loyalty will be the foundation of this union. ...Boss, I am proud to be the one doing this for you today, and–"

"Get on with it," said Dante, visibly growing a bit impatient too.

He and his second-in-command exchanged a glance, and Eden held in a little chuckle for poor Rolf who had done his best. Just then, the two pups, having recognized their usual feeder, began barking at Rolf. He put down his little piece of paper and grabbed the pups to carry them.

"Now," he sighed, "please join hands."

They obeyed, as they were already facing each other. Dante's hands were firm and hot on Eden's, and she smiled.

"Do you, Dante De Luca, Tiger among the Zodiac, agree to take this woman as your wife?"

"I do."

"Why the whole Zodiac thingy?" asked Jack with a frown.

"It's also a transfer of titles," whispered Circé. "The SINs will register Eden as his partner and thus, his only heir for his official position. Just an update in the database, sort of."

"Those hackers..."

"Do you, Eden..." started Rolf, hesitating.

"Newman."

"Eden Newman, leader of the Edge and daughter of the Architect, agree to take Dante De Luca as your spouse?"

Eden smiled.

"...Deal."

The Tiger smiled back, pleased. Her answer sent them back to how their relationship had started: a complex, intimate, and dangerous contract. This one didn't feel very different. They locked their fingers together, already very close.

"Well, I declare you husband and wife. You may..."

Their lips were already in contact before he got to finish that sentence. They kissed each other playfully, ignoring the embarrassed audience. Eden had never thought something so simple would make her so happy. She had a husband. It felt unreal to call Dante her husband, but there she was. It was such a quaint ceremony, but it was more than enough. She would have hated something grand and braggy. Just them, a few witnesses, a pretty dress, and comfy leather boots. She didn't need more. She only needed him.

"Alright, alright, my loves," said Jack. "I am all for fun and sex, but we still got a hell of a shitload a' storm coming right at us, so let's not jump in bed too soon. Damn, I thought this would be my one chance to get the bride's bouquet..."

"You can always grab one of those," chuckled Circé, pointing at the arrangements on the table.

"Oh no, lady. I have my pride. It's alright. I'll have the cute beta guy propose to me if I need."

With that, Jack winked in Rolf's direction and walked out, stretching and yawning. Circé chuckled, crossing her arms, and turned to the newlyweds.

"Sorry, guys, but we really don't have much time."

"We'll get changed and come down in a minute," said Eden, trying to elude Dante's restless kisses, "...or m-maybe a couple."

"See you downstairs, then. Ten minutes tops."

Circé and Rolf quickly walked out, taking the puppies with them, and Eden turned to Dante with a smile on her face, answering his kiss.

"Is it better kissing your wife or your bodyguard?" she asked playfully.

He sighed and finally stopped pursuing her with his kisses. He gazed down at her outfit, looking a bit sad.

"I wish you could stay like this the whole day. Or that I could undress you. In bed."

"I wish so too, but I need to change into something more comfortable if we want a chance to win this. ...I'll put the dress away for later, okay?"

"...I'll get you a better one."

"I like this one. It's custom-made."

"...I wanted to see you in a real wedding dress."

"It is a real wedding dress. I was wed in it. Stop being grouchy to stall for time, let's go get dressed."

"Hm..."

He didn't stop pouting, but at least he followed her to get changed. Eden got out of the dress with a bit of regret, took off most of the makeup, and traded Circé's hairpins for a high ponytail. To her surprise, once she stepped out of the bedroom, Dante, who had changed faster, moved forward and grabbed her hand. He put a ring on her finger and kissed her before she could say a word.

"At least wear this," he said.

Eden smiled, her eyes going down to the gorgeous piece of jewelry. She had no intention to take it off. It was gold, with little pink diamonds in a shape akin to a flower.

She loved it.

"Finally!" exclaimed Loir once they got downstairs. "My pair of Kitties!"

"You were faster than I thought," said Circé with a chuckle.

"Don't get me started," sighed Eden. "...How are things going?"

The tone immediately became serious in the room. They were all in Loir's room, the large Map of Chicago displayed ahead of that day's battle. Everyone was there, including Dante's lieutenants like George. It had rarely been so crowded, but Eden knew more men were getting ready to leave downstairs. The place was strangely quiet, though; they could even hear the pups grunting and playing in the corner. Jack, who would be staying there with Loir, was trying to entertain them, but even he looked a bit nervous, glancing repeatedly at the men present.

"Everyone is getting ready," said Rolf. "All the Zodiacs have already made contact to say they are almost or already in position."

"The Edge is ready as well," nodded Circé. "Nebty says good morning."

She gave her a quick wink. Just like Eden, the female hacker was geared up for battle under her usual purple kimono. They had both chosen skin-tight, black bodysuits, most fitting for this kind of mission. Unlike the others and Dante's men who would mostly be fighting in plain sight, their mission would be a stealthy one. Just as she was getting a bit more nervous, Dante wrapped his arm around her waist, and she naturally leaned against him. Everyone was used to their skinship by now. Since all of their eyes were focused on the Map to review the plan, she didn't feel too embarrassed.

Rolf glanced toward Loir, and with a big creepy smile as always, the hacker's fingers danced on his keyboard. Several colored lines appeared on the detailed Map of the Core. Eden remembered they needed her in the room for it to function, so they had probably waited for her and Dante to come down to start reviewing the plan...

"As discussed, the evacuations began around midnight, quietly so as not to get the Core's attention. The Goat is taking the non-fighting population to the various shelters, away from the fighting, and into hideouts where possible. We think the Core noticed, though; the air quality literally dropped this morning."

"The external temperature is at sixty degrees Fahrenheit, my Kitties," giggled Loir. "We have a warning of firepower, smoke, and rain about to piss on the Windy City, so everyone get your prettiest coats and masks out!"

"The plan is for the Dog and the Zebra to have the fight focused in the north first," continued Rolf, a part of the Map lighting up as he spoke. "They will make sure to get as much of the Core's attention as possible, and around an hour later, the Dragon and the Eagle will attack the south jointly. Each group has several targets to destroy, especially the towers used to amplify their communication and the Core's field of action. They also want to destroy the ventilation systems as soon as possible."

"Tell them to destroy the bridges that included former metro rails first," said Eden. "They are using them to convey their vehicles, but all of their means of transportation use electromagnets. If you destroy them, they won't be able to use them, unlike ours. We will have the advantage over them."

"We can use ram cars."

Eden was surprised to hear Nebty's voice in her ear already.

"Morning," she said.

"Morning, sleepyhead. I hope you're in tip-top shape, the fights are starting already."

"I'm not surprised..."

"The Edge has begun launching micro-attacks on the Core to support the Zodiacs on the ground, but it won't look like a coordinated attack yet, just a tad busier than the usual day."

Eden knew that to control the hundred-or-so hackers, she and Nebty would only be in contact with the eight team captains right below Nebty and Malieka, whose codename was Patience.

"Anubis is leading the hackers in the north with Mage," added Nebty. "Gluttony and Sapphire are in the south. Nekhbet and Crash will be with you as soon as you get into the Dark Reality, the two others are on stand-by and leading the scattered attacks. I've added some newbie Back Hackers to help Circé and Warlock, and everything else is going as planned. Everyone is waiting for your instructions."

"Got it." Eden nodded.

She had almost met them all virtually the previous day, but she already knew all of those hackers. Those with the names of the seven sins were actually Malieka's apprentices or peers, and those named after Egyptian gods had been trained and selected by Nebty. Mage was another survivor from the first generation of the Edge, who had never made it to Chicago and lived in a different city. The other hackers had been recruited separately, but all those named were top hackers of Chicago or other systems. It wouldn't be hard to remember for her or Loir.

Her attention went back to Rolf, who was still explaining the plan.

"...Our team is set to arrive from the west as soon as we meet up with the Rat's men, in less than half an hour from now. The Core's soldiers will already be busy on two other battlefields at each end of Chicago, so our attack has to be quick but brutal. Our goal is to pave the way into the Core for the hackers and as many of our group as possible. Our objective is this."

A large and tall building was lit up, and the Map zoomed into it. It was surprisingly close to the river, and in fact, just a few streets away from the border to the Suburbs. A chill went down Eden's spine. That large, dark tower had once been her home and a place to run away from.

"...The Arcadia Tower," she muttered.

"The Arcadia Tower," said Rolf at the same time. "This is the central power of the Chicago Core. Not only do all of the important leaders of the Core live on the upper floors, but it is known to contain all of the System's physical resources: data centers, main computers, and all the human resources that keep the Chicago Core's System functional."

"It requires a ton of space in the real world," said Eden.

"Can't we just... bomb the place?" George frowned.

"It wouldn't shut down the System," she shook her head. "There's a digital

471

backup, like everything. It will get triggered if we touch the System's physical parts, and most likely restore it to the latest backed-up version, perhaps even transfer it all to another city that has its data centers intact for a while. They may even have a spare copy ready of this place elsewhere in Chicago itself. If we want to really destroy it, we have to do it both in reality and in the Dark Reality simultaneously: trap it where it is and as it is so the data won't run elsewhere."

"Isn't there a risk they already have a digital backup elsewhere, then?"

"No," Circé said. "Chicago's Core is the most elaborate, and the most up-to-date. The other Cores aren't powerful enough to keep copies of it, and because it also stores each of the other Cores' former versions, it can't keep too many versions of itself, so it erases the former versions each time a new one is created, only keeping the latest for safety. That's why we have to hack this one, erase it, and prevent it from resetting itself. If we did the same to any other Core elsewhere, it would temporarily be shut down, but the Chicago Core would send its latest digital version and it would be a matter of minutes before it's back to normal. The Chicago Core is its own backup, though. So if we manage to take down this one, all the other Cores will be vulnerable too, with only their live versions left and no backup."

George grimaced.

"...Okay, I think I understood half of that."

"It's like a brain," sighed Eden. "If you lose an arm, you can still replace it since your brain will remember how the nerves work. But if your brain is... gone, you can't use anything else even if the rest of your body is intact."

"It's a no-brainer!" chuckled Loir.

"...Yeah, I think I got the image."

"*What's in your head, in your head?*" Loir sang terribly off-key. "*Zombie, zombie, zombie-ie-ie~!*"

"Warlock, shut up and move on, we're on a schedule here," sighed Circé.

"Yes, yes... Our ladies are all so bossy..."

Despite complaining, he zoomed in again on the building, showing its structure.

"Most of the lower floors are for entertainment," said Rolf. "There was a flood around a century ago, so they entirely redesigned the ten lowest floors to be for leisure, open to the public, and easy to evacuate. Getting there should be no issue. Above that, everything up to the fifty-ninth floor is private residences and offices. It's the sixtieth floor and up that we're aiming for."

"Better not be afraid of heights, my pretties!" chuckled Loir.

He zoomed in again, showing the upper floors Rolf was describing.

"According to our sources, these are all part of the Core data centers and offices for people working for the System. We need to get there to destroy it physically."

"So that's where we get to use explosives?" smirked George. "We better get out quick though..."

"Us hackers need to get there too," retorted Circé with a glare. "There's no way to access the System from the Dark Reality unless we are physically connected to those data centers."

"Oh, shit..."

"You have to get us there, then leave," said Eden. "Once a few of us get in, we can corrupt the System from the inside and get more hackers to take it down."

"I thought that was just for getting inside the Core!"

"It's the same principle," said Eden. "I can physically get inside the Core and open the way for the hackers into the Dark Reality because my SIN is different, but it still requires me to interact from the other side."

"Your hacking stuff is too complicated for me," George shook his head, "but I get the picture. You get in, everybody gets in, and we get the real shit started. Noted."

Rolf cleared his throat, gathering everyone's attention before the hackers and George began bickering again.

"Luckily for us, the tower is close to our point of entry. Still, we should expect some resistance. They would never leave this place unguarded, that's why we're going in strong and fast. We will use everything in this attack, and we are not expecting any backup from anyone but the hackers."

"Our main goal is to get Eden in," declared Dante. "She must survive and get to the Arcadia Tower alive, at any cost. If she dies before we get into the tower, everything will be lost."

Eden felt her throat clench a little. She wasn't afraid to die, she had decided to participate in this operation fully knowing the risk. The one thing that resonated strangely was hearing Dante talk about it. He had always been so strongly protective of her, the idea she might die being put out there with his voice felt... odd. She took a deep breath.

"...Once I am inside, I will let the hackers attack the Core so more of us can get in. Not only our group but all sides as well. I will basically force it to accept anyone with a SIN, corrupted or not, which is their current first form of defense. No one can get in until I am in, so all groups will have to endure at the border."

"How long will it take?"

"Given that the Edge will be helping me, it should only take a few minutes... I hope. However, after that, the System will try to push us back. There will be no use refusing our SINs once everyone is inside, but they can still target the corrupted SINs, one way or another. That's when the Edge will be the most useful. The hackers will fight back the System's attempts to attack every fighter with a SIN. It's a double-edged sword."

"They already have a limited impact on our SINs anyway," said Circé. "It's not like they wouldn't already have that advantage over us, but Eden's infiltration will give us a way to fight for control of it and confuse them."

"...Can they kill us using just our SINs?" frowned George, suddenly realizing. "...They can't, right?"

Loir suddenly erupted in creepy high-pitched laughter, making him jump in fright.

"...Theoretically, no," sighed Eden. "Most corrupted SINs have a basic line of defense to prevent explosions or something. But, once I get in and add the corrupted SINs to the System so they let us through, they might... try something similar."

"...Similar like what?"

"Deep-fried brains!" exclaimed Loir, a bit too enthusiastically.

Circé and Eden exchanged a grimace while George's expression fell.

"*Zombie, zombie~*"

"It won't get that far," said Eden. "We have to do everything we can to succeed."

Still, she felt a cold chill go down her back. Everything was going to change that day. Either they succeed and change their city for the better, perhaps even freeing everyone from the corrupt System of the Cores, or they fail and the consequences would be unfathomable... The first one would be their death, for sure. Perhaps some would be captured and tortured. She didn't even want to think about it. The Core would never forgive what they were about to do, but they had no choice. It was to preserve life in the Suburbs as they knew it.

"The Zodiac will do what it has to do," said Dante, stepping forward. "It is our way. No one backs down, and no one stops fighting until we've won."

His voice seemed to impact his men considerably, many of them raising their heads, determined looks in their eyes and their chests inflated. Eden suddenly realized she had barely interacted with any of them. She had only knocked out a handful on her first day here... She had only ever seen them as Dante's silent army, but now, his lieutenants had never looked more human. In each of their gazes, she could guess a personal history that had led them here. Through blood and tragedy, each of them had become a fighter, ready to put their life on the line for the Tiger's will.

She took a deep breath. The Zodiac was mostly seen as dangerous gangsters, heartless mafiosos, but right now, dozens of them were about to go to war and risk their lives for hundreds of others. Regardless of their reasons, this proved they had more heart than most people in the Core. She felt a bit more confident in this mission all of a sudden. She was a part of this too. The Edge was like the eleventh Zodiac.

"We strike, and Eden gets in. As soon as we can, we all get in behind her, and we escort her to the tower. She has to get to the top floors, or we are all as good as dead."

All the lieutenants nodded and Loir sighed.

"Kitty Boss, you suck at pep talks. Oh, well. You can't take the stripes off the Kitty."

"...Let's go," said Eden.

They turned around, all the lieutenants leaving the room first. Eden exchanged a look with Jack from across the room, but she didn't have time for goodbyes. He'd be staying here, anyway.

"Bring me a souvenir, my Kitty!" exclaimed Loir, waving his hand happily.

Right after that, Dante guided her outside of the room.

It was a strange ride, completely silent, holding each other's hand. Eden stared at the tall building for as long as she could see it, wondering if she'd sleep there again that evening. The streets of Chicago were strangely solemn and beautiful in the dawn light. The Italians' cars drove past deserted streets until they stopped in front of dozens of scooters and bikes, and even a tank parked in the middle of the street. Everyone was heavily armed with different models, their oxygen or gas masks on, making a strange assortment of people ready for an apocalypse.

"Good morning," smiled Thao, standing on the tank, excited. "Are we ready for a war?"

They could already hear the explosions and gunshots from afar. They weren't too far from the northern front. If she looked to her right, Eden could also see the large clouds of smoke in the south as well. Four of the Zodiacs were already fighting against the Core, and they wouldn't stop. They'd keep fighting and taking those walls and bridges down until she let them inside. Determined, her heart beating fast, she turned to Thao and nodded.

"Let's go."

"Yahoo!" exclaimed the Rat, shouting at her men. "Let's get going, boys! Turn this big boy around, we're going to wake this fucking Core with a bang!"

Eden was about to step away when Dante grabbed her wrist and lifted his mask to put a quick kiss on her lips.

"...Stay alive."

"You too," she muttered.

She put another kiss on his lips, and they put their masks on before walking together, getting to the point of attack. They were incredibly close to the border. Soon enough, the walls of the Core appeared in front of them. Large, tall, and wide walls of concrete, covered in tags, with heavy barricades in front of the entrance they were targeting, the Bryne West Door.

"Pan," she called out, sure he'd respond.

"...Good morning, Eden. See you soon."

# CHAPTER THIRTY-FIVE

"Get ready!" shouted Thao. "We're taking this door down, and hell's about to break loose right after, people!"

All the fighters were prepared, carrying their firearms and ready to shoot. The tank slowly moved up to the door, positioning its cannon. The wall of concrete was built over a former highway and was much thicker than they could see. One blow wouldn't be enough to take it down, but their goal was to force their way in as fast as possible. Because only Eden could get in, it didn't matter if it wasn't large enough for all the Zodiacs' men. Thao would probably enlarge it later. For now, Eden's only objective was to be ready to get in.

She found refuge behind the closest building, protecting her ears, Dante next to her with a gun in each hand. They all waited, and the tank's first blow resonated a few seconds later. An incredible cloud of smoke appeared, meaning at least a portion of the concrete had been hit. They probably hadn't succeeded in making an opening in one shot, but now, the Core was aware something was happening on this side too. It was beginning.

"Edge, update me on your position," she said.

"Anubis here. The fight's raging here; they've deployed assassination drones, fighting bots, and automated weapons from the wall. We're busy taking those over. Our radars have detected human fighters behind the doors, but they aren't opening it yet."

"Gluttony here! We haven't breached yet, but the casualties are increasing! We're closer to forcing our way in, and they've begun sending human soldiers already!"

"Pride here. Trying to keep up with that damn crazy Warlock, but we're intensifying the hacks on the Core. They'll notice it's more than the usually isolated attacks soon. We've got about fifteen—no, twenty Dive Hackers in already."

They all sounded busy and focused, but at least, so far, things were going more or less as planned. The fact that the Core had sent human soldiers to the south to face the Dragon and the Eagle meant they were overwhelmed already. If they could, they would have sent only their military robots, drones, and androids to deal with the attack rather than risking some of their citizens' lives. Eden even doubted those soldiers were really citizens; perhaps they were more like prisoners used for this purpose or something. She couldn't remember any citizen being involved in law enforcement in the Core...

Another detonation indicated the tank was still firing at the door.

"Nebty, the evacuations?"

"About eighty percent already, but some idiots are refusing to move. Lecky and A. are on it though. Focus on your side, Ghost, you're going to be the busy one in a minute..."

Another blow seemed to indicate she was right. Eden heard Thao shouting orders from far away, and suddenly, a rain of bullets showered them.

"Shit!"

Eden felt Dante's hand suddenly push her against the ground, his body covering her.

"Dante!"

"Don't move!"

The shooting continued, and more screams and gunshots were heard.

"Thao!" Eden shouted despite the deafening uproar.

"Drones!" the Rat hissed back, probably hiding too. "The fucking murder drones are here already!"

"Greed, Pride, get those bastards down!" she roared.

"On it."

Soon after, the gunshots lessened, and Eden heard several crashes. She and Dante moved at the same time, coming out of hiding and pointing their guns toward the sky. The hackers had already lessened the drones by a bunch. In one glimpse, Eden caught sight of at least a dozen of them crashing to the ground, or against the buildings near them, emitting smoke and strange sizzling sounds. The drones still flying looked like gigantic metallic stink bugs, with bodies the shape and size of a large tire, and several cannon legs firing in all directions.

*"Is it a bug? Is it a bat? Nope, it's a bot, bot, a cute little murder bot~"*

Eden shot, ignoring Loir's annoying singing, trying to destroy more of them. The drones were arriving from behind the wall, in ordering ranks, and scattered once they were over the Rat's and the Tiger's men, beginning to shoot randomly. Luckily, after the first wave of fire, the mafiosos were now firing back and shooting those things down before they were able to hit them. The drones were conceived to kill precise targets but were not used to said targets firing back. They had no dodging moves nor defense; two or three good hits were enough to destroy them or at least damage them enough so they would crash. Soon enough, things got back on track, with Thao ordering her men to shoot the doors in the wall again while Dante's men kept firing at the incoming drones. The hackers were also doing their part, taking control of the drones and forcing them to crash or shoot their peers. Their number was the only issue, and more kept coming.

Another blow was fired, this time followed by a loud collapse of the wall. The concrete was starting to suffer from all the damage, and caving in on itself.

"We need a proper opening!" shouted Dante.

"This isn't a precision weapon, in case you hadn't noticed!" Thao retorted, annoyed.

There was hope, though. With so much of the wall blasted, the concrete was collapsing, and they were now starting to see the tips of some of the buildings behind it. The question was, were they going to have to climb over that, or find a way in...

"Loir, does the Map show anywhere that could be easier for us to get through on this side?" frowned Eden.

"Did you forget? The Map isn't working without you, my Kitty!"

"Fucking Pan," she groaned.

"Eden," called out A.'s voice suddenly, "there used to be a large interchange in place of that door, according to the twenty-first-century maps. The bridges' columns should be in reinforced concrete and steel, they might be fine. I'll send you the columns' positions, but it might be worth checking if they didn't withstand the blows."

Eden nodded, and the next second, she felt her SIN react.

"SIN, show me the data received."

Immediately, her view changed to display a filter over what she was seeing. Now, Eden could actually see some three-dimensional representation of what this place used to be. On top of the wall they were now fighting, she could see what used to be a large highway, and a bit on her right, the columns that were supporting the former highway. A. was right. The Core had probably built the wall by simply filling between the raised highway and the one on the ground, but the columns were most likely still there, simply trapped in the construction.

"Thao, try firing a bit more to the right!" Eden shouted, pointing in the direction of the column.

The first shot was made right next to it, and the edge of the already-blown hole was probably almost exposing the column. If they tried blasting a couple more times, it would reveal it...

The Rat nodded and gave orders to her men, the tank's cannon shifting a few inches to the right where Eden had pointed. They resumed blasting shot after shot, and while she did her part shooting at the incoming drones, Eden kept an eye on the growing hole. Soon enough, the columns appeared, damaged but withstanding the blows better than the rest of the wall. Moreover, they were close enough to the door that if Eden left this way, the Core may not notice!

She exchanged a glance with Dante, next to her, who nodded, before pointing his guns toward the sky again.

"The north door has fallen! Ghost, they are sending human soldiers up there too!"

That was good news, but it was also too soon. Even if the doors had fallen, without Eden deactivating the Core's control barrier, no one with a corrupted SIN would be able to step inside. She had to go in first, alone.

"Ghost, they are sending more robots our way!"

She grimaced. The more robots they sent, the more men they would lose on this side. There were perhaps two or three hundred of Thao's and Dante's subordinates, but a lot of them were forced to hide because of the murder drones and the tank's blasts. They were losing time, and there was another issue that would be on the table soon: oxygen. With everyone forced to wear masks, it meant they were using a lot of stocked oxygen, and running around would make them consume more and more. Eden glanced up. The large ventilation fans at the top of the walls were barely damaged at all, and still releasing all sorts of toxic gas and carbon dioxide on their side of the wall.

"...Loir, can we hack the fans?"

"The fans? My Kitty is one hot lady! Let me see..."

"It's not like no one's tried before, Ghost," groaned Pride. "Those things only have a command for the speed force, there's nothing to do! They can't even spin enough to blow the other way!!"

"...Their own circuit means they need to have at least a portion of the physical system here."

"Oh, I like how my Kitty thinks! Get me in, get me in! A lady needs her fan, and I'm about to blow one tornado over the Windy City! Hurricane incoming, you bad bees!"

Eden began to run toward the wall, far enough that the tank's repeated blasts didn't risk harming her. The sounds were deafening and she couldn't see anything farther than an arm's length ahead because of all the dust, but at least she didn't have to worry about breathing in anything bad.

"Eden!" Dante called out as she ran farther away from him.

"Just cover me!"

Whether he agreed or not, Eden kept running, looking for a portion of the collapsed wall she could climb. It was dangerously close to the tank's fire, but she had no choice. They needed to attack the fans to buy some time for everyone and even the odds.

"We can't hack them," protested Greed. "There are over two hundred of those fans all around the Core, and—"

"I'm in!" exclaimed Loir.

"What?"

"You newbies are so narrow-minded! It's like a game of dominoes! One after the other, and boom! Boom! Boom! All down like dominoes!"

"What the heck is that crazy saying?! Even if you're in, we can only move these things side-to-side, or change the rotors' speed!"

"Badabadadadadadadam!" Loir was shouting in their ears, clearly overexcited.

Eden could hear him furiously typing on his keyboard, and his hysterical laughing didn't sound good at all, but one thing she was confident in was his crazy genius. Crazy for sure, but still genius. She finally found a decent enough pathway among the rocks and began climbing, as fast and safely as she could. Each of the tank's blows just a few meters away made every piece of concrete tremble and threaten to collapse around her, but she didn't have time to stop. She was thankful for her boots: the leather and soles were allowing her to grip a bit better against the rock, especially since she didn't have to bother about damaging or tearing them.

"Even if you get there, we can only control thirty of them at best! We can't focus so many hackers on the fans!"

"Greed, Pride, just fucking obey Ghost," said Nebty, "and don't mind Warlock!"

"Get ready to hack," grunted Eden, a bit thankful Nebty spared her the scolding.

She was having trouble breathing, climbing, and watching her surroundings at the same time, but her ascent was quick. She only regretted that the depth of the wall wouldn't allow her to simply cross over. She could climb up thanks to what had already been destroyed, but the hole hadn't pierced through the concrete enough for the other side to appear. Only perhaps a third or half of the wall was blasted apart; there was still a long way to go as Thao's tank kept firing.

"Ghost, Nebty, it's Anubis. They are retiring some of their forces in the north; chances are they are sending them your way!"

Eden grimaced, but that was predictable. Since the army in the north couldn't go in, they were stuck there no matter how much they fought, and with the west side being the closest to the Arcadia Tower, the Core had probably understood this side was going to be more bothersome.

"Sapphire here! We managed to even the odds a little here, but we won't last much longer without reinforcements; we've lost a lot of people! We could use more hackers!"

"Pride, go help the south," grunted Eden.

"Are you sure?"

"I have enough support from Warlock and Greed until I'm in. Focus your team on the south, for now. I'll let you know once we're in!"

"Crash just got into the Dark Reality, Ghost," said Nebty. "Nekhbet will

480

get there at the same time as you!"

"Good," she nodded.

She didn't have much oxygen left, but she was almost there. Suddenly, the tank fired another blast, and everything around Eden shook violently. She screamed involuntarily, grabbed a piece of concrete next to her, and stuck her body against the rocks, waiting for it to pass.

"Thao, for fuck's sake!" shouted Lecky in their ears.

"Once again, not a precision weapon! Stop whining! We're almost there!"

"Yeah, but we're still all dead if she doesn't make it!"

"Ghost, are you alright?" asked A.

"Yeah... Yeah, sorry, it surprised me. I'm almost at the fans. Thao, keep shooting, I'll be fine."

"Don't get yourself killed, Ghost," said Circé. "If you fall from that height..."

Eden rolled her eyes. She had tried not to think about it and not look down, but since she was almost at the top of the wall, she was indeed deadly high already. She forced herself not to look again and resumed her climb.

"Just... try not to shoot too close," she groaned.

"...If you hit near her again, I'm killing you."

"Just you try!"

"Dante, Thao, we really don't have time for this!" protested Lecky. "You can kill each other all you want after we're done, but please cooperate a little bit longer!"

Eden sighed. She couldn't believe they still had the time and air to argue down there. In fact, things were getting much harder for her as she approached the fans. She was closer to all those toxic gasses, and she began coughing despite her mask, which was having trouble filtering so much.

"Eden, you okay?" asked Dante.

"I'm going to have to jump right after Loir takes control. Circé, can you find me a way down that won't kill me?"

"...I may have an idea. Give me a minute!"

"...No problem," sighed Eden.

She still had at least that much time before reaching the top. With each of the tank's blasts, of which Thao was making an effort to not shoot too close to her, everything under her was on the brink of collapse, and twice, Eden had to hold on to the column itself. Finally, though, she reached the loud fans. They looked like gigantic fans with grids in front of them, but they were obviously controlled by advanced technology. Using the grid to hold on, Eden looked around for anything that could have been part of the System.

"Got it!" she exclaimed. "Loir, Crash, Greed, get ready, I'm opening this one up to hack!"

"Yahoo! Geronimo!"

She found one of the panels hiding several cables and took out a little device hidden in her leg. She had several of these, what Loir called his "little army." They were like digital keys that acted as beacons for the hacker to find and gain access through. She planted it, and right away, the little device began beeping. Loir was probably getting a similar signal on his computers, showing him a little back door into the closed circuit of the fans.

"Found you! Come here, little one!"

"Shit, that's a huge one," groaned Crash.

"See?" sighed Greed. "It's going to take us hours to... Wha-... What the fuck is that thing?!"

"Hey, hey, hey!" shouted Crash. "You can't plant a fucking cyber bomb while I'm in! Hey!"

Crash's voice stopped abruptly, making Eden concerned. Loir wouldn't really kill a Dive Hacker, would he? His hysterical laugh made her actually worry for the first time, and Greed had gone silent too.

"This fucker..." Greed's voice finally muttered. "He completely wiped the initial coding for that program! There's... pretty much nothing left!"

"No, there's the base one," sighed Crash. "Shit, I really thought he was going to wipe me too... He nearly blasted all the controls here. I didn't even know you could blast this many at once..."

"My baby!" squealed Loir. "Who's a good boy? Who's Daddy's favorite cyber bomb? Look at that! It looks like a mall spring cleaning after a Black Friday during a pandemic! Now, now, now, let's make a blast!"

"What the fuck is he gonna do now...?" muttered Greed, worried.

Eden was worried too. It was never good when Loir didn't let them know his intentions in advance, especially with no one to watch him. She could hear him type a new code, and all the fans suddenly spun on their own, the rotors working even faster. In a matter of seconds, the wind picked up, making her worry.

"Loir... Loir, I'm still up here!"

"*I believe I can fly~*" he was singing. "*My Kitty can touch the sky~*"

The fans spun, faster and faster. Not only that, but Loir was positioning them so all the fans were facing one another, not toward the Core or the Suburbs. She couldn't understand what he was doing. Now the gas was being released on both sides!

"Loir!"

"Eden, get ready to jump!" Circé's voice said.

"What?"

Eden panicked. She had no idea why Circé was telling her to jump, but she couldn't stay there. The fans were spinning like crazy, completely out of control, and as they were blowing against one another, the pressure was getting too strong in her direction. The gas wasn't the issue now; at this rate, she was going to be blown away!

"Now! Jump!"

Eden obeyed without a second thought, one second before her fingers couldn't hold on anymore. She jumped, praying she wasn't going to meet the hard ground far below. To her surprise, she landed much sooner than anticipated, on something unstable too. She looked down. Drones! They had taken control of two drones to catch her. The flying robots quickly took her farther away from the fans, and soon enough, she was able to jump to the ground, rolling down to safety. Eden raised her head, large gusts of wind still hitting her and everyone near the wall, but just then, they all heard a terrible ruckus. Two of the fans had just blown one another off of their bases, hitting each other and the ones next to them. Eden went white.

"Everybody, take cover!"

"Yahoo! Dominoes, bitches!"

There was no domino effect. Instead, the fans began exploding against one another, blowing large pieces of metal on all sides, causing immense damage to the wall and also to any building around. It rained debris on both sides, causing chaos on the ground, and everybody ran to take cover. A large piece of rotor brutally stabbed deep into the concrete, steps away from a panicked Eden. She rolled down again, taking cover under the drones, waiting for the rain of debris to stop. It lasted a while, and even after, nothing and nobody dared to move.

"He's insane," muttered Greed after a long silence. "He's... really, really insane."

"...I-I swear I thought they would fall like dominoes!" squealed Loir.

"Warlock, I'm blowing your fucking brains out the minute I'm back," groaned Circé.

"...Everyone okay over there?" asked Nebty.

"We lost some men," groaned Thao, "but I can't tell if it's from that crazy guy's actions or the drones... What a fucking mess..."

While everyone else updated Nebty on the situation, Eden let out a long sigh. She heard steps approach her, and a hand appeared to help her stand back up. Dante checked her out from head to toe, wiping some of the dust off her.

"...You alright?" he sighed.

Eden nodded.

"Seems like it..."

Everyone around them was doing the same, cautiously standing up or coming out of their hideouts. The explosions had sent dust flying everywhere, and now, all of the buildings were in shades of gray, covered in dust, blown asphalt, or blood. It looked like a war had just happened there, and that wasn't too far from the truth. Eden could feel a bitter taste on her tongue even with the mask still on.

"Guys, I think there's good news," said Circé, from somewhere behind them. "Look at the wall..."

The damages were considerable.

Because its structure had been fractured from the top, large portions of the wall had collapsed on themselves. As far as Eden could see, the wall had substantial sections missing everywhere. Mostly at the top, but it was still a huge improvement from what they had been trying to do. Thao's tank resumed with a few blows, and it was clear the wall was ready to collapse completely. It was only a matter of minutes now.

"The air quality is increasing," chuckled Nebty. "Looks like he blew away the toxic gas."

In fact, they could almost see that with their own eyes. Along with the dust, the thick gray mist was slowly disappearing, and above, the sky looked a bit clearer too. Had the fans provoked enough wind to clear out some of the gas? Eden was a bit relieved that Loir's crazy action hadn't only triggered bad news. She looked around, seeing some of the mafiosos taking off their masks to check the air, almost surprised to be able to breathe normally. In the sky, no more drones were coming either. The last ones that the explosions hadn't wrecked were quickly taken down by the hackers or the mafiosos, clearing the sky of any enemy drones.

"...Can you give us a warning next time crazy prepares something like that?" grunted Tanya's voice in their ears.

"I don't think that was anything remotely planned," sighed Nebty. "At least, it looks like it did help us a little. Their ventilation's destruction will keep the Core agitated for a little while; they need to purify their air and they can't just sweep it our way anymore. It's our chance. Rat?"

"We're almost in!" shouted Thao.

That was the truth. With a bit of excitement in her stomach, Eden could see the tunnel the tank's blows had dug, deep in the concrete; a hole to the other side would probably be appearing soon. More importantly for her, the part under the columns was now revealing several entries. If she climbed up and down again, she could definitely find a path to the other side somehow. As long as no one noticed, she could finally cross over. Eden turned to Dante again, who had his eyes riveted on the column, looking agitated.

"I won't be long," she promised.

"No. I'll be the one to find you soon."

Eden smiled and took off her mask. Indeed, they could breathe normally now. The air was still filled with dust, but it wasn't as bad as the toxic gas. Dante removed his too and immediately leaned in for a quick kiss. It probably wasn't their best, with their dry lips and a strange taste in between, but they needed a goodbye before parting, even if it was just for a short while. Eden smiled at him.

"...I want to show you," she muttered.

"What?"

"Who Ghost is."

Eden stepped back, still holding his hand, and deactivated her SIN manually. She turned the other one on, the one with Ghost's encoding. Her birth SIN. Slowly, her appearance changed, grabbing not only Dante's attention but that of everyone around who could witness it. Just like Circé had seen before, Eden's long blonde hair turned into a straight bob of extremely pale pastel pink hair, and her face became slimmer. Her hazel eyes turned to a dark golden brown, her nose a bit straighter, her lips fuller, and her cheekbones a bit more angular too. Her chin was more of a V shape, and her whole body appeared a bit leaner, longer. She sighed, looking down at her perfect hands and nails.

"...Holy shit," someone muttered.

"Is that the genetic encoding of the Core?" asked Greed. "That's... amazing. Creepy as fuck, but fucking amazing."

"Greed, show some respect," retorted Nebty. "You guys have different appearances on the Dark Web too."

"Yeah, but we can't take it to the real world!"

"It's not comfortable," said Eden, "and it's not... me. It's what the Core would have made me into if I had grown up there."

She was a bit worried about Dante's reaction, for some reason. For years, she had avoided using this appearance. It screamed "Core" so much, she would have stood out like a sore thumb in the Suburbs. Eden didn't like it, so she left it exactly as it was and only used that appearance in the Dark Reality for hacking purposes. She had never had any use for it in the real world until now.

She looked up at him, watching for his reaction, but it hadn't changed much. Instead, he was simply staring, as if looking for clues of the real Eden in this new appearance of hers. The dust still on her face and the thin cuts she had received from her earlier fall and rolling on the ground were still there, but everything underneath was a bit different. Her skin had even gone a bit paler, with no sign of imperfection anymore, not even the very thin and almost imperceptible freckles previously on her nose. Everything was lean, smooth, and too perfect. It wasn't Eden, indeed. A smile appeared on his lips, and he took the tips of her light pink hair between his fingers.

"Interesting," he muttered.

"You don't hate it?"

"No. But I prefer the other you."

Eden smiled. She would have been a bit disappointed if Dante had said anything to mean he preferred this appearance rather than her more real, imperfect self. He caressed her chin briefly.

"Get it done soon," he muttered. "I want my Eden back."

"I'll be quick," she nodded.

She put another kiss on his lips, and stepped back, their hands parting last.

Eden ran toward the wall, cautious of Thao's continuous blows on the side. Now, that part has almost completely collapsed. Even if there was a lot to climb over and down from, she was confident she'd get to the other side. Without looking back, Eden, as Ghost, quickly started climbing, twice as cautious about where she could grip onto. She didn't want the disagreeable experience of falling off again, and this time, she really had to be quick. The Core might not be able to notice her SIN, but anyone could spot her with their bare eyes now that the wall was almost completely down.

Somewhere behind and below her, the fight resumed. More drones had appeared over the wall, and Thao was close to blowing the entrance finally.

"Everyone make sure to keep them busy!" shouted Circé. "They must not notice her!"

Eden tried to stick as close to the rocks as possible, and under some when she could find small spots that partially hid her. She wasn't sure what kind of cameras the drones had to target people, but she didn't want to be caught by them; their lenses would definitely be able to recognize a human moving around. Thankfully, everyone on the ground was already keeping those things busy, hence the flying machines didn't have much time to figure out what she was doing. Moreover, the hackers were probably making sure to block the view or something with the drones they took control of. Eden was cautious not to talk and made as little noise as possible, but she was listening to everything that was going on.

"Anubis here, they are sending more men to our side again, and they have larger weapons too! I don't think they appreciated you blowing up their fans."

"Gluttony here. More of the Dragon's men have arrived, so we're doing alright. One of my teams has found a more efficient way to hack their battle bots, I'm sharing it now."

"Thanks, Gluttony," said Nebty. "I want everyone keeping those bastards as busy as possible and away from Ghost. Time to make some noise in the Dark Reality too. Someone get me a digital bomb on one of their servers, it will keep them busy until she can get more of us in!"

"It's Lecky. We're almost done evacuating, everyone is fine so far. The air pollution made it worse for a while, but it looks like it's dropping on our end too."

"Pride here. I confirm: the overall air purity is skyrocketing as we speak. The radars are showing it's basically evening out in both the Core and the Suburbs. They probably wanted the purest for themselves, but it's bearable for both sides this way."

"Haughty bastards..."

"...Any news from Prometheus yet?" asked A.

"He said he'd appear when he could to avoid raising suspicions."

"If we're talking about suspicions, I'm pretty sure Warlock made enough noise as it is... Aren't they going to pick up on his signature device?"

"Greed's right. Warlock, you should lay low for a while. Ghost doesn't need you just yet."

"What?" squealed Loir. "You're asking me to miss the action while my Kitties are running around? No way!"

"You just wrecked their ventilation system, they'll try to hunt you down. You should go offline for a while before the Core's people try to find you."

"They can go lick a battery's butt! I'm not hiding! This Warlock won't hide!"

Eden chuckled. It was the first time she had ever heard him say something like that...

"...Where in the world did you hear an expression like that?" sighed Circé.

"What? It's an expression? I just thought it had a funny taste when I tried!"

"So that's where you lost your last brain cells..."

Ignoring their bickering, Eden continued her climb as carefully and fast as she could. She could tell she was fairly high now, and she could see almost all of the Chicago skyline from where she was. On her right, there were still the columns from the former crossroad, holding strong despite all the explosions. A kind of platform above was probably the remnant of the former road's edge, and Eden did her best to stay hidden under that as she climbed over more of the wall. It was incredibly rough and unstable under her feet, and if it wasn't for her metal legs, she would have been covered in bruises already. Several times, she scratched her hands and arms, but it wasn't too bad. She focused on not falling and not stopping. Despite his jokes, Loir might really be in danger if the Core wanted revenge for their fans' destruction, and everyone was still fighting to buy her time. The pressure was good motivation to keep going despite the pain.

Soon enough, the rocks under her began crumbling. It was getting a bit more slippery, but Eden was more worried about how steep it would be on the other side of the wall, which should have certainly withstood most of the explosions.

Indeed, she reached the top of the wall, and despite having a large portion blown off, it was still far too high for her to simply jump. One, she would definitely be noticed, and two, she didn't want to risk breaking her neck. Eden looked to the side, considering her options. Unlike the Suburbs' side, a portion of the former highway that made up the other part of the crossroad was still there. It was at her height and looked to be going directly into the Core.

"...Nekhbet, I can't jump down. There's another highway next to me. ... Can I take this road?"

"Kitty! How dare you ask another Back Hacker?!"

"You should be laying low for a while and busy covering your tracks after that show," she sighed.

"Technically, you could, but you'll be completely exposed. It's the end of the former Interstate 290; it's closed to vehicles but it should still go as far as past the river. Anyone in the buildings around will be able to see you, though... Oh, no, wait. It goes under a building. If you make a run for it, you can probably hide and get down there. The building stops... bingo, right before the river. You should be able to reach the emergency stairs, and you'll be exposed for less than a minute."

"Perfect."

"Kitty!"

"Warlock, shut it, we said!"

Eden quickly climbed, and just as he'd said, found herself on a large, deserted highway. She looked back, impressed by the view of the Suburbs. She looked ahead again, the sunrise's colors appearing behind the buildings. She began running right away, glad that her legs didn't feel the fatigue.

"Our contact should be ready for you," said A. "Do you remember the address?"

"Don't worry, I'll find it," she answered in one breath.

It was a quick run, but she went as fast as she could, aware anyone spotting a human running on the deserted highway could signal her presence at any moment to the Core. If she was hunted from the get-go, it might jeopardize the whole operation... It took her less than a minute to reach the building and climb to the pedestrian walkway. There, a few steps away from the entrance, she caught her breath. She could hear the tank still blasting from the other side, and the sounds of many people fighting and shooting. They wouldn't stop and wouldn't be able to move until she actually got inside.

Just as she resumed walking, trying to find the door for an emergency exit, Eden heard something very loud above her head. By reflex, she retreated closer to the wall, checking both sides, and ran to hide behind a pillar when she spotted movement on the left. She crouched down, making herself as small as possible while they came through. Her heart was beating fast, but the vehicles were loud enough to cover everything.

"...Circé, you hear that?"

"Fuck. Is that an Overcraft?"

"Two," Eden corrected her. "They're coming your way."

"Shit! Warlock, forget about standing back, we're going to need you now! Everyone get ready! Overcrafts incoming!"

"We got one coming in the north too!" shouted Mage.

"Two in the south!"

Eden's heartbeat accelerated. Overcrafts meant more weapons, possibly more of the Core's soldiers too. She needed to hurry. As soon as she was sure the two vehicles had left her tunnel, she ran, quickly spotting an emergency exit. It hadn't been used in a while and she had to force it open, but it eventually broke under her kicks and she ran down the dusty stairs. Now, she needed to find a computer, or any sort of recent technology, to hack the Core from. She knew nothing like that would be easy to find here, which is why she needed to reach the safehouse first.

She finally reached the ground floor, still nervous but feeling safer now. The building looked almost completely abandoned, and it was early, so she was confident no one would have seen her; chances were too low. Moreover, if she had been spotted, she would know soon enough... She left the building, stepping onto open ground again, and for a second, she was blinded.

The first rays of sunlight streamed between the buildings as if to intensify this scene. She was back in the Chicago Core. She looked around, suddenly feeling very small, like that child years ago. The place was beautiful. The long paths of green grass on each side of the river, with a few wildflowers here and there, and trees bearing fresh fruit. Beyond the river were beautiful houses and white buildings without a speck of dust, with their superb lines and large windows. There were bright colors on the roofs, beautiful gardens behind small white fences, and the streets were impeccably clean. The light gray asphalt looked like it had been laid the previous day. She swallowed her saliva, feeling a bit strange. This place was so beautiful, and... peaceful. There were sounds of birds, a few morning radios streaming through the windows, and the gentle whirring of a few electric cars passing by.

She stepped on the grass, from the side of the river, staring at the view on the other side, feeling as if everything before had just been a strange dream. She couldn't hear any explosions, any sounds of fighting. Eden felt strange, really strange. She looked down at her dirty boots on the clean soil. The leather was ripped in so many places, the soles still had a few rocks caught in them. Eden took them off and put her feet down on the grass. She regretted not being able to feel it. After hesitating, she crouched down and laid her hand flat in the grass.

"...Eden."

Dante's voice brought her back to reality.

She glanced up and was met with the eyes of a stranger, a young woman who was running along the river in a white ensemble. A quick look at Eden, and she smiled at her, continuing on her way. Eden looked down. She must have looked as ragged as her boots after climbing. She waited until the jogging woman was far enough, and rushed to the turquoise-blue river, quickly washing her face and trying to get some dust off her clothes. She'd be spotted in no time if she was this dirty.

Once she was ready, a bit wet but ready, she stood back up and got back on the bridge, walking quickly. She couldn't hear the fight, but she could hear the voices of all the fighters still caught in it. Eden had to act quickly and bring the fight here...

# CHAPTER THIRTY-SIX

"...Has no one noticed you yet?"

"What are you whispering for, Circé?" sighed Eden. "...And I've only taken a few steps inside. It's not like alarms are going to start ringing on all sides."

"They would have already if it was anyone else," scoffed Nebty. "The barrier is still up. The fact that it hasn't gone off yet or that you aren't circled by dozens of murder bots already is enough proof you're still considered one of their citizens."

"My SIN is just coded that way. It's not like I really belong to this place."

"I didn't mean that in a bad way, Ghost, relax. That's exactly what we wanted, remember? Don't worry. We know which side you're on..."

Eden let out a long sigh. She wouldn't have gotten so defensive, usually, but she really was feeling out of place here, like a fish out of her pond. This was a beautiful but scary aquarium, in a way. As she kept walking, trying to act calm but moving fast, she couldn't help but feel like she was sticking out. She was worried about anyone she crossed paths with, even as they smiled at her. Perfect, pearl-white smiles with nothing out of place. Their hair and eyes were of all sorts of beautiful colors and shades, even the strangest ones, while their skin was precisely tanned to a specific shade. There wasn't a single hair out of place, not a bead of sweat, and Eden couldn't smell anything either. There was no smell. Perhaps she was too used to the Suburbs; over there, the air was always filled with smells of food, gas, human body odors, and so many things she both loved and hated.

Here, everything was... sterile. The air was so pure, she almost felt like she was breathing in an icy mist. Even while wearing her oxygen mask, she had never experienced such a strange thing. Eden kept trying to act normally while thinking how everything was different from what she knew. She walked along large, empty, yet pretty roads that were cleaner than Dante's place. Her boots felt much dirtier than the ground she was stepping on.

"You're almost there," said A. "Just a few more streets."

"I'm fine," muttered Eden.

She was feeling nervous, but if no one had noticed her presence or manifested any discomfort with her so far, she doubted any citizen of the Core would hold her back now. Because it was still early, she was barely crossing paths with anyone, except for a few morning runners, people with perfectly groomed dogs, and those who seemed to be headed somewhere, probably work. If anyone did glance at her, she was usually greeted with a smile, a word or two, and then they went on their way. Eden was surprised. Was her appearance really doing the trick, or were those people so worry-free that they couldn't imagine someone from the Suburbs being there? It was pretty disturbing. She kept walking, unable to stop looking all around her at the place she had been born in. Chrome white buildings with large windows, behind which she could see gorgeous living spaces, tons of green plants, and people exercising or having breakfast with their families. Everything was so quiet, so safe. So perfect, and yet so... empty. Eden wouldn't have been able to explain it, but she wasn't even feeling jealous of this. Those lives almost looked as if they were on display, too perfect to be true. Empty. There was no odor, no sound. No warmth at all...

"I'm almost there," she muttered for those who listened.

As opposed to what she was presently seeing, she could hear the ongoing fights happening on the other side of the wall. It was strange that only she could hear it. Because her SIN was still linked to everyone else's fights, she felt like she was still in the middle of the fight, gleaning information from all sides and hoping they'd make it. She accelerated a bit. The hackers were so busy, they barely talked anymore, while those on the ground and fighting against the Core's bots and human soldiers were continuously grunting and shouting. At least, it meant they were still alive. Fighting and overwhelmed, but alive...

Eden took a new right turn, trying to figure out the location of the address she had been given. She had seen it on a map and knew how to find the names of the streets, but she was worried she'd miss it or get the wrong place, as everything looked so alike. She was growing more nervous the longer she was here, and she was a bit doubtful about the place she was going, too. Allies within the Core? She didn't want to not trust A. and his network, but she still had her doubts.

Finally, Eden reached the place. Surprisingly, it was a simple house like most of the one or two-story buildings. A large, white square with a green roof, a few plants, and even a little garden. Eden stood at the entrance, hesitating for a second. All the windows had white curtains, so she had absolutely no idea what was going on behind them. The only clue about her secret ally was the perfectly kept vegetable garden and flowers.

She pressed the doorbell, her heart beating fast. What should she do if something went wrong? What if the information she had was false, or this was a trap? Or what if the person inside didn't recognize her?

To her surprise, a little door in the fence opened right away, and Eden walked into the garden. On the other side, a young woman opened the door to the house, greeting Eden.

"Good morning," she said with a large smile as if they were long-time friends. "Come in! You must be hungry, breakfast is ready."

"Good morning..."

This whole interaction felt incredibly odd, but Eden walked in quickly, aware there might be eyes watching. The young woman let her in, and sure enough, she quickly glanced left and right outside before closing the door behind them. She let out a faint sigh of relief after that, her orange irises going to Eden. She was wearing a turquoise sports ensemble, matching shoes, and her black hair was in a high ponytail as if she had just been ready to leave for a workout.

"Are you Eden?" she asked.

"Yes."

"Father is waiting for you. Come."

Her father? Eden nodded and followed the woman through the house. This place was styled differently from what Eden would expect all the houses to be. Despite its exterior, the interior was clearly decorated in an older fashion, as if everything was vintage or taken from an old movie. There was a green, leather sofa, some ugly carpets, very colorful decorations on the walls, an old retro TV, a gramophone, and just a few plants. Something about this place strangely put Eden at ease. She realized it was because the overall atmosphere was similar to Jack's bar... It had a familiar smell too.

"Father! Your guest is here!"

"Oh, is she?"

The voice coming from upstairs surprised Eden. She slowly watched him come down the stairs, completely stunned. No wonder she recognized the smells in this place!

"Mr. Charles?" she mumbled. "How...?"

"Good morning, dear," said the older man.

He smiled at her, but Eden was speechless. Her customer from the bar! How was Mr. Charles the contact? She hadn't imagined this scenario at all.

"Thank you, darling," he said to his daughter. "I'll take care of my guest now."

"Alright, I'm going for my run then! See you later!"

The young woman left, leaving the two of them there. Mr. Charles chuckled.

"She's a good girl," he said, "but she doesn't like to get involved in my business, which is a good thing... She's too much like her peers here."

"I don't understand. You're... the Edge's contact?"

"Oh, I would be careful with the words you use in here, dear."

The man nodded, and slowly moved around the apartment, going to what seemed to be a kitchen with little appliances. He started a coffee machine that immediately produced a rich, golden-brown coffee in two glass cups, and pushed a few buttons on another machine Eden didn't know.

"How do you like your eggs, dear?"

"I don't know..."

Eden couldn't remember ever having eggs before. Mr. Charles chuckled.

"Then I'll just do the same as mine."

"Mr. Charles, I didn't come here for breakfast. I need to access the Co–I mean, I need to do what I came for quickly."

"I know, dear, but it's upstairs and it will probably take a little while. Oh, you can go while I finish preparing breakfast. An old man has his habits, you see. I need a good organic breakfast and my coffee to function!"

Eden frowned, but without waiting any longer, she went upstairs. The upper floor was a bit different; there was still this vintage home decor, but there was also a large desk with plenty of technology on it. A couple of computers were already running, and Eden immediately recognized the programming language on it. She rushed to the keyboards and cables, trying to figure out how to use this model she's never seen before.

"Loir, I'm here. I have the technology in front of me. What do I do?"

"Oh, it's playtime!"

The Back Hacker guided her for a few minutes on how to use this piece of equipment she was unfamiliar with. Loir was having fun like a collector finding a rare piece of a collection, and from time to time, he'd throw in a direction for her, so Eden had to keep up with his endless rambling without interrupting him.

"They don't make such beauties like this anymore! Look at that definition! It might not have been perfect, but it had its charm! Can you believe they only had two-dimensional screens back then? Plus, those old ladies are a bit grumpy, but once you get to know them, they are so easy to use! Nowadays, computers are so heavily programmed they are only extremely good for the simplest tasks! That beauty there can hold her race! Here, select the fourth line of code and implement the one I just sent you. Ah, the old ones are the best. They know the road, are reliable, and have none of that wretched programmed obsolescence! It's like a fancy one with schizophrenia packed in it! I'd rather stick to my Rolls Royce! Oh, there, get ready for the nasty one... Yes, good timing! Oh, my gorgeous, you and I are going to play... Alright, I call her Marilyn! And Marilyn's mine now!"

493

"What next?" frowned Eden, seeing a charging bar on the screen.

"I need a few minutes to get my Marilyn up to date with my genius. She can handle it but it's going to take a few minutes! If you need to go to the loo, go now!"

Eden rolled her eyes. He really didn't care about how many people were listening to them... She sighed but stepped away from the newly-named computer Marilyn. Judging by how fast it was loading, she did have a few minutes. Eden decided to go back downstairs and see if there was time for that breakfast after all. She had done quite a lot of physical exercise that morning, and even if she was used to ignoring her hunger cues, it was harder to resist that smell coming from below...

"A.," she called out while going down, "I got in. Warlock's working on it."

"We know. Good job, but enjoy that break. After that, things will get rough..."

Eden thought so too.

"I'll cut off the feed for now," she said. "Just in case someone tries to patch in. Bring me back as soon as Warlock's ready, or if there's anything."

"Sure."

"...Dante? Are you alright?"

"Not really. Missing my wife and there isn't enough to keep myself busy with..."

Eden chuckled. His wife... With everything that had happened so far, she had forgotten they got married just this morning. In fact, so much had happened already that it didn't feel like it was only a short while ago.

"Well, we'd better catch up soon then," she smiled.

"Kitties flirting on the line! I repeat, Kitties flirting on the line!"

"SIN, cut off my communications," groaned Eden.

She arrived in the kitchen, a bit annoyed by Loir. She knew the communications weren't meant for this, but she couldn't help but miss Dante too. For once, she was being honest about her feelings, but it just happened to not be the right time or place for it...

To her surprise, Mr. Charles really had prepared breakfast, and quite an impressive one too. There was a full plate by the time she reached the table, even coffee and fruit juice. She had rarely seen such a pretty-looking breakfast. The older man smiled and pulled her chair out for her.

"An old man likes his habits," he said as she walked up. "I love a good breakfast to start the day. Especially ahead of an important battle."

Eden cautiously sat, her eyes going down to the breakfast and her stomach growled, expressing its appetite. Still, she had many questions in mind that wouldn't go away. She watched Mr. Charles sit on the other side and very gracefully sip his coffee. He was dressed almost the same as she had always seen him, with an outdated but elegant brown suit, except that his jacket was put aside on the couch, and she could see his suspenders.

"Mr. Charles... I don't understand," she muttered. "All this time?"

"Oh, of course! You'd be surprised how many of us remember the good times... and miss them. Of course, there is a lot of politics involved, things an old man like me should have retired from a while ago, but it's also the burden of a soldier to show up in times of war, isn't it?"

He chuckled and took his fork, opening up the egg. Eden was shocked at the gorgeous orange color hidden inside, and her stomach couldn't hold it anymore. She did the same, mimicking Mr. Charles and eating her eggs benedict with delight. Any other time, she would have eaten silently and all in one go, but the questions were too many. She ate as quickly as she could while spacing her sentences correctly so as not to speak with a full mouth.

"You were a... a soldier?"

"Oh, I speak figuratively, dear. Well, mostly. I once belonged to an intelligence agency, although I was much more often behind a desk than on the field. Each army needs their support like you need your partner, don't you, dear? How can one go into battle without backup?! There used to be many agencies. Data, human behavior, systems, numbers, populations, communication, military, anything that could be analyzed, we did. Naturally, we were often contacted to work for bigger corporations, including the Core itself."

He drank a bit of his fruit juice, delicately tapped his lips with his napkin, and grabbed his fork again. In front of his impeccable table manners, Eden felt like a starved barbarian, but he was kind not to say anything about it while she filled her mouth with as much food as she could. She had no idea how everything on this plate could be so pretty and so good, while she had no idea what most of it was. She could recognize the hash browns and beans, but there were also unidentified dark-red little slices, and green little tree-shaped vegetables.

"So how did you... shift to the other side?" Eden asked, careful about her words.

"Knowledge! One of the most secret but deadly weapons that came into my hands was information. No matter how hard a corporation or government tries to conceal it, information remains the most valuable asset of all. At least, in the right hands. I quickly came across some things that were meant to be forgotten and buried and would have cost me my neck if others knew... It also opened my eyes to the heavy price we've paid to live the life we are living now."

Mr. Charles sighed and stopped eating for a short while, taking his cup of coffee again.

"I am blessed to have raised my children in such a perfect place, Eden. My daughter has never eaten as you do now because she has no idea what it's like on the other side. No idea."

Eden slowed her chewing a bit, embarrassed. Was she really eating in such an unrestrained way? She was hungry for sure, but she was also just trying to

495

eat it all quickly before Loir's update was done... Mr. Charles chuckled, visibly amused by her confusion.

"It is quite alright. It makes me happy that I was able to help you a bit more..."

"Mr. Charles... Is it a coincidence that you were... my customer, on the other side?" Eden finally asked.

"Of course not," he chuckled. "There is no such thing as a coincidence, dear. No, I knew... about a lot of things. Your father was a complicated man, but he was my friend."

"...You knew my dad?"

"I sure did! Who do you think helped me survive and live until I reached this age, knowing what I know? I wouldn't be here if it wasn't for him, dear. Your father was many things, including a genius and a complicated man. But before anything, I believe he was a hero."

Eden choked up at those words. She hadn't even realized how hearing about her unknown father would make her react until she felt that tight knot in her throat. She tried to cough it up, grabbing her cup of fruit juice to drink it down, but the tears were already forming in her eyes.

"That's right, young lady," Mr. Charles smiled. "Your father was the bravest man I ever met..."

"I never got to meet him," muttered Eden.

Mr. Charles suddenly stood up and grabbed something out of his pocket. He handed a little picture to a confused Eden. It was a simple, aged square of paper, its colors having faded quite a bit.

"I know they don't print much of those these days, but... I am even more old-fashioned than my years would tell. This is a precious memento... I always keep it with me, no matter how dangerous that could be. I want to remember the man who saved my life."

There were only seven men in the picture. They were all posing in front of the camera, looking a bit tired but happy. They were all wearing shirts and formal outfits, but it looked like they had worn them for a while. The background looked like an office, or perhaps a lab. She couldn't tell, most of the light was on those men and everything behind was a bit dark and too common to spot any details. The seven men were more important in her eyes. She immediately recognized Mr. Charles amongst them; he hadn't changed much, even wearing suspenders. He looked to be in his forties in this picture, and one of the oldest. The man next to him looked about the same age, perhaps a bit older, but his white beard could have misled her. He was the only one barely smiling, his lips slightly outward, but he seemed to be more smiling with his eyes behind his glasses. The other men were in their thirties, and smiling wide, seemingly waving at the camera.

"Who are they...?"

"Those two were my colleagues," said Mr. Charles, pointing his index finger to show her. "They were captured shortly after the launch of the Core, tortured, and probably killed. This one was a bit luckier; he had an accident and died quickly. This one is still alive, I believe. He managed to leave for another Core. This one... He's still working for them."

The only man he hadn't pointed at was the man with the beard. Eden's heart dropped when she realized why this older man seemed familiar. They had the same nose and the same forehead...

"That's right. This is your father. This picture was taken a few years before you were born... before the Chicago Core was finalized and launched. When we were still just regular workers, hoping to protect the interests of our fellow citizens, thinking our ideas were going to change the world... We had just pulled an all-nighter working on a new data-treating system, one of the System's foundations today. Your father was leading the project. An incredibly smart man, he was. Always ahead of everyone. Even the brightest of us."

Eden was barely listening anymore. Her eyes were riveted on that man in the picture. Her father. Her real, biological father she'd never met... She felt a bit strange. Sometimes, she resented that man. He was a stranger to her when he was supposed to have been the most important person, at least for her childhood.

"...Why did he never... see me?" she muttered. "I've... I literally have no recollection of him."

"Oh, he wished he could, dear. But almost as soon as the Core was created, he knew all too well how dangerous that would be, and how they could use you against him. You and your mother. So he made a deal to keep you safe, far from him and from the Core's leaders. As long as he worked for them and had no interaction with you or your mother, you'd be safe. It may be complicated for you to understand, but... those times in which we lived, you couldn't trust anyone. The Core's leaders grew incredibly strong overnight, and everyone became prey in a manhunt. I am one of the few survivors that escaped."

"...Why did they try to kill you if you helped create the Core?"

"Because I knew too much, dear. It's as old as the world; one man can know too many secrets for his own sake! As soon as I realized they'd come for me too, I reached out to your father. He was one of the few they couldn't do without, so he helped me plan my escape. We completely changed my identity and used one of the very few advantages we had over the System to manipulate it to save my life. After that... I hid, for as long as I could, until our mutual friends found me."

"They led the Edge to you..."

"Exactly. Sir Prometheus gave them information about me and let them find me..."

"Wait. ...Prometheus did?"

"Of course. He was also working on the Core with us, for a long time. Although I never personally got to meet him, he was your father's very best assistant. He most likely was hidden for his own safety, which I surely can understand..."

Eden frowned. Hidden from the Core? She had a feeling he had always been within their sights, though. He had mentioned several times himself that he was in the Chicago Core... or was he deliberately working for them, as a double agent? There was still so much mystery about her master who had yet to appear, she was growing nervous. What if he had been caught and this was all a trap? Or if he had been working for the Core all along, merely playing around with her and the Edge?

"Marilyn!" Loir suddenly shouted in her ear. "Welcome to Loir's playground, my beauty baby! We're ready to roll, my Kitty!"

"Sorry," said Eden, standing up and grabbing another bite. "I have to go back upstairs, we're ready."

"Of course, dear. I'll clean this up, don't worry and go!"

Eden smiled and nodded, a bit embarrassed to have to leave in a rush when she had eaten almost all of it so fast, for free, and without helping out in any way. She gave back the picture hurriedly, trying not to think twice about it, and ran back upstairs.

As Loir had said, this old thing was now pretty much up to date, and already seemingly working on its own. She could recognize Loir's characteristic hectic style in the lines of codes that were appearing on the screen.

"Are we there yet?" she asked.

"Almost ready to jump, my Kitty! I hope you're ready for your first thrill ride behind enemy lines!"

"Ghost, we're ready for you," added Nebty. "Prepare yourself, though, this might be quite different from what you usually see. Just stay long enough to get us all in, and get out as soon as you can. They might not be able to find your SIN here, but in the System, you're going to pop up like the biggest anomaly they've seen that's escaping their grid..."

"Crash, Nekhbet?" she called out, getting a bit nervous.

"Ready to Crash the party! I'm almost there!"

"I'm with you guys," added Nekhbet.

Eden nodded and sat in front of the screen, jumping into the code to enter her own, typing fast on the keyboard. Loir was excited, and she could see it. Hacking the Core's System from the inside ought to be the boldest thing they had ever done... and the whole success of this war would depend on it too. If they failed, everyone would stay locked out of the Core, in a war that would go on until they were all suppressed. Plus, all three hackers would be in more danger than usual. They had to make it in and out through the System, and if it found them, they'd simply die right there. Brain dead.

She took a deep breath and relaxed, closing her eyes for a few seconds.

Once Eden opened them again, she was far from Mr. Charles' house. She blinked twice, looking around her cautiously. Loir did mention things would be different, but she had never expected something as simple as a waiting room. The velvet furniture and bottle-green walls with strange paintings all around showed terrible taste. She grimaced slightly, looking around her. There were a lot of other people seated just like her, on a comfy armchair, waiting patiently. Eden counted twenty armchairs, in rows of five, half of which were occupied. Those people looked normal for people from the Core. Her appearance as Ghost wasn't making her stand out in any way, which was a good thing. A lot of them had their eyes on a screen, the only thing to look at in the room. Eden glanced up. It showed numbers... Twenty-four, then twenty-five. Someone in the room stood up and went past a curtain of beads leading to somewhere she couldn't see. Eden hesitated. No one had stopped that person or checked anything, but it didn't mean she wouldn't get checked later. Maybe there was some sort of security behind that curtain... She glanced around, and there was an android on her right, looking at something on a screen. Eden hesitated. She couldn't wait until someone missed their turn, and she didn't have a number! Should she ask anyway? The robot hadn't even seemed to see her arrive. When someone else landed in the waiting room, the android went to them, greeting them by name and giving them their number.

Eden suddenly wondered. If that robot was part of the System, was she invisible to it too? ...It was worth trying. After someone else stood up, she counted to ten, and went after them, walking as naturally as possible. No one in the room reacted, and neither did the android. She walked past the curtain of beads, her heart beating insanely fast. She was so nervous, she could almost feel the sweat from her real body.

"Steady, my Kitty, you're playing in kindergarten right now! You should be fine..."

Despite his words, Eden could tell when Loir was nervous as well. They were both on a different field than their own, like in a foreign land. All their experience would be close to useless here; this wasn't the Dark Reality.

She kept walking down what seemed like a very long corridor. She would have been worried if she hadn't heard noises coming from the end of it. Could it be that easy? Just as she was about to enter, she heard voices on the other side. She tried to listen but quickly realized this corridor was made so she couldn't hear until she was actually at the entrance. She could see, though. It looked like a playroom. A place very loud, with lots of people, movement, and bright lights.

"...Loir," she muttered. "I might need something a bit more dressed up."

"Coming right up!"

Eden took a deep breath and looked down. She was now wearing a short and sexy black dress that hugged her curves, with a decent amount of cleavage and, for once, nothing was too insane about the outfit. She touched her head, and as she suspected, Loir had given her a little black headband with two triangles, probably meant to be cat ears... There was a scarf of soft and thick fur on her right shoulder too, and lace gloves on her hands, everything in a velvety black.

"Let's hope that's fine..."

"Getting kicked out because of the dress code would be a first!" chuckled

Loir.

Eden was still much too nervous to laugh. At least, everything about her should pass as a member of the Core...

Another problem arose just as the previous person left, and she could finally access the end of the corridor instead of walking endlessly. Two real people guarding the entrance. At least, they seemed real. For all she knew, they could have also been bots, but there were few ways to know...

"Loir? Those two..."

"Real people, Kitty. Sorry, hope you practiced your liar game!"

Eden broke out in a cold sweat. This was easily her most nerve-wracking Dive ever, or at least one of the worst she'd ever experienced. She tried not to slow down and walked confidently toward the man and woman at the entrance. The woman had red hair and was wearing a very over-the-top outfit, with lots of colored feathers, beads, and everything that could possibly shine on the fabric. There was so much that Eden's eyes could barely focus on her face. Next to her, the man was wearing a very simple tuxedo, his eyes hidden behind dark glasses.

"Welcome, my dear!" exclaimed the woman loudly. "Welcome to Pleasure Island! We have thirty-three of our fifty entertainment stations currently open for your entertainment, for as long as you want! All currencies are accepted and you can check the exchange rate on your personal assistant! As usual, we will ask you to respect the rules of security and privacy toward the other guests of the Island! Children are forbidden, but as I can see, you are not underage! Do you want to set a limit to your spending on the Island today?"

"N-no," Eden muttered, a bit lost.

"Amazing! Then, as soon as you have linked your money account with us, you will be free to go through!"

Eden panicked. She didn't have any money account they wouldn't pry into and find odd things! She waited for a second, hoping Loir would find a solution for that...

"There we go, perfect!" smiled the woman. "We will put you into the high bidders' category. Please remember to wear a privacy filter if you want to get into the adult pleasure stations, and you can also remove all the ads for the modest sum of five thousand credits for today's visit, or for all your next visits for only..."

Eden got a bit bored as she delivered this speech. She wanted to tell that woman to hurry up, but she was worried she'd do or say something that would give her away, so she remained quiet until the woman finished her speech, asking Eden if she had any questions.

"...Can I bring guests through my account?" Eden asked.

"Of course! Big spenders can have up to five guests allowed after they've spent a minimum of seventy-five thousand credits, and it's an additional five credits per guest after the second! You can go to the bar and ask for the company order, darling. Any other questions?"

"...No, thanks."

"Great, now we will finish the quick security check by analyzing your SIN. ...It seems to be your first connection on Pleasure Island, welcome!"

Eden nodded. This was the moment of truth. This was where they'd know if her SIN and all of her father's hard work to keep her safe would make this whole fight worth it. She glanced back at the corridor behind her. If things went wrong, there would be no use in running back. Everything would be over.

She turned her eyes back to the woman who was standing still, probably waiting for the check on Eden's information.

"...Oh," she said after a while, making Eden jump. "You really are a first-timer! How rare for your age! Most people come here for the first time around their teens!"

"...I don't go out often," Eden muttered.

"Indeed!" laughed the woman. "Let's see. Eden Newman, twenty-three years old, Chicago Core native... Oh, it seems you have extra privacy. Are you military?"

"My family works for the government."

"Oh, they can be so stiff on that, can't they? Well, better for your privacy! ...In any case, I don't see anything off here. Oh, you have a message that's been unread for... uh, almost twenty years, darling. You might want to check on that. You also have a private locker, it's going to be on the second floor, on your right. Anyway, everything is in order for me, Miss Eden. Welcome to Pleasure Island!"

Eden nodded and walked past them. She couldn't believe it had worked so easily. Her SIN was still completely working in the Core's System... Not only that, but she had some stuff left for her?

"Like a kitty in a dog park!" exclaimed Loir. "We're in! Oh, my pretty Marilyn, you did a good job, my pretty!"

"I still can't believe it," muttered Eden.

Now that she had walked past the security, some blurring filter came off, and she realized the room she had been seeing from afar was in fact a very, very large casino. Eden blinked twice, completely overwhelmed by the size of the place. There were money games as far as her eyes could see, and a sea of people playing around. As she looked up, she realized there were many, many floors above. At least a dozen, and a lot of doors with neon signs above. The floor above seemed to be restaurants, or at least she hoped, from the name.

"Wait, people eat in the Dark Reality?" exclaimed Loir.

"Rich people entertainment," scoffed Nebty. "They can trick their senses to believe they are eating, while their body won't take on a pound... Trust me, food isn't the only thing they cheat their brain into thinking they are experiencing for real, and you don't want to know what's behind the other doors."

Eden could easily believe that. Some words above the doors made her want to vomit. People probably came to this virtual paradise to experience what was illegal in the real world... She tried to ignore all of it and hurried to find the closest bar.

"Loir, do I really have that much money? They probably took an entrance fee too. How did you find an account so quickly? Did we hack one?"

"Excuse me!" squealed her partner. "You want to give me extra work? My Kitty married rich, may I remind you! Your hubby's healthy, thick wallet came in handy! There's still a few zeros left too, don't worry! Oh, shall we win it back? I'm very confident in Baccarat!"

Eden stopped and sighed.

"Oh, for the love of... Dante, I'm sorry."

"Don't worry about it. He's right, it's your money and assets now too... former Miss Newman?"

"Sorry to intrude on your chat, but I'm curious about that too," said Circé, sounding out of breath. "...Wasn't that... Pan's last name as well?"

"Eden, why didn't you tell us? What's your relationship to Pan?"

Eden sighed and sat at the bar, grabbing one of the screens used to take orders and quickly started typing to invite her guests and hacker partners.

"I wish I knew as well..."

"That can't be a coincidence," muttered Circé.

"My thoughts exactly," said Nebty, "or perhaps they simply put that name on Eden's SIN to make it easier? It might not be your real last name then. Or even Prometheus'. His whole name sounds more like a hacker's codename, anyway."

"Hey, hey," protested Loir. "You ladies get out of my Kitty's feed! I'm trying to work here!"

"We're just chatting, focus on your work, Warlock!" Circé shouted back. "I have time to shoot down murder bots while you're comfortably seated at the headquarters!"

"You should focus on doing an update, C.," he chuckled.

"What? An update of what?"

"An update of your brain, you old witchy!" he shouted.

Eden grimaced. With that, Circé began to scream and shout countless slurs at him. She had just as much flourish in her language as he did, and from the awful noise they could hear in the background, she was probably also taking out her anger on whatever she could around her.

Meanwhile, Eden was still busy making her way into the System's network. Luckily, the guest invitation program was exactly the kind of breach they had been looking for. If she could use this to have Nekhbet and Crash join her, those two would be able to help her corrupt this place even more from the inside. Then all of the Edge would be able to help them lift the invisible barrier outside, tricking the Core to let in all people regardless of their SIN's status. She had to be quick, though. She had been lucky to be getting through so effortlessly thanks to her Ghost SIN, but no one could tell how long it would take for the Core's Artificial Intelligence to pick up the anomalies of her SIN. And there probably were some. Eden kept glancing left and right secretly, hoping no one would question her. Most people walking around were most likely real-life people's avatars and didn't pay much attention to a young woman alone at the bar...

"Aren't you going to order anything?"

She jumped and turned around. She grimaced at the large figure with a bird's face, but it was definitely on a very sexy woman's body with Egyptian attire. Eden let out a long sigh.

"Nekhbet, don't fucking scare me like that... Nice to see you, though. I didn't think you were a woman..."

"Who said I am?"

"You're not a dude?!" exclaimed a voice coming from Eden's left.

With the appearance of a twentieth-century game character, Crash sat next to her at the bar, ordering a drink in just a couple of touches.

"I never said I was a man either," said Nekhbet, crossing their arms. "I don't identify as either of those, but feel free to call me whatever you'd like."

"...I see a lady," shrugged Crash, "but with your voice... Ugh, whatever."

"Got it," nodded Eden. "We don't have time to chat though, we gotta move."

Just as she said that, she noticed two people dressed in black, at one end of the room, pointing fingers in their direction. Crash grimaced.

"I think we might have lit up their Systems like a Christmas tree," he said. "Let's get moving and partying and crashing!"

"What do you need me to do?" frowned Eden.

"Distract them," said Nekhbet. "You and Crash should keep them busy while I wipe down their security with our Back Hackers. You two Divers need to buy us time before we get kicked out of here."

"Can't they kick us out already?"

"No. They let you in, it's too late to simply kick you out, or they'd have to kick out everyone else too. So let's use this to our advantage. Go!"

Eden and Crash nodded and got moving immediately, while Nekhbet took her seat and the screen at the bar to resume typing, probably working with the Back Hackers. Crash finished his drink in one go, and suddenly, he began spinning until there was only a large red tornado in the room, making an awful mess wherever he went. Eden jumped on the closest table and began wrecking everything she could under her feet, sending glasses and poker chips flying around. The guards of the System had begun moving to hunt them down, but it was already too late. More and more Dive Hackers were materializing directly in the room and immediately began participating in the rampage.

"Eden, my Kitty," said Loir. "You shouldn't stay around too long. They might have identified you as their black cat by now..."

"Don't worry and go," nodded Nekhbet, who had gotten close to her as soon as they were done. "This place is already ours to take, but they might try to locate you in the real world, and this time, we won't be able to help you until our people physically get there. We just opened the doors, so you should meet up with the Zodiacs and the others as soon as you can. Dive again when you reach Arcadia Tower."

Eden nodded and ran toward one of the doors. The casino was an absolute wreck already. The real guests had probably left as soon as they realized something was wrong, or perhaps they had been warned, while the Dive Hackers were hell-bent on making a mess of this place to overwhelm the System. Some doors she had seen earlier were closed or had completely disappeared. Some strange, large, black boxes had appeared at completely random places, floating or on something, beacons put there by the Back Hackers who were working hard at corrupting as much as they could. The casino itself was being modified as she walked out of there, walls moving and game tables being replaced by weapon units, large stocked chests, or simply deleted.

"Loir, pull me out," Eden said.

A couple of minutes later, she was back on the upper floor of Charles' house. Eden let out a long sigh. That had gone better than she thought... Luckily for them. Compared to the Zodiacs and their men fighting to get inside the Core, she'd had it easy so far. In fact, she realized how lucky she was that the path had been paved for her beforehand, both by her father and Pan. Eden wondered when her enigmatic master would make a dramatic appearance. She couldn't help but think the rest of this whole mission would be far from easy. They were still just getting started.

"Mr. Charles?" she called out while getting downstairs. "I'm done here, but we have to evacuate. They are going to..."

She stopped, shocked by the scene. Everything was just as she had left it before, except for the large, scary explosive device that had replaced the delicious breakfast on the table, and the equally scary jacket full of wires on Mr. Charles' chest.

"...What is this?" she muttered, her mouth a bit dry.

"Oh, do not worry," smiled the older man. "I expected them to find this place a long, long time ago. Everything is ready."

"You're going to bomb your own house?"

She couldn't believe it. This place was obviously full of memories and personal, sentimental items; this wasn't a ready-made house, but a real home, with things that had been accumulated over the years. Moreover, she had seen Mr. Charles' daughter just a moment ago!

"Yes," he nodded as if it was a simple question. "Do not worry, it should be contained to this house only. My neighbors will just enjoy the fireworks from their windows!"

"You can't be serious!"

"Oh, I'm much more than serious, Miss Eden. But I am an old man who is lucky to have survived this far already, young lady. I am glad I was able to help you, it makes living to this age all worthwhile..."

"But you have children!"

504

"Yes, I do," he chuckled. "I even have grandchildren! Which makes it all the more valuable. I am happy to leave the next generation to collect the fruits of what we accomplished today. But me? I expect nothing more. All of my things are in order, I can leave as peacefully as I want. The one thing I am afraid of is being captured by them. That, I can't let happen."

Eden was torn. She knew she should have said something to stop him, convince him to re-think this, but she just couldn't. In fact, she could tell it would all be useless. She could see it in Mr. Charles' eyes. He was determined and incredibly composed. There wasn't a hint of fear in his eyes. This wasn't the expression of a man about to commit suicide out of fear; Eden was facing an old man who lived a happy life and knew how he wanted to leave. As she looked around, she realized this place already looked empty. Everything was stored and cleaned, as if he had also wanted to give his house a decent last day before it all disappeared. She tried to think of something to say, but nothing was coming.

"Ghost! The barrier's down!"

"Anubis here, we're breaching in too."

"Same in the south!"

"Watch out for the murder bots!"

"We managed to blow up another door! We need more weapons at the front!"

"Rat, another blast!"

"Eden, hold on. I'll find you soon. Just a few minutes."

None of the voices that were pouring in her ears could take Eden out of there. She knew a lot was going on, on all sides of the wall. The city she had been born in was changing forever, their landscape was being rewritten by what would eventually become history. She knew lives were at stake, with an all-out war venturing inside the Core. The Edge's Back Hackers and Divers were all assaulting the System just as the Zodiacs were leading their armies in. Everything was going fast, big, and hard, but none of that seemed to reach the small room she was in, just yet. There was something unbelievably sad and solemn in this room. Eden was facing Mr. Charles, a man she'd even considered an old friend, and realized she was seeing him for the last time. He had done what he could to help her and even given her a bit of her enigmatic past back. This was a farewell.

With a tight throat and no words coming out, she slowly nodded. She couldn't find anything else to say, so she just didn't. He smiled and sat down at the breakfast table from earlier.

"Well, that's it, young lady. You probably should get going now. It won't be long before they get here."

Eden didn't know if he meant the Core or her allies, but she didn't have the luxury to wait for either of those. She slowly took a step back.

"...Thank you for everything," she muttered.

"Oh no, dear. Thank you. Now, you should get going. Run, Eden."

505

Eden turned around, and ran, without looking back. She got out of the house in mere seconds, finding herself back in the Core's street, but it wasn't enough. She kept running; something inside her urged her to leave, as fast as possible. Otherwise, she might turn around and do something foolish. She knew there was no one to save, but she still felt her heart clenching with that strange pain. A very loud uproar came from somewhere on her left, distracting her. She spotted several trails of dark smoke, and more importantly, the sound of gunfire. Large drones and Overcrafts had appeared a bit farther in the sky, charging in all directions to go and try to contain the invaders. They were already too late. Now that the people of the Suburbs were in the streets, they would have issues using any large-scale weapons without risking their own citizens' lives.

A siren began wailing, and red lights appeared. A loud, robotic voice resonated throughout the Core.

*"Citizens, stay home. This is an emergency situation. Citizens, stay home. This is an emergency situation."*

The voice kept repeating that, but a lot of people were already outside, in their gardens, looking around with worried expressions, some of them covering their mouths in shock or pointing toward the ruckus. While Eden ran, she spotted countless faces behind their windows, trying to catch a glimpse of what was going on. She couldn't help but feel a little bit sorry for those people. Most of them had never witnessed, let alone experienced, violence. Their perfect, choreographed lives were being completely blown off their course by the people of the Suburbs. Eden's pity for those people had to stop right there, though. There was enough misery on the other side that she couldn't help but resent them also. In fact, their blindness and self-indulgence were infuriating. If they knew so many people were outside, without ever getting fresh oxygen, even if they believed them to be criminals and delinquents, shouldn't they have expected children to be born there too? How did they never, ever doubt such a tight and controlled system? The answer was most likely that they never had to. Perhaps they were taught to never ever doubt anything. And thus, the fake paradise of the Core could go on while the Suburbs experienced everyday hell.

Eden's run through the streets was catching eyes, but not as much as the sky now filled with battle drones and Overcrafts, or the explosions coming from the south, north, and west. Every one of those citizens knew something was happening, something big. Eden even had to push her way through a few crowds to get closer to her allies.

"Eden, how far are you?" asked Dante's deep voice in her ears.

"Not too far. But there's... Oh, shit."

She jumped out of the main street right in time and into a private garden so as to not be seen. She could hear the sounds of the fight, but there was little to no chance she'd get there; two large vehicles were blocking the road ahead of her, with armed human soldiers patrolling, their weapons up and ready to shoot.

"Secure the perimeter. Make sure no one goes in, we have to contain those people. We have permission to shoot and kill."

"But our citizens–!"

"They should be off the streets. If they're not, their loss. The orders are clear. Shoot anything that moves. We can't take any chances with those kinds of people. They won't give us any either."

Eden felt a cold chill down her spine. They were even ready to kill their own citizens? This was getting insane! She crouched down, hoping the perfectly-cut green bushes of the garden would hide her. The street was quiet compared to the fight up ahead, but she had no idea how she'd be able to get by the two vehicles and all the soldiers with them. She had only caught a quick glimpse of them, but there were too many for sure. She looked around, but the garden didn't seem to have any other exit either. She was trapped in her hideout for now... She looked up, and in the house, there luckily seemed to be no one at the windows. Had no one spotted her jumping in the garden? Or had they gone to call the authorities already? Eden barely dared to breathe. If she made any sound, they'd shoot...

"My Kitty, you're just two blocks away from your favorite Big Kitty!"

"...Why is she not talking?" asked Nebty. "Ghost, can you hear us?"

Eden grimaced. Even whispering would have seemed too risky for now. She was glad years of Diving had taught her to keep her composure because the voices in her ear sounded so loud, it would have made her panic already. But she knew only she could hear them. There was no way the soldiers would pick up on this.

"Where is she?" asked A.

"Found her, near the Tiger's group's position. Why isn't she moving? She isn't hurt, is she?"

It was so frustrating not to be able to answer when they were all trying to understand her situation. Eden took deep, slow breaths to calm herself. There had to be a way out. She slowly moved to the end of the garden, to the corner that was on the same road as the crossroad those stupid vehicles were keeping her from. It was so frustrating. There was just an arm's length, thick bush between her and the way leading straight to Dante...

"My Kitty's playing moody. My Kitty is all pouty! I gotta find my favorite little Kitty..."

Eden tried to think. Would Loir be able to find the two vehicles if he had her position? Probably not. They looked like old-school army trucks, not something too technologically advanced. The Core had most likely decided not to send too many technology-reliant assets, given that the Edge was busy wrecking the System already...

"Eden," suddenly said Dante's voice. "If you can't join us, get to the tower first. You won't be noticed like we are, and I can find you. Just go."

She bit her lip. She knew the tower was on her right. She could definitely head there first and meet with them a couple of blocks farther down, but it

507

didn't solve her problem: she was stuck in this garden for now. She looked around. Could she try and ask the inhabitants of the house for help, if there were any? Perhaps they'd let her in, and she could get out through a window on the other side. The only issue was if the soldiers found her first, but she had to try it. There were few options left and no time to lose…

She moved, and a branch snapped; it was the scariest sound she'd ever heard.

"Over there!"

She heard the men shout, and ran toward the house's door. If they began firing, she'd be dead for sure…

However, no gunshot was fired. A second later, a loud, enormous bang shook the whole neighborhood. Eden was thrown across the garden and her body slammed against the door she'd hoped to reach. She fell to the ground, gusts of wind still sweeping her face. She looked up. From the fire and smoke right across the tall bushes, at least one of the vehicles had been hit by something. She jumped up onto her feet despite the pain radiating from her back, and looked around, looking for the source of the explosion. It didn't take long.

A massive cloud of dark smoke was coming up from where Mr. Charles' house once stood.

# CHAPTER THIRTY-SEVEN

Her heart ached, but sadly, she didn't have time to dwell on it. With tears running down her face, reflecting all her anger, frustration, and pain, Eden ran again. She knew this was her one shot. By the time the soldiers got back on their feet, realized what happened, and perhaps spotted her, Eden would already be far away. She decided not to go for the frontline; she would already be raising her chances of running into more soldiers, vehicles, or drones. Eden had no trouble spotting the tower; it was the tallest building of all. It easily stood behind the lines of houses, and even behind more buildings, the difference in height making it easy to see from any crossroad. This was her destination. If Dante had said he'd find her there, she trusted he would.

"I'm out," she said in one breath. "I'm going to the tower first…"

"My Kitty's back!"

"Ghost! Thank God, you're alive," sighed Nebty.

"What was that explosion?" asked A.

"Our ally… He blew his house up."

"Is he…?"

Eden didn't answer. She was saving her breath for her run, but she also didn't want to say the words. It felt horrible. She could hear explosions coming from the northeast ahead of her, from her left, and behind her, but the one that had come from Charles' house felt the scariest of all. She knew he had done this to be sure not to be hunted down, captured, and possibly tortured, but it just felt too unfair. They were fighting to save the people of the Suburbs, yet there would be more deaths than ever before…

She found a small alley between two buildings and squeezed in between to catch a break. She could hear the murder drones quickly flying above her head and to the front, but it was only a matter of time before those things tried to shoot her. She couldn't approach the tower just like that. If those things got commands to shoot on sight like the soldiers, they'd definitely shoot a foreign target running toward the Arcadia Tower. That place was going to be the most secure of all; they had to expect a lot of firepower that'd attempt to stop them. She hid for a few seconds and got to the end of the building, listening to the flow of information in her ear. Because everyone was using the same channel to get information across as fast as possible, it took focus just to listen. The sound was as good as if they were all standing in the same room, but everyone else was caught in action, gunshots and explosions resonating behind them.

"You bastards! See if you can handle that! Ha!"

Tanya's strong Russian accent and the flow of insults that ensued made Eden smile. The Zodiacs not using translating software had their accent come in even stronger than usual because of anger. Someone had probably muted Joaquin too, or maybe he didn't have a SIN himself because she could only hear him from afar as if his voice came from a different person's mic.

"Everyone's getting in," said Malieka, and her smile could be heard in her voice. "We're making great progress now that all the doors are down."

"They are sending Overcrafts to try and contain us," grunted Lecky. "No, wait… They are sending it past the frontline, to the Suburbs!"

Eden felt a chill down her spine. Were they going to aim at the population rather than the fighters? It didn't make sense. Even if it was the Core attacking them, the Overcrafts were made to carry humans rather than weapons. Why would they sacrifice human soldiers to contain them rather than use their fighting robots?

"They are trying to trap us where we are," Michael said suddenly. "Look at their positions. They will try to make sure no fighter escapes and kill us all as an example."

"…Damn, seems like you're right, King," groaned Nebty. "I'd congratulate you for being as smart as they say, but this is going to be a massive issue. We can't split our fighters!"

"Crash those damn Overcrafts before they land!" shouted Circé.

"Got it. Dive Hackers, I want everyone available to focus on those vehicles!"

"Crash them into one another, or to the ground," ordered Michael, "but make sure they land far away from us!"

Eden sighed. The variety of profiles among the Zodiacs was really showing: the smartest of them were giving orders and laying down strategic plans at incredible speed, while the most brazen were leading people into the fight and bringing them up. Since the beginning, no Zodiac had been useless or dragging behind. She was impressed by how well they cooperated with one another. Each duo in the north, west, and south were working together like she never thought they could, directing their men and making fast progress into the Core. From what she grasped, all teams were already in or the last of their men were coming inside now. At the very least, the fight was being taken to the Core's territory, which had been their main objective.

Eden glanced left and right. The streets were still calm where she hid. It looked like the Core's citizens had finally listened to orders and had all gone home; many doors and windows were already closed and covered. This time, she wouldn't be able to take refuge in any building if the Core spotted her.

"My Kitty, you're a dozen blocks away!"

"Anyone onto my position?"

"A couple of murder bots roaming around! Oh no, two more… Oopsie, looks like they are suspecting that we are coming for them! Let's bring the party to them, my Kitty!"

"I'd rather not get shot down…"

Despite her words, Eden quickly ran across the street to hide under a porch, the next hideout available heading toward the tower. This might be the last one for a while, though. She was in the heart of the city now. There would be more skyscrapers than houses and fewer places to hide. She knew a bit about murder bots. Those things were meant to fly high above the ground and used very simple movement detection cameras, so their bird's-eye view could be blocked by pretty much anything. However, they could fire extremely fast, and once they locked on to a target, they wouldn't stop.

From her hideout, Eden spotted one flying approximately one block away from her position. She crouched down, getting nervous. She was still far from her destination, and there would only be more of those as she got closer…

"…Can't you help me get rid of those things?"

"Oh, do I get to play Pac-Man?"

"Whatever you want, as long as they can't shoot me. Loir, if just one of those things hones in on me, the whole plan will be in jeopardy!"

"Yahoo! Let's see… Which one will I take to play with?"

Eden sighed, and while Loir was having fun, she glanced toward the tower. She was on the right street, but it still felt too far. Being alone should have allowed her to move quickly and unnoticed, but the backup was also limited, and she was getting worried she wouldn't make it.

"Eden, we're almost there," said Dante, as if he had heard her thoughts at that exact moment.

She could hear that. The gunshots and explosions were coming from almost all sides, but the closest ones were definitely from Dante's group. She could even recognize Thao's tank firing relentlessly. Seems like the Rat hadn't parted with her new favorite toy…

Suddenly, a loud noise coming from the opposite direction made Eden crouch down even lower, her chest almost on the ground. She witnessed the vehicle driving past her, a vehicle full of humanoid robots. She could tell right away that they were soldier bots. They were deactivated and still for now, but that wouldn't be the case for long. Those things were ten times stronger than a normal human and loaded with weapons. It was like a whole army in one truck. Eden glared at the truck going toward Dante's position.

She made up her mind at the last second. After a quick glance up, Eden jumped on the truck, her hands grabbing the back door. Her body slammed into the hard surface for the second time in the span of a few minutes, making her grimace in pain, but she held on, quickly finding a position she could maintain. She didn't plan on staying there long, though. Moving the best and fastest she could, she swung her leg and kicked the back door of the truck repeatedly. This was one of the most ridiculous positions, but she didn't have time and couldn't afford to be thrown off either; she only had a couple of seconds.

She heard a loud shot right after the next kick. A hole the size of a coin had appeared right above the handle. She forced herself not to move her upper body or look back. One of the murder bots had found her on the truck. Ignoring it, she kept kicking, doing her best to stick the rest of her body to the truck, hoping the bot would focus on her legs instead; those she could afford to have shot at. And indeed, shot they were. She kept kicking the door's lock, and a bullet hit her leg. She had to be careful as the bot would soon realize the foreign movement was part of a larger body. Those things were pretty dumb; they could recognize a moving vehicle, but not a human body, so they focused on the movement that seemed odd.

Luckily, the lock and handle fell off a couple of seconds later. Without anything to hold it, the door opened quickly, throwing Eden to the side, and all the soldier bots fell off the truck and rolled down the road. The murder bot opened fire right away on the massive amount of movement it didn't recognize.

While Eden ran as fast as her legs could carry her to her previous hideout, the bot made a massacre out of the soldier bots that were perfectly functional just seconds before. When she finally got back into a crouched position and looked at the damage, the robots were lying in a pool of their fuel, like dead bodies.

"Nice one, Kitty! Now, that's some action!"

Eden let out a long sigh of relief. Her legs were damaged, but at least, she had spared Dante's group from a militia of soldier bots.

"Please tell me you got rid of the other bots," she groaned, leaning her head against the wall.

"Yup! Just captured Blinky! Oh, my little bots, now you're all mine to play with!"

Eden nodded and carefully stepped out of her hiding place.

"Send them to Dante's side," she said. "How close–"

She heard the gunshot before she felt the bullet. Eden fell down to her knees, her breath caught in her throat while her arm was overcome by unbearable pain.

"Kitty!"

512

She quickly rolled to the side, her instincts taking over. She felt all her blood leave her upper body and a cold shiver, the wound sapping all of her strength. Still, Eden was a fighter and used to pain too. She knew she had to react quickly or she'd die in a blink. She threw herself behind a wall, checking to make sure there was nothing else waiting for her. But the steps of the soldiers were already running in her direction. She grimaced. She had made a stupid mistake. She looked down at her injury, her forearm covered in blood, but that sight only made things worse. She could already feel the lack of sensation in her right wrist and hand.

"Kitty shot! I repeat, Kitty shot!" Loir shouted.

"I'm alright," she managed to say.

"Thao, get fucking moving!" shouted Lecky. "We don't have time to take names!"

"...I'm going to need a gun," muttered Eden, realizing she'd lost hers.

She stuck herself against the wall, praying Dante would get to her before the Core's soldiers. It was a dead-end; she had nowhere to run.

"You're going to need medical attention first, Ghost," said Nebty. "We need to get the medical unit to her, fast!"

"Warlock, Thao, we're running out of time. De Luca and I are going to make a run to her," said Circé. "Cover us!"

"Inky, Blinky, Pinky, it's your moment, my babies!"

Eden groaned. She hated to be defenseless, and even worse, in need of being rescued. One thing was certain, though: Dante and Circé wouldn't make it to her before the Core's soldiers. She could hear their steps, just seconds away from her. She got closer to the end of the wall, trying to ignore the pain, and getting ready. Her hand and forearm had gone more numb than painful, which wasn't the worst outcome. She had to survive until they made it there. Perhaps only just a few more seconds...

"Here!"

She moved as soon as the soldier's silhouette appeared. Using her crouched position, Eden kicked her leg right in his stomach and pulled the gun from his hand with her valid hand, spinning it to take control of the weapon. She shot one, two, three times. The soldier fell back with a shocked expression still on his face, his mouth open. However, Eden didn't even let his body touch the ground, stepping right behind it and shooting again, toward his allies. There were three of them. Before they could even notice, she shot continuously in their direction, hitting two of them and forcing the last one to retreat away from her. She saw him dive behind a building, just like she had done, and shout for reinforcements.

Since she couldn't aim at him anymore, Eden stepped back into hiding, trying to take deep breaths. Her head was spinning. She was glad her legs could support her regardless of her condition because otherwise, they would probably have given up long ago. The pain in her arm was becoming unbearable again now that the effects of the adrenaline had passed.

513

"Dante," she called out, unable to think of anything else.

He didn't answer. She sighed. For once, she was the one waiting for him. She could hear Loir's voice from far away, playing with his new bots, and all the hackers, too busy hitting back at the Core's robots and people. It sounded like her getting injured had pushed all teams to get there even faster, but those in the south were experiencing major setbacks. She closed her eyes, leaning against the wall and trying to fight the urge to pass out. Focusing on the constant feed of voices helped, so she did that instead. Nebty was coordinating the attack on the System, which was apparently going as planned so far. Michael and Tanya were trying to blow through a building to force their way deeper inside the Core, while Old Man Long and Joaquin had apparently split ways to spread out the fight instead of allowing the Core to control it. They all knew the Core wasn't prepared to fight on their own ground, and couldn't use weapons too large within their streets with their own population watching from behind their windows. The sirens were getting louder, deafening even. Eden could hear machines coming from all sides to fight them now. They had probably realized this was a serious and coordinated attack that would require them to mobilize their entire army's strength. What was meant to be a bolt-like attack was turning into an all-out war.

"There! She's hiding behind the wall! Only one rebel woman spotted! Shoot her down!"

Eden opened her eyes. What rebel were they talking about? She realized she was still in her Ghost appearance. They probably thought she was one of their people that had suddenly gone rogue to help the Suburbs... She sighed and rolled her eyes.

"I'm coming!" shouted Loir. "Nobody touches my Kitty! Now you've done it! I'm going to attack you all like the small little fried squid you are!"

Eden chuckled. Somehow, a part of her brain that wasn't dealing with the pain found relief in Loir's antics. She heard shots being fired right after his words, and only thought of hiding the best she could without realizing those were coming from the other side of the building, not in her direction. She sighed.

Steps were heading toward her. She grabbed the gun again, hoping to be able to hold on for a while longer. She was a fighter, but her body had its limits no matter how far she pushed them. Eden was in automatic mode, and she was prepared to shoot at anything that appeared on her right. Her eyes were set in that direction, trying hard not to close them and ready to fire.

A silhouette appeared, and she shot.

The gun somehow left her hand, and she felt herself fall into someone's embrace. She looked up. Dante smirked, with blood coming down from his temple.

"Sorry I'm late," he muttered. "...I didn't think you'd be this mad."

"I injured you..."

"It's alright. Circé, how long?"

514

"Just a couple of minutes. It's just the anesthetics knocking her out for now. She'll be back in no time."

Eden did feel strange, mostly numb. She was aware of being in Dante's embrace somehow, but she could only focus on one thing at a time. Right now, it was the blood coming from his temple, and dripping slowly onto her chest. Thankfully, the wound was superficial. It had grazed him, deep enough to cut him and make him bleed a bit, but it was already drying by itself, and the Tiger didn't seem to care at all either.

The sounds of the fight seemed like they were coming from behind a wall. Eden was surrounded by Circé and Dante, and they were keeping her hidden against the wall while the little medical unit was doing its job. The small robot looked like a strange spider on her arm, spraying painkillers while cauterizing and stitching the wound quickly. Eden had only ever seen one of those on an online auction, and she knew how valuable they were. Perhaps about as much as a Part. She wondered how many of those the Zodiacs had brought to the fight.

She heard Dante sigh and put a kiss on her head.

"I really don't like it when you're where I can't see you..."

"Sorry..." muttered Eden.

She wouldn't have mumbled an apology if she wasn't half groggy and having a hard time keeping up with the conversation. Eden was enjoying this short-lived peace, though. Dante's arms might have been her only safe place ever.

Little by little, her senses began to come back. With the medical bot done treating her arm, her sensations were coming back in the rest of her body, her mind becoming clearer as well. She tried to wiggle her fingers and toes and took several deep breaths. It felt like the fight that had been kept at a distance until now was suddenly approaching from all sides.

"Everything alright?" asked Circé.

"What did I miss?" Eden groaned, accepting Dante's helpful hand to get back on her feet.

"Only a few minutes."

While she quickly stretched, she could see a lot had happened in those few minutes. They were still on the same block she'd been shot at, but now, all the surrounding areas had turned into a battlefield, with gunshots heard in all directions, random explosions, and dozens of voices shouting. There was gray smoke and an unpleasant, thick scent of powder, burnt asphalt, and gas filling the air. She almost regretted leaving their oxygen masks. All of Dante's and Thao's people had arrived with their heavy weapons and now, Eden was actually behind the frontline, while their little army was making the Core's robots slowly but surely back off.

"All you munchkins!" Loir shouted. "You'll see what I do to you, you empty expired cans on legs! Fear the army of the mighty Warlock!"

"Let's focus the fire on the main road!"

515

"Watch out for the windows! They have more units in the buildings," warned Nebty.

Dante handed Eden a pair of familiar twin guns. They were heavy, silver, and perfectly molded for her hands. He only gave her a quick smile.

"Ready for another round?"

"Always."

He turned around and, without adding a word, stood at the end of the wall, weapons in hand and ready to get back into the main fight. Eden got on her knees next to him, peeking at the main scene of the fight while staying carefully hidden. She found herself quite shocked. Three more trucks of soldier bots appeared while she was out. Those things were decent fighters, but even more fearsome because of their firepower. Thao's tank was now used as a shield by the fighters, the cannon having been destroyed somehow. Those who were running ahead to try and fight the humanoid robots one-on-one were getting killed each time. They were making very little progress and damage, and the only safe way to fight back seemed to be from behind some sort of shield. The fight appeared to be stuck, neither side making any progress. The problem was that the robots' only aim was defending the building, while Eden's side had to keep moving.

"Is there any way to hack those things?" she groaned.

"We tried," muttered Nebty, "but they aren't linked to the System by any way we know. They are most likely on auto-pilot, with orders to shoot anything that moves."

They were the same as the human soldiers of the Core, then.

Eden glanced up. The fight was just as intense in the sky. The murder bots that were already hacked and on their side were easy to spot, attacking their peers and the soldier bots, while the others were trying to get past the line of defense to shoot their fighters. In total, there were probably around fifty bots flying around, caught in their own space battle. The murder bots seemed to be focused on the sky, though, and their gunfire on the soldier bots didn't do enough damage. Eden frowned.

"...Loir, Nekhbet. I got an idea. Have you ever seen a game of bowling?"

"Worth a try!"

"What?" squealed Loir. "I can't sacrifice my babies! They have been such good little bots!"

"You can replace them," groaned Nebty. "It's not like the Core's going to run out of those damn things..."

"Ugh, you guys are so insensitive. All bots are the same to you? They are irreplaceable to me! My precious little ones!"

"...I'll let you play with the pups," sighed Eden.

"Geronimo!! Here comes the Kamikaze unit! Cowabunga!"

Suddenly, a rain of bots seemed to crash down. One by one, all the units dived, hitting the soldier bots at full speed and sending them flying. Because both types of robots were made of the same materials, the soldier bots didn't have a strong resistance to their flying peers. Not only that, but as Nebty had mentioned, those things were programmed to attack humans, not robots. Thus, they showed absolutely no resistance to the bots attacking them. In just a few seconds, the previously tight ranks of robots were full of holes.

"Strike! And strike! Take this!"

Loir wasn't the only one having fun. From the number of bots suddenly falling, all the Back Hackers had probably joined him, using the murder bots like cannonballs to hit the robots as fast and hard as possible. Some bots even survived to make a second hit, and quickly, the fight's pace was overthrown. Thao shouted an order, and everyone came out of their hideouts, firing all they could as they ran ahead.

Eden saw men fall, shot down, but no one stopped or turned back. They knew it would be a one-time-only kind of attack, and they had to use it to pierce an opening through the robots' defensive line. The opportunity wouldn't come twice. Eden ran like all of them, both guns up and firing ahead of her. She had no time to check on anyone she knew and cared about. It was simply run or die for everybody. A part of her was aware of Dante, near her and covering her open flank while she covered his, but they had no time to consult with each other. Their duo ran ahead, like everybody else, looking for the opening they needed.

When they finally crossed the first lines of robots, Eden kicked ahead, opening the gap more for those who followed them. She could hear the deafening shots of the soldier bots firing at her allies, and smell the blood flying in the air. This would be one of the deadliest attacks. Nebty's voice was encouraging all of them like an anthem guiding their troops forward. Seeing the soldier bots fall in front of them, overwhelmed by their number and heavy fire, Eden knew they'd succeed. The tower's mighty height was in sight, right in front of them. Without realizing, she had gone ahead, leading the way past their automated opponents with her powerful, metal legs, her blonde hair flying around her. In a way, Eden was more at ease when she fought than when she hid. Good fighters didn't need to think about their next move when they fought. Their body could move on its own, led by years of training and their survival instincts. She had always hated hiding, and now that she could fight in plain sight, knowing who she was fighting and why, Eden felt confident. Even though her arm still hurt, her body was tired, and there were people dying all around them, she felt braver than ever. Her confidence was flowing through her limbs, and she was unstoppable.

"Yes! Ghost, keep going!"

"The robots are confused and have stopped shooting!"

It made sense. They were armed to fire at human targets, but because all the humans were now amongst them, the robots were conflicted over whether to open the fire in their own ranks or not. The Core had chosen to keep them out of the System from fear of hacking attacks, but that meant they hadn't put any reflection process in those units, so they couldn't choose. Without the main artificial intelligence to guide them, those robots were impossible to hack, but too stupid to make the simplest decisions. Eden's side piercing through their defenses was a major win in itself. A portion of the fighters that had managed to get through with her stayed behind to help wipe out more robots; sadly, they had already lost many lives, but at least this fight was a small victory, and some had made it. That was all that mattered for now.

"Thank God," muttered Lecky.

"You're almost there," added Malieka. "Let's stay focused, everyone, we haven't–"

A major explosion shook them all. For a moment, Eden thought about hiding, but just like the people next to her, she realized they were far from where the detonation had originated from. All their eyes went to the south, where a frighteningly large, thick pillar of dark smoke was reaching the sky like a storm.

"…What the heck happened?" she managed to mutter, as everyone was still in awe.

"I don't know…" muttered Nebty. "I can't reach anyone there!"

"Sapphire?" Eden called. "Gluttony?"

Only silence answered. Around them, everyone had quickly hid or stopped running, unable to move because of what they were seeing in the south. The pillar of smoke was bigger than an entire building.

Eden felt Dante grab her arm and pull her behind him.

"Old Man Long," he said. "…Joaquin?"

"If there's anyone still hearing us in the south, answer now!" shouted Malieka with an angry voice.

"…They used a Hell Bomb."

The voice had come through a lot of noise, as if it was from too far away. Eden frowned.

"Who is that? …Greed, is that you?"

"Yeah… I just logged onto one of our Dive Hacker's SINs to see the last seconds of his feed. They used a Hell Bomb, Ghost. There's no one left there."

An icy chill ran down Eden's spine. There wasn't anyone part of the Zodiac or the Edge that didn't know what a Hell Bomb was. It wasn't even the real name, but a nickname everybody gave to that weapon, as if its effects needed an emphasis. They were supposedly forbidden by all Core Governments, at least officially. Those things were one of the worst weapons ever created and had been rendered inhumane and illegal to use by several foreign governments. The mere use of that thing was considered a crime against humanity and anyone who did use it would have been sentenced to centuries of imprisonment. Eden had only heard about that thing, but the little she knew was enough to give her nightmares. The Hell Bomb was a weapon dedicated to genocides and to ending human lives. It was a mixture of acids, fire, and all sorts of gasses, meant to not let its victims escape in any way, while causing less damage to anything non-organic. Perhaps the houses and streets still looked the same over there. That bomb could disintegrate flesh and bones in a blink, and leave absolutely nothing behind.

It was terrifying to think of the void that had become of the place their allies stood just one second before. Eden wanted to vomit, but she couldn't. Instead, those feelings of shock, horror, and disgust remained stuck in her throat. She glanced around at the stunned expressions.

"...Let's keep moving."

Dante's words felt like they were dragging everyone away from a strange nightmare. Many heads turned toward him, including Eden. He was right, of course, but his ability to overcome the sudden threat of instant death was mind-blowing.

"How many of those do they have?" gasped Nekhbet. "If they use them, they will be able to wipe us all out in just a few seconds!"

"They probably hoped to scare us that way."

Eden shook her head and turned her heels first. She was the first to resume running toward the building, closely followed by Dante once again. Many followed their lead. This time, the threat of the fighting robots had become secondary. The fear of a Hell Bomb was a hundred times worse; if the Core launched another one of those things here, they'd be wiped out without even a second to fight back. They had already lost one of their three groups in a blink. A third of all the people they had brought had been killed in an instant, with no chances of survival. She didn't want to imagine what the scene looked like on the ground, in the south, for the sky to have become so dark over there. It was that scary.

"...They can't possibly fire more of those," she muttered. "Not within their Core."

"Those bloody bastards just did!" shouted Tanya. "We're going to be next!"

"No, Ghost is right," muttered Michael. "First, they must have gathered a lot of unwanted international attention for using that thing. Second, they will have to justify the use of a mass murder weapon within a citizen safe zone. Finally, those things are much too expensive and rare for them to use two of them on us. They probably hoped to scare us with that, and thought we'd quietly go back if we realized they had such weapons. But you guys should be close enough to the Arcadia Tower, so don't slow down! That's one place they will never dare touch."

"He is right," added Tanya with her famous accent. "I am not taking my boys back to tell them this was all for nothing. I'm sorry for the Old Man and Joaquin, but the show must go on. Ghost's group is our current priority, and they both knew that."

Eden nodded. She was impressed with the Zodiacs' self-control and calm, given the situation, but she had to admit they were right: they had to keep going. Forcing the Core to use such a bomb was perhaps what would save them.

"Everybody hold on tight then," sighed A, "but Tanya's right. If they resorted to using a Hell Bomb on their own territory, that means we're seriously scaring them. It's a good sign."

"Say that to all the people who just died," grunted Circé, bitter.

The reality of the hundreds of deaths was still hovering over their heads like a silent threat. Eden was trying hard not to think about it too much, but it was impossible. Old Man Long, who had seemed so invincible before, had been killed in a blink. Even the hot-headed, heavily armed Joaquin. They really must have forced the Core to react... Were they trying to reduce their numbers and scare them in one go? Or was the Core scared by all the weapons that were coming from the south? Did they want to make an example out of them? There was no telling. Either way, the message was clear: there would be more casualties if they wanted to achieve their goal, and neither side would back down.

"Let's just get there," grunted Nebty. "Their admission lobby is already ours, there was nothing the System could do to stop us. After that, though, I have a feeling things will not be that simple, so let's get ready, everyone."

Even if she hadn't said so, Eden had no intention to stop or give up. The doors of the Arcadia Tower were just ahead of her now. That was the final stage of the fight, where they would have to climb up toward their victory. Because of the sirens and red lights all over the Core, people had most likely been evacuated already, except for the leaders that would be taken to the secure spaces, just as they had observed. Eden felt her fist clench as she sprinted for the last steps to the front door. She was almost there, and ready to uncover the truth. About her dad, about Pan, and finally, what had happened to her mother. She wanted to know why her family had been shattered, and why so many people had to suffer in the Suburbs. She had grown attached to those running alongside her, and she felt sorry for those who had died on the way here. She didn't dare to stop to count the casualties, but they were many. Eden could tell just from how the feed had been more silent than before, many voices had been lost on the way here.

"Let's go, my Kitty!"

She smiled, and jumped forward, ready to slam the door open with a kick.

# CHAPTER THIRTY-EIGHT

Their group barged in loudly, using firearms to force the doors open. Eden and Dante were some of the first to enter the Arcadia Tower, weapons drawn and ready to fire immediately.

To their surprise, they only found an empty lobby. The very entrance of the tower was completely deserted; not a single person was around. Eden had expected a bit of a fight, perhaps a few soldier bots, but there was literally nothing. She looked around, as confused as everyone else. The ground floor was clearly a commercial hall. Dozens of closed shops were lined up around them, all with their curtains drawn, some barricaded. Because of the lobby's high ceiling that was four or five floors tall, she could even see shops far above her, with some decorations still hanging on the rails of the balconies and advertising screens.

"...They really did evacuate the place," scoffed Circé.

"Makes sense," sighed Malieka. "According to the data we have, there are at least ten floors of only business, leisure, and commercial spaces. The Core probably thought there was no use losing some of their defensive lines on those floors and gave them up. I bet you're going to have much more of a challenge upstairs."

"Then let's establish a defense line here first," said Thao. "I'm staying down here. I bet they won't be late to send reinforcements toward the tower now that we've gotten here."

"Perhaps even the ones that were fighting south," muttered Greed. "Our people died, but the machines might have made it..."

He hadn't spoken very loudly, but everyone took on a very serious and determined expression. They would all be only too happy to vent the loss of their allies on the bots that had been partially responsible for the tragedy. Although they were only machines, at least it would provide a taste of revenge.

"...The one we need to go to is the... sixtieth floor?" said Eden, looking up. "Where are the elevators?"

"Are elevators safe?" frowned George, who emerged from the crowd as the group was splitting in two. "I mean, they are controlled by the System, right? What if they decide to crash them while we are inside?"

"That would be a pretty horrible way to die," nodded Circé, walking to a little electric box on one of the walls and opening it. "Nebty, can you get our guys working on that?"

She put in a tiny key like the ones Loir usually gave Eden, and the little device lit up a purple color right away.

"Already on it. Give us a minute."

That minute was enough for Thao to organize her defense line. Quickly, her men ransacked the nearby shops to prepare a barricade in front of the doors they had just wrecked.

Meanwhile, Dante's men regrouped around them. Eden suddenly realized how many people they had already lost. There were only about a hundred people left for each Zodiac, when there had been hundreds more starting this fight outside the wall. She spotted Rolf giving orders a bit further away too and re-distributing the weapons and ammunition among the men. Those who had made it here all looked relieved to be catching a break. Some had even brought over food from one of the shops and were trying to drink and feed themselves as quickly as possible, in case something else happened right away.

"Here."

With a surprised look, she took the little sandwich George handed her with a smug expression.

"You should, uh... eat something too."

With that, he simply turned around, his ears a bit red, leaving Eden there with her sandwich, a bit confused. ...Was that his way of making peace with her? They had never really seen eye to eye before, but that was the first time he was actually doing something somewhat nice for her. She smiled and began eating, only realizing then how hungry she'd been. The bit of breakfast earlier at Mr. Charles' apparently wasn't enough. It was true they had been running around, climbing, and fighting for a while, but she felt a bit guilty eating a whole sandwich while everyone else didn't have the food she had earlier. Luckily, it didn't look like they were holding back on ransacking the shops. She could see Thao's men going in and out non-stop, their arms filled with packages of food, water, and other things they'd probably make use of while waiting for the fight.

Suddenly, several of the elevators on the side opened with a ding sound.

"Your rides are safe and ready," announced Nebty. "Make sure you only take elevators one to six for now. We aren't done taking control of the others yet."

"...You absolutely sure?" muttered George.

Circé rolled her eyes and pushed him to go ahead and get in first. Eden got in the elevator with them but took a glance back at Thao and her men. They looked ready to hold a siege here, but who could predict when the fight would really get here, and how long they'd be able to hold it? She sighed, and the elevator doors closed on them.

The elevators were pretty large, enough to carry ten people. Eden felt Dante's hand smoothly wrap around her waist, and she couldn't resist taking a little step back to lean against him. Everyone around didn't seem to notice. They all had their eyes on the screens that composed the ceiling and walls of the elevator, and with good reason.

Those screens were obviously made for entertainment purposes, but for people of the Suburbs, what was displayed was probably mind-blowing. While showing a view of Chicago as if they were floating about the city, all kinds of ads were displayed of strangers with white smiles and amiable expressions. They were advertising pretty much everything: food, clothing, strange drinks, games, even plants. Eden, who had already seen similar things during her hacking missions, glanced around to see the expressions of her allies. Some were in absolute awe, their mouths open while they stared at the screens, captivated. Others looked more pissed off or annoyed by those screens. They were probably realizing that the people of the Core had access to everything, while their lives in the Suburbs were full of struggles, and just trying to make it to the next day with enough oxygen. They could probably never afford any of those things in this life, yet the people of the Core were benefiting from them daily with no idea of how valuable they were.

All of a sudden, the view changed. The ads all disappeared at once, while the view of Chicago was covered by a red, menacing filter. A loud, male voice came out of the elevators' speakers, and probably resonated throughout the whole building.

"*Intruders. You have decided to rebel against the Core, which took care of you. You have harmed citizens of the Core, destroyed their possessions, and committed a number of crimes against our peaceful citizens.*"

"You mean, your blind and privileged puppies," groaned Circé.

"*An order has been issued for your immediate arrest. Those who resist will be considered uncooperative by law enforcement representatives, and be executed on the spot. I repeat. Any attempt to resist or flee will be considered as an act of rebellion, and the death penalty will be immediately enforced.*"

"That's what happens when you're judge, jury, and executioner..."

"Circé, shut up," groaned Eden.

"*The attack on the Arcadia Tower is a Level One crime. Every non-citizen found there will be immediately executed. Those who have not caused any harm on the Core's territory and are willing to cooperate will be arrested, and sentenced upon their trial."*

Eden grimaced. There was no way there would be a trial. They only hoped to arrest those who decided to lay down their weapons more easily, but there was no doubt the Core would kill them all, as an example.

*"The cyber attack on the System is a Level One crime. All foreign hackers found on the Core's System are facing the immediate death penalty. The hackers that are identified committing illegal intrusion on the Core's System will be immediately executed."*

"As if you could catch us," hissed Nebty.

*"This is a warning. Immediately leave the Arcadia Tower, and surrender. We will use our law enforcement robots to arrest you and give you fair trials. Failure to comply will result in the immediate issue of a death penalty order..."*

"I don't understand," said Eden. "They already know we won't back down, and their robots have already fired at us. So why..."

Before she could end her sentence, the filter immediately changed from red to blue. This time, a female voice spoke, gently but firmly.

*"Dear citizens. A foreign attack began this morning on our Chicago Core. Violent non-citizens have intruded on our dear Chicago Core and have begun to cause havoc, destroying our homes, robbing our possessions, and murdering our own citizens. We urge all citizens of the Core to stay home, for your own safety, and report any suspicious movement. All the intruders are armed and extremely dangerous. Do not open your doors to these attackers. Do not interact with these attackers. If you have any information, immediately report it to the Core's emergency line. I repeat. The intruders are armed and extremely dangerous. Do not..."*

"People won't believe that," said Eden. "We only fought with robots, they won't believe we are really murdering citizens like that..."

"I think they will," muttered Greed. "...Look."

One of the elevators' panels suddenly changed, showing what looked like a very poor-quality video. Eden immediately recognized the scene, though. It was the one they had lived just minutes ago when their group had fought and pushed through the lines of soldier bots to get into the Arcadia Tower.

There was one major difference from what had really happened, though. Instead of fighting with soldier bots, Eden, Dante, Thao, and everyone else were shown to be firing at citizens. They had digitally replaced all the robots in that frame to make it look as if their group was firing at unarmed citizens. The murder bots were still shown in the sky, but once again, the ones that had been turned over to their side were digitally erased.

"Holy crap..."

"Yep," sighed Malieka. "They are showing their citizens a different narrative so they won't help us."

"We already picked up a dozen calls of people reporting Tanya's group advancing," added Nebty. "It won't do much, but now, we're really on our own."

It wasn't much of a change for their situation, but it was still pretty bad news for everyone. Until then, they had fought hard knowing what they were doing was for the sake of thousands of others. However, now, they were depicted as cold-blooded murderers, terrorists to the citizens of this city. Although it was not a big difference, the change of narrative was depressing, especially since the Core was doing this so easily.

"...Can we do something about this?" muttered Eden.

"I don't think so. Hacking their broadcast would take a while, and it's a waste of resources, Ghost. Let's just move on."

Eden nodded. She knew Nebty had to make the most efficient decisions, even if they weren't always fully satisfying.

Suddenly, the elevator did a little jump and stopped its course. It remained closed, though. Everyone looked at each other with worried expressions.

"...Greed?"

"Just a minute! They are fighting to take back control of the elevators... Don't do anything for now! I'm on it! Nekhbet, I could use some help here!"

Next to Eden, though, George didn't look too good. He had become more pale since they had gotten in there, and now, he was all fidgety, glancing toward the doors non-stop.

When the doors suddenly opened, on what was indicated as the fifty-fifth floor, he went to run outside. However, things didn't happen as planned. Dante grabbed him by the collar just in time, as George's body seemingly fell past the elevator. What seemed like one of the tower's shopping floors just a second before suddenly turned into a large, deep, black void. For a minute, it was chaos in the elevator, while Rolf, Eden, and Dante hurried to grab a part of George and pull him back inside.

"What part of 'don't move' did you not understand?!" Circé shouted at him.

"W-w-what... happened..." mumbled poor George, lying in the middle of the elevator.

"They used screens to create an illusion," sighed Eden. "There are some leisure centers in the tower; some probably include virtual entertainment rooms that are all screens. They probably stopped the elevators at one of those rooms, hoping a few of us would actually fall and die exactly like you almost did."

"Which is why I said not to move," grunted Greed. "I only have control of the elevators and the lower floors for now. They can put you through hell on any of the upper floors, guys, so stay inside, it's safer. I'll let you know when we arrive... if I can regain control of these damn things."

Eden frowned, and exchanged a glance with Circé over her shoulder. Greed seemed to be struggling to get back control. It was only to be expected. The Core probably wouldn't let them simply access their most important rooms like that.

"...What floor are we on right now?"

"Somewhere on the fifty-sixth and fifty-seventh, if I can trust what we have from Pan's Map."

"Of course you can trust the Map!" shouted Loir, sounding personally offended. "Why would you not be able to trust the Map?! This Map can even pinpoint a mole on your butt cheek, sir!"

"...Ugh, noted. My bad. Anyway, that's where you are."

"Do we have emergency stairs nearby?"

"Stairs? ...Yeah, but it's opposite from your position."

"It's alright. Land us where you can, even if it's on a lower floor. We should probably climb up the stairs instead of using the elevators, they will fight to the end to make sure these things don't reach the sixtieth floor."

"Got it."

The elevator moved again, going down this time. George grimaced, but lucky for him, Greed managed to stop them on the fifty-fourth floor. This time, he double-checked before taking a step out, but the whole floor around them was real this time. It seemed they had arrived at the front desk of some company's office, and Eden remembered Rolf had mentioned some floors were rented for such use too. They all left the elevator one by one. Just as the last of them got out, though, the screens of the elevator changed, visibly being tampered with.

"...Greed?"

"They have control of all the screens. I can't do a thing."

"How nice to meet you again, Eden," suddenly said a voice in the speakers. "Oh, you've grown, child."

Eden frowned, and turned to the elevator. A simplistic face was displayed there as if someone was talking using a white mask to cover their real face. Probably some strange filter, but it really made the whole thing creepier, especially as it had appeared on all three walls of the elevator.

"...Who are you?"

"I am the Governor," chuckled the voice, "and an old friend of your dear father, the Architect."

Eden's blood went cold. She felt Dante grab her hand and pull her back, away from the elevator, but she barely reacted to it. She was more shocked to hear what that voice was saying.

"...What do you know about my dad?"

"Your dad and I were very close, child. After all, he was the Architect. The man who built, shaped, and gave life to our current way of life!"

"...You killed my father?"

"Me? Oh, I would have never. Your father was too precious of a colleague for me. And, I told you, we were friends."

"...I don't believe you."

"I suspected you wouldn't. After all, you spent quite some time away from us, didn't you? Your little friends from the slums probably had all their time to give you some tragic narrative about how much of a villain the Core's people

526

are."

"Not the Core's people, only people like you. And it's not a lie. I've witnessed it myself."

"That aside, you didn't get the childhood and upbringing you deserved. It truly saddens me to think of everything you could have achieved if you had inherited your father's legacy properly. I'm sorry your poor mother's dementia was what forced you to such a life."

Her mother. Hearing her mentioned by this man made Eden even madder than before. She glared at the screen, taking one step forward.

"Don't you dare talk about my mother," she hissed. "Not after what you've done to her!"

"...What have we done? I'm afraid I don't understand, Eden. We've been doing our best all along to take care of your poor mother. I wish we could have reunited you two sooner, but... things did end up so tragically, didn't they."

"...What?"

Suddenly, the screens of the elevator changed. Eden took another step forward, without thinking. She couldn't believe her eyes. On the screens, a video surveillance of what looked somewhat like a hospital room was displayed. Everything was white, but in that room, a dark-haired woman was clearly noticeable. She was curled up in a corner, wearing some white hospital gown, visibly skinny and afraid. There were two women, looking like nurses, trying to talk to her, but that woman was curled up in a corner.

"...Your poor mother was so sad when you suddenly stopped calling her, Eden."

"...You're lying."

"Oh, I'm not. Why would I? After all, your mother is alive, and with us. ...Just like you should be, Eden."

"...Somebody check that video feed right away," said Dante.

"We can't," immediately answered Nebty. "We've been trying since earlier, but we can't even access the screens casting it. It's one of their inner broadcast lines."

"Keep trying anyway," said Eden. "I want to know if that bastard's lying to me."

"...Bastard? That's a bit rude, young lady," chuckled the Governor.

"You'll be less worried about my language when you see what else I can shoot at you, Governor. If my mom is truly alive and you do anything to her, I swear I will kill you."

"We'll see, Eden. We'll see."

After that, his face disappeared from the elevator screens, which went back to displaying the city of Chicago again.

"...Nebty, is there no way to–"

"No offense, Ghost, but your personal matter will have to wait. We've got all hands on deck right now, and I hate to be the bearer of bad news, but it's about to get ugly downstairs. You guys should hurry up, I don't know how

527

long Thao and her people will be able to hold them off."

After hearing this, Eden nodded, swallowing her feelings the best she could. Dante gently taking her hand helped a lot. They exchanged a glance, and he hugged her quickly as if to give her a bit of comfort. It was very welcome.

Meanwhile, behind them, Circé had run to one of the computers in that room, along with another of Dante's men who had to have some hacking background. They were both typing quickly, probably opening some doors for the Edge's people to barge in.

"...The stairs?" Eden asked.

"Right behind you guys. They should be safe to use. You also have another one farther ahead, but it might be a bit more risky. Too tight."

"Got it."

She was about to turn to said location when loud sounds suddenly came from above. They all crouched down, eyes on the ceiling, prepared for anything. They were clearly sounds of steps, steps made by several very heavy things.

"Oh, they are taking the party to you, my Kitty!"

"How many?"

"Uh, I'd say there's the whole class of soldier bots!"

"We don't have enough people here to face soldier bots," grunted Circé.

Eden nodded. There were still only the ten people that had arrived on this floor. She turned to the elevators behind her.

"What happened to the others?"

"Half are still downstairs, and two of the elevators we had to stop on the lower floors. They are on their way to you, so the reinforcements are coming."

"That's only twenty people at best," muttered Eden.

"We're sending the elevators back," sighed Greed. "Just hold on while you can. You're going to have to wait, the guys can't climb sixty floors like that. Plus, we should use the elevators while we still have a hold of them. At least... some of them."

"...What about six and seven?" asked Eden, who had just seen those two elevators' numbers light up.

"Not ours..."

"Oh, hold on to your seatbelt, my Kitties!"

A bell rang, and the doors of the elevators began to open. Dante, Eden, and everyone fired at them the second they spotted the soldier bots' shiny metal. For a few seconds, there was a blinding succession of shots fired, until everyone stopped. The robots fell right where they stood in the elevators.

"Oh, that was one nice firework!" exclaimed Loir, excited.

"And a lot of ammunition was used," sighed Eden. "Loir, we can't have more of those coming through the elevators. Get on it."

"Got you, my Kitty! Room service incoming!"

Just as he said that, the lights to all the elevators, up to the twelfth, lit up. All those above seven were coming from upstairs, the others from downstairs. Eden started to sweat. That was five more groups of robots incoming. She wasn't sure they'd be able to withstand that many, and the other elevators weren't there yet...

Suddenly, the number lights began to blink strangely, and the numbers on all the elevators changed from the floor number it was at to an ominous 404.

"There we go!" shouted Loir.

A terrible ruckus came from the elevators, causing everyone to step back with caution, more afraid of Loir's sudden override than the robots. The numbers on elevators eight through twelve all went crazy, and from the terrible noise she could hear, Eden was almost feeling sorry for the robots inside.

"*Up and down! Up and down!* Come on, my little canned sardines! *Shake it!*"

Eden glanced back to see Circé roll her eyes before going back to her screen. As long as Loir was in control... Suddenly, the elevators slowly went back to their floor, and the doors opened. The robots all fell down, flattened from the bottom and the top, and looked like dwarfed versions of themselves. Eden chuckled. The doors then closed and went downstairs, probably to let more of Dante's men in once they would have gotten rid of the robots.

"See, my Kitty? Easy peasy! *That's one less problem without ya~*" sung Loir.

Meanwhile, the other elevators finally arrived, and more of Dante's men barged in and spread out in the area. They also had more ammunition now, and everyone reloaded their weapons to prepare for what was coming next.

"Good job," said Eden to Loir, walking up to Circé. "...What do you have?"

"Not much. These are basic office computers, they don't have much access, but the Dive Hackers will take care of the rest... How are you holding up?"

"...I'm trying not to think about it."

Circé sighed, and stood back up to face her, done with the computer.

"Eden, you know how these people are. Either they don't have your mother and they are going to make you believe they do, or they do have her, and they are going to use her anyway. You might never know the truth. They will use whatever they've got against you. It's all up to what you choose to believe, and what you choose to fight for."

"...I know."

Eden nodded. In fact, she didn't want to discuss this anymore. She didn't want to even think about this. She knew that the Governor was going to use her, manipulate her because of what she was capable of. She brushed her hair back and nodded.

"Come on, let's move."

Dante arrived next to her, quickly reloading her guns for her. They exchanged a brief smile.

"Not tired yet?" she asked.

"Never. I'm considering this our honeymoon."

"You like it extravagant," she chuckled.

"Guns and bombs. Exactly our style," Dante nodded, giving her a quick kiss on her forehead.

Eden smiled, this little interaction immediately making her feel better. Ironically, that had been the same when they first met, and on their first date. Technically, today was even their wedding day... She sighed. If this was all over one day, she wondered if he'd find another way to cause trouble somewhere for their future dates.

"Let's go," said Dante, a bit louder for everyone. "Everyone split up between both sets of stairs."

His men nodded, and without another word, they split up. Rolf led one group to the smaller stairs Greed had mentioned, while Eden and Dante took the main ones, with Circé somewhere behind them. They could still hear some noise coming from above, so they were expecting more fighting soon.

"We just need to get to their computer systems," said Circé. "As long as we can get there, we will be able to Dive and take them down from the inside."

"We need to hold a siege on the sixtieth floor," nodded Eden. "If we can take control of the tower, the rest will probably be easy. I also need to reach Pan..."

Eden was worried that her master had been completely mute since the beginning of the fighting. She had a bad feeling about this, and a part of her was hoping he was alright.

"Tanya," Dante called.

"We are doing fine!" she grunted back. "Those pieces of crap have mostly left to defend their center, so they're bringing the party to you guys!"

"We're not far," said Michael. "We're going to get to one of their power sources soon, it might give you guys an advantage if we manage to disable it..."

"Disable it? It's a power generator, not a time bomb!" scoffed Tanya. "Let's just blow up the damn thing!"

"If that makes you happy," sighed Michael. "Either way, don't worry about us, guys. A., Lecky, how about you?"

"They sent missiles to the Suburbs, just as we had feared," replied Lecky. "Thank God we had evacuated everyone there. They haven't reached the slums yet, but... even if they don't go that far, I'm worried there won't be much left of the Suburbs if you don't hurry up, guys. We've got reports of more Overcrafts coming over here. If they send units to search the area, they will notice the buildings are empty."

The situation was more urgent in the Suburbs. While the other Zodiacs kept exchanging, Eden was listening, but also focused on their progression. They climbed the next couple of floors without too much trouble, but the noise was clearly coming from above, on the fifty-eighth floor. She was sure the robots were lying in wait upstairs, probably ready to shoot the second they appeared at the door. This time, the elevator or stairs wouldn't change a thing.

530

"They probably parked all their soldier bots above to keep us from going any farther," she muttered. "...What do we do?"

"We can't bomb the place," said Circé before Dante even opened his mouth. "That's a no. If we damage those units on the sixtieth floor, we won't be able to use them, and we don't know where the next floor with all their information units will be."

"We can't send a decoy," retorted Eden. "We don't have anything that could go up there and buy us time... We can't hack those damn soldier bots either."

"How about using the elevators? With a charge in them?"

"Dante, we just said we can't blow it up. We might have a few more floors to climb if we do–"

"Uh, excuse me..." suddenly muttered Nebty.

"What?"

"I have a bad feeling about this conversation you're having right now, and one Overcraft has literally just turned around. I mean, that thing was in the sky in the Suburbs, and it just... turned around like that. Two Overcrafts just began to follow it as if they are chasing–wait, shit, they are firing at it!"

The two women and Dante exchanged a look. They all ran to the closest floor and straight toward the windows to see what was happening. Indeed, from afar, they saw the three flying vehicles, one of them busy doing some very strange dance in the sky, while two others were chasing and firing at it. It was like witnessing a space fight, except that the chased vehicle seemed to have gone completely crazy, making impossible flight movements and not even bothering to fight back against its pursuers.

"What the–"

That's when Loir's singing came into their ears. Eden and Circé went white at the same moment.

"...Loir, please tell me you're not the one controlling that thing," muttered Eden.

"*Come and fly away with me, come and fly away with me-e-e-e-e~*"

"Warlock, stop it! You're going to kill us all, you crazy piece of shit!"

"*We're rising, we're falling, we'll make it through~*"

He was not listening. Either he had put the volume of his music too high on purpose or he was simply ignoring them, there was no way to tell. They saw the flying vehicle come right toward the building, looking like it was going to crash into them.

Everyone on their floor turned around and ran at the same time. They ran, as fast and far as they could, completely overtaken by the idea that Loir's madness was going to kill them.

The shock was violent and brutal. The whole building trembled. Eden felt a terrible pain in her ears, and her whole body vibrated under the shock, even as Dante's body was covering her. It felt like it lasted for a long, long while.

"Eden, Eden, open your eyes."

She did, surprised to even be alive. There were thick curtains of dark smoke covering the windows outside, a loud alarm ringing, and red lights blinking everywhere.

"...What happened?"

"The Overcrafts' wing brutally hit a good portion of the hundredth floor," replied A., "far above you, and it crashed much farther away, luckily. Only several floors above you guys were touched. You should be fine, including the ten or so floors above you. Hoping it doesn't collapse... I don't think so, though. We're quickly checking the predictions of the structure, the building itself doesn't appear to be in danger. The chances of it collapsing are below five percent. But he still did a lot of damage. The whole building went into security mode."

Eden turned around. Indeed, all of the doors were thrown wide open, and the elevators were all disabled. It was a common emergency program for any building with basic security, but it was only triggered when the building could detect a large danger. Not something like a few exchanges of fire, but a fire itself, or an aerial attack, could definitely set it off... and it meant all the robots were going to get the message of an emergency situation. Some would reset themselves, turn off, or try to attach themselves to the System, where their hackers would be able to override them.

"It's amazing!" exclaimed Malieka. "Now we can try to take complete control of the building!"

"Warlock, you insane, fucking nutjob!" shouted Circé, her hair in a complete mess around her. "We were inside!"

"Hehehe~" he chuckled, visibly very proud of himself. "Now, we get to play fair!"

As she could hear his voice coming from different speakers around them, not just her own ear, Eden guessed he was already making his way into the System. The whole Arcadia Tower had joined the System to try and protect itself, as the defense systems would have it, but it was putting the whole building at Loir's mercy, and he was already deep inside.

"Oh," said the Governor's voice suddenly. "A familiar presence. If it's not dear Warlock coming back from the dead. Of course you have to be a massive annoyance. Again."

"How are you, you dirty, smelly, old bag of shit?!" chuckled Loir. "I hope you missed me?"

"Not one bit."

Eden was shocked. Loir and the Governor knew each other? Not only that, but they seemed to know each other well, although it was not on the best terms. She glanced toward Circé, but the witch had a complex expression on, glaring at the speakers above.

"Eden."

On the other side, Dante pulled her hand, and she immediately understood. With the current confusion, it was a golden opportunity to go upstairs. Eden followed after him, and they quickly made their way to the stairs, followed by Dante's men. Despite the strange situation, they couldn't lose their objective. They swiftly progressed, but she couldn't help but listen to the ongoing conversation coming through the speakers.

"I had the faintest hope you had died in whichever hole you found yourself."

"Nope. I ate pizza and I got to have plenty of fun!" chuckled Loir. "I missed you, though. I'm sad I didn't get to pay you back for the last time."

"It's annoying to hear. You should have surrendered yourself, Warlock. You caused us a lot of trouble."

"Oh, the pleasure is all mine, old fart. Damn, how old are you now? A hundred and sixty or something? You should be dead, buried, and all eaten up by cute little worms by now."

"Not a chance. People like me live long lives and die young. You, however, need to come and get that death penalty you escaped."

"No thanks. I'll pass. But I can send you another Overcraft if you want! Come on, Gogo, which floor are you on? I'm sure I can hit you right where it hurts next time..."

"I strongly advise you to stop. I have your little friends in the building too. It would be regrettable if something happens to them, wouldn't it? After all, you already lost all your friends once, did you not?"

Eden froze, glancing at Circé. This time, she didn't look mad at Loir. They were clearly talking about the Edge. Loir and Circé's time in the Edge.

"Ah..." sighed Loir. "You really know how to annoy people. It's hard to believe nobody killed you in your sleep yet!"

The more she listened, the more Eden had a hard time recognizing Loir. It was his voice, but it was as if he had a whole different personality, far from the usually insane Loir. More... angry and desperate. Like something had suddenly switched in him. On the other end, the Governor chuckled.

"Oh, Warlock... The rebel, the survivor. It's sad you and your little group of friends convinced yourselves you could really accomplish this madness. I don't really have the patience for terrorists. I was thinking of being understanding toward Eden, but you? I have no patience left for you."

"Come and get me, old rat," chuckled Loir. "My Kitty will take care of you. Unless I find you first..."

"Nebty, what are they doing?" asked Circé.

"Warlock just hacked another Overcraft."

"Loir, stop it! You're going to kill us all!"

"They will get your location," said Malieka. "Those kinds of hacks are too brutal and ri–"

"Ah... There you are. The Emerald Tower. Oh, you set yourself up quite nicely, didn't you?" chuckled the Governor's voice. "I thought you'd be in a bunker, or perhaps in some sewer. Too bad. Your arrogance is going to kill you."

"Like I said," said Loir, a rictus in his voice. "Come and get me..."

"De Luca," said Nebty. "I hate to give you bad news, but they just launched a missile from one of the Overcrafts. And it's headed right to your territory. Less than one minute away."

"Loir, get out of there!" shouted Eden.

"No can do, Kitty."

"Loir!"

"Sorry, my Kitty, there's this little thing I've postponed for a long while. I'll help you while I can, but I think you're going to have to pick another Back Hacker."

"...You can't be serious," muttered Circé, going white. "...Warlock, it's not worth it, get out!"

"Sorry, Witchy, you know I can't. It's alright. I'll get to be with her."

Eden and Circé exchanged another look, more and more alarmed.

"...Non~" he sang. "*Rien de rien... Je ne regrette rien...*"

"Loir, stop singing and fucking get out!" Eden screamed. "I said get out!"

"...De Luca, the missile is ten seconds away."

"*Ni le bien, qu'on m'a fait...*"

"Loir!"

"Warlock, leave!"

"*Ni le mal...*"

"LOIR!"

"...Five seconds."

"*Tout ça m'est bien ég–*"

The sound was suddenly cut off.

# CHAPTER THIRTY-NINE

A long, heavy silence ensued. She could only hear her loud and thundering heartbeat, and some chaos, coming from far away. But in there, time had stopped. Eden turned around, trying to find a window oriented southwest. She ran toward it, trying to see past the already dark sky filled with smoke. She squinted her eyes, forcing herself to see past the fog, past the first buildings, her eyes desperately looking for where she knew Dante's building to be.

There was nothing there, though. Just another tall, thick column of dark smoke, and the tips of flames she could spot from time to time behind the tall wall splitting the Suburbs and the Core.

"...It can't be," she muttered. "...Loir?"

"Warlock?" Circé called behind her. "...Nebty, please tell me someone has..."

"I'm sorry, girls," muttered Nebty's voice.

Tears appeared in Eden's eyes. She wiped them furiously, unable to believe it. It couldn't be. There was no way Loir was gone just like that. Not so fast, not so easy. To think he had just been... blown up, in a second. It was just too much and too hard to endure.

"...Check again," she cried out, her voice breaking. "Nebty, check again..."

"I'm really sorry, Ghost. There's nothing to check, hun. Nothing to pick up there."

Eden felt the tears pouring from her eyes. She covered her mouth so as not to shout, unable to stop it. She had never thought Loir could even die. He was always hidden, so careful, so secretive, and so enigmatic. She had never imagined he'd be gone, even for a second. There was always a way out for him. How could he be gone so easily? With... not even a real fight. Not chatting his way out with his craziness... Just a stupid song, and an apology? Eden was mad at him for dying like that. She felt... abandoned. Again.

Gentle arms came to hug her from behind. It wasn't Dante, but Circé's thin arms, the long sleeves of her kimono-like outfit covering Eden like a blanket.

"It's alright, Eden. He left the way he wanted to... Free."

Eden choked up even more. Was that really why he had left his position open so easily? She just couldn't talk anymore. Everything was just too much of a shock.

"Come on," Circé gently pulled her away. "Let's... just keep going."

Eden was having a hard time understanding how they could just keep going without Loir. She hadn't even imagined his death would be possible, despite all this. She was sure he was the one who'd survive, even if everything went down. How could he be among those who wouldn't make it? She was still expecting his stupid high-pitched laugh any second in her ears...

"Eden."

This time, it was Dante's voice that came to pull her out of her despair. She nodded weakly, and wiped her tears and snot, trying to repress her crying. She didn't care at all about how ugly she must have looked right now, and that she was the only one crying. Circé had red eyes, but everyone else looked horribly indifferent. After all, Loir was the last one in an already long list of dead people... How many more would she lose?

Suddenly, it hit her. Jack. Jack was in the tower too with the pups. She felt like a second dagger had just pierced her heart. She couldn't believe it. Had Jack died too? Or did he have the time to evacuate... Everything had happened so fast. She couldn't even confirm anything right now. She was too far away, and there was too much left to be done. Eden took several deep breaths, letting Dante pull her in the right direction, and tried to bury her worries for now. She knew Circé was right. Loir had chosen how he wanted to die, and for one good reason. Amongst all of them, he was probably one of those who hated the Core the most.

"...I'll be your Back Hacker for now, Ghost," muttered Greed, sounding terribly sorry.

Eden nodded, before realizing he couldn't see her right now.

"Thanks..."

In fact, the whole channel had gone strangely silent since the building had been blown up. Perhaps Loir, or Warlock, was a lot more respected than she had initially thought, because the hackers, in particular, seemed to have gone from extremely chatty to completely mute. Only Nebty was still talking because she had to coordinate things, but the answers she got were brief and disheartened. Somehow, it comforted Eden a bit to think she wasn't the only one grieving him. They may not have known the crazy punk as she did, but

536

Warlock was truly a hacker the others looked up to.

"We can probably make it upstairs before they get to us," declared Circé. "There must be several floors of computers, and the robots will avoid fighting there. If we can just get Ghost and me on the right floor and win some time, I bet we will be able to do some damage."

"Wasn't it all about getting to that sixtieth floor in the first place? Why do you sound like you're not sure if we're going to get this done?" groaned Tanya.

"Because we don't know how much security they really have on those floors," Malieka answered for them. "There might be computers for lower levels of the System, in which Ghost and Circé will have limited access to things. What we really need is to get to the Core. It's like stepping into some random area of a maze and trying to get to the center. The closer we land, the less work we will have to do, and every minute is incredibly precious in there."

"Agreed," nodded Nebty. "We really need to make sure Ghost has the most direct access to our target. Go upstairs, we will see what we can do about those robots. For now, they seem focused on the fight downstairs. It's going to start blowing up at any mi–"

Before she could finish her sentence, a loud detonation came from under them, shaking the whole building. For a second, everyone in the room froze, a bit worried.

"...nute. I guess it just started."

"Those bastards are here!" Thao shouted.

"We noticed," said Dante.

He exchanged a look with his men, and everyone resumed their course toward the stairs, as quickly as possible. The chatter had resumed in their ears. There was no time left to mourn now, everyone was either defending their position or trying to make their way closer to the System.

Despite her grief and her tears, Eden was doing her best to keep up, both with her group and everything that was said in her ears. The hackers were apparently struggling to get past the System's defenses, just like they had predicted. It was a massive attack like never before, but they were like ants attacking a mountain. Eden was even starting to worry there wouldn't be enough of them. The hackers in the System that were trying to help were exposed, and their numbers were getting reduced bit by bit. All of Nebty's lieutenants were reporting non-stop, trying to keep up. Eden realized Loir's absence had left a void in the ranks. She only had notions of Dive Hacking, but she could tell they were struggling twice as hard as before, some of them constantly asking for more backup. A dark feeling began to grow in her heart. They couldn't slow down, not now. This time, she genuinely decided she'd find the time to grieve later if she got any. Right now, Loir would have been telling her to get her kitty paws going.

She climbed the stairs behind Circé, trying to hold it all in. She was comforted by the fact that Dante was right behind her, and they weren't alone climbing those stairs. It was surprisingly narrow and empty, and with those thick walls meant to protect from a probable fire, they could barely hear the fight going on outside. They had gotten high too now that they were a few dozen floors above the ground. Eden couldn't understand how people could possibly have the time to evacuate a building from such a height, but she kept climbing anyway. Every time they heard an odd sound, they would stop, ready for the enemy to come from above or downstairs.

Luckily, they got to the floor above, or at least, they thought so. The door to the sixtieth floor was secured with a heavy lock, and a large, yellow warning sign too. Circé rolled her eyes and stepped forward with one of her hairpins to try and pick the lock.

"Of course it wouldn't be so easy," she grumbled. "They probably thought they should watch out for possible spies as well... Shit!"

They heard her hairpin break. The difference in size compared to the lock was obvious, and Circé rolled her eyes, turning to Eden and Dante.

"Your turn," she grumbled.

The two of them exchanged a quick glance, before Eden raised her leg, and immediately began kicking the lock furiously. In fact, it felt good. She could vent her frustrations on the little piece of metal, and not even feel the pain from the shock. All she could feel was the strength she was furiously putting into each kick, as if unleashing all of her anger and bottled-up feelings from before. The door was creaking loudly, even starting to bend under the pressure. The lock itself was just looking more and more damaged but still closed. After a few more seconds, Dante grabbed Eden's arm for her to stop, and gently pulled her back. She had barely realized she was sweating and making an angry grimace. He suddenly grabbed one of his subordinates' larger guns and began firing at the annoying lock. It happened so quickly, the closest people had to take a step back to not get hit too. For a couple of seconds, the bullets seemed to do nothing, until they heard the lock finally give up and fall loudly. Dante stopped right away.

"Finally," groaned Circé, pushing the door.

She opened it, into what seemed like a small office, with another door on the other side. Their little group of twenty people crossed the room, Circé opening the next door again.

This time, they found what they wanted: rows and rows of large columns with hundreds of wires and colored lights on them, all protected by thin, glass doors. Eden and Circé ran inside together, looking for the best possible access point.

"What are we looking for?" asked Dante.

"Ideally, there should be a serial number that could help us find the oldest and newest units... but it looks like they erased them all. Damn it, how are we supposed to find the closest access point? How do the people working here even know what to look for? There is no classification, no alley number, nothing. Each and every one is exactly the same!"

"Can't you just pick one?"

"No, we can't. Remember the maze thing? We need to use the one that's not going to take us hundreds of hours to hack once we get in. One with simple access, but deep in the System. ...Nebty, I'm putting in one of my hack keys; give me something worthwhile."

Circé quickly found an access port, and plugged her little key into it. They waited for a second, then all the little lights on the unit she had picked turned purple.

"Access open," she muttered to herself.

"It would have been faster if we had more Dive Hackers," groaned Nebty, "and more Back Hackers. We're starting to lose too many people, and that's all the Edge has got. We really need to sort out these units quickly, it's so infuriating. Oh, crap. You got an old one... but we might be able to do something with it. I'm on it."

A loud sound came from above them, like something very heavy was moving. Eden grimaced.

"I think we're really running out of time in here too. The soldier bots are right above us. Whichever one you pick, it's going to have to be on this floor."

"You are not making my shopping session easy... I need at least a couple of minutes to find their classification. It's gotta be somewhere."

"We might have to Dive in randomly," grimaced Circé. "We don't have time to pick the right one..."

"No," said Malieka. "You can't just pick randomly, it would be too risky. What if you get on a useless one, or worse, a trapped one? We can't put you two at risk. Ghost will need a second Dive Hacker to help her inside. No one else will be able to join you until you both get inside and give us access. You know how this works."

"Fine, fine... but hurry up. I don't want to be shot while I'm Diving..." grimaced Circé, eyes on the ceiling.

"We will block the entrances," said Dante, gesturing for his men to move.

Immediately, the Italians scattered, running to block the doors on each side with what they had, or what they could find. Only Dante stayed by Eden's side, quietly. He grabbed her hand, squeezing it gently, but he didn't say anything. They were both standing next to each other, waiting for an answer.

"...You are so stubborn, child," suddenly said the Governor's voice.

Eden had almost forgotten about that man. She glanced around, trying to find where the voice came from, furious. She didn't want to hear his voice anymore. Not after what he had done to Loir.

"You should give up on that strange idea of yours. You and your friends will only get yourselves killed... and that is not what I want, trust me. You should be able to live among your people, with us, in the Core. You're not like them, Eden. However you were raised is not the future your father had planned for you."

"On the contrary," Eden raised her gun. "I think my father wanted me to see exactly what I needed to see."

She fired at each of the speakers she spotted in the room. Whenever she heard his voice again, she lifted her arm and made sure whichever device the sound came from was destroyed.

"Uh... S-sorry to interrupt the search, but... is anyone else seeing what I'm seeing?" suddenly asked Pride.

"Wait... What the heck is going on?" muttered Greed.

One after the other, several of the hackers were heard, surprised. The chat became so busy and loud, Eden grimaced and had to cover one of her ears.

"Hey, hey!" shouted Nebty. "Everybody shut up for a second! What the heck is going on in there? What is that..."

"I have no idea," muttered A. "There are... It's like hundre–no, thousands of connections are entering the System. What are those... Are those online auctions?"

"Yeah, I'm picking them up too," said Greed. "What the heck is that? Free cat plushie to win... Online games, free movies... What are those? There are dozens popping up everywhere!"

Circé and Eden immediately raised their heads and glanced at each other. Could it be...?

"And everyone is logging online to get that stuff," muttered Malieka. "There's... Wait, there are even some in the Dark Reality? Open sources? Classified information? How to get past the guardian falcon of the Russian Data Library... Holy crap, these are hacking programs! And... hundreds of classified hacks... There are even tips for beginner hackers!"

"It's in the other Cores too!" shouted Crash. "I'm getting signals from New York, London, Cape Town, New Delhi, Tokyo... even Neo Shanghai!"

"Hey, hey, I found something," said Nebty. "I found the source of the breach. Looks like some idiot just poured all of their details out, or their security portal just got blown open. Looks like someone got their private servers completely hacked and put out there... Oh, wow! Hey, what's this? Shut it down, shut it down!"

"Nebty?"

"Sorry, that... that's fucking Pandora's Box opened and poured into the System. No wonder the System is crashing, everyone is getting online to grab something!"

"...The Anarkia program."

Circé chuckled nervously.

"Hey, how did you know that?" asked Greed. "That word is everywhere, in all the auctions, all the data for sale, and the programs! It's hidden in all of the code we're running into!"

"...It's Loir?" Eden muttered.

Circé nodded, a smirk on her face.

"It was one of his crazy ideas... I never thought he'd do it. I mean, what kind of crazy pours years of work, hacking, and research just out there in the System? No hacker would sacrifice their stuff, and sell everything they got.

540

Even less for free. That's a perfect way to be completely vulnerable and get... killed."

"He... triggered this with his death," muttered Malieka. "I don't know how he did it, but the second he got offline, all his servers were opened wide and onto the System."

"...That's exactly how he did it," Eden chuckled. "...He never went offline."

She found herself chuckling nervously. She was half crying, half laughing. So he really had one last crazy plan... the craziest plan of all. No one else would have done such a thing, or even prepared such an insane idea. Yet, he had done it. He was emptying everything, absolutely everything, all of his crazy genius out there, not only for everyone to see, grab, and take, but to give one last middle finger to the System. All of Loir's knowledge was now going to be in the open, for any new hacker to learn. All the information they had stolen, for years, was just left out for everyone to see, like on a giant billboard to the world. No wonder the entire world was trying to get online. It was open season on the mastermind of this century's craziest genius.

"...It's working," exclaimed Greed, his smile could be heard in his voice. "The System is starting to slow down from the insane amount of visitors. All the hackers are getting online and finding breaches too!"

"It's not only the Edge now," said Nebty. "Every single hacker will want to get into that System with us. The Anarkia program just blew a massive hole in their security!"

Eden smiled, wiping her tears once again. That was Loir's final goodbye. "...Thank you, you crazy cat."

"Girls," said Nebty. "I'm loving this overload of the System, but the mess isn't going to last more than a few minutes before they fight back and put everything back in line. We need to find your entry point, and soon!"

Circé and Eden exchanged a quick glance and a nod and went back to scouring through the aisles of the data center, trying to look for a sign, a number, or something, anything that would indicate one of them was useful.

"I-I think I got one," said Greed. "Number six-hundred–"

"Greed," groaned Circé, "unless you missed the last ten minutes of us roaming around, there is still no number on these stupid data centers!"

"Oh, sorry, sorry. I don't have eyes in the room so... Oh, got it. It's two aisles behind the one you picked, the fourth one on the left."

Circé and Eden ran to said block, and even confirmed it once more with Greed.

"It can only pull one person," Greed warned them. "There's a second one you can use, just three more down to your right, opposite side."

"I'm going there," said Circé, following his directions. "Nebty, get me a decent Back Hacker!"

"I'm on you," chuckled Malieka. "Hope I will suffice... Greed, ready?"

"Ready anytime for you, ladies... Nekhbet, Crash, try to join us. I'm sending you the location point, if you manage to get there..."

"It's going to take us time to load over there," sighed Crash. "Everything is so freaking slow... Damn, three minutes of downloading time! What is this, the twentieth century?!"

"Stop complaining and get on it," retorted Eden.

They waited a few seconds, and she turned to Dante, who had followed her all along. When their eyes met, he wrapped his arm around her waist gently.

"...You ok?"

"I'm holding up. I think... I might need a minute when this is over."

Her eyes were still red, feeling dry and a bit stingy from all her earlier crying. She sniffled once, feeling her equally dry throat and lips. This was a freaking long day indeed.

"...You stay by my side," she muttered.

"I'm not leaving you," he promised. "I'll guard you, don't worry."

"Aren't I supposed to be the bodyguard..."

"We can watch each other's backs. Get in there and make them pay."

This was so like Dante, she thought. He never showed when he was sad or angry. At least, not in his facial expressions. But, he could express himself more violently, with words and actions. She was a bit glad to hear that he was pissed off about Loir's death too, enough to tell her to get back at their enemies for it. She held his hand with one of hers, while the other grabbed the cables necessary from the data center to connect herself, waiting for Greed's signal. This was different from Mr. Charles' computers; she needed a direct connection.

"...I'm sorry about your house," she muttered.

"I'll buy a new one. One you'll like."

"I liked that one."

"Then I'll get the same one."

Eden smiled bitterly, but her heart wasn't ready for his kind words, this time. It didn't make much sense anyway... That place was probably a grave and a mess right now. No comfort Dante could give her would be enough to take away her pain, and Eden just couldn't help but feel like crying again. She closed her eyes, and as soon as Greed gave her the signal, she connected her SIN.

She reopened her eyes in an elevator. Her reflexes taking over, she put one knee down, checking her surroundings; she was in a very old-style elevator, like in those old movies with a manual door, and a simple grid to cut her off from the outside world. A ding was heard, and the little list of numbers next to her had the number five lit up. Eden frowned, but as nothing happened, she opened the door and stepped out. This place was far from what she had expected. In fact, it looked a bit like Dante's building's ground floor, with very old-fashioned decor; this time, it had a monochrome theme, all in shades of beige, brown, and camel, with thick mats, and leather and suede furniture. What caught her eye first, though, were the impressively tall bookshelves.

Eden's lateral vision was filled with oakwood shelves. Most of them were packed with boxes or thick notebooks, all perfectly lined up.

"...A data archive room," she muttered.

"Yep," said Greed. "It's a more recent room than it looks, though, I promise. You're in one of the most recent archives rooms of the System, but the security is lower here. We couldn't have found a more recently saved version of this room without triggering a whole bunch of security... but at least, the central room of the System is very close. We only need to get to the latest version of that place to get there."

"What about C.?"

"She landed two floors below you, she's on her way to the elevators."

"Alright... Where to now?"

"Third aisle on your left, the one with the boxes that start with a B. We need to navigate through this archive to jump to another, more recent one... Normally, they isolate each archive, but because they take up so much space on the server, they tend to delete the rooms they have no use for. Which means the old rooms have lower security but using them, we can get to another room that's more recent with the access we–"

"Greed, stop chatting, just tell me where to go," said Eden. "I know how archived data rooms work..."

Having a different Back Hacker than Loir was making her nervous and a bit annoyed too. It wasn't Greed's fault, though. Dive and Back Hacker teams generally worked better after years and years of cooperation. If anyone other than Eden had worked with Loir, they would have gone crazy with his antics, but she knew he was more reliable than he let on. She forced herself to take a deep breath and pushed those thoughts aside to find said box.

"Got it," she said, opening it.

"Get the red folder... No, the dark red one, sorry. I need the numbers inside."

She opened it up, and as soon as Greed saw it, Eden heard a snapping sound, and the environment around her changed. It looked like exactly the same room, but this time, the shelves were made of black metal, the floor was all wood, and there was no other furniture, only more shelves.

"...More recent version," she guessed.

"Nope, older. 2104, but I promise we're getting closer. Just a few more jumps... Oh, I need you to go upstairs this time."

Eden hesitated, looking around her. Meanwhile, Circé appeared next to her, in her hacker appearance. She was wearing a more modern version of her usual kimono, with swords crossed on her back, platform heels, and twin high ponytails. Her face was covered by a strange demon-like mask.

"Catching a break?" she asked Eden.

"No, it's just... This is the backup of the server from my birth year."

"Oh..."

"Do you want me to do a quick check, Ghost?" asked Malieka's voice.

"Just in case."

"Yes, please."

Meanwhile, Circé and Eden began to head upstairs, going back to the elevator they had come from. Navigating through the archives to find an access point they could exploit could take a while, but Eden couldn't help but get an odd feeling from knowing that this was her birth year's archive. This place contained everything the System had twenty-three years ago... The world her father had created at its early stages. More files here than in the one before meant a lot of it had been wiped out afterward, to make space for more, surely.

"I got something. Keyword Newman... Oh, right next to the one we were headed for, actually. Same shelf but on the far left."

Intrigued, Circé and Eden headed there. She couldn't help but walk fast, curious.

"Everything alright outside?" asked Circé.

"Girls, you've been in there less than a minute," said Greed. "Relax. It's going to get really annoying soon enough..."

Eden didn't listen to him, only focused on the box. She found it. It looked strangely older than the others, like an old cardboard box, with a serial number on it. She grabbed it without hesitation, opening it.

"It's all video files," said Greed. "Surveillance videos... from what looks like a house."

"Show me," said Eden, her heart beating fast.

Her environment changed in a blink, obliviating everything, even Circé. Suddenly, she was inside a large living room. She frowned and turned around. There was an empty baby's crib, next to a small couch. A little colored carpet was laid down, meant for a small child, with toys scattered around. There was no sign of life, though. Only the furniture and the decor of a warm home, with pictures on the walls, and plants. Eden turned around, spotting three doors.

"On your left," said Greed.

Eden moved, and she was suddenly pushed into the next room. This time, it was an office. A very disorderly office. There were papers absolutely everywhere. On the floor, on the furniture, and even pinned all the way up on the walls. She couldn't understand anything on it, it was all blurred. The things she was most attracted to were the very large computer and its screen, and the man sitting in front of it. She jumped in surprise; there was a dog next to the chair, chewing a dog toy with its tail wagging. She had no idea she used to have a dog... Eden turned to the man. He was speaking to the screen, with a serious expression.

"Why is there no sound?" she asked, annoyed.

"There really isn't, Ghost," said Greed, a bit apologetic. "It seems like they recorded without audio in the first place... They probably didn't need it for a security camera."

Now that she thought about it, all the colors around her looked less vivid than they should have been, a bit grayish. The recording wasn't of the best quality... which explained why she couldn't read the papers or see the details well. She turned to the man again. His traits weren't well captured either. He had a large, long beard that was poorly taken care of, equally messy hair, and round glasses. Even without the high quality, she recognized the man from Mr. Charles' picture. Her dad.

She stepped closer, realizing he was carrying something in his arms. There was a small baby, with its eyes half-opened. Eden stared at the scene for a few seconds. Despite the absolute mess around him, the man was holding the baby securely against his chest, his thumb gently rubbing its little chubby leg.

"...Sorry, Eden, but we've got to go," said Circé.

"I've seen enough. Thanks."

Another snap, and she was back in the large library with Circé. Her partner tilted her head.

"Seen anything interesting?"

"Not really... but it was nice."

"Good for you then. Come on, girl, let's get moving."

Eden nodded. Without audio, she would only have watched the scene in a loop, with no idea who her father was chatting with through that screen. Yet, she was a bit glad she had gotten to see him, even if it wasn't real. For the first time, she felt a bit close to that man who had been a stranger most of her life... and she felt somewhat happy about that too. She had never known how her father felt toward his daughter that had to flee her home, and she always thought they had never really met... yet, she had just seen otherwise. The baby could have been in her crib, but instead, her father had her in his arms, holding her tenderly. They really did have a bond, even if she had forgotten it...

Circé found the next box and grabbed it to open it. Eden glanced one last time at the cardboard box, and it disappeared. They had moved to a different archive.

"How many more of those?" groaned Circé. "We don't have time to run through archives all day, you said this was a close entry point!"

"Hey, it's not like I can parachute you guys into the middle of the System! The closest doesn't mean it's right there, okay? The whole thing is damn huge, and I promise, we're already freaking close compared to all the other hackers taking the long, long way to even get where you are, alright? Stop bitching."

"You're lucky you're hidden somewhere and not where I can slap you," groaned Circé.

"Come on, ladies," said Malieka. "Two floors down, northeast aisle, fourth shelf on the right. The box starting with a twelve. I promise we're trying to make this as fast as possible."

Eden and Circé exchanged a glance, and with a nod, ran together to the closest balcony, jumping over it. They dove for a couple of seconds, before both grabbing the rail two floors below.

"...Show-offs," chuckled Greed.

"We're on the clock," retorted Circé.

"It does go faster this way. Please try not to kill yourselves too fast, though, that would be stu–wait. ...Greed, you caught that?"

"Yep. Ladies, jump and run all you want, but you have to move quickly. You've been spotted."

"In a freaking archive?!" exclaimed Circé, running beside Eden. "You're kidding me?"

"Don't ask me, I'm not the one who spent money on a stupid security program... I mean, at least it shows they are aware of their security breaches, props to them."

"How bad, Greed?"

"Bad... Not good. Really not good. I can't catch it... Malieka?"

"I see it. It's malign software. They are sending a wiper, ladies, you better hurry up, it's a big one!"

"They are wiping out their own archives?!" exclaimed Circé.

"Well, maybe they really don't care about 2123... or they don't like you in their archives. Anyway, don't stop. They sent a mean one."

"Give me some weapons!" groaned Eden.

"Coming, coming..."

They suddenly heard it. A large, loud groan, coming from behind them. The System could send anything to try and scare intruders, and from the noise, they could tell this one was going to be big indeed.

"Greed!"

"There!"

Pink leather gloves suddenly appeared on Eden's hands, with claws as long as daggers. She raised an eyebrow.

"Loir-craft?"

"Yeah. He left a bunch of stuff on your back data inventory... Just going through it now, I'll send you more if I can sort it out."

"Thanks."

Eden was a bit glad Loir had left some weapons behind for her... He was a lot more meticulous than she gave him credit for, after all. As if he had everything prepared just in case.

The monster appeared. A large, monstrous reptile, its head shaped like a triangle, with impressive fangs. It had six legs and was moving like a mix of a snake and a spider, climbing on the shelves while making strange groaning noises.

"Ugh," groaned Circé. "They don't even bother to make them realistic now, they just go for ugly monsters."

"They probably sent us a non-elaborated one," said Eden, studying the monster.

She glanced ahead. They were only ten steps away from the box they needed. Unfortunately, the monster had jumped in between them and their target. Circé took out one of her swords.

"You run," she said. "I'll cover you."

"Are you going to be alright...?"

"Yeah. Just a minute and I'm going to make a damn handbag out of this thing."

"Got it."

Dive Hacking required quick decisions and a lot of trust in her partner. Eden knew this thing was probably going to be a handful for Circé, but she was at least as experienced as her. They both knew the risks, and what they had really come all this way for. They couldn't lose time, nor risk her getting injured so soon.

"Nekhbet is almost there," said Malieka. "He's in the previous file. You'll get a sidekick in a minute, C..."

"I call dibs on the handbag. Eden, get ready to go."

Eden nodded, preparing herself to run, claws up. She evaluated the space between the monster, Circé, and their surroundings; she could get to it in a high jump, only if the monster attacked Circé instead of her. They waited, for a second, and finally, Nekhbet appeared on the other end of the aisle, a long spear in hand. He attacked first, and the creature screeched in surprise, turning around to attack.

"Now!"

Eden and Circé jumped at the same time, each on their target. Eden's hands grabbed the box, but she felt a vivid pain in her leg. She opened it.

She landed painfully on her butt, onto a strange grassy ground, and immediately rolled, prepared for another attack. This time, though, she was alone, and in a garden-like version of the archive.

"Greed?"

"...They are busy with that thing. Get to the floor below. Same aisle, green box at the bottom. Hurry, there's more coming."

Eden nodded and got back on her feet. She glanced down, annoyed. She was feeling pain in her leg... That damn SIN. She took a deep breath, forcing herself to remember it wasn't real. She jumped to the floor below again, prepared to find the box. To her surprise though, there was a silhouette already there. Eden immediately lifted her claws, ready to fight.

This monster was different though. It had two legs and looked like a child, a simple child with a monochromatic, gray outfit. In fact, there was nothing monstrous about it, only an angelic face, and a body that looked entirely made of strangely vivid colors... as if lights were projected from all sides, almost blinding. The feeling Eden had in her gut made her approach cautiously. It was a feeling of déjà vu. Why did she feel like this? She knew she couldn't trust one of the System's illusions. It wouldn't be the first time it used such a trick to suddenly attack her. There was definitely something odd about this one, though. She couldn't even sense any hostility, and it seemed to be simply... waiting there, for her.

"...Hi, Eden."

She froze. That voice. Was that a trick, again? She hesitated, staring into his bright eyes and gentle smile.

"...Pan?"

# CHAPTER FORTY

He chuckled and nodded, slowly stepping forward as if not to scare her.

"Yes," the child smiled. "I'm surprised you even recognized me in this form!"

"What are you... How did you get here?"

"Ah... Sorry, I only managed to find this way to interact with you. The System's archives are always useful, aren't they? You can dig some old things out, and just when everyone was thinking they wouldn't be useful again... But here we are."

"What are you doing here, Pan?" frowned Eden.

"I said I would help you, didn't I?" he smiled. "I'm not really here, sadly. I only took this physical appearance temporarily, to speak to you... I'm so glad you made it this far, Eden."

"...My friend is dead," she suddenly blurted out, angry. "Loir is dead, Pan. He's dead and I couldn't do anything to save him."

His expression fell, and he nodded, lowering his head with a sorry expression.

"I know... I'm really sorry I couldn't prevent it. I know he was a really good and close friend of yours... He was one of my friends too."

"Why weren't you there?" she asked angrily. "Why didn't you come out to help us sooner? This plan was half yours, so why are you only appearing now?! I needed you, Pan! Why weren't you there when I really needed you? They killed Loir. They even killed Old Man Long, the Eagle, and so many other people! ...Even now, there are people out there, still fighting, risking their lives, and dying as we speak. Everyone is in danger. ...It was your plan, Pan."

He took a deep breath, and nodded again.

"I know... I knew there would be lives sacrificed, and I am... really sorry about that. But... I truly will do what I can, Eden, but it's not much. In fact, I'm taking a huge risk just to speak to you right now. If they discover what I am up to, they could get rid of me before you even get to me. I don't really care about my own death. I was ready to die as soon as this plan was launched, but... it's true you still need me. I don't want to go before I'm sure you've succeeded."

Eden hesitated. She couldn't even check she was actually talking to the real Pan right now. She had a gut feeling it was him, but a gut feeling was never enough.

"...Greed?" she called out. "Hey, Greed!"

"Oh, finally! I was worried sick for a second, I couldn't hear you... Where are you?"

Eden blinked twice, surprised. She looked around, but nothing had changed. How come her Back Hacker couldn't see her? He should have had eyes on her at all times!

"I'm... in the same space, looking for the green box you told me. ...You really can't see me?"

"No, nothing. It's like you're in a Blank. The whole area is invisible to me, and... Damn, the whole coding is getting wonky. Whoever's doing that is good... Give me a minute, I'll try to bypass it!"

Eden turned to Pan, who nodded. He had created a Blank to talk to her? Blanks were like a safety bubble, something some hacker pairs had invented to try and throw people off their trail; it was creating a sort of intended glitch generated from the Dive Hacker's SIN, a hole to create a gray area where the code was impossible to see for any external eye or messing with the other hackers in there. It usually required an extremely high-level Back Hacker, and the connection to the SIN of the Dive Hacker they were trying to hide in this Blank. If Greed couldn't see her, then it means Pan was behind it and doing an amazing job too... It looked like the conversation was even muted.

"You don't trust Greed?" she frowned.

"Oh, no, I don't trust anyone. But, to be fair, no one should trust me either. I'm so symbiotically linked to the System that I'm a threat to everyone else. It's also how I can move around the archives so easily like this... although it won't be long before it finds me. I'm like a virus that lives in its body and does a bit of damage once in a while."

He chuckled, visibly proud of whatever mess he could cause. Eden hesitated. She was still mad at him, but the more she spoke to him, the more she felt like it was no use; Pan knew his wrongs and limits perfectly well.

"...Can you help us or not?" she muttered.

"I will do my best," he said with a low, sad voice, "but I told you, I'm limited. You too. There's only so much you can do by messing around in these archives."

"I saw my dad."

Her sentence seemed to truly surprise him. The boy opened his eyes wide and, after a second, a faint but genuine smile appeared on his lips.

"...Really?"

"It was old footage from a surveillance camera... I saw him when he was younger, and I was a child. He was talking to someone, but I didn't get the audio."

"Oh... I see."

His enigmatic words that didn't answer anything annoyed her. Since the beginning, Eden was dying to know the relationship between Pan and her dad. She had always had a feeling it was something complicated, but the more she knew about either of them, the more enigmatic the other was...

"It must have been nice," he said with a sad smile, "for you to see him. I also come down here sometimes... to rewatch a few things."

"Like what?"

"Like that one you saw. Memories of when you were still here, in the Core... as a child. Of the happy days before I was trapped here, before what they did to your parents. I hope you'll be able to see it all someday. Sadly, we don't have time for that right now, do we?"

Eden swallowed her saliva and her mixed, torn feelings. She just couldn't figure out Pan at all. There were a million questions she wanted to ask him, but none that she could decide on first. She glanced down at her leg, realizing she had forgotten the fake pain already. She glanced to the side. No monsters were coming, and the box she had come to get was right there. Was that thanks to Pan protecting and hiding her?

"...Where are you?" she finally muttered.

"Fifteen floors above you. The seventy-fifth one. You'll get in trouble for getting there, my Eden."

Eden's heart felt a pinch. Just fifteen floors above her? Only fifteen floors? This was the closest she had ever been to meeting the real Pan, all this time... She was so curious and suddenly dying to see his physical self. Whoever he was, whatever he was, she wanted to see the real Pan. She tried to breathe, but to her surprise, he suddenly grabbed the box she had come for and handed it to her with a smile.

"Come on, pretty songbird," he said. "You still have a lot to do."

"What did you call me?" she asked.

"I told you. I've been watching you from up close for a while... See you soon."

Before she could protest, Pan grabbed her hand and put it on the box. Immediately, everything around Eden changed. She dropped the box as soon as she could, but he was already gone, and everything around her had changed. She gasped, feeling like she had just finished a marathon. She turned around, analyzing her surroundings by reflex.

"Ghost? Ghost? Oh, that damn thing... Come on. Ghost, please? If you hear me, can you–"

"I hear you," she sighed. "Sorry, Greed, I hear you now."

"Oh, thank God! I had half the Edge about to tear me apart and that was not cool at all, lady. What the heck happened? Who did that?"

"Pan."

"Pan? You mean... Prometheus?"

"You saw Prometheus?" suddenly asked Lecky.

"Yeah. He said his real body is upstairs, in this building. On the seventy-fifth floor."

"Oh, we should have expected so..."

Eden was torn. She had come here to find the safest way into the System, ruin the Core's plan, and destroy them from the inside. They were supposed to bomb everything, in the Dark Reality and in the real world alike, but what about Pan? She couldn't help but glance above her again. He was upstairs, just upstairs...

"I need to get to him," she suddenly declared.

"Oh, uh... okay... Really? I mean, no offense, but that's a whole lot of floors to get there, and nothing nice on the way, Ghost. I know we've been playing it safe that way, but I'm sure that was what we all agreed on to begin with. Get to the servers, destroy what we could, and get out of there. If you really want to go upstairs, we're putting the whole plan in jeopardy..."

"Nebty?" Eden asked with a sigh.

She knew it was selfish of her, but now, she just couldn't get it out of her head. Perhaps she would change her mind if literally everyone was against it, but...

She heard Nebty sigh on the other end, and chat with Lecky, Malieka, and A. for a few seconds.

"...Okay," she sighed. "I would have said no, but frankly speaking, you're just going to keep circling around in the archives for nothing if we keep going like this, and we need to be more decisive. The seventy-fifth floor is also where one of their biggest servers is. If you get there, this time we can really get to them, without the archive maze bullshit."

"Thanks for saying that only now!" groaned Circé.

"Circé! How are you doing?" asked Eden.

"I'm still alive, thanks... but unplugging now, if nobody minds. I have no intention to stay around if we're not going to use these stupid archives, and you're already too far ahead. There are more and more monsters coming my way, and we don't have all day to play with them."

"I can keep going on my own," Eden nodded. "...Greed, I want the Edge to make copies of these archives. We need to take control of everything here."

"Wait, what?"

"They have surveillance camera records here. If we get all of them, it could help us."

552

"We're not trying to make a point," said Nebty. "The plan was always to destroy them!"

"Yes, but no one says we will succeed, and regardless of if we do or not, they could be useful."

"Could be? Come on, Ghost, we don't have the time or the resources for that!"

"Why not?" asked Lecky. "All of the Edge should be focusing on the System's hacking right now. As soon as Eden opens it up for them, just let them dig out all they want in there. Ghost, just find a way to give us access to that place. We will do the rest."

"Excuse me, are you in charge or am I?"

Ignoring Nebty's angry tone, Eden nodded and turned around, running to the balcony from earlier. She wondered how recent the garden version was... Greed guided her twice more into different versions, and Eden forgot about fighting any of the nightmarish creatures that appeared; Nekhbet appeared to support her, but now, it was a race against the clock. Eden didn't want to lose one more second. She ran, grabbing box after box, visiting two more versions of this world, following Greed's instructions to the letter. Their communication wasn't as fluid and intuitive as with Loir, but it was starting to get easier.

"I found it!" he exclaimed a minute later. "A forgotten back door, 2072 version. Next box, second aisle to the right, top shelf with a blue... no, indigo blue. Come on, come on... Yeah, it's going to be the one, Ghost. Just get there, and we can open a fucking highway in there!"

Eden nodded and ran as fast as she could. She felt like she hadn't Dived in so long, she was having trouble picking up her legendary speed in there. Luckily, she soon got out of the elevator on the said version and began running again to get that final box.

Suddenly, she heard a bang on the side.

"...Greed, what was that?"

"Your signal to run!"

She didn't wait, and kept running, headed right to the box. She could hear him furiously typing on his keyboard, so fast and loud it sounded like music. Greed's typing was angrier and louder than Loir, and she could hear him swear and groan.

"What's going on?" she asked as soon as she got enough breath for it.

"Nothing good. We've been discovered, they are trying to wipe those servers clean! Oh, damn it, damn it... Shit, they are going crazy fast and deleting every fucking thing. Looks like you were right, they got a few dirty secrets they want to keep..."

Eden didn't need to ask any further; it was clear now, the Core was trying to wipe it all out because of her. Or was it because they had found Pan wandering in there? Either way, she was running out of time. She jumped in front of the shelf she needed and began searching for that box, but this one was scarily full. She had to throw a few of them out of the way before she finally spotted it.

"Found it!"

"Thank God. We just lost all of the fifties..."

She opened the box and suddenly, the floor shook violently under her. Eden got down on her knees, holding on to the shelf, when she realized nothing around her was moving. Instead, she was the one off balance. She felt a strange sensation in her arm.

"What's going on?"

"Eden, come back," suddenly said Dante's voice. "We have to move."

"Go," said Greed. "I got what I need here, girl, Nekhbet and I will finish. Good job, and stay alive! See you for the next and last one, I hope..."

Eden left the Dark Reality and blinked twice.

Immediately, the sounds of gunshots made her jump to her feet, but a hand grabbed her shoulder to make her lay low again.

"Welcome back," grunted Dante.

They were hidden between two of the data centers, and from what she could see and hear, there were gunshots coming from all sides. Dante was busy trying to shoot back, moving his head, shoulder, and arm only when he could get clear shots at them. Eden grimaced, massaging her stiff neck.

"How bad is it?"

"I've seen worse. They sent five soldier bots our way. I guess we were found out."

"You should have told me earlier!"

"It wasn't that bad."

Eden rolled her eyes. Perhaps it wasn't much to him, but she wasn't fond of knowing she had been completely unconscious with her body stuck in the crossfire while she was Diving. A loud bang came from the other side, and Dante quickly used his height to glance above the large block of metal.

"...Our last grenade," he sighed, quickly reloading his gun. "How about you? Do we need to go up?"

"To the seventy-fifth floor, to save Pan, or whatever. If we can..."

"We can," he nodded confidently. "...Rolf, can you cover us?"

"Sure."

"You're going up, just the two of you?" exclaimed Circé. "Have you gone mad?!"

"We don't need more," said Dante, grabbing Eden's hand, visibly ready to move.

"My ass, you don't need more! This is a fucking battle and all of the floors above are filled with more of those fucking soldier bots! This is war, you crazy punk, not a date just for the two of you!"

Dante smirked, sending a quick wink to Eden. Despite the situation, he somehow had the guts to find amusement here... She sighed, and glanced above the data centers too to assess the risks. For once, though, she was more of Circé's opinion. There were more bots coming down from the elevators that Greed didn't have control of. The only thing was that the stairs were visibly clear. Eden guessed those things either had protocols to stay away from them, or their legs couldn't climb them. After all, they were rather basic robots...

"Greed, how is it going?"

"Getting there," he said. "We're halfway through the download on our own servers... which I hope we're not filling with a bunch of useless crap."

"What about the control of the tower?"

"Oh, that. Give me a second."

Dante suddenly pulled her for them to change positions, and fired at one bot that had appeared at the end of their aisle. Eden kept her gun up, but he was standing between her and the threat on purpose, so that she didn't even get to properly see that robot until it miserably fell down, full of Dante's bullets.

"We have control over half of the elevators, and luckily, we got enough control on the lower floors as well, they completely abandoned it. We were able to secure Thao's group, so we're focusing on Tanya and Michael's... They are still attacking the Suburbs with their Overcrafts, though. ...Shit, I'm glad we emptied those buildings. It's a wreck out there, Ghost."

"It's only a matter of time before they realize they are attacking empty buildings," said Malieka. "Nebty, I think they really need to go upstairs. The Edge is still stuck because of the protocols, we only have access to the protocols and the lower levels of their security, but it won't be enough. ...Pan could get us all the access we need."

"I know, but I'm still worried. If Ghost gets killed, it's all over, you realize that?"

"...You just need me to log on and open up," sighed Eden. "I'll do it the second I get on the main security levels, and Pan can just catch up. If we free him..."

"It's not a question of freeing Pan, Ghost! He never was a priority, alright? You're the priority, and we need you to get to where the System is vulnerable."

"The System is more vulnerable upstairs," Eden retorted. "...I swear I'll get there and open it up for the Edge to fight for control, no matter what. I'll go through each floor if needed."

"...You may not have to," suddenly said Pride. "I'm with Crash, and we just found something useful. The center of the System is exactly on the seventy-fifth floor Pan is apparently on. It's... the heart, literally. If we get Ghost there, we win. The Edge can access all of it and win. Even Ghost could just rewrite it all, it's the neurologic center of the System!"

Eden and Dante exchanged a glance, and a nod. They began moving before Nebty even gave them any permission, both of them rushing toward the stairs again, guns up to shoot at anything in their way.

"Fine," groaned Nebty. "But for God's sake, everyone who can, stay with the rogue pair!"

"...We're married."

"Nobody asked, De Luca! Nobody!"

Despite the moniker, Eden could only chuckle briefly; this situation was way worse than she had ever experienced. Dante was pulling her hand once again and running ahead of her while shooting left or right as the situation called for it. She could hear the gunshots flying above her head or brutally hitting some of the servers.

"You damn Italians!" groaned Pride. "Can you please leave some of those servers intact if we're supposed to copy them? You're doing more damage to those archives than the Core itself, and they are intentionally trying to wipe them!"

"We don't exactly have time for neat cleaning, Pride!" retorted Circé, annoyed.

Indeed, it was raining fire from all sides. Several times, they had to dodge them by diving down or staying hidden behind one of the dark towers for a couple of seconds. Eden glanced over her shoulders, and indeed, more soldier bots were coming down from the elevators. Luckily, their arrival was predictable, so Dante's men would fire as soon as the doors opened. One of the elevators was even stuck where it was because of the pile of soldier bots preventing the doors from closing. Still, their firepower was enough to force them all to stay in hiding and wait for the right window to fire back. They should have been grateful those central units separating them from the robots were in some sort of reinforced steel for their own protection, otherwise, it would have been a massacre in the room.

Finally, they reached the stairs and climbed up as fast as they could to get out of sight. Eden was brutally pushed forward, and she heard Dante groan, sending a chill down her spine.

"Dante!"

"I'm fine. Keep going!"

His voice didn't sound fine, but she had no time to disobey. Biting her lip furiously, Eden climbed the stairs. Circé and more of Dante's men ran into the stairwell behind them, but there was no sign of Rolf. He was staying behind to lead the fight against the robots, and Eden could still hear him shout orders to the men. She tried not to think too much about it; if everything went well, those robots would be deactivated in a matter of minutes now, hopefully...

She held Dante's hand a bit more firmly, and they progressed together up the stairs, only slowing down when they got close to the doors for the next floors. Behind each, a terrible ruckus could be heard, but it seemed like the robots were staying far away from the emergency stairs. The more they kept climbing unbothered, the more suspicious Eden got; even if the robots were initially prevented from accessing the emergency stairs, the Core should have bypassed those protocols and told them to fire at anything moving by now... Was that Pan's doing once again? Eden couldn't help but think he was scarily powerful at times.

Suddenly, the stairs trembled, and they stopped moving, eyes riveted above them.

"...What's that?" asked Circé behind them.

Eden frowned, and put her head in the hole between the stairs, trying to see what was going on farther above. She removed her head right before a gunshot resonated in the stairwell.

"Soldiers!" she shouted. "And they saw me."

"I thought so!"

They couldn't send soldier bots, so the Core sent their human soldiers after them. Eden could now very clearly hear steps rushing from above.

"What do we do?" she asked Dante.

They glanced at the door they had just passed. The seventy-third floor! They were so close to their goal. Dante grimaced, but turned around and fired several shots at the door's lock, slamming it open with a kick. They all ran inside, guns up and ready to fire at anything that comes. They only found more rows of central units inside, although this room was in the dark for some reason. Quickly, Greed remotely turned the light on for them. Eden sighed and turned around, watching two of Dante's men push the door closed. On the left, she realized Circé was busy wiping her shoe on the carpet with a grumpy expression.

"Whoever's bleeding, you could try not to spill it everywhere..."

Eden's blood suddenly went cold. She turned back around, her intuition suddenly clicking. Dante. Her lover didn't seem bothered at all, but she had him spin around and lifted his shirt. That's where the blood came from. A very fresh, blood-dripping bullet injury was located in his lower back, and not a minor one either.

"Dante, you're bleeding!"

"I'm fine."

"Hell no, you're not!"

Eden immediately ripped his sleeve to try and soak up the blood that was coming out. She couldn't believe someone was incapable of feeling their body bleeding out like that, but Dante was definitely unaware of it. He glanced over, not shocked at all, even when his eyes got down to the blood-soaked fabric. His inability to feel pain was turning into a terrible and cruel weakness.

"Let me see," said Circé, pushing Eden over. "Oh, shit, they really didn't miss..."

She took out one of those little first aid medical bots and applied the carbonic ice spray all over the injury, but even if it was enough, they wouldn't have been able to tell. Dante was still standing, looking perfectly fine despite that hole in his back. He only grimaced when the robot began pulling a little string to stitch the injury.

"Damn it..."

"You can't feel pain, but stitching bothers you?"

"The sensation is annoying."

Eden sighed. In other circumstances, she could have laughed at him losing his temper over getting stitched, but this wasn't the time. Now, she was worried her lover could die from blood loss and not have the smallest clue

557

about his own condition. Eden kept staring at the medical bot, almost annoyed at how that thing could only do first aid and basic care. Sadly, they wouldn't have much time to worry about Dante's condition. They could already hear the soldiers banging against the door, and the elevators coming their way. Dante's men were rounding up around them, trying to establish a safe perimeter, but either way, things wouldn't go well. They were only two floors away from Pan...

"Greed, anything from Pan?"

"Nothing that I know of. But there are Blanks appearing left and right on the System. It's seriously messing them up... It's like miniature bombs put on their secured servers, all going off at the same time. I have no idea what's going on there except that it is not coming from our side. The Edge is already fucking busy enough as it is..."

"We need that help," muttered Malieka, sounding worried. "There are more Overcrafts heading for the Suburbs, Ghost, and they are getting closer to our location. They are scanning the buildings again, and they will soon–"

Before she ended her sentence, a loud noise was heard as an echo. Eden heard it on her side too, and although she was too far to check out the windows, she had clearly recognized the sound of a bomb going off.

"...They've just begun blowing up buildings," muttered Malieka. "That one was hit by a rocket in the south. And there are more coming. They are targeting the largest buildings first."

"Most likely to flatten everything before they rebuild," scoffed Michael, sounding out of breath. "Since they couldn't evacuate the Suburbs themselves, they decided to kill two birds with one stone: getting rid of anyone whom their radars might have missed, while starting the building site for their future extension..."

It sounded all too gloomy for those who lived in the Suburbs. Eden couldn't help but think about the neighborhoods she used to go to eat or to work. The Dragon had fallen, and now all neighborhoods starting from the south were in danger. At least the inhabitants were evacuated and in hiding, but they were losing the few things they had... It was just too sickening. She closed her fists, and quickly reloaded her guns out of anger, ready for the next fight.

"Will you be alright?" she asked Dante, resolute.

"Of course."

It wasn't very reassuring, but at least his wound had received medical care, and he wasn't suffering at all. She nodded, vaguely trying to convince herself. Everyone was worn out, wounded, and running out of ammunition. They needed to bring this fight to an end as soon as possible.

"...Let's get them in the crossfire," she suddenly declared.

"What?"

"Greed, can you cut out the lights in this room?"

"I can, but as far as I know, the robots will have night vision! Even if the soldiers don't, you guys will be caught in a mean crossfire!"

"We only need them to go out for a few seconds, to blind them," explained Eden. "The elevators are a no, so we have to get back to the stairs, alone. If we can trap both the robots and the soldiers here, we will be good to go..."

"...That's one crazy plan if I've ever heard one," sighed Greed, "but I got you. I need thirty seconds to get ready, so hide well and give me the go-ahead whenever you're ready... Oh, boy, this one's going to be ugly..."

"Sadly, I don't think we have any other good options," groaned Circé. "We're trapped here."

"If I get control of the elevators, that might be a better escape route. I'll try to get them running as soon as I can!"

Before Eden could even react, Dante grabbed her first and pulled her between two units to hide, close to the stairwell door they had just come out of, which was now barricaded but ready to give out soon. She closed her eyes, trying to imagine the situation. The soldiers were going to open fire at will. With a bit of luck, they wouldn't care about the robots, so they would take out some of their own soldier bots in the process.

To her surprise, she felt his lips on hers, and reopened her eyes, answering his short kiss a bit reluctantly. Then, she pushed him, blushing, confused, and a bit angry.

"Do you think it's really the moment?"

"It feels like a now-or-never moment, actually," he chuckled.

Eden sighed. She couldn't say he was fully wrong, but his timing was more than dauntless.

"Fine..." she muttered.

A smile appeared on his lips, and they exchanged another short but more intense kiss before splitting again. Her heartbeat couldn't have gone any faster anyway...

"You two are really nasty," grumbled Circé, who happened to be hiding right across from them.

Blushing, Eden ignored her, glancing at the door again. They were all hiding and ready now, and the banging against the door was leaving hints that their barricade wouldn't hold much longer.

"Greed, on my count," she muttered.

"Ready when you are."

Eden took a deep breath, trying to calm herself, her eyes on the door. She could see the joints about to give way. She had to find the perfect timing. This wasn't very different from all her previous hacks. She had to follow her gut, and trust her allies...

"3... 2... Now!"

The lights went off, and back on two seconds later. A wave of gunfire picked up right away, all shots fired in both directions. It was deafening and blinding. Eden was doing her best to keep her shooting precise, but everything was happening so fast. She had to move quickly, keep firing, try to protect herself, and not shoot an ally.

"Ghost, the elevator! Now!"

She stumbled back, trying to cover both sides while dashing to the elevators, and kept running while grinding her teeth to ignore the pain. In the real world at least, she knew her legs weren't going to give way. She had to keep going. She rushed, worried for Circé, Dante, and everyone, but right now, it was shoot and run. She knew they were all rushing to get to the safety of the elevators under Greed's control. They had bought perhaps seconds by turning the lights off and back on, but now, it was all a matter of who would make it to the elevators...

She felt her body being violently pushed against the metallic walls of the elevators, and somebody screaming. Something heavy fell on her, and the cabin suddenly moved, with the strangely familiar *ding!* of an elevator closing its doors. Eden grimaced. Her hips were killing her. She tried to move and suddenly realized, the dead weight on top of her was a body... and the hot liquid underneath her was blood. A lot of blood.

"Oh, no..." she muttered, unable to utter anything else.

She panicked and tried to turn around, contorting herself in the small cabin. She felt like she was covered in the horrible and haunting stench of blood now that she was catching her breath. She managed to look behind her, and her breathing stopped.

The elevator was filled with bodies. Six bodies, on top of one another. Only six. Eden realized at least two were already dead, as they had fallen face-first against the floor, and their backs were full of bleeding holes... She went to cover her mouth with her hand, shocked, but realized a second too late it was covered in blood too. She grimaced, and grabbed the handrail above her, trying to find a more stable and less painful position. She couldn't see it under the bodies that had fallen on her, but she could guess one of her Parts had been torn off her thigh. The pain was violent, but strangely numbing at the same time. Eden guessed her SIN had taken over to help her manage the pain, but it wasn't enough. She felt pearls of cold sweat dripping down her temple and nape.

"D-Dante?" she called out.

Despite her disgust and shock, she tried to push the body that was on her leg, and she found him: Dante was under his men, who had probably died to protect them after they had made it into the elevator. Eden panicked. She grabbed his arm, shaking and pulling it.

"Dante! Dante! Dante, answer me! Dante!"

She began crying as she called his name again and again. Finally, she heard a familiar groan, and let out a sigh of relief. He was alive... unconscious and probably injured, but alive. She looked around, but from what she could see, the two other men in the elevator were either dead or dying.

"G-... Greed?" Eden called out, panicked. "Greed?"

She realized the complete silence around her. She couldn't hear anything from her SIN, which was a strange sensation for someone who had been connected to dozens of others for the past hour... Was it damaged? Why was the connection out? She slowly reached her hand up to touch where her SIN was. Her fingers suddenly touched an area, sending a wave of pain through her body. The hole she had found left her speechless. Somehow, her SIN had been fired at, and damaged, if not destroyed... No more communication with the outside. Eden tried to stop crying, wiping her snot with her wrist and looking up. The elevator they were in had stopped on the seventy-fifth floor, but it didn't open. She repressed the urge to scream. Was Greed still in control? ... What had become of the others? She couldn't even reach out to Circé, Nebty, or anyone. She had never felt so terribly alone... She grabbed Dante's shirt and tried shaking him again. For a few seconds, Eden only focused on pushing the men off his back, pulling him, shaking him. She just couldn't stop crying, but moving was helping her calm down. Plus, she was worried he was going to die of suffocation... Finally, with the bodies pushed to the side, she managed to turn him over, and Dante instinctively took a breath in. Eden let out a sigh of relief. He was alive... He was alive. She tried to swallow her crying, and shake him again.

"Dante, wake up," she muttered. "Please. Please..."

Without Loir, without Dante, Circé, or anybody else to answer, she felt so utterly alone. Never had she felt so horribly alone. It made no sense, but right now, she was confined in a box with dead bodies and her unresponsive lover. The panic was starting to take over her rational mind, and Dante was the last piece of sanity she was holding on to.

"Dante!"

She suddenly slammed his torso, out of anger, and he coughed, waking up right away. He sat up, coughing loudly, and Eden let out a long sigh of relief.

"Eden?"

She didn't say anything and dove into his arms, relieved. She just really, really needed someone to hug her right now. She heard him sigh, and answer her hug, patting her back.

"...Are you alright?"

"I'm not," she cried angrily. "I... I can't reach out to Greed, or anybody. I don't know what happened to the others..."

"You're alive," he calmly answered.

As if that explained everything. Eden shook her head. She was getting tired of everyone counting on her being alive, to survive this. As if nothing else mattered... She understood the stakes, but she just couldn't accept how many people had died or were dying right now, all for her to end this. It was just too much on the shoulders of one person. Luckily, she wasn't alone for now. Dante gently helped her calm down, hugging and patting her. He even took off his already pretty-much-ruined shirt to wipe as much blood as he could off her face and hands. It felt like time had stopped, for a few seconds, in this elevator for the two of them.

It was all Eden really needed to finally calm down. Her panic from before was withdrawing, and instead, a strange sensation of cold was coming over her, as if her whole body was calming down. Dante suddenly realized something was off about her leg being so far from her body. He frowned and pushed his men, searching for it. He found the piece, torn off and covered in Eden's blood. He glanced at her leg. Her hip was covered in blood where it had been forcefully ripped off.

"...Can you put it back on?"

"I don't know."

Dante pulled it over, close to her leg, to see if they could put it back on somehow...

Suddenly, the doors behind him opened. Dante immediately grabbed a gun, ready to fire, but the bright light shining blinded them both.

"Welcome," said the Governor's voice, "I have been waiting for you!"

Dante fired immediately.

# CHAPTER FORTY-ONE

Despite Eden covering her ears, his shots echoed loudly, wherever he was shooting at. Then, he stopped, out of ammunition. A sinister laugh was heard, echoing and seemingly coming from everywhere around them.

"Sorry, but you are wasting your bullets, young man."

While Dante was searching the elevator's floor and through his men's pockets for another weapon, Eden grabbed his shoulder to try and glance over. The voice was telling the truth; the room behind him seemed to be completely empty. She could tell from the echo of each sound. Using the elevator's handrail to pull herself up onto one leg, Eden painfully got up, observing the area they had arrived at. Contrary to her expectations, the seventy-fifth floor was nothing like the previous ones.

It looked like a gigantic laboratory. It was all white, with tiles on the floor, the furniture made of a material that seemed to be clear glass, and strange, large columns filled with enigmatic liquids. Before even stepping out of the elevator, Eden got an ominous feeling about this place. It felt... off, and somewhat unreal. She even checked the floor before stepping on it, making sure that this wasn't some sort of illusion, but she could feel something was different. This place felt like one of those cold hospital rooms she had been in once or twice. Cold, sterile, and with no scent but chemicals. Whatever was in there was unnatural, artificial. She took a deep breath and balanced on her leg to get closer, ignoring the pain.

"Come on, child, don't be shy," said the voice coming from invisible speakers around them. "After all, this is part of your legacy as well..."

Eden didn't like that at all. What legacy was he talking about? She felt her heartbeat accelerate, her nervousness on the rise. She hated that the Governor's voice was hovering over them, like some deity controlling the place. She wished she could have asked Greed to disable whatever mic that man was using... Sadly, there was still no news from anyone else. She could hear a faint sizzle, perhaps her SIN trying to reboot itself, or whatever was left of it finally giving up. They were completely on their own for now.

Just as she was struggling to stay up, all her weight on one leg, Dante appeared by her side, grabbing her around the waist and supporting her. Eden leaned on him, but she felt sorry for doing so. She knew he would have even carried her if he wasn't in such a bad state himself... Things were much worse than one gunshot injury now. Eden had only been preoccupied with having him wake up before, but now that they were both standing, she glanced over at her partner. She could see that he had another hole in his left shoulder, his ear on the same side was partially missing, and his pants were covered in blood... He had even lost a shoe. If he had been able to feel pain, she wondered if he would have stood perfectly calm like this, a gun in hand and helping her walk.

"Dante..." she muttered, worried.

"I'm alright."

He clearly wasn't, but to him, it probably made little to no difference. Eden was worried, but at the very least, he wasn't in pain, whether that was a curse or a blessing... He helped her get out of the elevator, and together, they stepped inside the very strange, wide all-white room.

Eden realized what it was that felt really odd about this room to her: it was quiet, but not void of life. One of the columns closest to them had a large, square, glass window, which allowed them to see something floating in it. Eden tried to approach, recognizing some large reptile-like creature, apparently asleep, floating around in some liquid that was too thick and too green to be water. She had no idea what that thing was, if it was an unknown species or another Chimera that the Core had created. There was a little console attached to that strange aquarium, with vitals confirming that thing was alive. Eden felt a chill down her spine. What was this place? She glanced around and, against the walls on her left and right, finally saw the large central units, although they were white, unlike the previous ones. It wasn't the most interesting thing, though. Right ahead of them, on the other end of the room, was the largest computer she had ever seen. Even Loir's installations were only a third of that. There was a large screen and dozens of keyboards, buttons, handles, and measuring instruments she didn't even know the use for. It seemed to be displaying several surveillance cameras at once, mostly the ongoing fights. Eden's heart sank as she recognized Tanya, Michael, and their group still fighting valiantly against the soldier bots, all of them visibly injured and tired. Thao's men were regrouping, and she could recognize the Rat's silhouette from afar, shouting orders and pointing at her men.

The rest of the screens were showing the Suburbs, but it took Eden a minute to recognize the places. Not because the screens were a few steps away, or the fact that she hadn't been to those places often, but because those neighborhoods looked nothing like she had remembered anymore. Each looked like a battlefield or a war zone. A devastated land, with large piles of crumbled buildings, ruined streets, and thick clouds of dust covering everything. Eden's breathing was getting erratic, she was too shocked to calm down. They were really wiping out the Suburbs with their bombs. The last buildings that had stood tall were now miserable clusters of concrete, some pieces even burning. It was utter chaos out there, and as she started to recognize the many different places, she began to panic. How much had really been wiped out already? She couldn't hear the bombs anymore, but it was as if she could feel them through the screen. Fury and despair dropped from the sky on the places she'd always known. Eden felt Dante's embrace around her tighten a bit, either to comfort her or share her anger, she couldn't tell.

"...What the heck is this place?" she muttered, furious.

"Oh, child," chuckled the Governor. "You're standing in the middle of the future. This room was one of those your father worked in the most. In fact, half of what is in here was his life's work!"

Eden felt disgusted. Whatever this place was, she couldn't believe it used to be her father's. There were dozens of columns around them, with living creatures trapped. A lot of them were visibly mutilated or had some of their body parts held open by cables while they were still alive. She could see a monkey's rib cage, the skin torn off to the sides and held open by a dozen hooks pulling it apart, with its lungs moving and heart pulsating, while the poor creature's face expressed sheer terror. In another, there was a strange marine creature swimming around frantically, trying to escape some weird little bot that was constantly cutting its limbs. Eden watched in horror as the poor creature would desperately try to swim away before the bot grabbed it, cut off its leg, and let it go. The little creature writhed in pain, but to Eden's surprise, the cut-off limb regrew right away, and the circle of hunting began again. There were hundreds of its little limbs on the floor of the aquarium... all belonging to that one creature. This wasn't an experiment; it was torture.

"What... What are you doing here...?" she muttered, disgusted everywhere she looked.

"Science! Tomorrow starts here, child. We create and prepare the future of our civilization in this room. A future where there will be no more pain, no more suffering we humans have been enduring for so long. Our citizens won't even know pain, diseases, hunger, wars. The absolute, perfect world."

"Fuck you and your shitty perfection," groaned Eden. "You're torturing innocent creatures for this!"

"This is science, child. It comes at a cost, but sacrifices have to be made. While Mother Nature is healing on her own, we shall work hard to heal ourselves too. Those creatures are only a few among millions! They are expendables."

"...Like the people in the Suburbs?" hissed Eden.

"You're mistaken! The Suburbs were only meant to be temporary, child. We just couldn't be ready in time for all our citizens to live in this utopia we've been working on. We had to get rid of the bad apples for better seeds to grow! Look at the Core you saw today. Isn't it close to what they call Paradise? No crimes, no poverty, no suffering. Every citizen gets to live the dream our ancestors had in mind! They don't need to worry about tomorrow, but only ride this train of everyday bliss!"

"Bullshit," retorted Eden.

This room was the opposite of Paradise. If anything, it was hell, and she didn't want to accept that anything good could come out of that. She kept looking around, desperate to find Pan. He had said he was here, so where was he? She couldn't see any living creatures other than those in strange cages, and she couldn't bear to look at them any longer. Still, Dante helped her move forward, walking through the aisles full of dead or tortured creatures. The closer they got to that console, the worse it got. There were fewer and fewer living creatures, and more and more bodies floating, or even just body parts she wouldn't have been able to recognize.

They finally reached the console, and Eden stared at the keyboard, trying to figure out how that thing was used. It had to be the heart of the Core Pan had mentioned, the main part. So how could she operate it? She used her hands to support herself on the console, while Dante grabbed one of the strange glass stools for her to sit on. From the way he was walking, even if he wasn't feeling any pain, Eden could tell he was having trouble moving normally. His leg seemed to give way, and his body was strangely leaning to the side too as if his injury was keeping him from standing upright... She tried to push her worries about him to the back of her mind and focus. They were so close to the end. If they could turn this thing around and have the Edge take control, it would all be over.

"Dante, go and plug this into one of the central units," she muttered upon sitting down. "Any of them. Alright?"

He nodded, grabbed it, and turned around. Eden looked at his figure moving away, her heart getting heavier with each step he took. She took a deep breath and turned to the console, quickly trying to turn it on and understand how the hell this thing was supposed to work. It didn't look like any of the systems she knew, or it was ten times more complicated than a normal computer. There were too many keypads with the strangest commands, and that thing even seemed to resist any attempt she made to control it. She was a decent Back Hacker, but this was harder than anything she had ever tried. There were dozens of protections and protocols keeping her out of the System. She had the machine right under her fingers, but it was stubbornly keeping her out.

"Come on," she groaned.

"Ah... How nostalgic to see his daughter's hands on her father's brightest creation."

Eden glared at the ceiling since she didn't know any better. That voice was infuriating beyond anything. Still, she ignored it, trying to find her way into the more-than-reluctant computer. She had never seen such a complicated programming language, nor such a protected system ever. Perhaps she would have been more efficient if she could Dive in, but with her Ghost SIN damaged, it was out of the question. She hoped it would somehow begin working again, and allow her to Dive just enough to find a way in for the others...

"Your father was the smartest man that lived in this century, Eden," the Governor continued. "He imagined, conceived the world we live in today. Can you imagine? He literally shaped the world and paved the future for the next century. While humanity gives time for our mother planet to heal, we will continue to thrive in those bubbles he created, looking for our own evolution! And when nature is ready for us humans to come back to her, we will return, stronger, smarter than ever. Perfect citizens who each belong here, and know what to do. Each one of them treasuring their city, working hard for their peers' sake–"

"You just shut up," groaned Eden. "You shut up about this so-called utopia of yours. There is no paradise built on the thousands of people you killed. Your quiet little sheep won't be any different. They deserve their own mind, their own choices. You can't possibly control every citizen in this city to do your bidding and buy into this bullshit you're serving them!"

"You're not seeing the larger picture, child. Those sacrifices are necessary. Haven't you learned about the ways of the world, of the animal reign since the beginning of time? Only the strongest, fittest survive. The others are nothing but the losing, expendable links of the food chain. They are simply bound to disappear, for the species to survive. We are so close to achieving the perfect human colony!"

Eden decided to stop answering him. She was convinced this man was mad, insane, and his belief in his fantasy just disgusted her all the same. She kept furiously typing on the keyboard, her anger and frustration on the rise. She couldn't believe she was being slowed down by this stupid machine when hundreds–no, thousands of lives were on the line. The psychopath on the speakers was like a horrible reminder of what was going on outside, and she wasn't going to lose her focus, especially when the surveillance cameras were displaying the ongoing battle the entire time.

"Your father had that vision too. I can only be sorry those worthless people convinced you they were worth all the suffering you have gone through, child. You deserved better than them. You are one of us, and we are different. Better, and turned toward the future. They are merely living on the scraps of the past we allow them to feed on. But not for much longer. Soon, there will be none of those pathetic reminders of what humans used to be, and we will move on to this gorgeous, perfect utopia humanity has always thrived for! ...Can't you see it? We're so close to the end, to achieving long, pain-free lives! Even immortality is no longer just a fantasy!"

The poor creature having its limbs cut off and regrown constantly came to Eden's mind. This was probably one of the few ideas they had in mind for that so-called utopia he was rambling about... Just the idea of it made her shiver. She already knew what relying on fake legs could do to one's mind. The trauma was part of her, and those two robotic pieces weren't. She grieved for the legs she had lost, but not for that piece of junk that had been left in the elevator. She didn't want to believe humans would ever lose the ability to grieve at all. How would they learn to treasure their bodies when it would be so easy to heal and regrow them? Eden knew how long, painful, but necessary the process of healing was. However, it was what had made her stronger, much stronger than before.

"You're going to create monsters," she answered. "Monsters void of feelings. We need pain, we need to suffer, and we need to know what loss is like. Your utopia is never going to be anything but sterile bullshit. Living in a dream isn't living."

"...So stubborn," sighed the Governor. "I'm sure you will change your mind, though, Eden. Once you see the miracles we have already accomplished, that your father accomplished! Can't you see? He did it all for you! For his child to live in a better, stronger world. You should have never experienced the hell you went through, and I am the most sorry about that horrible life you've been subjected to. You should have lived like us, so carefree and happy!"

Eden closed her fists on the keyboard. If she hadn't needed this thing so badly, she would have punched that damn console already. She was fed up hearing him use her father as an argument. She hadn't known the man, but everything was telling her the Governor was lying. Whatever her father had accomplished, he had also turned around. He had changed, and he had created the Edge himself to stop that Core he had created. It just didn't add up; she didn't have to listen to those sugar-coated lies.

She glanced to the side. Dante was already plugging in the pirate key to the central units. Soon, the Edge would be able to reach her again and solve all this.

"You're so mistaken, child. Your father shared this vision! Can't you see it?"

"My father was wrong, and he knew it!" she shouted. "He and Mr. Charles gave their lives to stop this! He died because he refused to listen to you anymore, but he left enough of a legacy to stop you..."

"Ah... You're talking about the Edge, aren't you?"

Eden's hands froze.

"That's... the most beautiful part of it all. Your father created the Edge, child."

"...Yes, he did. To stop all this!"

"Oh, no, no, no, that's where you're wrong. Your dear father was such

568

a smart man, Eden. Do you think we would have captured and destroyed the Edge so easily if he had truly meant for them to stop him...? We knew about the Edge's creation and existence all along! It was your father's idea, not to stop our project, but to test it!"

"...What?"

Suddenly, the screen in front of her changed, showing a dozen faces. Eden's heart sank. The original Edge. She immediately recognized Circé among them, looking much younger, with her hair a bright purple color, black lips, and heavy eyeshadow. There was also Pratiti, with long black dreadlocks, and no bandages... All of those people were wearing gray uniforms in the images, and glaring at whoever had taken those shots.

"That's right, Eden. Your father had planned the destruction of the Edge from the minute he created it. It was all part of another of his genius plans. He knew people would try to stop the Core, so why not invite them to do it, and see how far they could go? And just when they were about to succeed... we got rid of the biggest threats! Ah... Truly, Eden, your father was a genius."

"...Or the worst, cold-blooded bastard," Eden cried.

She felt the urge to scream. She couldn't believe her father had done such a horrible thing, not to the Edge. Eden kept staring at the faces, feeling almost as if they were glaring at her. She couldn't see Loir among them, but it didn't matter. In fact, perhaps seeing his face now would have made it all worse... Unable to repress the tears that were coming, Eden forced herself to keep looking at those images, as if to carve them into her mind, along with that horrible feeling of guilt. She couldn't fathom that her father could have done that to those people who believed in him.

"Your father personally selected each one of them. He fetched the very best hackers, and worst people, to create the biggest threat his creation would ever face, to test it. He scoured to the ends of the Dark Web, to every corner of the globe, to create his own enemy. You've probably heard it already, haven't you? The Edge was sent to attack each Core, one by one. With each attack, we were carefully watching how they did it, the vulnerable parts of our System they exposed, to see what we had to fix next! We had to make a few sacrifices for that, but... eventually, it was the best way to reveal our biggest weaknesses."

Eden slowly shook her head, unable to believe it.

"No... No, you're lying..."

"Of course not. I understand, it's hard. But do you really think he could have created such an impressive team of hackers without us knowing? After all the attacks they made on the Cores? Some of them were truly impressive. We knew about them and pretty much let those young people do it. How terrifying would it have been if we hadn't been aware all along! Sadly, we had to end this project as soon as the last version of the Chicago Core was completed, the most perfect one we had ever created: flawless, magnificent, and this time, virtually invulnerable. Plus, we got rid of all the biggest threats at once!"

Eden clenched her fists, furious. They had played around with the Edge like they were toys and threw them away when they were done. No, they had exterminated them. She felt like throwing up, disgusted. She was almost glad Nebty and Circé probably weren't hearing this...

"Well, it would have been a flawless plan if a few of them hadn't escaped, but... Oh, well, mistakes do happen, even for the most brilliant of us. I was honestly hoping to even recruit one or two among them, you know! After all, your father had hand-picked them himself. Sadly, almost none of them were very... open to our offers. In fact, I was sad to hear the only one we could recruit hadn't really come to our side of their own volition."

Eden felt a vicious feeling of relief. Yes, some of the Edge had survived. Nebty, Circé, Loir. They had survived, even long enough to betray the Core and bite back. Loir had died today, but if she could at least avenge him, she knew she'd be able to hear his crazy laugh from the other side.

"This is just another example of how fickle humans are," said the Governor. "Unreliable. Emotional. If they had understood our vision, we would have welcomed them with open arms!"

"...But none of them wanted to give up their freedom."

Eden jumped. Pan's voice! She looked all around, almost excited to see him, but instead, the Governor's voice chuckled.

"That's right... That is why humans need proper guidance and focused vision. The more options they are given, the less they know what to do! However, when we let them only see this utopia we are working for, they are bound to follow us. The Edge and those people in your precious Suburbs are not part of this vision, Eden. We only need to keep the very best, and we have to leave the rotten apples out of the basket..."

Eden kept glancing all around, her heart beating like crazy. Where was he? Where was Pan? She couldn't wait to see him. She needed to see that there was still someone left on their side, someone who knew the Core was wrong.

Suddenly, she heard a very faint bell sound and turned her head back to the computer. In one corner of the screen, a very basic, black chat tab appeared with only a few words.

"Hi, Eden."

"...Pan," she muttered.

"Don't be scared. I'm here."

"Ah, yes," said the Governor. "You two haven't seen each other in such a long time, have you? Are you surprised to find him here? You see, Pan is the most important part of your father's vision. He is the one who keeps his legacy alive!"

Eden hesitated. ...Did the Governor see that chat tab? It didn't seem like he did. He just kept rambling about his utopia, his vision, while Eden's hazel eyes were riveted on that little chat tab. After a hesitation, her fingers found the keyboard. She felt like her heart was going to explode with excitement.

"Where are you?"

"Right on your left."

She frowned and slowly turned to the left. She was expecting to see a human figure pop out somewhere, but everything was just as still as before. She knit her eyebrows. Was there something she was missing...?

Suddenly, her eyes naturally went to the columns of liquid. She hesitated, now worried. It couldn't be, right...? After some hesitation, she approached the closest of them. This one's liquid was of a misty gray, and much foggier, thicker than the others. The closer she got, though, the better she saw what was inside. After a few seconds, she stopped, hesitating. She felt like her entire blood flow was pulsating like crazy in her ears. There was a silhouette in there. A humanoid one, too small to be a human adult but big enough to be younger... When Eden finally saw it, she gasped, covering her mouth in shock.

She had witnessed many horrors, in real life and in the Dark Reality, but this wasn't even close to anything she had seen before. There was a child. No, perhaps a boy in his pre-teens, but his whole body was incredibly skinny, with no visible muscles, literally only skin and bones. That wasn't all. His eyes were wide open and completely inexpressive with the top of his head cut open. Eden felt the urge to throw up, and she did, falling on her valid knee, unable to stop it. The boy's head was opened up, the brain clearly visible and moving, with hundreds of little cables attached to it. It looked like an upside-down, terrifying half-machine medusa. The little cables even emitted small lights that seemed to be running to and away from the brain at regular intervals. Eden couldn't even process what she was seeing. Who would do such a horrible thing to a child? That brain was clearly alive, but that child was... not living at all. The whole body seemed to be floating around, completely inanimate. Eden realized one of his hands had two fingers missing, and the left leg ended with a strange lump of flesh instead of a foot. She wiped her mouth, trying to stand back up. She noticed a little console under the column. Gathering all her strength and bravery, she forced her only valid leg to make the jump to the console. She landed brutally on her knee, but her hands managed to grab the console to hold on to. It was sparkling clean and clearly used often... There was something about the temperature inside, his vitals... and a name. Prometheus Angel Newman... It really was her Pan.

"Ah, yes... Pan's old envelope," sighed the Governor. "I regret the suffering that child had to go through, but it was inevitable."

"What... What did you do to him?" Eden cried, furious.

"Oh, we didn't do anything! If anything, we saved his life. You see, sometimes, we humans simply aren't born as... perfect as we should be. In fact, it's been a secret for a few decades now, but I suppose there is no use hiding it from you now that you've seen it. See, your older brother was... one of those children that should have never been allowed to come to life."

"...My older brother?" muttered Eden. "N-no... I don't understand."

"Well, we made an exception because, of course, he was your father's son. Moreover, your mother was some strange woman who refused technology... That child was born despite the surveillance we usually used to ensure our children are born with the very best potential! For a few years now, we have already been doing proper sorting so that every child born into the Core is truly fit for this marvelous life of wonders!"

Eden couldn't hear anymore. With a grunt, she turned around, going back to the computer with all the anger and strength she could muster. The trail of blood she left behind seemed terribly messy on the sparkling white tiles, but Eden didn't care about all of that or her injuries. She was fed up with his bullshit, with those crazy ideas of his. The only one she wanted to hear was Pan, and Pan alone. She used the strength in her arms to get back to the keyboard, looking for that chat tab again.

"I hope you weren't scared, or too shocked."

"Pan, what is going on?" she managed to type, guessing the Governor somehow couldn't see it.

"That is my real body."

"That's a dead child! What is this shit about you being my brother?"

"...Let me show you."

Suddenly, the screen in front of her changed again. It seemed like another surveillance video like the one Eden had watched just minutes before in the archives. She recognized the same office her father had been in, but it looked very different. This time, the place was a complete mess, although there were a lot fewer papers all around, and the computer seemed smaller too, with fewer screens. Her father too seemed somewhat different. Younger, she guessed. He was in one corner of the room, his head in his hands, visibly... crying. Eden checked the date in the corner. It was a few years before her birth... What had happened back then? She glanced at the chat tab again.

"A few weeks before my birth."

Eden frowned. That was before Pan was even born? ...Did that mean he really was her older brother?

Suddenly, a square on the console made a snapping sound and opened, revealing a little device connected to a long cable that was coming from the supercomputer. Eden didn't recognize it, but she grabbed it. It extended pretty far, and the end of it looked like a SIN, but bigger...

"Put it on your SIN."

She hesitated. She didn't even know what that thing was supposed to do. Eden glanced toward Dante, but he was still leaning against one of the central units, visibly doing something with the cables. Had he managed to establish a connection with the Edge? Was he getting directions from A. or Nebty? Eden turned her eyes back to the console.

"Trust me. It will only help you use your SIN."

Eden took a deep breath. Pan was her last ally at the moment, anyway... Grimacing after touching her damaged and injured SIN area several times, she finally managed to somehow plug that thing into it. It wasn't the best sensation. It felt like an electric shock ran from her nape and throughout her whole body, making her grimace. It was a similar feeling to putting on her Parts.

Suddenly, she felt her SIN activating again. So did the computer in front of her. In fact, everything changed. In a second, everything about her surroundings changed, and she was pulled into the System.

It took a couple of seconds for the room around her to stabilize enough for her to recognize the place. It was the same environment as before. Her father's office, with her father on the ground. Except this time, she could hear the poor man weeping, muffled cries. She instantly felt sorry for him, unable to understand why he was crying so much. Suddenly, the image paused, and something bright appeared next to her.

A silhouette, and then, the familiar appearance of a boy. Eden let out a faint sigh. Pan had used his real appearance but gave it a more... healthy look. He looked like what that child in the column would have looked like if it had been able to grow for a few more years. He had more meat on his bones, a youthful appearance, gorgeous hazel eyes, and blonde hair.

"...Hello," he said with a chuckle.

"It's not funny at all," cried Eden.

"I know. I'm sorry you had to go through so much."

His eyes went down to her legs. In this reality, her legs were perfectly fine and made of flesh. The cable was probably tricking her brain into thinking her legs were fine because she couldn't feel the pain anymore and had no issue standing up either. Then, Pan's eyes went back to their father.

"...That night, he had learned I would be a sick child," he muttered.

"What do you mean?"

"...Soon after the first version of the Core was created, and a lot of people were forced to live in the Suburbs, the Core leaders quickly understood they would still have to control the growth of the population, or the Cores would be overpopulated in just a few generations' time. A lot of the global population had been decimated by wars all over the world, but that wasn't enough if they wished to let our Mother Earth heal in peace. So, they made a decision to control all the upcoming births."

Pan slowly approached their father, looking at him from above.

"For a couple of centuries, women always sought doctors and medical assistance for giving birth. It was a natural process that was heavily monitored, from the conception of the child to its birth. With technical advancements, they were able to ensure a safer delivery, but also predict things such as the baby's gender, health, and so on. During the twenty-first century, people began to be able to foretell the child's physical appearance, personality traits, intellectual capacities, and... the diseases they carried."

Eden was hearing that for the first time. In the Suburbs, most women gave birth alone, at home, without medical assistance. No one trusted hospitals and doctors, which were incredibly expensive and belonged to the Core. No one in the Suburbs ever made it to the level of knowledge a doctor would have, so they all relied on what womanhood could teach them...

"Our mother was a purist," chuckled Pan. "Ironically, Dad had fallen

573

for a woman who didn't like machines, and still believed in the old world, when our routines weren't regulated by politicians and their robots. She hid her pregnancy for as long as she could until I reached a certain size and it wasn't possible anymore. But when they took her in for a test... They realized the child she carried wouldn't pass the criteria for the Core's newborns. That night, they told our parents I wouldn't be allowed to come into this world."

Eden's heart sank. How could they say such a terrible thing... She remembered the child's appearance, in his cage of water. His deformed foot, his missing fingers. Was that what the Core had rejected? ...There were hundreds of people born with disabilities in the Suburbs! How did it make sense that the Core killed children that would have been born with the slightest issue when they had the technology to cope with it?!

The video suddenly resumed. To Eden's surprise, their father suddenly lifted his eyes, looking almost as if he saw them. She almost stepped back in surprise. However, he quickly got on his feet and jumped on an old-looking red phone on the opposite wall. They saw him visibly crying and shouting into the little device, although they couldn't hear the sound of it anymore.

"...That night," Pan muttered, "Father begged the Governor to let me live. He didn't care that I would be born disabled; he had the money to help me live a good life. My brain showed no issues, and even great intellectual capacities. If only it wasn't for my appearance... They negotiated for a long time. The Governor refused to have any imperfect child out in the world when the rest of the Core wasn't allowed such mercy. He was afraid of riots if people knew they killed unborn babies. Normally, they only pretended we died of natural causes in the womb, you see. But Father was too close to all their secrets to not know what was really happening. He had probably never imagined he'd be another victim of their cruel ways."

Eden felt disgusted too. She remembered their parents had quite an age gap... Had their father tolerated this, until he had met their mom, and given birth to his own children?

"...Eventually, they came to an agreement. I was to be kept in Father's lab or house as an experiment. I was born, but my body was completely... unusable. Perhaps the Core wanted to make sure I wouldn't be able to ever get out, or it was truly fate. Either way, our parents really considered me a living being. In fact, Father did his best to keep me alive... but it's hard when the body isn't properly functioning, you see. I never even really lived like a human being. I was born, but I never had any experience of the real world, I didn't grow up as a baby should. I was immediately taken and subjected to this strange thing that's not even a half decent life. So, he tried to save what was left of my consciousness using what he was the best at: machines. Always more and more machines. Machines meant to teach me about the human world, to feed me knowledge of dozens of software and retain everything. I began to learn... to grow, to get smarter and smarter. Until he realized, my brain was getting smarter than what most human intellectual capacities ever naturally reached. I was still growing, and conscious, but much, much faster than any other entity, or even a normal human, going beyond the known limits of the human brain."

Pan smiled, and turned to her, distracting Eden from the figure of their sobbing father.

"...Do you understand now? I'm not... completely human, but I am no computer either. I'm something in between, an abnormal mutation, another Chimera created by despair. But, for the first years of my life, I was mostly Father's assistant, and the one who helped him create the very first System."

"So... you're... some sort of... artificial intelligence?" Eden muttered.

"No, Eden, I'm still human. I am your older brother. And I am the smartest, first brain-powered computer intelligence. I am the System's mind, if it has one."

# CHAPTER FORTY-TWO

Eden almost staggered, not from a lack of balance this time, but from the shock. She had an older brother, a half-dead child her father had somehow saved and turned into a computer's conscience... It sounded like fiction, and yet, in the world they lived in, she knew exactly how this was possible. No, she had actually seen it herself. Pan's appearance... So they had simply kept him here, and connected his brain like a central unit? They had simply preserved his body all these years, so they would retain the smartest machine ever... a machine with a real, human conscience. She could barely begin to fathom it.

"...I don't understand," she muttered. "How come... If that's true, why did Father..."

"There's a lot you still don't know," he said with a gentle expression. "Let me show you."

The decor changed. It was their father's office again, but a later version. This time, their father was excitedly walking around, speaking out loud to himself, grabbing a paper to take notes, running to the computer, and chewing on a pen before doing some calculations.

"That's the evening we figured out how to store and duplicate the Core's version we had been working on," smiled Pan. "See? I'm here."

Eden looked where he was pointing at. There was one screen, among the six on her father's desk, with someone there. She approached. The film quality was bad, but if she focused, she could vaguely recognize someone with Pan's traits.

576

"I liked to appear like this," he explained. "It helped Father a lot when he could think of me as being alive, only... trapped behind a screen. Sadly, he wasn't the only one allowed to manipulate me. The Core was my master... Everyone controlling the Core could control me. Bit by bit, I started to become more of a machine, as someone who had never really been human."

"...What about Mom?"

"...Mother never forgave Father for what they had done to me. You see, when she realized she would never get to hold me, she considered her child killed at birth, and I was merely a computer mimicking what that child could have been. I think it was too painful for her. I didn't resent her for that... She didn't hate me, and she eventually came around too. Luckily, they soon got pregnant again."

He turned his eyes to her, with a bright smile on. Eden felt a bit uneasy. After everything that had happened, how could Pan seem so happy about her birth? He had basically been rejected by their mom... Eden couldn't blame her or their dad. She didn't know if she could have imagined that body was ever a human being. Pan's real eyes looked... dead.

"...Everything changed after your birth," he said.

The decor changed again. This time, it looked a lot closer to that scene she had seen, and her baby self was there, in her father's arms. Except he was pacing around in his office, with a frustrated expression.

"You know, our parents almost separated, until they realized Mother was pregnant. Then, they got back together, stronger than before. Mother finally agreed to talk to me… sometimes. I don't really know what she thought of me, but at least she acknowledged my existence a little. She was all about you, of course. They both were. For me, though, your birth was an even more pivotal moment."

"...Why?" Eden asked, trying to follow her father's constant pacing with her eyes.

Something inside her made her not want to miss a second of their dad's gaze on her. For a man she couldn't quite remember, he seemed completely enamored with his newborn. He was holding her little hand and talking to her, pacing around in the room, perhaps to soothe her into sleep. From the tiny and only window in the room's ceiling, she could guess it was nighttime.

"See, as I began to outsmart every human, I became more and more... machine-like," sighed Pan. "The fact was that I had never experienced the most basic human needs. I didn't know what food tasted like, or that things have different scents. I had no idea what human touch felt like, nor warmth, nor cold. I didn't even sleep or dream. All I did, 24/7, was study even more, as if I ate an entire library every day. But the more the Core manipulated me, integrated me into its System, the less... human I was. It began to worry Father a lot. He was scared he would lose the being he thought of as his son to a computer. So, he did his very best to let me experience those human emotions I was lacking. We watched all sorts of movies together. He tried to describe each sensation, each taste, everything a human was supposed to feel that I couldn't."

"But... if a Dive Hacker's brain can be tricked like I am now, thinking my legs are fine when I know they aren't, why didn't it work for you? I can feel the heat or cold when I Dive, I can be... tricked into tasting something that doesn't exist."

"That's because you know those sensations already," smiled Pan. "Your brain remembers, and the System goes into your memories to pull it and trick you to relive it. Moreover, that kind of technology is very recent. Back then, Father had no way to let me experience all those things. He could only attempt and let me try to experience it through him, as a proxy. What is it, what makes you human, if everything you do and are capable of can be done by a computer as well? Your emotions, your feelings. Your sensations, and your experiences. I wasn't able to get all that. And the more days passed, the less... human I was."

They both turned their eyes back to their father. He had now gone to sit on the large, comfortable chair in one corner of the room. Eden didn't remember that piece of furniture from before, so maybe it had been added because of her... Her father was still hugging her gently, his index finger caught in her tiny hand, but his expression was still upset, and staring at the screens at the opposite end of the room.

"I don't think Father expected your birth to be what would finally... trigger my emotions again."

The scene changed again. This time, they were transported into what was clearly a nursery. Eden hadn't expected the little room to look so... full. All the furniture was in pale wood, and there was a large, pink teddy bear in a corner. The pink carpet seemed very thick, and there were little wooden toys left on a play mat. Her baby self was in her bed, although completely awake. From the bright sunlight, it was early morning, and she was alone, visibly chattering to herself and moving her arms around, making little smiles and coos. Eden blushed, finding herself surprisingly cute...

"...What's special about this scene?" she frowned, confused.

"Nothing," he chuckled, "but it is one of my favorite memories of you. We can't hear it, but I was playing music for you... While our parents slept, you were always awake early. If nothing was going on in the room, you were bored, and immediately cried, so I would always play some music for you. I was... fascinated by your baby self. I had seen thousands of children before, but you were my little sister, you see. Something about you made me... feel different. I was experiencing new things for the first in a very long time. Not through you, but because of you. There is something adorable about how unpredictable babies are. Adults were almost boring to me, but you... you were my everyday favorite distraction."

Seeing the baby smile happily to whatever music was playing in the nursery, Eden found herself smiling too. The scene changed again without warning, and baby Eden was now lying on her stomach on the play mat while a little screen was put next to her in the room with Pan's face on it. The baby seemed busy with another toy, but Pan was visibly talking to her, and from time to time, she'd turn her head to him and giggle.

"I'm proud to say I was your favorite babysitter," chuckled Pan. "Those were the happiest times of my life... When I was less computer and only Eden's big brother. I could forget about all those calculations, the System, and whatever they were doing to me. All I wanted was to spend time with you. Father had to explain to me those sensations I felt because all the software in the world was lacking knowledge about love."

Pan sighed and turned his head just as the scene changed again. They were now back in their father's office, but Eden was gone, and he was simply chatting with someone on the computer, perhaps Pan.

"...The changes in me didn't please a lot of people," muttered Pan, his smile gone. "As I got... more human, and more interested in my baby sister than the System we were supposed to improve, the Core's leaders grew impatient. With me, and with Father. They urged him to revert the changes in me, as my conscience had grown. I wasn't agreeing to a lot of things they wanted to implement in the System anymore and, unfortunately for them, I was still stronger, so they couldn't make me change like that. I refused to do some things that I found hateful, ruining some of their plans. One day, knowing very well the story behind my own birth, I even wrote in the very core of the System a rule, that they should never kill a child, unborn or not. It made them furious, as you can imagine... They couldn't punish me, so they directed their anger toward Father. It only made him realize how wrong the new System was turning out to be. Your birth had changed both of us, and he wasn't willing to be part of that corrupted System anymore. Men like him, and his friend Charles that you have met, began looking for a way out of that future the Core was building. They felt sorry for the people in the Suburbs and even more sorry for the future generations that would be bound to that corrupted System."

"Why couldn't he just... stop everything?" Eden asked. "Why not just destroy it all, start all over?"

Pan turned to her, and Eden suddenly understood.

"...Because of you," she muttered. "...It would have meant killing you."

"Exactly," nodded Pan. "Father wasn't ready to make that sacrifice. He sought a way to destroy the System he had built, but all the ways he thought of implied destroying me one way or another. That was a thought that terrified him, but it was sadly true. I had become too close to the System, we were—no, we still are two parts of the same machine. Father couldn't find a way to get rid of it without also damaging or killing me."

"...But now, you've found a way, right?" said Eden. "It's been years. That's why you called me here, isn't it? You know how to deactivate the System without killing yourself!"

Pan stared at her for a very, very long time without answering. And it took that long for the reality to sink into Eden's mind. Her heart dropped, slowly realizing the truth.

"...You haven't," she muttered. "You mean... You want me to kill you with it?"

"It's alright, Eden," he said. "You're not making that choice, I am. I swear I have tried everything, but... since Father's death, the Core has been the only one to modify me. I'm... closer to the System than ever. I've tried to fight back, but the System is still heavily reliant on me. If you deactivate what keeps me alive, you'll end the System that easily."

"No," she retorted, stepping away from him. "No, Pan, no way. I refuse. You can't ask me to do that!"

"I understand you're upset," he nodded very calmly. "I expected that reaction from you. It's funny how your reactions are easier to predict now..."

"Don't read me!" she shouted. "Both you, and Father, I am so fed up with you making all these decisions for me! I don't care what you say, I can't... I can't kill you!"

"It's not killing me. Not really. I'm sorry you think of it like that. But really, I'm not–"

"Not alive?" Eden retorted. "You're here! You're talking to me! You've been right by my side, ever since I was born! You said it yourself, you felt love for me! You've been protecting me! You can see, you can hear me! You can feel feelings! If that's not being alive, then what the fuck is?!"

This time, Pan seemed really surprised, staring at her with wide eyes as if it had just hit him. He remained silent for a few seconds, then his eyes went around as if looking at the room for the first time. He chuckled nervously, then turned to her again, that smile still on his lips.

"I guess... you're right."

He hid his mouth with his hand, looking strangely happy.

"I never... I mean, I had a rough idea of what being human, and alive, was supposed to be but, I... Eden, you..."

He walked up to her, looking as if he was about to hug her, but he brutally stopped himself, his hands hanging mid-air, inches away from her. His expression slowly fell, into a bitter-sweet one. Eden was still staring at him, confused. Was he meaning to hug her? ...Could he hug her? However, Pan seemed to renounce it, with a sad smile.

Eden hesitated and suddenly stepped up to him, hugging him anyway. It was a strange sensation. His body was warm, but it felt like... something a bit different from the warmth of a human body. Warmer, even. Was the computer struggling to represent her brother's virtual figure? She heard him chuckle, and the warmth suddenly embraced her back too.

"Thank you, Eden."

"Don't thank me yet," she sighed, letting him go. "We still haven't found out how we're going to save you while destroying the Core."

"No, you can't," he shook his head. "I understand what you feel, and I really appreciate it, but your need to save me just can't be measured up to the importance of shutting the System down. You came here for that, remember? Thousands of lives depend on it as we speak."

Eden kept shaking her head, stubborn. There had to be another way. She couldn't even fathom losing someone else today, but of all people, her own brother, and after everything he had endured...

"Tell me more," she said, "about... Dad. I need to know. The Governor said... he betrayed the Edge and he chose the Core. It doesn't make sense, right? If he knew, all along... Why did Mother and I have to leave, to run? What happened to Father? How did things... I don't understand why he did this to them. I need to know."

"Don't worry," Pan smiled. "Father... He knew the Core better than anyone, right? What was the best way to create a counter-attack force that even the Core wouldn't find, and try to destroy?"

Eden frowned, trying to wrap her head around this.

"Wait... You mean... He lied to both the Core and the Edge? He made the Core believe he was manipulating the Edge, but he was really... manipulating them? But... the Edge failed."

"Did it?" smiled Pan, tilting his head.

Everything changed around them again. Eden was now in an empty room with Pan, completely white, with only a large screen next to them. The twelve mugshots from before were brought back.

"Don't worry," said Pan. "The Governor has no idea you're in here with me. He still has no idea about the truth behind the Edge's creation."

"What truth?" asked Eden. "They didn't make it. Almost all of them died, and Circé was even forced to work for them!"

"Father knew how risky it would be to create the Edge. He knew he would have no choice but to gather the best hackers in plain sight of the Core, making them think it was all a large-scale test. In fact, he did absolutely everything in plain sight and didn't risk it by hiding any of what the Edge was doing. The only thing he was counting on was the actual people he had chosen."

Pan turned to the figures, and four of them were brought forward, strangers Eden didn't know.

"These four were the less... reliable ones. Where Father recruited them from, they were known as criminal hackers, but also committed crimes such as money extortion, slaughter, murder, and an even longer list of crimes. In other words, he wasn't counting on them at all."

"In other words, they were expendable?"

Pan shrugged, visibly not sorry at all.

"The others... Father hoped they would survive. He knew how risky things were, and he just couldn't help them. He instilled the idea of an Edge that would perdure past the first generation... and I was to watch the other survivors. It didn't matter who, as long as just one of them made it. I could give them the information to start over, and rally more hackers."

"...I don't understand. How was he so sure some of them would make it?"

Pan smiled and brought one of the portraits forward. It was a young man among the Edge, visibly one of the youngest. He was the only one who wasn't just glaring at the camera that had taken his picture but was smirking with a haughty expression. The prison-like outfit looked a bit large on him, and he was wearing it messily, a shoulder out. He had red hair in a two-inch-long mess, a small nose with some freckles on it, clear blue eyes, and a little silver earring. The more Eden stared at him, the more she felt like she knew him. After a few seconds, it finally hit her.

"...No fucking way," she muttered.

"Ah," smiled Pan. "Do you recognize him?"

"That's... Loir?"

Never in a million years would she have identified that young man as Loir, if not for the hints dropped before. The Loir she knew was much, much skinnier than that, and covered in dark tattoos on most of his visible skin. She had never seen the real color of his eyes either under the screen of dark ink that covered them. His head was shaved too. Who would have known he used to be a redhead... She even wondered how he had never joked about that when he had told her a hundred times about his missing toes.

"...What happened to him?"

"You should already have heard," sighed Pan. "After the Edge was stopped, your friend and the others were captured and tortured... He was the most stubborn of all and went through much worse as a result. He was incredibly successful in pissing off his jailers."

Eden smirked without thinking. Yeah, Loir definitely had that effect on people...

"He was the one in which Father had the most hope."

"...What do you mean?"

Pan smiled and stepped closer to Loir's image, looking as if he was staring at the portrait of a friend. Eden suddenly remembered: Pan was the one who had led her to find Loir. Her friend had been such a recluse, she would have never been able to find him if it hadn't been for Pan guiding her to his hideout. Even their first encounter had been rowdy. Loir wasn't so ready to trust anyone, and she had been the one to insist on them becoming partners, persuaded by Pan. To think their bond was actually so much more complicated than that.

"Of all the aliases we have known him by," said Pan, "the one most likely to be his real name is Yulian Laskin."

"...Yulian?"

Pan nodded.

"At least, that's the name that was on his official papers... From what I found, Loir was born in a now-destroyed country in Eastern Europe. Parents unknown. Year, city, and date of birth unknown. He was probably an orphan among many, many more. What is known for sure was that his official trace was first found in some old paperwork about a growing group of young hacktivists that was opposing the military and dictatorial regime. After that, he has a long,

long list of short stays in all sorts of carceral establishments. Funny enough, his age and name vary in each establishment he visited, so despite my best efforts, I hardly ever managed to actually find the next piece of information about him. He did cross paths several times with the Russian Mafia, working for or against them, transiting groups very frequently. I even once found traces of him working for two opposite sides at the same time. God knows which one he was actually rooting for..."

Eden was stunned. Somehow, it felt like Pan was talking about a stranger, yet all those pieces were perfectly fitting into the strange puzzle that was Loir... She was mesmerized, and, somehow, also a bit happy to hear more about her friend, even if it was too late.

"One of his most remarkable talents was jail-breaking," said Pan, an amused smile on his lips. "Out of all the times he was incarcerated, I found him to have a surprisingly high rate of successful evasion attempts. Only the most cruel and strict prisons too, as if he had been comfortable staying in the low-level ones."

"...Free food and bed," chuckled Eden, not even surprised.

"I think so too," her brother smiled. "He stopped escaping facilities a couple of decades back, though. In fact, it seemed like Loir had found a more stable group to stay in. They weren't particularly remarkable, actually. Just another young group of hacktivists, protesting against the local figures of power. Their members got arrested a few times and released. Each time, Loir was among those caught, and waited until his release, up to six months later."

"Only six months?"

Pan shrugged.

"From what I saw, small crimes overfill prisons. Back then, hacking crimes weren't properly regulated yet, so half the time they got arrested, the penal system didn't know what to do or how to properly punish their crimes, so a legal gray area got them out in no time. Sadly, that ended with the first appearance of the Cores."

"...When they updated all the cyber criminal legal systems," muttered Eden.

As a Dive Hacker, she knew all too well about the risks of the job. Being a hacker meant exposing herself to dozens of cyber laws with each Dive. The creation of the System had been a good occasion for an old and decadent legal system to update itself on the latent issue of cyber criminality. They hadn't just found proper punishments for all the crimes that weren't even identified before; they made them much stricter and implemented all sorts of schemes for the System to be the judge of the hackers' wrongs. While hackers weren't often caught by the System itself, being caught in the real world meant dealing with very real, physical consequences of what had been done on the other side. Eden was too young to have known a time when cyber criminality wasn't regulated, but now, she was all too aware of the laws that existed, although she ignored them all daily...

"Exactly. It was a turning point for all hackers."

"What happened to Loir? And his group?"

"...I am not sure," sighed Pan. "I believe they went dark for a while, but the emergence of the Core also meant each country tightened its borders, and there are some files even I couldn't get access to. It is most likely that they fought on a much safer scale, or caused enough trouble that it was hidden by the local authorities. Either way, your friend eventually found himself in a very high-security level prison, again. Sadly, some people from his group ended up there as well and received the death penalty after their judgment."

"Oh, shit..."

Pan sighed and slowly nodded.

"I felt sorry for them too," he muttered. "In fact, his fleeting identity was most likely what saved his life. Because they couldn't find Yulian in the records, they considered his arrest as his first, and he got a more lenient sentence... Life imprisonment in that same high-security prison. According to the archives I found, it wasn't just any kind of prison, but one where they also mentally broke down people to then turn them into their own spies..."

"Into their own hackers."

"Exactly. ...I am unable to explain how Yulian... I mean, how Loir resisted the treatments he received. The information I found in his file as a patient of theirs is frightening even for my mostly insensitive self."

"He was tortured," whispered Eden.

"Yes. When Father found his trace, he was already much more like the Loir you knew than this young boy. At least, mentally. I recall he barely passed most of the psychological tests they put him through before admitting him into the Edge. Yet, Father was adamant about recruiting him."

"...He knew a broken-down Loir would never work for the Core."

"That was his bet."

Eden tried to recall what Loir had told her, but from what she could gather, their father had most likely been right about him. That whole story about Loir being the one that got the Edge captured was completely wrong; they hadn't been caught because he had been an idiot and called the Governor, but because the Governor actually knew about the Edge all along. It was all mixed up, even perhaps because he had willingly taken the blame rather than defending himself.

"Wait," she said. "So... the Governor captured the Edge, and forced some to work for them, killed others, but... Dad thought Loir would be able to escape?"

"Oh, he didn't just suspect he would be able to," chuckled Pan. "He actually knew. See, I told you Loir had worked for many different groups, alienating or befriending them. He even managed to make enemies here. Enemies whom, once they knew the most wanted criminal would be in the Chicago Core..."

"...Were eager to get him out and punish him," said Eden. "It was the Russian Mafia, wasn't it? Tanya helped him break out of the Core's prison, and, uh... punished him herself. He was captured and physically tortured by rival groups, but he eventually was among the ones who made it out."

"His jailbreak didn't just free him," chuckled Pan. "It caused the perfect distraction to free the survivors next to him. Not only the Edge hackers but a few people who had been arrested by the Core. It was a perilous plan, but Father had calculated everything precisely so key people would be able to use Yulian's jailbreak to escape too."

Eden took a minute to let all that sink in. Not only had her father not actually betrayed the Edge all along, but he had even ensured some of their survival. Loir was a much deeper and more complex hacker than she had thought, with a past darker than all of the tattoos on his skin. It turned out that there had been such a crazy and complicated conspiracy going on against the Core all along... That was just an awful lot to take in. She knew time worked differently in that room, in a reality that Pan was controlling, but she still needed a full minute to calm down and quietly take it all in. She took a deep breath, and let herself sit down, her head in her arms and her arms crossed on her folded knees. After she felt her heart calm down a bit, she raised her head.

"So... I was right," she finally said, covering her lips. "Dad was on our side, right? On the Suburbs' side."

"Father was always on the side of life," smiled Pan, lowering himself to her level with a gentle smile. "He was one of the smartest humans, right? He had that crazy plan in mind, all just to save you."

"Okay, so... what went wrong? Why did Mother and I have to run all of a sudden?"

Pan's expression sank. He sighed, and slowly got back up, turning to the mugshots of the Edge again.

"It was a risky plan... A very risky plan, with low rates of success. When Loir and some of the others managed to escape, things went awfully wrong here. It was clear it had been an inside job, and the Core's leaders immediately sought the culprits. It didn't take them long to point to me and Father."

Eden felt herself choke up a bit. Now that she had seen her father as a man loving her baby self, she couldn't help but feel much more attached to him, and fear for his final fate. It wasn't so much because he had, according to Pan, changed because of her, but because he had once been that man in his office, completely devoted to the two of them. She was even mad at herself for having doubted him; he was nothing but a hero who had tried to save both of his children with all he could.

"...What did they do to him?"

"They knew they couldn't touch me, and if they touched Father, I would still be able to retaliate; so, they threatened the ones that were most vulnerable and dear to us: you and Mother. Father saw it coming long before it happened. He knew things would eventually take a turn for the worse, so he had a plan to have you both run. He had prepared everything. Fake identities, even your Ghost SIN, and he knew I could locate Loir and the other Zodiacs anytime and compel them to help us hide you."

"But what about Dad?" Eden cried. "Didn't he try to save himself? He had you, and you knew they couldn't get rid of you. Couldn't you and Dad have worked something out..."

Pan slowly shook his head.

"Dad was a scientist, Eden. If anything, he knew his chances of survival, how hard it would be for him to escape... You know, a part of him really wanted to be with you, but he was also very... consumed by guilt."

"Guilt?"

Pan sighed and extended his hands. The mugshots disappeared, and meanwhile, they were suddenly projected into the air, far above the Chicago Core. It was so abrupt that Eden almost lost her balance, her feet seemingly standing above nothing but air, and below them, the smaller-scale version of the Core. It was a live feed of the ongoing battles on the ground. Eden felt dejected once again. It was a horrible sight. From the height, they were probably seeing what was gathered by the cameras at the top of the Arcadia Tower or from drones, but it was all too precise and real for her. Several portions of the wall between the Suburbs and the Core had been blown up, and near each hole, dozens of bodies were lying on the ground. It was a war scene on every street she laid her eyes on. Their groups had already spread inside the Core. Tanya and Michael's group had clearly decided to take the fight into multiple streets, hiding between houses and trying to hold their ground until they reached Thao. The Rat Zodiac was also doing her very best; Eden could see thick clouds of smoke coming up from the entrance of the Arcadia Tower, which had most likely been blown up already.

That wasn't all; far in the Suburbs, the skyline wasn't the same anymore. So many buildings she used to see from the roof of her own were already gone, reduced to a ridiculous mountain of bricks and rubble. The Core's Overcrafts were everywhere in the Suburbs, shooting at random and collapsing two more buildings while she watched, helpless, the city she knew completely ravaged.

"...This wasn't what he wanted."

Pan's voice brutally took her back to where they were. Eden realized she was crying, already shaken up by the devastation outside. She rubbed her cheeks, well aware her tears were probably pouring out in the real world as well.

"Dad didn't do this," she muttered.

"That's not for us to decide anymore," sighed her brother. "...But, there is one last thing I have to show you. It's important."

The scene changed again around them. They were brought back to her dad's office. This place was now almost familiar to her, but to Eden's surprise, this particular scene was even more so.

It was the one she had seen in the archives, exactly the same scene this time. Her father, facing a computer, with his baby girl in his arms. She had wondered who he was speaking to, but now, she could see his face on the

586

screen he was facing. Eden frowned, and approached. Pan resumed the video for her to hear what was happening.

She heard her father nervously cough a couple of times, adjust his position, and clear his throat again.

"Hello, Eden," he finally said, with a clearer voice than she had thought. "It's, uh... W-well, it's Dad. Ah, I am not going to be really good at this... Ah, that's you. See? You're just a baby right now. You're very small. You're only two days old. Quite a sleeper too! I envy you that..."

His eyes went down to the baby in his arms, immediately softening up. He smiled at her and scratched his beard, clearly nervous again. She even saw him wipe his palm's sweat on his shirt before putting his hand around his baby again and looking back at the screen, or more precisely, at the camera filming him.

"I wonder how old you will be when you watch this. I hope you're not too disappointed... I-I am not a very smart man. I mean, I build things, but... being a dad is so much more complicated than codes and physics. There's no formula for that..."

He scratched the curls of his hair, visibly a little embarrassed. It was a bit funny to watch this. She had always known he was a very smart and respected man, but seeing him like this, the Architect looked like any awkward new parent... He kept nervously moving his hand that wasn't holding her, scratching his hair or messy beard, wiping his sweat again and holding her gently, his palm on her tummy or grabbing her little feet for no reason.

"See, this is... the last time I will be holding you like this," he finally said with a sad smile. "After this, I will hide you and your mom, for your security. I don't want to send you away, but... as your dad, I have made this decision. I hope... you will understand. I have made mistakes, you see. I told you, your dad is not so smart... but I do hope to set them straight. Meanwhile, Prometheus will watch over you. He is your older brother, you see! I-I would like to say I saved him, but... I think it would be more accurate to say we saved each other. I created him while saving who should have been my son... I was also hoping to find a way to make a computer with the feelings of a human, and so far, he is doing well. I just hoped the machines we use could know what it's like... I don't know. I thought that perhaps if they were more human, we humans would be less heartless in response..."

He sighed, and leaned back, his eyes automatically drifting back to his baby girl. Eden had rarely interacted with children or newborns, so she was a bit shocked at how small she was... did he say two days old? Wasn't she small, even for a newborn? ...She couldn't say. At least, she was at an age at which she wouldn't remember this; her father had sent her and her mom away to hide before she could remember him at all...

"You know, Prometheus is very interested in you, my Eden. I think he doesn't understand it yet, but he loves you. And he'll watch over you, always. He's just a screen away. Your big brother will be there, and I hope you two will get to grow together... so that, even in the future, without me, you will never truly be alone, my daughter."

He smiled and leaned forward.

"See, you were born from me and your mother, but out there, so many people are waiting to meet you. You will see." He nodded. "I have never seen anything as fascinating as human connections... I sincerely wish you will grow to meet so many people, my Eden. Right now, we might be locked in tiny bubbles, but I want to show you there are a lot more people out there. We can never truly be alone on this planet. You will never be alone, my Eden. Even if you're not with me..."

He took a deep breath and turned to his baby again. He sighed, and gently, put his forehead against her, making baby Eden whine a bit in her sleep. He leaned back, staring at her again, before turning back to the camera.

"...This is my goodbye, but this world out there is here for you, Eden. Don't stay alone. Go out there, meet a lot of people. I promise you'll find humans so amazing, you'll find others you can love, and be loved. I'm sure you'll be alright. I will make this whole world safer for you. Better for you, and kinder. ...I love you, my Eden. Your dad loves you."

The video recording stopped abruptly, along with the sound, making Eden notice how much she was crying. Embarrassed, she rubbed her cheeks, before realizing she was still in the Dark Reality, and probably crying anyway in the real world; she tried to breathe in and out and turned to Pan.

"Th-thank you for showing me this," she said.

"I knew you'd be happy to see it," he smiled, tilting his head. "...And I'm sorry you didn't get much time with Dad."

"So... he knew?"

Pan nodded.

"After what had happened to me, he and Mother had figured out that the Core might try to use you... Not only that, but it had already been a few years since my birth and the new Core, and as time passed, Father was getting more and more upset with what the Core's leaders were doing. He was arguing more and more with them every day, about all sorts of things they wanted to do, both to the people and to the System. He was outraged by the Suburbs and the way they handled the citizens too: the harsh treatment of prisoners, and the heavy surveillance placed everywhere inside the Core. He strongly opposed the use of orphans for scientific experiments... He knew things would reach a breaking point. So, he and Mother had devised a plan, even before you were born. He prepared that special SIN, just for you, as extra security, so they wouldn't ever be able to kick you off the System... In other words, they'd never be able to fully cut you off from me."

"So you could watch me..."

"Exactly," nodded Pan. "After that video... During the night, Dad sent you and Mother away. We staged a fire and pretended you were both killed in that fire. Father even burned himself to make it all more believable, while you and Mother were rehomed under different identities, still inside the Core, but farther away from here, close to the border with the Suburbs. I don't know if they believed Dad, but it didn't really matter. He was arrested just months after, under a bundle of accusations the Core had made against him. If anything happened, Mother had to run to the Suburbs and hide, but as you already know, sadly, when that happened a few years later, she didn't make it... Father couldn't create a different SIN for her like he had done for you, because you were a newborn. So, she was captured almost too easily by the Core as soon as she tried to flee to the Suburbs with you."

Eden could only nod, a bit bitter. Finally, the puzzle of the tragedy that had affected her family was falling into place. Why she had never met her father. Her double SIN. Her failed attempt to flee with her mother, and finally, Pan... Despite how sad this all was to hear, a part of her was finding a strange relief in learning all this. As if she could find some closure for her past and put all of her nostalgic but unresolved feelings to rest.

"Thank you, Pan... No, Prometheus," she chuckled.

"I think I like it better when you call me Pan," he said with a joyous expression. "...I know the situation isn't ideal for it, but I am happy you finally know it all... and we got to properly meet too."

Eden could understand his joy, but unlike her brother, she had to go back to the real world soon and deal with the harsh reality of it. She took a deep breath, trying to calm herself; that was indeed a lot all at once...

"How long has passed? Since I came in here?"

"Four minutes, and a bit over thirty seconds."

Less than five minutes. Eden nodded. It meant there was still plenty of time, or at least, she shouldn't have missed too much of what had happened in the real world.

"Pan, I came here to stop them. To stop the Core."

"I know. As soon as you deactivate me, there will be a–"

"I am not deactivating you!" she shouted. "I came here to stop the bastards who did this to our family, I'm not going to bloody kill my own big brother! And no, I don't care what you think you are or not! You're alive to me and I still need you!"

"...I understand," sighed Pan, surprisingly calm, "but you are running out of time either way. So... what do you want to do? I don't think there's another way, Eden. I know you want to save me, but the System is heavily reliant on me. My death would be the quickest way."

"It doesn't mean there isn't another way then, right? We have to find it, Pan. Please."

He stared at her for a long while, and she wondered if, behind those pretty hazel eyes, his computer brain was actually looking through thousands of pieces of data to find a solution... Would she ever reconcile with having a half-computer brother? In a way, she knew she already had. Her own legs were already those of a robot. This was the kind of strange world they lived in, where they had to be one with the machines.

Which got her thinking. Did they really need to take down the machines? Eden, better than most, knew what disabling the System would mean. They had to cut off all of the smartest computers. It would disable all the computers, but also the Parts and all the bots the Core's people relied upon daily. Was that really the best solution? It had sounded so simple when she had discussed it with the Zodiac because it was the only sure way to disable all the weapons the Core had...

"Pan, bring me back."

"What?"

"Bring me back to the real world. You can still communicate with me from there, right? From that computer. I want to go back, check on Dante, and see if I can liaise with the rest of the Edge. I need to check up on everyone, and perhaps, we'll find a solution if there's more of us to think about it..."

"I understand," he nodded, "but Eden, just know it's alright if you don't find another way, alright? I'm prepared for it."

"...I'm not."

Just a blink later, she was back to facing the large computer. The pain suddenly hit her like a violent wave, making her lose her balance and start to fall. Surprisingly, two strong arms gently caught her, and she felt his torso like a cushion under her back.

"Dante!"

"Welcome back," he said, putting a kiss on her temple. "Anything new?"

"A lot of new things... Are you alright?"

"I'm fine."

She wanted to roll her eyes. As if he'd ever say anything else... Still, she let out a sigh, and for a second, leaned herself into his embrace. It was almost cruel how they had no time for even a moment of tenderness. She felt Dante's gentle breathing against her ear, so comforting and warm, but she could also feel the blood from his injuries. She only had to glance to the side to see the long trail that he had left behind him from the data centers to here...

"The Edge is on," he said. "They are already investigating the server as we speak."

"So much effort, for so little!"

Eden grimaced at the annoying voice. The Governor. She had almost forgotten about him...

"You children are so clueless about the world we live in. The humanity of today needs the System, more desperately than you can see! Can you imagine how many lives rely on this? The System of today regulates our everyday lives. We simply cannot go back to a time when there wasn't any!"

Eden knew there was a portion of truth in this, but she refused to believe there was no way to reconcile living with machines and people's free will.

"You can fuck off," she groaned, trying to get herself up again.

Dante helped her, visibly completely oblivious to his own wounds. Eden could barely look at him. There was literally blood all over his suit... It was impressive he could even stand and act so calmly right now. She tried not to think too much about it. The sooner this would be over, the sooner they could treat him.

"Eden, look."

She followed his finger, pointing at the screen. Pan! The chat tab was still there and telling her to go to the back-left corner of the room, behind them. Eden found a spark of hope. Had he found an answer?

Dante helped her go over there, both of them struggling a lot. She could hear the voice of the Governor laughing above them.

"This is quite a sight! Oh, Eden, young Eden... How did it feel to finally meet your... sibling? I know he isn't quite the ideal older brother, but what an impressive, remarkable achievement your father created with him! Men were so obsessed with artificial intelligence for years, but your father simply turned the problem around, making human intelligence into a computer instead! I have to admit, dealing with an actual human brain has its challenges at times. It can be quite difficult, and sometimes, I'm baffled about how an entity which has never known a physical existence can reason over ethical problems or societal issues..."

"Don't call my brother an entity or an object, you greedy bastard," hissed Eden.

"Oh, but Prometheus is far more than that, of course! Prometheus... Do you know your brother was named after the brave Titan that brought fire to the humans?"

"...I'm pretty sure he got his guts eaten up by an eagle for that," groaned Dante.

"Well then, we know who's the eagle," said Eden.

# CHAPTER FORTY-THREE

They finally reached the spot Pan had indicated, but Eden quickly understood this wasn't about the System. Instead, there were three rows of Parts. All kinds of Parts: hands, arms, feet, fingers, and legs. Eden sighed. She was a bit glad, and also a bit disappointed it wasn't the solution she had hoped for. Still, she quickly searched through the Parts assembled to find some that would fit her legs. Dante helped her grab a pair of dark matte ones, made of some very advanced tech. Eden put them on, immediately finding some relief in being able to stand by herself. Those were the most advanced Parts she had ever set her eyes on, probably the kind she'd never be able to afford by herself in this life... Perhaps that model wasn't even on the market as she had never seen anything quite like it. She guessed there were analgesic needles in the joining parts, as her hips went from painful to strangely numb. She practiced moving around, grateful that Pan had somehow managed to repair her SIN a bit, at least enough for her to use Parts again.

Once she was set and able to walk by herself again, Eden dove further into the shelves, hoping to find something for Dante, more pain relievers or a healing bot perhaps. But there wasn't anything. Those people weren't very concerned with the pain they inflicted on others in this room... At least, now she didn't have to lay on him, she could support him instead. Eden turned to Dante, grabbing his arm.

"You alright?" she asked again, unable to put her worries aside.

He nodded, and gently kissed her on the top of the head again, annoying

Eden a bit. She wished they had more time together, but all of a sudden, she had a bit of regret that it was only the two of them up there. Some of Dante's men would have been good reinforcements, and a way to drag their injured boss to safety...

Sadly, she had no time to think about that. With her legs functional again, and with two new Parts, the previous one ditched without an ounce of regret, she then focused on her SIN. If she could use Parts again, that meant she was back in the System. Somehow, Pan had healed her SIN while she was in there with him.

"A.? Nebty? Somebody?" she called.

"Finally!" exclaimed Greed. "What's up, Ghost? You missed the war!"

"Shut up. What did I miss? Are you in?"

"We're like... halfway in. It's so freaking complicated, the System is not happy at all with us being here, and Nebty gave us orders to wait before we touch anything."

"Yes I did," said Nebty's voice. "Eden, I'm looking at the heart of the System right now, and it's really, really complicated. Everything is nested together; if we touch anything, I'm worried we're going to trigger a chain reaction and do a lot more damage than good. Please tell me you've found a way to deactivate this hell!"

Eden took a deep breath, and slowly shook her head. She turned around, analyzing the room, trying to search for answers, but nothing here seemed to help.

"I-I found it," she said. "The heart... no, the brain of the System. It's not a data center, Nebty, or even a central unit. It's a brain."

"...A brain?" said Circé. "What the... Are you talking about something figuratively? Is that a code name or something...?"

"No, I'm talking about a real, actual human brain. It's a human brain that's generating all of the System's abilities. He was born disabled many years ago, so the Core used a... a child's brain to juice the whole System. That's why it's so intelligent, but it's no artificial intelligence, it's actual human intelligence, only enhanced by the machines. He's the one making all the decisions, the one who's been trying to stop the Core from the beginning. Pan. Pan is the System's heart."

"Holy fuck..."

"...Shit," grunted Nebty. "So... you're telling me if we... deactivate the System, we have to actually... stop Pan?"

"We have to kill him," grunted Eden, "and that's what he thinks too."

"You sound like you've got a different idea, Ghost," said A.

"I don't have another idea," she retorted. "I simply hate the idea of killing him. Pan is... my older brother. And not just that, he's the Architect's son and the only one who's been trying to stop the Core so far. He's... he's basically everything that is actually good about the System! The moral sense of it!"

"...I admit, the more I hear you, girl, the more I don't like it either," said

Malieka.

"I get that too, but is there no way to dissociate the two?" asked Nebty. "Eden, we have to stop these people no matter what; we're talking about hundreds of lives at stake at this very moment. I totally get that you don't want to... sacrifice Pan, but if you got another option, I need to hear it right now."

"I don't have one! ...Yet."

There had to be another solution. Eden kept looking around, desperate, looking for the one idea she really needed.

"Are we really hesitating to kill one non-real person to save all of the Suburbs?!" exclaimed Pride. "All due respect, Ghost, but that guy is the one who came up with that plan! If he's fine with dying, perhaps we're wasting time for nothing!"

"Pride!"

"What? I'm telling the truth! We already lost Warlock to these guys, how many more of our friends are we going to fucking watch die before we do the right thing?!"

"It's not the right thing," retorted A.

"It's a fucking computer to unplug!"

"It's not just that!" retorted Eden. "If we do this, all of the technology stops. You understand? Everything will stop. The Governor just said it, and Pan confirmed it too. He is the one that literally keeps the Core's System functioning. If we cut everything now, every piece of modern technology we know will cease to function, we're throwing everyone back into the twentieth century."

"...There's been worse," muttered Crash.

"You think?" groaned Circé. "How do you think your Dives work? What cleans the air we breathe? The money system? All the medical robots? Even the security systems could trap people in their own homes!"

"The Parts will stop working too," added Greed.

"...You're right, I'm starting to really not like this situation either," said Nebty.

For a while, everybody went silent on the channel, and Eden was just glad they weren't pushing her to kill her older brother... She turned to the column where his body was and went back to the large computer. There wasn't anything new on the chat tab, but she knew he was watching. One of the screens in the corner was displaying the room's surveillance camera's live footage, with Eden right in the center of it.

"...Pan, you have to help us," she muttered.

"Tough choice, isn't it?" chuckled the Governor.

"...I know that bastard's voice," hissed Circé. "Don't let yourself be swayed by him, Eden!"

Eden suddenly realized something. She stepped back from the computer, and looked up, finding the camera itself. If Pan could see her, the Governor was probably watching too.

"You're in the building, aren't you?" she said. "Governor. I want to meet you, face to face."

"Ah! Fine, child. After all, I owe you that much..."

Behind them, one of the elevator doors suddenly opened.

Eden stared at that empty elevator with a bad feeling. What was she going to find upstairs? Or more like... who? She took a deep breath to try to calm herself down. Even if she got killed as soon as she stepped in, there was still the Edge who had access to the System. If anything happened to her, no way were they going to let the Core win. She had already played her part in this, and she also trusted Pan would take things into his own hands if anything happened to his little sister. She could at least trust him this much for the little bit of time she had spent with him.

"Eden."

Dante held her hand a bit tighter, his eyes set on the elevator with a determined expression.

"I'm coming with you," he said.

"...I know."

She smiled back at him. That only felt right, now. She wasn't going to push her lover away anymore, certainly not at this moment. She needed him, and she knew Dante wouldn't ever let go of her, no matter the price. If this was going to be the end, she was glad that she was with him, whatever would happen next.

They stepped inside the elevator together, firmly holding hands, and the doors closed. She heard Dante chuckle.

"What?"

"...I think I really like elevators, actually. It brings back some nice memories."

She blushed, knowing which memories he was referring to... This scene did feel oddly familiar. She smiled a bit, glad they were together in this box going up. She held his hand a bit tighter. Just a few floors, closer to the sky, and closer to the end. Now, it was all about looking for that last solution; Eden could give up on many things, but she refused to give up on a better world. Ironically, it looked as if this elevator had the same settings as the others, showing them scenes of present-day Chicago as if it was simply made of glass. She wished she could have seen such a view when the city wasn't ravaged by soldier bots, guns, and bombs sent by the Core. All of the streets were covered in dark smoke, some places were blown up as she watched, and countless fires had started. Not to mention the bright, red, flashing lights that were layering the whole city under a strange, scary filter. It was as if red was the last visible color, everything else in shades of dark gray up to the line of trees beyond the Suburbs. The green, vast forests that were forbidden to humankind for decades now... Eden missed the view from the top of the roof she lived on. She used to hate that place, but now, she wished she could go back in time and enjoy one more sunrise there.

"You're going to be okay."

Dante's words took her away from her dark thoughts. She turned around, frowning.

"Shouldn't you say 'we'?" she asked, upset.

But her lover only answered with a smile, making her heart hurt even more. Eden's throat tightened. Dante never made promises he couldn't keep... She let out a pained sigh, and leaned against him again, immediately finding his comfortable embrace.

"I'll stay with you," he simply said.

Eden found herself so selfish for wanting his presence more than anything at this very moment. Wherever they were going, she wasn't expecting to come back alive, and neither did Dante. However, she was feeling strangely... fine. She was nervous, but not in a state of panic like she would have expected. It was as if she had been running away her whole life, but now she was about to confront the very root of all of her fears: the Core itself. She wasn't afraid; she was ready.

"...Pan?"

"I'm here, little sister. I will hear and see everything. Worry not."

"I have a request for you."

"I'm listening."

The elevator finally stopped a minute later and opened unbearably slowly.

Eden would have been prepared to see anything, but the room that awaited them was unusually... normal. It looked like a large office, tied together with a vintage-meets-urban theme. It reminded her of Jack's bar because of the old, criminal Chicago theme, with black, leather seats and oak wood furniture, but more spacious and bright. There were dozens of big, dazzling light bulbs hanging from a high industrial ceiling, and a black marble floor that made their steps resonate throughout the whole room. On their right and behind them, the walls were covered in green plants, while the rest was nothing but large windows, giving a perfect view of Chicago once again. It wasn't the actual Chicago, though. Whatever the screens were showing behind those fake windows, it belonged to a different time, with no explosions, and not even the wall separating the Suburbs. There were many more buildings and much more green too. Eden even wondered if this was a scene from the past or an entirely virtual representation. Either way, she couldn't help but be fascinated.

The city behind the windows was... utopic. The sky was bluer than she had ever seen, the buildings pearl white, and even the asphalt of the roads looked spotless. Eden could even spot little birds on the roofs, happily hopping and flying around. It was as if everywhere her eyes stopped, there was a little bit of life that captivated her with its unique and simple beauty.

"...Magnificent, isn't it?"

She turned to the corner of the room where the voice had come from.

There was a long, long table with a dozen chairs around it, but at the very end, a unique, large, throne-like seat. The man was standing next to it, smiling at her. Eden was shocked at how young he was. From his voice and words, she had imagined a man in his fifties, perhaps older. However, the gentleman facing her with a bright smile and gorgeous brown curls looked under thirty. He was wearing a simple white shirt too, although it was buttoned to the top and had shiny cufflinks.

"Surprised?" he asked, visibly amused by her expression.

"...I had imagined more of an old fart," Eden grumbled.

"Oh, I am old indeed. Older than your father was. But I'm a rich old fart."

So, this all came from money... and it was scary. If Eden had crossed paths with that man in the streets, she would have had no idea he was two, or perhaps three times older than she was. His youthful appearance was very convincing, with that toned body, bright blue eyes, and perfect smile. He chuckled and stepped close to the window, just like her, but on the other end of the large glass.

"I can never get tired of this view," he declared, looking fondly at the landscape. "It's not real, as you've probably already realized, but it could be one day. At the very least, that is my vision for the future."

"That will be hard to do if you keep blowing up buildings and murdering people," Eden hissed.

"Oh, I do not think so. See, the biggest obstacle in this vision coming true is... people."

She frowned, lost by his words, but the Governor kept staring at the screens with an enigmatic smile.

"Ha... I always thought we left them with way too much leeway. Look at your precious Suburbs. Rebellious, unruly... so many criminals too. See, one thing that we should have learned, from centuries of fighting each other, is that humans aren't meant to be left to their own devices. We are guilty of all seven sins, on a daily basis, and yet we always persist, we keep going, like the entitled, self-absorbed, and greedy creatures that we are."

"...I don't think many people would see things that way."

"They would be wrong, child. Look at the Suburbs, look at the Core. Which one is better right now? Once we have purged all the sinners, the criminals, and the... faulty out of our city, what do we have?"

He smiled and sighed with happiness, his eyes looking around at the buildings.

"A working society. Each member in their designated spot, working just as they need to be so the machine can keep going. No one stepping out of line, no one undoing the hard work of the community. No troublemakers. Granted, the people of the Core might not be perfect yet, but... we are getting there."

"By not leaving them any free will?"

The Governor chuckled.

"Free will is only a sweet disguise for chaos, Eden. It is what makes men want more, and sadly, ambition makes them crush others on their way to that. Look at history. How many times did men's ambition get fulfilled at the expense of others?"

"Oh, so you're telling me you got to your position by being a nice guy and sharing your paycheck with the rest of the city?"

The Governor laughed.

"I see where you come from. Something such as money is such a difficult discussion. But, I can assure you, I don't earn more than I need, and I actually invested quite a lot into–"

"Into looking like a freaking kid half your age?" scoffed Eden. "I'm sorry to break it to you, but money isn't a difficult discussion in the Suburbs. It's an actual, factual need. We don't get to chat and argue about what we do with it; every single human being that works, works because they need to. And every single credit we earn, we need to survive. There is no discussion needed because everyone in the Suburbs knows exactly what their neighbor goes through, on a daily basis, to survive. We can't afford to complain about such things as looking young or old, about the color of the damn furniture, or what clothes we can put on our backs!"

Eden's anger visibly cooled the Governor's enthusiasm. The man sighed and turned to her. His eyes briefly went to Dante, with a much clearer disgust for him. Still, Dante didn't avoid his eyes at all, putting a hand on Eden's waist, and although he was standing behind her, his eyes looked like a guard dog ready to bite at any time to defend its master.

"...The Suburbs is the result of a chaotic society. They are the remains of the failure of the previous generations to keep society under control. The Core is our best chance of survival. ...Do you know how many human beings are alive, on this planet, at this moment?"

Eden frowned, unable to understand where he was going.

"A little under two point three billion," announced Pan through the speakers.

Eden glared at the ceiling, a bit mad at her brother for playing along with the Governor, but the old man had visibly expected this much. He didn't look surprised and simply extended his arms.

"Just a century ago, we were almost four times as many, and suffocating our own planet! ...Mother Earth was rotting under men's blind ambitions. We killed hundreds of other species to build our cities, fill our stomachs, and procreate, always destroying more. Evolution only taught us how to break the food chain, making ourselves the apex predator of a whole planet! Our own kind was our worst enemy, and naturally, we began destroying each other."

Suddenly, the screens around them changed into a very different vision.

Eden even stepped away in shock. War. Not like the war she had seen outside, but an absolutely terrifying war scene was playing on the screens. Every single building burning, explosions everywhere, dozens of vehicles flying or in the streets, spitting fire and smoke at every corner of the ground. Planes were flying in all directions, shooting at each other and crashing into buildings. And bodies. Hundreds of bodies filling the streets with blood and flesh, only a handful of people still alive, busy killing each other. She couldn't even tell if this city was Chicago or another; it was ravaged. If there had been any sounds, she could imagine how terrifying and deafening it would have been.

"...This, Eden, is war. The real, hideous, and vile side of what our kind is capable of. Destruction, nothing but destruction, for miles and years on end. We didn't just lose two-thirds of all living things in just a couple of decades. We lost countries, civilizations, continents. Two of the seven continents were entirely annihilated. Half of Europe and Asia were blown up, and whatever countries were left, on any land, were devastated by war. And finally, natural disasters from years of ignorance destroyed what our weapons couldn't."

He sighed.

"...If not controlled, left to their own devices, men become the best artisans at destruction. They do not even mean the evil they cause, it is their ignorance that becomes both their best argument and their weapon of choice. We chose to ignore how sick we made our planet, how we dumped our trash in the weakest countries. Men chose to blame those they couldn't reach, for it was easier to deflect their mistakes onto someone else and feign ignorance... Thus, men like your father and I had no choice but to rise up and take control to prevent the final destruction of our civilization!"

"Do not put my father and yourself in the same damn basket," groaned Eden. "You can find whatever excuse you want, you are still a mass murderer. You killed thousands of children, and all those people that didn't fit in your utopia!"

"It was necessary," retorted the Governor, perfectly composed. "I understand a child like yourself might have trouble seeing the greater vision we had. But, without the proper leader to take the reins, our kind is doomed to self-destruct."

"How the fuck do you justify murdering unborn children?!"

"Natural selection, nothing else! Eden, you do not understand. How would our planet be able to handle eight billion humans again? It would die in the next century. Thus, we have no choice but to regulate our population. Look at the Core! The sacrifices made allow those people to live in harmony! In peace! Not only that, but all the Cores are on the same level of equity! No more poor countries, no more apex predators preying on the weak! The sacrifices are made for the greater good, for the sake of preserving our civilization! If only the good, healthy genes survive, under the right supervision, humans will be able to keep on living for centuries on this planet! Earth will be green and blue again!"

"And what gives you the right to make that choice?" muttered Eden.

She laughed bitterly, annoyed by all that she was hearing.

"I get that we destroyed half the planet with our bullshit. I get that humans are the smartest and cruelest kind. I already know all that. We all know what happened. But you know what? ...Truthfully, I do not care if our kind is bound

599

to go extinct in a century or two. I don't care if we all end up dying of hunger, lack of oxygen, or from fighting. As horrible as it is, at the very least, we get to fight for our own survival. ...What I can't handle is listening to one old rotten bastard, alone in his fucking tower, deciding who gets to live or die!"

The Governor's expression darkened.

"Careful, child. You do not–"

"I don't understand?" Eden interrupted him. "Go ahead, keep patronizing all of Chicago because you know so much better! You think nobody knows? We aren't blind or deaf! We all see what our world is like, in the Suburbs, past your white fences and perfect roads! ...So you think free will is a threat? You think blindsiding people is going to make them any better? I don't see any of your so-called perfect people fighting for their beliefs! Look at Chicago! Half of them are fighting for their survival, and the other half are completely numb and lobotomized for the sake of a utopia that will never truly exist! Your precious citizens can't even process what is going on in their streets, you've made them utterly ignorant of the suffering of others! I hear you saying men destroyed the planet, but all I can see is a bastard like you, building walls between people and choking up one side and feeding the other with lies!"

"...That is the only way for our kind to survive," retorted the Governor, anger in his eyes. "A child like you cannot understand. It takes resolve to be the one to shoulder such precious ambition!"

"I can understand it is wrong to kill a baby against their parents' wishes."

The anger rose in the Governor's eyes, and this time, he did look a bit older. But Eden continued, feeling herself become colder and more resolved than ever.

"You're a wretched person who hides behind shitty excuses," she continued, "you murder babies that don't fit your utopia, and you get rid of people with a will to live another way. You torture children to feed a science that allows old farts like you to cheat death. Don't lecture me about the natural order of things. I've seen what you do down there."

"Science will be the solution for our kind to survive!"

"No," said Eden. "It should be used to save lives, to help people. What you're doing is mass murder with a needle. Children like Adam or Prometheus are used as your science experiments when you should have used all that technology to make their lives better, not enslave them to technology!"

"Do you have any idea how many lives we have saved thanks to the research we do here?"

"And how about how many you've destroyed thanks to it? You can't choose to be accountable only for your successes, Governor. Let me guess. How many of your precious citizens are aware of all your little experiments? Of all the children, adults, and creatures you've tortured in their name? I bet they don't even realize how dirty of a business you've got going on..."

"They shall thank me for their survival! After all, aren't you glad that your precious brother survived? How about the man standing next to you? Do you have any idea how many different bodies are allowing him to be alive, right now?!"

Eden's heart sank.

"So it was all you. ...I always wondered how the previous Tiger got that technology," she muttered. "Now it all makes sense. ...Where better to hide your horrors than in the giant dumpster where you banished everything else. It was you, all along. You used men like the previous Tiger to do your dirty work."

"Yes," he said. "I used rodents to get rid of vermin! And that man next to you is nothing but the result of another successful experiment! You should be thanking me, Eden! Without me, both he and your brother would be dead!"

Eden took a deep breath. She was growing more and more disgusted with this man at every word that came out of his mouth. It was all coming back, under a new light. Adam's murder, the truth behind Dante's very existence. The shadow of the previous Tiger. Her dad. All of it was a result of the Governor pulling strings behind the scenes.

"Your brother wouldn't have lived a single minute in this world if it wasn't for our technology!" exclaimed the Governor, annoyed.

"Yeah," scoffed Eden. "So instead of saving a baby's life, you decided that it would be so much better to use my father's newborn as a fucking piece of technology. My father dedicated his whole life to making our world a better place for the next generations, and when he finally had his own children, you tried to use the both of us as fucking bargaining tools!"

"Your father was like any other self-absorbed man out there! As soon as he saw an opportunity to use that technology for his own greed, he used it! He tried to break our principles for–"

"He tried to save his only son, you selfish bastard!" Eden shouted back. "He did what any other decent human being capable of love would have done out there! He did exactly what all those machines should have ever been used for! To save lives!"

The Governor slowly shook his head, visibly annoyed. Their argument echoed throughout the whole room, and despite the distance between them, they didn't need to shout. He sighed, massaging his temple as if he was dealing with a temperamental child that refused to listen.

"...Your father knew the final goal would be to enhance all forms of life, but also to merge humans and machines. Your brother isn't the only miracle we have achieved between these walls! Do you understand how I can look so young at over eighty years old? We are on our way to unveiling the true immortality men have only dreamed of, all this time! We can preserve humans through machines! Look at yourself, child. Those legs of yours, don't they allow you to walk and run faster than your real ones? ...That man behind you is a prime example! The first human Chimeras are already spreading!"

"No," hissed Eden. "What was done to him should never be done to anybody else!"

601

"Oh, it will be," chuckled the Governor. "You should be grateful. In exchange for all of the ones he provided us, I allowed the Tiger to keep some of the defective ones... I shouldn't have, now that I realize he made his own Chimera, a walking failure standing here in my office! He claimed he had always wanted a son, and our program allowed him to create the very best killer, by meshing together all the boys he had kept. That cunning bastard only got what he deserved."

Eden's blood was growing cold in disgust. So it was true. Dante was nothing but the blend of the boy she had known in the streets, Adam the orphan, and other boys... She remembered he had talked about training with other boys. Had his memories gotten mixed up from all the different memories of those boys? It was impressive he was even able to retain his own self, most would have gone crazy by now. Perhaps that also explained why he was so inexpressive. He didn't just have no sense of pain, he also didn't seem to carry many emotions. Unless that was the previous Tiger's doing, in his hope to create the perfect killing machine... If so, his attachment to her was probably part of his imperfections. A part of Adam had remained, the part that was dedicated to protecting Eden.

While she got lost in her bitter thoughts, the Governor kept talking, shaking his head with an almost theatrically disappointed expression. She just felt utterly disgusted at this man, and at the previous Tiger Zodiac too. To think about how many orphans they had probably swiped from the Suburbs and murdered for their experiments was just revolting.

"...That was one of our most ambitious projects, but of course, there were bound to be some mistakes! After the first successful Chimeras, we realized we would be able to do the same with humans. Synthesizing several bodies into one to create superhumans, something all countries had been dreaming of for a while! There was nothing we wouldn't be able to do to raise them to perfection. Physically enhanced, smart as a man could be, and yet, less emotionally involved, less risk. The cognitive part was the hardest, of course, but it wasn't like it had never been experimented on before... Truly, that was an over-a-century-old project of humanity. Of course, this was only the start of many other projects and an unlimited path to future achievements. Can you imagine, if instead of Parts, we managed to transfer whole body parts into living humans? We could replace every failing piece one by one, like any machine, and live forever! Our ancestors had found ways to transplant organs, but with our current capacities, we can replace absolutely everything! That was for the medicinal part, of course, but we needed to consider the military aspects as well. As I said, many were sold on the idea, but this one was much harder than merely replacing organs or limbs. If only we figured out how we could change a human's deep nature, how to rewire and program the human brain, we could create nothing short of a killing machine! That goal made it all worth it. We could get as many orphan boys as we needed from the streets, and put them through the trials–"

"My God," muttered Eden. "You're just disgusting. Do you even realize what you're talking about?! Kidnapping and murdering defenseless children for experiments! To turn them into absolute monsters too! You can't use humans like freaking mindless robots! Like bloody weapons! You think you're so good and know so much better? You're just another self-entitled, old prick launching bombs and committing mass murder from his ivory tower!"

"This selfish prick is the reason that man is even standing next to you," hissed the Governor, "and your dear brother Prometheus himself was a huge stepping stone in this next achievement. I am the change necessary for our people's survival. Of course, some of our deeds weren't the most commendable, but that was all for the sake of many more! Those children wouldn't have survived the streets anyway!"

"You know nothing of that!" Eden shouted, furious.

"There was no stopping us," continued the Governor, as if he couldn't hear her. "Once we understood we could make a human brain into a machine... Ah, how much easier would it be, if we could control all of the population directly? No more half-access through the SINs; we could create our own army! ... Look at him. Even for a failure, he's quite impressive! You should be grateful, Eden, for this man is a survivor, just like you. But he will be the last walking failure. The next generation of his kind is already in the making! The first generation of superhumans, entirely devoted to this Core! No feelings, only their cognitive abilities, absolute loyalty, and of course, bodies that can endure anything without ever experiencing pain! ...Isn't it beautiful? We won't have to sacrifice our own citizens or use stupid robots that could fail us at any time. We're almost there, another age of unchallenged peace and power! It's the beauty of progress! Imagine, if we gain full control of an army of soldiers? Not faulty ones like him. Those that would be rewired to be completely emotionless, painless! Entirely devoted to the Core, the perfect soldiers! Look at him! Isn't it amazing! Even with his body full of bullets, he's still standing, and alive! ...Adam–no, Dante, is that his new name? He survived, but he's imperfect, seeing how he seems to have feelings toward you."

"...He's dying."

The words had left Eden's lips before she could stop them, just like her tears.

"Adam already died, and now, Dante's dying," she repeated. "He's dying, and... he can't even feel it."

She could feel Dante's body, standing right behind her, still there, but she could also feel how he was not doing well. His hand, still holding hers, was getting colder and colder. His grip was getting weaker. Eden's tears kept slowly falling, as she held onto him while glaring at the Governor who had made her lover like this.

"You're creating nothing but ghosts of humans," she continued. "You have no idea of the real value of life and death."

"Death will be the least of our concerns once we find the path to immortality!" he shouted. "The best of our citizens deserve everything, even the power to live, for as long as they need! We can heal and replace everything!"

"You can't numb everything that makes us humans!" Eden shouted even louder. "People like you have no fucking idea of the value of one's life! You kill and cheat death as you please! How can you be fine with murdering newborns, and claim you're giving yourself extra decades for the sake of humanity? You're just another self-centered, selfish bastard! You're murdering thousands of people, and the rest of the Chicago population doesn't even know what it's like to survive, every day, on a handful of credits, scraps, a mattress against the asphalt, and breathing nothing but polluted air!"

"They do not need to know!" retorted the Governor. "Progress is the new natural selection! Those who deserve to be our citizens shouldn't have to worry about the life of vermin! Do you care for the lives of rats? Of ants? Do not lecture me when you've been surviving on that same technology you loathe!"

"...I don't loathe the technology," said Eden. "That's the difference between me and you. I don't hate the machines, I hate what you've done with them. If I murder someone, nobody blames the gun for it. So why are you pushing all the blame on those who only fight to survive? You're not fighting for survival. You're only praying for supremacy."

"...Wouldn't you do it?"

A cold chill ran down Eden's spine. She hated the way this man smiled, that creepy way he looked down at her, with those eyes that were way too young to belong to an eighty-year-old man... He chuckled again and combed his brown curls back.

"Greed, Eden. Every single human knows about this. So, let's discuss it. Speak honestly, child, if you had a chance to save him, would you take it?"

"...What?"

"Look around you. This is the top of this world. You've seen the lab your brother is in, haven't you? We can accomplish miracles of technology there. We could save that man you love so much. Everything. It is doable. His whole body, all as good as new... Wouldn't you agree to that?"

"No."

Eden's response had been so quick, the Governor's expression sunk briefly before he chuckled.

"...You're lying. He is dying," he muttered as if assuming she hadn't understood, "and we can save him. This isn't merely hypothetical. I'm offering you."

"...Then what?" she muttered. "It would be somebody else again?"

Gently, she felt Dante's hand move to hug her a bit tighter. Eden was still crying, but in her heart, she had never been so sure about something. She wouldn't do that to him. She took a deep breath and grabbed Dante's hand tighter against her waist. She could feel how weak he was from the way his body was gradually leaning more and more on hers. She was trembling in fear, at the thought that he could fall or collapse at any second. She had no idea how he was even able to still stand. But she was certain. Perhaps she would have made a very different decision if it had been two hours ago. Yet, after all she had seen, after all she had heard, she couldn't.

Eden slowly shook her head, ignoring her tears running down.

"Dante is not Adam," she cried. "Whatever happened to that boy... Whatever you did to him and the others, he died that day. And Dante De Luca was born, but he is not the boy I met in the Suburbs. Dante is someone else. Perhaps... Perhaps his infatuation with me began with whatever was left of Adam inside his brain, but I am sure of one thing. He and Adam are not the same. The sweet boy from the Suburbs died. And now, the only man I want is Dante. And whatever you want to do to him... He won't be my Dante anymore."

She felt Dante gently kiss the back of her head.

"...You foolish girl," hissed the Governor, taking a couple of steps back. "...Fine, die with your boyfriend then! You may have come all the way here, but what have you accomplished? You cannot shut down this System! Even if you sacrifice your brother, you'll be condemning all of Chicago with it! That's right. All of the Core's citizen's SINs are bound to the System. If you shut it down, they will automatically suffer brain damage! You'll murder all of the Core with hundreds of cases of strokes! You claim to be some righteous woman, like your dad, but you're just as powerless as he was, in the end. You and your friends will accomplish nothing, and you will be wiped out for more of our citizens to be able to thrive! Soon, there will be nothing left of the Suburbs. It will all be over, and no one will cry for that vermin!"

"My dad was a hero," said Eden, "and you murdered him because he was going against what you wanted. You murdered him like you murdered the Edge and everyone who stood in your way. You're right. The System cannot be shut down, but I've realized it doesn't need to be. The System isn't wrong; you are. You and all those bastards who control it for their own sakes. I am ending this today."

Eden raised her weapon, suddenly aiming it toward the Governor. Her gun pointing directly at his head made the old man suddenly step back.

"...Ha!" he exclaimed. "As expected! You're just another terrorist! What are you going to do, Eden? Kill me? This won't end anything. I may control the Core, but even if I die, somebody else will take after me. You won't be able to get rid of the whole chain of command, child!"

"I can always start with you."

Eden fired. The gunshot loudly hit the glass, making the Governor jump back in fright. The gunfire set off a loud alarm in the room, a strident sound assorted with beeping red lights. Luckily, it was immediately deactivated after only ringing twice, most likely by Pan, but in this short amount of time, the Governor had already run toward a cabinet on the side, grabbing a gun himself.

Dante reacted first, pulling Eden to dive behind the closest piece of furniture, which was the other end of the large, wooden table. Luckily, it seemed to be secured to the ground by a large concrete base; in other words, a decent shield. While keeping her hidden, Dante moved to start firing above the table too.

"I want all soldier bots here!" shouted the Governor, furious. "Get them all up here!"

"Sorry, sir," said Pan's calm voice. "I cannot do that."

"You wretched thing! I should have gotten rid of you long ago!"

The Governor kept firing, but he obviously had no talent. He shot every single piece of furniture around them but never hit the table even once. Dante, on the other hand, was a much better shot, and after a couple of tries, he hit the Governor's shoulder. The man screamed in pain while Eden grabbed Dante's shirt to pull him back into hiding with her.

"Are you okay?" she asked.

He didn't answer, only peeking at the status of his gun while the screams of pain from the Governor could be heard in the background. Eden glanced at the hand that had grabbed his shirt. It was covered in blood. She cried even more.

"Dante, stop..."

Once sure his gun was reloaded, he tried to get back on his feet, but, unexpectedly, he wasn't able to. His legs gave out, and he fell next to her, looking almost surprised himself. Eden watched, helpless, as Dante struggled against his own body, trying hard to get back up. It was no use. Even his hands suddenly dropped the gun on her lap, his fingers completely unresponsive. She could tell he was trying to move them again, in vain. They were merely shaking.

"Stop," she muttered.

"He's going to shoot at you again," he said, as if more bothered by that than his own situation.

He groaned again, his eyes glaring at the gun he couldn't grab. She saw his shoulder moving, his eyebrows frowning under the effort, but everything else was completely still. His own body had given up, and she couldn't stand to watch him struggle anymore.

"Dante, stop it!"

He froze, visibly surprised by her cry. Eden sniffled, and leaned against him, hugging him. She knew it was already too late. She could only hang on to him, hug him tightly. Eventually, she heard him sigh.

"...Sorry."

"Don't be sorry," she cried. "Don't be..."

"I wanted to protect you until the end. ...Don't get shot, okay?"

"I won't. I promise I won't..."

"Shit, I think I'm... cold."

Eden trembled. He wasn't just cold; his whole body was as cold as ice. She was trying hard to hug him, all of him, but Dante wasn't hugging her back. His arms were simply lying there, against the floor. She hugged him even tighter, her tears silently soaking his shirt.

"Hug me."

She nodded, and hugged him even tighter, hoping even just a little part of him could feel that. He sighed again against her neck.

"Sorry, my songbird," he muttered. "I think I just need to rest. Just... a minute."

"It's okay. Don't worry. ...I'll be alright."

Eden waited, and hugged him as hard as she could. Never had Dante's body felt smaller, weaker than hers. She hugged him as if she was hugging herself, holding on to what she could, and letting herself cry silently. She could still hear the Governor grunting and screaming in pain, somewhere farther up front, but she couldn't have cared less. Right now, she just wanted to hold on to Dante, for one more minute.

One last minute.

# CHAPTER FORTY-FOUR

"You bastard!" shouted the Governor. "I should have gotten rid of you long ago!"

His words woke Eden up. She hadn't even realized she had passed out, perhaps for a few seconds. She slowly sat up and glanced down at Dante's body in her arms. He was truly gone. She could feel her tears, still hanging on her cheeks, and that tight throat choking her up with sadness. Her hands moved, from around him to grab his shirt so tightly, the blood squirmed in between her fingers.

"Dante..." she cried.

He was simply laying there with his eyes closed. It looked as if he was merely sleeping, aside from his cold body and the lack of breathing. Eden sniffled, staring at him with that deep feeling of loss inside her heart. She could see Dante, but what she felt was a large void. A horrible, deep, and large void that was threatening to consume her whole being with sadness. She had lost people before, but this time felt even more cruel. He hadn't even felt the pain, but the way he was gone felt just absolutely unfair. Inhuman.

Bit by bit, she felt the anger rise in her heart. She was sad, sad beyond words, but so many emotions were right behind that sadness, knocking on the back of her mind like a storm about to pick up. Anger. Rage. Madness. Determination. Boldness. Bravery. It was as if his strength was passing on to her. One of her trembling hands slowly moved, letting go of Dante's shirt to grab his gun instead. The other refused to move, but it didn't matter. Eden only had to raise her head a bit to see the man responsible for all this. She could hear him, his vociferous voice reaching her like an annoying crow in the back.

"You failures from the Suburbs have no idea what we are capable of! You're nothing but the remains of a deceased world! The waste of a generation!"

Eden closed her eyes. She was so frustrated, she couldn't even utter a single word. This man was mad. Just... mad. He had murdered hundreds of people from where he stood, and now, from a single bullet, he had completely lost it. A bitter smirk perked up her lips. There were still some men made of flesh in his world, after all. Eden was glad he could suffer. Someone like him who was entirely numb to the pain of others deserved every single bit of pain he endured.

Her teary, hazel eyes went back to Dante. He was gone, but her hand just would not let go. She took a deep breath. She had to keep her promise and survive this, somehow. She didn't want to die here with him. Eden herself realized how strong her own will to survive had grown now, and moreover, that would have been the opposite of what Dante wanted. She couldn't do that to him, not after his sacrifice. No, in fact, he had given her the willpower she had always lacked. With another wave of tears, she reluctantly let go of the blood-soaked shirt. As soon as her fingers had let go, she was dying to grab it again, but she kept herself from it. A part of herself already couldn't endure the sight of his inert body, and she didn't want this, those sensations of his cold body, to be the ones that remained engraved in her head. Dante was gone. Eden took a deep breath and grabbed the gun with both hands. It was time she ended this.

After glancing above the table that separated her from the Governor, she realized he was hiding behind the other end, and a medical bot had come out of nowhere, probably healing him at record speed.

"Are you alright?" suddenly asked Pan's voice.

"I'm not."

Eden was telling the truth. She was in a whole storm of emotions right now and wasn't sure she could handle much more. All she wanted was to end all of this.

Having heard her, the Governor reappeared, carefully leaning against his leather seat. His eyes went to the gun in Eden's hand, but seeing that she wasn't pointing at him, he probably felt confident. He smirked, glaring at her while the medical bot was still working on his shoulder. In fact, there was already pretty much nothing left of that injury.

"You've accomplished nothing by coming here, child," he said. "Even if you kill me, it will all be for nothing. You can't stop those fights with my death. You'll only lead your precious Suburbs to be destroyed for good. You think the Core's citizens are innocent? They aren't. They voted for this. They approved every single project we sent them! This isn't just my doing, Eden. It is human nature speaking. When we told them we could increase life expectancy, they wanted it. When we told them we could drop criminality in their streets to zero percent, they voted. Oh, and of course, they all voted for me, every time, for the last fifty years! They put their future in me. If you kill me now, you'll only be a terrorist girl from the Suburbs who took the life of their leader. Someone else will be chosen to replace me, and everything will go on, just as before. Minus the Suburbs, of course. Retaliation would be the right way."

"You blindside them, don't you?"

Despite her tears, Eden's voice was unexpectedly clear. She wiped her nose and cheeks, but her hazel eyes stayed on the Governor, with unresolved anger in them.

"You don't tell them the cost. If you told your citizens how many lives you sacrificed, would they still vote for you? Would they really vote if they heard their own children are killed in the womb?"

The Governor's expression gradually fell. She had touched a sensitive chord. He let out an annoyed groan and glanced at the medical bot that was trying to heal him.

"They did not need to know," he said. "They only needed to know the results, not everything we had to pay for it. Does that make any difference? They want immortality. They want safety, wealth, and peace of mind."

"You're choosing the truths that suit you," Eden muttered. "...If you only show one portion of the truth, you're making that choice for them. This isn't democracy. Your citizens are no better than puppets."

"They are happy puppets! Look outside, Eden. Your Suburbs are the ones who came and wrecked that heaven we had put in place! Look at the destruction! The deaths they are causing!"

Eden didn't need to glance outside. The blood on her hands, clothes, and face was enough already. There wasn't a single Core civilian's blood spilled outside, she was sure of that. It was nothing but the Core's doing, the Governor's system parodying the truth to suit their needs.

"You're lying," she muttered. "All the time. You won't even show them the truth!"

Suddenly, the glass windows around them changed. Pan was now displaying two versions of what was going on outside of the tower; from one window to the other, things were only slightly different. Eden immediately recognized the tweaked version that the Core was displaying, where the people of the Suburbs were seemingly murdering their citizens, while on the other side was the truth: the robots killing the fighting members of the Zodiac and the ones behind them. She didn't even flinch; she had already seen the chaos in those streets. She vaguely recognized Tanya and Michael, both hiding behind what looked like tanks, screaming orders to their people and holding on, just a few streets away from the tower. In the fake version, there were some of the Core's citizens' houses on fire, while in real life, most were unscathed. Of course, the people from the Suburbs had no reason to attack them when they could barely defend themselves.

"...You're nothing but a liar," she muttered.

She turned to the Governor again. Her eyes weren't crying anymore, but expressing a deep sadness either way.

"You lie," she said. "You lie to the people, to your citizens so you can push the weight of your own choices on them. You only let them see the Suburbs you see, and you build walls so they have no idea of the nightmare it is outside. You call it a paradise? It's a fucking cage you got them all in!"

"You think your dear Suburbs are any better?" scoffed the Governor. "Look at them! Thieves, murderers, rapists! All of them are committing crimes on a daily basis without blinking! You think your precious Zodiac are decent leaders? They are nothing but gangsters! We knew what kind of scum would breed when we left the Mafia to reign over, but we didn't care! The vermin preying on the vermin! We figured you'd eventually all murder each other!"

"Look outside," retorted Eden. "You don't have the slightest idea of who those people really are. Do you think it's only fear that keeps us moving, behind those criminals? No. It's the will to survive. I didn't become a hacker to commit crimes, I did it to survive. Every single day, every hour, hundreds of people in the Suburbs only have one thing in mind. They want to stay alive, they want to be safe. It's true. We kill, we steal. But we don't do it for pleasure! We do it to survive! Even children have no choice but to steal when they are starving, and everyone in the Suburbs is starving!"

"Human nature is ugly," hissed the Governor. "If we don't provide for them, our citizens will end up just the same. Hence, we need to keep a portion of the population fed plenty, comfortable, and thriving, and leave the others to naturally disappear."

"...Naturally disappear? It's mass murder!" shouted Eden. "There are thousands of innocent people dying for the comfort of a few hundred! How can you claim you're saving the population when old farts like you literally plan to live forever? There's no way there will be resources to keep us immortal, so you just chose to reduce the number of births so you can keep on living! It's just disgusting!"

"You children don't know anything! Your generation will perdure until Mother Earth is ready to have us again! And then–"

"And then what? You'll keep selecting who lives and who dies? Who can be born? You'll keep nurturing insensitive people with no idea what it's like to be hungry just for a day? ...Those people outside, your precious Core citizens, are just blind and deaf to the cries coming from beyond the wall. But the truth is, you just don't have the guts to actually give them their free will back. They are more your prisoners than the Suburbs are. They vote for a despot because they have no idea they are voting for the death of thousands of others, and their own children!"

"That's right!" shouted the Governor, jumping on his feet. "And everything works better this way! Humans are incapable of making choices for the greater good unless directed by a higher power! I am the one that governs them all, I am the one who makes the right choices for their sake! It takes men like me

611

to save humankind from its own madness! To save our future! And all our citizens only need to see the results, and thank me for it! Yes, your precious Suburbs are expendable, and they will disappear rightfully so! What happened today will only be their downfall!"

"And once they're gone, who is going to fill your next Suburb, Governor?" scoffed Eden. "You can't expect that the garden you've cultivated all this time won't ever create rotten apples. There will always be criminals. Misfits. People who just don't belong to that so-called perfect paradise! It can't work. There will always be someone who steps out of the lines. Always. As long as humans are left with their own willpower..."

A vicious smile appeared on the Governor's lips. He chuckled, but this time, he didn't look young or charming anymore. Eden could see past what he looked like. Inside, he was nothing but an old man, trapped in his own visions, entirely insensitive to the pain of others. He could still feel pain, but he wouldn't even blink at the massacre going on outside. It didn't bother him a single bit. It was as he said. He saw the humans that didn't belong in his vision as vermin, disposable. And he would dispose of everyone that hindered his plans.

"That's exactly my point," he chuckled. "We can always sort the bad apples, Eden. ...Isn't it ironic? Your father named you this, but the child grew to be the vicious, devilish snake that wanted to push ignorant Adam and Eve to take a bite of the forbidden fruit. But I am the god of this world, Eden, and as long as I want it, humans will never get to see the truth. Their only truth will be the one I show them, and just like this, I will be the maker and savior of our future. I will keep on living, just to save humanity, just to show them, in a century or two, what we have accomplished together. I will live to see it; I will be adored as the savior, as the one who guided them through the dark ages of this planet. And one day, when I am sure my vision will go on forever, I will peacefully die, adored and mourned by all."

"...Damn, you were right, Eden," chuckled a voice. "He really is one hell of a crazy piece of shit!"

The Governor's face whitened. He looked up, and the screens around them changed. One by one, several windows opened, showing the faces of the current Edge. Dozens of hackers, men and women, appeared, with their headphones on and their eyes riveted on screens. Soon, their faces covered all of the windows around them, and Eden glanced around, a bit relieved to see so many familiar faces. She couldn't even tell who was who, but she had recognized Greed's voice coming from her right. On the left, a window appeared, with Nebty's face at the very center.

"You rotten bastard," she hissed.

The Governor was completely surprised by the Edge appearing around him. He kept turning around, staring at all the windows that were opening and gradually covering the fake visions of Chicago. After a while, he chuckled, turning to Nebty's face.

"Ah! The rats are coming out of their hideouts!"

"We're not coming out of anywhere, you bastard," hissed Malieka. "Your System is ours. We are in every inch of those servers."

The Governor's expression sank for a second, but then, he laughed again.

"You think you won?" he chuckled. "You foolish vermin, you think you can scare me like this? I know how the System works! It is only controlled by the Core, and I am the Core! The fact that you are in it doesn't change anything! I am the man in charge! Even Prometheus cannot stop my doing! Every single new system that is implemented has to be validated by the Core's citizens, and you have no say in this! Their SINs are not corrupted, all it takes is one vote, and all of you will be kicked out, the System will be reset, and all that hard work of yours will have been for nothing! I will be the only one left! I was elected by the Core's citizens! I rule over all of the Core, and as soon as I tell them, you all will be hunted down like the criminals you are!"

"Yeah, you know, I wouldn't be so sure about that, old man," chuckled Greed.

The windows displaying the hackers all disappeared, one after the other, freeing the windows and were now just blank. The Governor frowned, staring around the disappearing tabs, completely lost, until one of the window panels changed. Instead of becoming a window, this one was showing a surveillance camera of this very room. Eden glanced that way too. They could both see the Governor's stunned expression, visibly unable to understand. Still, he kept staring, and the nervousness was clear in his eyes. The old man wasn't gloating anymore. Another window was replaced with his face again, another angle this time. One by one, all the panels were gradually replaced by live footage of the room's surveillance cameras, showing him from different angles. The only window that remained was the one with Nebty in it, staring down at him as if she wanted to watch this until the very end.

"This one's for the Edge, you piece of shit," she groaned.

"You... So what if you hacked the cameras in this room?!" he shouted. "You can't do anything to me!"

"Oh, we didn't hack those cameras," chuckled Nebty, relishing in his panic. "Pan gave us access to them. We wouldn't have just gone through all that trouble for the sake of seeing your ugly face!"

"W-what..."

"On the way here, I asked Pan to record everything happening in this room in real-time," said Eden, "and then, he gave the Edge access to all the cameras here. So they could broadcast everything."

"B-broadcast..."

The Governor's face sunk, bit by bit. He kept turning around to see his own shocked face, plastered in high quality on every panel of the walls. The sheer panic could be seen on each screen, the truth suddenly dawning on him. Then, one panel changed. Instead of a large version of the live footage of the room, one could see a blonde woman, standing in her living room with a shocked expression, her hands covering her mouth. The background showed the sparkling white furniture and green plants of a house in the Core as if they needed extra confirmation as to who that woman was. Right next to her, the panel changed, splitting in two to show more houses, one with a family seated around their table and their baffled expressions riveted toward him. The other one was a middle-aged couple on their couch with a similar shocked expression.

One by one, all the windows changed, splitting into dozens of squares, all live footage of his citizens' homes, with those people staring in his direction with utter shock on their faces. There wasn't a single person not staring at their screens with faces of disgust or horror. Some were even crying already.

"N-no," the Governor muttered. "No, no..."

"It's too late," said Eden. "They heard and saw everything. ...No more lies, no more secrets, Governor."

"What... What have you done?!" screamed the Governor, furious.

"What should have been done long ago," declared Eden. "Showing the truth to your citizens. The kind of rotten old man they are all voting for and hiding behind."

The Governor kept spinning around, his eyes wide open and staring at all the screens in shock and disbelief. Whether he believed it or not, it was far too late. Eden glanced around too. All of the citizens on the screen looked so shocked, there was no way they hadn't heard and seen it all. The cameras corrupted by the Edge were zooming in on the Governor's furious and shocked face, following his every step. They had never shown Eden at all, so even now, the citizens had no idea what she looked like, they had most likely only heard her voice. Eden took a deep breath, calming down a little. This was it. Pandora's box was now wide open, and the citizens of the Core were exposed to the truth. Not only that, but while they stood in this tower, the rest of the Edge was working hard to restore what was shown from the streets and establish the truth, not the modified images. Eden watched the shock in every one of those people's eyes. With relief, she saw fear, anger, shock, disgust, and even sadness. Many of them were rendered speechless or crying. It was one brutal awakening for sure, after the decades they had all spent thinking only good things happened in this tower, and thinking of the Suburbs as only a zone for criminals... Yet, their leader had just exposed his own crimes, including the murder of countless children, and their own unborn babies. Perhaps that explained why some couples or middle-aged people looked more shocked than others.

"I-it's... It's a lie!" he shouted. "They are lying! Th-they modified my voice! I-I didn't..."

"It's going to be hard to get out of that one, Governor," said Nebty. "We're not done here."

The screens showing the Governor changed to images of the ravaged Suburbs this time. Eden realized those shots were most likely taken from the

614

Overcrafts or bots they had hacked; it wasn't like surveillance cameras, but recorded images, the time stamps proving they were from less than two hours ago. The Edge didn't have anything to hide, and they truly showed everything: the blown-up buildings, the bodies scattered around the streets. The Core's destroyed robots, those who fired against them in the previous fight. Then, they showed the worst part: the Hell Bomb detonating in the south. Eden forced herself to watch too, the brutal end of the Dragon and the Eagle. It was just a large flash on the screen, followed by a cloud of thick, dark smog. And then, as the wind gently blew away the darkened air, they saw it: the void left by the Hell Bomb, with only blasted buildings, and sinister shadows, like silhouettes burnt on the ground. There were no bodies left, but one could easily see where they had stood, just seconds before their horrible end. It was so terrible, just to imagine that someone's whole body could literally be blasted until there was nothing left.

"...You did this," hissed Eden, glaring at the Governor. "You did this without even batting an eye."

"N-no, it's fake! It's fake!"

"Your citizens can just go out of their houses to see if it's real or not," she retorted. "All it takes is for them to go outside, into their streets, and see for themselves. We brought the fight to your turf, and they will see for themselves that their screens were showing nothing but lies, like everything else you've ever shown them!"

"Stop it!" he shouted. "Stop it! ...I will hunt you all down! I'll eradicate the Suburbs! You are nothing but vermin that's been surviving on our backs all this time! You don't get a say in this! The Core doesn't need people like you, we were showing mercy to let you live off our scraps for this long! How dare you do this?!"

His anger got him shouting, sweating, and panicking. He was stumbling around, his eyes going in every direction as if he couldn't decide which screen was the least worst to watch. Nebty and the rest of the Edge were leaving them no time to think at all. Bit by bit, they were showing absolutely everything about the destruction and death going on. The screens were now split into dozens of separate windows, showing either reality or the Core's citizens still shocked by what they were discovering. From time to time, someone would run out of the frame, and Eden guessed they were following her advice of going out to see for themselves.

"...You!"

As if he had regained his senses, the Governor's eyes suddenly went back to her, filled with anger. He lifted a finger in Eden's direction, slowly stepping away, toward his desk.

"This is all your doing. This is all your fault! I showed mercy already, but your wretched father had to betray me, and you had to pursue his madness even further! You and your brother should have never been allowed to live! All because I was lenient! You're what happens when a single mistake gets out!"

"I'm what happens when one of your citizens has their own free will, you old bastard," hissed Eden. "Father knew about all the wrongdoings you were desperate to hide, and he tried to get the truth out too. Every single person who found out about this refused to follow you any longer, didn't they?! You're just a cunning, selfish, lying, old scoundrel!"

"You don't get to lecture me, you brat!" he shouted back, furious. "You've ruined decades of hard work! Everything is ruined because of you!"

"Your airtight bubble of lies just popped," muttered Eden. "It's about time the Core's people woke up from that tasteless dream you were drugging them with. No matter what you believe, humans deserve to make their own choices. Even if they reject the Suburbs' people, they deserve to know what the world is really like outside. How we starve, how we barely survive, how we can't even breathe freely. If they make that choice again, then so be it. But I won't leave an old wretched liar like you to decide a thousand people's fate from this tower."

"You... You swine!"

His eyes went to the screens again. The Governor closed his fists, but there was nothing he could do other than watch. The surveillance cameras were now showing the Core's citizens, all going into the streets. Eden saw some of them at the entrance of their gardens, watching the ravaged streets in shock. Many now looked scared of all the robots and were taking detours to avoid them. She even spotted some people running toward the injured, intending to help them. Most looked completely shocked by the number of bodies and the soldier bots' presence. Although those things were programmed not to attack the Core's citizens, it didn't stop them from firing. In the north, where Michael and Tanya were still hanging on, Eden could see some people at their windows, looking completely speechless at the battle happening there. This was the truth they would have never seen through their System-manipulated screens. Perhaps they never even would have believed it if they didn't take that extra step to go out and see for themselves. Eden let out a long sigh of relief. So, this hadn't all been done in vain after all. Now, at least, the Suburbs' fate would be known. Those who had died wouldn't be forgotten, erased from history by mindless, heartless machines.

"Trust me, we won't leave anything out," said Nebty. "We're digging deep into your rotten System and putting everything in the open, Governor. All your dirty secrets, everything you've tried to hide. There won't be a single thing left."

"P-Prometheus!" shouted the Governor, suddenly turning to the cameras. "You traitor! You're supposed to help the System!"

"Sorry, Governor, I'm afraid I cannot follow your directions anymore."

"You don't have to think, you stupid brain! I am your master! I decide what you get to do or not!"

"I've been hacked," chuckled Prometheus. "The Edge is now all over the System, what can I possibly do? Plus, remember, Governor, I may be just a

616

brain, but I still have my free will. And my will is to follow my precious little sister's wish."

"You don't get to decide who your master is! You don't get to disobey me!"

"You're mistaken, Governor. My master is the System. If the System is hacked, so am I. Moreover, my programming prevents me from doing anything that would harm my little sister."

Pan's face suddenly appeared on one of the screens, giving a little wink to Eden. She somehow managed to gather a faint smile, despite all of her sadness and anger. At the very least, Pan was still with her. Eden was so glad they had found a way that would allow her older brother to keep living. He was already merely the shadow of what his life should have been. How unfair would it have been for him to disappear in such a way too? She refused to do that, not with everything it would have implied. Of course, she knew this alternative might have also brought a more... finite solution. Perhaps things would have gotten better, over time, without any technology left. Still, Eden couldn't agree to that. Not with everything technology had brought her. Not just her brother, but also everyone she had met. The Edge, and all of the people that were assisting her in this. How many of them would have never been able to meet, see the light of the day, or even get to know one another if it wasn't for their ability to navigate through the System and the Dark Reality? Eden was just starting to understand. Technology was man-made and controlled by men too. The issue wasn't with the fighting robots or the System. It was with the people behind it. And right now, she had just made half of Chicago realize how wrong things could go if that technology was placed in the wrong hands.

The Governor seemed to be slowly realizing it too. His shock was still painted all over his face, but gradually, he was visibly recovering from it, his anger taking over with a distorted grimace on his face. The charming young man from before was gone and now, Eden was truly starting to see this man for who he was underneath: a rotten old man.

"You... All of this is because of you!"

He suddenly dove at the table and opened a drawer. Eden's instincts immediately took over. She got back behind the table, hiding herself the best she could. She heard the first shot right after, although it was far above her head. More followed, all just as poorly aimed, filling the opposite wall with holes, some bullets even bouncing back off of the elevator door. His gun was just firing non-stop. She grimaced. The Governor was the worst shooter she'd ever seen, but if he kept shooting like a madman, she wouldn't be able to take a single step toward the elevators.

"Ghost!" shouted Circé. "What's going on?!"

"That bastard started firing at her," hissed Nebty. "Stay hidden, we're going to find a solution to get you out of there! Thao, Tanya, we're going to need an escape route!"

"I'm fine," groaned Eden.

"We're fleeing?" protested the Russian woman. "For real?"

"We did what we had come here for. Whatever happens next..."

"Wait," said Circé. "...Nebty, something's off. Those damn robots stopped firing here!"

"Here too," said Michael.

Eden glanced at the screen above her while staying hidden behind the table. What was going on? She could see all the robots had stopped moving, everywhere. They didn't seem offline, just... frozen.

"Pan, is that you?" asked Lecky.

"No... But look."

Eden turned her head to see the new window he had just opened displaying another camera's footage. She didn't recognize the room it was showing, but there were a lot of men and women, either in white coats or suits, running around to computers and visibly arguing out loud.

"What are they doing?!" shouted the Governor.

Suddenly, the audio matching the surveillance camera was turned on, and a man and a woman, both looking in their thirties, with very elegant allures but upset expressions, walked up to the cameras.

"The Council has made the decision to temporarily halt the System while we deal with the situation. Our citizens are gravely upset, and we are flooded with their appeals about the current situation. Governor, you are currently relieved of all of your administrative functions. The authority over the System and the Pan Unit will be transferred to us for the time being. Please know that your actions will be put on trial."

"You can't do that! I am the Governor! I am the highest authority! How dare you do this?!"

"I regret, Governor," said the woman, "the citizens are the highest authority of the Core, and, at the moment, we have a ninety-five percent rate of unpopularity toward you. According to our Constitution, this allows the Council to take over all official decisions regarding the Chicago Core and System. All military operations launched under your command will be immediately canceled to prevent any further outbreaks."

"The Scientific Community aligns with those decisions," added the man, who was glaring behind his glasses. "Your actions are nothing but intolerable, and we will see that you pay for all your crimes, including toward our peers that tried to oppose you. We will also reach out to the Suburbs' current leaders to find a way to settle the damages you caused."

"We are not negotiating with those criminals!" shouted the Governor, furious.

"You are the criminal, Governor. We ask that you remain in your building until you're officially prosecuted. There's an awful lot of mess for us to deal with, but, given the situation, we first need to appease our citizens and at least lessen the incommensurable damages you've caused. Not to mention the major leak of data. But I promise we will get to your case!"

618

He looked absolutely disgusted with the Governor, and the communication was immediately cut off right after that. Eden tried to ease her breathing a bit since he had stopped shooting. That rotten old man was probably too shocked by how low he had now fallen that he had forgotten about her. Eden eyed the elevator. Could she make it? She glanced down at Dante's body. ...She didn't want to leave without him. She wanted to at least be able to give him a proper funeral. More than anything, the idea of leaving him here with that man disgusted her beyond anything. She took a deep breath. Her new Part legs would be able to carry her without trouble, but would she be able to carry Dante and get to the elevator before she got shot? She grabbed his gun, only to realize that thing was out of bullets. She had left her weapon god knows where too... She sighed. Either she made it to that elevator, or they'd both die here, together.

"Eden, it's alright."

She suddenly raised her head, only to see Pan was still there, on the screen, gently smiling at her.

"Don't worry, little sister," he said. "You'll be alright. Take him. Go."

Eden nodded. If Pan said so, she had to believe him. Either way, she couldn't think of another solution. With a deep breath, she dropped the gun, and pulled Dante the best she could, preparing herself to run. Just steps away from her, the doors to the elevator suddenly reopened. Eden stood up right away, heading there as fast as she could.

"Oh no, you're not!" shouted the Governor.

From the corner of her eye, she saw him aim in her direction. This time, no matter how bad of a shot he was, he'd hit her somehow. Still, she didn't stop. Eden knew she wouldn't have a second chance to get them to that elevator. She kept running, waiting for the sound of gunshots any second now.

They didn't come, though. She heard the Governor swear furiously.

"Why won't it work!"

"Did you forget, Governor? The System is programmed so no harm can be done to a child..."

"That bitch is not a child!"

"...Even if it's still unborn."

Eden finally reached the elevator doors, and fell forward, on all fours, Dante's body falling next to her. Her hands fell on something familiar. She grabbed the gun, turned around, and shot, several times, until the doors closed.

She stayed like this for several long seconds, seated in the middle of the elevator, her hands still trembling on the gun. All of a sudden, she felt unwell. Dizzy. The elevator spun around her. She leaned back, unable to even sit anymore. It was as if her body was suddenly catching up with all the madness of the last two hours.

"...Pan?"

"I'm here."

"Did I get him...?"

619

"Yes."

"Good..."

"You did well, little sister."

Eden wasn't so sure of that. Right now, she had a metallic taste in her mouth, her head spun like crazy, and she knew she was about to pass out any second. She vaguely felt the elevator going down until it stopped, and the doors suddenly opened.

"Stop! Stop! Don't shoot! It's Ghost!"

She vaguely heard people running, stomping around her, and many voices. Eden didn't even realize she had closed her eyes, but the darkness was inviting her gently. She felt familiar hands gently grabbing her.

"Oh shit, he's... Take him. ...Eden? Eden, it's Circé, can you hear me? Are you injured? Help me carry them, you idiots! We need to get her out of there. Nebty, we're ready to go. ...Hold on, girl, just a bit longer. I got you. We got you."

# CHAPTER FORTY-FIVE

Something was grunting and gently biting her hand. She heard a little bark. Her dry mouth was the first sensation that came to her... along with a mild headache. She tried to breathe in, but something was bothering her, making her want to scratch her nose.

"Easy now, you silly pup! I want her to wake up too, but she ain't your freakin' toy... Come on, stop bitin', I said! You're cute, but you're a pain in the butt, you know that?"

Eden slowly managed to open her eyes. The light blinded her for a second, so she closed them again. Then, she reopened them, more easily this time. She felt... heavy, and incredibly tired. Numb, even. She forced herself to breathe through her mouth and moved her head.

"Oh, shit! Eden? You up, honey?"

"...Jack?"

Eden wondered if she was dreaming. Would she have felt like this in a dream? Perhaps. She blinked and Jack was still right next to her, looking worried, his large body leaning forward. He was wearing a fuzzy white jacket over his colored overalls and had a blanket on his lap. He smiled, visibly relieved.

"It's me, honey! Oh damn, I'm so happy to see your pretty eyes again!"

Eden moved her head, a bit unsure about everything. She was in a white-gray room, with what sounded like a lot going on around her, but most of it was in the distance. She could hear voices, but not what they were saying...

She recognized the aseptic scent of a hospital first. She frowned and heard another bark.

She turned her head and spotted the puppy playing with her hand on the side of the bed, its little tail wagging. Bullet? Upon seeing the naughty pup, everything came back to her all at once. She felt and heard her own heartbeat accelerate through the beeping of some machine.

"Jack, how did you... and the pups... What happened?"

He sighed.

"Well, uh... that... crazy guy, Loir, he told us to go get him something from a room, and... well the lad must have known what he was doin' cuz it turned out to be a safe room. So... the pups and I made it, along with the Italian boys that were with us..."

"...A-and Loir?"

Jack slowly shook his head.

"I think the poor lad knew he wouldn't have the time, hun. When someone came to help us get out, everything around had been... blasted."

Her heart sank. If Jack was there, she had hoped Loir had possibly made it too... Eden let out a faint sigh and looked at the pup playing with her hand. The other one was napping at the end of the bed, its round belly exposed without a care in the world. At least those three were fine... She tried to remember the previous events, but her memory was blurry as soon as she got to the Governor's part. The sadness was still there, though, and rushed over her like a wave as soon as she remembered her lover. She knew Dante was gone. She didn't even need to ask Jack, she just knew.

"So... How did it end?" she asked. "How am I here...?"

"Our Circé witchy babe got you out of there," said Jack. "Believe it or not, the Core actually let the Zodiac drawback without a fuss! All their soldier robots were disabled and still are as of now. They withdrew all the Overcrafts from the Suburbs too, and let us use those the Edge had taken control of to carry the ones with minor injuries back home. So, pretty much everyone else was brought back here, to the general hospital. Never thought I'd ever get to put my feet here, to be honest. But apparently, the Core suspended all the medical fees as a token of goodwill, so everyone is getting healed and cared for, for free! Well, not that we trust the medical bots or what, but at least they are doin' a decent job."

"I see... Did anyone else..."

"Uh, a few people died, but no one that we know, I think... except for those unlucky lads who were blasted down south..."

"Oh my goodness, she's up! Jack, you were supposed to call me!"

Eden turned her head again to see Circé rushing up to her. Her purple hair was braided over one shoulder, and she had changed into a surprisingly simple black kimono too. She went to the other side of the bed, grabbing Eden's hand gently with her fingers and pushing the pup aside.

"She literally just woke up seconds ago, babe!" retorted Jack.

"How are you?" asked Circé, frowning a bit. "Does anywhere hurt? They gave you a bunch of anesthetics and some blood too..."

"I'm good. ...You?"

"I'm alright. They stitched me up just fine, so I'm just hanging around to help... A lot of people needed a bed more than I did."

She made a brief pause, looking a bit sorry.

"Eden... do you remember what... happened?"

"...Yeah," nodded Eden.

She knew exactly what she was referring to with such a cautious expression. Circé looked terribly sorry and pressed her hand gently.

"...I'm so sorry."

"It's... I'm alright."

"We... retrieved his body," Circé added.

"C.!" protested Jack, but she ignored him.

"We have it here, it's with the Italians. We wanted to know what you'd want to do, we thought we should wait... for you to wake up."

"Thank you. I just... want to hold a proper ceremony. ...How long have I been unconscious?"

"Just about two days, it's evening now."

"How is the situation outside?"

"Well, we–"

"Girl, can't you just rest?!" exclaimed Jack, annoyed.

"I'm alright, Jack. ...Circé, please. Tell me what's happening."

"Everything's fine," she immediately replied. "As in, the fight's over, and we've got nothing to fear so far. Well, needless to say, the Suburbs are still wrecked and many people couldn't get home, but we're setting up camps and putting people wherever there's space, and distributing food for free too. Many people opened their restaurants to help distribute food and the Zodiac is paying for most of it. ...In fact, the Zodiac is negotiating with the Core as we speak. They arrested the Governor, as they promised, but the guy died from your gunshot within the next couple of hours. Honestly, I suspect they didn't try hard to save him..."

Eden sighed. She wondered how hard they would have charged him for his crimes... Her bullet probably spared them from digging any further into the huge pile of shit their Governor left behind.

"...You said the Zodiac is negotiating with them? Now?"

"Yeah. Well, it started over an hour ago, so..."

"I want to go."

"What?"

"Hun, no!" protested Jack. "You literally just woke up, you should stick to this bed!"

"Jack, I'm going. I want to go."

Jack turned to Circé with angry eyes, visibly seeking her help, but she simply shrugged.

623

"Well, technically, you have a right to be there. I'll go grab you a wheelchair."

She quickly left before Jack could get mad at her, so he turned to Eden with furious eyes instead.

"Are you insane?!" he shouted. "Girl, you should just stick to this bed and take the damn year off after all the bullshit you went through!"

"I'm really fine, Jack, the drugs are just making me tired. Also, I'll regret it if I don't attend those negotiations, I should be there."

"You should stay in a damn bed! Eden, you almost freakin' died!"

"I promise I'm fine."

"What about your baby, then?"

She froze.

"My... what?"

"Yes, girl, your Tiger left a cub in there! You're pregnant! ...You really didn't know?"

Eden was speechless. Pregnant? ...She had no idea. No, she hadn't even imagined this possibility... She felt strange. She really was pregnant with Dante's child? Well, there had been plenty of opportunities for her to get pregnant, for sure. Eden simply hadn't even thought about it ever happening. Their relationship was already so unusual in itself. How would she have even imagined they'd conceive a child together? That she would... become a mother?

"Is it alright?" she suddenly asked, coming back to her senses. "The... baby?"

"Y-yeah, it is. But it would be better if its mommy didn't move around!"

She nodded, a bit relieved. Meanwhile, Circé came back already, pushing a wheelchair, and with some people who seemed to be the medical staff behind her. Despite Jack's protests and best arguments, Eden was cleared to get into the wheelchair and attend the negotiations that were occurring just a block away. Jack insisted on acting as her caretaker, and once she was carefully covered with a blanket and his jacket, he personally took her out of the hospital, the pups on Eden's lap. They had removed her Parts, but she wasn't in a hurry to get them back.

While she played with the puppies on her lap, relieved they had both made it, she was taken several floors up into a large room. It seemed to be a regular apartment living room, although quite big for one in the Suburbs. It was visibly used as a temporary HQ for the Zodiac. All of those who had survived the battle were there, plus Nebty, Malieka, and a few unknown faces. Many turned heads when Eden arrived, and either gave her a nod or muttered a greeting. However, no one wanted to interrupt A., who was seated alone in the middle of the large couch, elbows on his knees, fingers crossed, and leaning toward the large screen in front of him with a serious expression.

"...The details of the losses next week. However, I'm sure you're more than capable of doing the math yourself, considering how your Governor illegally surveyed our neighborhoods."

"We will be sure all the data that was obtained by illegal means will be destroyed or handed to you," answered a male voice from the screen.

Eden recognized that voice, and the face on the screen. It was the man who had gotten mad at the Governor back in the Arcadia Tower. He was currently occupying most of the screen, but there were several windows open, with other faces apparently attending the meeting. A woman took over in his stead.

"As soon as we can establish the exact amount of the damages, we will repair the buildings exactly as they were, and transfer the agreed sum to the families as compensation. Regarding the wall..."

"No more wall."

All eyes turned to Eden. Jack gently pushed her wheelchair so she would face the screen too.

"...Miss Newman," said the scientist, visibly surprised.

"We don't need that wall anymore," continued Eden. "If you truly regret what happened, stop trying to separate the Suburbs from the Core. We don't need the wall to be rebuilt, we need to destroy what's left."

"...Miss Newman," said the woman, frowning. "I am afraid you don't quite understand the impact of what would happen if we did."

"I don't think you understand it either. Whatever you fear, however, will not happen. Look at the fight that took place. Did any of your civilians get harmed?"

"No, but—"

"Then you know living together is possible."

"Even if we agree to this, taking down the wall will have too many consequences!"

"If you're so afraid of taking down one border, you should be more worried about what could happen if you keep it up. In light of what happened, it was the natural response to the Suburbs being choked up. This is bound to happen again if you don't offer a way out. People will keep getting hungrier, poorer, more desperate."

"Miss Newman, you don't understand. If we take down the wall, our citizens will feel threatened. Not physically perhaps, but financially, and on many other levels! What if they get their jobs taken, their houses taken—"

"And you think the people living in the Suburbs moved there of their own free will? I'm not asking you to kick out the Core's people. Realistically, it will take years for the people in the Suburbs to catch up to the Core. They don't have the skills to get high-end jobs, and they don't have the finances to get those properties either. However, taking down the wall and reopening those roads will be the first step in letting them back in."

"What about the crime rate? If our citizens are harmed because of your decision—"

"You have all the Mafia Leaders in this very room," said A. "We have always kept the fights between us, and those who don't belong to our mafia live their lives just fine. Do you think any of us would risk going against the

Core again on our own? If there are crimes committed, I promise we will take care of them. We won't oppose you arresting those who harm your citizens, either."

"We all lost a lot of people already," added Thao. "If we can get a chance to not need guns and violence anymore, most of our people will happily take that. We can't promise you perfect citizens, but if you want the crime to stay between the worst and out of the Core, we can guarantee that."

All of the present Mafia Leaders nodded in agreement. Eden realized the few unknown faces were replacing the Dragon and the Eagle, and Tanya, who wasn't there. She spotted Rolf, leaning against the wall too, probably here to represent the Italian Mafia...

"...I see," said the woman. "This is not a decision we can make right away, but we will consider it and give you an answer in the next forty-eight hours with our own conditions. Anything else?"

"Don't repair the buildings exactly as they were," said Eden. "...Build new ones, better ones."

"Aren't you pushing it?!"

"Your robots did the damage," Eden retorted. "None of your citizens were harmed, but for us, many lost their homes they could already barely afford. If you really want to show goodwill, do it right. Don't put people back into slums, but into proper homes, as any human being deserves."

"I like the sound of that," nodded Michael, seated in an armchair. "Don't pretend you guys don't have the money for it. It's about payback too. You can add that to the proper oxygen fans and new roads we agreed on."

"And, gentle reminder, we still have the codes to destroy those fans if you put the former ones in," added Nebty with a grin. "I suggest you update your System and don't leave us out of it this time. Even if you try, it will only give you at best a few years before we take control again. And Pan's still on our side."

The woman sighed.

"...Fine. Miss Newman, your... brother asked us to be particularly understanding and is currently holding our Systems hostage. I need to say, we are not fond of his attitude."

"He can keep doing that," said Eden. "We need someone who watches both sides. He might be partial to me, but he won't suffocate the Core. He was programmed to save humankind, after all. He isn't your enemy. ...I'll talk to him later."

"I'll look forward to that," Pan's voice suddenly echoed in the room. "I'm glad you're alright."

"Thanks. Speak to you later."

"Then we'll leave you to discuss our new offer," said A., standing up. "We will resume this tomorrow."

The communication was cut off.

"...I don't trust them," grunted Thao.

"Neither do they, but as long as Pan's on our side, they probably don't have much of a choice," sighed Lecky.

"...Glad to see you, Ghost," said Michael with a gentle smile. "We were hoping you'd join those negotiations."

"Why?"

"Technically, we consider you part of the Zodiac as well," said A.

Rolf walked up to her, quietly nodding, and, to her surprise, he placed himself on her right, joining his hands together like a bodyguard.

"De Luca didn't have an official successor, in case of his death," calmly explained A. "So, technically, as his wife, you are the new Tiger. Although, your position is a bit more special, thanks to your connection to Pan. Either way, we would like you to remain with the Zodiac, regardless of the official title you pick. We plan to shift to a more... official and less conflicting organization."

"Gotta work on that crime rate," scoffed Thao.

"...I understand," said Eden. "But... I'll only do it for six months until we settle things around here with the Core. That's it. After that, I just want to be left in peace."

"I guess we could... arrange for you to take a step back," nodded Lecky. "A consultant role to the Zodiac should suffice after the negotiations and repairs are settled. You deserve a break indeed. Can I ask why six months though?"

"She's got a baby Tiger on the way," chuckled Circé.

"Oh!"

One by one, all of the Zodiac and Edge gave her some congratulations, but Eden could only receive them with a half-bitter smile. First, because it didn't feel real to her, and second, because she was still too upset about the death of her baby's father. After that, most of the Zodiac left. Nebty chatted with Eden for a short bit, but as the leader of the Edge, she was still busy coordinating with her hackers to dig up all of the crap they could find on the Governor to have the Core's leaders take responsibility for it.

The two women chatted until they left the building, which was apparently only requisitioned for this. Then, Rolf, Jack, and Circé decided to take her back to the hospital together.

"...Rolf, can I ask you a favor?" she asked on their way back

"Anything," he answered without hesitation.

"...I want to hold some sort of ceremony for Dante."

"They are planning to do a mass one, for everyone who died..."

"No, I want to hold a small one, a private one. Just for him."

"...I understand. I'll make the preparations."

"Are you sure it's alright? For me to... become the Tiger? Shouldn't it be you?"

"I can act as your proxy all you want, but you're his next of kin. Moreover, the Zodiac respects you more. Truthfully, I was never ready to take over, madam. I'm happy to assist you."

"...I see."

627

Eden had no intention to take over for Dante, though. She had already decided she wanted another life. A different life, with her baby. She felt like she had done exactly what she had been prepared for, her whole life, but now, she really needed a new chapter to start. One where she could be really, truly free. She wanted Dante's funeral to be her last goodbye to her previous life. Her last goodbye to Ghost, and his Songbird. Although Dante's death should have probably kept her depressed for days, she couldn't find that sadness in her heart. Perhaps it would come later, at night, when she was left alone. Right now, she was surrounded by Jack, Circé, and Rolf, all three acting very caring and protective.

They got her back in her hospital room, sitting her upright this time, so she could see everything going on outside the large window next to her bed. From there, she could see all of the destruction that had ravaged the already ugly neighborhoods. It was a lot. It would probably take months to rebuild everything, and she hoped it would be built into something much, much better. That was the only reason Eden had agreed to temporarily become part of the Zodiac, so she could see that the promises to them were kept and a new dawn in Chicago. One where her child would have no idea about sleeping on an old mattress, holding a gun, or risking death during a Dive. Where their baby could breathe clean air, eat fresh fruits, and see trees grow.

Hours later, a tear would go down her cheek, and she would smile, imagining that future, with Dante's child in it.

Their love child.


*The End*

# EPILOGUE

"Kids, time to eat! Come down! Now! …Don't make me repeat myself!"

He put the plate on the table, checking that he hadn't forgotten anything. The table was set for six people and was already filled with big plates full of food to share over a colored tablecloth. It smelled wonderful throughout the room. He snapped his fingers and turned around to grab what he always forgot: the water pitcher. After double-checking a second time, he made a satisfied nod. Then, he walked over to the old gramophone sitting in a corner of the room, sparkling clean. He pulled open the large drawer under it and slowly looked through the records to pick one. He chose one, took the large record out of its vintage packaging, and put it on. After a few seconds of lazy spinning, gentle jazz music began to play, filling the room with the smooth sound of a saxophone and a soprano voice. The man hummed along with a faint smile.

"Oh my God, it smells divine! My husband is the best cook," chuckled a pretty blonde woman upon walking in.

He turned around, finding her on the doorstep in that pretty blue dress that suited her so well, her long hair in a bun. She put down the fresh baguette on the table.

"Of course," he smiled. "That's what it takes to be married to the best wife!"

He received his wife in his arms as she walked up to him, putting a gentle kiss on her cheek. Then, he moved his hands to her slightly round tummy, caressing it.

"Is he moving?" he asked, his eyes sparkling with excitement.

"Not yet. You know it's too early..."

"I can't help it. I can't wait to meet this one."

"I know! Speaking of children, did you call the others?"

"I just did. How long do you think it will take them?"

"If they don't want to be forbidden from playing in the White Reality for a week again, less than five minutes," she sighed.

"Good. I'll go get Mom, can you feed the birds?"

"Will do, chef."

The man smiled at his wife, hugging her once more before she turned around, walking up to one of the kitchen cabinets. Their kitchen was beautifully set up, all in clear wood and white counters, with a lot of natural light and dozens of plants in every corner. The cooking space was already back to being spotless, dishes drying on a rack, and a hint of lemon floating in the air. There were all sorts of spices and dried herbs displayed in glass jars on wooden shelves, a pot with wooden cooking utensils, and flowers in bloom in the white vase by the window. Family pictures were displayed across the wall, with the same smiling faces looking a bit older in each one. The whole room screamed warmth and happiness.

"Uncle, can you set the timer to five minutes? If the kids aren't here by then, no Diving for them this week!"

"They just turned off their game, they are on the way," chuckled a voice echoing in the room.

The man nodded with a satisfied expression, and after exchanging a wink with his wife, made his way to the garden.

It was a beautiful garden, perhaps the best on the street. Like the rest of the residential area they lived in, it was pretty quiet, except for all the birds they could hear. It had been the main reason why he bought this house: he wanted to offer his mom her dream garden, and now, the place truly blossomed. There were trees, bushes, and all sorts of plants, with the vegetable garden being the main center of focus. It wasn't the perfect type of garden with any precise spacing, but one could tell all the flowers and plants were well attended and happily blooming in response. A pretty calico cat greeted him by rubbing itself against his ankle as soon as he stepped out.

"Hi, there," he said.

Right after the calico cat, another one came up to him, meowing for a treat or a pet. The man sighed, and ignored the cats, walking toward the back of the garden. Cautious not to step on the green grass, he followed the stone path to the end of the garden, near the little pond. Right beside the pond, there was a pretty white gazebo with wooden furniture he had made all by himself, and colored cushions.

There, a woman was reading a book out loud to the little girl on her lap, and seemingly, to the four dogs and twice as many cats gathered around them. He sighed with a faint smile. The dogs were each of a different breed, and the

630

cats had all moved from the street to their garden permanently. His mother just had this habit of spontaneously adopting any stray she found, and nobody ever tried to stop her either. It had started with two pups when he was young, and since, she had never turned away anything that had fur and a hungry stomach. Now it seemed like all the local strays knew where to come if they ever felt hungry. He had grown up surrounded by pets, and he loved it. As soon as he got close enough, the dogs reacted, three of them running to him with happy barks and wagging tails.

"Daddy!"

The little girl jumped down from her grandma's lap and ran to her dad, pushing through the gathered canines. He laughed and greeted her with open arms.

"So that's where you were, baby tiger! Hiding with Grandma, huh?"

"Grandma was reading me a story..."

"Was it a good story?"

"Yes! Grandma's the best at telling stories! But we haven't finished it yet..."

"You can finish after lunch, honey. Come on, go get your big brothers, I made your favorite."

"Pasta!" exclaimed the baby girl. "Yes!"

Then, she ran toward the house, followed by the excited dogs. Meanwhile, he turned toward the older lady left behind. With the little girl gone, the only dog left moved to her lap, and she petted him on the head.

"You made your father's pasta?" she asked as he approached.

"To make my mom happy," he said. "I know your favorite..."

He sat next to her, giving her a smile. Eden caressed his cheek, gently.

"Thank you, Julian."

"Of course. Anything for the best grandma ever."

"Oh," she chuckled. "I'm a better grandmother than I was a mom..."

"I don't know who you're talking about, my mom was the best mom."

Eden chuckled, and he leaned to give her a kiss against her blonde hair. She was starting to get a few more white hairs, but it strangely blended in well with the platinum blonde. She was a young grandmother and, even with a few wrinkles she refused to ever hide, she was still as beautiful as he had always known her to be. After exchanging a knowing look, he leaned his head against her shoulder, taking her hand.

"...I mean it, you know," he said.

"Thank you, my love. But you don't know how many times I almost killed you."

He laughed.

"Mom! You're not supposed to say stuff like that to your kids."

"Oh, you're big enough. And you know too."

"Of course, I know. I still remember the time you and Uncle Jack fought for about an hour about your non-existent cooking skills."

"He thought I was starving you," she rolled her eyes. "How could I have known my son was a picky eater?"

"I'm not picky, Mom, you are a terrible cook. Which is why I had to learn."

"That was all according to my plan, to have you feed me when I'm older."

"Nice plan. I'm never going to be able to leave you alone."

"See? Your mom is the smartest."

He chuckled, and they stayed like this for a little while. From the couch, they could see the entire house and the skyscrapers in the background. It was definitely her favorite spot, she could spend all day there. Which is why he had built this whole patio, and even a small coffee table to put her tea on.

"...I loved when you sang to me the most," he muttered. "Even when I was sad, as long as I heard you sing, everything seemed to be fine. I know why my daughter loves to hear you."

"Your dad loved it too," said Eden.

"Dad had good taste. ...Do you miss him?"

She took a little while to answer, although this wasn't his first time asking. Perhaps because she was truly pondering the question every time, Eden always took an extra minute to sincerely question herself. She turned to look at her son. He had grown up to look more like her than his dad. Still, she could see parts of Dante in him sometimes, more in his character. He was stubborn, headstrong, and very protective of her and their family. He had the exact same smile too.

"Not when I look at you," she smiled.

"Thank God he left you such a handsome and capable son."

"You grew up alright," Eden laughed, ruffling his hair. "...Oh, it smells so good."

"I made all your favorite foods for today."

"I can smell it. Thank you, my love."

They remained silent for a little while, but, after some hesitation, Julian slowly turned toward her.

"Mom... can I ask you something?"

"Anything," she replied without hesitating.

"Why... did I never get a stepfather?"

"What?" Eden chuckled. "Didn't you have enough father figures already? Jack and Rolf would be hurt to hear that!"

"No, I'm not talking about me, you know I was fine, but... why did you never remarry? I understand why it was just the two of us when I was a kid, but... it's not like you couldn't have. I mean, as you said, there were plenty of men around you, and I saw how some of them looked at you. I had the prettiest mom on the block! Why did you never even... try to find yourself someone else?"

Eden remained silent for a few seconds. Her hand gently petted the dog on her lap, and she eventually smiled faintly.

632

"...Because none of them looked at me the way your father did, I guess. I told you what kind of job I had before he appeared. There were many, many men around me, but even so, I kept them all at bay, and I always felt so lonely no matter what. But when your dad barged into my life, he made me realize I didn't have to be lonely. So, even when he left... I never felt lonely again."

She let out a faint sigh.

"To be honest, there were times I did wonder if it wouldn't be better for you if I remarried... but every time I thought about it, I felt like I couldn't. Hell, I imagined your dad coming back from the dead to take me away! He was so jealous."

Julian laughed.

"I'm glad I managed to do it on my own," she continued. "Well, I had a lot of help. Everyone took care of me, even when I thought I didn't need it. Every time things got hard, somebody would show up to help. That's how I knew. That our family didn't have to be perfect, it had to be just a bit bigger than usual. I was the same. I grew up without my dad, and when my mom left me too, there was always someone to take my hand. There are some bonds that go beyond blood and family ties. We have a warm, caring community of people around us, and that's worth more than any family out there."

"...I see. Well, thank God for them, or I would have probably died of starvation before the age of five!"

Eden laughed. She was proud of her son beyond words, and at the same time, shocked how he had turned out to be such a fine man. Technically, he had been pretty much raised by mafiosos, criminal hackers, a drag queen godmother... and a cyber uncle. If that wasn't the most unexpected mix to make a handsome and talented young man! She smiled and held his hand gently. He reminded her of Dante every single day, and she loved that. It was as if he had known, and left a part of him to look after her until her later years... Although she had tried many times to send him away to live his life, telling him she'd be fine on her own, Julian always came back to her, no matter what; he was as stubborn as his dad. Eden had given up. Even her daughter-in-law had the best relationship with her and was the first to get mad whenever Eden suggested she got her own place. They had naturally taken her to live with them in their new house, and she suspected they had chosen this one to accommodate her.

"Let's go," declared Julian with a sigh. "It wouldn't be great if Grandma arrives after the kids..."

He helped her into her hoverchair, next to the patio. It was the most recent model that could go on all sorts of surfaces and was very comfortable. Eden had chosen to never put her Parts back on again after the battle. Although it was less convenient at times to take care of her son, this was a choice she had made for herself. It was another way to say farewell to her previous life, and she had never regretted it. It was as if, after spending her lifetime running, a new chapter had begun, where she could simply take her time, and not just try to survive.

She had Dived a few more times, but only when she was still working for the Zodiac, or to spend time with Prometheus. It had taken a few years, and many negotiations, but the current Chicago was so much more peaceful than what she had once known, and now, there was no need for Ghost anymore. There was still some disparity between the people, but there were no more walls, no more oxygen masks. Eden was still in touch with some of the former Zodiac and the Edge, but she was only acting as a consultant from time to time. She and Pan had worked together to take over some of her father's abandoned research, while also making sure the wrongs the Governor had done were repaired and no crimes could be committed again in the name of science. Truthfully, she could have spent the rest of her life without working at all. To her surprise, Dante had left more than enough money to provide for her and her son, and Eden hadn't needed to act as the Tiger for long. As soon as somebody else had taken over, she had happily taken a step back to dedicate herself to Julian. The crime rate and gunfights had significantly dropped, just as promised. The Zodiac wasn't gone completely but had changed into some kind of global organization, probably still very mafia-like, but they did not touch the citizens. Most of the Zodiac Eden once knew had passed or were retired, the same as the Edge. It did feel like a new generation had taken over, with, hopefully, the means to do even better than they had.

"Ah... That song," Eden muttered, surprised, as they were almost at the entrance of the house.

"One of your favorites," smiled Julian.

She couldn't help but smile as they crossed the threshold. All three children turned their hazel eyes to their grandmother but, before any of them could say a word, they noticed the nostalgic expression in her eyes, and saw her lips open.

"*Stars fading but I linger on, dear, still craving your kiss... I'm longing to linger till dawn, dear... Just saying this–Sweet dreams till sunbeams find you; sweet dreams that leave all worries behind you... But in your dreams whatever they be, dream a little dream of me...*"

"*Dream a little dream of me,*" repeated the little girl, with a pretty voice.

She ran to her grandmother, taking her hand.

"I love it, Grandma! Your voice is so pretty!"

"...Yours too, my little Songbird. Yours too."

# Bio

Jenny Fox is a French author, born in Paris in 1994.
She reads alone for the first time at 6 years old, Harry Potter and the Philosopher Stone, and writes her very first story at 9 years old. Her teacher reads it in front of the whole class, and from then on, she will never stop writing, from short stories to fanfiction.

His Blue Moon Princess is her first story to be entirely written in English, inspired by her experience overseas and her love for Fantasy Novels.

Follow her at @AuthorJennyFox on her Social Media.

# Also By Jenny Fox

## THE SILVER CITY SERIES
His BlueMoon Princess
His Sunshine Baby
His Blazing Witch

*

## THE DRAGON EMPIRE SAGA
The War God's Favorite
The White King's Favorite
The Wild Prince's Favorite (Coming soon)

*

## STAND-ALONE STORIES
Lady Dhampir
The Songbird's Love
A Love Cookie
Hera, Love & Revenge
The HellFlower
Dhampir Knight (Coming Soon)
A Love Cookie 2 (Coming Soon)

*

## THE FLOWER ROMANCE SERIES
Season 1
Season 2

Made in the USA
Las Vegas, NV
19 August 2023

76295823R10370